PENGUIN CLASSICS

GENERAL EDITOR, POETRY: CHRISTOPHER RICKS

TROILUS AND CRISEYDE

GEOFFREY CHAUCER was born in London, the son of a wine-merchant, in about 1342, and as he spent his life in royal and government service his career happens to be unusually well documented. By 1357 Chaucer was a page to the wife of Prince Lionel, second son of Edward III, and it was while in the prince's service that Chaucer was ransomed when captured during the English campaign in France in 1359–60. Chaucer's wife Philippa, whom he married c. 1365, was the sister of Katherine Swynford, the mistress (c. 1370) and third wife (1396) of John of Gaunt, Duke of Lancaster, whose first wife Blanche (d. 1368) is commemorated in Chaucer's earliest major poem, *The Book of the Duchess*.

From 1374 Chaucer worked as controller of customs on wool in the port of London, but between 1366 and 1378 he made a number of trips abroad on official business, including two trips to Italy in 1372–3 and 1378. The influence of Chaucer's encounter with Italian literature is felt in the poems he wrote in the late 1370s and early 1380s – *The House of Fame*, *The Parliament of Fowls* and a version of *The Knight's Tale* – and finds its fullest expression in *Troilus and Criseyde*.

In 1386 Chaucer was member of parliament for Kent, but in the same year he resigned his customs post, although in 1389 he was appointed Clerk of the King's Works (resigning in 1391). After finishing *Troilus* and his translation into English prose of Boethius' *De consolatione philosophiae*, Chaucer started his *Legend of Good Women*. In the 1390s he worked on his most ambitious project, *The Canterbury Tales*, which remained unfinished at his death. In 1399 Chaucer leased a house in the precincts of Westminster Abbey but died in 1400 and was buried in the Abbey.

BARRY WINDEATT is Professor of English in the University of Cambridge, and a Fellow of Emmanuel College. His books include a critical introduction to *Troilus and Criseyde* and a parallel-text edition of the poem, designed to show Chaucer at work on his principal source, Boccaccio's poem *Il Filostrato*. He has also translated *The Book of Margery Kempe* for Penguin Classics and has edited other writings of the medieval English mystical tradition.

GEOFFREY CHAUCER

Troilus and Criseyde

Edited with an Introduction and Notes by
BARRY WINDEATT

PENGUIN BOOKS

PENGUIN BOOKS

Published by the Penguin Group
Penguin Books Ltd, 80 Strand, London WC2R ORL, England
Penguin Putnam Inc., 375 Hudson Street, New York, New York 10014, USA
Penguin Books Australia Ltd, 250 Camberwell Road, Camberwell, Victoria 3124, Australia
Penguin Books Canada Ltd, 10 Alcorn Avenue, Toronto, Ontario, Canada M4V 3B2
Penguin Books India (P) Ltd, 11, Community Centre, Panchsheel Park, New Delhi – 110 017, India
Penguin Books (NZ) Ltd, Cnr Rosedale and Airborne Roads, Albany, Auckland, New Zealand
Penguin Books (South Africa) (Pty) Ltd, 24 Sturdee Avenue, Rosebank 2196, South Africa

Penguin Books Ltd, Registered Offices: 80 Strand, London WC2R ORL, England

www.penguin.com

This edition first published 2003
1

Introduction and Notes copyright © Barry Windeatt, 2003
All rights reserved

The moral right of the editor has been asserted

Set in 10.25/12.25 pt PostScript Adobe Sabon
Typeset by Rowland Phototypesetting Ltd, Bury St Edmunds, Suffolk
Printed in England by Clays Ltd, St Ives plc

Contents

Troilus and Criseyde

Acknowledgements

For the original suggestion that I undertake this companion volume to her forthcoming Penguin edition of *The Canterbury Tales*, and for much generous collaboration ever since in a common endeavour, I am greatly indebted to Jill Mann. A number of magnanimous friends and colleagues have helped me with advice and information, and it is a pleasure to record here my thanks to Derek Brewer, Christopher Cannon, Helen Cooper and Jacqueline Tasioulas. To Ruth Morse, who has read and commented upon much of this edition, I am especially grateful for all her help and encouragement. It has also been my inestimable good fortune that this book has had such a superlative copy-editor as Monica Schmoller.

Editor's Note

The text of *Troilus and Criseyde* in this edition is accompanied by glosses, at the foot of each page, of those words and phrases with which modern readers may need immediate help. For definitions of parts of speech, and for a word's possible range of meanings, readers are referred to the Glossary. The on-page glosses also include the modern spelling of proper names where these differ in Chaucer's text. Cross-references from on-page glosses to items in the Notes are indicated by 'n.' Not every subject of annotation can be signalled by means of the glosses, however, and readers are referred to the Notes for a full commentary on Chaucer's poem.

References in the apparatus of this edition are in short form by author name and date of publication (e.g. Windeatt 2003) to the Bibliography, where full bibliographical information is to be found for all works cited. Readers are referred to the headnote to the Notes for some further conventions pertaining to citations of frequently cited works. Complementing the Bibliography, a select list of Further Reading has also been provided as a guide for readers to some contemporary criticism devoted to Chaucer's *Troilus and Criseyde*.

Chronology

c. **1342** Born in London, son of John Chaucer, a well-to-do wine-merchant, and his wife Agnes. John Chaucer holds office (1347–9) as the king's deputy-butler in the port of Southampton, supervising wine shipments from Bordeaux for the royal cellars.

1357 In service as a young 'page' in the household of Elizabeth, Countess of Ulster, wife of Prince Lionel, second surviving son of Edward III. (The Countess's household expense accounts record payments to Chaucer at Easter 1357 for a paltock (short cloak), a pair of black and red hose and a pair of shoes, and at Whitsun and Christmas for other necessities.)

1359–60 In service as a *valettus* or yeoman in Prince Lionel's retinue in France; captured at the siege of Rheims and ransomed for £16 (payment from the King's Wardrobe, 1 March 1360; see 15 October 1386, below).

1360 *October*: paid by Prince Lionel for carrying letters to England from Calais.

1361–6 Prince Lionel in Ireland as Viceroy; Chaucer's life in these years is unrecorded; presumably in service in a royal household.

1365/6 Marries Philippa, eldest daughter of Paon de Roet (of the household of Queen Philippa) and sister of Katherine Swynford, who became mistress (*c.* 1370) and third wife (1396) of John of Gaunt, Duke of Lancaster.

1366 Chaucer's father dies; his mother remarries.

1366 *February–May*: receives a safe-conduct from the King of Navarre; possibly on pilgrimage to Santiago, or on diplomatic business. Perhaps previously in Acquitaine with the Black Prince.

1367 *20 June*: granted an annuity of 20 marks as an esquire of the royal household.

c. **1367** Chaucer's son Thomas born.

late 1360s Translates (part of) the *Roman de la Rose*.

1368 *July–September*: abroad on the king's service.

12 September: death of Blanche, Duchess of Lancaster, John of Gaunt's first wife. *The Book of the Duchess* written not long after.

1369 *September*: in France with John of Gaunt's expeditionary force.

1370 *June–September*: in France again, presumably in connection with the annual military campaign.

1372 *30 August*: Philippa Chaucer granted an annuity of £10 by John of Gaunt for service in the household of his second wife, Constance of Castille (through whose right he claimed the throne of Castille).

1371–3 Payments for winter and summer robes to Chaucer as an 'esquire of the King's chamber', i.e. Edward III's inner household.

1372–3 *1 December–23 May*: in Italy (Genoa and Florence), as a member of a trading and diplomatic mission.

1373 *20 August*: Chaucer receives a royal commission to travel to Dartmouth to arrange for the restoration to its master of an arrested Genoese merchant ship.

1374 *23 April*: granted a pitcher of wine a day for life by the king (commuted in 1378 for an exchequer annuity of 20 marks).

10 May: granted lease for life of rent-free dwelling above the city gate at Aldgate.

8 June: appointed controller of the customs of hides, skins and wools in the port of London (annual income £16 13s. 4d.), with requirement to keep the records in his own hand.

13 June: receives an annuity of £10 from John of Gaunt.

1375–7 Writing *The House of Fame*; probably completed by 1378.

1376–7 In France on several occasions, deputed from the

customs to serve on diplomatic commissions negotiating for peace and for the marriage of Richard II.

late 1370s Writing *Anelida and Arcite*.

1378 *May–September*: in Lombardy on diplomatic business to Bernabò Visconti, lord of Milan, and Sir John Hawkwood (an English mercenary adventurer in Italy).

1380 Birth of Chaucer's son Lewis (said to be aged eleven when Chaucer writes the *Treatise on the Astrolabe* for him in 1391).

4 May: released by Cecily Champain from any legal action in respect of what the deed of release terms her *raptus* (a term used in legal documents to refer both to abduction and/or rape).

c. **1380** Writes *The Parliament of Fowls*.

c. **1380–81** Writes *Palamon and Arcite* (later *The Knight's Tale*).

1381 Chaucer's mother dies.

c. **1381–6** Writing *Troilus and Criseyde*; perhaps simultaneously with, or shortly after, the *Boece*, his prose translation of Boethius.

1382 Appointed controller of the petty custom in the port of London.

1383 *23 June–1 November*: obtains permission to appoint a deputy in his principal controllership (pleading pressure of unspecified other business).

1385 *17 February*: obtains permission to have a permanent deputy at the wool customs.

c. **1385** *The Complaint of Mars* written.

1385 The French poet Eustache Deschamps sends a poem of praise to Chaucer with the refrain 'Grand translateur, noble Geoffroy Chaucier!'.

10 September: receives livery of mourning as an esquire of the King's Household upon the death of the king's mother, Joan of Kent.

12 October: appointed a member of the commission of the peace in Kent; appointment renewed 28 June 1386, possibly with occasional service until 1389; probably now living in Kent.

1386 *1 October–28 November*: Member of Parliament for Kent at one session, the 'Wonderful Parliament' (held in the chapter-house of Westminster Abbey); one minor petition presented by the Commons requested that life-appointed controllers of customs be removed from office, on suspicion of financial irregularities, and that in future no such life appointments be made.

By 5 October: gives up lease on Aldgate dwelling.

15 October: a witness before the High Court of Chivalry (meeting in the refectory of Westminster Abbey) in the Scrope–Grosvenor trial, a dispute over the right to bear certain arms. Chaucer gives evidence that he saw the said arms borne by Sir Richard Scrope when he was himself in arms before the town of Rethel, near Rheims, during the campaign of 1359–60. Testifies to being forty years of age 'and more'.

4 December: resigns his two controllerships at the customs.

c. 1386–7 Writing *The Legend of Good Women*.

1387 Philippa Chaucer dies.

c. 1387 Begins *The Canterbury Tales*.

1388 *3 February–4 June*: the 'Merciless Parliament', hostile to the King's Household and personal patronage, and to the practice of granting life annuities.

1388 *1 May*: transfers his two exchequer annuities to John Scalby.

1389 *12 July*: appointed Clerk of the King's Works.

1390s Appointed deputy-forester of North Petherton in Somerset (possibly a legal appointment while the estate's owner was a minor).

1390 *3 September*: robbed by highwaymen of his horse and of £20 6s. 8d. of the king's money at the 'Fowle Ok', Hatcham, in Deptford, probably on his way to pay workmen's wages at the royal manor of Eltham. (Also recorded as the victim on 6 September of further robberies of £10 in Westminster and of £9 and 43d. at Hatcham.)

1391 Writes *Treatise on the Astrolabe*; continues work on *The Canterbury Tales*.

17 June: resigns as Clerk of the King's Works.

1392 *The Equatorie of the Planetis*, possibly by Chaucer.

1394 *28 February*: granted royal annuity of £20 for life.

Death of Anne of Bohemia (Queen Consort of Richard II).

1394–5 Revises Prologue to *The Legend of Good Women* (and removes a reference to Queen Anne).

1395/6 Receives a gown of scarlet with fur trimming from Henry, Earl of Derby (the future Henry IV).

1396? *Envoy to Bukton* (mentioning the Wife of Bath).

1397 *1 December*: royal grant of a tun (a large cask) of wine per year.

1398 Moves back to London from Kent? (Responsibility for collecting from Chaucer a debt incurred in 1389 is transferred from the Sheriff of Kent to the Sheriff of London.)

1399 24 *December*: takes fifty-three-year lease on a house in the precincts of Westminster Abbey.

1400 *The Complaint of Chaucer to his Purse* with an envoy to Henry IV, who became king upon the deposition of Richard II on 30 September 1399; Henry IV renews payment of Chaucer's annuities.

25 October: Chaucer's death, according to a now illegible inscription on his tomb, recorded in 1606 (Crow and Olson 1966: 548); buried in Westminster Abbey at the entrance to St Benedict's Chapel; moved in 1556 to a new tomb set against the east wall of the south transept, in what has subsequently become 'Poets' Corner'.

Introduction

Troilus and Criseyde, Geoffrey Chaucer's most ambitious single achievement, his masterpiece, is a great humanist poem. Its theme is human love, with all its potential for ecstasy and for anguish in body and mind: love as desire and its fulfilment; love at its most idealizing and transcendent. A vindication of the rights of women, Chaucer's poem is also a compassionate exploration of their wrongs. One of the supreme narrative poems in English, it is set during the siege of Troy and tells how Troilus, son of King Priam, falls in love with Criseyde, a beautiful widow. Through the intervention of Criseyde's uncle, Pandarus, Troilus and Criseyde become lovers, until Criseyde is obliged to leave Troy for the camp of the besieging Greeks, where she forsakes Troilus for the Greek warrior Diomede. By the time that Chaucer wrote *Troilus* Criseyde's infidelity was already a byword, with her story well known in England from Continental sources written in French and Latin centuries before. It was a story that focused on the end of an affair, and one novelty of *Troilus and Criseyde* for Chaucer's early readers was to begin from the beginning with a prequel of how love started and came to fulfilment. Nor had any other work in English yet addressed love – other than the love of God – with such sympathetic understanding, and Chaucer's insight into character invites comparison with the modern novel in its sustained attention to inward feeling and motive. Although the story's sad end in love betrayed was a commonplace, Chaucer's genius for comedy and dramatic speech, and his exploration of love in its philosophical and metaphysical dimensions, produce a profoundly original reading that both celebrates and questions conventions and traditions to make them new.

Traditions of Troilus and Criseyde

In classical tradition Troilus was an emblem of early death, and Troy's fate was identified with his. According to Virgil's *Aeneid* Achilles slew the young prince during the long siege ('unfortunate youth and ill-matched in conflict with Achilles', 1.475), but in earlier classical tradition Achilles ambushed Troilus at a fountain, then pursued and slaughtered him on a temple altar of Apollo. Tradition gave Achilles two motives: an unreciprocated passion for Troilus, and also a prophecy that if Troilus reached the age of twenty Troy could not be destroyed, whereas his death would presage Troy's downfall. By implication, this Troilus dies almost before he can live, and before he can love.

Later, two influential forgeries developed the role of Troilus as one of the pre-eminent Trojan warriors: the sixth-century Latin *De excidio Troiae historia* (The Fall of Troy, A History) by Dares Phrygius, and the fourth-century *Ephemeridos belli Troiani libri* (A Journal of the Trojan War) by Dictys Cretensis, both of which purport to be eye-witness accounts of the siege of Troy.[1] Dares describes the main Trojan and Greek characters, including Troilus as warrior (rather than lover), Diomedes, and Briseis (the concubine of Achilles). In some conspicuous name-dropping, Chaucer refers those who wish to read more about the Trojan War to the accounts in Homer, Dares and Dictys (1.146n.), and later urges them to read Dares (5.1771), but these are probably flourishes for effect. Chaucer himself apparently relied on a fuller revision of Dares, the *Frigii Daretis Ylias* (The Iliad of Dares the Phrygian) by the Anglo-Latin poet Joseph of Exeter (*c.* 1185).[2] Chaucer's 'portraits' of Diomede, Criseyde and Troilus (*Troilus*, 5.799–840) derive from Joseph's text, and by including those portraits (curiously belatedly, in the case of Troilus and Criseyde), Chaucer collects and interleaves some of the earliest sources for the story ('Lo, trewely, they writen that hire syen . . .', 5.816).

While Troilus derives ultimately from classical sources,

Criseyde first appears in medieval romance linked with her lover Troilus. The story of Troilus's love for 'Briseida' and his displacement by Diomede is first found in Benoît de Sainte-Maure's 'Romance of Troy', the *Roman de Troie* (c. 1155–60), as one of a series of love stories interwoven with a narrative of the Trojan War, beginning with Jason and Medea, and including Paris and Helen, and Achilles and Polyxena.[3] Benoît's is one of a number of contemporary French romances on classical subjects, the *romans d'antiquité*; his poem claims to be based on a text of Dares discovered in a cupboard in Athens by a nephew of the Roman historian Sallust (*Troie*, 75–144). Unlike the other affairs he narrates, Benoît's narrative of this one begins only near its end, at the point when Briseida is about to be sent from Troy to the Greek camp (and so corresponds to the events of the fifth book of Chaucer's *Troilus*). It says nothing of how Troilus gained Briseida's love, and Benoît's focus is at least as much on her developing involvement with Diomede as on her abandonment of Troilus. Thus the earliest-known appearance of the love of Troilus and Criseyde is presented only in the context of its painful disillusionment and disintegration. The lovers' grief at their parting, Diomede's wooing and Briseida's soliloquies in her lonely dilemma are passages displaying Benoît's knowing combination of courtly speech and psychological insight, and Chaucer draws closely on these passages in his last book (see 5.107–89 and nn.).

To his Briseida Benoît assigned her original Homeric role of a woman passed involuntarily from one man to another, absorbing aspects of both Chryseis, daughter of a Trojan priest, and of Briseis, a beautiful widow (who puts her own side of the story in Ovid's *Heroides*). Benoît evidently did not understand 'Briseida' in Dares as a patronymic of Hippodamia, daughter of Brises, the concubine whom Agamemnon confiscated from Achilles with fateful consequences for the Trojan War. Not recognizing that Hippodamia (whose story he borrowed from Dictys elsewhere in the *Roman*) was the 'Briseida' whom he found described in Dares, Benoît made his Briseida the object of that rivalry in battle between Troilus and Diomede already sketched in Dares. In his heroine Benoît established an enigmatic combination of attractiveness and changeability, and invented the circumstances in which her constancy would be most cruelly tested by insecurity. Although Chaucer sets aside Benoît's explicitly antifeminist critique, the *Roman de Troie* furnishes a model in presenting the heroine at once understandingly but critically: as early as *c.* 1230 a Provençal poem alludes to the heroine as a type of female fickleness ('Briseida, who so shamed herself because her heart was changeable, for she left Troilus to love the son of Tideus').[4]

The story of Troilus and Criseyde became much more widely known when Benoît's vernacular verse 'Romance of Troy' was repackaged in the Latin prose of *Historia destructionis Troiae* (The History of the Destruction of Troy) by the Sicilian judge Guido de Columnis of Messina (1287).[5] In his moralizing 'history' (which enjoyed greater influence than the *Roman de Troie*), Guido puts an unsympathetic gloss on the experience of Briseida and her lovers; he removes any ambiguity about her motives and denigrates as lechery and lust what Benoît had motivated by romantic love. It is symptomatic of Guido's antifeminist hostility that his Briseida's affections desert Troilus on the very day that she leaves him and arrives in the Greek camp, and that she shows no remorse. Chaucer is more directly indebted to Benoît – he uses passages from the *Roman de Troie* which Guido omits or abbreviates unsympathetically. Guido's significance for *Troilus* is more for the *Historia*'s baleful influence on the heroine's reputation, for when Chaucer's Criseyde foresees that books will ruin her (5.1060), she could be speaking of the *Historia*. So, in a French poem of 1389, Jean de Chambrillac can use Criseyde's fickleness as justification for male inconstancy in love:

I know all about Troilus – handsome, valiant and of high birth – who was Briseida's lover and had no wish for any other love. All the good he got out of that was to remain without a lover, because when she left Troy, Diomede took possession of her. She was his lady; he was her lover. That teaches me to avoid fixing my heart in one place – I'm not afraid this'll do me any harm![6]

With the lovers' story well established, Giovanni Boccaccio made the love affair of Troilus and Criseida (as he renamed Briseida) the subject of his early narrative poem *Il Filostrato* (The One Overwhelmed by Love), written *c*. 1335.[7] As its title suggests, the focus of *Filostrato* centres on the male hero's emotional experience in his affair with Criseida, whom Boccaccio makes a widow rather than the unattached girl of the earlier narratives. Boccaccio's originality included his making the Troilus and Criseyde story the sole subject of an extended independent work, and particularly in inventing the story of how their love started and developed until their enforced separation, the very point at which earlier accounts had only begun. It is also Boccaccio who introduces the new figure of Pandaro, here expressly a young nobleman, cousin of Criseida and confidant of Troiolo, but not especially talkative, interventive or humorous. However Chaucer first encountered Boccaccio's poem – whether on his own travels to Italy on official missions or from the various Italians he met in the course of his job as a Customs official in London[8] – it is unlikely that *Filostrato* was well known in England when Chaucer made it his principal source for *Troilus*, so that there was all the more novelty in an account of the whole love affair of Troilus and Criseyde from beginning to end.[9] With so many literary forebears, no wonder Chaucer's Troilus and Criseyde both have a sense of themselves inhabiting the pages of books yet to be written (5.583–5, 1058–60).

Contexts and Dates

Troy and Trojans were central to the imagined genealogy of medieval London, so that the Trojan setting of *Troilus* would have struck a chord for Chaucer's contemporaries. Tradition had it that London was founded after the sack of Troy by a refugee Trojan noble, Brutus, who gave the land his name and built London as his capital with the name of 'New Troy', later corrupted to 'Trinovantum'.[10] The contemporary poet, John Gower, to whom *Troilus* is co-dedicated (5.1856–7), repeatedly refers to London in his works as 'New Troy'; a Latin poem of

1392 by Richard of Maidstone calls King Richard II 'Troilus' or 'Little Troy'; and in the mid-1380s Nicholas Brembre (several times mayor of London, and Chaucer's associate in the Customs service) was reported to be planning to change the name of London to 'Little Troy', and to become 'Duke of Troy' himself.[11] The *Liber Albus*, a fifteenth-century handbook of City of London customs, claims that London possessed and enjoyed the liberties, rights, customs and institutions of the ancient city of Troy.[12] For the first audiences of *Troilus*, Trojans are both ancestors and contemporaries, ancient and modern.

Chaucer probably composed *Troilus and Criseyde* during the early and mid 1380s. It must have been completed by early 1387 at the latest, for Ralph Strode – the philosopher and lawyer to whom *Troilus* is submitted with a request for correction (5.1857) – died in that year. Thomas Usk, a Londoner who was executed for treason on 4 March 1388, already shows some familiarity with the text of *Troilus* in his prose *Testament of Love*, where his allegorical figure of Love refers to Chaucer as 'the noble philosophical poete in Englissh', on account of the 'tretis that he made of my servant Troilus'.[13] If the declaration early in *Troilus* that 'oure firste lettre is now an A' (1.171) is indeed an allusion to the fact that 'now' (following the marriage of Richard II to Anne of Bohemia on 14 January 1382) the initial of the Queen of England was an 'A', this may indicate when Chaucer was working on his poem, as may the possible punning allusion (4.184) to Jack Straw and the Peasants' Revolt of 1381. The synchronizing in the third book of the union of Troilus and Criseyde with a conjunction of Jupiter, Saturn and the moon in the sign of Cancer (3.624–5) – a rare and portentous conjunction that occurred in the early summer of 1385 for the first time since AD 769 (and was associated with 'great upheaval of realms'[14] by contemporary commentators) – may help date *Troilus*. However, the conjunction would not actually need to have taken place for someone as interested in astrology as Chaucer to be mindful of it when writing his poem about characters living not long before the fall of Troy.

It was with *Troilus and Criseyde* that Chaucer, by then in his early forties, established his contemporary reputation (his earlier and shorter *Book of the Duchess* and *House of Fame* may have made less impact, for they survive only in limited numbers of manuscripts).[15] This was a pivotal point in Chaucer's career as a poet. Just before, or even simultaneously with, his composition of *Troilus*, he was also working on his translation into English of *De consolatione philosophiae* (The Consolation of Philosophy) by the late Roman writer Boethius (d. AD 524), and *Troilus* is shaped and informed by the philosophical concerns, the idioms, images and poetry of Boethius. Only a little earlier (*c.* 1380), in his philosophically inflected dream poem *The Parliament of Fowls*, Chaucer had first explored the seven-line rhyme royal stanza that he was shortly to employ in *Troilus*.[16] Here, too, in the *Parliament*, he made an assured use of Boccaccio. Chaucer's imagination was evidently seized by Boccaccio's early narrative poems, the *Teseida* and *Filostrato*, in which the course of love is represented with lyric immediacy within the classical settings of ancient Thebes and Troy. It was also from the three great medieval Italian authors, Dante, Petrarch and Boccaccio, that Chaucer could derive an exalted sense of poetic vocation and confidence in what might be accomplished in a vernacular language. The sheer scale of *Troilus* was like nothing Chaucer had previously attempted, and no single later poem of his would surpass it. Indeed, for several centuries *Troilus and Criseyde* remained the most admired of Chaucer's works.[17]

Nonetheless, in his very next poem, in the Prologue to *The Legend of Good Women*, Chaucer casts himself as if responding defensively to a recent controversy stirred up by *Troilus*, fictionalizing himself as punished by the God of Love for having made men less trusting of women by his tale of Criseyde (F 332–5). The poet's defence is that he should not be blamed by faithful lovers 'Thogh that I speke a fals lovere som shame' (F 467), and that his intention was to further the cause of fidelity in love and to warn by example against faithlessness (F 471–4). In this episode in a later work, referring back to the capacity of *Troilus* to invite multiple questions and contrary interpretations, it is notable that Chaucer's poem seems to be entitled simply 'Creseyde' (F 441; G 431: 'Crisseyde'). The very name of the poem is elusive. Since the fifteenth century it has come to be entitled

Troilus and Criseyde, but Chaucer names it differently in different contexts elsewhere in his writings, and no title is indicated within the text itself.[18]

Genres and Structure: 'Amerous auncyent hystory'

Versions of the Troilus and Criseyde story before Chaucer tend to identify with such particular genres as romance or history, but Chaucer's *Troilus and Criseyde* brings together a variety of generic elements in a conjunction that challenges any single definition and is uniquely its own.

Although *Troilus* is often termed a romance, its narrative focus and setting preclude much of the customary material, shape and concerns of medieval romance. *Filostrato* had already reached beyond romance to a kind of post-romance novella. Boccaccio's version presented the tale of a worldly hero's affair with a not unwilling widow, conducted in a distinctly urban, domestic setting (ostensibly Trojan, but with a modern feel), and with no place for the supernatural or marvellous, or for branchingly episodic knightly adventures, or for much that is idealizing. Chaucer broadly accepts *Filostrato*'s undigressive structure and focus, but not all its exclusions. Instead, *Troilus* places itself in a referential relation to romance tradition, just as its Trojan setting plays with the texture and tone of historical narrative. For all its worldly knowingness, *Filostrato* still presents a narrative of falling in love and winning love, but in concluding with the irretrievable loss of the lady it departs from customary romance patterns in the hero's elegaic sorrow, disillusionment and death. Taking this much further, Chaucer juxtaposes the unsustainable nature of human idealisms with an intensity of eventual disappointment and pathos which evokes explicit comparison with tragedy ('go, litel myn tragedye': 5.1786).

In drawing on *Filostrato*, Chaucer constantly adapts, augments and deepens Boccaccio's version: *Troilus* can only be called a 'translation' if that is understood as consistently transforming incident and character into a transvaluation, reimagined and retold. A copy of *Filostrato* was evidently in front of

Chaucer as he worked on *Troilus*: he often matches the Italian text stanza for stanza.[19] Boccaccio's scene-structure (defined by exits, entrances and narrative transitions) underlies the *Troilus* narrative, which Chaucer has often developed into something like a dramatic script through his expansion of scenes of direct speech.[20] These scenes – with one or other of the lovers alone, or with Pandarus, or occasionally together – place in the foreground some vivid, quasi-dramatic exchanges of dialogue, and much first-person expression in songs, letters, soliloquies, testament and complaint, for Chaucer has extended and built on a model in *Filostrato* that moves fluently between narrative and lyric.[21] Chaucer's first three books augment the sense of distance and absence   separation, gazing through windows, dreaming – and with it the need for mediation, a go-between, messages and letters, so that his English narrative focuses on what long remains an imagined love and an object of aspiration.

Such idealizing in absence and imagining across distance gives a markedly lyrical dimension to *Troilus*, with its many pretexts for composition and performance of a sequence of lyric genres. Chaucer's Troilus is acutely sensitive to music (5.442–6, 459–62), and nothing suggests he is not singing his own songs, uttering his own petitions and complaints, or – with some tips from Pandarus – writing his own courtly epistles ('How he may best discryven hire his wo', 5.1314). For her part, Criseyde sends Troilus more than the letters quoted or paraphrased in the text (5.470–71); she is twice entertained with performance of songs (2.824–6; 3.614) and explicitly questions how the sentiments expressed in Antigone's song relate to the character and experience of its female author (2.878, 883–6); in her absence Troilus recalls his special delight in hearing Criseyde sing (5.576–80). With its various lyric pieces inset into the narrative, *Troilus* gives the impression of being at once a narrative poem and a sonnet sequence. A pattern of lyric clusters creates an almost operatic interaction between narrative and aria which can pause over lyric pieces within its onward momentum. Despite its uniform versification, the lyric moments are pointedly signalled and demarcated within the text, as if intimate documents have been collected up and presented as verbatim testimony within a historically minded text ('and whoso list it here, | Loo, next this vers he may it fynden here', 1.398–9; 'He wrot right thus and seyde, as ye may here', 5.1316; cf. 5.1589). The whole of the third book (redolent in places of an epithalamium or nuptial song) is structured by a sequence of formal and expressive set-pieces – petitions, invocations, hymns, aubades or dawn-songs – while the lyric middle of the poem finds a counterpoint in an elegaic pattern of formal complaint or lamentation in the last two books. In a courtly context the plangent act of making 'complaint' ('Somtyme a man mot telle his owen peyne', 2.1501) prompts songs and epistles, and becomes part of the lovers' characteristic disposition both before their union and after the change in their fortunes. Courtship itself is expressed through complaint (3.53, 104; cf. 5.160–61); the hero's character grows in definition as a plaintiff, against love or misfortune, although Criseyde too is allowed her moments of extended complaint (e.g. 3.813–40; 4.827–47; 5.689–707, 1054–85), lamenting some anguish or quandary that, like other lyric contexts in *Troilus*, may challenge the possibility of expression ('How myghte it evere yred ben or ysonge, | The pleynte that she made in hire destresse?', 4.799–800). In a poem shaped by the story of a 'double sorwe', complaint becomes one of the poem's defining generic components, central both to its form and its eventually tragic theme.[22]

Although there had been no inevitable shape to the story of Troilus and Criseyde, Chaucer's opening anticipation of a 'double' sorrow gives an overview of the structure to come and insists from the beginning that a knowledge of the whole poem's shape is integral to its meaning throughout. In this double sorrow, where joy once won is lost but cannot (as in romance) be retrieved, there is a doleful reflex of traditional romance in the construction of the narrative. Chaucer's creation in *Troilus* of a single fifth book out of the four separate Parts 5–8 of *Filostrato*, and his expansion of the third book, establish a symmetrical structure, tracing the fundamental pattern of the poem, the rise and fall of Troilus's fortunes ('Fro wo to wele, and after out of joie', 1.4). The symmetry of a five-book structure had many classical precedents, not least Horace's prescription for five-act plays in the *Ars Poetica* (189–90), and the regularly classical, architectural symmetry of its form sets *Troilus* apart, both from Chaucer's other poems and from previous romance in England.

The poem's structure is further articulated through its apparatus of proems and book-division, with Latin incipits and explicits (ambitious and formal for a work in English at this date). These emphasize each book as an entity, while also contributing to the overall symmetry in which the central experience of the lovers' union becomes the mid-point of a concentric structural pattern of recurring and mirroring features and episodes throughout the whole poem's span of double sorrow:

Prayer	First proem
Smile	Troilus mocks lovers (1.194)
Lollius	(1.394)
Canticus Troili	(1.400–420)
Ride past	Troilus rides past (2.619ff., 1247ff.)
Dream	Criseyde's dream (2.925–31)
Letter	Troilus's first letter (2.1065–85)
Letter	Criseyde's first letter (2.1219–25)
Venus	Third proem
Hymn to Love	Third proem (from *Filostrato*)
Consummation	(3.1254ff.)
Hymn to Love	Troilus's song (3.1744–71, from Boethius, 2.m.8)
Venus	Address to Venus (3.1807–13)
Ride past	Troilus rides past (5.519–60)
Canticus Troili	(5.638–44)
Dream	Troilus's dream (5.1233–41)
Letter	Troilus's last letter (5.1317–1421)
Letter	Criseyde's last letter (5.1590–1631)
Lollius	(5.1653)
Laughter	Troilus laughs from the spheres (5.1821)
Prayer	Concluding prayer (5.1863–9).

In this design the lovers' union occurs near the very centre of the total number of lines in the poem. The mid-point of the 8239 lines of *Troilus*, with its structure of rise and fall, comes at 3.1271 (the 4120th line), in a prayer by the hero praising Love for having 'me bistowed in so heigh a place'. The centre of the poem has thus been aligned with the hero's conception of the highest point of his fortune, while references to the revolving of the wheel of Fortune near the beginnings of the first and fourth books (1.138–40; 4.6–11) import the structural analogy of the arc traced by the hero's rising and falling fortunes on the rim of Fortune's wheel, with the earlier books 'ascending' and the latter two 'descending'. In the Prologue to the *Monk's Tale*, tragedy is defined as a fall (VII.1973–7), and Troilus apparently interprets his own misery comparably ('wrecche of wrecches, out of honour falle | Into miserie, in which I wol bewaille', 4.271–2). However, there are differences from the Monk's definition which point to the modified understanding of tragedy in *Troilus* (see 5.1786n.). If the nature of the end defined a medieval tragedy of fortune, the ending of *Troilus* does not match well: the personal and emotional loss that Troilus suffers through Criseyde's infidelity does not equate with a loss of worldly power or prosperity, nor does it coincide with the end of his life, and (unlike in *Filostrato*) his love for Criseyde is never said to end. Tragedy lies in the whole pattern of the poem's action, rather than in the characters of Troilus or Criseyde, and the last two books, in their poignant sense of the pathos and pity of their theme, embody a Boethian understanding of tragedy as an elegaic art of complaint and lamentation.

In *Troilus* Chaucer is among the first to use such terms as 'tragedy' and 'comedy' in English, and this reflects his readiness to experiment with a serio-comic narrative shifting 'bitwixen game and ernest' (3.254) in ways that set tragic and comic in relation to each other ('Were it a game or no, soth for to telle', 3.650). The belated classification of *Troilus* as 'litel myn tragedye' is inseparable from self-deprecating mock modesty and is at once succeeded by Chaucer's hope to write comedy (5.1786–8), even though the whole of *Troilus* has been energized by a comic sense. A terrible pathos and pity near the close receives its due in the association with tragedy, yet that is not left to stand alone and unqualified as the sole retrospect on the story. In making an end, *Troilus* presses beyond tragedy by including its hero's apotheosis to the spheres above. To follow the hero's spirit beyond death, and to show him laughing at complaint, laughing at the mourning of those he sees lamenting his death, invokes tragedy, only to redefine the concept by juxtaposing it with the comic perspective of divine comedy.

Telling Tales: Narrative and Audience

Just as Chaucer plays upon the rhythms of romance, so he relates his book to the authority of history. Medieval authors customarily presented themselves not as inventors but as interpreters of established sources, so as to invest their fictions with the authority that came with traditional associations. Chaucer twice claims to be following a fictitious author 'Lollius' (1.394; 5.1653), and in his second proem misleadingly pretends that *Troilus* is being translated from a Latin source (2.14). Lollius is included in the *House of Fame* (1465–72), along with Homer and other attested authorities on Trojan history, which suggests that Chaucer did believe there was an ancient authority on Troy called Lollius. Such a misconception may genuinely have arisen through misconstruing a line in the Roman poet Horace (see 1.394n.), yet Chaucer knew that the poem in Italian on his desk was not by the ancient author Lollius, although he may have imagined that *Filostrato* derived from his work. Like the author of the *Roman de Troyle* (a French prose translation of *Filostrato*),[23] Chaucer may possibly have thought that the Italian poem was by Petrarch, although in his *Clerk's Tale*, far from concealing his source, Chaucer would make prominent acknowledgement of Petrarch (IV.31–3), just as in his *Monk's Tale* he makes much of the name of Dante (VII.2460–62). It remains possible that Chaucer simply did not know the identity of *Filostrato*'s author, since medieval manuscripts often omit such information (but he knew its title, which he introduced as 'Philostrate', a name taken by a lover when in disguise in his *Knight's Tale*, I.1428). Boccaccio was Chaucer's principal source for three of his major poems set in pagan antiquity – *The Knight's Tale, The Franklin's Tale* and *Troilus and Criseyde* – yet Chaucer nowhere acknowledges him by name. To present *Troilus* as a translation of Lollius – a book some might have heard of but none had so far read – ostensibly pretends to be making available a major literary discovery of a lost work (and the medieval accounts of Troy already represented a series of fabrications of authority, including invented 'discoveries' of texts). It may be a spoof or a private joke (in his *Fall of Princes* Lydgate already knows that *Troilus* derives from an Italian source: 'In youthe he made a translacioun | Off a book which callid is Trophe | In Lumbard tunge, as men may reede & see'[24]), but that Chaucer so obscures and fictionalizes the nature of his indebtedness suggests how compelling it was for him to accommodate the novelty of his material with the claim to authority that medieval poets craved for their work.

Troilus consistently maintains the fiction of itself as slavishly following its ancient source, implying its undeviating subjection to that authority even where Chaucer is actually writing independently. The second proem implies that the humble author's role is restricted merely to translating from Latin, and versifying into English rhyme, the historical subject matter of his source. This fiction of dependence on sources can include some convenient suppressions of material they actually contain, especially concerning Criseyde. The source is claimed not to divulge Criseyde's age (5.826) or whether she had children (1.132–3), although *Filostrato* describes her as young and childless. It is claimed that no authority discloses how long it took before Diomede succeeded with Criseyde, and readers are challenged to check in their own libraries (5.1086–90), although the length of time in question can be calculated from Benoît's account. The imputed reticence of the source (but actually Chaucer has no source here) on what Criseyde really thought of the assurance that Troilus would not be at her uncle's house if she went there ('Nought list myn auctour fully to declare | What that she thoughte whan he seyde so', 3.575–6) only draws attention to information which becomes all the more intriguing when it is declared to be missing from the source. Nor can the

Troilus author be criticized ('How sholde I thanne a lyne of it endite?') if the source – not that Chaucer has one here in fact – has edited out certain documents from the record, like the lost letter, mentioned yet perforce unincluded (3.501–4). Chaucer invents a problem of gaps and lacunae in the supposed source to allow himself the opportunity both to raise and reject the possibility that the narrative might represent some kind of transcript of the lovers' every word and look, or could be other than a selective abridgement of the experience and time-span that it depicts (3.491–7). By the same token, the very idea that Criseyde falls in love a trifle hastily is protested against – possibly a little too much – on the grounds that only the beginning can be narrated of what was necessarily a lengthy process (2.666–79), which again only highlights, and perhaps questions, the match between narrative form and the sequence it represents. At one point (3.967–73) it is stressed that the narrative cannot claim to know why Criseyde did not do something, although it can record her actions. Yet at another point, without explaining how, the text claims to be able to include (with allowance for translation) the very words of Troilus's first song, where the source in Lollius provided only the gist (1.393–9).

Such pervasive fictionalizing of *Troilus*'s relation with its supposedly ancient source draws attention to the question of authority and its problematic nature. A professed outsider to love, the author figure disclaims any intention or ability to write about his subject matter with inside knowledge ('That of no sentement I this endite', 2.13). He apparently abjures authorial authority, or rather, he plays a game with his fictionalized audience, abdicating and sharing authority. The narrative defers to an implied audience of lovers: their knowledgeability is flattered by a narrator who presents himself as excluded from their experience and makes a play of submitting the poem's treatment of love for their expert stylistic appraisal (3.1324–36). It is a witty fiction, for a poet who ends by praying that no scribe miscopy his text in any particular and submits his work to the correction of two named contemporaries – an erudite poet and a prominent lawyer and philosopher – is not actually inviting any audience of lovers to step in and adjust the text in the light

of their experience. Nonetheless, the poem addresses its implied
audience as if recited in their presence, for *Troilus* dramatizes
within itself a distinctive concurrence of identities and deliveries.
The poem can present itself as both the written pages of a book,
which the bookish author is still in the midst of composing, and
as the script for a performance which is in the act of being
delivered. In the opening lines these identities in performance
and composition are superimposed (1.5–7), although, as the
leaves of the book accumulate, the sense of a performance gives
way rather to that of composition, and in the final book it is for
the first time an imagined solitary reader who is addressed
('Thow, redere . . .', 5.270). Any individual reading of the poem
in solitude still has the power to re-create an imagined occasion
on which the poem is recited, during which possible objections
at certain points from critical members of an audience are
anticipated in a way that prompts alertness to the authority and
appropriateness of the narrator's account ('Now myghte som
envious jangle thus', 2.666; cf. 2.12, 29–35). This layered sense
of the text as the product at once of a bookworm and a performer
allows the narrative its concurrence of well-wrought, crafted
formality with anxious immediacy and open-endedness. There
remains the paradox that in this recital of the story of a secret
love, to hear is to overhear: the narrative addresses its audience
as if including the reader or listener as an accomplice in the
action ('Us lakketh nought but that we witen wolde', 3.531), or
as if imparting confidences ('. . . the manere and the wise |
Reherce it nedeth nought, for ye ben wise', 2.916–17).

Playing Love's Game

Just as *Troilus* constructs an implied audience of sophisticatedly
knowing and discerning lovers – and thereby flatteringly associ-
ates all and any readers with such an audience – so too the
anticipated reactions of such an implied audience shape percep-
tions of how love is to be conducted in the poem. The *Filostrato*
proem had cast the poet as lover, addressing to his absent
mistress a poem about Troilus and Criseyde as an emblem of
his desolation in her absence and his longing for her return. In

the *Roman de Troie* Diomede looks forward to sleeping with Briseida, and in *Filostrato* the physical nature of the satisfaction that Troiolo foresees for his love is as evident to readers as it is to Criseida. In *Troilus*, by contrast, a prolonged process of talking, thinking and theorizing about love never acknowledges in advance a goal in physical consummation, but insists mysteriously on its sense of purpose ('For for o fyn is al that evere I telle', 2.1596). In Chaucer's poem, a narrator who disclaims any personal experience of love writes about his similarly inexperienced hero's first encounter with love, while deferring to the judgement of knowledgeable lovers quick to notice divergences from their ideas of how the art of love is to be pursued (2.22–35). The love affair between Troilus and Criseyde is conducted through the serio-comic fictions and pretences of the 'game of love'. Such 'courtly love' offered an idiom of styles and conventions, and opportunities for role-play, that could be interpreted literally, or less than wholly seriously, according to context. At one moment Pandarus seemingly commends on principle a lover's unceasingly devoted service (1.816–19), but at another he twits the prince kneeling to his lady ('Nece, se how this lord kan knele!', 3.962); he can ring the changes on the language of love as a quasi-religious observance; he can take at face value, depending on context, the fictions of the lover as sick or even dying for love.

To Pandarus all such role-play is an aspect of courtship conducted with and through style as a type of game, but what for Pandarus can be a manner of speaking, Troilus will take literally, to express the processes and aspirations of his secret life as a lover. Through the conventional idiom of love as a form of feudal service, all the striving commitment of Troilus's inner self can be given form and ceremony.[25] This is love as the diligent service Troilus promises Criseyde at their first meeting (3.143–4), and in which he sees his life fulfilling its created purpose (3.1290), although serving implies deserving and hopes for an earned reward. Such love as service remains a fictional role-reversal in the lovers' private life together – where the prince, renouncing his royal rank, swears himself his lady's vassal, and where Criseyde pointedly discounts his princely status (1.432–

4; 3.169–75) – but this only emphasizes how the poem inhabits an inward world that is remade by the lovers' imagination and desire. Here is service as an open-ended commitment within love's suffering, which is also traditionally compared with illness or even madness (1.419–20).[26] Part of the game is that love is a sickness for the lover which his lady, as if she were a kind of doctor, may heal with the medicine that is herself, as Criseyde privately acknowledges (2.1582). Some medieval medical writings did recognize the lover's malady as a form of illness, and throughout *Troilus and Criseyde* there is much play with the ambivalence of illnesses pretended and real (for example, 2.1527–30). As he waits patiently or restlessly for his lady to administer the 'cure' that is her sexual surrender, sickness represents the fretful suspense of the lover's life as a waiting game.[27] The well-worn fiction that a man might sicken and actually die for love was another of the gambits available in playing love's game, and the threat that Troilus might die is a ploy that Pandarus seemingly takes seriously in exerting pressure on Criseyde (see 2.320–22n.).[28] Yet if her circumstances dictate that Criseyde must react largely to others' moves, she does not give the impression of being an unknowing player ('It nedeth me ful sleighly for to pleie', 2.462).

Moves and role-playings are available to be taken at face value, or otherwise, by players, as by readers in this game, and this is also true of the tradition in which the lover's devotion to his lady mirrors the observance of a religious devotion. First comes conversion (1.308, 1002–8) and, after confession and repentance (1.932–8; 2.525), the lover, with the zeal of the convert, counts himself a member of a quasi-religious order of lovers and builds his hopes on salvation. Within love's game, however, the lover's salvation is at his lady's disposition, dependent on her favour (or 'grace') rather than his merits. The lover's standing with his lady is understood in terms of the Christian theology of grace (3.1261–7), while arrival at sexual fulfilment goes in parallel with allusions to entering heaven (3.704, 1204, 1251, 1322, 1599, 1657). Patterns of religious observance and doctrine function as a correlative to the devotion within a love affair, apparently identifying the rewards and fulfilments of passion with those of religious devotion, but always with the possibility that worldly, bodily passions may not sustain all that such religious parallels imply. 'Though ther be mercy writen in youre cheere, | God woot, the text ful hard is, soth, to fynde!' (3.1356–7), as Troilus exclaims to Criseyde, and that 'text' which takes the form of courtly expression, manner and demeanour can be the most equivocal to read.

Not the least playful aspect of this game of love and its fictions in *Troilus* is that there seems little practical reason for it. Such love in medieval texts has often been called 'courtly love', referring both to its intrinsic courtliness as conduct and to its context in the very unprivate social circumstances of medieval courts, where necessarily love might often be illicit and furtive. Unlike many such affairs in medieval romance, however, the love of Troilus and Criseyde offends no third party (and as ancient pagans their extra-marital affair is not directly the concern of Christian morality). There is no adultery: both lovers are single and free, and as a widow Criseyde, unlike some romance heroines, does not need to conceal her love from a disapproving family. Instead, in this story, the potential objection comes from the man's family. In versions before Chaucer, the treacherous defection of Calchas to the enemy, as well as the disparity in rank between the prince and the astrologer's daughter, had made a liaison between Troilus and Criseyde politically and socially unacceptable, and so made its secrecy a defining aspect. In *Troilus and Criseyde*, however, Criseyde's social status is much more elevated than in earlier versions: her home is called a palace (2.76, 1094; 5.523), and is luxuriously appointed (2.1228–9); she is socially accomplished and mixes easily with the Trojan royal family, by whom she is esteemed (3.211–17). In *Troilus*, the principal anxiety about secrecy stems from Criseyde's concern for her reputation, her 'name' and honour – ironically, given her subsequent notoriety as a byword for unfaithfulness.[29] The text proceeds by never explaining, as if it were self-evident, why such an affair would be hidden,[30] yet both the obsessive secrecy and the sense of ceremonious form with which the affair is conducted seem less the outcome of necessity than symptoms of how playing love's game interacts

with the lovers' characters. This is a courtly love, not because
the significant action takes place within a court, but because it
is practised through the ambivalent observances of courtli-
ness, by which Troilus as a lover can be celebrated at once for
his discretion and his consummate dissimulation (3.428–34).
Criseyde evidently fears that any wider knowledge of their secret
game will destroy society's endorsement of her, upon which her
sense of identity depends.

'Manhod' and 'Wommanhede'

Almost all reference to the 'wommanhede' and womanly aspects
of Criseyde, or to manly qualities and 'manhod' in relation to
Troilus, represent Chaucer's additions. How the lovers' be-
haviour conforms to – or conflicts with – gender stereotypes
and codes is built into the texture of Chaucer's poem about a
love affair in time of war, and sets one gender into dialogue
with another. From her very first sighting Criseyde is stressed
to be definingly and quintessentially womanly, radiating not
simply an incomparable beauty but 'wommanly noblesse'
(1.282–7); Troilus hails her as a kind of model or pattern of
womanliness (3.106, 1296), which includes gaiety and laughter
(4.866; 5.569).[31] Pandarus extols her moral virtues, her com-
passion and (apparently paradoxically) commends her to her
would-be lover Troilus precisely because of her womanly con-
cern for honour (1.888–9). The value that Criseyde sets on what
society will think of her – her honour and good name, and
hence her social identity – determines her compliance with the
exchange and eventually her loss of reputation. Yet although
antifeminist tradition had already typecast Criseyde as a loose
woman, Chaucer sets out to make this 'fallen' woman deeply
sympathetic and understandable in her nature as a woman and
in the context of the 'tresoun that to wommen hath ben do'
(2.793). Her justifiable fears and anxieties as a woman alone
express, without wholly explaining, her character: the remark-
able inward debate with herself in Book 2 about the pros and
cons of love ('Therto we wrecched wommen nothing konne, |
Whan us is wo, but wepe and sitte and thinke', 2.782–3) draws

readers closely into her stream of consciousness, while her Book 5 soliloquy conveys her anguished quandary ('And wommen moost wol haten me of alle', 5.1063). The old story cannot change its course, but Chaucer has intervened decisively in his sources so as to divide his poem's attention much more equally between Criseyde and Troilus.[32] To understand more of Criseyde's circumstances is to be more understanding of her conduct and to be more conscious of how narrative may remake the history it claims to report.

If Criseyde's defining womanliness is complemented in the poem by someone quintessentially and conventionally masculine, that person is less Troilus than Diomede, for in terms of gender there is nothing uncertain about Diomede. As soon as he sees Criseyde, and at once intuits her relationship with Troilus, Diomede sets out to try his luck with her, and that bold, assertive, competitive nature which makes him an effective warrior is translated directly into his role as a suitor. By contrast, Troilus's masculinity is placed much more at question by his experience and circumstances in the narrative. Although Troilus is a great warrior in the Trojan War, his martial identity has to be taken largely by report in Chaucer's poem, as in the melodramatic frisson of Pandarus's account to Criseyde of Troilus hunting down Greeks ('Whil that he held his blody swerd in honde', 2.203). As long as the battlefield remains off-stage, the narrative focuses on the indoor world of a private, personal life where the hero's conventional stature as a warrior stands him in little stead. A hero in his capacity to feel, his abundant emotions, although in so many ways to his great credit, paralyse him into ineffectual passivity, and hence into questionable reliance on another man's duplicitous mediation in his most intimate concerns. There is comedy in Troilus's inability to take any sexual initiative for himself and – Troilus has solemnly foresworn any more jokes about love (1.936–8) – there is some fond burlesque of the elaborate sufferings of the courtly lover, here taken to almost absurd extremes, yet perhaps all the more admirable in their idealism. Passivity and tearful languishings may try the modern reader's patience, yet in their sensitivity they are intrinsically positive, emphasizing that gentleness and considerateness by which conventional male characteristics (rawly asserted in Diomede) are modified for the better by partaking of qualities more traditionally associated with women (and which Troilus has praised in Criseyde). This Troilus is on new terrain where conventional male roles as defender, provider and initiator give him few advantages. The woman he desires is in control of her own space, resources and movements. 'I am myn owene womman' (2.750) Criseyde reminds herself: as a widow, she does not need Troilus; she can stipulate her own terms, and hence is not dependent upon him.[33]

In daring a more understanding reading of a woman already prejudged as promiscuous, *Troilus* does not evade the issue of Criseyde's sexual nature. If her uncle oversteps the mark and looks forward to the lovers' union ('Wel in the ryng than is the ruby set . . . Whan ye ben his al hool as he is youre', 2.585–7), Criseyde at once censors his innuendo with a nervous laugh, yet implies he is ruining everything by insisting on talking about it (2.589–90). The text conveys just how much she is aroused soon afterwards by the sight of Troilus, fully armed from battle, riding home past her window, the vision of a youthful conquering hero, but also a bashful one: she is attracted by the thought of his qualities and an impression of his physique, prowess and vigour. She blushes at her own thoughts (2.652), but it is 'his manhod and his pyne' (2.676), a suffering masculinity, that works an effect on her heart ('his manly sorwe to biholde | It myghte han mad an herte of stoon to rewe', 3.113–14). Concluding and silencing all Criseyde's sensible objections to a love affair comes the message of the unconscious: her dream of a male eagle (a royal creature like Troilus and white, perhaps like his innocence) tearing her heart from her breast and inserting his own, an emblem of penetration which neither frightens nor hurts her (2.925–31). Criseyde's dream is probably refashioned from the later dream in *Filostrato* (7.23–4), in turn much altered in *Troilus* (5.1233–41), in which Troiolo sees a boar (family emblem of Diomede) goring Criseida's breast with its tusks, seemingly to her enjoyment. Eagle and boar, both Criseyde's lovers are associated with fierce male animals, yet her sexual partnership with Troilus is also strikingly described as one of mutual obedience to the other's pleasure (3.1690); they repair to bed for any couple's mixture of love-making and dialogue (4.1430–35), and in her ringing commendation of the 'gentil herte and manhod' (4.1674) of Troilus on their last night together, Criseyde values his moderation in gratifying his desires ('And that youre resoun bridlede youre delit', 4.1678).

In order for anything to happen between an inexperienced Troilus and a cautious Criseyde, Chaucer developed the role of Pandarus. He becomes a stage-manager, a kind of surrogate author within the narrative: he invents a plot by arranging correspondence, meetings and transitions; he generates action from feeling, invents motivation for the characters (as in the fiction of Troilus's jealousy of Horaste: 3.792–8), and seems to see further into them than they see themselves (2.1373–9, 1506–12). Yet his material is the personal lives of other people with whom his feelings are intimately involved – his niece and a close male friend – while his own nature is curiously unresolved. The narrative provides no description of this apparently unattached man, by implication older than Troilus and Criseyde (although his age, like his appearance, remains unspecified), and full of opinions about love which have evidently not brought him personal success. Pandarus jokes about his lack of achievement in love (1.666–9); Troilus knows whom he loves (1.715–18), and Criseyde teases him about his mistress (2.98). But according to Pandarus his own failures need make him no less capable of advising others successfully: he becomes the go-between and arranger who not only brings the lovers together and contrives to introduce Troilus into Criseyde's bed, but who also seems to be present in their bedroom for much of the time (his noticed presence is more significant than his unnoticed departure). It is Pandarus who looks forward to the pleasure of not two people but three ('And so we may ben gladed alle thre', 1.994). It is Pandarus himself who both voices the questionable nature of his pandering role yet also locates that role 'bitwixen game and ernest' (3.254), something which, if serious, is only half in earnest and half in jest.

Why does Pandarus invest so much energy and go to such inordinate trouble? What is the impetus for his excited engagement, his close bodily contact with each of the lovers, his conversations with both of them after they have first made love? If it is for some kind of voyeuristic satisfaction in other people's intimacy, does that not also raise the problem of the reader's own witnessing of intimate moments? With his niece – privately, he takes a condescending view of her intelligence (2.267–73) – Pandarus is always given to bantering about love in ways that may threaten to become invasive, and only thinly disguise his underlying resolution. In a striking gesture he thrusts Troilus's letter down into her bosom when she scruples to accept it (2.1154–5), and as he feels Criseyde's interest in Troilus becoming aroused Pandarus is likened to a smith striking while the iron is hot (2.1275–6). In visiting his niece in her bedroom on the morning after her first night with Troilus, his jaunty innuendo and invasive gestures – thrusting his arm under her bedclothes, calling it a sword and inviting her to behead him – combine with an opaque narrative ('And Pandarus hath fully his entente', 3.1582) to suggest the oppressive implications of his manipulative expertise, and at least open up the possibility (unspecified and unprovable) that his interest in his niece might go beyond flirtatious banter.

Just as Pandarus visits Criseyde after the lovers' first night together, so he also visits Troilus, who now speaks directly to him about his desire ('I hadde it nevere half so hote as now', 3.1650). When Pandarus arrives, Troilus kneels to him gratefully 'with al th'affeccioun | Of frendes love that herte may devyse', 3.1590–91), so acknowledging the accomplishment of a mission whose undertaking had been marked earlier by similar body language ('Tho Troilus gan doun on knees to falle, | And Pandare in his armes hente faste', 1.1044–5). There is physical closeness between these friends: Pandarus can come by chance into Troilus's bedchamber unannounced (1.547–9); he literally tries to shake the truth out of Troilus about his love (1.869–70); he watches his friend rest after they have exercised together (2.512–18); and, unlike in *Filostrato*, Troilus and Pandarus sleep in the same room sometimes, which allows them opportunities for private conversation rare in the unprivate world that *Troilus* depicts (3.229–38). In these extensive conversations Troilus's inexperience makes him so singularly dependent on Pandarus's direction of his intimate life as to make their relationship unusual, and Troilus's rather unlikely offer to reciprocate by gaining for Pandarus any of his sisters (3.407–13) only emphasizes how their friendship involves a one-sided and unequal influence by the friend who – with inexhaustible goodwill and the closest interest and attention to detail – procures for the other. 'Brother' is how they often and affectionately address each other, in a bonding that no less implies the extent of Pandarus's feelings for his friend by focusing on Troilus's feelings for Criseyde.

Multiple perspectives, simultaneous evocation of disparate emotions, contexts and genres come together in the exploration of 'manhod' and 'wommanhede' in the consummation scene, which Chaucer has radically rewritten from *Filostrato* (where the lovers have arranged directly between themselves to spend the night together at Criseida's house). In *Troilus* Pandarus must stage-manage the meeting by means of a plot where farcical comedy underscores the point that Troilus arrives in Criseyde's bed through no initiative of his own. This scourge of the Greeks promptly falls down in a swoon when Criseyde reproves him for his unfounded jealousy, and Pandarus can seize the moment to strip and heave the unconscious Troilus into Criseyde's bed. Once the lovers reach the bedroom in *Filostrato* (3.31–2) Boccaccio has this exchange:

> They undressed and got into bed, where the lady, who still had one last piece of clothing on, asked him charmingly: 'Shall I take everything off? Newly wed brides are shy on the first night!'
>
> Troiolo responded: 'Light of my life, I beg you to – so that I may hold you naked in my arms, as my heart desires!'
>
> And she replied: 'Look how I rid myself of it!' And throwing off her shift she at once entwined herself in his arms . . .

After this, *Filostrato* simply declares that they experienced the full force of love and leaves the rest to the imagination, whereas in *Troilus* the bodily nature of love is acknowledged more fully, yet without archness or titillation in the lovers. (Archness is the male onlooker's: 'take every womman heede | To werken thus, if it comth to the neede', 3.1224–5.) Troilus's delight in exploring Criseyde's naked body is presented with no sense of anything embarrassing or shameful, but rather as something frankly natural, pleasurable and without inhibition (3.1247–53). Instead of the Italian Criseida's arch reference to the newly married (which she is not), Chaucer's English Troilus invokes Hymen, pagan god of marriage, so investing his sexual encounter with Criseyde with a quasi-matrimonial solemnity and committal (3.1258). Yet where *Filostrato* had shown only Criseida undressing for Troiolo, *Troilus* precedes this scene of the man's exploring the woman's already undressed body with the burlesque earlier scene in which it is the man who has been stripped of his clothes, but by his male best friend, and his unconscious body, passive and helplessly exposed to the gaze of others, is then wetted and chafed by Pandarus and Criseyde in their attempts to revive Troilus from his swoon. It is in this scene that both Pandarus and Criseyde query whether Troilus is acting like a man ('is this a mannes herte?', 3.1098; 'Is this a mannes game?', 3.1126). After this, Troilus's demand that Criseyde submit herself to him, and the narrative's likening of Troilus to the fierce sparrow-hawk, with Criseyde as the hapless, trembling lark caught in its talons (3.1191–2), read like curiously belated reassertions of an archetypal male role which comic context and circumstance in *Troilus* have already understood anew. To Troilus's demand ('Now yeldeth yow, for other bote is non!', 3.1208), Criseyde can calmly retort that if she hadn't already yielded she wouldn't be there, quietly making the point that her decision has already been taken on her own terms and in her own time.

If 'manhod' explores new terrain in the lovers' personal lives in the first three books, it encounters different and difficult territory after the diplomatic exchange of prisoners is agreed: Criseyde will not accept that Troilus should put their private world of love before his public role and the Trojan polity ('God forbede, | For any womman that ye sholden so!', 4.1556–7). While to Pandarus the obvious solution is for Troilus simply to assert his will and abduct Criseyde ('But manly sette the world on six and sevene', 4.622), Troilus still regards himself as bound to submit his will to Criseyde's wishes (4.172–5), and also bound to obey the law in a context already tainted by earlier abductions of women (4.547–60). Nor can he quite believe that the traditional wiles of women will rescue them ('Ye shal nat blende hym for youre wommanhede', 4.1462). His deference to his lady and to the rule of law, his discretion and self-control, bring him only endless further trials of that self-control, together with the more usually feminine role of being abandoned to helpless complaint. The poem's exceptional understanding of the nature of Criseyde as a woman is complemented by the way that her lover is understood to be a better man because his 'manhod' includes some of the qualities of 'wommanhede'.

Knowing Better

> '. . . al that evere is iknowe, it is rather comprehendid and knowen, nat aftir his strengthe and his nature, but aftir the faculte (that is to seyn, the power and the nature) of hem that knowen' (*Boece*, 5.pr.4.137–41)

A story of disappointment and betrayal in love becomes inseparable in *Troilus* from larger questions prompted by the narrative about a world where any human commitment or ideal is tested against time and change.[34] Chaucer's characters relate their experience to Fortune so prominently as to alert the reader's attention to the appropriateness of their understanding, and hence to an element of debate in the poem about love, fate and freedom, recurrently echoing the argument and phrasing of Boethius's *Consolation of Philosophy*, in a sustained dialogue between the worlds of romance and philosophical debate.[35] An enquiry into how human freedom is qualified by fallible and partial ability to know and to remember what is known – which is one of the legacies to *Troilus* of the *Consolation* – lends impetus to a fictional narrative in which the characters are disposed (rightly or wrongly) to interpret what befalls them in their lives and loves in terms of destiny, fortune and chance. The majority of Chaucer's borrowings from Boethius derive from the earlier books of the *Consolation*, and this pattern of allusion points to the limits and boundaries of the characters' understanding. In the *Consolation* a dialogue with the allegorical figure of Philosophy leads a condemned prisoner towards enlightenment and serenity: the action is in the dialogue and its spiritual and intellectual development, in which Boethius progresses by retrieving the memory of wisdom once known but forgotten. Reflections belonging in the *Consolation* to the retrospective review of a life with no certain earthly future are quoted in *Troilus* within the open-ended perspective of a romance still being lived through by its hopeful protagonists, in what develops into at once a celebration and a critique of our human loves, a sustained debate about love that informs many scenes and episodes in *Troilus*.

In that debate *Troilus* quotes from one side of the Boethian argument: the lamentations and questionings, sometimes fragmentary and taken out of context, but generally not the answers and explanations. That Troilus is disposed to see whatever happens to him as predestined, and makes fatalistic speeches, does not necessarily mean that the poem as a whole is endorsing a sternly predestinarian reading of its story. Much of what is uttered on such themes has to be weighed in context rather than taken at face value. The rhetorical eloquence of astrological references to configurations of the heavens at significant junctures in the plot (all Chaucer's additions to *Filostrato*) make space in the poem for a powerful sense of the possibility that the characters' actions are determined by planetary influences. In the orthodox medieval distinction, planetary influences incline but do not compel, although (in the medieval understanding of ancient pagan belief) the Trojan characters of *Troilus* might be predisposed to take a fatalistic view of their subjection to the stars, even if the poem's Christian readers know better.[36] The starry dimension and planetary parallels to the poem's action need not be read deterministically, yet they keep before us the mystery of possible connection. A sense of predetermined pattern coexists with the open-endedness of chance, accident and coincidence that further the action, although readers will know better that in some cases what seems like chance depends on point of view.

The story's unalterable ending in betrayal might seem to deny its characters freedom of action, yet this is not how *Troilus* reads. To give the old ending a new beginning is to rethink the freedom, consistency and predictability of characters. The fuller the poem's characterization and its focus on the characters' 'entente' and self-consciousness, the more a sense of potential autonomy is in debate with an alertness both to the fated and chance nature of events. An important difference from *Filostrato* is that Chaucer has written out of *Troilus* all the worldly wisdom that enables Boccaccio's experienced lovers to know better than to commit themselves very deeply to anything. Chaucer's poem opens with a Troilus who thinks he knows better than to fall in love, yet once he becomes a lover all his prior detachment and reason are as if forgotten, until disillusion and death teach him to know better about everything in this world. For Troilus the most acute challenge to his freedom comes with his quandary over the political deal to exchange Criseyde. It is this dilemma over whether or how to act that proves the moral pivot of the poem in its exploration of the lovers' freedom. There is irony in the representation of an individual freely arguing himself out of the freedom he actually possesses, and Troilus's soliloquy (markedly more predestinarian than its Boethian original) captures through its stylistic awkwardness the hero's sense of helplessness. That there is no Lady Philosophy to engage with Troilus as she does with Boethius and explain why he is not predestined (although Pandarus may partly impersonate her role) only serves by its onesidedness to emphasize how the characters' opinions about fortune and freedom are to be seen as partial. Troilus is shown declining to exercise the possible choices that are open to him, declining to request openly that his mistress not be exchanged, and submitting to the will of his lady a decision on whether to ambush and abduct her. Such an option he has, as a successful soldier, but chooses not to take, and this chosen inaction is very much the expression of the hero's identification with the courtly ideal of service in love. Troilus refuses to exercise 'sovereignete . . . in love' (3.171–2) over his 'lady sovereigne' (4.316); his refusal happens to be fatal, but despite all the fatalistic rhetoric presenting the hero as powerless, the poem shows Troilus – caught in a mesh of circumstantial and cultural factors – giving up choice and freedom rather than never possessing them.

In complement to this is Criseyde's concern with her own freedom of action. On balance, her Book 2 monologue suggests she knows better than to risk letting into her settled and respectable lifestyle the turmoil of a love affair, but she is overcome by a mixture of events, pressures and something in herself. In both of the bedroom interviews with Troilus she is taken advantage of, yet it is also clear that she retains some initiative, not least in the implication that she has anticipated more than – for appearances' sake – she would be prepared to admit openly. Even in the later books Criseyde resists Troilus's plans for an escape which she dreads would exclude them permanently from that social identity, honour and good name in which her sense of self has been constructed (4.1555–82). Instead she argues for trying to evade seeming necessity by stratagem and ingenuity; the tone is sceptical (4.1406–11), expressing confidence that the human will may overcome apparent necessity and be lord over fortune (4.1587–9). Inventing futures and foreseeing escapes, her speech is the antithesis of the hero's despairing fatalism. With whatever mistaken confidence, Criseyde determines to choose her own way of reconciling the demands of love, secrecy and her reputation with a willed acquiescence in the outward necessity to go to the Greek camp. The collapse of her inward resolve to act so as to get the better of circumstance is poignantly accompanied by the recognition of necessity by both Criseyde and Troilus in the fifth book. Here she admits and repents her miscalculation, lamenting human inability to foresee the future (5.743–9). In a curious play with time the narrative looks forward to her foreknown betrayal without precisely including the moment it occurred, so that Criseyde's abandonment of Troilus, like her earlier decision to submit to him (3.1210–11), remains mysteriously outside the narrative and beyond its power to know or explain.

Characteristically, Chaucer frames the lovers' tendency to see their lives in relation to the workings of fortune by the way in which the narrative through its own processes explores the theme of freedom and predestination. All the play made about 'myn auctour' only adds to the sense that a form of predestination is being illustrated through the poem's claims to be subject to its sources, yet all the while the narratorial frame and the management of the reader's response is designed to dramatize the coexistence of freedom and constraint. The narrating voice of *Troilus* grows fondly, even foolishly, involved with his material, sharing the language and seemingly the aims and values of the lovers, and of Pandarus too. Such narratorial engagement and partiality can become a surrogate for the audience's identification with the lovers, both inhabiting their point of view and knowing better, forgetful of the known ending until inevitably it makes itself felt. Yet the old story's end is already established and in its outward events unalterable, so that the future of Troilus and Criseyde is foreknown and, as it were, predestined. That the reader knows (as past) what is future (and therefore unknown) to the characters effectively puts the reader in God's place. Indeed, it might be argued that the whole poem is a dramatization or practical example of that debate between Philosophy and the prisoner that Troilus uses for his soliloquy, as to whether the author's, or reader's, or onlooker's knowing a thing to be true – whether present, past or future – necessitates its happening.

'Th'ende is every tales strengthe'

Translated to the skies after death, Troilus knows better at last. All the poem's imagery of sight and blindness culminates in his moment of vision from on high, a bold emblem of the insight that experience in the poem brings both hero and reader. The pagan lover's spirit rises above limited earthly understanding, so as to gain a perspective on love in this world that his soul can only have merited by its power of loving. Only in a love for God – truth and reality itself, beyond time and change – may the aspirations of the human power to love be fulfilled, and the rest and peace found in God can make 'love celestial' both spiritually and aesthetically an apt point of resolution and renewal at the poem's close. The story's setting in pagan antiquity allows all the joyful potential in human love to be explored to the full, while the poem's ending can look back on that past love's ultimate limitations, without needing to press a moral or pass judgement on pagan lovers. To open up spiritual perspectives without condemnation of individuals: such is the openness of approach, and charity of spirit, that the ending commends not by injunction but in a question ('And syn he best to love is, and most meke, | What nedeth feynede loves for to seke?', 5.1847–8).[37]

Yet a conclusion to *Troilus* that not only spurns the Trojan world of its story but also urges its audience to turn to the love of God, in a seeming renunciation of the love of Troilus and Criseyde, has challenged and pained many modern readers. Disappointed or not, some readers accept that, in concluding, *Troilus* reverts to a more conventionally 'medieval' and ortho- dox approach to the pagan past and to the enjoyment of sexual love than prevails in the body of the narrative, as prior illusions are disabused in hero, narrator and reader. A shift of perspective and transference of allegiance convey the exaltation of resurgent devotion, with all the momentum of a journey home and a reaffirmation. For other modern readers, it is this very reversion into conventionality of sentiment (after a poem that has explored the limits of convention), and a moral assertiveness at variance with the narrative technique earlier in the poem, that allow such an ending to be regretted and disregarded as some- thing more prescribed by his culture than made by the poet. Another view, by contrast, insists on unity between poem and ending whereby the other-worldly dimension to the conclusion has always been implicit, by means of irony, throughout the presentation of a love affair that announces its doleful end in its beginning. Yet however much the ending may become implicit through a cumulative structure of ironies in the narrative, it retains its power to surprise. Boccaccio could close *Filostrato* smartly with advice for young men to beware of women (before sending the poem to his mistress with a graceful envoy), but Chaucer attempts something more complex and more com- passionate.

Of its nature the story of Troilus and Criseyde offered no

single event to serve as a climactic ending: the precise moment when Criseyde forsakes Troilus is occluded by a chivalrous narrative; the end of Troilus is not synchronized with his betrayal by Criseyde, and he lingers on in anguish; his death in battle, reported in a single line, is something of an anticlimax; nor did tradition as yet specify the end of Criseyde (although the fifteenth-century Scottish poet Robert Henryson would later invent one in his *Testament of Cresseid*). As he neared the point of Troilus's death, Chaucer faced the challenge of finding a conclusion not only to a story line that faded away like the reciprocal love it chronicled, but also to the abundance of implication invested in his narrative. If the story ended mutedly without climax, might there be a climax to the poem, a climax of interpretation and understanding? Endings of story and poem in *Troilus* become distinct: the performative quality of the closing stanzas dramatizes the problematic process of making an ending, so that the artifice makes the conclusion. The variety and flurry of closural devices represents both an attempt at comprehensiveness and an uncertain accumulation of alternatives. Here is a professedly selective account, and readers are referred elsewhere to 'Dares' or 'other bokes' for alternative readings of Troilus's career or Criseyde's guiltiness (5.1765–78), but in closing its version of Troilus and Criseyde (and Pandarus) the text defies traditional interpretation, identifying itself with betrayed women, and bids them 'Beth war of men . . . !' (5.1779–85). Here the text is retrospectively aligned with tragedy and, even while cast as humbly following in the footsteps of the greatest classical poets, it makes a proud claim for itself that could be made for no contemporary English poem (5.1786–92). Yet its writerly concerns about miscopying and misunderstanding reflect a larger unease over interpretation (5.1793–8), pressing in even before the hero's death is reported and his soul's ascent to the spheres. Here is a succession of different endings that denies any single vantage-point from which the poem is to be explained as a whole.[38]

If 'th'ende is every tales strengthe' (2.260) as Pandarus declares, the 'strengthe' of the ending of *Troilus* lies in its continuing capacity to prompt questions about the ends and design of the poem. 'By his contrarie is every thyng declared' (1.637), as Pandarus remarks to Troilus, and in continuing 'Ech set by other, more for other semeth' (1.643), he enunciates what may be seen as one of the informing principles of contrast and interrelation in *Troilus*, in which at last 'of two contraries is o lore' (1.645). Not least because of Pandarus, facilitator and wordsmith, the impetus of the narrative often lies in dialectic: alternatives are ever in debate. To accumulate so many possibilities for interpretation discovers a wholeness in the poem more through inclusion than exclusion, more in process than in product. A juxtaposition of contrasts and antitheses in continuing debate typifies the structure and poetic texture of *Troilus* to the end; in juxtaposition one element modifies and is seen in relation to another, promoting a kind of multiconsciousness in which any interpretation of the text must necessarily be offset by its opposite or contain its contrary within itself. Seen in this light, the poem's ending offers a final retrospect yet not necessarily a total view. Indeed, if the poem's celebration of love in this world were simply gainsaid by its prayerful conclusion, *Troilus* might not have been revoked, along with other works, as a 'worldly vanitee' (in the 'Retractation' at the close of *The Canterbury Tales*). 'Ye knowe ek that in forme of speche is chaunge | Withinne a thousand yeer . . .' (2.22–3), and if it is the ending's rhetoric of timeless verities that now may seem to exemplify the poem's earlier lesson about cultural change over time, this only serves to pose afresh the questions always implicit in the intensity of love's joy and pain in the 'double sorwe' of Troilus and Criseyde:

> for of thinges that han ende may ben maked comparysoun, but of thynges that ben withouten ende to thynges that han ende may be makid no comparysoun (*Boece*, 2.pr.7.106–9).

NOTES

1   Dares Phrygius, in Meister 1873; Dictys Cretensis, in Eisenhut 1958; both translated in Frazer 1966.

2   Joseph of Exeter, in Gompf 1970; translated in Roberts 1970.

3   Benoît de Sainte-Maure, in Constans 1904–12. For extracts, see
     Gordon 1934 and Havely 1980.
4   For the verse letter from Azalais d'Altier to Clara d'Anduza, see
     Crescini 1890.
5   Guido de Columnis, in Griffin 1936; translated in Meek 1974.
     Cf. also Benson 1980.
6   Jean de Chambrillac, in Raynaud 1905: 203–4:

> Bien ay oÿ de Troÿluz
> Le beau, le preux de hault pouoir,
> Qui a Brisaÿda fu druz,
> Ne d'autre amer n'ot nul vouloir.
> Le bien qu'il en pot recevoir
> Fu qu'il demoura sans amie;
> Car quant de Troie fu partie,
> Dyomèdes en fu saisiz:
> Sa dame fu, il ses amis.
> Cela m'aprent que je m'atieigne
> Qu'en lieu seul soit mon cuer assiz;
> Je ne creing pas que mal m'en vieigne.

7   *Il Filostrato*, in Branca 1964– : vol. 2; translated in Havely
     1980.
8   See Wendy Childs, 'Anglo-Italian Contacts in the Fourteenth
     Century', in Boitani 1983: 65–87:

> Surviving customs accounts give us the names of twenty-nine
> Italians Chaucer certainly met trading through London in 1380–1
> and 1384–5 as they were wool-exporters for whom he sealed cockets
> [customs certificates] at the custom house ... the twenty-nine
> included at least seven Florentines, five Lucchese, three Venetians,
> two Genoese, two from Pistoia and one from Bologna.

9   See A Table of Parallels.
10   See Wright 1985: 14–15: 'There then he built his city and called
     it Troia Nova. It was known by this name for long ages after,
     but finally by a corruption of the word it came to be called
     Trinovantum.' See also Clark 1981: 135–51.
11   See Gower's *Confessio amantis*, prologue 37* and *Vox clamantis*,
     1.993–6, in Macaulay 1899–1902: vols. 2 and 4, and Stockton
     1962; for Richard of Maidstone, see Wright 1838: 31, 32, 35. On
     Brembre's ambitions, see the chroniclers Thomas Walsingham,

Historia Anglicana, in Riley 1863–4: 2:174, and Henry Knighton, in Martin 1995: 500–501.

12 *Liber Albus*, in Riley 1861: 54.

13 Thomas Usk, *The Testament of Love*, in Skeat 1897: 123.

14 Walsingham, in Riley 1863–4: 2.126 ('maxima regnorum commotio').

15 For discussion of the date of *Troilus and Criseyde*, see Kittredge 1909; Lowes 1908; McCall and Rudisill 1959; O'Connor 1956; Robertson 1985; Tatlock 1935.

16 On rhyme royal, see Metre and Versification.

17 In *An Apologie for Poetrie* (1581) Sir Philip Sidney declared:

> Chaucer undoubtedly did excellently in hys *Troylus and Cresseid*; of whom, truly I know not, whether to mervaile more, either that he in that mistie time, could see so clearly, or that wee in this cleare age, walke so stumblingly after him. Yet had he great wants, fitte to be forgiven, in so reverent antiquity.

However, John Dryden's influential praise of Chaucer in the Preface to his *Fables* (1700), in which he has little to say of *Troilus*, decisively shifted the basis for appreciation of Chaucer towards *The Canterbury Tales*.

18 The final Latin explicit ('Here ends the Book of Troilus and Criseyde') is attested by half the manuscripts that include the poem's ending (see 5.1869n.), but may not be authorial. In his 'Retractation' at the close of *The Canterbury Tales* Chaucer refers to 'the book of Troilus' (X.1085–6), and in his short poem to his scribe, *Adam Scriveyn*, Chaucer calls it simply 'Troylus'. It is John Lydgate (in his *Fall of Princes* of 1431–8) who claims Chaucer entitled the poem 'Troilus and Criseyde': 'And in our vulgar, longe or that he deide, | Gaff it the name off Troilus & Cresseide' (Bergen 1924–7: Prologue, 286–7). In his 1517 edition Wynkyn de Worde entitles the poem: 'The noble and amerous auncyent hystory of Troylus and Cresyde in the tyme of the syege of Troye. Compyled by Geffraye Chaucer.'

19 For Chaucer at work on his Boccaccio source, see the text of *Troilus and Criseyde* in parallel with *Il Filostrato*, in Windeatt 1984. Cf. also Lewis 1932 and Meech 1959.

20 In some *Troilus and Criseyde* manuscripts marginal glosses, signalling speakers' names and beginnings of speeches, reflect contemporary readers' sense of the poem's markedly dialogic texture. MS H5 (see List of Manuscripts) adds speakers' names in the

margin by their speeches as at these points: 1.568, 'Troylus'; 1.582–3, 'Pander'; 1.596–7, 'Troylus'; 1.617, 'Pandare'; 1.820, 'Troylus'; 1.829, 'Pandarus'; 1.834, 'Troylus'; 1.841, 'Pandarus'. In H4 speech units and dialogue are also often highlighted by marginal commentary, e.g. at 4.827, 'Verba Cressaidis P.'; 4.1527, 'Responsio .C.'; 5.218–19, 'Verba T. in absentia C.' S1 also contains much signalling of speakers by marginal notes.

21 In addition to the rubrics for songs and letters which probably derive from the poet, manuscript glosses also reveal contemporary interest in identifying lyric units (see 1.653–8n.; 5.295n.).

22 Some manuscripts' marginal commentaries pick up on the incidence of complaint, e.g. at 1.547, 'How Pandar fond Troilus compleynyng' (R); 2.526, 'How Pandar tolde Crisseide that Troilus pleind to love' (R); 4.260, 'Here maketh Troylus his compleynt upon fortune' (S1); 4.729, 'How Cresseyde compleynyd for she shuld departe oute of Troye' (R); 4.743, 'lamentacio .C.' (H4 Ph S2); 5.1674, 'Nota bene de Troily how he complenit' (S1).

23 *Le Roman de Troyle*, in Moland and d'Hericault 1858. The text is of uncertain date but has been attributed to the fifteenth century. On Chaucer's possible use of a French translation of *Filostrato*, see Hanly, 1990.

24 Lydgate, *Fall of Princes*, in Bergen 1924–7: Prologue, 283–5.

25 For love as 'service' in *Troilus and Criseyde*, see 1.427, 468; 2.678–9, 838–40, 1150–51; 3.440–41, 1288, 1815.

26 For the theme of Troilus's sickness and healing, see also 1.1087–91; 2.571, 1066, 1527–30, 1582. For some references to madness, not in *Filostrato*, see 1.499; 3.793–4; 4.230, 238, 348, 917, 1539; 5.206, 1213. Cf. also Green 1979, Beecher and Ciavolella 1990, Wack 1990.

27 Notions of love as sickness and the lady as its physician are at least as old as this Ancient Egyptian poem of around 1300 BC, cited in Dronke 1968:1.10:

> I shall lie down at home
> As though I were ill.
> Then my neighbours will come in to see me,
> And my beloved will be with them.
> She will make the doctors unnecessary,
> For she knows my malady.

28 When Shakespeare's Rosalind makes light of the convention of

dying for love, Troilus is her first example: 'The poor world is almost six thousand years old, and in all this time there was not any man died in his own person, videlicet, in a love-cause. Troilus had his brains dashed out with a Grecian club, yet he did what he could to die before, and he is one of the patterns of love ... Men have died from time to time and worms have eaten them, but not for love' (*As You Like It*, IV.i.89–103).

29 On Criseyde's concern with her honour, see especially 2.470–80, 703–7, 738, 760–63; 3.159–66, 943–4; 4.1328–9, 1665–6; 5.1058–66, 1077; and also 1.888–9; 4.159, 564–71.

30 From its inception love is associated with secrecy and concealment: see 1.322, 329, 354, 379–85, 488–91, 581, 744.

31 For some other references (not in *Filostrato*) to Criseyde's womanly qualities, see 3.1302, 1740; 5.244, 473, 577.

32 For Chaucer's more equal attention to both Troilus and Criseyde, see notes to 2.78–595, 813–931, 1093, 4.1369, 1667–87, 5.1100.

33 For other references to Troilus's manhood, masculinity and manly behaviour, see 2.1263; 3.428, 1098, 1126; 4.529, 622, 1674; 5.30.

34 On time in *Troilus and Criseyde*, see 1.156n.; on commitment to life-long devotion, see 1.468, 536–7; 3.1607; 4.677, 1680.

35 For the absence from some *Troilus and Criseyde* manuscripts of Troilus's Boethian song (3.1744–71), his soliloquy on predestination (4.953–1085), and his soul's ascent to the spheres (5.1807–27), see A Note on the Text.

36 For references in *Troilus and Criseyde* to pagan belief, custom and worship, generally not in *Filostrato*, see 1.153, 162–4; 2.372–3; 3.383–4, 539–46; 4.946–52, 1401–11; 5.302–22; for some references to classical deities, often explained within the text, see 2.77, 435–6, 443; 4.22–5, 1079–82, 1116–17, 1149.

37 T. S. Eliot, reviewing R. K. Root's edition of *Troilus* in *The Times Literary Supplement* of 19 August 1926, reflected the twentieth-century's renewed attention to *Troilus* ('The centre for critical judgment of Chaucer is not the Prologue to the *Canterbury Tales* ... but decidedly *Troilus and Criseyde*') as well as his own interest in Chaucer as a medieval Catholic and European poet like Dante:

> For Chaucer's religious attitude is implicit nowhere more than throughout the poem of *Troilus* ... [T]he eventual elevation of the soul of Troilus to the eighth sphere ... is not, as it may appear to

many readers, simply the hurried combination of a tired story-teller aided by conventional piety. Troilus is not hoisted to heaven in a machine; his ascent is an explicit and required statement of the sense of the whole poem.

38 In her 'The Pastons and Chaucer', in *The Common Reader* (1925), Virginia Woolf remarked of Chaucer (McNeillie 1994: 31):

> Questions press upon him; he asks questions, but he is too true a poet to answer them; he leaves them unsolved, uncramped by the solution of the moment, and thus fresh for the generations that come after him.

Further Reading

Aers, David, *Chaucer, Langland, and the Creative Imagination* (London, 1980), ch. 5.

—, *Community, Gender and Individual Identity* (London, 1988), ch. 3.

Barney, Stephen A. (ed.), *Chaucer's 'Troilus': Essays in Criticism* (London, 1980).

Benson, C. David, *Chaucer's 'Troilus and Criseyde'* (London, 1990).

— (ed.), *Critical Essays on Chaucer's 'Troilus and Criseyde' and his Major Early Poems* (Milton Keynes, 1991).

Bishop, Ian, *Chaucer's 'Troilus and Criseyde': A Critical Study* (Bristol, 1981).

Boitani, Piero (ed.), *Chaucer and the Italian Trecento* (Cambridge, 1983).

— (ed.), *The European Tragedy of Troilus* (Oxford, 1989).

Boitani, P. and Mann, J. (eds.), *The Cambridge Chaucer Companion* (Cambridge, 1986), chs. 2, 4, 5, 13.

Brewer, Derek, *A New Introduction to Chaucer* (2nd edn; Harlow, 1998).

Burnley, J. D., *Chaucer's Language and the Philosophers' Tradition* (Cambridge, 1979).

Davenport, W. A., *Chaucer: Complaint and Narrative* (Cambridge, 1988), ch. 6.

David, Alfred, *The Strumpet Muse: Art and Morals in Chaucer's Poetry* (London, 1976), ch. 2.

Dinshaw, Carolyn, *Chaucer's Sexual Poetics* (Madison, WI, 1989), ch. 1.

Donaldson, E. Talbot, *Speaking of Chaucer* (London, 1970), chs. 4, 5, 6.

Fleming, John V., *Classical Imitation and Interpretation in Chaucer's 'Troilus'* (Lincoln, Nebr., 1990).

Gordon, I., *The Double Sorrow of Troilus* (Oxford, 1970).

Hansen, Elaine Tuttle, *Chaucer and the Fictions of Gender* (Los Angeles, 1992), ch. 6.

Havely, Nicholas (trans.), *Chaucer's Boccaccio* (Cambridge, 1980).

Kelly, Henry Ansgar, *Love and Marriage in the Age of Chaucer* (Ithaca, NY, 1975).

—, *Ideas and Forms of Tragedy from Aristotle to the Middle Ages* (Cambridge, 1993).

—, *Chaucerian Tragedy* (Cambridge, 1996).

Knight, Stephen, *Geoffrey Chaucer* (Oxford, 1986), ch. 2.

Lawton, David, *Chaucer's Narrators* (Cambridge, 1985), ch. 4.

McAlpine, Monica E., *The Genre of 'Troilus and Criseyde'* (Ithaca, NY, 1978).

Mann, Jill, *Feminizing Chaucer* (Woodbridge, 2002).

Margherita, Gail, *The Romance of Origins: Language and Sexual Difference in Middle English Literature* (Philadelphia, PA, 1994), ch. 5.

Martin, Priscilla, *Chaucer's Women: Nuns, Wives and Amazons* (2nd edn; Basingstoke, 1996), ch. 9.

Mehl, Dieter, *Geoffrey Chaucer: An Introduction to his Narrative Poetry* (Cambridge, 1986), ch. 6.

Muscatine, Charles, *Chaucer and the French Tradition* (Berkeley, 1957), ch. 5.

Nolan, Barbara, *Chaucer and the Tradition of the Roman Antique* (Cambridge, 1992).

Patterson, Lee, *Chaucer and the Subject of History* (London, 1991), ch. 2.

Pearsall, Derek, *The Life of Geoffrey Chaucer: A Critical Biography* (Oxford, 1992).

Salter, Elizabeth, *English and International: Studies in the Literature, Art and Patronage of Medieval England*, ed. D. Pearsall and N. Zeeman (Cambridge, 1988), chs. 10, 11, 15.

Salu, Mary (ed.), *Essays on 'Troilus and Criseyde'* (Cambridge, 1979).

Shoaf, R. A. (ed.), *Chaucer's* Troilus and Criseyde*: 'Subgit to alle Poesye': Essays in Criticism* (Binghamton, NY, 1992).

Spearing, A. C., *Chaucer: 'Troilus and Criseyde'* (London, 1976).

—, *Readings in Medieval Poetry* (Cambridge, 1987), ch. 5.

—, *The Medieval Poet as Voyeur* (Cambridge, 1993).

Strohm, Paul, *Social Chaucer* (Cambridge, MA, 1989)

Taylor, Karla, *Chaucer reads 'The Divine Comedy'* (Stanford, CA, 1989), chs. 2 and 3.

Wetherbee, Winthrop, *Chaucer and the Poets: An Essay on 'Troilus and Criseyde'* (Ithaca, NY, 1984).

Wimsatt, James I., *Chaucer and his French Contemporaries* (Toronto, 1991).

Windeatt, Barry, *The Oxford Guides to Chaucer: 'Troilus and Criseyde'* (Oxford, 1992; repr. 1995).

— (trans.), *'Troilus and Criseyde': A New Translation* (Oxford, 1998).

Wood, Chauncey, *The Elements of Chaucer's 'Troilus'* (Durham, NC, 1984).

List of Manuscripts

A Additional MS 12044, British Library. Fifteenth-century vellum manuscript written in two hands, containing only *TC*.

Cl Pierpont Morgan Library MS M.817 (The Campsall MS). Early fifteenth-century decorated vellum manuscript, containing only *TC*, with a border decoration including the arms of Henry V while Prince of Wales, i.e. before 1413. (See Krochalis 1986.)

Cp Corpus Christi College, Cambridge, MS 61. Early fifteenth-century vellum manuscript containing only *TC*; remarkable frontispiece picture and spaces for other illustrations never executed (see Parkes and Salter 1978; Hardman 1997); possibly commissioned for Charles d'Orléans, held prisoner in England 1415–40 after his capture at Agincourt (Scott 1996: 2.182–5).

Dg MS Digby 181, Bodleian Library. Late fifteenth-century paper manuscript, containing a fragment of *TC* (ends, mid-page, at 3.532) in a miscellany of other poems by Chaucer, Hoccleve, Lydgate and others.

D University Library, Durham, Cosin MS V.II.13. Fifteenth-century vellum manuscript, containing *TC*, Hoccleve's *Letter of Cupid*, and another short poem.

Gg Cambridge University Library MS Gg.4.27. Early fifteenth-century vellum manuscript, containing *TC* (lacks openings and endings of some books), along with a miscellaneous collection of Chaucer's works and Lydgate's *Temple of Glass*. (See Parkes and Beadle 1979–80.)

H1 MS Harley 2280, British Library. Fifteenth-century vellum manuscript, containing only *TC*.

H2 MS Harley 3943, British Library. Fifteenth-century vellum manuscript written in four hands, containing only *TC*.

H3 MS Harley 1239, British Library. Mid-fifteenth-century vellum manuscript written in three hands, containing *TC* and selections from *The Canterbury Tales*.

H4 MS Harley 2392, British Library. Fifteenth-century paper and vellum manuscript, containing only *TC*.

H5 MS Harley 4912, British Library. Fifteenth-century vellum manuscript, containing only an incomplete copy of *TC* (ends at 4.686).

J St John's College, Cambridge, MS L.1. Mid-fifteenth-century vellum manuscript, containing *TC* and (in a sixteenth-century hand) Henryson's *Testament of Cresseid*. (See Beadle and Griffiths 1983.)

Ph Huntington Library HM 114 (formerly Phillipps MS 8252). Early fifteenth-century paper and vellum manuscript, containing *TC* and a collection of verse and prose. (See Hanna 1989.)

R MS Rawlinson Poet. 163, Bodleian Library. Fifteenth-century paper manuscript written in four hands, containing only *TC* and the unique copy of Chaucer's *To Rosemounde*.

S1 MS Arch. Selden. B.24, Bodleian Library. Late fifteenth-century paper manuscript; contains *TC* along with a miscellany of English and Scottish verse, including the unique copy of *The Kingis Quair*. *TC* probably copied *c.* 1488 by the Scottish scribe James Gray, protégé of Henry Sinclair, 3rd Earl of Orkney, whose arms appear after the colophon of *TC*. (See Boffey and Edwards 1997.)

S2 MS Arch. Selden Supra 56, Bodleian Library. Paper manuscript containing only *TC*; dated in the colophon to 1441.

References to no longer extant MSS of *TC*: in a 1487 inventory of the Duke of Burgundy's possessions at Brussels (Hammond 1911); in an inventory, not later than 1479, of books belonging to John Paston II (Davis 1971: 517).

Early editions:

Cx Caxton's edition (*c.* 1483); apparently only lightly edited; possibly printed, with little or no collation with other

manuscripts, from a lost manuscript related to the R+ tra-
dition.

W Wynkyn de Worde's edition (1517); after 1.546 a reprint of
Cx, but up to 1.546 W reproduces a now-lost manuscript of
the Ph+ tradition.

Th Thynne's edition (1532); based on some collation of manu-
scripts, in addition to Cx; generally a corrected text of the
Cp+ type, with some agreements with Ph+ in Book 1.
(For R+, Ph+ and Cp+, see A Note on the Text.)

A Note on the Text

No autograph copies of *Troilus and Criseyde* survive, nor were any of the sixteen extant manuscripts written before the early decades of the fifteenth century, at least twenty or thirty years after the time of the poem's composition. The manuscripts fall into three groups defined by shared scribal errors, and a number of manuscripts hold throughout the poem with one group (called 'γ', or Cp+, because the Corpus manuscript is one of those in this group). The other two manuscript groups are usually termed 'α' and 'β', or Ph+ and R+ respectively, after the Phillipps and Rawlinson manuscripts, which in each case are the sole manuscripts to hold consistently with these groups throughout the poem. The text has not been seriously corrupted, but scribal confusions may have transmitted in edited form the difficulties in Chaucer's working copy (or copies) of his poem.[1]

The principal differences between the manuscripts fall into three categories:

1. omission by the Ph+ manuscripts of three 'philosophical' passages: Troilus's Boethian song (3.1744–71) and 'predestination' soliloquy (4.953–1085), and his ascent to the spheres (5.1807–27);

2. variants in the Ph+ manuscripts which are closer to the parallel Italian lines in Chaucer's main narrative source, Boccaccio's *Filostrato*, while the other manuscripts also have apparently authentic versions of the same lines;

3. other variations between manuscript groupings over several possibly authentic versions of the same line.

What the three 'philosophical' passages have in common is that they are extracts closely translated from sources other than

Chaucer's main source, *Il Filostrato*, and are all incorporated at points in *Troilus* where Chaucer is following *Filostrato* closely. This suggests that their absence from some manuscripts may go back to the processes of the poem's composition. Troilus's song and the ascent to the spheres are both passages interpolated between two successive and closely translated *Filostrato* stanzas, while the 18-stanza predestination soliloquy is actually interpolated into the middle of a single *Filostrato* stanza (4.109). In all three contexts (which show signs of subsequent scribal editing and conflation) it would be possible, even likely, that the poet's working draft did not read on completely smoothly from his main *Filostrato*-derived narrative to any such incorporated passage and back again. Such passages might have been put together separately from the work on *Filostrato* and then perhaps added physically to the main draft on extra slips marked for inclusion, always with the possibility of scribal misinterpretation and omission.[2] The three 'philosophical' passages were manifestly 'added' to *Troilus* (in common with numerous other passages) in the sense that they do not derive from *Filostrato*, but whether their absence from some manuscripts means that they were added significantly later in the poem's existence than its composition process remains an open question. Authorial revision through distinct versions is not clearly indicated by the manuscripts, whose history needs to be distinguished from the possible history of the poem. Whether or not Chaucer intended his poem to have any completed, published existence without the predestination soliloquy, his devoted admirer Thomas Usk (executed, 4 March 1388) had already absorbed the Boethian qualities of *Troilus* into his *Testament of Love*, where he evidently refers to 4.953–1085. Indeed, without this soliloquy, which so affects the overall philosophical tone of the whole poem, there would have been rather less aptness in Chaucer's submitting the poem for correction to 'philosophical Strode' (5.1857), a form of dedication present in all extant manuscripts.

If the absence of the 'philosophical' passages from the Ph+ manuscripts derives from some scribal interpretations of Chaucer's working copy, this is also the likely origin of the survival in those manuscripts of sporadic variants (mostly

confined to single lines or even single words) which more closely
resemble the parallel lines in Chaucer's Italian source than the
different (but evidently authentic) versions of the lines in other
Troilus manuscripts. Several lines in Books 1 and 4 are among
the more striking cases (see notes to 1.83, 85; 4.247), and it is
in these books, where Chaucer is often working most closely
from the Italian, that other cases cluster (see notes to 1.111,
169; 4.258, 590, 596, 820, 882, 906; cf. also notes to 3.1482;
4.290, 318, 724). Few such variants in Ph+ affect character or
event (but see notes to 4.590, 596, 820); a few are more Latinate
(e.g. 4.37, 1218), and in one rare case of variation extending
over more than a single line, a stanza (4.750–56) is copied
in Ph+ in a sequence corresponding to the parallel stanzas in
Filostrato, while all other manuscripts have the stanzas in a
different, but equally authentic, ordering.

Overall, however, most readings of the Ph+ group may be
explained as deriving from characteristic scribal error,[3] as may
the variant readings that differentiate the other two *Troilus*
manuscript groups, Cp+ and R+. Although Cp+ and R+ gener-
ally agree in the course of the poem as against Ph+, in a limited
run of variants in Book 3 Cp+ and Ph+ agree as against R+.
With a few of these R+ variants – notably at 3.1324–37, 1392–
3 and 1438–9 – there will be room for argument as to which
version of the lines, or both, may be authentic, although the
larger run of R+ readings through the poem may be explained
as scribal in origin. In sum, the *Troilus* manuscript groups
do not represent distinct authorial versions, and the text of
Chaucer's poem has to be established in each line by weighing
the manuscript evidence in accordance with the editorial prin-
ciple of preferring the harder reading in the context of observ-
able patterns of characteristic scribal error.

Cp+ is the group with the firmest identity and with the largest
number of early manuscripts that maintain a consistent metri-
cality within a broader accuracy. It is significant that Cl, the
copy made before 1413 for the future Henry V, is of the Cp+
type, and that those who planned a magnificent illuminated
copy of *Troilus*, the Corpus MS itself, also chose this textual
tradition. One of the earliest extant examples of the *Troilus*

text, a single-leaf fragment now at Hatfield House (Campbell 1958) is not only of the Cp+ type but was written by the same scribe who copied both the Ellesmere and Hengwrt MSS, the two earliest and most authoritative texts of *The Canterbury Tales* (Doyle and Parkes 1978: 170). That a scribe who had access to *Canterbury Tales* texts very closely linked to Chaucer should use a text of the Cp+ type in copying *Troilus* offers a notable endorsement of the contemporary status of that text.

The text in this edition is based on the three best manuscripts of the Cp+ tradition, Cp, Cl and H1, together with the very good early copy J, the best manuscript that is not of the Cp+ group. Cp has been used as copy-text, emended as necessary for sense and metre from one or more of the other three manuscripts. Divergences by one or more of these four manuscripts from the others are not generally recorded in the notes, which do, however, record where a substantive reading in the text is not based on one or more of these four authorities. The metrical principles governing editorial emendation are set out in Metre and Versification, and the notes do not record emendations for metrical reasons of the text found in these four manuscripts which involve characterizable scribal error.[4] Most Ph+ readings which appear closer to *Filostrato* are recorded in the notes (but for a corpus of variants, see Windeatt 1984).

The text has not been modernized except in the following details. *I/J*, *i/j*, *U/V* and *u/v* have been normalized according to modern practice, and initial *ff* appears as *F* or *f*. Abbreviations and contractions are silently expanded. Obsolete letter forms have been modernized: *yogh* is represented as *gh* or *y* or final *z*, and *thorn* is represented as *th*. Capitalization, word-division and punctuation (including diacritical marks) are editorial.

NOTES

1   On the textual problems of *Troilus*, see Root 1916; Brewer 1981; Hanna 1984, 1992; Windeatt 1979a, 1984, 1992: 12–36.

2   See also 2.1750n. The lines immediately before Troilus's first song (itself derived from a Petrarch sonnet and interpolated into Chaucer's *Filostrato*-based narrative) seem to acknowledge an

inset status which the song may have had, literally, in Chaucer's working copy: '. . . and whoso list it here, | Loo, next this vers he may it fynden here' (1.398–9).

3   There is, for example, almost always something unsatisfactory about Ph+ variants involving classical allusions:

Ph+ 'wight' for 'Furie', 1.9; Ph+ omit 'Palladion', 1.164; Ph+ 'Sisyphus' for 'Ticius', 1.786; Ph+ 'the god' for 'Apollo', 3.543; Ph+ 'god' for 'Mars', 4.25; Ph+ omit 'Edippe', 4.300; Ph+ 'any aungel' for 'Jove', 4.644; Ph+ 'Ther Pluto regneth' for 'That highte Elisos', 4.790.

4   Such errors would include unmetrical readings caused by:

presence or absence of final -n in verbal inflections, infinitives, past participles, and words such as 'bitwixe(n' and 'withoute(n' (e.g. 2.1617: myghten] myghte Cp; 5.1618: Comen] Come Cp; 3.995: founde] founden Cp; 2.1280: Withoute] Withouten Cp; 5.856: Bitwixe] Bitwixen Cp);

presence or absence of final -e (see Metre and Versification) in adjectives and verbal inflexions (e.g. 2.383: goode] good Cp; 2.851, 1065: righte] right Cp; 3.417: moste] most Cp; 3.481: goode] good Cp; 5.232: righte] right Cp; 5.1521: false] fals Cp; 2.701: thoughte] thought Cp; 3.440: myghte] myght Cp; 3.958: kouthe] kouth Cp; 3.1603: myghte] myght Cp; 4.431: roughte] rought Cp; 5.172: myghte] myght Cp; 5.356: dred] drede Cp).

Metre and Versification

Chaucer is apparently the first writer in English to make sustained use of the 10-syllable line (beginning with his early poem *An ABC*), and the first to use the 7-line rhyme royal stanza in English (in his *Parliament of Fowls*, usually thought to predate *Troilus*). One model for Chaucer would have been the syllabic regularity in French verse, although the model closest to hand for *Troilus* was the 11-syllable lines of the 8-line stanzas in Boccaccio's *Filostrato* (Duffell 1996). The metre of *Troilus* is based on a line of ten syllables arranged in a broadly alternating pattern of unstressed and stressed syllables (sometimes with an eleventh final syllable).

To maintain such a decasyllabic pattern in Chaucer's lines, certain conventions are observed: some words are to be pronounced with more syllables than their modern derivatives, such as *cre-a-ture*, nouns ending in *i-oun*, verbs and nouns ending *-ie* or *-ye* (e.g. *multipl-i-e*, 1.486), or the name *Tro-i-lus*, which is usually trisyllabic. Some additional syllables, beyond ten or eleven per line, can be accommodated within an established range of variation, as with the unstressed *-e* sometimes found in lines before the caesura or pause. Within this 10-syllable line, it is only the general perception of relative stress and unstress that concerns the establishment of a metrical pattern, not the many degrees of rhetorical stress naturally arising in spoken English. There is much flexibility and variety, and in some words, chiefly of French origin, the stress may fall later than in modern English (e.g. *natúre, honoúr, matére, servíse*), and some loan words may be variably stressed.

Chaucer was writing in a period of rapid linguistic change in

English, and near the close of *Troilus* he foresees that scribes might mistranscribe his poem and so ruin its metre through 'defaute of tonge' (5.1796). Chaucer's remarks about language here imply a conservative attitude to the metre dependent upon it, and from a metrical perspective the greatest 'diversite | In Englissh and in writyng of oure tonge' (5.1794) is the fast-fading scribal understanding of the role of final *-e*, particularly in the declension of adjectives. In Old English, as still in Chaucer's written English, monosyllabic adjectives in the singular were declined according to the weak declension with a final *-e* when preceded by (1) the definite article, (2) a possessive pronoun, (3) a demonstrative pronoun, and (4) when modifying a following noun in the vocative case or a proper noun, as in these examples:

> Ibounden in the blak*e* bark of care (4.229)
> That hir behelden in hir blak*e* wede (1.177)
> 'Have here a light, and loke on al this blak*e*' (2.1320)
> 'O blak*e* nyght, as folk in bokes rede' (3.1429)

Adjectives following the noun are uninflected ('Nor under cloude *blak* so bright a sterre', 1.175), but there was also an inflectional *-e* in the plural form of adjectives.

Although the declensions were not always observed by Chaucer's time, and less so thereafter when the *Troilus* manuscripts were being copied, preservation of the weak declension for monosyllabic adjectives ending in a consonant (adjectives of more than one syllable being uninflected) is instrumental in the metrically regular pattern of many *Troilus* lines (Samuels 1972, 1988; Burnley 1982a; Pearsall 1999b). The way in which early manuscripts (Cp, Cl, H1, J) have consistently provided so many final *-e*'s which are etymologically correct in the history of each word where used and which, if pronounced, achieve lines of regular syllabic content and stress pattern, establishes the usage of such manuscripts, in the context of linguistic change and patterns of scribal copying, as the harder and better reading.[1]

The best manuscripts also maintain an understanding, represented in their spelling, of the contractions and elisions

required for lines to read metrically, such as the contracted
verb forms (sometimes found only in *Troilus* among Chaucer's
poems), which preserve metrical regularity:

'Hym *tit* [= tideth] as often harm thereof as prow' (1.333)
'*Ret* [= redeth] me to love, and sholde it me defende?' (2.413)
'Lo, yond he *rit* [= rideth]!' 'Ye,' quod she, 'so he doth!' (2.1284)
'I write, as he that sorwe *drifth* [= driveth] to write' (5.1332)

It is also such manuscripts that carefully maintain the spelling
of the various contracted forms and elisions necessary to a
metrical reading:

'So lat *m'alone*, and it shal be thi beste' (1.1028)

Of which *th'effect* rehercen yow I shal:
Th'embassadours ben answerd for fynal;
Th'eschaunge of prisoners and al this nede (4.144–6)

He *nyst* how best hire herte for *t'acoye*;
'But for *t'asay*,' he seyde, 'it naught ne greveth,
For he that naught *n'asaieth* naught *n'acheveth*' (5.782–4)[2]

and observe the different spellings of the same word that may
be metrically necessary in different contexts:

But *wheither* that she children hadde or noon (1.132)
God woot *wher* [= whether] he was lik a manly knyght (2.1263)

Indeed, these spelled forms in the manuscripts point to the need
to make such elisions when reading lines where the requisite
elision may not be represented in the spelling of extant manu-
scripts. The *e* in inflectional endings (-*ed*, -*es*, -*eth*, etc.) often
needs to be elided or slurred for the metre:

'A kynges herte sem*e*th by hyrs a wrecche' (1.889)
'And yet m'athenk*e*th that this avant m'asterte' (1.1050)

and also when medially before liquids and nasals (*l, r, m, n*), as in *owene* (= *ow'ne*), *every* (= *ev'ry*), or *evere* (= *e're*):

> So muche, day by day, his owene thought (1.442)
> In every peril which that is to drede (1.84)
> For evere it was, and evere it shal byfalle (1.236)

In addition, final -*e* is regularly elided before an initial vowel or before *h* which is either silent (as in *honour*) or not strongly aspirated (such as *he, his, him, hem, hadde*):

> And seyde, 'Ywis, whan thow art horned newe' (5.650)
> 'And that ye deigne me so muche honoure' (3.139)
> 'And seyde hire, 'Now cast it awey anon' (2.1156)

It is also the case that certain common words were often pronounced as monosyllables: e.g. the possessive pronouns (*hire, oure*, etc.), the verb forms *have* and *come*, the past tense of auxiliary verbs (*hadde, nolde, koude, were*, etc.), and the plural demonstrative *thise*.

However, a working definition for the metre of *Troilus* must include the openness to variation that characterizes Chaucer's metrical practice. Important variations from the norm include 9-syllabled lines which lack the first unstressed syllable (the so-called 'headless' line):

> Trewe as stiel in ech condicioun (5.831)
> Sholden spille a quarter of a tere (5.880)

Not infrequent, and attested by early manuscripts (whereas scribes will sometimes introduce an extra syllable to regularize), such 'headless' lines were evidently part of a metrical variety that Chaucer's poem accommodates, and other authentic lines are also found with fewer than ten syllables ('Yong, fressh, strong, and hardy as lyoun', 5.830). In some such lincs, a trochaic pattern may reverse the expected unstress-stress sequence ('Graunted on the morwe, at his requeste', 5.949). A further variation occurs in evidently authentic lines which omit an unstressed syllable after the caesura or pause; this is sometimes termed the 'broken-backed' or 'Lydgatean' line, after John Lydgate, Chaucer's fifteenth-century follower ('Of that he spak no man heren myghte', 2.1119).

A different kind of variation is represented by lines with four stressed syllables – e.g. 'With hauk on honde and with an huge route' (5.65) – where the fifth syllable would not normally bear an equivalent stress to the other four, although it may take some form of half stress (the second 'with' in 5.65 stands in what would normally be a stressed position, whereas the first does not). The occurrence of these lines is not such as to modify the expectation of five relatively stressed syllables in most lines. Any resemblance to the four-stress lines of the English alliterative tradition (as in *Piers Plowman* or *Sir Gawain and the Green Knight*) would seem to arise more by default than by design, reflecting local accommodations between larger metrical expectation and natural speech pattern. It is such accommodations that also characterize the variousness of Chaucer's deployment of the caesura within his demandingly elaborate stanzaic form, together with his use of enjambement (Killough 1982; Youmans 1996: 195–7).[3]

Chaucer's *Complaint of Venus* laments 'Syth rym in Englissh hath such skarsete' (80), and it is an astonishing achievement to maintain the ABABBCC rhyme royal pattern throughout his 1177-stanza *Troilus* (Stevens 1979). There are only a few cases where Chaucer falls back on rhyming two lines with the same word (*fro/fro*, 2.513, 516; *was/was*, 5.975, 978); or where there may be an unsatisfactory rhyme (*sike/endite/white*, 2.884–7; *riden/abiden/yeden*, 2.933–6); or where Chaucer has evidently rhymed the open and close *o* or *e* (*agoon/doon*, 2.410, 411) between which he usually distinguishes scrupulously (e.g. 5.15–19). Although it may appear that Chaucer sometimes rhymes a word with itself, if the two words are used in different senses or represent different parts of speech, this was regarded as a special metrical accomplishment and termed 'rime riche'. Such other features as Chaucer's deployment of Kentish forms in rhyme,[4] or his use of so-called 'broken' rhyme – when one word in one line rhymes with two in another[5] – witness to the demands of observing the rhyme scheme, and the art that Chaucer brings to satisfying such demands. Some sounds or particular words may be noted to recur in rhyme, and some for particular effect (*Troye/joie* and *trouthe/routhe* being especially evocative), but there is no sense of undue repetition. A rare moment of self-consciousness in *Troilus* about the demands of rhyme ('as I may my rymes holde', 3.90) only serves to invite admiration for a demanding task, and the larger impression is of Chaucer's graceful accomplishment 'To ryme wel this book til I have do' (2.10).

NOTES

1   For the grammar of Chaucer's final *-e* in relation to editorial problems of metre, see Cowen and Kane 1995: 112–23. Chaucer's literary disciple Thomas Hoccleve shows in the holographs of his poems a meticulous concern to maintain decasyllabic lines (Jefferson 1987; Burrow 1999).

2   Cf. 'For *noldestow* of bownte hem socouren' (3.1264); 'Why *nad* I swich oon with my soule ybought' (3.1319); 'For whom that the al this *mysaunter* [misaventure] ailleth' (1.766). Use of the forms 'Pandarus' or 'Pandare' in different lines also reflects metrical considerations.

3   Pauses occur near the beginnings and ends of lines, as well as at or near the more familiar mid-line position, and some lines contain more than one pause: e.g. 1.533–4; 2.1103; 4.493, 640, 1349; 5.219, 376–7.

4   For example: *a-fere*, 1.229; *lest*, 1.330; *fulfelle*, 3.510; *feere*, 3.978; *keste*, 3.1129.

5   Cf. *Troye/joie/fro ye*, 1.2–5; *tolis/scole is/foolys*, 1.632–5; *vices/vice is*, 1.687, 689; *newe is/hewis*, 2.20–21; *fowles/owles/foul is*, 5.380–83; *welles/helle is/ellis*, 5.1374–7.

Troilus and Criseyde

BOOK 1

The double sorwe of Troilus to tellen
That was the kyng Priamus sone of Troye,
In lovynge, how his aventures fellen
Fro wo to wele, and after out of joie,
My purpos is, er that I parte fro ye.   5
Thesiphone, thow help me for t'endite
Thise woful vers, that wepen as I write.

To the clepe I, thow goddesse of torment,
Thow cruwel Furie, sorwynge evere in peyne:
Help me, that am the sorwful instrument,   10
That helpeth loveres, as I kan, to pleyne;
For wel sit it, the sothe for to seyne,
A woful wight to han a drery feere,
And to a sorwful tale, a sory chere.

For I, that God of Loves servantz serve,   15
Ne dar to Love, for myn unliklynesse,
Preyen for speed, al sholde I therfore sterve,

1 **double:** twofold **sorwe:** sorrow   2 **kyng Priamus sone of Troye:** son of
King Priam of Troy   3 **aventures:** fortunes **fellen:** befell   4 **wo:** sorrow
wele: happiness   5 **er that:** before **ye:** you (unstressed form of *yow*)
6 **t'** (= *to*) **endite:** compose   7 **woful:** sorrowful **vers, that:** verses which
8 **the:** you **clepe:** call   9 **sorwynge:** sorrowing **peyne:** suffering
10 **sorwful:** sorrowful   11 **pleyne:** lament   12 **wel sit it:** it is very fitting
sothe: truth **seyne:** tell   13 **wight:** person **han:** have **drery:** sad
feere: companion   14 **sory:** sad **chere:** expression   16 **Ne dar:** dare not
for: because of **unliklynesse:** unsuitability   17 **speed:** success **al sholde
I:** even if I were to **sterve:** die

So fer am I from his help in derknesse.
But natheles, if this may don gladnesse
20 To any lovere, and his cause availle,
Have he my thonk, and myn be this travaille!

But ye loveres, that bathen in gladnesse,
If any drope of pyte in yow be,
Remembreth yow on passed hevynesse
25 That ye han felt, and on the adversite
Of othere folk, and thynketh how that ye
Han felt that Love dorste yow displese,
Or ye han wonne hym with to gret an ese.

And preieth for hem that ben in the cas
30 Of Troilus, as ye may after here,
That Love hem brynge in hevene to solas;
And ek for me, preieth to God so dere
That I have myght to shewe in som manere
Swich peyne and wo as Loves folk endure,
35 In Troilus unsely aventure.

And biddeth ek for hem that ben despeired
In love, that nevere nyl recovered be,
And ek for hem that falsly ben apeired
Thorugh wikked tonges, be it he or she;
40 Thus biddeth God, for his benignite,
So graunte hem soone owt of this world to pace,
That ben despeired out of Loves grace.

18 **fer**: far **derknesse**: obscurity   19 **natheles**: nonetheless **don**: give
20 **availle**: be of use to   21 May he have the thanks due to me, and let mine
be this labour   22 **bathen**: bask   23 **pyte**: pity   24 **passed**: past
hevynesse: sadness   25 **adversite**: misfortune   27 **dorste**: dared, was bold
28 **Or**: or else **with to gret an ese**: too easily   29 **hem**: them **cas**: situation
30 **here**: hear   31 **solas**: joy   32 **ek**: also   33 **myght**: power **shewe**: express
manere: way   34 **peyne**: suffering **wo**: misery **folk**: followers
35 **unsely**: unhappy **aventure**: misfortune   36 **biddeth**: pray **despeired**: in
despair   37 **nyl** (= *ne wyl*): will not   38 **falsly**: unjustly **apeired**: injured
39 **Thorugh**: by means of **wikked**: malicious   40 **benignite**: graciousness
41 **pace**: pass   42 **despeired out of**: in despair of **grace**: favour

And biddeth ek for hem that ben at ese,
That God hem graunte ay good perseveraunce,
And sende hem myght hire ladies so to plese   45
That it to Love be worship and plesaunce.
For so hope I my sowle best avaunce,
To prey for hem that Loves servauntz be,
And write hire wo, and lyve in charite,

And for to have of hem compassioun,   50
As though I were hire owne brother dere.
Now herkneth with a good entencioun,
For now wil I gon streght to my matere,
In which ye may the double sorwes here
Of Troilus in lovynge of Criseyde,   55
And how that she forsook hym er she deyde.

   Yt is wel wist how that the Grekes stronge
In armes with a thousand shippes wente
To Troiewardes, and the cite longe
Assegeden, neigh ten yer er they stente,   60
And in diverse wise and oon entente,
The ravysshyng to wreken of Eleyne,
By Paris don, they wroughten al hir peyne.

Now fel it so that in the town ther was
Dwellynge a lord of gret auctorite,   65
A gret devyn, that clepid was Calkas,

43 **at ese**: content   44 **ay**: always **perseveraunce**: continuance
45 **myght**: ability **hire**: their   46 **worship**: honour **plesaunce**: delight
47 **avaunce**: make prosper   48 **Loves servauntz**: servants of Love
49 **charite**: state of Christian love with others, loving kindness   50 **have of
hem compassioun**: sympathize with them   52 **herkneth**: listen
entencioun: will   53 **streght**: directly **matere**: subject   54 **here**: hear
56 **forsook**: deserted **er**: before **deyde**: died   57 **wist**: known   59 **To
Troiewardes**: towards Troy   60 **Assegeden**: besieged **neigh**: nearly
stente: ceased   61 **diverse wise**: different ways **oon entente**: single purpose
62–3 They devoted all their efforts (*peyne*) to avenge (*wreken*) the abduction
(*ravysshyng*) of Helen (n.), committed (*don*) by Paris (son of Priam of Troy)
64 **fel it**: it happened   65 **gret**: great **auctorite**: authority   66 **devyn**: divine,
soothsayer **clepid**: named **Calkas**: Calchas (n.)

That in science so expert was that he
Knew wel that Troie sholde destroied be,
By answere of his god, that highte thus:
70   Daun Phebus or Appollo Delphicus.

So whan this Calkas knew by calkulynge,
And ek by answer of this Appollo,
That Grekes sholden swich a peple brynge,
Thorough which that Troie moste ben fordo,
75   He caste anon out of the town to go;
For wel wiste he by sort that Troye sholde
Destroyed ben, ye, wolde whoso nolde.

For which for to departen softely
Took purpos ful this forknowynge wise,
80   And to the Grekes oost ful pryvely
He stal anon; and they, in curteys wise,
Hym diden bothe worship and servyce,
In trust that he hath konnynge hem to rede
In every peril which that is to drede.

85   The noise up ros whan it was first aspied
Thorough al the town, and generaly was spoken,
That Calkas traitour fled was and allied
With hem of Grece, and casten to be wroken
On hym that falsly hadde his feith so broken,

67 science: knowledge expert: learned, skilled   69 highte: was called
70 Lord Phoebus or Apollo of Delphi   71 calkulynge: (astrological)
computation, reckoning   72 peple: army   74 fordo: destroyed
75 caste: determined anon: at once   76 wiste: knew sort: (divination by)
casting of lots   77 ye: yes, indeed wolde whoso nolde: whether anyone
wished it or not, willy nilly   78–9 For which reason this foreseeing
(forknowynge) wise man firmly resolved (Took purpos ful) to leave quietly
80 oost: army, host pryvely: secretly   81 stal: stole curteys wise: courteous
fashion   82 diden: accorded, paid worship: honour   83 konnynge: skill,
understanding rede: advise   84 drede: be feared   85 noise up ros: rumour
arose aspied: noticed   86 generaly: everywhere   87 traitour fled was: had
fled as a traitor allied: joined   88 hem of Grece: the Greeks casten: (they)
determined wroken: avenged   89 falsly: treacherously

And seyden he and al his kyn at-ones   90
Ben worthi for to brennen, fel and bones.

Now hadde Calkas left in this meschaunce,
Al unwist of this false and wikked dede,
His doughter, which that was in gret penaunce,
For of hire lif she was ful sore in drede,   95
As she that nyste what was best to rede;
For bothe a widewe was she and allone
Of any frend to whom she dorste hir mone.

Criseyde was this lady name al right:
As to my doom, in al Troies cite   100
Nas non so fair, forpassynge every wight,
So aungelik was hir natif beaute,
That lik a thing inmortal semed she,
As doth an hevenyssh perfit creature,
That down were sent in scornynge of nature.   105

This lady, which that alday herd at ere
Hire fadres shame, his falsnesse and tresoun,
Wel neigh out of hir wit for sorwe and fere,
In widewes habit large of samyt broun,
On knees she fil biforn Ector adown   110

90 **seyden:** (they) said **kyn:** family **at-ones:** at once 91 **brennen:** burn
fel: skin 92 **meschaunce:** misfortune 93 **Al unwist:** quite unaware
false: disloyal **dede:** deed 94 **penaunce:** misery 95 **hire:** her **ful:** very
sore: deeply **drede:** fear 96 **As she that:** for she **nyste** (= *ne wiste*): knew not
best to rede: the best advice 97–8 **allone Of:** without 98 **dorste:** dared **hir
mone:** tell her troubles 99 **lady:** lady's **al right:** exactly 100 **As to my
doom:** in my opinion 101 **Nas** (*ne was*): (there) was not
forpassynge: surpassing **wight:** person 102 **aungelik:** angelic **natif:** natural,
inborn 103 **thing inmortal:** immortal creature 104 **hevenyssh:** heavenly
perfit: perfect 105 **in scornynge of nature:** to put Nature to scorn
106 **alday:** continually **at ere:** in her ear 107 **fadres:** father's
shame: dishonour **falsnesse:** treachery **tresoun:** treason 108 **Wel neigh:** very
nearly **wit:** mind **fere:** fear 109 **habit large:** flowing garments
samyt: samite (a costly silk) **broun:** dark 110 **fil:** fell **Ector:** Hector (n.)
adown: down

With pitous vois, and tendrely wepynge,
His mercy bad, hirselven excusynge.

Now was this Ector pitous of nature,
And saugh that she was sorwfully bigon,
115   And that she was so fair a creature;
Of his goodnesse he gladede hire anon,
And seyde, 'Lat youre fadres treson gon
Forth with meschaunce, and ye youreself in joie
Dwelleth with us, whil yow good list, in Troie.

120   'And al th'onour that men may don yow have,
As ferforth as youre fader dwelled here,
Ye shul have, and youre body shal men save,
As fer as I may ought enquere or here.'
And she hym thonked with ful humble chere,
125   And ofter wolde, and it hadde ben his wille,
And took hire leve, and hom, and held hir stille.

And in hire hous she abood with swich meyne
As til hire honour nede was to holde;
And whil she was dwellynge in that cite,
130   Kepte hir estat, and both of yonge and olde
Ful wel biloved, and wel men of hir tolde –
But wheither that she children hadde or noon,
I rede it naught, therfore I late it goon.

111 **pitous**: pitiful, sad **tendrely**: in a heartfelt way   112 Begged for his
mercy, exonerating herself   113 **pitous**: compassionate   114 **saugh**: saw
sorwfully bigon: overwhelmed with unhappiness   116 **gladede**: comforted
118 **Forth with meschaunce**: to the devil   119 **whil yow good list**: as long as
you please   120 **th'onour**: the honour **don yow**: cause you to   121 **As
ferforth as**: as much as if   122 **save**: protect   123 **fer**: far **ought**: in any way
enquere: find out **here**: hear   124 **chere**: expression   125 **ofter**: more often
wolde: would (have done) **and**: if   126 **hom**: (went) home **held hir
stille**: lived quietly   127 **abood**: remained **meyne**: retinue   128 As her
position made it necessary to maintain   130 **Kepte hir estat**: lived
appropriately to her station   132 **or noon**: or not   133 **rede**: read (in the
source) **late**: let **goon**: pass

The thynges fellen, as they don of werre,
135 Bitwixen hem of Troie and Grekes ofte;
For som day boughten they of Troie it derre,
And eft the Grekes founden nothing softe
The folk of Troie; and thus Fortune on lofte
And under eft gan hem to whielen bothe
Aftir hir course, ay whil that thei were wrothe. 140

But how this town com to destruccion
Ne falleth naught to purpos me to telle,
For it were here a long digression
Fro my matere, and yow to long to dwelle.
But the Troian gestes, as they felle, 145
In Omer, or in Dares, or in Dite,
Whoso that kan may rede hem as they write.

But though that Grekes hem of Troie shetten,
And hir cite biseged al aboute,
Hire olde usage nolde they nat letten, 150
As for to honoure hir goddes ful devoute;
But aldirmost in honour, out of doute,
Thei hadde a relik, heet Palladion,
That was hire trist aboven everichon.

134 fellen: happened of werre: in war 135 Bitwixen: between hem of
Troie: Trojans 136 som: one boughten . . . it derre: had the worst of it they
of Troie: Trojans 137 eft: another time nothing: not at all softe: weak,
yielding 138 on lofte: on high, above 139 under: below whielen: wheel,
turn (on Fortune's wheel) 140 Aftir hir course: in accordance with her
custom ay whil that: as long as wrothe: at odds 141 com: came
142 falleth naught to purpos me: is no part of my intention
144 matere: subject matter dwelle: detain 145 gestes: exploits, stories
felle: happened 146 Omer: Homer Dares: Dares Phrygius Dite: Dictys
Cretensis 147 Whoso: whoever 148 though that: although
shetten: penned in 149 al aboute: on every side 150 They (the Trojans)
would not discontinue their ancient custom 151 devoute: sacred
152 aldirmost: most of all honour: respect out of doute: certainly
153 heet: called Palladion: Palladium (an image of Pallas) 154 In which
they put their trust more than anything

155   And so bifel, whan comen was the tyme
         Of Aperil, whan clothed is the mede
         With newe grene, of lusty Veer the pryme,
         And swote smellen floures white and rede,
         In sondry wises shewed, as I rede,
160   The folk of Troie hire observaunces olde,
         Palladiones feste for to holde.

         And to the temple, in al hir beste wise,
         In general ther wente many a wight,
         To herknen of Palladion the servyce;
165   And namely, so many a lusty knyght,
         So many a lady fressh and mayden bright,
         Ful wel arayed, both meeste, mene, and leste,
         Ye, bothe for the seson and the feste.

         Among thise othere folk was Criseyda,
170   In widewes habit blak; but natheles,
         Right as oure firste lettre is now an A,
         In beaute first so stood she, makeles.
         Hire goodly lokyng gladed al the prees.
         Nas nevere yet seyn thyng to ben preysed derre,
175   Nor under cloude blak so bright a sterre

         As was Criseyde, as folk seyde everichone
         That hir behelden in hir blake wede.
         And yet she stood ful lowe and stille allone,

155 **bifel:** it happened   156 **mede:** meadow   157 **grene:** greenery
lusty: delightful **Veer:** springtime **pryme:** beginning   158 **swote:** sweetly
159–60 In various ways, as I read, the Trojans performed their ancient
ceremonies   161 **feste:** festival **holde:** observe   162 **hir:** their
wise: fashion   163 **In general:** together, in a body **wight:** person
164 **herknen:** listen to   165 **namely:** especially **lusty:** gallant
166 **fressh:** lovely **bright:** beautiful   167 **arayed:** dressed **meeste, mene and
leste:** highest, middling and lowest (in rank)   168 **Ye:** yes, indeed
170 **natheles:** nonetheless   171 **Right:** just   172 **makeles:** matchless
173 **goodly:** beautiful **lokyng:** looks **gladed:** cheered **prees:** crowd   174 **Nas**
(= *ne was*): (there) was not **seyn:** seen **preysed:** praised **derre:** more highly
175 **sterre:** star   177 **behelden:** saw **wede:** clothing   178 **ful lowe:** very
humbly **stille:** quietly, motionless

Byhynden other folk, in litel brede,
And neigh the dore, ay undre shames drede,   180
Simple of atir and debonaire of chere,
With ful assured lokyng and manere.

This Troilus, as he was wont to gide
His yonge knyghtes, lad hem up and down
In thilke large temple on every side,   185
Byholding ay the ladies of the town,
Now here, now there; for no devocioun
Hadde he to non, to reven hym his reste,
But gan to preise and lakken whom hym leste.

And in his walk ful faste he gan to wayten   190
If knyght or squyer of his compaignie
Gan for to syke, or lete his eighen baiten
On any womman that he koude espye.
He wolde smyle and holden it folye,
And seye hym thus, 'God woot, she slepeth softe   195
For love of the, whan thow turnest ful ofte!

'I have herd told, pardieux, of youre lyvynge,
Ye loveres, and youre lewed observaunces,
And which a labour folk han in wynnynge
Of love, and in the kepyng which doutaunces;   200
And whan youre prey is lost, woo and penaunces.

---

179 in litel brede: in a little space   180 neigh: near ay: always undre: subject
to shames drede: fear of disgrace   181 atir: attire, clothes debonaire: gentle
chere: demeanour   182 assured: composed lokyng: look
183 wont: accustomed gide: lead, direct   184 lad: led   185 thilke: that
(same) on every side: in all directions   187 devocioun: devotedness,
inclination   188 reven: deprive   189 preise: praise lakken: find fault with
hym leste: he pleased   190 faste: intently wayten: watch   192 syke: sigh
eighen: eyes baiten: feast   193 koude: could espye: descry
194 holden: consider folye: foolishness   195 woot: knows
softe: comfortably   196 the: you turnest: toss and turn   197 pardieux: by
God lyvynge: way of life   198 lewed: foolish, ignorant   199 which: what
labour: effort wynnynge: obtaining   200 kepyng: retention (of love)
doutaunces: uncertainties   201 prey: prey, victim woo: sorrow
penaunces: miseries

O veray fooles, nyce and blynde be ye!
Ther nys nat oon kan war by other be.'

And with that word he gan caste up the browe,
205 Ascaunces, 'Loo! is this naught wisely spoken?'
At which the God of Love gan loken rowe
Right for despit, and shop for to ben wroken.
He kidde anon his bowe nas naught broken;
For sodeynly he hitte hym atte fulle –
210 And yet as proud a pekok kan he pulle.

O blynde world, O blynde entencioun!
How often falleth al the effect contraire
Of surquidrie and foul presumpcioun;
For kaught is proud, and kaught is debonaire:
215 This Troilus is clomben on the staire,
And litel weneth that he moot descenden –
But alday faileth thing that fooles wenden.

As proude Bayard gynneth for to skippe
Out of the weye, so pryketh hym his corn,
220 Til he a lasshe have of the longe whippe –
Than thynketh he, 'Though I praunce al byforn
First in the trays, ful fat and newe shorn,
Yet am I but an hors, and horses lawe
I moot endure, and with my feres drawe' –

202 **veray:** true **nyce:** foolish   203 **nys nat** (= *ne is nat*): is not **oon:** one person (who) **war by other be:** be warned by another's example   204 **caste up:** raise **browe:** eyebrow   205 **Ascaunces:** as if to say **Loo!:** look!   206 **rowe:** angrily   207 **for despit:** through resentment **shop:** planned **wroken:** avenged   208 **kidde:** showed **nas** (= *ne was*): was not   209 **sodeynly:** suddenly **atte fulle:** squarely   210 **yet:** to this day **pekok:** peacock **pulle:** pluck   211 **entencioun:** intention, purpose   212 **falleth:** happens **effect:** consequence **contraire:** contrary, opposite   213 **surquidrie:** pride **foul presumpcioun:** vile arrogance   214 **debonaire:** meek   215 **is clomben:** has climbed **staire:** stairs   216 **weneth:** supposes **moot:** must   217 **alday:** all the time **faileth:** fails to occur, falls short **wenden:** expected   218 **Bayard:** typical name for a horse (n.) **gynneth:** begins **skippe:** jump, spring   219 **weye:** (right) way **pryketh hym his corn:** he feels his oats   221 **Than:** then   222 **trays:** traces **newe:** newly   223 **but:** only   224 **feres:** fellows **drawe:** pull

So ferde it by this fierse and proude knyght: 225
Though he a worthy kynges sone were,
And wende nothing hadde had swich myght
Ayeyns his wille that shuld his herte stere,
Yet with a look his herte wex a-fere,
That he that now was moost in pride above,   230
Wax sodeynly moost subgit unto love.

Forthy ensample taketh of this man,
Ye wise, proude, and worthi folkes alle,
To scornen Love, which that so soone kan
The fredom of youre hertes to hym thralle;   235
For evere it was, and evere it shal byfalle,
That Love is he that alle thing may bynde,
For may no man fordon the lawe of kynde.

That this be soth, hath preved and doth yit:
For this trowe I ye knowen alle or some,   240
Men reden nat that folk han gretter wit
Than they that han be most with love ynome;
And strengest folk ben therwith overcome,
The worthiest and grettest of degree –
This was, and is, and yet men shall it see.   245

And trewelich it sit wel to be so,
For alderwisest han therwith ben plesed;
And they that han ben aldermost in wo,

---

225 **ferde it by:** it turned out with **fierse:** bold   226 **worthy:** noble
227 **wende:** supposed   228 **Ayeyns:** against **stere:** steer, control (or stir,
disturb)   229 **wex:** became **a-fere:** on fire   230 **above:** superior
231 **Wax:** became **subgit:** subject   232 **Forthy:** therefore **ensample
taketh:** learn by the example   234 **To scornen:** with regard to scorning
235 **thralle:** enslave   237 **bynde:** bind, fetter   238 **fordon:** abrogate
kynde: nature   239 **soth:** true **preved:** proved (true) **yit:** still
240 **trowe:** believe **alle or some:** one and all   241 **reden:** suppose
gretter: greater **wit:** intelligence   242 **han be:** have been **ynome:** seized
243 **strengest:** strongest **therwith:** by that   244 **degree:** rank
246 **trewelich:** truly **sit** (= *sitteth*) **wel:** is most appropriate
247 **alderwisest:** the wisest of all   248 **aldermost:** most of all

With love han ben comforted moost and esed;
250   And ofte it hath the cruel herte apesed,
And worthi folk maad worthier of name,
And causeth moost to dreden vice and shame.

Now sith it may nat goodly ben withstonde,
And is a thing so vertuous in kynde,
255   Refuseth nat to Love for to ben bonde,
Syn, as hymselven liste, he may yow bynde;
The yerde is bet that bowen wole and wynde
Than that that brest, and therfore I yow rede
To folowen hym that so wel kan yow lede.

260   But for to tellen forth in special
As of this kynges sone of which I tolde,
And leten other thing collateral,
Of hym thenke I my tale forth to holde,
Bothe of his joie and of his cares colde;
265   And al his werk, as touching this matere,
For I it gan, I wol therto refere.

Withinne the temple he wente hym forth pleyinge,
This Troilus, of every wight aboute,
On this lady, and now on that, lokynge,
270   Wher so she were of town or of withoute;
And upon cas bifel that thorugh a route

249 **esed**: made happy   250 **apesed**: appeased, assuaged
251 **name**: reputation   252 **dreden**: shun   253 **sith**: since **may nat
goodly**: can hardly **withstonde**: resisted   254 **kynde**: nature
255 **bonde**: enslaved   256 **Syn**: since **as hymselven liste**: as he pleases
257 **yerde**: stick, sapling **bet**: better **bowen**: bow **wynde**: bend
258 **brest**: breaks **rede**: advise   259 **lede**: lead   260 **in special**: particularly
262 **leten**: leave aside **collateral**: subsidiary, subordinate
263 **thenke**: intend **holde**: continue   264 **cares**: miseries **colde**: chill/ing,
painful (see n.)   265 **werk**: conduct **as touching**: concerning   266 **For I it
gan**: because I began (to tell of it) **therto**: to it **refere**: return
267 **pleyinge**: making fun   270 **Wher so**: whether **of withoute**: from out of
town   271 **upon cas**: by chance **bifel**: it happened **route**: crowd

His eye percede, and so depe it wente,
Til on Criseyde it smot, and ther it stente.

And sodeynly he wax therwith astoned,
And gan hir bet biholde in thrifty wise.   275
'O mercy, God,' thoughte he, 'wher hastow
    woned,
That art so feyr and goodly to devise?'
Therwith his herte gan to sprede and rise,
And softe sighed, lest men myghte hym here,
And caught ayeyn his firste pleyinge chere.   280

She nas nat with the leste of hire stature,
But alle hire lymes so wel answerynge
Weren to wommanhod, that creature
Was nevere lasse mannyssh in semynge;
And ek the pure wise of hire mevynge   285
Shewed wel that men myght in hire gesse
Honour, estat, and wommanly noblesse.

To Troilus right wonder wel with alle
Gan for to like hire mevynge and hire chere,
Which somdel deignous was, for she let falle   290
Hire look a lite aside in swich manere,
Ascaunces, 'What, may I nat stonden here?'

272 **percede:** gazed through   273 **smot:** hit **stente:** stopped
274 **wax:** became **therwith:** because of that **astoned:** astonished   275 **in
thrifty wise:** prudently   276 **hastow** (= *hast thow*): have you **woned:** dwelt
277 **feyr:** fair **goodly:** beautiful **devise:** look upon
278 **Therwith:** thereupon **sprede:** swell **rise:** feel exalted   279 **lest:** in case
280 **caught ayeyn:** recovered, resumed **firste:** former **pleyinge:** jesting
chere: expression   281 **with:** among **leste:** shortest **of:** as to **stature:** height
282 **hire lymes:** parts of her body **answerynge:** corresponding
283 **wommanhod:** womanliness   284 **lasse:** less **mannyssh:** like a man,
unwomanly **semynge:** appearance   285 **pure wise:** sheer manner
mevynge: way of moving   286 **gesse:** infer   287 **estat:** dignity
noblesse: nobility (of character)   288 **wonder:** marvellously **with
alle:** indeed   289 **like:** be pleasing **chere:** demeanour
290 **somdel:** somewhat **deignous:** haughty   291 **lite:** little
292 **Ascaunces:** as if to say

And after that hir lokynge gan she lighte,
That nevere thoughte hym seen so good a syghte.

295   And of hire look in him ther gan to quyken
So gret desir and swich affeccioun,
That in his hertes botme gan to stiken
Of hir his fixe and depe impressioun.
And though he erst hadde poured up and down,
300   He was tho glad his hornes in to shrinke:
Unnethes wiste he how to loke or wynke.

Lo, he that leet hymselven so konnynge,
And scorned hem that Loves peynes dryen,
Was ful unwar that Love hadde his dwellynge
305   Withinne the subtile stremes of hire yen;
That sodeynly hym thoughte he felte dyen,
Right with hire look, the spirit in his herte –
Blissed be Love, that kan thus folk converte!

She, this in blak, likynge to Troilus
310   Over alle thing, he stood for to biholde;
Ne his desir, ne wherfore he stood thus,
He neither chere made, ne word tolde;
But from afer, his manere for to holde,
On other thing his look som tyme he caste,
315   And eft on hire, whil that servyse laste.

293 **lokynge:** look **lighte:** brighten   294 **nevere thoughte hym seen:** it seemed
to him he had never seen   295 **quyken:** arise   297 **his hertes botme:** the
bottom of his heart **stiken:** stay fast   298 **fixe:** unchangeable
impressioun: image   299 **erst:** before **poured:** stared **up and
down:** everywhere   300 **tho:** then **in to shrinke:** to draw in
301 **Unnethes:** hardly **wiste:** knew **wynke:** close his eyes   302 **Lo!:** see!
leet: considered **konnynge:** knowledgeable   303 **dryen:** suffer
304 **unwar:** unaware   305 **subtile:** ethereal **stremes:** beams **yen:** eyes
306 **hym thoughte:** it seemed to him   307 **Right:** just **spirit:** vital spirit
309 **this:** this (person) **likynge:** pleasing   311 **wherfore:** why   312 **chere
made:** revealed by his expression   313 **afer:** afar **manere:** (usual) manner
holde: maintain   314 **caste:** directed   315 **eft:** again **laste:** lasted

And after this, nat fullich al awhaped,
Out of the temple al esilich he wente,
Repentynge hym that he hadde evere ijaped
Of Loves folk, lest fully the descente
Of scorn fille on hymself; but what he mente,   320
Lest it were wist on any manere syde,
His woo he gan dissimilen and hide.

Whan he was fro the temple thus departed,
He streght anon unto his paleys torneth,
Right with hire look thorugh-shoten and   325
          thorugh-darted,
Al feyneth he in lust that he sojorneth;
And al his chere and speche also he borneth,
And ay of Loves servantz every while,
Hymself to wrye, at hem he gan to smyle,

And seyde, 'Lord, so ye lyve al in lest,   330
Ye loveres! For the konnyngeste of yow,
That serveth most ententiflich and best,
Hym tit as often harm therof as prow:
Youre hire is quyt ayeyn, ye, God woot how!
Nought wel for wel, but scorn for good   335
          servyse –
In feith, youre ordre is ruled in good wise!

316 fullich: entirely awhaped: confounded   317 esilich: unhurriedly
318 ijaped: made fun   319 folk: followers, devotees descente: falling,
lighting   320 fille: should fall what: whatever mente: meant
321 wist: known on any manere syde: in any way   322 dissimilen: conceal
324 streght: immediately torneth: returns   325 thorugh-shoten: shot
through thorugh-darted: pierced   326 Al feyneth he: although he pretends
lust: pleasure sojorneth: continues   327 chere: manner speche: talk
borneth: polishes   328 ay: always every while: constantly   329 Hymself to
wrye: to cover himself   330 so: how lest: delight
331 konnyngeste: cleverest   332 ententiflich: diligently   333 Hym tit (= hym
tydeth): there befalls him therof: from that prow: advantage   34 Youre hire
is quyt: you are repaid ye: yes woot: knows   335 wel for wel: one good
thing for another   336 ordre: (religious) order

'In nouncerteyn ben alle youre observaunces,
But it a sely fewe pointes be;
Ne no thing asketh so gret attendaunces
340   As doth youre lay, and that knowe alle ye;
But that is nat the worste, as mote I the!
But, tolde I yow the worste point, I leve,
Al seyde I soth, ye wolden at me greve.

'But take this: that ye loveres ofte eschuwe,
345   Or elles doon, of good entencioun,
Ful ofte thi lady wol it mysconstruwe,
And deme it harm in hire oppynyoun;
And yet if she, for other enchesoun,
Be wroth, than shaltow have a groyn anon.
350   Lord, wel is hym that may ben of yow oon!'

But for al this, whan that he say his tyme,
He held his pees – non other boote hym gayned –
For love bigan his fetheres so to lyme
That wel unnethe until his folk he fayned
355   That other besy nedes hym destrayned;
For wo was hym, that what to doon he nyste,
But bad his folk to gon wher that hem liste.

---

337 **In nouncerteyn**: without certainty   338 **But**: unless **sely**: trifling
pointes: details   339 **asketh**: requires **attendaunces**: attentions
340 **lay**: devotion   341 **as mote I the**: as I may prosper   342 **tolde I**: if I told
leve: believe   343 **Al seyde I soth**: although I spoke the truth **at me greve**: feel
annoyed with me   344 **take**: consider **that**: that which **eschuwe**: avoid
(doing)   345 **elles**: else **entencioun**: will   347 **deme**: consider
harm: wrong   348 **enchesoun**: reason   349 **wroth**: angry **shaltow** (= *shalt
thow*): you shall **groyn**: scolding   350 **wel is hym**: he is fortunate **of yow
oon**: one of you   351 **for**: despite **say**: saw   352 **held his pees**: kept quiet
boote: remedy **hym gayned**: was of help to him   353 **lyme**: smear with
birdlime (to catch him)   354 **wel unnethe**: scarcely **until**: to
fayned: pretended   355 **nedes hym destrayned**: affairs pressed on him
356 **wo was hym**: he was unhappy **nyste** (= *ne wiste*): did not know
357 **bad**: told **hem liste**: they pleased

And whan that he in chambre was allone,
He doun upon his beddes feet hym sette,
And first he gan to sike, and eft to grone,   360
And thought ay on hire so, withouten lette,
That, as he sat and wook, his spirit mette
That he hire saugh a-temple, and al the wise
Right of hire look, and gan it newe avise.

Thus gan he make a mirour of his mynde   365
In which he saugh al holly hire figure,
And that he wel koude in his herte fynde,
It was to hym a right good aventure
To love swich oon, and if he dede his cure
To serven hir, yet myghte he falle in grace,   370
Or ellis for oon of hire servantz pace;

Imagenynge that travaille nor grame
Ne myghte for so goodly oon be lorn
As she, ne hym for his desir no shame,
Al were it wist, but in pris and up-born   375
Of alle lovers wel more than biforn –
Thus argumented he in his gynnynge,
Ful unavysed of his woo comynge.

359 **his beddes feet**: the foot of his bed **hym sette**: sat   360 **sike**: sigh
eft: likewise   361 **lette**: ceasing   362 **wook**: remained awake
mette: dreamed   363 **a-temple**: in the temple **wise**: manner
364 **Right**: exactly **newe**: anew **avise**: contemplate   366 **holly**: wholly,
completely **figure**: person   368 **aventure**: fortune   369 **swich oon**: such a
one **dede his cure**: did his best   370 **yet myghte he**: he might yet **falle in
grace**: win favour   371 **ellis**: else **for . . . pace**: pass for   372 **travaille**: effort
grame: suffering   373 **goodly oon**: excellent a one **lorn**: lost, wasted
374 **ne hym for his desir no shame**: nor any disgrace to him because of his
desire   375 **Al were it wist**: even if it were known **in pris**: (he would be)
esteemed **up-born**: exalted   377 **argumented**: reasoned
gynnynge: beginning   378 **Ful**: completely **unavysed**: unaware

Thus took he purpos loves craft to suwe,
380   And thoughte he wolde werken pryvely,
First to hiden his desir in muwe
From every wight yborn, al outrely,
But he myghte ought recovered be therby,
Remembryng hym that love to wide yblowe
385   Yelt bittre fruyt, though swete seed be sowe.

And over al this, yet muchel more he thoughte
What for to speke, and what to holden inne;
And what to arten hire to love he soughte,
And on a song anon-right to bygynne,
390   And gan loude on his sorwe for to wynne;
For with good hope he gan fully assente
Criseyde for to love, and nought repente.

And of his song naught only the sentence,
As writ myn auctour called Lollius,
395   But pleinly, save oure tonges difference,
I dar wel seyn, in al, that Troilus
Seyde in his song, loo, every word right thus
As I shal seyn; and whoso list it here,
Loo, next this vers he may it fynden here.

379 **took he purpos:** he decided **craft:** art **suwe:** follow
380 **pryvely:** secretly, discreetly   381 **in muwe:** in secret   382 **yborn:** born,
alive **outrely:** completely   383 **But:** unless **ought recovered:** in any way
benefited **therby:** by that   384 **to:** too **yblowe:** broadcast   385 **Yelt** (=
yeldeth): yields **sowe:** sown   386 **over:** in addition to **muchel:** much
387 About what to say and what to leave unsaid   388 **arten:** induce
389 **anon-right:** immediately   390 **on . . . wynne:** complain about
392 **repente:** feel regret   393 **sentence:** sense   394 **writ** (= *writeth*): writes
auctour: authority   395 **pleinly:** fully **save:** except for **tonges:** language's
396 **in al:** entirely **that:** that which   398 **list it here:** wishes to hear it
399 **next:** next to **vers:** line

Canticus Troili

'If no love is, O God, what fele I so?   400
And if love is, what thing and which is he?
If love be good, from whennes cometh my woo?
If it be wikke, a wonder thynketh me,
When every torment and adversite
That cometh of hym may to me savory thinke,   405
For ay thurst I, the more that ich it drynke.

'And if that at myn owen lust I brenne,
From whennes cometh my waillynge and my
      pleynte?
If harm agree me, wherto pleyne I thenne?
I noot, ne whi unwery that I feynte.   410
O quike deth, O swete harm so queynte,
How may of the in me swich quantite,
But if that I consente that it be?

'And if that I consente, I wrongfully
Compleyne, iwis. Thus possed to and fro,   415
Al sterelees withinne a boot am I
Amydde the see, bitwixen wyndes two,
That in contrarie stonden evere mo.
Allas, what is this wondre maladie?
For hete of cold, for cold of hete, I dye.'   420

Canticus Troili: Troilus's song   400 **no love is**: love does not exist
402 **whennes**: whence   403 **wikke**: bad **thynketh me**: it seems to me
405 **savory thinke**: seem pleasant   406 **ay thurst I**: I am always thirsty
ich: I   407 **lust**: desire **brenne**: burn   408 **waillynge**: wailing
pleynte: lament   409 **harm**: pain, suffering **agree**: be pleasing to
wherto: why **pleyne**: complain   410 **noot** (= *ne woot*): do not know
unwery: without being tired **feynte**: become exhausted, grow faint
411 **quike**: living **queynte**: curious   412 **may**: can there be   413 **But
if**: unless   415 **Compleyne**: lament **iwis**: certainly **possed**: tossed
416 **sterelees**: rudderless **boot**: boat   417 **Amydde**: in the middle of
418 **contrarie**: opposite directions **stonden**: are set **evere mo**: perpetually
419 **wondre**: strange **maladie**: illness   420 I die of cold when I have a fever,
and of a fever when I am cold

And to the God of Love thus seyde he
With pitous vois, 'O lord, now youres is
My spirit, which that oughte youres be.
Yow thanke I, lord, that han me brought to this.
425   But wheither goddesse or womman, iwis,
She be, I not, which that ye do me serve;
But as hire man I wol ay lyve and sterve.

'Ye stonden in hir eighen myghtily,
As in a place unto youre vertu digne;
430   Wherfore, lord, if my service or I
May liken yow, so beth to me benigne;
For myn estat roial I here resigne
Into hire hond, and with ful humble chere
Bicome hir man, as to my lady dere.'

435   In hym ne deyned spare blood roial
The fyr of love – the wherfro God me blesse –
Ne him forbar in no degree, for al
His vertu or his excellent prowesse,
But held hym as his thral lowe in destresse,
440   And brende hym so in soundry wise ay newe,
That sexti tyme a day he loste his hewe.

So muche, day by day, his owene thought,
For lust to hire, gan quiken and encresse,
That every other charge he sette at nought.

---

422 pitous: piteous   **426 not** (= *ne wo(o)t*): do not know **do me:** cause me
to   **427 sterve:** die   **428** In her eyes you stand very high
429 vertu: excellence **digne:** worthy   **431 liken:** please **beth:** be
benigne: well disposed   **432 estat:** rank   **433 chere:** manner
434 man: servant (in love), vassal   **435–6** The fire of love did not deign to
spare the royal blood in him   **436 the wherfro:** from which **blesse:** protect
437 forbar: spared **in no degree:** in no way   **438 vertu:** excellence
prowesse: valour   **439 held hym . . . lowe:** kept him in a humbled state
thral: servant   **440 brende:** burned **soundry wise:** various ways **ay**
newe: constantly   **441 sexti:** sixty **hewe:** colour   **443 lust to:** desire for
quiken: kindle **encresse:** increase   **444 charge:** responsibility **sette at**
nought: counted as nothing

Forthi ful ofte, his hote fir to cesse,   445
To sen hire goodly lok he gan to presse;
For therby to ben esed wel he wende,
And ay the ner he was, the more he brende.

For ay the ner the fir, the hotter is –
This, trowe I, knoweth al this compaignye;   450
But were he fer or ner, I dar sey this:
By nyght or day, for wisdom or folye,
His herte, which that is his brestez yë,
Was ay on hire, that fairer was to sene
Than evere were Eleyne or Polixene.   455

Ek of the day ther passed nought an houre
That to hymself a thousand tyme he seyde,
'Good goodly, to whom serve I and laboure
As I best kan, now wolde God, Criseyde,
Ye wolden on me rewe, er that I deyde!   460
My derc herte, allas, myn hele and hewe
And lif is lost, but ye wol on me rewe!'

Alle other dredes weren from him fleddc,
Both of th'assege and his savacioun;
N'yn him desir noon other fownes bredde,   465
But argumentes to his conclusioun:
That she of him wolde han compassioun,

445 **Forthi:** therefore **fir:** fire **cesse:** put an end to   446 **sen:** see
goodly: pleasing **lok:** appearance **presse:** push forward   447 **therby:** by this
esed: relieved **wende:** supposed   448 **ay:** always **ner:** nearer
brende: burned   449 **ner:** nearer   450 **trowe:** believe
452 **folye:** foolishness   453 **his brestez yë:** the eye of his breast
454 **ay:** always (fixed) **sene:** see   455 **Polixene:** Polyxena (n.)
458 **goodly:** pleasing one   459 **wolde God:** would that God (would grant
that)   460 **rewe:** have pity **er that:** before **deyde:** died   461 **hele:** health
hewe: colour, looks   462 **but:** unless   463 **dredes:** anxieties
464 **th'assege:** the siege **savacioun:** safety   465 Nor in him did desire breed
any other progeny (*fownes*)   467 **of . . . han compassioun:** take pity on

And he to ben hire man while he may dure.
Lo, here his lif, and from the deth his cure!

470 The sharpe shoures felle of armes preve
That Ector or his othere brethren diden
Ne made hym only therfore ones meve;
And yet was he, where so men wente or riden,
Founde oon the beste, and longest tyme abiden
475 Ther peril was, and dide ek swich travaille
In armes, that to thenke it was merveille.

But for non hate he to the Grekes hadde,
Ne also for the rescous of the town,
Ne made hym thus in armes for to madde,
480 But only, lo, for this conclusioun:
To liken hire the bet for his renoun.
Fro day to day in armes so he spedde
That the Grekes as the deth him dredde.

And fro this forth tho refte hym love his slep,
485 And made his mete his foo, and ek his sorwe
Gan multiplie, that, whoso tok kep,
It shewed in his hewe both eve and morwe.
Therfor a title he gan him for to borwe
Of other siknesse, lest men of hym wende
490 That the hote fir of love hym brende,

---

468 **man**: servant **dure**: endure   470 **sharpe**: furious **shoures**: attacks
felle: terrible **of armes preve**: the proof of combat   472 Left him unmoved
on that account   473 **where so**: wherever **wente or riden**: walked or rode
474 **Founde**: discovered (to be) **oon the beste**: the very best **longest tyme
abiden**: (to have) remained the longest time   475 **swich travaille**: such great
deeds   476 **thenke**: think of **merveille**: a marvel   477 But not on account of
any hatred he had for the Greeks   478 **rescous**: rescue   479 **madde**: rage
480 **conclusioun**: purpose   481 **liken**: please **bet for**: better because of
renoun: fame   482 **spedde**: was successful   483 **the deth**: the plague (or
simply, death; cf. 536) **dredde**: feared   484 **fro this forth**: from this time on
tho: then **refte hym love**: love deprived him of   485 **mete**: food **foo**: enemy
486 **whoso**: whoever **tok kep**: took notice   487 **hewe**: complexion **eve and
morwe**: all the time   488 **title**: name **borwe**: borrow   489 **wende**: supposed

And seyde he hadde a fevere and ferde amys.
But how it was, certeyn, kan I nat seye,
If that his lady understood nat this,
Or feynede hire she nyste, oon of the tweye;
But wel I rede that, by no manere weye,   495
Ne semed it as that she of hym roughte,
Or of his peyne, or whatsoevere he thoughte.

But thanne felte this Troilus swich wo
That he was wel neigh wood; for ay his drede
Was this, that she som wight hadde loved so,   500
That nevere of hym she wolde han taken hede,
For which hym thoughte he felte his herte blede;
Ne of his wo ne dorste he nat bygynne
To tellen hir, for al this world to wynne.

But whan he hadde a space from his care,   505
Thus to hymself ful ofte he gan to pleyne;
He seyde, 'O fool, now artow in the snare,
That whilom japedest at loves peyne.
Now artow hent, now gnaw thin owen cheyne!
Thow were ay wont ech lovere reprehende   510
Of thing fro which thou kanst the nat defende.

'What wol now every lovere seyn of the,
If this be wist, but evere in thin absence
Laughen in scorn, and seyn, "Loo, ther goth he
That is the man of so gret sapience,   515
That held us loveres leest in reverence.

---

491 **ferde amys:** felt unwell   492 **certeyn:** certainly   494 **feynede
hire:** pretended **tweye:** two   495 **manere weye:** means   496 **roughte:** cared
498 **thanne:** then   499 **wel neigh:** very nearly **wood:** mad   500 **som:** a
certain **wight:** (other) man   501 **of . . . taken hede:** paid attention to
502 **hym thoughte:** it seemed to him **blede:** bleed   503 **dorste:** dared
504 **for al this world to wynne:** though all this world were the reward
505 **space:** respite **care:** sorrow   506 **pleyne:** lament   507 **artow** (= *art
thow*): you are   508 **That whilom japedest:** you who formerly mocked
509 **hent:** caught   510 **ay:** always **wont:** accustomed **ech:** each
reprehende: reproach   511 **the:** yourself   514 **goth:** goes
515 **sapience:** wisdom   516 **leest:** least **reverence:** respect

Now, thanked God, he may gon in the daunce
Of hem that Love list febly for to avaunce."

'But, O thow woful Troilus, God wolde,
520   Sith thow most loven thorugh thi destine,
That thow beset were on swich oon that sholde
Know al thi wo, al lakked hir pitee!
But also cold in love towardes the
Thi lady is as frost in wynter moone,
525   And thow fordon as snow in fire is soone.

'God wold I were aryved in the port
Of deth, to which my sorwe wol me lede!
A, Lord, to me it were a gret comfort –
Than were I quyt of languisshyng in drede;
530   For, be myn hidde sorwe iblowe on brede,
I shal byjaped ben a thousand tyme
More than that fol of whos folie men ryme.

'But now help, God, and ye, swete, for whom
I pleyne, ikaught, ye, nevere wight so faste!
535   O mercy, dere herte, and help me from
The deth, for I, whil that my lyf may laste,
More than myself wol love yow to my laste;
And with som frendly lok gladeth me, swete,
Though nevere more thing ye me byheete.'

517 **thanked**: thanks be to **gon**: join **daunce**: dance   518 **list**: is pleased,
wishes **febly**: half-heartedly **avaunce**: advance, promote   519 **God
wolde**: would to God   520 **most**: must **thorugh**: because of   521 **beset were
on**: had bestowed your affections upon **swich oon**: such a person   522 **al
lakked hir pitee**: even if she lack compassion   523 **also**: as
525 **fordon**: done for   526 **wold**: grant   528 **A**: ah   529 **were I**: I would be
quyt: free **languisshyng**: suffering **drede**: doubt, uncertainty   530 For if my
hidden sorrow be made widely known   531 **byjaped**: mocked   532 **fol**: fool
whos: whose **ryme**: compose rhymes   533 **ye, swete**: you, dear one
for: because of   534 **pleyne**: lament **ikaught**: in captivity **ye**: indeed
faste: firmly   537 **to my laste**: till death   538 **lok**: look **gladeth me**: make me
happy   539 **more**: greater **byheete**: should promise

This wordes, and ful many an other to,   540
He spak, and called evere in his compleynte
Hire name, for to tellen hire his wo,
Til neigh that he in salte teres dreynte.
Al was for nought: she herde nat his pleynte;
And whan that he bythought on that folie,   545
A thousand fold his wo gan multiplie.

Bywayling in his chambre thus allone,
A frend of his that called was Pandare
Com oones in unwar, and herde hym groone,
And say his frend in swich destresse and care: 550
'Allas,' quod he, 'who causeth al this fare?
O mercy, God! What unhap may this meene?
Han now thus soone Grekes maad yow leene?

'Or hastow som remors of conscience,
And art now falle in som devocioun,   555
And wailest for thi synne and thin offence,
And hast for ferde caught attricioun?
God save hem that biseged han oure town,
That so kan leye oure jolite on presse,
And bringe oure lusty folk to holynesse!'   560

This wordes seyde he for the nones alle,
That with swich thing he myght hym angry maken,
And with an angre don his wo to falle,

540 **to**: in addition   541 **spak**: spoke   543 **neigh**: nearly **dreynte**: drowned
544 **for nought**: in vain **pleynte**: lament   545 **bythought**: reflected
546 **fold**: times   547 **Bywayling**: (while he was) lamenting   549 **Com oones in**: came in once **unwar**: unexpectedly **groone**: complain   550 **say**: saw
551 **quod**: said **fare**: to do, fuss   552 **unhap**: misfortune **meene**: signify
553 **leene**: thin   554 **hastow** (= *hast thow*): do you have **remors**: remorse, compunction   555 **devocioun**: piety, prayerfulness
556 **offence**: transgression   557 **for ferde**: because of fear **caught**: developed **attricioun**: (a mild form of) contrition   559 **leye . . . on presse**: shelve **jolite**: cheerfulness   560 **lusty**: lively, spirited **holynesse**: piety
561 **nones**: occasion, purpose   563 **angre**: fit of anger **don**: cause **falle**: decrease

As for the tyme, and his corage awaken.
565   But wel he wist, as fer as tonges spaken,
Ther nas a man of gretter hardinesse
Thanne he, ne more desired worthinesse.

'What cas,' quod Troilus, 'or what aventure
Hath gided the to sen me langwisshinge,
570   That am refus of every creature?
But for the love of God, at my preyinge,
Go hennes awey; for certes my deyinge
Wol the disese, and I mot nedes deye;
Therfore go wey, ther is na more to seye.

575   'But if thow wene I be thus sik for drede,
It is naught so, and therfore scorne nought.
Ther is another thing I take of hede
Wel more than aught the Grekes han yet wrought,
Which cause is of my deth, for sorowe and thought;
580   But though that I now telle it the ne leste,
Be thow naught wroth; I hide it for the beste.'

This Pandare, that neigh malt for wo and routhe,
Ful ofte seyde, 'Allas, what may this be?
Now frend,' quod he, 'if evere love or trouthe
585   Hath ben, or is, bitwixen the and me,
Ne do thow nevere swich a crueltee
To hiden fro thi frend so gret a care!
Wostow naught wel that it am I, Pandare?

564 As for the tyme: temporarily corage: spirit awaken: arouse   565 But he
well knew, as was reported far and wide   566 hardinesse: daring   567 ne: nor
(one who) worthinesse: honour   568 cas: accident aventure: chance
569 the: thee, you   570 refus of: rejected by   571 preyinge: request
572 hennes: from here certes: certainly deyinge: death   573 the disese: distress
you mot: must nedes: necessarily   574 wey: away na: no   575 wene: suppose
sik: ill drede: fear   576 scorne nought: do not jeer   577 take of hede: care
about   578 Wel: very much aught: anything wrought: done
579 thought: anxiety   580 But though I don't wish to tell you of it now
581 wroth: angry   582 malt: melted routhe: pity   584 trouthe: loyalty
586 crueltee: cruel act   587 care: sorrow, trouble   588 Wostow naught: don't
you know it am I: it is me

'I wol parten with the al thi peyne,
If it be so I do the no comfort,   590
As it is frendes right, soth for to seyne,
To entreparten wo as glad desport.
I have, and shal, for trewe or fals report,
In wrong and right iloved the al my lyve:
Hid nat thi wo fro me, but telle it blyve.'   595

Than gan this sorwful Troylus to syke,
And seide hym thus: 'God leve it be my beste
To telle it the, for sith it may the like,
Yet wol I telle it, though myn herte breste –
And wel woot I thow mayst do me no reste;   600
But lest thow deme I truste nat to the,
Now herke, frend, for thus it stant with me.

'Love, ayeins the which whoso defendeth
Hymselven most, hym alderlest avaylleth,
With disespeyr so sorwfulli me offendeth,   605
That streight unto the deth myn herte sailleth;
Therto desir so brennyngly me assailleth,
That to ben slayn it were a gretter joie
To me than kyng of Grece ben and Troye.

'Suffiseth this, my fulle frend Pandare,   610
That I have seyd, for now wostow my wo;
And for the love of God, my colde care,

589 **parten**: share   590 **If**: (even) if **do**: bring   591 **frendes right**: a friend's
prerogative **soth for to seyne**: to tell the truth   592 **entreparten**: share
desport: pleasure   593–4 **I have . . . iloved**: I have loved and shall (love)
593 **for**: despite **fals**: untrue   595 **Hid nat**: don't hide **blyve**: quickly
596 **syke**: sigh   597 **leve**: grant **beste**: best course   598 **the like**: please you
599 **breste**: should break   600 **do**: bring   601 **deme**: should suppose **to
the**: in you   602 **herke**: listen **it stant**: things stand   604 **hym alderlest
avaylleth**: it is of least of all use to him   605 **disespeyr**: despair
sorwfulli: sadly **offendeth**: assails   607 **Therto**: also **brennyngly**: ardently
me assailleth: attacks me   610 **Suffiseth this**: this is enough **fulle**: true, firm
611 **wostow** (= *wost thow*): you know

So hide it wel – I tolde it nevere to mo,
For harmes myghten folwen mo than two
615   If it were wist – but be thow in gladnesse,
And lat me sterve, unknowe, of my destresse.'

'How hastow thus unkyndely and longe
Hid this fro me, thow fol?' quod Pandarus.
'Paraunter thow myghte after swich oon longe,
620   That myn avys anoon may helpen us.'
'This were a wonder thing,' quod Troilus;
'Thow koudest nevere in love thiselven wisse.
How devel maistow brynge me to blisse?'

'Ye, Troilus, now herke,' quod Pandare;
625   'Though I be nyce, it happeth often so,
That oon that excesse doth ful yvele fare
By good counseil kan kepe his frend therfro.
I have myself ek seyn a blynd man goo
Ther as he fel that couthe loken wide;
630   A fool may ek a wis-man ofte gide.

'A wheston is no kervyng instrument,
But yet it maketh sharppe kervyng tolis;
And there thow woost that I have aught myswent,
Eschuw thow that, for swich thing to the scole is;
635   Thus often wise men ben war by foolys.

613 **mo**: others   614 **harmes**: misfortunes **folwen**: follow **mo**: more
616 **unknowe**: unknown   617 **hastow**: have you **unkyndely**: cruelly
618 **fol**: fool   619 **Paraunter**: perhaps **after swich oon longe**: long for such a
one   620 **avys**: advice **anoon**: at once   621 **wonder**: amazing
622 **thiselven wisse**: manage your own affairs   623 **How devel**: how the
devil **maistow** (= *mayst thow*): are you able **blisse**: happiness   624 **Ye**: yes
herke: listen   625 **nyce**: foolish   626 **excesse doth ful yvele fare**: excess (of
emotion) causes to fare badly   627 **counseil**: advice **therfro**: from that
628 **goo**: walk   629 Where he who had good eyesight fell over
631 **wheston**: whetstone **kervyng**: cutting   632 **tolis**: tools
633 **there**: where **woost**: know **aught**: in any way **myswent**: gone wrong
634 **Eschuw**: avoid **to the scole is**: is a lesson to you   635 **ben war
by**: beware by the example of

If thow do so, thi wit is wel bewared;
By his contrarie is every thyng declared.

'For how myghte evere swetnesse han ben knowe
To him that nevere tasted bitternesse?
Ne no man may ben inly glad, I trowe,   640
That nevere was in sorwe or som destresse.
Eke whit by blak, by shame ek worthinesse –
Ech set by other, more for other semeth,
As men may se, and so the wyse it demeth.

'Sith thus of two contraries is o lore,   645
I, that have in love so ofte assayed
Grevances, oughte konne, and wel the more,
Counseillen the of that thow art amayed;
Ek the ne aughte nat ben yvel appayed,
Though I desyre with the for to bere   650
Thyn hevy charge; it shal the lasse dere.

'I woot wel that it fareth thus be me
As to thi brother, Paris, an herdesse
Which that icleped was Oënone
Wrot in a compleynte of hir hevynesse.   655
Yee say the lettre that she wrot, I gesse?'
'Nay, nevere yet, ywys,' quod Troilus.
'Now,' quod Pandare, 'herkne, it was thus:

636 **bewared**: employed   637 Everything is defined by its opposite   640 **Ne no man may**: nor may anyone   **inly**: wholly   642 **Eke**: also   643 **Ech** each thing   **for other**: because of the other   644 **demeth**: judges   645 **is o lore**: there is one lesson   646 **assayed**: experienced
647 **Grevances**: hardships   **oughte konne**: ought to know how
648 **Counseillen the**: to counsel you   **amayed**: dismayed   649 **the ne aughte nat**: you ought not   **yvel appayed**: displeased   650 **bere**: bear
651 **charge**: burden   **the lasse dere**: harm you less   652 **woot**: know
fareth: turns out   **be**: concerning   653 **herdesse**: shepherdess
654 **icleped**: called   **Oënone**: nymph deserted by Paris for Helen (n.)
655 **compleynte**: letter of complaint   **hevynesse**: unhappiness   656 **Yee say**: you saw   657 **ywys**: to be sure   658 **herkne**: listen

'"Phebus, that first fond art of medicyne,"
660   Quod she, "and couthe in every wightes care
        Remedye and reed, by herbes he knew fyne,
        Yet to hymself his konnyng was ful bare,
        For love hadde hym so bounden in a snare,
        Al for the doughter of the kyng Amete,
665   That al his craft ne koude his sorwes bete."

        'Right so fare I, unhappyly for me.
        I love oon best, and that me smerteth sore;
        And yet, peraunter, kan I reden the
        And nat myself; repreve me na more.
670   I have no cause, I woot wel, for to sore
        As doth an hauk that listeth for to pleye;
        But to thin help yet somwhat kan I seye.

        'And of o thyng right siker maistow be,
        That certein, for to dyen in the peyne,
675   That I shal nevere mo discoveren the;
        Ne, by my trouthe, I kepe nat restreyne
        The fro thi love, theigh that it were Eleyne
        That is thi brother wif, if ich it wiste:
        Be what she be, and love hire as the liste!

659 **Phebus:** Phoebus Apollo **fond:** invented   660 **couthe:** knew **every wightes care:** the care of every patient   661 **reed:** advice **herbes:** medicinal plants **fyne:** thoroughly   662 **konnyng:** skill **ful bare:** completely useless
664 **Amete:** Admetus   665 **craft:** skill **bete:** cure
666 **unhappyly:** unfortunately   667 **oon:** one **me smerteth sore:** pains me grievously   668 **peraunter:** perhaps **reden the:** advise you
669 **repreve:** reproach   670 **sore:** soar   671 **listeth:** wishes
672 **somwhat:** something   673 **o:** one **siker:** certain **maistow:** you may
674 That certainly, though I were to die under torture (*in the peyne*)
675 **discoveren the:** give you away   676 **by my trouthe:** on my word **kepe nat restreyne:** don't care about restraining   677 **theigh that:** even though
678 **brother:** brother's **ich it wiste:** I knew it   679 Love her as you please, whoever she may be

'Therfore, as frend, fullich in me assure,   680
And tel me plat now what is th'enchesoun
And final cause of wo that ye endure?
For douteth nothyng, myn entencioun
Nis nat to yow of reprehencioun
To speke as now, for no wight may byreve   685
A man to love, tyl that hym list to leve.

'And witteth wel that bothe two ben vices:
Mistrusten alle, or elles alle leve.
But wel I woot, the mene of it no vice is,
For for to trusten som wight is a preve   690
Of trouth; and forthi wolde I fayn remeve
Thi wrong conseyte, and do the som wyght triste
Thi wo to telle; and tel me, if the liste.

'The wise seith, "Wo hym that is allone,
For, and he falle, he hath non helpe to ryse";   695
And sith thow hast a felawe, tel thi mone;
For this nys naught, certein, the nexte wyse
To wynnen love – as techen us the wyse –
To walwe and wepe as Nyobe the queene,
Whos teres yet in marble ben yseene.   700

680 **fullich**: completely **assure**: trust   681 **plat**: bluntly **th'enchesoun**: the
reason   682 **final**: ultimate   683 **douteth nothyng**: don't be afraid   684 **Nis
nat**: is not **reprehencioun**: reproach   685 **as now**: now **byreve**: prevent
686 **hym list**: he wishes **leve**: leave off   687 **witteth**: know **vices**: faults
688 To mistrust everything or else believe everything (*alle leve*)
689 **mene**: mean, middle way   690 **For**: because **for to**: to **preve**: proof
691 **trouth**: loyalty **forthi**: therefore **fayn**: gladly **remeve**: remove
692 **wrong conseyte**: misconception **do the som wyght triste**: make you trust
someone   693 **the liste**: you wish   694 **wise**: wise man (i.e. Solomon) **Wo
hym**: woe is him   695 **and**: if   696 **felawe**: friend **tel thi mone**: tell (him)
what's making you moan   697 **nexte wyse**: most direct way   698 **the
wyse**: wise folk   699 **walwe**: writhe **as Nyobe the queene**: like Queen Niobe
(n.)   700 **yseene**: (to be) seen

'Lat be thy wepyng and thi drerynesse,
And lat us lissen wo with oother speche;
So may thy woful tyme seme lesse.
Delyte nat in wo thi wo to seche,
705   As don thise foles that hire sorwes eche
With sorwe whan thei han mysaventure,
And listen naught to seche hem other cure.

'Men seyn, "To wrecche is consolacioun
To have another felawe in hys peyne."
710   That owghte wel ben oure opynyoun,
For bothe thow and I of love we pleyne.
So ful of sorwe am I, soth for to seyne,
That certeinly namore harde grace
May sitte on me, for-why ther is no space.

715   'If God wol, thow art nat agast of me,
Lest I wolde of thi lady the bygyle!
Thow woost thyself whom that I love, parde,
As I best kan, gon sithen longe while.
And sith thow woost I do it for no wyle,
720   And seist I am he that thow trustest moost,
Tel me somwhat, syn al my wo thow woost.'

Yet Troilus for al this no word seyde,
But longe he ley as stylle as he ded were;
And after this with sikynge he abreyde,
725   And to Pandarus vois he lente his ere,
And up his eighen caste he, that in feere

701 **drerynesse**: gloominess   702 **lissen**: alleviate   704 **seche**: seek
705 **foles**: fools **eche**: increase   706 **mysaventure**: misfortune   707 **listen
naught**: do not desire   708 **to wrecche is**: to a person in misery it is
709 **felawe**: companion   711 **pleyne**: complain   712 **soth for to seyne**: to tell
the truth   713 **harde grace**: bad luck   714 **for-why**: because
715 **wol**: wishes (it) **agast**: afraid   716 **the bygyle**: defraud you
717 **woost**: know **parde**: by God   718 **gon sithen longe while**: for a long
time now   719 **wyle**: guile   720 **seist**: (you) say   721 **somwhat**: something
syn: since   723 But for a long time he lay as still as if he were dead
724 **sikynge**: sighing **abreyde**: started up   725 **lente his ere**: listened
726 **eighen**: eyes **caste**: rolled **in feere**: afraid

Was Pandarus, lest that in frenesie
He sholde falle, or elles soone dye;

And cryde 'Awake!' ful wonderlich and sharpe;
'What! Slombrestow as in a litargie?   730
Or artow lik an asse to the harpe,
That hereth sown whan men the strynges plye,
But in his mynde of that no melodie
May sinken hym to gladen, for that he
So dul ys of his bestialite?'   735

And with that, Pandare of his wordes stente;
And Troilus yet hym nothyng answerde,
For-why to tellen nas nat his entente
To nevere no man, for whom that he so ferde;
For it is seyd, 'Man maketh ofte a yerde   740
With which the maker is hymself ybeten
In sondry manere,' as thise wyse treten,

And namelich in his counseil tellynge
That toucheth love that oughte ben secree;
For of himself it wol ynough out sprynge,   745
But if that it the bet governed be.
Ek som tyme it is a craft to seme fle
Fro thyng whych in effect men hunte faste –
Al this gan Troilus in his herte caste.

727 **frenesie**: madness   729 **cryde**: shouted   **wonderlich**: incredulously
sharpe: shrilly   730 **Slombrestow**: are you sleeping   **litargie**: lethargy
(see n.)   731 **artow** (= *art thow*): are you   **to**: at the sound of
732 **sown**: sound   **plye**: pluck   734 **sinken**: penetrate   **gladen**: make happy
735 **dul**: dull-witted   **bestialite**: animal nature   736 **stente**: ceased
738–9 Because he did not intend to tell anyone on whose account he was
behaving like this   740 **yerde**: rod   741 **ybeten**: beaten
742 **sondry**: various   **wyse**: wise people   **treten**: tell   743 And especially in
divulging his secret   744 **That**: that which   **toucheth**: concerns
secree: secret   745 **himself**: itself   **ynough out sprynge**: (soon) enough come
to light   746 **But if**: unless   **governed**: controlled   747 **craft**: clever move
seme fle: appear to flee   748 **in effect**: actually   749 **caste**: consider

750   But natheles, whan he hadde herd hym crye
        'Awake!' he gan to syken wonder soore,
        And seyde, 'Frend, though that I stylle lye,
        I am nat deef. Now pees, and crye namore,
        For I have herd thi wordes and thi lore;
755   But suffre me my meschief to bywaille,
        For thy proverbes may me naught availle.

        'Nor other cure kanstow non for me;
        Ek I nyl nat ben cured; I wol deye.
        What knowe I of the queene Nyobe?
760   Lat be thyne olde ensaumples, I the preye.'
        'No,' quod tho Pandarus, 'therfore I seye,
        Swych is delit of foles to bywepe
        Hire wo, but seken bote they ne kepe.

        'Now knowe I that ther reson in the failleth.
765   But tel me, if I wiste what she were
        For whom that the al this mysaunter ailleth,
        Dorstestow that I tolde in hire ere
        Thi wo, sith thow darst naught thiself for feere,
        And hire bysoughte on the to han som routhe?'
770   'Why, nay,' quod he, 'by God and by my trouthe!'

        'What, nat as bisyly,' quod Pandarus,
        'As though myn owene lyf lay on this nede?'
        'No, certes, brother,' quod this Troilus,

751 **syken:** sigh **wonder:** amazingly **soore:** grievously   753 **pees:** be quiet
crye: shout   754 **lore:** advice   755 **suffre:** permit, allow
meschief: misfortune **bywaille:** bewail   756 **availle:** avail, help '
757 **kanstow** (= *kanst thow*): you know   758 **nyl** (= *ne wil*) **nat:** will not
deye: die   760 **Lat be:** leave be **ensaumples:** exemplary stories **the preye:** beg
you   762 **delit of foles:** fools' pleasure **bywepe:** weep over, lament
763 **seken bote:** to seek for remedy **ne kepe:** are unconcerned   764 You're
being unreasonable about this   765 **what:** who   766 For whom all this
misfortune afflicts you   767 **Dorstestow:** would you dare   768 **darst:** dare
for: because of   769 **bysoughte:** begged **routhe:** pity   770 **trouthe:** troth,
pledged word   771 **nat as bisyly:** not (if I besought her) as earnestly
772 **lay:** depended **nede:** business

'And whi?' – 'For that thow scholdest nevere spede.'
'Wostow that wel?' – 'Ye, that is out of drede,'   775
Quod Troilus; 'for al that evere ye konne,
She nyl to noon swich wrecche as I ben wonne.'

Quod Pandarus, 'Allas! What may this be,
That thow dispeired art thus causeles?
What! Lyveth nat thi lady, bendiste?   780
How wostow so that thow art graceles?
Swich yvel is nat alwey booteles.
Why, put nat impossible thus thi cure,
Syn thyng to come is oft in aventure.

'I graunte wel that thow endurest wo   785
As sharp as doth he Ticius in helle,
Whos stomak foughles tiren evere moo
That hightyn volturis, as bokes telle;
But I may nat endure that thow dwelle
In so unskilful an oppynyoun   790
That of thi wo is no curacioun.

'But oones nyltow, for thy coward herte,
And for thyn ire and folissh wilfulnesse,
For wantrust, tellen of thy sorwes smerte,
Ne to thyn owen help don bysynesse   795
As muche as speke a resoun moore or lesse,

---

774 **For that**: because **spede**: succeed   775 **Wostow**: do you know **Ye**: yes
out of drede: beyond doubt   776 **konne**: can do   777 **wrecche**: despicable
creature **wonne**: won   779 **dispeired**: in despair **causeles**: without cause
780 **bendiste**: bless you!   781 **graceles**: out of favour   782 **yvel**: trouble
booteles: without remedy   783 **put nat**: do not suppose   784 **Syn**: since **in
aventure**: in doubt   785 **graunte**: admit   786 **Ticius**: Tityus (n.)
787 **foughles**: birds **tiren**: tear   788 **hightyn**: are called **volturis**: vultures
789 **dwelle**: continue   790 **unskilful**: unreasonable   791 **curacioun**: cure
792 **oones nyltow** (= *ne wylt thow*): won't you even once   793 **ire**: bad
temper **folissh**: foolish **wilfulnesse**: obstinacy   794 **wantrust**: distrust
sorwes smerte: painful sorrows (or, sorrow's pain)   795 **don bysynesse**: make
an effort

But list as he that lest of nothyng recche –
What womman koude loven swich a wrecche?

'What may she demen oother of thy deeth,
800   If thow thus deye, and she not why it is,
But that for feere is yolden up thy breth,
For Grekes han biseged us, iwys?
Lord, which a thonk than shaltow han of this!
Thus wol she seyn, and al the town attones:
805   "The wrecche is ded, the devel have his bones!"

'Thow mayst allone here wepe and crye and knele –
But love a womman that she woot it nought,
And she wol quyte it that thow shalt nat fele:
Unknowe, unkist, and lost that is unsought.
810   What, many a man hath love ful deere ybought
Twenty wynter that his lady wiste,
That nevere yet his lady mouth he kiste.

'What sholde he therfore fallen in dispayr,
Or be recreant for his owne tene,
815   Or slen hymself, al be his lady fair?
Nay, nay, but evere in oon be fressh and grene
To serve and love his deere hertes queene,
And thynk it is a guerdon hire to serve,
A thousand fold moore than he kan deserve.'

797 **list** (= *liest*): you lie here **as he that**: as does a man who **lest**: wishes **of nothyng recche**: to care about nothing   799 **What . . . oother**: what else **demen**: suppose   800 **not** (= *ne wot*): does not know   801 But that, out of fear, you've given up breathing   802 **For**: because   803 Lord, what sort of thanks shall you then receive for this!   804 **attones**: at the same time 805 **the devel have**: may the devil have   807 **that**: in such a way that 808 **quyte it that**: requite it so that   809 (To remain) unknown (is to remain) unkissed, and what is not sought after is lost   810 **ful deere ybought**: paid very dearly for   812 **lady**: lady's   813 **What**: why   814 **be recreant**: admit defeat **tene**: grief, vexation   815 **slen**: slay **al be his lady fair**: even though his lady be beautiful   816 **evere in oon**: constantly **fressh**: tireless **grene**: eager   818 **guerdon**: reward   819 **fold**: times

And of that word took hede Troilus,   820
And thoughte anon what folie he was inne,
And how that soth hym seyde Pandarus,
That for to slen hymself myght he nat wynne,
But bothe don unmanhod and a synne,
And of his deth his lady naught to wite;   825
For of his wo, God woot, she knew ful lite.

And with that thought he gan ful sore syke,
And seyde, 'Allas! What is me best to do?'
To whom Pandare answered, 'If the like,
The beste is that thow telle me al thi wo;   830
And have my trouthe, but thow it fynde so
I be thi boote, er that it be ful longe,
To pieces do me drawe and sithen honge!

'Ye, so thow seyst,' quod Troilus tho, 'allas!
But, God woot, it is naught the rather so.   835
Ful hard were it to helpen in this cas,
For wel fynde I that Fortune is my fo;
Ne al the men that riden konne or go
May of hire cruel whiel the harm withstonde;
For as hire list she pleyeth with free and bonde.'   840

Quod Pandarus, 'Than blamestow Fortune
For thow art wroth; ye, now at erst I see.
Woost thow nat wel that Fortune is comune

---

822 **soth hym seyde Pandarus**: Pandarus was telling him the truth   823 **for to slen hymself**: by killing himself   **wynne**: gain anything   824 **don unmanhod**: commit an unmanly act   825 **naught to wite**: (would be) not to blame   826 **lite**: little   827 **sore**: grievously   **syke**: sigh   828 **me**: for me 829 **the like**: you please   831 **have my trouthe**: take my word for it **but**: unless   832 **I be**: (that) I am   **boote**: remedy, help   **er that**: before 833 Have me torn to pieces and afterwards hanged!   835 **rather**: sooner 836 **cas**: situation   837 **fo**: foe   838 **riden konne or go**: are able to ride or walk   839 **whiel**: wheel   **withstonde**: resist   840 **hire list**: she pleases **pleyeth**: toys   **free and bonde**: free man and serf (i.e. everyone) 841 **blamestow**: you blame   842 **For**: because   **wroth**: angry   **now at erst**: only now, for the first time   843 **comune**: in common, shared

To everi manere wight in som degree?
845 And yet thow hast this comfort, lo, parde,
That, as hire joies moten overgon,
So mote hire sorwes passen everechon.

'For if hire whiel stynte any thyng to torne,
Than cessed she Fortune anon to be.
850 Now, sith hire whiel by no way may sojourne,
What woostow if hire mutabilite
Right as thyselven list wol don by the,
Or that she be naught fer fro thyn helpynge?
Paraunter thow hast cause for to synge.

855 'And therfore wostow what I the biseche?
Lat be thy wo and tornyng to the grounde;
For whoso list have helyng of his leche,
To hym byhoveth first unwre his wownde.
To Cerberus yn helle ay be I bounde,
860 Were it for my suster, al thy sorwe,
By my wil she sholde al be thyn to-morwe.

'Look up, I seye, and telle me what she is
Anon, that I may gon about thy nede.
Knowe ich hire aught? For my love, telle me this.
865 Thanne wolde I hopen rather for to spede.'
Tho gan the veyne of Troilus to blede,
For he was hit, and wax al reed for shame.
'Aha!' quod Pandare; 'Here bygynneth game.'

844 To every sort of creature to some extent   845 **parde**: indeed
846 **moten overgon**: must pass away   847 **everechon**: every one
848 **stynte**: were to stop **any thyng**: at all   849 **cessed she**: she would
cease   850 **sojourne**: stop   851 **woostow**: do you know
mutabilite: changeableness   852 **thyselven list**: you wish **by the**: in your
case   853 **fer**: far **helpynge**: aid   854 **Paraunter**: perhaps **synge**: sing (for
happiness)   855 **biseche**: beg   856 **Lat be**: leave be, give up
tornyng: turning, facing   857 **whoso list**: whoever wishes **leche**: physician
858 **To hym byhoveth**: he must **unwre**: uncover   859 **be I**: may I be
860 **Were it**: if it were   862 **what**: who   863 **gon about**: attend to
nede: business, affair   864 **aught**: at all   865 **rather**: sooner **spede**: succeed
867 **wax**: turned **reed**: red   868 **Here bygynneth game**: now the fun begins!

And with that word he gan hym for to shake,
And seyde, 'Thef, thow shalt hyre name telle.'   870
But tho gan sely Troilus for to quake
As though men sholde han led hym into helle,
And seyde, 'Allas, of al my wo the welle,
Thanne is my swete fo called Criseyde!'
And wel neigh with the word for feere he deide.   875

And whan that Pandare herde hire name nevene,
Lord, he was glad, and seyde, 'Frend so deere,
Now fare aright, for Joves name in hevene:
Love hath byset the wel; be of good cheere!
For of good name and wisdom and manere   880
She hath ynough, and ek of gentilesse –
If she be fayr, thow woost thyself, I gesse,

'N'y nevere saugh a more bountevous
Of hire estat, n'a gladder, ne of speche
A frendlyer, n'a more gracious   885
For to do wel, ne lasse hadde nede to seche
What for to don; and al this bet to eche,
In honour, to as fer as she may strecche,
A kynges herte semeth by hyrs a wrecche.

'And forthi loke of good comfort thow be;   890
For certeinly, the ferste poynt is this
Of noble corage and wel ordeyné,
A man to have pees with hymself, ywis.
So oghtist thow, for noht but good it is

---

870 **Thef:** wretch   871 **sely:** poor **quake:** tremble   872 **sholde:** were to
873 **welle:** source   874 **fo:** foe   875 **wel neigh:** very nearly **deide:** died
876 **nevene:** named   878 **fare aright:** do well   879 **byset the:** bestowed you
880 **name:** reputation   881 **gentilesse:** nobility   883 **N'y nevere saugh:** nor
did I ever see **bountevous:** generous   884 **estat:** rank **n'a gladder:** nor a more
cheerful   885 **gracious:** well-disposed   886 **do:** act **seche:** take thought
887 **al this bet to eche:** to make all this better still   888 In the full extent of
her concern for honour   889 **by hyrs a wrecche:** despicable in comparison
with hers   890 **forthi:** therefore **loke:** make sure, see to it   891 **ferste:** most
important   892 **corage:** disposition **ordeyné:** regulated   893 **pees:** peace

895   To love wel, and in a worthy place;
         The oghte not to clepe it hap, but grace.

         'And also thynk, and therwith glade the,
         That sith thy lady vertuous is al,
         So foloweth it that there is some pitee
900   Amonges alle thise other in general;
         And forthi se that thow, in special,
         Requere naught that is ayeyns hyre name –
         For vertu streccheth naught hymself to shame.

         'But wel is me that evere that I was born,
905   That thow biset art in so good a place;
         For by my trouthe, in love I dorste have sworn
         The sholde nevere han tid thus fayr a grace.
         And wostow why? For thow were wont to chace
         At Love in scorn, and for despit him calle
910   "Seynt Idiot, lord of thise foles alle."

         'How often hastow maad thi nyce japes,
         And seyd that Loves servantz everichone
         Of nycete ben verray Goddes apes;
         And some wolde mucche hire mete allone,
915   Liggyng abedde, and make hem for to grone;
         And som, thow seydest, hadde a blaunche fevere,
         And preydest God he sholde nevere kevere.

896 **The oghte**: you ought **clepe**: call **hap**: chance **grace**: divine favour
897 **glade the**: rejoice 898 **al**: entirely 900 **other**: other (virtues) **in general**: not specifically 901 **se**: see **in special**: especially 902 **Requere**: ask for **ayeyns**: contrary to **name**: reputation 903 For virtue does not stretch so far as to include anything shameful 904 **wel is me**: I am happy
905 **biset**: bestowed 906–7 For upon my word I would have sworn so favourable a fortune in love should never have befallen you 908 **wostow**: do you know **wont**: accustomed **chace**: rail 909 **despit**: insult
911 **hastow**: have you **nyce**: foolish **japes**: jokes 913 **Of nycete**: through foolishness **verray**: true, veritable **Goddes apes**: born fools
914 **mucche**: munch **mete**: food 915 **Liggyng**: lying **abedde**: in bed **make hem for to grone**: pretend to groan 916 **som**: one **blaunche fevere**: 'white fever', i.e. love-sickness (which makes lovers pale) 917 **kevere**: recover

'And som of hem took on hem, for the cold,
More than ynough, so seydestow ful ofte;
And som han feyned ofte tyme, and told   920
How that they waken, whan thei slepen softe;
And thus they wolde han brought hemself alofte,
And natheles were under at the laste –
Thus seydestow, and japedest ful faste.

'Yet seydestow that for the moore part   925
Thise loveres wolden speke in general,
And thoughten that it was a siker art,
For faylyng, for t'assaien overal.
Now may I jape of the, if that I shal;
But natheles, though that I sholde deye,   930
That thow art non of tho, I dorste seye.

'Now bet thi brest, and sey to God of Love,
"Thy grace, lord, for now I me repente,
If I mysspak, for now myself I love."
Thus sey with al thyn herte in good entente.'   935
Quod Troilus, 'A, lord! I me consente,
And preye to the my japes thow foryive,
And I shal nevere more whyle I live.'

'Thow seist wel,' quod Pandare, 'and now I hope
That thow the goddes wrathe hast al apesed;   940
And sithen thow hast wopen many a drope,

918 **took on hem:** put on (clothing) **for:** on account of   919 **seydestow:** you
said   920 **feyned:** pretended   921 **waken:** remain awake, keep vigil
softe: comfortably   922 **alofte:** to an advantageous position
923 **under:** unsuccessful **at the laste:** in the end   924 **japedest:** joked
925 **for the moore part:** mostly   926 **in general:** in general terms   927 **siker
art:** sure method   928 **For faylyng:** against failure **t'assaien overal:** to try
everywhere   929 **jape of:** joke about **shal:** would   931 **tho:** those (kinds of
lovers) **dorste:** would dare   932 **bet:** beat   934 **mysspak:** said something
amiss **myself I love:** I myself am in love   935 **in good entente:** willingly, with
good will   936 **me consente:** submit   937 **japes:** jests   938 **nevere
more:** never (speak amiss) again   940 **apesed:** assuaged   941 **sithen:** since
wopen: wept

And seyd swych thyng wherwith thi god is plesed,
Now wolde nevere god but thow were esed!
And thynk wel, she of whom rist al thi wo
945 Hereafter may thy comfort be also.

'For thilke grownd that bereth the wedes wikke
Bereth ek thise holsom herbes as ful ofte;
Next the foule netle, rough and thikke,
The rose waxeth swoote and smothe and softe;
950 And next the valeye is the hil o-lofte;
And next the derke nyght the glade morwe;
And also joie is next the fyn of sorwe.

'Now loke that atempre be thi bridel,
And for the beste ay suffre to the tyde,
955 Or elles al oure labour is on ydel:
He hasteth wel that wisely kan abyde.
Be diligent and trewe, and ay wel hide;
Be lusty, fre; persevere in thy servyse,
And al is wel, if thow werke in this wyse.

960 'But he that parted is in everi place
Is nowher hol, as writen clerkes wyse.
What wonder is, though swich oon have no
          grace?
Ek wostow how it fareth of som servise –
As plaunte a tree or herbe, in sondry wyse,

942 **wherwith**: with which   943 Now may God never wish anything but that
you be comforted (*esed*)   944 **rist** (= *riseth*): arises   946 **thilke**: that same
wikke: noxious   947 **holsom**: wholesome   948 **Next**: next to **foule**: vile
949 **waxeth**: grows **swoote**: sweet   950 **o-lofte**: above   951 **glade**: happy
morwe: morning   952 **fyn**: end   953 **loke**: take care **atempre**: restrained
bridel: bridle   954 **suffre to the tyde**: wait patiently until the right time
955 **on ydel**: in vain   956 **hasteth**: hastens **abyde**: wait   957 **trewe**: loyal
hide: conceal   958 **lusty**: cheerful **fre**: generous **servyse**: love-service
959 **werke**: act **wyse**: way   960 **parted**: divided   961 **hol**: whole   962 **is**: is
it **though swich oon**: that such a person **grace**: favour   963 You also know
how it turns out with some love-service   964 **As plaunte**: like planting
herbe: plant **sondry**: various

And on the morwe pulle it up as blyve!   965
No wonder is, though it may nevere thryve.

'And sith that God of Love hath the bistowed
In place digne unto thi worthinesse,
Stond faste, for to good port hastow rowed;
And of thiself, for any hevynesse,   970
Hope alwey wel; for, but if drerinesse
Or over-haste oure bothe labour shende,
I hope of this to maken a good ende.

'And wostow why I am the lasse afered
Of this matere with my nece trete?   975
For this have I herd seyd of wyse lered:
Was nevere man or womman yet bigete
That was unapt to suffren loves hete,
Celestial, or elles love of kynde –
Forthy som grace I hope in hire to fynde.   980

'And for to speke of hire in specyal,
Hire beaute to bithynken and hire youthe,
It sit hire naught to ben celestial
As yet, though that hire liste bothe and kowthe;
But trewely, it sate hire wel right nowthe   985
A worthi knyght to loven and cherice,
And but she do, I holde it for a vice.

965 **on the morwe**: next day **as blyve**: at once   968 **digne**: worthy
worthinesse: excellence   969 **faste**: firm **hastow**: you have
970 **for**: notwithstanding **hevynesse**: unhappiness   971 **Hope alwey**
wel: always be hopeful **but if**: unless **drerinesse**: dejection   972 Or over-
hastiness ruin (*shende*) the work of both of us   973 **maken a good**
ende: bring about a good result   974 **lasse afered**: less afraid   975 Of . . .
trete: to discuss   976 **lered**: learned men   977 **bigete**: begotten
978 **unapt**: undisposed **hete**: ardour, fever   979 **Celestial**: heavenly, spiritual
love of kynde: natural, earthly, love   980 **Forthy**: therefore   981 **in**
specyal: particularly   982 **bithynken**: consider   983 **sit** (= *sitteth*): suits
984 As yet, although she both would and could   985 **sate**: would befit
nowthe: now   986 **cherice**: hold dear   987 **but she do**: unless she does so
holde: consider **for**: as, to be **vice**: fault

'Wherfore I am, and wol ben, ay redy
To peyne me to do yow this servyse;
990   For bothe yow to plese thus hope I
Herafterward; for ye ben bothe wyse,
And konne it counseil kepe in swych a wyse
That no man shal the wiser of it be –
And so we may ben gladed alle thre.

995   'And, by my trouthe, I have right now of the
A good conceyte in my wit, as I gesse,
And what it is, I wol now that thow se:
I thenke, sith that Love, of his goodnesse,
Hath the converted out of wikkednesse,
1000   That thow shalt ben the beste post, I leve,
Of al his lay, and moost his foos to greve.

'Ensample why, se now thise wise clerkes,
That erren aldermost ayeyn a lawe,
And ben converted from hire wikked werkes
1005   Thorugh grace of God that list hem to hym
              drawe,
Thanne arn thise folk that han moost God in awe,
And strengest feythed ben, I undirstonde,
And konne an errowr alderbest withstonde.'

Whan Troilus hadde herd Pandare assented
1010   To ben his help in lovyng of Cryseyde,
Weex of his wo, as who seith, untormented;

988 **Wherfore**: for which reason **redy**: ready   989 **peyne me**: take pains
990 **bothe yow**: you both   991 **Herafterward**: after this   992 **konne**: can,
know how to **it counseil kepe**: to keep it secret   994 **gladed**: made happy
996 **conceyte**: notion **wit**: mind   1000 **post**: pillar, supporter **leve**: believe
1001 **lay**: religion, faith **moost**: most **foos**: enemies **greve**: injure
1002 **Ensample why**: for example   1003 **erren**: transgress **aldermost**: most
of all **ayeyn**: against   1005 **that list**: whom it pleases **hem to hym drawe**: to
draw them to himself   1006 **arn**: are **han . . . in awe**: fear   1007 **strengest
feythed**: of strongest faith   1008 **errowr**: heresy, mistaken belief
alderbest: best of all **withstonde**: resist, refute   1010 **help**: helper
1011 **Weex**: (he) became **as who seith**: as one might say **untormented**: free of
torment

But hotter weex his love, and thus he seyde,
With sobre chere, although his herte pleyde:
'Now blisful Venus helpe, er that I sterve,
Of the, Pandare, I mowe som thank deserve.   1015

'But, deere frend, how shal my wo be lesse
Til this be doon? And good, ek telle me this:
How wiltow seyn of me and my destresse,
Lest she be wroth – this drede I moost, ywys –
Or nyl nat here or trowen how it is?   1020
Al this drede I, and ek for the manere
Of the, hire em, she nyl no swich thyng here.'

Quod Pandarus, 'Thow hast a ful gret care
Lest that the cherl may falle out of the moone!
Whi, Lord! I hate of the thi nyce fare!   1025
Whi, entremete of that thow hast to doone!
For Goddes love, I bidde the a boone:
So lat m'alone, and it shal be thi beste.'
'Whi, frend,' quod he, 'now do right as the leste.

'But herke, Pandare, o word, for I nolde   1030
That thow in me wendest so gret folie,
That to my lady I desiren sholde
That toucheth harm or any vilenye;
For dredeles me were levere dye

1013 **sobre**: serious **chere**: manner **pleyde**: was light   1014 **blisful**: blessed
1015 That from you, Pandarus, I might deserve some thanks (i.e. for a favour
such as you are now doing me)   1017 **doon**: done **good**: good friend
1018 **wiltow seyn**: will you speak   1019 **wroth**: angry **drede I moost**: I fear
most   1020 **here**: hear **trowen**: believe   1021 **for the manere**: for
appearances' sake (n.)   1022 **Of the**: from you **em**: uncle   1023 **hast a ful
gret care**: are worrying a lot   1024 In case the man (*cherl*) in the moon may
fall out   1025 **nyce**: foolishly scrupulous **fare**: behaviour   1026 **entremete
of**: concern yourself with   1027 **bidde the a boone**: ask you a favour
1028 **thi beste**: best for you   1029 **the leste**: you please   1030 **o**: one **nolde**
(= *ne wolde*): would not wish   1031 **wendest**: should suppose
1033 **That**: that which **toucheth**: involves **harm**: wrong **vilenye**: dishonour
1034 For without doubt (*dredeles*) I would rather (*me were levere*) die

1035   Than she of me aught elles understode
         But that that myghte sownen into goode.'

         Tho lough this Pandare, and anon answerde,
         'And I thi borugh? Fy! No wight doth but so.
         I roughte naught though that she stood and herde
1040   How that thow seist! but farewel, I wol go.
         Adieu! Be glad! God spede us bothe two!
         Yef me this labour and this bisynesse,
         And of my spede be thyn al that swetnesse.'

         Tho Troilus gan doun on knees to falle,
1045   And Pandare in his armes hente faste,
         And seyde, 'Now, fy on the Grekes alle!
         Yet, parde, God shal helpe us atte laste.
         And dredelees, if that my lyf may laste,
         And God toforn, lo, som of hem shal smerte;
1050   And yet m'athenketh that this avant m'asterte!

         'Now, Pandare, I kan na more seye,
         But, thow wis, thow woost, thow maist, thow
                 art al!
         My lif, my deth, hol in thyn hond I leye.
         Help now!' Quod he, 'Yis, by my trowthe, I shal.'
1055   'God yelde the, frend, and this in special,'
         Quod Troilus, 'that thow me recomande
         To hire that to the deth me may comande.'

1035 **aught**: anything **understode**: would believe   1036 **that that**: that
which **sownen into**: tend towards, be conducive to   1037 **Tho lough**: then
laughed   1038 And with me as your surety? Pooh! No one does anything
else   1039 **roughte naught**: would not care   1040 **seist**: speak
1041 **Adieu**: farewell **God spede**: may God grant success to   1042 **Yef**: give
bisynesse: undertaking   1043 **spede**: success   1045 **hente**: clasped
faste: tightly   1046 **fy on**: I scorn   1047 **parde**: by God **atte**: at the
1048 **dredelees**: without doubt   1049 **God toforn**: before God (I swear)
smerte: feel pain   1050 **m'athenketh**: I regret **avant**: boast
m'asterte: escaped my lips   1052 **wis**: wise one **woost**: know **maist**: can do
1053 **hol**: wholly   1054 **Yis**: yes indeed!   1055 **yelde**: reward **this in
special**: particularly for this   1056 **recomande**: commend

This Pandarus, tho desirous to serve
His fulle frend, than seyde in this manere:
'Farwell, and thenk I wol thi thank deserve!   1060
Have here my trowthe, and that thow shalt wel
     here.'
And went his wey, thenkyng on this matere,
And how he best myghte hire biseche of grace,
And fynde a tyme therto, and a place.

For everi wight that hath an hous to founde   1065
Ne renneth naught the werk for to bygynne
With rakel hond, but he wol bide a stounde,
And sende his hertes line out fro withinne
Aldirfirst his purpos for to wynne.
Al this Pandare in his herte thoughte,   1070
And caste his werk ful wisely or he wroughte.

But Troilus lay tho no lenger down,
But up anon upon his stede bay,
And in the feld he pleyde the leoun;
Wo was that Grek that with hym mette a-day!   1075
And in the town his manere tho forth ay
Soo goodly was, and gat hym so in grace,
That ecch hym loved that loked on his face.

For he bicom the frendlieste wight,
The gentilest, and ek the mooste fre,   1080
The thriftiest, and oon the beste knyght

1058 **tho**: then **desirous**: eager   1059 **fulle**: true, firm   1060 **thenk**: believe
thank: gratitude   1061 **Have here my trowthe**: here is my pledge, take my
word for it   1064 **therto**: for it   1065 **founde**: build   1066 **renneth**: runs
1067 **rakel**: rash, hasty **bide**: wait **stounde**: while   1068 **line**: (builder's or
mason's measuring) line (n.)   1069 **Aldirfirst**: first of all **wynne**: achieve
1071 **caste**: planned **or**: before **wroughte**: acted   1073 **stede bay**: bay (i.e.
reddish-brown) horse   1074 **feld**: field of battle **pleyde the leoun**: acted the
lion   1075 **mette**: encountered **a-day**: by day   1076 **tho forth ay**: always
thenceforth   1077 **goodly**: pleasant **gat hym so in grace**: won such favour
for himself   1078 **ecch**: everyone   1079 **bicom**: became
1080 **gentilest**: noblest **fre**: generous   1081 The most admirable (*thriftiest*)
and the very best (*oon the beste*) knight

That in his tyme was or myghte be;
Dede were his japes and his cruelte,
His heighe port and his manere estraunge,
1085   And ecch of tho gan for a vertu chaunge.

Now lat us stynte of Troilus a stounde,
That fareth lik a man that hurt is soore,
And is somdeel of akyngge of his wownde
Ylissed wel, but heeled no deel moore,
1090   And, as an esy pacyent, the loore
Abit of hym that gooth aboute his cure;
And thus he dryeth forth his aventure.

Explicit liber primus.

1083 **Dede:** (as if) dead **japes:** jokes, jests **cruelte:** heartlessness   1084 **heighe
port:** lofty bearing **estraunge:** distant   1085 And each of those turned into a
virtue   1086 **stynte:** cease (speaking) **stounde:** while   1087 **fareth:** behaves
soore: grievously   1088 **somdeel:** somewhat **akyngge:** (the) aching
1089 **Ylissed:** relieved **no deel:** not a bit   1090 **esy:** compliant
loore: advice   1091 **Abit** (= *abideth*): awaits **gooth aboute:** occupies himself
with   1092 **dryeth forth:** continues to endure **aventure:** lot   *Explicit liber
primus*: Here ends the first book

BOOK 2

Owt of thise blake wawes for to saylle,
O wynd, O wynd, the weder gynneth clere;
For in this see the boot hath swych travaylle,
Of my connyng, that unneth I it steere.
This see clepe I the tempestous matere   5
Of disespeir that Troilus was inne –
But now of hope the kalendes bygynne.

O lady myn, that called art Cleo,
Thow be my speed fro this forth, and my Muse,
To ryme wel this book til I have do;   10
Me nedeth here noon other art to use.
For-whi to every lovere I me excuse,
That of no sentement I this endite,
But out of Latyn in my tonge it write.

Incipit prohemium secundi libri: Here begins the proem of the second book
1 **wawes**: waves   2 **gynneth**: begins **clere**: to clear   3–4 **boot . . . Of my**
connyng: boat of my skill **travaylle**: difficulty   4 **unneth**: hardly   5 **clepe I**: I
call **tempestous matere**: tumultuous subject   6 **disespeir**: despair
7 **kalendes**: first day of month (hence, beginning)   8 **Cleo**: Clio (n.)   9 **Thow**
be: may you be **speed**: help   10 **ryme**: compose in rhyming verse **do**: done
11 **Me nedeth**: I need **use**: employ   12 **For-whi**: for which reason **me**
excuse: beg pardon   13 **of no sentement**: not out of personal feeling,
experience (of love) **endite**: compose   14 **tonge**: language

15   Wherfore I nyl have neither thank ne blame
     Of al this werk, but prey yow mekely,
     Disblameth me if any word be lame,
     For as myn auctour seyde, so sey I.
     Ek though I speeke of love unfelyngly,
20   No wondre is, for it nothyng of newe is;
     A blynd man kan nat juggen wel in hewis.

     Ye knowe ek that in forme of speche is chaunge
     Withinne a thousand yeer, and wordes tho
     That hadden pris, now wonder nyce and straunge
25   Us thinketh hem, and yet thei spake hem so,
     And spedde as wel in love as men now do;
     Ek for to wynnen love in sondry ages,
     In sondry londes, sondry ben usages.

     And forthi if it happe in any wyse,
30   That here be any lovere in this place
     That herkneth, as the storie wol devise,
     How Troilus com to his lady grace,
     And thenketh, 'So nold I nat love purchace,'
     Or wondreth on his speche or his doynge,
35   I noot; but it is me no wonderynge.

     For every wight which that to Rome went
     Halt nat o path, or alwey o manere;
     Ek in som lond were al the game shent,

15 **Wherfore:** for which reason **thank:** thanks **blame:** censure
16 **Of:** for **mekely:** meekly 17 **Disblameth:** excuse **lame:** halting
19 **unfelyngly:** insensitively 20 **No wondre is:** it is no surprise **of**
newe: novel 21 **juggen:** discriminate **hewis:** colours 22 **forme:** manner
speche: language 23 **tho:** then 24 **pris:** currency **wonder:** amazingly
nyce: ludicrous **straunge:** unusual 25 **Us thinketh hem:** they seem to us
26 **spedde:** prospered 27 **sondry:** different 28 **londes:** countries
usages: customs 29 **forthi:** therefore **happe:** happen 31 **herkneth:** hears
devise: tell 32 **lady:** lady's 33 I would not go about winning love like
that 34 **wondreth on:** is amazed at 35 **noot** (= *ne woot*): do not know **me**
no wonderynge: no cause for amazement to me 36 **went** (= *wendeth*): goes
37 **Halt** (= *holdeth*): holds, keeps to **o:** the same 38 **shent:** ruined

If that they ferde in love as men don here:
As thus, in opyn doyng or in chere,   40
In visityng in forme, or seyde hire sawes;
Forthi men seyn, 'Ecch contree hath his lawes.'

Ek scarsly ben ther in this place thre
That have in love seid lik, and don, in al;
For to thi purpos this may liken the,   45
And the right nought; yet al is seid or schal;
Ek som men grave in tree, some in ston wal,
As it bitit. But syn I have bigonne,
Myn auctour shal I folwen, if I konne.

Explicit prohemium secundi libri.

Incipit liber secundus.

In May, that moder is of monthes glade,   50
That fresshe floures, blew and white and rede,
Ben quike agayn, that wynter dede made,
And ful of bawme is fletyng every mede,
Whan Phebus doth his bryghte bemes sprede
Right in the white Bole, it so bitidde,   55
As I shal synge, on Mayes day the thrydde,

39 **ferde:** proceeded   40 **opyn doyng:** overt act **chere:** demeanour,
expression   41 **in forme:** formally, correctly **seyde hire sawes:** (in the way
they) uttered their speeches (n.)   42 **Ecch:** every **contree:** country **his**
lawes: its rules   43 **scarsly:** scarcely   44 **lik:** the same **in al:** completely
45 **liken the:** please you   46 **the right nought:** you not at all **schal:** shall be
47 **grave:** carve **tree:** wood   48 **bitit** (= *bitideth*): happens
49 **auctour:** author, authority   *Explicit, etc.*: Here ends the proem of the
second book   *Incipit, etc.*: Here begins the second book   50 **moder is:** is the
first **monthes glade:** the pleasurable months   52 **quike:** alive **dede**
made: killed   53 **bawme:** balm, balsam **fletyng:** overflowing
mede: meadow   54 **Phebus:** Phoebus, the sun   55 **Bole:** bull (the zodiacal
sign of Taurus) **bitidde:** happened   56 **Mayes day the thrydde:** the third day
of May

That Pandarus, for al his wise speche,
Felt ek his part of loves shotes keene,
That, koude he nevere so wel of lovyng preche,
60   It made his hewe a-day ful ofte greene.
So shop it that hym fil that day a teene
In love, for which in wo to bedde he wente,
And made, er it was day, ful many a wente.

The swalowe Proigne, with a sorowful lay,
65   Whan morwen com, gan make hire waymentynge
Whi she forshapen was; and ever lay
Pandare abedde, half in a slomberynge,
Til she so neigh hym made hire cheterynge
How Tereus gan forth hire suster take,
70   That with the noyse of hire he gan awake,

And gan to calle, and dresse hym up to ryse,
Remembryng hym his erand was to doone
From Troilus, and ek his grete emprise;
And caste and knew in good plit was the moone
75   To doon viage, and took his way ful soone
Unto his neces palays ther biside –
Now Janus, god of entree, thow hym gyde!

Whan he was come unto his neces place,
'Wher is my lady?' to hire folk quod he;
80   And they hym tolde, and he forth in gan pace,

57 **for al**: despite   58 **part**: portion **shotes keene**: sharp arrows   59 **koude he**: although he could **of . . . preche**: discourse about   60 **hewe**: complexion **a-day**: by day **greene**: sickly   61 **So shop it**: it so happened **hym fil**: there befell him **teene**: affliction   63 **made . . . ful many a wente**: tossed and turned very many times   64 **Proigne**: Procne **lay**: song   65 **morwen**: morning **waymentynge**: lamentation   66 **forshapen**: transformed   67 **slomberynge**: slumber   68 **cheterynge**: twittering   69 **forth . . . take**: abduct   71 **calle**: call (for a servant) **dresse hym**: prepare himself   72 **erand**: mission   73 **emprise**: enterprise   74 **caste**: made an astrological calculation **good plit**: favourable position   75 **doon viage**: undertake a project   76 **palays**: palace **ther biside**: nearby   77 **entree**: entrance **thow hym gyde**: may you guide him!   80 **pace**: proceed

And fond two othere ladys sete and she,
Withinne a paved parlour, and they thre
Herden a mayden reden hem the geste
Of the siege of Thebes, while hem leste.

Quod Pandarus, 'Madame, God yow see,   85
With al youre book and al the compaignie!'
'Ey, uncle myn, welcome iwys,' quod she;
And up she roos, and by the hond in hye
She took hym faste, and seyde, 'This nyght thrie –
To goode mot it turne – of yow I mette.'   90
And with that word she doun on bench hym sette.

'Ye, nece, yee shal faren wel the bet,
If God wol, al this yeer,' quod Pandarus;
'But I am sory that I have yow let
To herken of youre book ye preysen thus.   95
For Goddes love, what seith it? telle it us!
Is it of love? O, som good ye me leere!'
'Uncle,' quod she, 'youre maistresse is nat here.'

With that thei gonnen laughe, and tho she seyde,
'This romaunce is of Thebes that we rede;   100
And we han herd how that kyng Layus deyde
Thorugh Edippus his sone, and al that dede;
And here we stynten at thise lettres rede –
How the bisshop, as the book kan telle,
Amphiorax, fil thorugh the ground to helle.'   105

81 **fond**: found **sete**: seated   82 **parlour**: private chamber, off a main hall
83 **mayden**: girl **geste**: story   84 **hem leste**: they pleased   85 **God yow
see**: may God watch over you   87 **Ey**: ah!   88 **roos**: rose **in hye**: quickly
89 **thrie**: thrice   90 May something good come of it, I dreamed (*mette*) of
you   91 **hym sette**: made him sit   92 **faren wel**: prosper **bet**: better
93 **wol**: wishes it   94 **let**: hindered   95 **preysen**: praise, commend   97 Is it
about love? Please teach me something useful!   99 **gonnen**: began
100 **of**: about   101 **Layus**: Laius, king of Thebes (n.)
102 **Edippus**: Oedipus **dede**: deed   103 **stynten**: stopped **lettres
rede**: rubrics   105 **Amphiorax**: Amphiaraus (n.) **fil**: fell

Quod Pandarus, 'Al this knowe I myselve,
And al th'assege of Thebes and the care;
For herof ben ther maked bookes twelve.
But lat be this, and telle me how ye fare.
110   Do wey youre barbe, and shew youre face bare;
Do wey youre book, rys up, and lat us daunce,
And lat us don to May som observaunce.'

'I! God forbede!' quod she. 'Be ye mad?
Is that a widewes lif, so God yow save?
115   By God, ye maken me ryght soore adrad!
Ye ben so wylde, it semeth as ye rave.
It satte me wel bet ay in a cave
To bidde and rede on holy seyntes lyves;
Lat maydens gon to daunce, and yonge wyves.'

120   'As evere thrive I,' quod this Pandarus,
'Yet koude I telle a thyng to doon yow pleye.'
'Now, uncle deere,' quod she, 'telle it us
For Goddes love – is than th'assege aweye?
I am of Grekes so fered that I deye.'
125   'Nay, nay,' quod he, 'as evere mote I thryve,
It is a thing wel bet than swyche fyve.'

'Ye, holy God,' quod she, 'what thyng is that?
What! Bet than swyche fyve? I! Nay, ywys!
For al this world ne kan I reden what
130   It sholde ben; some jape I trowe is this;
And but youreselven telle us what it is,

107 **th'assege**: the siege **care**: sorrow, grief 108 **herof**: concerning this
109 **lat**: leave **fare**: get on 110 **Do wey**: put aside **barbe**: wimple (n.)
112 **don . . . observaunce**: pay respect 113 **I!**: ah! 114 Is that how a widow
should live, as God may save you? 115 **soore**: extremely **adrad**: afraid
116 **wylde**: impassioned **rave**: are raving 117 **satte me wel bet**: would befit
me much better 118 **bidde**: pray 120 **evere thrive I**: I may ever prosper
121 **doon yow pleye**: make you happy 123 **aweye**: over
124 **fered**: frightened 125 **mote**: may 126 **wel bet**: much better **swyche
fyve**: five such things 129 **reden**: understand 130 **jape**: trick, joke
trowe: believe 131 **but**: unless

My wit is for t'arede it al to leene.
As help me God, I not nat what ye meene.'

'And I youre borugh, ne nevere shal, for me,
This thyng be told to yow, as mote I thryve!'   135
'And whi so, uncle myn? Whi so?' quod she.
'By God,' quod he, 'that wol I telle as blyve!
For proudder womman is ther noon on lyve,
And ye it wiste, in al the town of Troye.
I jape nought, as evere have I joye!'   140

Tho gan she wondren moore than biforn
A thousand fold, and down hire eyghen caste;
For nevere, sith the tyme that she was born,
To knowe thyng desired she so faste;
And with a syk she seyde hym atte laste,   145
'Now, uncle myn, I nyl yow nought displese,
Nor axen more that may do yow disese.'

So after this, with many wordes glade,
And frendly tales, and with merie chiere,
Of this and that they pleide, and gonnen wade   150
In many an unkouth, glad, and depe matere,
As frendes doon whan thei ben mette yfere,
Tyl she gan axen hym how Ector ferde,
That was the townes wal and Grekes yerde.

132 **wit**: wits, intelligence **t'arede**: to explain **leene**: slender   133 **not nat** (=
ne woot nat): do not know   134 **And I youre borugh**: as I am your surety
(i.e. I give you my word)   135 **mote**: may   137 **as blyve**: immediately
138 **on lyve**: alive   139 **And**: if **wiste**: knew   140 **evere have I**: I may ever
have   141 **wondren**: be curious   144 **faste**: eagerly   145 **syk**: sigh **atte
laste**: finally   147 **axen**: ask **do yow disese**: upset you   148 **glade**: joyful
149 **tales**: conversation **merie chiere**: cheerful mood, high spirits
150 **pleide**: enjoyed themselves **wade**: venture   151 **unkouth**: unfamiliar
glad: pleasant **depe**: profound   152 **ben mette yfere**: have met together
153 **ferde**: was getting on   154 **townes wal**: city's defence **Grekes
yerde**: scourge of the Greeks

155   'Ful wel, I thonk it God,' quod Pandarus,
'Save in his arm he hath a litel wownde –
And ek his fresshe brother Troilus,
The wise, worthi Ector the secounde,
In whom that alle vertu list habounde,
160   As alle trouthe and alle gentilesse,
Wisdom, honour, fredom, and worthinesse.'

'In good feith, em,' quod she, 'that liketh me
Thei faren wel; God save hem bothe two!
For trewelich I holde it gret deynte
165   A kynges sone in armes wel to do,
And ben of goode condiciouns therto;
For gret power and moral vertu here
Is selde yseyn in o persone yfeere.'

'In good faith, that is soth,' quod Pandarus.
170   'But, by my trouthe, the kyng hath sones
        tweye –
That is to mene, Ector and Troilus –
That certeynly, though that I sholde deye,
Thei ben as voide of vices, dar I seye,
As any men that lyven under the sonne:
175   Hire myght is wyde yknowe, and what they
        konne.

'Of Ector nedeth it namore for to telle:
In al this world ther nys a bettre knyght
Than he, that is of worthynesse welle,

---

156 **Save**: except   157 **fresshe**: spirited, lively   158 **Ector the secounde**: second Hector   159 **list habounde**: is pleased to abound
160 **trouthe**: constancy **gentilesse**: nobility   161 **fredom**: noble generosity
162 **em**: uncle **that liketh me**: I am pleased that   164 **trewelich**: truly
holde: consider **gret deynte**: highly honourable   165 **armes**: deeds of arms, warfare   166 And to possess excellent qualities (*condiciouns*) in addition
(*therto*)   168 Are seldom seen (*selde yseyn*) together (*yfeere*) in one person
169 **soth**: true   171 **mene**: signify   173 **voide**: devoid   175 **myght**: strength
wyde yknowe: widely known   **konne**: are capable of   178 **welle**: source, fount

And he wel moore vertu hath than myght –
This knoweth many a wis and worthi wight.   180
The same pris of Troilus I seye;
God help me so, I knowe nat swiche tweye.'

'By God,' quod she, 'of Ector that is sooth.
Of Troilus the same thyng trowe I;
For, dredeles, men tellen that he doth   185
In armes day by day so worthily,
And bereth hym here at hom so gentily
To everi wight, that alle pris hath he
Of hem that me were levest preysed be.'

'Ye sey right sooth, ywys,' quod Pandarus;   190
'For yesterday, whoso had with hym ben,
He myghte han wondred upon Troilus;
For nevere yet so thikke a swarm of been
Ne fleigh, as Grekes for hym gonne fleen,
And thorugh the feld, in everi wightes eere,   195
Ther nas no cry but "Troilus is there!"

'Now here, now ther, he hunted hem so faste,
Ther nas but Grekes blood – and Troilus.
Now hem he hurte, and hem al down he caste;
Ay wher he wente, it was arayed thus: 200
He was hire deth, and sheld and lif for us,
That, as that day, ther dorste non withstonde
Whil that he held his blody swerd in honde.

181 pris: praise   182 swiche tweye: two such men   183 sooth: true
185 dredeles: without doubt doth: performs   186 armes: warfare, fighting
worthily: nobly   187 bereth hym: conducts himself gentily: courteously
188 pris: praise   189 From those by whom I would most like (*me were
levest*) to be praised   190 sey right sooth: speak truly
192 wondred: marvelled   193 been: bees   194 fleigh: flew for: because of
gonne fleen: fled   195 wightes eere: person's ear   196 nas no cry but: was no
other shout except   198 nas: was nothing   199 hem ... hem: these ...
those caste: threw   200 Ay wher: wherever arayed: destined   201 hire
deth: the death of them (the Greeks) sheld: shield   202 as: as concerns ther
dorste non: no one dared withstonde: resist   203 swerd: sword

'Therto he is the frendlieste man
205   Of gret estat that evere I saugh my lyve;
And wher hym lest, best felawshipe kan
To swich as hym thynketh able for to thryve.'
And with that word tho Pandarus, as blyve,
He took his leve and seyde, 'I wol gon henne.'
210   'Nay, blame have I, myn uncle,' quod she thenne.

'What aileth yow to be thus wery soone,
And namelich of wommen? Wol ye so?
Nay, sitteth down; by God, I have to doone
With yow, to speke of wisdom er ye go.'
215   And everi wight that was aboute hem tho,
That herde that, gan fer awey to stonde,
Whil they two hadde al that hem liste in honde.

Whan that hire tale al brought was to an ende,
Of hire estat and of hire governaunce,
220   Quod Pandarus, 'Now tyme is that I wende.
But yet, I say, ariseth, lat us daunce,
And cast youre widewes habit to mischaunce!
What list yow thus youreself to disfigure,
Sith yow is tid thus fair an aventure?'

225   'A, wel bithought! For love of God,' quod she,
'Shal I nat witen what ye meene of this?'
'No, this thing axeth leyser,' tho quod he,

---

204 **Therto**: in addition   205 **estat**: rank **my lyve**: in my life   206 And
where he wishes, knows how (to show) greatest friendliness   207 **able for to
thryve**: worthy of success   208 **tho**: then **as blyve**: forthwith   209 **took his
leve**: said goodbye **henne**: from here   210 **blame have I**: I am at fault
211 **aileth yow**: is the matter with you **wery**: weary
212 **namelich**: especially   213 **have to doone**: have some business to do
214 **wisdom**: a wise course of action   215 **aboute**: near   217 While the two
of them transacted whatever business they wished   218 **tale**: conversation
219 **estat**: position **hire governaunce**: the conduct of her affairs   220 **tyme
is**: it is time **wende**: go   222 **habit**: clothes **to mischaunce**: to the devil
223 **What list yow**: why do you want   224 **yow is tid**: there has befallen you
fair: favourable **aventure**: good fortune   225 **wel bithought**: that subject
again!   226 **witen**: know   227 **axeth leyser**: requires time

'And eke me wolde muche greve, iwys,
If I it tolde and ye it toke amys.
Yet were it bet my tonge for to stille   230
Than seye a soth that were ayeyns youre wille.

'For, nece, by the goddesse Mynerve,
And Jupiter, that maketh the thondre rynge,
And by the blisful Venus that I serve,
Ye ben the womman in this world lyvynge –   235
Withouten paramours, to my wyttynge –
That I best love, and lothest am to greve;
And that ye weten wel youreself, I leve.'

'Iwis, myn uncle,' quod she, 'grant mercy!
Youre frendshipe have I founden evere yit.   240
I am to no man holden, trewely,
So muche as yow, and have so litel quyt;
And with the grace of God, emforth my wit,
As in my gylt I shall yow nevere offende;
And if I have er this, I wol amende.   245

'But for the love of God I yow biseche,
As ye ben he that I love moost and triste,
Lat be to me youre fremde manere speche,
And sey to me, youre nece, what yow liste.'
And with that word hire uncle anoon hire kiste,   250
And seyde, 'Gladly, leve nece dere!
Tak it for good that I shal sey yow here.'

228 **me wolde muche greve**: I would be very upset   229 **amys**: amiss,
wrongly   230 **stille**: hold still   231 **soth**: true thing   232 **Mynerve**: Minerva
(n.)   233 **Jupiter**: king of the classical gods **thondre**: thunder
rynge: resound   236 **Withouten paramours**: not counting lovers **to my
wyttynge**: to the best of my knowledge   237 **lothest**: most reluctant
greve: distress, vex   238 **weten**: know **leve**: believe   239 **grant mercy**: thank
you   241 **holden**: obliged   242 **quyt**: repaid   243 **emforth my wit**: to the
extent of my understanding (as far as I am able)   244 **As in my gylt**: by my
fault **offende**: displease   245 **amende**: make amends   247 **moost**: most
triste: trust   248 **Lat be**: give up **to**: towards **fremde**: distant **manere**: kind
of   249 **liste**: please   250 **kiste**: kissed   251 **leve**: dear   252 **for
good**: well

With that she gan hire eighen down to caste,
And Pandarus to coghe gan a lite,
255 And seyde, 'Nece, alwey – lo! – to the laste,
How so it be that som men hem delite
With subtyl art hire tales for to endite,
Yet for al that, in hire entencioun
Hire tale is al for som conclusioun.

260 'And sithe th'ende is every tales strengthe,
And this matere is so bihovely,
What sholde I peynte or drawen it on lengthe
To yow, that ben my frend so feythfully?'
And with that word he gan right inwardly
265 Byholden hire and loken on hire face,
And seyde, 'On swich a mirour, goode grace!'

Than thought he thus: 'If I my tale endite
Aught harde, or make a proces any whyle,
She shal no savour have therin but lite,
270 And trowe I wolde hire in my wil bigyle;
For tendre wittes wenen al be wyle
Theras thei kan nought pleynly understonde;
Forthi hire wit to serven wol I fonde' –

And loked on hire in a bysi wyse,
275 And she was war that he byheld hire so,
And seyde, 'Lord! so faste ye m'avise!

254 **coghe**: cough, clear his throat **lite**: little   255 **to the laste**: in the end
257 **subtyl**: ingenious **endite**: compose   258 **for**: in spite of **in hire
entencioun**: as far as their aim is concerned   259 **conclusioun**: end
260 **th'ende**: the conclusion   261 **bihovely**: beneficial   262 **What**: why
peynte: embellish **drawen**: draw out **on lengthe**: at length
263 **feythfully**: loyally   264 **inwardly**: intently   266 **mirour**: paragon **goode
grace**: (may there be) good fortune   267 **my tale**: what I have to say
endite: compose   268 **Aught**: in any way **proces any whyle**: long story of it
(n.)   269 **savour**: delight **therin**: in that **lite**: little   270 **trowe**: (she will)
believe **wil**: intention **bigyle**: deceive   271 For impressionable minds (*tendre
wittes*) suppose everything is trickery   272 **Theras**: where **pleynly**: fully
273 Therefore I shall try (*fonde*) to adjust (what I say) to her (level of)
intelligence   274 **in a bysi wyse**: attentively   275 **war**: aware   276 **so faste
ye m'avise**: how intently you are staring at me

Sey ye me nevere er now? What sey ye, no?'
'Yis, yys,' quod he, 'and bet wole er I go!
But be my trouthe, I thoughte now if ye
Be fortunat, for now men shal it se.   280

'For to every wight som goodly aventure
Som tyme is shape, if he it kan receyven;
But if that he wol take of it no cure,
Whan that it commeth, but wilfully it weyven,
Lo, neyther cas ne fortune hym deceyven,   285
But ryght his verray slouthe and wrecchednesse;
And swich a wight is for to blame, I gesse.

'Good aventure, O beele nece, have ye
Ful lightly founden, and ye konne it take;
And for the love of God, and ek of me,   290
Cache it anon, lest aventure slake!
What sholde I lenger proces of it make?
Yif me youre hond, for in this world is noon –
If that yow list – a wight so wel bygon.

'And sith I speke of good entencioun,   295
As I to yow have told wel herebyforn,
And love as wel youre honour and renoun
As creature in al this world yborn,
By alle the othes that I have yow sworn,
And ye be wrooth therfore, or wene I lye,   300
Ne shal I nevere sen yow eft with yë.

277 Sey . . . sey: saw . . . say   278 bet wole: will do so better   279 be my trouthe: upon my word thoughte now if: was wondering just now whether
280 fortunat: favoured by fortune   281 goodly aventure: good fortune
282 shape: allotted it kan receyven: knows how to be receptive to it
283 take of it no cure: pay no heed to it   284 wilfully: purposely
weyven: neglect   285 cas: chance   286 ryght: precisely verray: sheer
slouthe: indolence wrecchednesse: meanness of spirit   288 aventure: fortune
beele: fair   289 lightly: easily and: if   291 Cache: seize slake: fail, abate
293 Yif: give   294 wel bygon: happy   295 of: with   296 herebyforn: before
this   297 renoun: reputation   298 yborn: living   299 othes: oaths
300 And: if wrooth: angry therfore: because of it wene I lye: think I am
lying   301 eft: again yë: eye

'Beth naught agast, ne quaketh naught! Wherto?
Ne chaungeth naught for feere so youre hewe!
For hardely the werst of this is do;
305   And though my tale as now be to yow newe,
Yet trist alwey ye shal me fynde trewe;
And were it thyng that me thoughte unsittynge,
To yow wolde I no swiche tales brynge.'

'Now, my good em, for Goddes love, I preye,'
310   Quod she, 'come of, and telle me what it is!
For both I am agast what ye wol seye,
And ek me longeth it to wite, ywys;
For whethir it be wel or be amys,
Say on, lat me nat in this feere dwelle.'

315   'So wol I doon; now herkeneth! I shal telle:

'Now, nece myn, the kynges deere sone,
The goode, wise, worthi, fresshe, and free,
Which alwey for to don wel is his wone,
The noble Troilus, so loveth the,
320   That, but ye helpe, it wol his bane be.
Lo, here is al – what sholde I moore seye?
Doth what yow lest to make hym lyve or deye.

'But if ye late hym deyen, I wol sterve –
Have here my trouthe, nece, I nyl nat lyen –
325   Al sholde I with this knyf my throte kerve.'
With that the teris breste out of his yën,
And seide, 'If that ye don us bothe dyen

302 **Beth naught**: don't be **agast**: afraid **quaketh**: tremble **Wherto**: why?
303 **hewe**: colour   304 **hardely**: certainly   **do**: done, over   306 **trist**: trust
307 **were it**: if it were **unsittynge**: unsuitable   310 **come of**: come on, hurry
up   312 And also I long to know it, indeed   314 **Say on**: speak out
317 **wise**: prudent, discreet **worthi**: honourable **fresshe**: spirited **free**: noble
318 Who is wont always to act well   320 **but**: unless **bane**: destruction
322 **lest**: please, wish   323 **late**: let **sterve**: die   324 **Have here my trouthe**: I
give you my word   325 **Al sholde I**: even if I had to **kerve**: cut
326 **teris**: tears **breste**: burst **yën**: eyes   327 **don**: make

Thus gilteles, than have ye fisshed fayre!
What mende ye, though that we booth appaire?

'Allas, he which that is my lord so deere,   330
That trewe man, that noble, gentil knyght,
That naught desireth but youre frendly cheere,
I se hym dyen, ther he goth upryght,
And hasteth hym with al his fulle myght
For to ben slayn, if his fortune assente.   335
Allas, that God yow swich a beaute sente!

'If it be so that ye so cruel be
That of his deth yow liste nought to recche,
That is so trewe and worthi, as ye se,
Namoore than of a japer or a wrecche   340
If ye be swich, youre beaute may nat strecche
To make amendes of so cruel a dede:
Avysement is good byfore the nede.

'Wo worth the faire gemme vertulees!
Wo worth that herbe also that dooth no boote!   345
Wo worth that beaute that is routheles!
Wo worth that wight that tret ech undir foote!
And ye, that ben of beaute crop and roote,
If therwithal in yow ther be no routhe,
Than is it harm ye lyven, by my trouthe!   350

328 **gilteles**: innocent **fisshed fayre**: made a fine catch   329 **What mende
ye**: what do you gain by it **appaire**: perish   331 **trewe**: faithful
332 **cheere**: look   333 **ther he goth upryght**: i.e. on his feet   334 **hasteth
hym**: hurries   338 **nought to recche**: to care nothing   340 **japer**: trickster
341 **strecche**: prove adequate   343 **Avysement**: deliberation **nede**: necessity
344 **Wo worth**: woe be to, a curse on **vertulees**: without special powers
345 **dooth no boote**: effects no healing   346 **routheles**: without compassion
347 **tret** (= *tredeth*): treads **ech**: everyone   348 **crop and roote**: top (of a
plant) and root (i.e. the whole)   349 **therwithal**: along with that (beauty)
routhe: pity   350 **is it harm**: it is a pity

'And also think wel that this is no gaude;
For me were levere thow and I and he
Were hanged, than I sholde ben his baude,
As heigh as men myghte on us alle ysee!
355   I am thyn em; the shame were to me,
As wel as the, if that I sholde assente
Thorugh myn abet that he thyn honour shente.

'Now understond, for I yow nought requere
To bynde yow to hym thorugh no byheste,
360   But only that ye make hym bettre chiere
Than ye han doon er this, and moore feste,
So that his lif be saved atte leeste;
This al and som, and pleynly, oure entente –
God help me so, I nevere other mente!

365   'Lo, this requeste is naught but skylle, ywys,
Ne doute of resoun, pardee, is ther noon.
I sette the worste, that ye dreden this:
Men wolde wondren sen hym come or goon.
Ther-ayeins answere I thus anoon,
370   That every wight, but he be fool of kynde,
Wol deme it love of frendshipe in his mynde.

'What, who wol demen, though he se a man
To temple go, that he th'ymages eteth?
Thenk ek how wel and wisely that he kan

351 **gaude:** trick   352 **me were levere:** I would rather that
353 **baude:** pimp   354 **ysee:** see   357 **abet:** incitement **shente:** damaged
358 **requere:** require, ask   359 **bynde yow:** commit yourself
byheste: promise   360 **make hym bettre chiere:** look more favourably upon
him   361 **moore feste:** (treat him) more encouragingly   363 This is the
whole matter (*al and som*) and, in full (*pleynly*), our intention   365 **is naught
but skylle:** is only reasonable   366 **doute of resoun:** reasonable grounds for
fear   367 **sette the worste:** postulate the worst possibility **dreden:** fear
368 **wondren:** be curious **sen:** to see   369 **Ther-ayeins:** in reply to that
370 **but:** unless **fool of kynde:** a congenital idiot   371 **deme:** suppose **love of
frendshipe:** affection between friends (n.)   373 **th'ymages eteth:** is eating the
idols

Governe hymself, that he no thyng foryeteth,   375
That where he cometh he pris and thank hym geteth;
And ek therto, he shal come here so selde,
What fors were it though al the town byhelde?

'Swych love of frendes regneth al this town –
And wre yow in that mantel evere moo;   380
And God so wys be my savacioun,
As I have seyd, youre beste is to do soo.
But alwey, goode nece, to stynte his woo,
So lat youre daunger sucred ben a lite,
That of his deth ye be naught for to wite.'   385

Criseyde, which that herde hym in this wise,
Thoughte, 'I shal felen what he meneth, ywis.'
'Now em,' quod she, 'what wolde ye devise?
What is youre rede I sholde don of this?'
'That is wel seyd,' quod he. 'Certein, best is   390
That ye hym love ayeyn for his lovynge,
As love for love is skilful guerdonynge.

'Thenk ek how elde wasteth every houre
In ech of yow a partie of beautee;
And therfore er that age the devoure,   395
Go love; for old, ther wol no wight of the.
Lat this proverbe a loore unto yow be:
To late ywar, quod Beaute, whan it paste;
And Elde daunteth Daunger at the laste.

---

375 Conduct himself, so that he forgets nothing   376 **pris**: praise
377 **therto**: also **selde**: seldom   378 **What fors were it**: what would it matter
byhelde: should see   379 **regneth**: prevails in   380 **wre yow**: conceal
yourself **mantel**: cloak   381 And, as God may surely be my salvation
382 **beste**: best course   383 **stynte**: stop   384 **daunger**: disdain, reserve
sucred: sweetened **lite**: little   385 **wite**: blame   387 **felen**: find out
indirectly   388 **devise**: suggest   389 **rede**: advice   391 **ayeyn**: in return
392 **skilful**: reasonable **guerdonynge**: reward   393 **elde**: ageing, advancing
years **wasteth**: lays waste   394 **partie**: part   395 **the devoure**: consumes
you   396 Go and love; for when you are old, no one will want you
397 **loore**: maxim   398 'Aware too late,' said Beauty when it was past
399 **daunteth**: tames, subdues **at the laste**: in the end

400   'The kynges fool is wont to crien loude,
       Whan that hym thinketh a womman berth hire hye,
       "So longe mote ye lyve, and alle proude,
       Til crowes feet be growe under youre yë,
       And sende yow than a myrour in to prye,
405   In which that ye may se youre face a-morwe!"
       I bidde wisshe yow namore sorwe.'

       With this he stynte, and caste adown the heed,
       And she began to breste a-wepe anoon,
       And seyde, 'Allas, for wo! Why nere I deed?
410   For of this world the feyth is al agoon.
       Allas, what sholden straunge to me doon,
       Whan he that for my beste frend I wende
       Ret me to love, and sholde it me defende?

       'Allas! I wolde han trusted, douteles,
415   That if that I, thorough my dysaventure,
       Hadde loved outher hym or Achilles,
       Ector, or any mannes creature,
       Ye nolde han had no mercy ne mesure
       On me, but alwey had me in repreve.
420   This false world – allas! – who may it leve?

       'What, is this al the joye and al the feste?
       Is this youre reed? Is this my blisful cas?
       Is this the verray mede of youre byheeste?

401 **hym thinketh**: it seems to him **berth hire hye**: behaves haughtily
402 **mote**: may **proude**: proud people   404 **crowes feet**: lines, wrinkles,
around the eyes   404 **prye**: peer   405 **a-morwe**: in the morning   406 Niece,
I would not wish any greater distress upon you (or possibly: I pray, wish for
yourself no more sorrow)   407 **stynte**: stopped **caste adown**: lowered
408 **breste**: burst **a-wepe**: into weeping   409 **Allas, for wo**: how unhappy I
am! **nere I** (= *ne were I*): aren't I **deed**: dead   410 **agoon**: gone
411 **straunge**: strangers   412 **wende**: supposed   413 **Ret** (= *redeth*) advises
defcnde: forbid   414 **douteles**: without doubt
415 **dysaventure**: misfortune   416 **outher**: either   417 **mannes**: human
418 **mesure**: moderation   419 **repreve**: reproach   420 **leve**: trust
421 **feste**: rejoicing   422 **reed**: advice **blisful**: happy **cas**: situation
423 **verray**: true **mede**: fulfilment **byheeste**: promise

Is al this paynted proces seyd – allas! –
Right for this fyn? O lady myn, Pallas!   425
Thow in this dredful cas for me purveye,
For so astoned am I that I deye.'

Wyth that she gan ful sorwfully to syke.
'A, may it be no bet?' quod Pandarus;
'By God, I shal namore come here this wyke,   430
And God toforn, that am mystrusted thus!
I se wel that ye sette lite of us,
Or of oure deth! Allas, I woful wrecche!
Might he yet lyve, of me is nought to recche.

'O cruel god, O dispitouse Marte,   435
O Furies thre of helle, on yow I crye!
So lat me nevere out of this hous departe,
If that I mente harm or vilenye!
But sith I se my lord mot nedes dye,
And I with hym, here I me shryve, and seye   440
That wikkedly ye don us bothe deye.

'But sith it liketh yow that I be ded,
By Neptunus, that god is of the see,
Fro this forth shal I nevere eten bred
Til I myn owen herte blood may see;   445
For certeyn I wol deye as soone as he.'
And up he sterte, and on his wey he raughte,
Til she agayn hym by the lappe kaughte.

424 **paynted**: highly coloured **proces**: discourse   425 **Right**: precisely, just
fyn: purpose **Pallas**: Pallas Athene   426 Look after me in this frightening
situation   427 **astoned**: bewildered   428 **syke**: sigh   429 Is this the best you
can do?   430 **wyke**: week   431 **God toforn**: before God (I swear)
432 **sette**: reckon **lite**: little   434 If only he might survive – it doesn't matter
about me!   435 **dispitouse**: pitiless **Marte**: Mars (n.)   436 **on yow I crye**: I
invoke you   438 **vilenye**: dishonour   439 **mot**: must **nedes**: necessarily
440 **me shryve**: make my (last) confession (before dying)
441 **wikkedly**: maliciously **don . . . deye**: cause to die, kill   442 **it liketh
yow**: it pleases you, you wish   443 **Neptunus**: Neptune, god of the sea
444 **this forth**: henceforth   445 **herte**: heart's   447 **sterte**: leaped
raughte: started   448 **lappe**: fold, hem (of clothing)

Criseyde, which that wel neigh starf for feere,
450   So as she was the ferfulleste wight
That myghte be, and herde ek with hire ere
And saugh the sorwful ernest of the knyght,
And in his preier ek saugh noon unryght,
And for the harm that myghte ek fallen moore,
455   She gan to rewe and dredde hire wonder soore,

And thoughte thus: 'Unhappes fallen thikke
Alday for love, and in swych manere cas
As men ben cruel in hemself and wikke;
And if this man sle here hymself – allas! –
460   In my presence, it wol be no solas.
What men wolde of it deme I kan nat seye:
It nedeth me ful sleighly for to pleie.'

And with a sorowful sik she sayde thrie,
'A, Lord! What me is tid a sory chaunce!
465   For myn estat lith now in jupartie,
And ek myn emes lif is in balaunce;
But natheles, with Goddes governaunce,
I shal so doon, myn honour shal I kepe,
And ek his lif' – and stynte for to wepe.

470   'Of harmes two, the lesse is for to chese;
Yet have I levere maken hym good chere
In honour, than myn emes lyf to lese.

449 **wel neigh**: very nearly **starf**: died   450 **ferfulleste**: most timorous
452 **sorwful**: melancholy **ernest**: seriousness of purpose   453 **preier**: request
noon unryght: nothing wrong   454 And to prevent anything worse
happening   455 **rewe**: repent **dredde hire wonder soore**: became amazingly
fearful   456 **Unhappes**: misfortunes **thikke**: frequently
457 **Alday**: continually **manere cas**: kind of situation
458 **hemself**: themselves **wikke**: bad   459 **sle**: should kill
460 **solas**: consolation   461 **deme**: think   462 **sleighly**: cunningly **pleie**: play
my part   463 **sik**: sigh **thrie**: thrice   464 Ah, Lord! What an unhappy fate
has befallen me (*me is tid*)!   465 **estat**: position **lith**: stands **in jupartie**: at
risk   466 **emes**: uncle's **in balaunce**: at risk   467 **governaunce**: guidance
468 **so doon**: act in such a way **kepe**: preserve   469 **stynte**: stopped
470 **harmes**: evils **lesse**: lesser **for to chese**: to be chosen   471 Yet I would
rather treat him kindly   472 lese: lose

Ye seyn, ye nothyng elles me requere?'
'No, wis,' quod he, 'myn owen nece dere.'
'Now wel,' quod she, 'and I wol doon my peyne;   475
I shal myn herte ayeins my lust constreyne.

'But that I nyl nat holden hym in honde,
Ne love a man ne kan I naught ne may
Ayeins my wyl, but elles wol I fonde,
Myn honour sauf, plese hym fro day to day.   480
Therto nolde I nat ones han seyd nay,
But that I dredde, as in my fantasye;
But cesse cause, ay cesseth maladie.

'And here I make a protestacioun
That in this proces if ye depper go,   485
That certeynly, for no salvacioun
Of yow, though that ye sterven bothe two,
Though al the world on o day be my fo,
Ne shal I nevere of hym han other routhe.'
'I graunte wel,' quod Pandare, 'by my trowthe.   490

'But may I truste wel therto,' quod he,
'That of this thyng that ye han hight me here,
Ye wole it holden trewely unto me?'
'Ye, doutelees,' quod she, 'myn uncle deere.'
'Ne that I shal han cause in this matere,'   495
Quod he, 'to pleyne, or ofter yow to preche?'
'Why, no, parde; what nedeth moore speche?'

473 **me requere**: ask of me   474 **wis**: certainly   475 **Now wel**: all right then
doon my peyne: do my utmost   476 **lust**: inclinations **constreyne**: compel
477 **holden hym in honde**: deceive, cajole, with false hopes
479 **elles**: otherwise **fonde**: try   480 **Myn honour sauf**: without prejudice to
my honour **plese**: to please   481 I would never once have said no to that
482 **But**: except **dredde**: was afraid **fantasye**: imagination   483 But if the
cause should cease, the illness always ceases   484 **protestacioun**: avowal,
declaration   485 **proces**: business **depper**: further   486–7 **salvacioun Of
yow**: saving of your lives   487 **though that**: even though **sterven**: die
488 **on o**: in one **fo**: enemy   489 **routhe**: compassion   490 **graunte
wel**: assent   492 **hight**: promised   493 **holden**: keep **trewely**: faithfully
494 **doutelees**: without doubt   496 **pleyne**: complain **ofter**: more often

Tho fellen they in other tales glade,
Tyl at the laste, 'O good em,' quod she tho,
'For his love, which that us bothe made,
Tel me how first ye wisten of his wo?
Woot noon of it but ye?' He seyde, 'No.'
'Kan he wel speke of love?' quod she; 'I preye
Tel me, for I the bet me shal purveye.'

500

Tho Pandarus a litel gan to smyle,
And seyde, 'By my trouthe, I shal yow telle.
This other day, naught gon ful longe while,
In-with the paleis gardyn, by a welle,
Gan he and I wel half a day to dwelle,
Right for to speken of an ordinaunce,
How we the Grekes myghten disavaunce.

505

510

'Soon after that bigonne we to lepe,
And casten with oure dartes to and fro,
Tyl at the laste he seyde he wolde slepe,
And on the gres adoun he leyde hym tho;
And I afer gan romen to and fro,
Til that I herde, as that I welk alone,
How he bigan ful wofully to grone.

515

'Tho gan I stalke hym softely byhynde,
And sikirly, the soothe for to seyne,
As I kan clepe ayein now to my mynde,
Right thus to Love he gan hym for to pleyne:
He seyde, "Lord, have routhe upon my peyne,

520

498 **tales glade:** cheerful talk   501 **wisten:** knew   502 **Woot noon:** does no
one know   504 Tell me, so that I may the better prepare myself   507 **gon ful
longe while:** very long ago   508 **In-with:** within   510 **ordinaunce:** plan
511 **disavaunce:** repulse   512 **lepe:** rush   513 **dartes:** spears
515 **gres:** grass   516 **afer:** afar **romen:** roam   517 **welk:** walked
518 **wofully:** sorrowfully   519 **stalke:** creep up   520 **sikirly:** certainly
soothe: truth   521 **clepe ayein:** recall   522 **pleyne:** complain, lament
523 **routhe:** pity

Al have I ben rebell in myn entente;
Now, *mea culpa*, lord, I me repente!   525

'"O god, that at thi disposicioun
Ledest the fyn by juste purveiaunce
Of every wight, my lowe confessioun
Accepte in gree, and sende me swich penaunce
As liketh the, but from disesperaunce,   530
That may my goost departe awey fro the,
Thow be my sheld, for thi benignite.

'"For certes, lord, so soore hath she me wounded,
That stood in blak, with lokyng of hire eyen,
That to myn hertes botme it is ysounded,   535
Thorough which I woot that I moot nedes deyen.
This is the werste, I dar me nat bywreyen;
And wel the hotter ben the gledes rede,
That men hem wrien with asshen pale and dede."

'Wyth that he smot his hed adown anon,   540
And gan to motre, I noot what, trewely.
And I with that gan stille awey to goon,
And leet therof as nothing wist had I,
And com ayein anon, and stood hym by,
And seyde, "Awake, ye slepen al to longe!   545
It semeth nat that love doth yow longe,

524 **Al have I**: although I have **rebell**: rebellious **entente**: mind   525 *mea culpa*: (I confess) my fault   526 **disposicioun**: disposal   527 **Ledest**: directs **fyn**: end **purveiaunce**: providence   528 **lowe**: humble   529 **in gree**: favourably   530 **disesperaunce**: despair   531 **goost**: spirit **departe**: separate   532 May you be my protection (*sheld*), out of your kindness   533 **certes**: certainly   535 **myn hertes botme**: the bottom of my heart **ysounded**: sunk   536 **moot nedes**: must necessarily 537 **werste**: worst part **me . . . bywreyen**: reveal my thoughts 538 **gledes**: glowing coals   539 **wrien**: cover **asshen**: ashes **dede**: dead 540 **smot his hed adown**: hung his head   541 **motre**: mutter 542 **stille**: quietly   543 And pretended as though I knew nothing about it 544 **ayein**: back   546 **longe**: pine (or, pertain to)

'"That slepen so that no man may yow wake.
Who sey evere or this so dul a man?"
"Ye, frend," quod he, "do ye youre hedes ake
550   For love, and lat me lyven as I kan."
But though that he for wo was pale and wan,
Yet made he tho as fresshe a countenaunce
As though he sholde have led the newe daunce.

'This passed forth til now, this other day,
555   It fel that I com romyng al allone
Into his chaumbre, and fond how that he lay
Upon his bed; but man so soore grone
Ne herde I nevere, and what that was his mone
Ne wist I nought; for, as I was comynge,
560   Al sodeynly he lefte his complaynynge.

'Of which I took somwat suspecioun,
And ner I com, and fond he wepte soore;
And God so wys be my savacioun,
As nevere of thyng hadde I no routhe moore;
565   For neither with engyn, ne with no loore,
Unnethes myghte I fro the deth hym kepe,
That yet fele I myn herte for hym wepe.

'And God woot, nevere sith that I was born
Was I so besy no man for to preche,
570   Ne nevere was to wight so depe isworn,
Or he me told who myghte ben his leche
But now to yow rehercen al his speche,

548 sey: saw or: before   549 do ye youre hedes ake: give yourself a
headache   551 wan: pale, sickly   552 made: assumed fresshe: joyous
countenaunce: appearance   553 led the newe daunce: undertaken the latest
thing   554 passed forth: went on   555 fel: happened
556 chaumbre: bedroom   558–9 what that was his mone Ne wist I
nought: what he was lamenting about, I did not know   562 ner: nearer
563 wys: surely   565 engyn: ingenuity loore: learning
566 Unnethes: hardly   569 no: any preche: lecture   570 Nor ever was to
anyone so deeply sworn (to secrecy)   571 Or: before leche: physician
572 rehercen: recount

Or alle his woful wordes for to sowne,
Ne bid me naught, but ye wol se me swowne.

'But for to save his lif, and elles nought,   575
And to noon harm of yow, thus am I dryven;
And for the love of God, that us hath wrought,
Swich cheer hym dooth that he and I may lyven!
Now have I plat to yow myn herte shryven,
And sith ye woot that myn entent is cleene,   580
Take heede therof, for I non yvel meene.

'And right good thrift, I prey to God, have ye,
That han swich oon ykaught withouten net!
And be ye wis as ye be fair to see,
Wel in the ryng than is the ruby set.   585
Ther were nevere two so wel ymet,
Whan ye ben his al hool as he is youre –
Ther myghty God yet graunte us see that houre!'

'Nay, therof spak I nought, ha, ha!' quod she;
'As helpe me God, ye shenden every deel!'   590
'O, mercy, dere nece,' anon quod he,
'What so I spak, I mente naught but wel,
By Mars, the god that helmed is of steel!
Now beth naught wroth, my blood, my nece dere.'
'Now wel,' quod she, 'foryeven be it here!'   595

With this he took his leve, and home he wente,
And, Lord, so he was glad and wel bygon!
Criseyde aros, no lenger she ne stente,

573 **sowne:** repeat   574 Don't ask me, unless you wish to see me swoon
575 **elles nought:** for no other reason   576 **dryven:** impelled
577 **wrought:** created   578 Show him such encouragement that he and I can go
on living!   579 **plat:** flatly **shryven:** confessed   580 **cleene:** pure   581 **non yvel
meene:** intend nothing wrong   582 **thrift:** luck   **have ye:** may you have   584 **be
ye wis:** if you be as wise   586 **ymet:** met   587 **al hool:** completely **youre:** yours
588 **Ther . . . graunte:** may . . . grant   590 **shenden every deel:** spoil everything
592 **What so:** whatever   593 **helmed is:** wears a helmet   594 **wroth:** angry
blood: kin   595 **foryeven be it:** let it be forgiven   597 **wel bygon:** in a happy
situation   598 **stente:** delayed

But streght into hire closet wente anon,
600   And set hire doun as stylle as any ston,
And every word gan up and down to wynde
That he had seyd, as it com hire to mynde,

And wex somdel astoned in hire thought
Right for the newe cas; but whan that she
605   Was ful avysed, tho fond she right nought
Of peril why she ought afered be.
For man may love, of possibilite,
A womman so, his herte may tobreste,
And she naught love ayein, but if hire leste.

610   But as she sat allone and thoughte thus,
Ascry aros at scarmuch al withoute,
And men criden in the strete, 'Se, Troilus
Hath right now put to flighte the Grekes route!'
With that gan al hire meyne for to shoute,
615   'A, go we se! Cast up the yates wyde!
For thorwgh this strete he moot to paleys ride;

'For other wey is fro the yate noon
Of Dardanus, there opyn is the cheyne.'
With that com he and al his folk anoon
620   An esy pas rydyng, in routes tweyne,
Right as his happy day was, sooth to seyne,
For which, men seyn, may nought destourbed be
That shal bityden of necessitee.

599 **streght:** directly **closet:** private room, bedroom 600 **set hire doun:** sat
down 601 **wynde:** turn over (in the mind) 602 **com hire to mynde:** came to
her mind 603 **wex:** became **somdel:** somewhat **astoned:** astonished
604 **newe cas:** novel event 605 **Was ful avysed:** had fully considered
606 **afered:** afraid 607 **man:** a man **of possibilite:** possibly
608 **tobreste:** be shattered 609 **ayein:** in return **but if hire leste:** unless she
wishes 611 **Ascry aros:** (a) clamour went up **scarmuch:** skirmish
withoute: outside 613 **route:** host 614 **meyne:** household 615 **go we:** let
us **Cast:** throw **yates:** gates 616 **paleys:** palace 618 **cheyne:** chain (across
city gateway) 620 **An esy pas:** at a slow pace **routes tweyne:** two
companies 621 **Right as:** just as if **happy:** fortunate **was:** it was
622 **destourbed:** impeded 623 **That:** that which **bityden:** happen

This Troilus sat on his baye steede
Al armed, save his hed, ful richely;   625
And wownded was his hors, and gan to blede,
On which he rood a pas ful softely.
But swich a knyghtly sighte trewely
As was on hym, was nought, withouten faille,
To loke on Mars, that god is of bataille.   630

So lik a man of armes and a knyght
He was to seen, fulfilled of heigh prowesse,
For bothe he hadde a body and a myght
To don that thing, as wel as hardynesse;
And ek to seen hym in his gere hym dresse,   635
So fressh, so yong, so weldy semed he,
It was an heven upon hym for to see.

His helm tohewen was in twenty places,
That by a tyssew heng his bak byhynde;
His sheeld todasshed was with swerdes and   640
      maces,
In which men myghte many an arwe fynde
That thirled hadde horn and nerf and rynde;
And ay the peple cryde, 'Here cometh oure joye,
And, next his brother, holder up of Troye!'

For which he wex a litel reed for shame   645
When he the peple upon hym herde cryen,
That to byholde it was a noble game

---

624 **baye steede**: brown horse   627 **a pas**: at walking pace **softely**: slowly
628–30 But to look on Mars, god of war, was truly not such a knightly sight
to see as he was, for certain (*withouten faille*)   632 **to seen**: to look upon
fulfilled: full   634 **hardynesse**: daring, boldness   635 **gere**: armour **hym
dresse**: arm himself   636 **fressh**: eager **weldy**: vigorous   638 **helm**: helmet
tohewen: hacked to pieces   639 **tyssew**: band of rich cloth **heng his bak
byhynde**: hung behind him on his back   640 **todasshed**: shattered
maces: spiked clubs   641 **arwe**: arrow   642 **thirled**: pierced **horn and nerf
and rynde**: horn and sinew and hide   644 **next**: next to **holder
up**: mainstay   645 **reed**: red **shame**: modesty   646 When he heard the
people acclaiming him   647 **game**: sport

How sobrelich he caste down his yën.
Criseyda gan al his chere aspien,
650   And leet it so softe in hire herte synke,
That to hireself she seyde, 'Who yaf me drynke?'

For of hire owen thought she wex al reed,
Remembryng hire right thus, 'Lo, this is he
Which that myn uncle swerith he moot be deed,
655   But I on hym have mercy and pitee.'
And with that thought, for pure ashamed, she
Gan in hire hed to pulle, and that as faste,
Whil he and alle the peple forby paste,

And gan to caste and rollen up and down
660   Withinne hire thought his excellent prowesse,
And his estat, and also his renown,
His wit, his shap, and ek his gentilesse;
But moost hire favour was, for his distresse
Was al for hire, and thought it was a routhe
665   To sleen swich oon, if that he mente trouthe.

Now myghte som envious jangle thus:
'This was a sodeyn love – how myght it be
That she so lightly loved Troilus
Right for the firste syghte, ye, parde?'
670   Now whoso seith so, mote he nevere ythe!
For every thyng a gynnyng hath it nede
Er al be wrought, withowten any drede.

648 **sobrelich:** modestly   649 **aspien:** take note of   651 **yaf:** gave
654 **deed:** dead   655 **But:** unless   656 **for pure ashamed:** for very shame
657 **and that as faste:** and did so very fast indeed   658 **forby paste:** went by
659 **caste:** consider **rollen up and down:** turn over   661 **estat:** rank
662 **wit:** intelligence **shap:** figure **gentilesse:** noble graciousness   663 **moost**
hire favour: what found most favour with her **for:** because
664 **routhe:** pity   665 **sleen:** kill **oon:** a man **mente trouthe:** had honourable
intentions   666 **envious:** ill-willed person **jangle:** chatter
667 **sodeyn:** sudden, impetuous   668 **lightly:** easily   670 **mote:** may
ythe: prosper   671 **a gynnyng hath it nede:** must have a beginning
672 **wrought:** accomplished **drede:** doubt

For I sey nought that she so sodeynly
Yaf hym hire love, but that she gan enclyne
To like hym first, and I have told yow whi;   675
And after that, his manhod and his pyne
Made love withinne hire herte for to myne,
For which by proces and by good servyse
He gat hire love, and in no sodeyn wyse.

And also blisful Venus, wel arrayed,   680
Sat in hire seventhe hous of hevene tho,
Disposed wel, and with aspectes payed,
To helpe sely Troilus of his woo.
And soth to seyne, she nas nat al a foo
To Troilus in his nativitee: 685
God woot that wel the sonner spedde he.

Now lat us stynte of Troilus a throwe,
That rideth forth, and lat us torne faste
Unto Criseyde, that heng hire hed ful lowe
Ther as she sat allone, and gan to caste   690
Where on she wolde apoynte hire atte laste,
If it so were hire em ne wolde cesse
For Troilus upon hire for to presse.

And, Lord! So she gan in hire thought argue
In this matere of which I have yow told,   695
And what to doone best were, and what eschue,

---

674 **enclyne:** be inclined   676 **manhod:** manliness **pyne:** torment
677 **myne:** penetrate, undermine (as in a siege)   678 **by proces:** in course of
time   679 **gat:** obtained   680 **blisful:** beneficent **arrayed:** positioned
681 **Sat:** was positioned **hous:** one of the twelve divisions of the celestial
sphere   682 Favourably inclined, and made propitious (*payed*) by the
dispositions (*aspectes*) of the signs and heavenly bodies   683 **sely:** poor
684 **al a foo:** entirely an enemy   685 **his nativitee:** position of the planets at
his birth   686 **sonner:** sooner **spedde he:** he succeeded   687 **stynte of:** stop
speaking about **throwe:** while   689 **heng:** hung   690 **Ther as:** where
caste: consider   691 **Where on:** on what **apoynte hire:** settle, decide
692 **cesse:** cease   693 **presse:** exert pressure, be pressing   696 **eschue:** avoid

That plited she ful ofte in many fold;
Now was hire herte warm, now was it cold;
And what she thoughte somwhat shal I write,
700   As to myn auctour listeth for t'endite.

She thoughte wel that Troilus persone
She knew by syghte, and ek his gentilesse,
And thus she seyde, 'Al were it nat to doone
To graunte hym love, yet for his worthynesse
705   It were honour with pley and with gladnesse
In honestee with swich a lord to deele,
For myn estat, and also for his heele.

'Ek wel woot I my kynges sone is he,
And sith he hath to se me swich delit,
710   If I wolde outreliche his sighte flee,
Peraunter he myghte have me in dispit,
Thorugh whicch I myghte stonde in worse plit.
Now were I wis, me hate to purchace,
Withouten need, ther I may stonde in grace?

715   'In every thyng, I woot, ther lith mesure;
For though a man forbede dronkenesse,
He naught forbet that every creature
Be drynkeles for alwey, as I gesse.
Ek sith I woot for me is his destresse,
720   I ne aughte nat for that thing hym despise,
Sith it is so he meneth in good wyse.

697 plited: folded, turned back and forth fold: ways (or, folds) 700 As my
source is pleased to write 701 Troilus persone: Troilus's physical
appearance 703 Al were it nat to doone: although it wouldn't do 704 for
his worthynesse: on account of his nobility 705 pley: amusement
gladnesse: joy 706 honestee: honour deele: have to do 707 estat: position
heele: well-being 710 outreliche: utterly 711 Peraunter: perhaps have me
in dispit: bear a grudge against me 712 plit: position, state 713 Now
would I be wise to bring hatred upon myself 714 ther: where stonde in
grace: find favour 715 lith: lies mesure: moderation 716 forbede: should
forbid 717 forbet (= forbedeth) enjoins 718 drynkeles: without a drink
720 aughte: ought despise: disdain 721 meneth in good wyse: has good
intentions

'And eke I knowe of longe tyme agon
His thewes goode, and that he is nat nyce;
N'avantour, seith men, certein, is he noon –
To wis is he to doon so gret a vice;   725
Ne als I nyl hym nevere so cherice
That he may make avaunt, by juste cause,
He shal me nevere bynde in swich a clause.

'Now sette a caas: the hardest is, ywys,
Men myghten demen that he loveth me.   730
What dishonour were it unto me, this?
May ich hym lette of that? Why, nay, parde!
I knowe also, and alday heere and se,
Men loven wommen al biside hire leve,
And whan hem leste namore, lat hem byleve!   735

'I thenke ek how he able is for to have
Of al this noble town the thriftieste
To ben his love, so she hire honour save.
For out and out he is the worthieste,
Save only Ector, which that is the beste;   740
And yet his lif al lith now in my cure –
But swich is love, and ek myn aventure.

'Ne me to love, a wonder is it nought;
For wel woot I myself, so God me spede –
Al wolde I that noon wiste of this thought –   745

722 **agon**: past   723 **thewes**: qualities **nyce**: foolish   724 **N'avantour . . . is
he noon**: nor is he any boaster **seith men**: people say **certein**: certainly
726 **als**: as (or, also) **cherice**: hold dear   727 **avaunt**: boast **by juste
cause**: with good reason   728 **bynde**: tie **clause**: stipulation, condition (as in
a legal contract)   729 **sette a caas**: put a case (for the sake of argument)
hardest: worst (case)   732 **lette**: prevent   733 **alday**: continually   734 **al
biside hire leve**: entirely without their permission   735 **hem leste**: they please,
they wish **byleve**: leave off   737 **thriftieste**: most admirable
738 **so**: provided **save**: preserve, maintain   739 **out and out**: altogether
740 **Save**: except   741 **al lith**: lies entirely **cure**: power   742 **aventure**: lot
743 Nor is it surprising that I should be loved   744 **spede**: help
745 Although I would not want anyone to know of this thought

I am oon the faireste, out of drede,
And goodlieste, whoso taketh hede,
And so men seyn, in al the town of Troie:
What wonder is though he of me have joye?

750   'I am myn owene womman, wel at ese –
I thank it God – as after myn estat,
Right yong, and stonde unteyd in lusty leese,
Withouten jalousie or swich debat:
Shal noon housbonde seyn to me "Chek mat!"
755   For either they ben ful of jalousie,
Or maisterfull, or loven novelrie.

'What shal I doon? To what fyn lyve I thus?
Shal I nat love, in cas if that me leste?
What, pardieux! I am naught religious.
760   And though that I myn herte sette at reste
Upon this knyght, that is the worthieste,
And kepe alwey myn honour and my name,
By alle right, it may do me no shame.'

But right as when the sonne shyneth brighte
765   In March, that chaungeth ofte tyme his face,
And that a cloude is put with wynd to flighte,
Which oversprat the sonne as for a space,
A cloudy thought gan thorugh hire soule pace,
That overspradde hire brighte thoughtes alle,
770   So that for feere almost she gan to falle.

746 oon the: the very drede: doubt   747 goodlieste: most beautiful
748 seyn: say   749 of me have joye: be pleased with me   750 myn owene: an
independent at ese: content   751 as after myn estat: with respect to my
position in life   752 unteyd in lusty leese: free, without ties, in pleasant
pasture   753 debat: dispute   754 Chek mat: checkmate   755 they: i.e.
husbands   756 maisterfull: domineering novelrie: novelty   758 in cas: in
the event me leste: pleases me   759 pardieux: by God religious: a nun
760 sette at reste: settle, fix   762 name: good name   763 By alle right: in all
justice, rightly do: cause   767 oversprat (= *overspredeth*): covers
space: while   768 pace: pass   770 falle: collapse

That thought was this: 'Allas! Syn I am free,
Sholde I now love, and put in jupartie
My sikernesse, and thrallen libertee?
Allas, how dorst I thenken that folie?
May I naught wel in other folk aspie   775
Hire dredfull joye, hire constreinte, and hire
    peyne?
Ther loveth noon, that she nath why to pleyne.

'For love is yet the mooste stormy lyf,
Right of hymself, that evere was bigonne;
For evere som mystrust or nice strif   780
Ther is in love, som cloude is over that sonne.
Therto we wrecched wommen nothing konne,
Whan us is wo, but wepe and sitte and thinke;
Oure wrecche is this, oure owen wo to drynke.

'Also thise wikked tonges ben so prest   785
To speke us harm; ek men ben so untrewe,
That right anon as cessed is hire lest,
So cesseth love – and forth to love a newe!
But harm ydoon is doon, whoso it rewe:
For though thise men for love hem first torende,   790
Ful sharp bygynnyng breketh ofte at ende.

'How ofte tyme hath it yknowen be
The tresoun that to wommen hath ben do!
To what fyn is swich love I kan nat see,

773 **sikernesse:** security **thrallen:** enslave **libertee:** freedom of action
774 **dorst I:** did I dare **thenken:** think of **folie:** foolishness
775 **aspie:** observe 776 **dredfull:** fearful **constreinte:** distress 777 There is
no one in love who does not have reason to complain 779 **of hymself:** in
itself 780 **nice strif:** foolish contention 782 We unhappy women can do
nothing about it 783 **us is wo:** we are miserable 784 **wrecche:** misery
drynke: drink up, endure 785 **wikked:** malicious **prest:** ready 786 **us
harm:** harm of us **untrewe:** faithless 787 **right anon as:** just as soon as **hire
lest:** their desire 788 **forth:** onwards, on the way **a newe:** someone new
789 **ydoon is doon:** (that is) done is done **whoso it rewe:** whoever may regret
it 790 **hem first torende:** tear themselves apart at first 791 Too keen a
beginning often leads to break-up in the end 793 **tresoun:** treachery

795 Or wher bycometh it, whan it is ago –
    Ther is no wight that woot, I trowe so,
    Where it bycometh. Lo, no wight on it sporneth;
    That erst was nothing, into nought it torneth.

    'How bisy, if I love, ek most I be
800 To plesen hem that jangle of love, and dremen,
    And coye hem, that they seye noon harm of me!
    For though ther be no cause, yet hem semen
    Al be for harm that folk hire frendes quemen;
    And who may stoppen every wikked tonge,
805 Or sown of belles whil that thei ben ronge?'

    And after that, hire thought gan for to clere,
    And seide, 'He which that nothing undertaketh,
    Nothyng n'acheveth, be hym looth or deere.'
    And with an other thought hire herte quaketh;
810 Than slepeth hope, and after drede awaketh;
    Now hoot, now cold; but thus, bitwixen tweye,
    She rist hire up, and wente hire for to pleye.

    Adown the steyre anonright tho she wente
    Into the gardyn with hire neces thre,
815 And up and down ther made many a wente –
    Flexippe, she, Tharbe, and Antigone –
    To pleyen that it joye was to see;
    And other of hire wommen, a gret route,
    Hire folowede in the gardyn al aboute.

795 **wher bycometh it**: what becomes of it **ago**: past   797 **on it
sporneth**: trips over it (i.e. it is too small)   798 **That erst was nothing**: what
was nothing before   800 **jangle**: chatter **dremen**: dream up things
801 **coye**: cajole   802 **hem semen**: it seems to them   803 All that people do
to please (*quemen*) their friends is for some harmful purpose
804 **stoppen**: cause to stop wagging   805 **sown**: sound   806 **clere**: become
clear   808 **be hym looth or deere**: whether he like it or not   811 **bitwixen
tweye**: between the two   812 **rist hire up**: gets up **pleye**: relax
813 **Adown**: down **steyre**: staircase **anonright**: immediately   815 **made . . . a
wente**: took a turn   818 **route**: company

This yerd was large, and rayled alle th'aleyes,   820
And shadewed wel with blosmy bowes grene,
And benched newe, and sonded alle the weyes,
In which she walketh arm in arm bitwene,
Til at the laste Antigone the shene
Gan on a Troian song to singen cleere,   825
That it an heven was hire vois to here.

Cantus Antigone

She seyde, 'O Love, to whom I have and shal
Ben humble subgit, trewe in myn entente,
As I best kan, to yow, lord, yeve ich al
For everemo myn hertes lust to rente;   830
For nevere yet thi grace no wight sente
So blisful cause as me, my lif to lede
In alle joie and seurte out of drede.

'Ye, blisful god, han me so wel byset
In love, iwys, that al that bereth lif   835
Ymagynen ne kouthe how to be bet;
For, lord, withouten jalousie or strif,
I love oon which that moost is ententif
To serven wel, unweri or unfeyned,
That evere was, and leest with harm desteyned.   840

'As he that is the welle of worthynesse,
Of trouthe grownd, mirour of goodlihed,
Of wit Apollo, stoon of sikernesse,

820 **yerd**: garden **rayled**: fenced **th'aleyes**: the paths   821 **shadewed**: shaded
blosmy: flowery **bowes**: boughs   822 **benched newe**: furnished with new
benches (n.) **sonded**: sanded **weyes**: paths   824 **shene**: fair   825 **cleere**: clearly
826 **an heven**: heavenly *Cantus Antigone*: Antigone's song   827–8 **have and**
shal Ben: have been and shall be   828 **subgit**: subject   829 **yeve ich**: I give
830 **lust**: desire **to rente**: as a tribute   831 For your grace never sent anyone
833 **seurte**: security   834 **byset**: bestowed   835 **bereth lif**: are alive
836 **bet**: better   838 I love one who is most diligent   839 **unweri**: without
weariness **unfeyned**: unfeigned, sincere   840 **desteyned**: sullied
841 **welle**: fount   842 **grownd**: foundation **mirour**: model, paragon
goodlihed: excellence   843 An Apollo of wisdom, a rock of steadfastness

Of vertu roote, of lust fynder and hed,
845   Thorugh which is alle sorwe fro me ded –
Iwis, I love hym best, so doth he me;
Now good thrift have he, wherso that he be!

'Whom shulde I thanken but yow, god of Love,
Of al this blisse, in which to bathe I gynne?
850   And thanked be ye, lord, for that I love!
This is the righte lif that I am inne,
To flemen alle manere vice and synne:
This dooth me so to vertu for t'entende,
That day by day I in my wille amende.

855   'And whoso seith that for to love is vice,
Or thraldom, though he feele in it destresse,
He outher is envyous, or right nyce,
Or is unmyghty, for his shrewednesse,
To loven; for swich manere folk, I gesse,
860   Defamen Love, as nothing of hym knowe:
Thei speken, but thei benten nevere his bowe!

'What is the sonne wers, of kynde right,
Though that a man, for feeblesse of his yen,
May nought endure on it to see for bright?
865   Or love the wers, though wrecches on it crien?
No wele is worth, that may no sorwe dryen.
And forthi, who that hath an hed of verre,
Fro cast of stones war hym in the werre!

---

844 **roote**: root, origin **of lust fynder and hed**: originator and source of
pleasure 845 **fro me ded**: slain in me 847 Now may he have good luck (*thrift*),
wheresoever he be! 849 **bathe**: bask **gynne**: begin 852 **flemen**: banish
853 **t'entende**: to be inclined 854 **amende**: improve 856 **thraldom**: servitude
though: even though 857 **outher**: either **nyce**: foolish 858 **unmyghty**: unable
for: because of **shrewednesse**: wickedness 860 **Defamen**: slander 861 **benten
nevere his bowe**: i.e. never tried it themselves 862 **What**: in what way
wers: worse **of kynde right**: in its own proper nature 863 **for**: because of
feeblesse: weakness 864 **for bright**: because of (its) brightness 865 **on it
crien**: condemn it 866 **wele is worth**: good fortune is of value **dryen**: endure
867 **who that**: he who **verre**: glass 868 **cast**: throwing **war hym**: let him
beware **werre**: war

'But I with al myn herte and al my myght,
As I have seyd, wol love unto my laste   870
My deere herte and al myn owen knyght,
In which myn herte growen is so faste,
And his in me, that it shal evere laste.
Al dredde I first to love hym to bigynne,
Now woot I wel, ther is no peril inne.'   875

And of hir song right with that word she stente,
And therwithal, 'Now nece,' quod Cryseyde,
'Who made this song now with so good entente?'
Antygone answerde anoon and seyde,
'Madame, iwys, the goodlieste mayde   880
Of gret estat in al the town of Troye,
And let hire lif in moste honour and joye.'

'Forsothe, so it semeth by hire song,'
Quod tho Criseyde, and gan therwith to sike,
And seyde, 'Lord, is ther swych blisse among   885
Thise loveres, as they konne faire endite?'
'Ye, wis,' quod fresshe Antigone the white,
'For alle the folk that han or ben on lyve
Ne konne wel the blisse of love discryve.

'But wene ye that every wrecche woot   890
The parfit blisse of love? Why, nay, iwys!
They wenen all be love, if oon be hoot.
Do wey, do wey, they woot no thyng of this!
Men mosten axe at seyntes if it is
Aught fair in hevene (Why? For they kan telle),   895
And axen fendes is it foul in helle.'

870 **laste**: last day   872 **faste**: firmly   874 **Al dredde I first**: although I was afraid
at first   875 **inne**: in it   876 **stente**: stopped   877 **therwithal**: thereupon
878 **so good entente**: such admirable sentiments   880 **goodlieste**: most
excellent   881 **estat**: rank   882 **let** (= *ledeth*): leads   883 **Forsothe**: truly
884 **sike**: sigh   886 **konne faire endite**: are able to express so beautifully
887 **wis**: certainly   **white**: fair   888 **han or ben**: have (been) or are
889 **discryve**: describe   890 **wene ye**: do you suppose   891 **parfit**: perfect
893 **Do wey**: enough of this   894 **mosten**: would have to   **axe at**: enquire of
895 **Aught**: at all   896 **fendes**: fiends, devils

Criseyde unto that purpos naught answerde,
But seyde, 'Ywys, it wol be nyght as faste.'
But every word which that she of hire herde,
900   She gan to prenten in hire herte faste,
And ay gan love hire lasse for t'agaste
Than it dide erst, and synken in hire herte,
That she wex somwhat able to converte.

The dayes honour, and the hevenes yë,
905   The nyghtes foo – al this clepe I the sonne –
Gan westren faste, and downward for to wrye,
As he that hadde his dayes cours yronne,
And white thynges wexen dymme and donne
For lak of lyght, and sterres for t'apere,
910   That she and alle hire folk in went yfeere.

So whan it liked hire to go to reste,
And voided weren thei that voiden oughte,
She seyde that to slepen wel hire leste.
Hire wommen soone til hire bed hire broughte.
915   Whan al was hust, than lay she stille and
          thoughte
Of al this thing; the manere and the wise
Reherce it nedeth nought, for ye ben wise.

A nyghtyngale, upon a cedre grene,
Under the chambre wal ther as she ley,
920   Ful loude song ayein the moone shene,
Peraunter in his briddes wise a lay
Of love, that made hire herte fressh and gay.

---

897 **purpos**: argument, subject   898 **as faste**: very soon
900 **prenten**: imprint **faste**: firmly   901 **t'agaste**: to frighten
902 **erst**: before **synken in**: penetrate   903 **able**: inclined **converte**: change
(her mind)   904 **yë**: eye   905 **foo**: foe **clepe**: call   906 **westren**: move
westwards **wrye**: turn   907 **yronne**: run   908 **thynges**: objects **wexen**: grew
donne: dun, grey-brown   910 **yfeere**: together   911 **to reste**: to bed
912 **voided**: withdrawn   913 **hire leste**: she wished   915 **hust**: hushed
917 **Reherce**: to repeat   918 **cedre**: cedar   919 **Under**: close by   920 Sang
very loudly in the moonlight   921 **briddes wise**: bird's fashion **lay**: song
922 **gay**: cheerful

That herkned she so longe in good entente.
Til at the laste the dede slep hire hente.

And as she slep, anonright tho hire mette   925
How that an egle, fethered whit as bon,
Under hire brest his longe clawes sette,
And out hire herte he rente, and that anon,
And dide his herte into hire brest to gon –
Of which she nought agroos, ne nothyng   930
    smerte –
And forth he fleigh, with herte left for herte.

Now lat hire slepe, and we oure tales holde
Of Troilus, that is to paleis riden
Fro the scarmuch of the which I tolde,
And in his chaumbre sit and hath abiden   935
Til two or thre of his messages yeden
For Pandarus, and soughten hym ful faste,
Til they hym founde and broughte hym at the
    laste.

This Pandarus com lepyng in atones,
And seyde thus: 'Who hath ben wel ibete   940
To-day with swerdes and with slynge-stones,
But Troilus, that hath caught hym an hete?'
And gan to jape, and seyde, 'Lord, so ye swete!
But ris and lat us soupe and go to reste.'
And he answerde hym, 'Do we as the leste.'   945

923 **herkned**: listened **in good entente**: willingly   924 **dede**: dead
hente: seized   925 **slep**: slept **hire mette**: she dreamed   926 **fethered**: with
feathers **bon**: bone   928 **rente**: tore   929 **dide**: caused   930 **agroos**: was
frightened **ne nothyng smerte**: nor felt any pain   931 **fleigh**: flew
932 **holde**: continue   933 **riden**: ridden   934 **scarmuch**: skirmish   935 **sit** (=
sitteth): sits **abiden**: waited   936 **messages**: messengers **yeden**: went
939 **lepyng**: bounding **atones**: at once   940 **ibete**: beaten
941 **slynge-stones**: stones hurled from slings (as missiles in warfare)
942 **hete**: fever, temperature   943 **jape**: joke **so ye swete**: how you are
sweating   944 **ris**: get up **soupe**: sup, take supper   945 **Do we as the
leste**: let's do as you wish

With al the haste goodly that they myghte
They spedde hem fro the soper unto bedde;
And every wight out at the dore hym dyghte,
And where hym liste upon his wey hym spedde.
950   But Troilus, that thoughte his herte bledde
For wo, til that he herde som tydynge,
He seyde, 'Frend, shal I now wepe or synge?'

Quod Pandarus, 'Ly stylle and lat me slepe,
And don thyn hood; thy nedes spedde be!
955   And ches if thow wolt synge or daunce or lepe;
At shorte wordes, thow shal trowen me:
Sire, my nece wol do wel by the,
And love the best, by God and by my trouthe,
But lak of pursuyt make it in thi slouthe.

960   'For thus ferforth I have thi werk bigonne
Fro day to day, til this day by the morwe
Hire love of frendshipe have I to the wonne,
And therto hath she leyd hire feyth to borwe –
Algate a foot is hameled of thi sorwe!'
965   What sholde I lenger sermoun of it holde?
As ye han herd byfore, al he hym tolde.

But right as floures, thorugh the cold of nyght
Iclosed, stoupen on hire stalke lowe,
Redressen hem ayein the sonne bright,

946 **goodly**: with propriety, properly   947 **spedde hem**: hurried   948 **hym dyghte**: departed   949 And he hurried on his way wherever he wished   951 **tydynge**: piece of news   954 **don thyn hood**: put on your hood, call it a day (n.)   **spedde be**: are provided for   955 **ches**: choose   **lepe**: leap   956 **At shorte wordes**: briefly   **trowen me**: take my word for it   957 **do wel by the**: treat you well   959 Unless a lack of perseverance make it (turn out otherwise) because of your inertia   960 **ferforth**: far   **werk**: business   961 **this day by the morwe**: this morning   962 **love of frendshipe**: affection as a friend, friendship   963 **leyd hire feyth**: given her word   **to borwe**: as a pledge   964 At any rate one foot of your sorrow has been crippled (and so cannot pursue you as quickly)   965 **sermoun**: discourse   **holde**: maintain   968 **Iclosed**: folded up   **stoupen**: drooping   969 **Redressen hem**: recover   **ayein**: in

And spreden on hire kynde cours by rowe,   970
Right so gan tho his eighen up to throwe
This Troilus, and seyde, 'O Venus deere,
Thi myght, thi grace, yheried be it here!'

And to Pandare he held up bothe his hondes,
And seyde, 'Lord, al thyn be that I have!   975
For I am hool, al brosten ben my bondes.
A thousand Troyes whoso that me yave,
Ech after other, God so wys me save,
Ne myghte me so gladen; lo, myn herte,
It spredeth so for joie it wol tosterte!   980

'But, Lord, how shal I doon? How shal I lyven?
Whan shal I next my deere herte see?
How shal this longe tyme awey be dryven
Til that thow be ayein at hire fro me?
Thow maist answer, "Abid, abid," but he   985
That hangeth by the nekke, soth to seyne
In gret disese abideth for the peyne.'

'Al esily, now, for the love of Marte,'
Quod Pandarus, 'for every thing hath tyme.
So longe abid til that the nyght departe,   990
For also siker as thow list here by me,
And God toforn, I wol be ther at pryme;
And forthi, werk somwhat as I shal seye,
Or on som other wight this charge leye.

970 **spreden:** open **kynde cours:** natural course **by rowe:** in a row
973 **yheried:** praised 975 **al thyn be:** yours be all 976 **hool:** unhurt, in
health **brosten:** broken **bondes:** fetters 977 Whoever gave me a thousand
Troys 978 **wys:** surely 979 **gladen:** make happy 980 **spredeth:** swells
tosterte: burst 983 **awey be dryven:** be passed 985 **Abid:** be patient
987 **disese:** distress, discomfort **abideth:** awaits, remains **for:** because of
988 **Al esily:** take it easy, relax **Marte:** Mars 990 **So longe abid:** wait just so
long 991 **also siker as:** as surely as **list** (= *liest*): lie 992 **pryme:** 9.00 a.m.
(n.) 993 **werk:** do, act 994 **charge:** task

995   'For, pardee, God woot I have evere yit
      Ben redy the to serve, and to this nyght
      Have I naught feyned, but emforth my wit
      Don al thi lust, and shal with al my myght.
      Do now as I shal seyn, and far aright,
1000 And if thow nylt, wite al thiself thi care:
      On me is nought along thyn yvel fare!

      'I woot wel that thow wiser art than I
      A thousand fold, but if I were as thow,
      God help me so, as I wolde outrely
1005 Right of myn owen hond write hire right now
      A lettre, in which I wolde hire tellen how
      I ferde amys, and hire biseche of routhe.
      Now help thiself, and leve it nought for slouthe!

      'And I myself wol therwith to hire gon;
1010 And whan thow woost that I am with hire there,
      Worth thow upon a courser right anon –
      Ye, hardily, right in thi beste gere –
      And ryd forth by the place, as nought ne were,
      And thow shalt fynde us, if I may, sittynge
1015 At som window, into the strete lokynge.

      'And if the list, than maystow us salue,
      And upon me make thow thi countenaunce;
      But by thi lif, be war and faste eschue
      To tarien ought – God shilde us fro meschaunce!
1020 Rid forth thi wey, and hold thi governaunce;

996 **to:** up until   997 **feyned:** held back   **emforth my wit:** as far as I am able
998 **Don al thi lust:** accomplished all you wished   999 **far aright:** do well
1000–1001 And if you don't want to (*nylt*), blame (*wite*) your trouble only
on yourself: your faring badly is not due to me   1004 **outrely:** absolutely
1007 **ferde amys:** suffered   1008 **leve:** postpone   **for slouthe:** out of laziness
1009 **therwith:** with it   1011 **Worth:** mount, get   **courser:** war-horse
1012 **hardily:** certainly   **gere:** apparel   1013 **as nought ne were:** as though
there were nothing in it   1016 **the list:** you wish   **maystow:** you can
salue: greet   1017 And direct your look at me   1018 **be war:** take care
eschue: avoid   1019 **tarien:** hang about   **ought:** at all   **God shilde:** may God
protect   1020 **hold thi governaunce:** keep your self-control

And we shal speek of the somwhat, I trowe,
Whan thow art gon, to don thyn eris glowe!

'Towchyng thi lettre, thou art wys ynough:
I woot thow nylt it dygneliche endite,
As make it with thise argumentes tough;   1025
Ne scryvenyssh or craftyly thow it write;
Biblotte it with thi teris ek a lite;
And if thow write a goodly word al softe,
Though it be good, reherce it nought to ofte.

'For though the beste harpour upon lyve   1030
Wolde on the beste sowned joly harpe
That evere was, with alle his fyngres fyve
Touche ay o stryng, or ay o werbul harpe,
Were his nayles poynted nevere so sharpe,
It sholde maken every wight to dulle,   1035
To here his glee, and of his strokes fulle.

'Ne jompre ek no discordant thyng yfeere,
As thus, to usen termes of phisik
In loves termes; hold of thi matere
The forme alwey, and do that it be lik;   1040
For if a peyntour wolde peynte a pyk
With asses feet, and hedde it as an ape,
It cordeth naught, so nere it but a jape.'

1022 **don**: make **eris**: ears   1023 **Towchyng**: concerning   1024 I know you
won't write it in haughty fashion   1025 **make it . . . tough**: show off
1026–7 Nor write it like a professional scrivener, or artfully; blot it a little
too with your tears   1028 **softe**: tender   1029 **reherce**: repeat
1030–33 For if the best harpist (*harpour*) . . . were to . . . pluck one string
1030 **upon lyve**: alive   1031 **beste sowned**: finest sounding **joly**: merry
1033 **ay o werbul harpe**: always harp one tune   1034 **Were his nayles**: even if
his fingernails were **poynted**: filed into points   1035 **dulle**: become bored
1036 **glee**: music **strokes**: strummings **fulle**: fed up   1037 **jompre**: jumble
discordant: dissonant   1038 **As thus**: for example, such as **termes**: technical
terms **phisik**: medicine   1039 **hold**: preserve **matere**: subject
1040 **forme**: proper form **do**: ensure **lik**: consistent   1041 **peyntour**: painter
pyk: pike (the fish)   1042 **hedde it as an ape**: give it the head of an ape
1043 It is not at all fitting, unless it were only a joke

This counseil liked wel to Troilus,
1045   But, as a dredful lovere, he seyde this:
'Allas, my deere brother Pandarus,
I am ashamed for to write, ywys,
Lest of myn innocence I seyde amys,
Or that she nolde it for despit receyve;
1050   Than were I ded: ther myght it nothyng weyve.'

To that Pandare answered, 'If the lest,
Do that I seye, and lat me therwith gon;
For by that Lord that formede est and west,
I hope of it to brynge answere anon
1055   Right of hire hond; and if that thow nylt noon,
Lat be, and sory mote he ben his lyve
Ayeins thi lust that helpeth the to thryve.'

Quod Troilus, 'Depardieux, ich assente!
Sith that the list, I wil arise and write –
1060   And blisful God prey ich with good entente,
The viage, and the lettre I shal endite,
So spede it; and thow, Minerva, the white,
Yif thow me wit my lettre to devyse.'
And sette hym down, and wrot right in this
      wyse:

1065   First he gan hire his righte lady calle,
His hertes lif, his lust, his sorwes leche,
His blisse, and ek thise other termes alle
That in swich cas thise loveres alle seche;
And in ful humble wise, as in his speche,

1044 **liked wel**: much appealed   1045 **dredful**: anxious   1048 **seyde amys**: said something amiss   1049 **for despit**: out of resentment 1050 **weyve**: avoid   1051 **the lest**: you wish   1053 **formede**: created **est**: east   1055 **of hire hond**: from her   **nylt noon**: don't want to 1056–7 Forget it, and may anyone who helps you to prosper against your will regret it for the rest of his life!   1058 **Depardieux**: by God   1060 **prey ich**: I pray   1061 **viage**: undertaking   1062 **spede it**: cause it to prosper **white**: fair   1063 **Yif**: give   **devyse**: compose   1065 **righte**: true   1066 The very life of his heart, his delight, the healer of his sorrows   1068 **seche**: seek out

He gan hym recomaunde unto hire grace –   1070
To telle al how, it axeth muchel space.

And after this ful lowely he hire preyde
To be nought wroth, thogh he, of his folie,
So hardy was to hire to write, and seyde
That love it made, or elles most he die,   1075
And pitousli gan mercy for to crye;
And after that he seyde – and leigh ful loude –
Hymself was litel worth, and lasse he koude;

And that she sholde han his konnyng excused,
That litel was, and ek he dredde hire soo;   1080
And his unworthynesse he ay acused;
And after that than gan he telle his woo –
But that was endeles, withouten hoo –
And seyde he wolde in trouthe alwey hym
        holde;
And radde it over, and gan the lettre folde.   1085

And with his salte teris gan he bathe
The ruby in his signet, and it sette
Upon the wex deliverliche and rathe.
Therwith a thousand tymes er he lette
He kiste tho the lettre that he shette,   1090
And seyde, 'Lettre, a blisful destine
The shapyn is: my lady shal the see!'

1070 **recomaunde**: commend **grace**: favour   1071 To recount everything
about how he did so would require a great deal of space
1072 **lowely**: humbly **preyde**: begged   1074 **hardy**: bold
1075 **made**: caused **most**: must   1076 **pitousli**: pitiably **crye**: beg
1077 **leigh**: lied **ful loude**: quite palpably   1078 **lasse he koude**: could do
(even) less   1079 **han his konnyng excused**: pardon his (lack of) intelligence
1081 **unworthynesse**: undeservingness **acused**: blamed   1083 **hoo**: halt
1084 **trouthe**: faithfulness **holde**: keep   1085 **radde**: read
1087 **signet**: signet ring (with a seal set in it)   1088 **wex**: wax
deliverliche: deftly **rathe**: soon   1089 **lette**: left off   1090 **shette**: closed up
1092 **The shapyn is**: is allotted to you

This Pandare tok the lettre, and that bytyme
A-morwe, and to his neces paleis sterte,

1095 And faste he swor that it was passed prime,
And gan to jape, and seyde, 'Ywys, myn herte,
So fressh it is, although it sore smerte,
I may naught slepe nevere a Mayes morwe;
I have a joly wo, a lusty sorwe.'

1100 Criseyde, whan that she hire uncle herde,
With dredful herte, and desirous to here
The cause of his comynge, thus answerde:
'Now, by youre fey, myn uncle,' quod she, 'dere,
What manere wyndes gydeth yow now here?

1105 Tel us youre joly wo and youre penaunce:
How ferforth be ye put in loves daunce?'

'By God,' quod he, 'I hoppe alwey byhynde!'
And she to laughe, it thoughte hire herte brest.
Quod Pandarus, 'Loke alwey that ye fynde

1110 Game in myn hood; but herkneth, if yow lest:
Ther is right now come into town a gest,
A Greek espie, and telleth newe thinges,
For which I come to telle yow tydynges.

'Into the gardyn go we, and ye shal here,

1115 Al pryvely, of this a long sermoun.'
With that they wenten arm in arm yfeere
Into the gardyn from the chaumbre down;
And whan that he so fer was that the sown

1093 **bytyme**: early   1094 **A-morwe**: next morning **sterte**: hurried
1097 **sore smerte**: feels terrible pain   1098 **Mayes morwe**: May morning
1099 **joly wo**: merry misery **lusty**: cheerful   1101 **dredful**: apprehensive
desirous: eager   1103 **by youre fey**: upon your honour
1105 **penaunce**: suffering   1106 **ferforth**: far **put**: advanced **loves
daunce**: the dance or game of love (n.)   1108 **to laughe**: laughed
thoughte: seemed **brest**: burst   1109 **Loke**: make sure   1109–10 **fynde
Game in myn hood**: find me amusing   1111 **gest**: visitor   1112 **espie**: spy
newe thinges: news   1113 **tydynges**: news   1114 **go we**: let us go
1115 **pryvely**: confidentially **sermoun**: tale

Of that he spak no man heren myghte,
He seyde hire thus, and out the lettre plighte: 1120

'Lo, he that is al holy youres free
Hym recomaundeth lowely to youre grace,
And sente yow this lettre here by me.
Avyseth yow on it, whan ye han space,
And of som goodly answere yow purchace,   1125
Or, helpe me God, so pleynly for to seyne,
He may nat longe lyven for his peyne.'

Ful dredfully tho gan she stonden stylle,
And took it naught, but al hire humble chere
Gan for to chaunge, and seyde, 'Scrit ne bille,   1130
For love of God, that toucheth swich matere,
Ne bryng me noon; and also, uncle deere,
To myn estat have more reward, I preye,
Than to his lust! What sholde I more seye?

'And loketh now if this be resonable,   1135
And letteth nought, for favour ne for slouthe,
To seyn a sooth; now were it covenable
To myn estat, by God and by youre trouthe,
To taken it, or to han of hym routhe,
In harmyng of myself, or in repreve?   1140
Ber it ayein, for hym that ye on leve!'

1120 **plighte**: plucked   1121 **holy**: wholly **free**: freely
1122 **lowely**: humbly   1124 **Avyseth yow on it**: consider it carefully
space: opportunity   1125 **goodly**: gracious **yow purchace**: provide for
yourself   1126 **helpe me God**: God help me **pleynly**: frankly
1127 **longe**: long, for long   1128 **dredfully**: fearfully   1130–32 Bring me no
writing . . . on such a subject   1130 **Scrit**: writing **bille**: letter, petition
1131 **toucheth**: concerns   1133 **estat**: position **reward**: regard
1134 **lust**: pleasure   1135 **loketh**: consider   1136 **letteth nought**: do not
hesitate **favour**: partiality   1137 **sooth**: true thing **covenable**: suitable
1140 **in repreve**: to my own reproach   1141 **Ber it ayein**: return it **for**: for
the sake of **on leve**: believe in

This Pandarus gan on hire for to stare,
And seyde, 'Now is this the grettest wondre
That evere I seigh! Lat be this nyce fare!
1145 To dethe mot I smyten be with thondre,
If for the citee which that stondeth yondre,
Wolde I a lettre unto yow brynge or take
To harm of yow! What list yow thus it make?

'But thus ye faren, wel neigh alle and some,
1150 That he that most desireth yow to serve,
Of hym ye recche leest wher he bycome,
And whethir that he lyve or elles sterve.
But for al that that ever I may deserve,
Refuse it naught,' quod he, and hente hire faste,
1155 And in hire bosom the lettre down he thraste,

And seyde hire, 'Now cast it awey anon,
That folk may seen and gauren on us tweye.'
Quod she, 'I kan abyde til they be gon';
And gan to smyle, and seyde hym, 'Em, I preye,
1160 Swich answere as yow list, youreself purveye,
For trewely I nyl no lettre write.'
'No? than wol I,' quod he, 'so ye endite.'

Therwith she lough, and seyde, 'Go we dyne.'
And he gan at hymself to jape faste,
1165 And seyde, 'Nece, I have so gret a pyne
For love, that everich other day I faste –'
And gan his beste japes forth to caste,

1144 **seigh**: saw **Lat be**: give up **nyce fare**: foolish behaviour
1145 **mot**: may **smyten**: struck 1146 **yondre**: over there 1147 **take**: give,
hand over 1148 To your detriment! Why are you pleased to take it this
way? 1149 **faren**: proceed **alle and some**: one and all 1151 You care least
what becomes of him 1152 **sterve**: die 1153 **for al that that**: for the sake of
everything that 1154 **hente**: took hold of 1155 **thraste**: thrust
1156 **cast**: throw 1157 **gauren on**: stare at 1160 **purveye**: provide
1162 **so**: provided that **endite**: compose, dictate 1163 **lough**: laughed **Go
we dyne**: let us have dinner 1165 **pyne**: torment 1166 **other**: alternate
faste: go without food 1167 **forth to caste**: to reel off

And made hire so to laughe at his folye,
That she for laughter wende for to dye.

And whan that she was comen into halle,   1170
'Now, em,' quod she, 'we wol go dyne anon.'
And gan some of hire wommen to hire calle,
And streght into hire chambre gan she gon;
But of hire besynesses this was on –
Amonges othere thynges, out of drede –   1175
Ful pryvely this lettre for to rede;

Avysed word by word in every lyne,
And fond no lak, she thoughte he koude good,
And up it putte, and wente hire in to dyne.
But Pandarus, that in a studye stood,   1180
Er he was war, she took hym by the hood,
And seyde, 'Ye were caught er that ye wiste.'
'I vouche sauf,' quod he. 'Do what you liste.'

Tho wesshen they, and sette hem down, and ete;
And after noon ful sleighly Pandarus   1185
Gan drawe hym to the wyndowe next the strete,
And seyde, 'Nece, who hath araied thus
The yonder hous, that stant aforyeyn us?'
'Which hous?' quod she, and gan for to byholde,
And knew it wel, and whos it was hym tolde;   1190

And fillen forth in speche of thynges smale,
And seten in the windowe bothe tweye.
Whan Pandarus saugh tyme unto his tale,

1168 **folye**: nonsense   1169 **wende for to dye**: thought she would die
1174 **besynesses**: occupations **on**: one   1176 **pryvely**: secretly
1177 **Avysed**: (having) considered   1178 **fond**: (having) found **lak**: fault
koude good: knew how to behave properly   1179 **up**: away
1180 **studye**: reverie   1181 **war**: aware   1183 **vouche sauf**: admit it
1184 Then they washed, and sat down, and ate   1185 **sleighly**: cunningly
1186 **Gan drawe hym**: went   1187 **araied**: done up   1188 **stant** (= *standeth*):
stands **aforyeyn**: opposite   1191 **fillen forth in speche**: (they) began to speak
smale: trivial   1192 **seten**: sat   1193 **tyme unto his tale**: the right moment
for what he had to say

And saugh wel that hire folk were alle aweye,
1195   'Now, nece myn, tel on,' quod he; 'I seye,
How liketh yow the lettre that ye woot?
Kan he theron? For, by my trouthe, I noot.'

Therwith al rosy hewed tho wex she,
And gan to homme, and seyde, 'So I trowe.'
1200   'Aquite hym wel, for Goddes love,' quod he;
'Myself to medes wol the lettre sowe.'
And held his hondes up, and sat on knowe;
'Now, goode nece, be it nevere so lite,
Yif me the labour it to sowe and plite.'

1205   'Ye, for I kan so writen,' quod she tho;
'And ek I noot what I sholde to hym seye.'
'Nay, nece,' quod Pandare, 'sey nat so.
Yet at the leeste thonketh hym, I preye,
Of his good wille, and doth hym nat to deye.
1210   Now, for the love of me, my nece deere,
Refuseth nat at this tyme my prayere!'

'Depardieux,' quod she, 'God leve al be wel!
God help me so, this is the firste lettre
That evere I wroot, ye, al or any del.'
1215   And into a closet, for t'avise hire bettre,
She wente allone, and gan hire herte unfettre
Out of desdaynes prison but a lite,
And sette hire down, and gan a lettre write,

1194 **aweye**: out of the way   1197 **Kan he theron**: is he knowledgeable about
such matters? **noot**: do not know   1198 **hewed**: coloured
1199 **homme**: hum   1200 **Aquite**: repay   1201 **to medes**: in return
sowe: sew   1202 **sat on knowe**: knelt   1203 **lite**: little   1204 **plite**: fold
(n.)   1209 **doth**: cause   1211 **prayere**: request   1212 **Depardieux**: by God
leve: grant   1214 **al or any del**: entirely or in part   1215 **closet**: small private
room **for t'avise hire**: to consider, deliberate   1216 **unfettre**: unshackle
1217 **desdaynes prison**: the prison of disdain **but a lite**: only a little
1218 **sette hire**: sat

Of which to telle in short is myn entente
Th'effect, as fer as I kan understonde: 1220
She thanked hym of al that he wel mente
Towardes hire, but holden hym in honde
She nolde nought, ne make hireselven bonde
In love; but as his suster, hym to plese,
She wolde ay fayn to doon his herte an ese.   1225

She shette it, and to Pandare in gan goon,
Ther as he sat and loked into the strete,
And down she sette hire by hym on a stoon
Of jaspre, upon a quysshyn gold-ybete,
And seyde, 'As wisly help me God the grete,   1230
I nevere dide a thing with more peyne
Than writen this, to which ye me constreyne,'

And took it hym. He thonked hire and seyde,
'God woot, of thyng ful often looth bygonne
Comth ende good; and nece myn, Criseyde,   1235
That ye to hym of hard now ben ywonne
Oughte he be glad, by God and yonder sonne;
For-whi men seith, "Impressiounes lighte
Ful lightly ben ay redy to the flighte."

'But ye han played the tirant neigh to longe,   1240
And hard was it youre herte for to grave.
Now stynte, that ye no lenger on it honge,

1219 **in short**: briefly   1220 **Th'effect**: the purport   1222 **holden hym in
honde**: play him along   1223 **bonde**: enslaved   1224 **suster**: sister
1225 **fayn**: gladly   **doon . . . an ese**: please, gratify   1226 **in gan goon**: went
in   1228 **stoon**: stone window-seat   1229 **jaspre**: jasper   **quysshyn**: cushion
gold-ybete: embroidered with gold   1230 **wisly help**: surely as may help
grete: great   1231 **peyne**: effort   1232 **constreyne**: compel
1233 **took**: handed   1234 **looth**: reluctantly   1235 **Comth ende good**: comes
a good outcome   1236–9 He should be happy that you are only won over to
him with difficulty; that's why people say, 'Impressions easily made are
always likely to fade away very easily'   1240 **played the tirant**: acted the
despot   **neigh**: almost   **to**: too   1241 **grave**: engrave (with Troilus's
impression)   1242–3 Now stop, that you may remain undecided no longer
about it, even though you wish to preserve the outward appearance of reserve

Al wolde ye the forme of daunger save,
But hasteth yow to doon hym joye have;
1245   For trusteth wel, to longe ydoon hardnesse
Causeth despit ful often for destresse.'

And right as they declamed this matere,
Lo, Troilus, right at the stretes ende,
Com rydyng with his tenthe som yfere,
1250   Al softely, and thiderward gan bende
Ther as they sete, as was his way to wende
To paleis-ward; and Pandare hym aspide,
And seyde, 'Nece, ysee who comth here ride!

'O fle naught in (he seeth us, I suppose),
1255   Lest he may thynken that ye hym eschuwe.'
'Nay, nay,' quod she, and wex as red as rose.
With that he gan hire humbly to saluwe
With dredful chere, and oft his hewes muwe;
And up his look debonairly he caste,
1260   And bekked on Pandare, and forth he paste.

God woot if he sat on his hors aright,
Or goodly was biseyn, that ilke day!
God woot wher he was lik a manly knyght!
What sholde I drecche, or telle of his aray?
1265   Criseyde, which that alle thise thynges say,
To telle in short, hire liked al in-fere,
His persoun, his aray, his look, his chere,

1244 **hasteth yow:** hurry **doon:** cause   1245 For believe me, hardheartedness
maintained too long   1246 **despit:** resentment   1247 **declamed:** discussed
1249 **his tenthe som:** his party of ten   1250 **softely:** slowly
thiderward: towards there **bende:** turn   1251 **sete:** sat   1252 **To**
paleis-ward: towards the palace **aspide:** noticed   1253 **ysee:** see
ride: riding   1254 **suppose:** believe   1255 **eschuwe:** avoid
1257 **saluwe:** salute   1258 **dredful:** timid **hewes muwe:** colour changes
1259 **debonairly:** modestly   1260 **bekked on:** nodded at **forth he paste:** he
passed on   1261 **aright:** properly   1262 **goodly:** good-looking **biseyn:** in
appearance **ilke:** same   1263 **wher:** whether   1264 **What:** why
drecche: delay **aray:** apparel, gear   1265 **say:** saw   1266 **in short:** briefly **al**
in-fere: all together   1267 **persoun:** figure, appearance

His goodly manere, and his gentilesse,
So wel that nevere, sith that she was born,
Ne hadde she swych routh of his destresse;   1270
And how so she hath hard ben here-byforn,
To God hope I, she hath now kaught a thorn,
She shal nat pulle it out this nexte wyke –
God sende mo swich thornes on to pike!

Pandare, which that stood hire faste by,   1275
Felte iren hoot, and he bygan to smyte,
And seyde, 'Nece, I pray yow hertely,
Telle me that I shal axen yow a lite:
A womman that were of his deth to wite,
Withoute his gilt, but for hire lakked routhe,   1280
Were it wel doon?' Quod she, 'Nay, by my
        trouthe!'

'God help me so,' quod he, 'ye sey me soth.
Ye felen wel youreself that I nought lye.
Lo, yond he rit!' 'Ye,' quod she, 'so he doth!'
'Wel,' quod Pandare, 'as I have told yow thrie,   1285
Lat be youre nyce shame and youre folie,
And spek with hym in esyng of his herte;
Lat nycete nat do yow bothe smerte.'

But theron was to heven and to doone:
Considered al thing, it may nat be;   1290
And whi? For shame; and it were ek to soone

1268 **goodly**: kind   1271 **how so**: although **here-byforn**: before this
1272 **To God hope I**: I devoutly wish **kaught**: come by   1273 **wyke**: week
1274 **mo**: others (possibly an adjective: 'more') **pike**: pull out   1275 **hire**
faste by: close to her   1276 **iren hoot**: hot iron **smyte**: strike
1277 **hertely**: earnestly   1278 **that**: what   1279 **wite**: blame   1280 He
being guiltless, but because she lacked compassion   1283 **felen**: understand
1284 **yond**: yonder, over there **rit** (= *rideth*): rides   1285 **thrie**: thrice
1286 **nyce shame**: foolish modesty   1287 **esyng**: comforting   1288 Don't
let silly scruples (*nycete*) cause you both pain   1289 But on this matter there
was much that called for hard work and had to be done
1290 **Considered**: considering   1291 **For**: on account of **to**: too

To graunten hym so gret a libertee.
For pleynly hire entente, as seyde she,
Was for to love hym unwist, if she myghte,
1295   And guerdoun hym with nothing but with sighte.

But Pandarus thought, 'It shal nought be so,
Yif that I may; this nyce opynyoun
Shal nought be holden fully yeres two.'
What sholde I make of this a long sermoun?
1300   He moste assente on that conclusioun,
As for the tyme; and whan that it was eve,
And al was wel, he roos and tok his leve.

And on his wey ful faste homward he spedde,
And right for joye he felte his herte daunce;
1305   And Troilus he fond allone abedde,
That lay, as do thise lovers, in a traunce
Bitwixen hope and derk disesperaunce.
But Pandarus, right at his in-comynge,
He song, as who seyth, 'Somwhat I brynge,'

1310   And seyde, 'Who is in his bed so soone
Iburied thus?' 'It am I, frend,' quod he.
'Who, Troilus? Nay, help me so the moone,'
Quod Pandarus, 'Thow shalt arise and see
A charme that was sent right now to the,
1315   The which kan helen the of thyn accesse,
If thow do forthwith al thi bisynesse.'

1294 **unwist**: undetected   1295 **guerdoun**: reward
1299 **sermoun**: discourse, speech   1300 **moste**: must   1301 **As for the tyme**: for the time being   **eve**: evening   1302 **roos**: got up
1306 **traunce**: state of abstraction, daze   1307 **derk**: gloomy
disesperaunce: despair   1309 **song**: sang   **as who seyth**: as if to say
1312 **help me so the moone**: so help me the moon   1314 **charme**: charm,
spell   1315 **helen**: heal   **accesse**: fever   1316 **do ... thi bisynesse**: apply
yourself, make an effort

'Ye, thorugh the myght of God,' quod Troilus,
And Pandarus gan hym the lettre take,
And seyde, 'Parde, God hath holpen us!
Have here a light, and loke on al this blake.'   1320
But ofte gan the herte glade and quake
Of Troilus, whil that he gan it rede,
So as the wordes yave hym hope or drede.

But finaly, he took al for the beste
That she hym wroot, for somwhat he byheld   1325
On which hym thoughte he myghte his herte reste,
Al covered she tho wordes under sheld.
Thus to the more worthi part he held,
That what for hope and Pandarus byheste,
His grete wo foryede he at the leste.   1330

But as we may alday oureselven see,
Thorugh more wode or col, the more fir,
Right so encrees of hope, of what it be,
Therwith ful ofte encresseth ek desir;
Or as an ook comth of a litil spir,   1335
So thorugh this lettre which that she hym sente
Encrescen gan desir, of which he brente.

Wherfore I seye alwey, that day and nyght
This Troilus gan to desiren moore
Thanne he did erst, thorugh hope, and did his   1340
     myght
To preessen on, as by Pandarus loore,
And writen to hire of his sorwes soore.

1318 **gan . . . take**: gave   1319 **holpen**: helped   1320 **blake**: black (i.e. ink,
writing)   1321 **glade**: be glad **quake**: tremble   1323 **So as**: according to
whether **yave**: gave   1326 **hym thoughte**: it seemed to him   1327 Even if
her words were guarded   1328 **worthi**: appropriate **held**: clung
1329 **byheste**: promise   1330 **foryede**: abandoned **at the leste**: at least
1331 **alday**: all the time **oureselven**: ourselves   1332 **wode**: wood **col**: coal
1333 **of what it be**: for whatever it may be   1335 **ook**: oak **spir**: shoot
1337 **brente**: burned   1340 **erst**: before **did his myght**: exerted himself
1341 **preessen on**: press forward **loore**: instruction   1342 **soore**: painful,
agonizing

Fro day to day he leet it nought refreyde,
That by Pandare he wroot somwhat or seyde;

1345   And dide also his other observaunces
That til a lovere longeth in this cas;
And after that thise dees torned on chaunces,
So was he outher glad or seyde 'Allas!'
And held after his gistes ay his pas;
1350   And after swiche answeres as he hadde,
So were his dayes sory outher gladde.

But to Pandare alwey was his recours,
And pitously gan ay tyl hym to pleyne,
And hym bisoughte of reed and som socours.
1355   And Pandarus, that sey his woode peyne,
Wex wel neigh ded for routhe, sooth to seyne,
And bisily with al his herte caste
Som of his wo to slen, and that as faste;

And seyde, 'Lord, and frend, and brother dere,
1360   God woot that thi disese doth me wo.
But wiltow stynten al this woful cheere,
And, by my trouthe, er it be dayes two,
And God toforn, yet shal I shape it so,
That thow shalt come into a certeyn place,
1365   There as thow mayst thiself hire preye of grace.

1343 **refreyde**: grow cold   1345 **dide**: performed **observaunces**: rites
1346 **til a lovere longeth**: befits a lover   1347 And according to how the luck
of the dice fell   1348 **outher**: either   1349 And always paced himself
according to progress (n.)   1350 **after**: according to   1351 **outher**: or
1352 **recours**: resort   1354 **bisoughte**: begged **reed**: advice **socours**: help
1355 **sey**: saw **woode**: mad   1356 **Wex wel neigh ded**: very nearly died
1357 **bisily**: diligently **caste**: planned   1358 **slen**: put an end to **as faste**: very
quickly   1360 **disese**: distress **doth me wo**: makes me unhappy
1361 **wiltow**: if you will **stynten**: stop   1363 **shape**: arrange   1365 **There
as**: where

'And certeynly – I noot if thow it woost,
But tho that ben expert in love it seye –
It is oon of the thynges forthereth most,
A man to han a layser for to preye,
And siker place his wo for to bywreye;   1370
For in good herte it mot som routhe impresse,
To here and see the giltlees in distresse.

'Peraunter thynkestow: though it be so,
That Kynde wolde don hire to bygynne
To have a manere routhe upon my woo,   1375
Seyth Daunger, "Nay, thow shalt me nevere wynne!"
So reulith hire hir hertes gost withinne,
That though she bende, yeet she stant on roote;
What in effect is this unto my boote?

'Thenk here-ayeins: whan that the stordy ook,   1380
On which men hakketh ofte, for the nones,
Receyved hath the happy fallyng strook,
The greete sweigh doth it come al at ones,
As don thise rokkes or thise milnestones;
For swifter cours comth thyng that is of wighte,   1385
Whan it descendeth, than don thynges lighte.

'And reed that boweth down for every blast,
Ful lightly, cesse wynd, it wol aryse;
But so nyl nought an ook, whan it is cast;

1367 **tho that**: those who   1368 **forthereth most**: that most advances (one's
suit)   1369 **layser**: opportunity **preye**: beseech (his lady)   1370 **siker**: safe
bywreye: reveal   1371 **impresse**: imprint, urge   1372 **giltlees**: innocent
1373 **Peraunter thynkestow**: perhaps you are thinking   1374 **Kynde**: nature
don: cause   1375 **manere**: kind of   1376 **Daunger**: disdain, reserve
wynne: conquer   1377 **gost**: spirit   1378 **bende**: may bend **yeet**: still **stant**
(*standeth*): stands **on roote**: firmly rooted   1379 **What in effect**: of what use
boote: remedy   1380 **here-ayeins**: in reply to that **stordy**: sturdy, stout
1381 **for the nones**: for the purpose   1382 **happy**: fortunate **fallyng**
strook: stroke that fells it   1383 **sweigh**: momentum **come**: fall
1384 **milnestones**: mill stones   1385 **of wighte**: heavy   1387 **reed**: a reed
blast: gust   1388 **lightly**: readily **cesse wynd**: if the wind cease
1389 **cast**: felled

1390   It nedeth me nought the longe to forbise.
        Men shal rejoissen of a gret empryse
        Acheved wel, and stant withouten doute,
        Al han men ben the lenger theraboute.

        'But, Troilus, yet telle me, if the lest,
1395   A thing now which that I shal axen the:
        Which is thi brother that thow lovest best,
        As in thi verray hertes privetee?'
        'Iwis, my brother Deiphebus,' quod he.
        'Now,' quod Pandare, 'er houres twyes twelve,
1400   He shal the ese, unwist of it hymselve.

        'Now lat m'alone, and werken as I may,'
        Quod he; and to Deiphebus wente he tho,
        Which hadde his lord and grete frend ben ay –
        Save Troilus, no man he loved so.
1405   To telle in short, withouten wordes mo,
        Quod Pandarus, 'I pray yow that ye be
        Frend to a cause which that toucheth me.'

        'Yis, parde,' quod Deiphebus, 'wel thow woost,
        In al that evere I may, and God tofore,
1410   Al nere it but for man I love moost,
        My brother Troilus; but sey wherfore
        It is; for sith that day that I was bore,
        I nas, ne nevere mo to ben I thynke,
        Ayeins a thing that myghte the forthynke.'

1390 **the**: you **forbise**: instruct by examples   1391 **empryse**: undertaking
1392 **Acheved**: accomplished **stant withouten doute**: '(which) stands
securely' or '(it) stands . . .' (i.e. there can be no doubt)   1393 Even if people
have taken that much longer about it   1397 **privetee**: inmost recess (i.e. in
confidence)   1399 **er houres twyes twelve**: within twenty-four hours
1400 **the ese**: give you relief **unwist**: unaware   1401 **werken**: to act
1403 **grete**: close   1407 **toucheth**: concerns   1409 **God tofore**: before God (I
swear)   1410 **Al nere it but for**: unless it were to do with
1411 **wherfore**: why   1412 **bore**: born   1413 **nas** (= *ne was*): was not
thynke: intend   1414 **the forthynke**: displease you

Pandare gan hym thanke, and to hym seyde,   1415
'Lo, sire, I have a lady in this town,
That is my nece, and called is Criseyde,
Which some men wolden don oppressioun,
And wrongfully han hire possessioun;
Wherfore I of youre lordship yow biseche   1420
To ben oure frend, withouten more speche.'

Deiphebus hym answerde, 'O, is nat this,
That thow spekest of to me thus straungely,
Criseyda, my frend?' He seyde, 'Yis.'
'Than nedeth,' quod Deiphebus, 'hardyly,   1425
Namore to speke, for trustcth wel that I
Wol be hire champioun with spore and yerde;
I roughte nought though alle hire foos it herde.

'But telle me, thow that woost al this matere,
How I myght best avaylen.' – 'Now lat se,'   1430
Quod Pandarus; 'if ye, my lord so dere,
Wolden as now do this honour to me,
To preyen hire to-morwe, lo, that she
Come unto yow, hire pleyntes to devise,
Hire adversaries wolde of it agrise.   1435

'And yif I more dorste preye as now,
And chargen yow to han so gret travaille,
To han som of youre bretheren here with yow,
That myghten to hire cause bet availle,
Than wot I wel she myghte nevere faille   1440

1418 **Which**: to whom **oppressioun**: wrong   1419 **possessioun**: possessions
1420 **lordship**: protection, patronage   1423 **straungely**: as if she were a
stranger   1425 **hardyly**: assuredly   1427 **champioun**: defender **spore**: spur
yerde: staff, spear   1428 **roughte nought though**: would not care if
foos: enemies   1430 **avaylen**: help   1434 **pleyntes**: grievances **devise**: set
out   1435 **adversaries**: enemies **agrise**: tremble, shudder with fear
1436 **more dorste preye**: dared beg a further favour   1437 And impose on
you to put yourself to so much trouble   1439 **availle**: assist

For to ben holpen, what at youre instaunce,
What with hire other frendes governaunce.'

Deiphebus, which that comen was of kynde
To alle honour and bounte to consente,
1445   Answerd, 'It shal be don; and I kan fynde
Yet grettere help to this in myn entente.
What wiltow seyn if I for Eleyne sente
To speke of this? I trowe it be the beste,
For she may leden Paris as hire leste.

1450   'Of Ector, which that is my lord, my brother,
It nedeth naught to preye hym frend to be;
For I have herd hym, o tyme and ek oother,
Speke of Cryseyde swich honour that he
May seyn no bet, swich hap to hym hath she.
1455   It nedeth naught his helpes for to crave;
He shal be swich, right as we wol hym have.

'Spek thow thiself also to Troilus
On my byhalve, and prey hym with us dyne.'
'Syre, al this shal be don,' quod Pandarus,
1460   And took his leve, and nevere gan to fyne,
But to his neces hous, as streyght as lyne,
He com; and fond hire fro the mete arise,
And sette hym down, and spak right in this wise:

He seide, 'O verray God, so have I ronne!
1465   Lo, nece myn, se ye nought how I swete?
I not wher ye the more thank me konne.

1441 **holpen:** helped **what at:** what with **instaunce:** urging
1442 **governaunce:** guidance   1443 **comen was of kynde:** was by nature
disposed   1444 To agree to everything honourable and good
1446 **entente:** opinion   1447 **wiltow:** would you   1449 **leden:** govern **hire**
leste: she pleases   1451 **nedeth naught:** is unnecessary **preye:** ask   1453 **swich**
honour: so highly   1454 **hap to:** favour with   1455 **helpes:** assistance
crave: request   1456 **swich, right:** just exactly   1460 **gan to fyne:** stopped
1461 **lyne:** a plumb line   1462 **fro the mete arise:** rising from dinner
1464 **verray:** true **so have I ronne:** how I've run!   1465 **swete:** sweat
1466 I don't know whether you're any the more grateful to me

Be ye naught war how false Poliphete
Is now aboute eftsones for to plete,
And brynge on yow advocacies newe?'
'I, no!' quod she, and chaunged al hire hewe.   1470

'What is he more aboute, me to drecche
And don me wrong? What shal I doon, allas?
Yet of hymself nothing ne wolde I recche,
Nere it for Antenor and Eneas,
That ben his frendes in swich manere cas.   1475
But, for the love of God, myn uncle deere,
No fors of that; lat hym han al yfeere –

'Withouten that I have ynough for us.'
'Nay,' quod Pandare, 'it shal nothing be so,
For I have ben right now at Deiphebus,   1480
At Ector, and myn oother lordes moo,
And shortly maked ech of hem his foo,
That, by my thrift, he shal it nevere wynne,
For aught he kan, whan that so he bygynne.'

And as thei casten what was best to doone,   1485
Deiphebus, of his owen curteisie,
Com hire to preye, in his propre persone,
To holde hym on the morwe compaignie
At dyner, which she nolde nought denye,
But goodly gan to his preier obeye.   1490
He thonked hire, and went upon his weye.

1467 **Be ye naught war:** aren't you aware **Poliphete:** Polyphoetes (see n.)
1468 **eftsones:** immediately **plete:** go to law   1469 **on:** against
advocacies: charges   1470 **I:** ah   1471 **What:** why **drecche:** trouble
1473 **recche:** care   1474 **Nere it:** if it were not **Eneas:** Aeneas   1477 **No fors
of:** it does not matter about **al yfeere:** everything   1481 **oother . . .
moo:** many other   1482 **shortly:** in short time **foo:** enemy   1483 **by my
thrift:** I swear   1484 **aught:** anything **kan:** is able to do
1485 **casten:** considered   1486 **owen curteisie:** characteristic courtliness
1487 **in his propre persone:** in person   1488 **holde:** keep
1489 **denye:** refuse   1490 **goodly:** graciously **preier:** request

Whan this was don, this Pandare up anon –
To telle in short – and forth gan for to wende
To Troilus, as stille as any ston;
1495   And al this thyng he tolde hym, word and ende,
And how that he Deiphebus gan to blende,
And seyde hym, 'Now is tyme, if that thow konne,
To bere the wel tomorwe, and al is wonne.

'Now spek, now prey, now pitously compleyne;
1500   Lat nought for nyce shame, or drede, or slouthe!
Somtyme a man mot telle his owen peyne.
Bileve it, and she shal han on the routhe:
Thow shalt be saved by thi feyth, in trouthe.
But wel woot I that thow art now in drede,
1505   And what it is, I leye, I kan arede.

'Thow thynkest now, "How sholde I don al this?
For by my cheres mosten folk aspie
That for hire love is that I fare amys;
Yet hadde I levere unwist for sorwe dye."
1510   Now thynk nat so, for thow dost gret folie;
For I right now have founden o manere
Of sleyghte, for to coveren al thi cheere.

'Thow shalt gon over nyght, and that bylyve,
Unto Deiphebus hous as the to pleye,
1515   Thi maladie awey the bet to dryve –
For-whi thow semest sik, soth for to seye.
Sone after that, down in thi bed the leye,

1492 **up anon:** got up at once   1495 **word and ende:** beginning and end, all
1496 **blende:** deceive   1498 **bere the:** conduct yourself   1500 **Lat
nought:** don't refrain   **nyce shame:** foolish modesty   1501 **telle:** speak
about   1502 **the:** you   1503 **feyth:** loyalty   1505 **leye:** bet   **arede:** guess
1507 **cheres:** looks, manner   **mosten folk aspie:** people must notice
1508 That it is because of love for her that I'm suffering   1509 **hadde I
levere:** I would rather   1510 **dost gret folie:** are behaving very foolishly
1511 **o manere:** one kind   1512 **sleyghte:** trick   **coveren:** act as a cover for
1513 **over nyght:** the night before   **bylyve:** quickly   1514 **as the to pleye:** as if
to amuse yourself   1516 **For-whi:** because   **semest sik:** look ill   1517 **the
leye:** lie down

And sey thow mayst no lenger up endure,
And lie right there, and byd thyn aventure.

'Sey that thi fevre is wont the for to take   1520
The same tyme, and lasten til a-morwe;
And lat se now how wel thow kanst it make,
For, parde, sik is he that is in sorwe.
Go now, farwel! And Venus here to borwe,
I hope, and thow this purpos holde ferme,   1525
Thi grace she shal fully ther conferme.'

Quod Troilus, 'Iwis, thow nedeles
Conseilest me that siklich I me feyne,
For I am sik in ernest, douteles,
So that wel neigh I sterve for the peyne.'   1530
Quod Pandarus, 'Thow shalt the bettre pleyne,
And hast the lasse need to countrefete,
For hym men demen hoot that men seen swete.

'Lo, hold the at thi triste cloos, and I
Shal wel the deer unto thi bowe dryve.'   1535
Therwith he took his leve al softely,
And Troilus to paleis wente blyve;
So glad ne was he nevere in al his lyve,
And to Pandarus reed gan al assente,
And to Deiphebus hous at nyght he wente.   1540

1518 **up endure**: bear to stay up   1519 **byd thyn aventure**: await what befalls
you   1520 **fevre**: fever **wont**: accustomed   1521 **a-morwe**: next morning
1522 **make**: fake   1524 **Venus here to borwe**: with Venus present as a
guarantor   1525 **and**: if **holde ferme**: keep resolutely
1527 **nedeles**: needlessly   1528 Advise me that I pretend to be ill   1529 **in
ernest**: genuinely   1530 **sterve**: die   1532–3 And you have the less need to
pretend, because people suppose a man they see sweating is hot   1534 **hold
the**: keep yourself **triste**: hunting station **cloos**: concealed
1535 **unto**: towards   1537 **blyve**: quickly   1539 **reed**: advice

What nedeth yow to tellen al the cheere
That Deiphebus unto his brother made,
Or his accesse, or his sikliche manere –
How men gan hym with clothes for to lade
1545 Whan he was leyd, and how men wolde hym glade?
But al for nought; he held forth ay the wyse
That ye han herd Pandare er this devyse.

But certayn is, er Troilus hym leyde,
Deiphebus had hym preied over-nyght
1550 To ben a frend and helpyng to Criseyde.
God woot that he it graunted anon-right,
To ben hire fulle frend with al his myght.
But swich a nede was to preye hym thenne,
As for to bidde a wood man for to renne!

1555 The morwen com, and neighen gan the tyme
Of meeltid, that the faire queene Eleyne
Shoop hire to ben, an houre after the prime,
With Deiphebus, to whom she nolde feyne;
But as his suster, homly, soth to seyne,
1560 She com to dyner in hire pleyne entente –
But God and Pandare wist al what this mente.

Com ek Criseyde, al innocent of this,
Antigone, hire suster Tarbe also.
But fle we now prolixitee best is,

1541 **yow to tellen:** to tell you about **cheere:** welcome 1543 **accesse:** sudden
illness **sikliche:** sickly 1544 **clothes:** bedclothes **lade:** load 1545 **leyd:** in
bed **glade:** cheer up 1546 **for nought:** in vain **held forth ay the wyse:** always
kept on behaving in the way 1548 **hym leyde:** lay down
1549 **over-nyght:** the night before (Criseyde's arrival)
1550 **helpyng:** supporter 1552 **fulle:** true 1553 There was as much need to
ask him 1554 **bidde:** ask **wood:** mad **renne:** run 1555 **neighen**
gan: approached 1556 **meeltid:** mealtime 1557 **Shoop hire:** intended **an**
houre after the prime: 10.00 a.m. 1558 **feyne:** dissemble 1559 **suster:** i.e.
sister-in-law **homly:** informally 1560 **in hire pleyne entente:** willingly
1561 **But:** only 1564 But it is best we now avoid longwindedness

For love of God, and lat us faste go   1565
Right to th'effect, withouten tales mo,
Whi al this folk assembled in this place;
And lat us of hire saluynges pace.

Gret honour did hem Deiphebus, certeyn,
And fedde hem wel with al that myghte like;   1570
But evere mo 'Allas!' was his refreyn,
'My goode brother Troilus, the syke,
Lith yet' – and therwithal he gan to sike;
And after that, he peyned hym to glade
Hem as he myghte, and cheere good he made.   1575

Compleyned ek Eleyne of his siknesse
So feythfully that pite was to here,
And every wight gan waxen for accesse
A leche anon, and seyde, 'In this manere
Men curen folk.' – 'This charme I wol yow leere.'   1580
But ther sat oon, al list hire nought to teche,
That thoughte, 'Best koude I yet ben his leche.'

After compleynte, hym gonnen they to preyse,
As folk don yet whan som wight hath bygonne
To preise a man, and up with pris hym reise   1585
A thousand fold yet heigher than the sonne:
'He is, he kan, that fewe lordes konne.'
And Pandarus, of that they wolde afferme,
He naught forgat hire preisynge to conferme.

1566 th'effect: the point tales: talk   1568 saluynges: (exchange of) greetings
pace: pass over   1570 like: please   1572 syke: sick man   1573 Lith yet: is
still confined to bed therwithal: thereupon sike: sigh   1574 peyned
hym: took pains glade: make happy   1575 cheere good he made: was in
good spirits   1577 feythfully: sincerely pite was: it was pitiful   1578–9 And
everyone immediately turned into a doctor on the subject of fever
1580 charme: charm, spell leere: teach   1581 oon: one person al list hire
nought: although she did not wish   1582 Who thought, 'I know best how to
be his doctor.'   1585 pris: praise reise: exalt   1587 kan, that: knows how to
do what

1590   Herde al this thyng Criseyde wel inough,
           And every word gan for to notifie;
           For which with sobre cheere hire herte lough –
           For who is that ne wolde hire glorifie,
           To mowen swich a knyght don lyve or dye?
1595   But al passe I, lest ye to longe dwelle;
           For for o fyn is al that evere I telle.

           The tyme com fro dyner for to ryse,
           And as hem aughte, arisen everichon,
           And gonne a while of this and that devise;
1600   But Pandarus brak al that speche anon,
           And seide to Deiphebus, 'Wol ye gon,
           If it youre wille be, as I yow preyde,
           To speke here of the nedes of Criseyde?'

           Eleyne, which that by the hond hire held,
1605   Took first the tale, and seyde, 'Go we blyve';
           And goodly on Criseyde she biheld,
           And seyde, 'Joves lat hym nevere thryve
           That doth yow harm, and brynge hym soone of lyve,
           And yeve me sorwe, but he shal it rewe,
1610   If that I may, and alle folk be trewe!'

           'Tel thow thi neces cas,' quod Deiphebus
           To Pandarus, 'for thow kanst best it telle.'
           'My lordes and my ladys, it stant thus:

1591 notifie: take note of   1592 sobre: serious   cheere: outward expression
lough: laughed   1593 hire glorifie: be proud of herself   1594 To be able
(mowen) to cause (don) such a knight to live or die   1595 passe: pass over
dwelle: delay   1596 For: because   o fyn: one end, purpose   1598 hem
aughte: they ought   arisen everichon: everyone got up
1599 devise: converse   1600 brak: interrupted   speche: conversation
1601 gon: proceed   1603 nedes: urgent affairs   1605 Took first the
tale: was the first to speak   1606 goodly: kindly   1607 Joves: Jove
1608 brynge ... of lyve: kill   1609 yeve: give   rewe: regret   1613 stant (=
stondeth): is

What sholde I lenger,' quod he, 'do yow dwelle?'
He rong hem out a proces lik a belle   1615
Upon hire foo that highte Poliphete,
So heynous that men myghten on it spete.

Answerde of this ech werse of hem than other,
And Poliphete they gonnen thus to warien:
'Anhonged be swich oon, were he my brother –   1620
And so he shal, for it ne may nought varien!'
What shold I lenger in this tale tarien?
Pleynliche, alle at ones, they hire highten
To ben hire help in al that evere they myghten.

Spak than Eleyne, and seyde, 'Pandarus,   1625
Woot ought my lord, my brother, this matere –
I meene Ector – or woot it Troilus?'
He seyde, 'Ye, but wole ye now me here?
Me thynketh this, sith that Troilus is here,
It were good, if that ye wolde assente,   1630
She tolde hireself hym al this er she wente.

'For he wol have the more hir grief at herte,
By cause, lo, that she a lady is;
And, by youre leve, I wol but in right sterte
And do yow wyte, and that anon, iwys,   1635
If that he slepe, or wol ought here of this.'
And in he lepte, and seyde hym in his ere,
'God have thi soule, ibrought have I thi beere!'

1614 **What**: why **do yow dwelle**: cause you to delay   1615 **rong hem
out**: rang out, proclaimed, to them **proces**: case   1616 **highte**: was called
1617 **heynous**: hateful **spete**: spit   1618 Each of them responded to this
worse than the other   1619 **warien**: curse   1620 May such a person be
hanged, even if he were my brother!   1621 **varien**: be otherwise
1622 **tale**: discourse **tarien**: delay   1623 **Pleynliche**: simply, unreservedly
highten: promised   1624 **hire help**: of help to her   1626 **ought**: at all
1632 **grief**: trouble   1634 And, with your permission, I will just pop in
1635 **do yow wyte**: let you know   1636 **ought**: anything
1638 **ibrought**: brought **beere**: bier

To smylen of this gan tho Troilus,
1640   And Pandarus, withouten rekenynge,
Out wente anon to Eleyne and Deiphebus,
And seyde hem, 'So ther be no taryinge,
Ne moore prees, he wol wel that ye brynge
Criseyda, my lady, that is here;
1645   And as he may enduren, he wol here.

'But wel ye woot, the chaumbre is but lite,
And fewe folk may lightly make it warm;
Now loketh ye (for I wol have no wite
To brynge in prees that myghte don hym harm,
1650   Or hym disesen, for my bettre arm)
Wher it be bet she bide til eft-sonys?
Now loketh ye that knowen what to doon is.

'I sey for me, best is, as I kan knowe,
That no wight in ne wente but ye tweye,
1655   But it were I, for I kan in a throwe
Reherce hire cas unlik that she kan seye;
And after this she may hym ones preye
To ben good lord, in short, and take hire leve.
This may nought muchel of his ese hym reve.

1660   'And ek, for she is straunge, he wol forbere
His ese, which that hym thar nought for yow;
Ek oother thing that toucheth nought to here

1640 **rekenynge:** (time for) calculation   1642 **So:** provided that
taryinge: delay   1643 **prees:** crowd   1645 **as:** for as long as   **here:** listen
1646 **lite:** small   1647 **lightly:** easily   1648 **loketh:** think, consider
wite: blame   1650 **hym disesen:** cause him discomfort   **bettre arm:** right
arm   1651 Whether it would be better that she wait until another time
1652 **to doon is:** is best to do   1653 **for me, best:** for my part, the best thing
1655 **But:** unless   **throwe:** short time   1656 **Reherce:** go over   **unlik**
that: differently from what (i.e. better than)   1657 **ones:** once
1658 **lord:** i.e. patron, protector   1659 **muchel:** much   **ese:** comfort
reve: deprive   1660 **for:** because   **straunge:** a stranger, not a relation
forbere: forgo   1661 **which that hym thar nought:** which he need not
1662 **toucheth nought to here:** does not concern her

He wol yow telle – I woot it wel right now –
That secret is, and for the townes prow.'
And they, that nothyng knewe of his entente,   1665
Withouten more, to Troilus in they wente.

Eleyne, in al hire goodly softe wyse,
Gan hym salue, and wommanly to pleye,
And seyde, 'Iwys, ye moste alweies arise!
Now faire brother, beth al hool, I preye!'   1670
And gan hire arm right over his shulder leye,
And hym with al hire wit to reconforte;
As she best koude, she gan hym to disporte.

So after this quod she, 'We yow biseke,
My deere brother Deiphebus and I,   1675
For love of God – and so doth Pandare eke –
To ben good lord and frend, right hertely,
Unto Criseyde, which that certeynly
Receyveth wrong, as woot wel here Pandare,
That kan hire cas wel bet than I declare.'   1680

This Pandarus gan newe his tong affile,
And al hire cas reherce, and that anon.
Whan it was seyd, soone after in a while,
Quod Troilus, 'As sone as I may gon,
I wol right fayn with al my myght ben oon –   1685
Have God my trouthe – hire cause to sustene.'
'Good thrift have ye!' quod Eleyne the queene.

1664 **prow**: advantage   1667 **softe**: gentle   1668 **salue**: greet **pleye**: jest
1669 **alweies**: at any rate, in any event **arise**: get up, get well
1670 **faire**: dear **beth al hool**: get well   1672 **reconforte**: comfort
1673 **koude**: knew how to do **disporte**: cheer up   1674 **biseke**: beg
1677 **hertely**: cordially   1680 **declare**: set out   1681 **newe**: afresh **affile**: file,
polish   1684 **gon**: walk   1685 **oon**: one (of her supporters)   1686 **Have
God my trouthe**: may God receive my pledge, I swear to God
sustene: support   1687 **Good thrift have ye**: may you have good luck

Quod Pandarus, 'And it youre wille be
That she may take hire leve, er that she go?'
1690   'O, elles God forbede it,' tho quod he,
'If that she vouche sauf for to do so.'
And with that word quod Troilus, 'Ye two,
Deiphebus and my suster lief and deere,
To yow have I to speke of o matere,

1695   'To ben avysed by youre reed the bettre –'
And fond, as hap was, at his beddes hed
The copie of a tretys and a lettre
That Ector hadde hym sent to axen red
If swych a man was worthi to ben ded,
1700   Woot I nought who; but in a grisly wise
He preyede hem anon on it avyse.

Deiphebus gan this lettre for t'onfolde
In ernest greet; so did Eleyne the queene;
And romyng outward, faste it gonne byholde,
1705   Downward a steire, into an herber greene.
This ilke thing they redden hem bitwene,
And largely, the mountance of an houre,
Thei gonne on it to reden and to poure.

Now lat hem rede, and torne we anon
1710   To Pandarus, that gan ful faste prye
That al was wel, and out he gan to gon
Into the grete chaumbre, and that in hye,
And seyde, 'God save al this compaynye!
Com, nece myn; my lady queene Eleyne
1715   Abideth yow, and ek my lordes tweyne.

1688 Pandarus said, 'Is it your wish . . .'   1690 God forbid it should be
otherwise   1691 **vouche sauf**: agree   1693 **lief**: dear   1695 **avysed**: advised
reed: counsel   1696 **as hap was**: as it chanced   1697 **tretys**: document
1698 **red**: advice   1699 If so-and-so deserved to die   1700 **Woot I nought**: I
do not know   **grisly wise**: grim manner   1701 **avyse**: consider   1703 **In
ernest greet**: very seriously   1704 **romyng outward**: strolling outdoors
faste: intently   1705 **Downward a steire**: down a staircase   **herber**: garden
1706 **ilke**: same   1707 **largely**: fully   **mountance**: length, space
1708 **poure**: pore   1710 **prye**: spy out   1712 **in hye**: hastily

'Rys, take with yow youre nece Antigone.
Or whom yow list – or no fors; hardyly
The lesse prees, the bet – com forth with me,
And loke that ye thonken humblely
Hem alle thre, and whan ye may goodly   1720
Youre tyme se, taketh of hem youre leeve,
Lest we to longe his restes hym byreeve.'

Al innocent of Pandarus entente,
Quod tho Criseyde, 'Go we, uncle deere';
And arm in arm inward with hym she wente,   1725
Avysed wel hire wordes and hire cheere;
And Pandarus, in ernestful manere,
Seyde, 'Alle folk, for Goddes love, I preye,
Stynteth right here, and softely yow pleye.

'Aviseth yow what folk ben hire withinne,   1730
And in what plit oon is, God hym amende!'
And inward thus, 'Ful softely bygynne,
Nece, I conjure and heighly yow defende,
On his half which that soule us alle sende,
And in the vertu of corones tweyne,   1735
Sle naught this man, that hath for yow this
          peyne!

'Fy on the devel! Thynk which oon he is,
And in what plit he lith; com of anon!
Thynk al swich taried tyde, but lost it nys:

1717 **whom**: whomsoever **no fors**: it doesn't matter **hardyly**: certainly
1718 **prees**: crowd   1720 **goodly**: courteously   1722 **restes**: times of rest
hym byreeve: deprive him of   1725 **inward**: in   1726 **Avysed**: having
considered   1727 **ernestful**: serious   1729 **Stynteth**: stop **softely yow
pleye**: amuse yourselves quietly   1730 **Aviseth yow**: take thought
hire: here   1731 **plit**: plight, state **oon**: one person **amende**: make well
1732 **And inward**: and (he said) on the way in (or, privately)
1733 **conjure**: implore **heighly yow defende**: strictly forbid you
1734 **half**: behalf **sende**: sent   1735 And by the power of two crowns
(see n.)   1736 **Sle naught**: do not kill   1737 **Fy**: scorn **which oon**: who
1738 **com of**: come on, hurry up   1739 **taried tyde**: time spent delaying

1740   That wol ye bothe seyn, whan ye ben oon.
        Secoundely, ther yet devyneth noon
        Upon yow two; come of now, if ye konne!
        While folk is blent, lo, al the tyme is wonne.

        'In titeryng, and pursuyte, and delayes,
1745   The folk devyne at waggyng of a stree;
        And though ye wolde han after mirye dayes,
        Than dar ye naught. And whi? For she, and she
        Spak swych a word; thus loked he, and he!
        Las, tyme ilost! I dar nought with yow dele.
1750   Com of, therfore, and bryngeth hym to hele!'

        But now to yow, ye loveres that ben here,
        Was Troilus nought in a kankedort,
        That lay, and myghte whisprynge of hem here,
        And thoughte, 'O Lord, right now renneth my sort
1755   Fully to deye, or han anon comfort!'
        And was the firste tyme he shulde hire preye
        Of love – O myghty God, what shal he seye?

                    Explicit secundus liber.

1740 **oon**: united   1741 In the second place no one yet suspects anything
1743 **blent**: deceived **wonne**: gained   1744 **titeryng**: vacillation
pursuyte: prolonged entreaty   1745 People are suspicious at the moving of a
straw   1746 **wolde han**: would wish to have **after**: afterwards
mirye: happy   1747 **dar ye naught**: you dare not **she, and she**: this woman
and that   1749 **Las**: alas **dele**: have dealings   1750 **hele**: health, well-being
1752 **kankedort**: dilemma (n.)   1754 **renneth**: approaches **sort**: fate, lot
1755 **Fully**: absolutely   1757 **shal he seye**: is he to say   *Explicit, etc.*: Here
ends the second book

BOOK 3

Incipit prohemium tercii libri.

O blisful light of which the bemes clere
Adorneth al the thridde heven faire!
O sonnes lief, O Joves doughter deere,
Plesance of love, O goodly debonaire,
In gentil hertes ay redy to repaire!   5
O veray cause of heele and of gladnesse,
Iheryed be thy myght and thi goodnesse!

In hevene and helle, in erthe and salte see
Is felt thi myght, if that I wel descerne,
As man, brid, best, fissh, herbe, and grene tree   10
Thee fele in tymes with vapour eterne.
God loveth, and to love wol nought werne,
And in this world no lyves creature
Withouten love is worth, or may endure.

Incipit, etc.: Here begins the proem of the third book   1 **blisful**: fair
bemes: beams, rays **clere**: brilliant   2 **thridde heven**: third planetary sphere
(that of Venus) **sonnes lief**: darling of the sun **Joves doughter**: i.e. Venus
4 **Plesance**: delight **debonaire**: gracious one   5 **gentil**: noble-spirited
repaire: find a home   6 **veray**: true **heele**: health, well-being
7 **Iheryed**: praised   9 **descerne**: discern, perceive   10 **brid**: bird **best**: beast
herbe: plant   11 **in tymes**: at (certain) seasons **vapour**: emanation, influence
eterne: everlasting   12 **werne**: deny   13 **lyves**: living   14 **worth**: of value

15 Ye Joves first to thilke effectes glade,
    Thorugh which that thynges lyven alle and be,
    Comeveden, and amorous him made
    On mortal thyng and, as yow list, ay ye
    Yeve hym in love ese or adversitee,
20 And in a thousand formes down hym sente
    For love in erthe, and whom yow liste he hente.

    Ye fierse Mars apaisen of his ire,
    And as yow list, ye maken hertes digne;
    Algates hem that ye wol sette a-fyre,
25 They dreden shame, and vices they resygne;
    Ye do hem corteys be, fresshe and benigne;
    And heighe or lowe, after a wight entendeth,
    The joies that he hath, youre myght it sendeth.

    Ye holden regne and hous in unitee;
30 Ye sothfast cause of frendship ben also;
    Ye knowe al thilke covered qualitee
    Of thynges, which that folk on wondren so,
    Whan they kan nought construe how it may jo
    She loveth hym, or whi he loveth here,
35 As whi this fissh, and naught that, comth to were.

    Ye folk a lawe han set in universe,
    And this knowe I by hem that lovers be,
    That whoso stryveth with yow hath the werse.

15-17 **Ye Joves first . . . Comeveden:** you first moved Jove   ·15 **thilke:** those
effectes: consequences   17 **amorous:** enamoured   19 **Yeve:** gave
ese: success   **adversitee:** misfortune   20 **formes:** shapes   21 **hente:** took
22 **apaisen:** appease, assuage   **ire:** anger   23 **digne:** honourable, noble
24 **Algates:** especially   25 **resygne:** renounce   26 **do hem . . . be:** cause them
to be   **corteys:** courtly   **fresshe:** full of life   **benigne:** considerate   27 **heigh or
lowe:** in all respects   **after a wight entendeth:** according to how a person is
inclined   29 **regne:** kingdom   **hous:** household   30 **sothfast:** true
31 **covered:** hidden   **qualitee:** nature   32 **on wondren so:** are so curious
about   33 **construe:** explain   **jo:** happen   34 **here:** her   35 **were:** weir, a
fish-trap   36 You have established a law for people universally (*in universe*)
38 **stryveth:** contends   **hath the werse:** comes off worse

Now, lady bryght, for thi benignite,
At reverence of hem that serven the,   40
Whos clerc I am, so techeth me devyse
Som joye of that is felt in thi servyse.

Ye in my naked herte sentement
Inhielde, and do me shewe of thy swetnesse.
Caliope, thi vois be now present,   45
For now is nede: sestow nought my destresse,
How I mot telle anonright the gladnesse
Of Troilus, to Venus heryinge?
To which gladnesse, who nede hath, God hym brynge!

Explicit prohemium tercii libri.

Incipit liber tercius.

Lay al this mene while Troilus,   50
Recordyng his lesson in this manere;
'Mafay,' thoughte he, 'thus wol I sey, and thus;
Thus wol I pleyne unto my lady dere;
That word is good, and this shal be my cheere;
This nyl I nought foryeten in no wise.'   55
God leve hym werken as he kan devyse!

And, Lord, so that his herte gan to quappe,
Heryng hire come, and shorte for to sike!
And Pandarus, that ledde hire by the lappe,

39 **lady bryght**: radiant lady **benignite**: graciousness 40 **At reverence of**: in
honour of 41 **clerc**: scribe **devyse**: relate 42 **joye of that**: of that joy
which 43–4 Pour (a capacity for) feeling into my bare, empty heart, and
make me express your sweetness 45 **thi vois be**: may your voice be
46 **sestow nought**: do you not see 48 **to Venus heryinge**: in praise of Venus
49 May God bring to such happiness whoever needs it *Explicit, etc.*: Here
ends the proem of the third book *Incipit, etc.*: Here begins the third book
51 **Recordyng**: going over **his lesson**: what he had prepared 52 **Mafay**: by
my faith 54 **cheere**: expression 55 **foryeten**: forget **in no wise**: on any
account 56 **leve**: grant **werken**: to act **devyse**: plan. 57 **so that**: how
quappe: pound 58 **shorte for to sike**: to pant 59 **lappe**: hem or fold (of a
garment)

60 Com ner, and gan in at the curtyn pike,
And seyde, 'God do boot on alle syke!
Se who is here yow comen to visite:
Lo, here is she that is youre deth to wite.'

Therwith it semed as he wepte almost.
65 'Ha, a,' quod Troilus so reufully,
'Wher me be wo, O myghty God, thow woost!
Who is al ther? I se nought trewely.'
'Sire,' quod Criseyde, 'it is Pandare and I.'
'Ye, swete herte? Allas, I may nought rise,
70 To knele and do yow honour in som wyse.'

And dressed hym upward, and she right tho
Gan bothe hire hondes softe upon hym leye.
'O, for the love of God, do ye nought so
To me,' quod she, 'I! What is this to seye?
75 Sire, comen am I to yow for causes tweye:
First, yow to thonke, and of youre lordshipe eke
Continuance I wolde yow biseke.'

This Troilus, that herde his lady preye
Of lordshipe hym, wax neither quyk ne ded,
80 Ne myghte o word for shame to it seye,
Although men sholde smyten of his hed.
But Lord, so he wex sodeynliche red,
And sire, his lessoun, that he wende konne
To preyen hire, is thorugh his wit ironne.

60 **Com ner**: drew near **curtyn**: bed-curtains **pike**: peep 61 **God do boot
on**: may God heal **syke**: sick people 63 **youre deth to wite**: to blame for
your death 65 **reufully**: pitifully 66 **Wher me be wo**: whether I am
unhappy 71 **dressed hym**: raised himself **right**: just 72 **softe**: gently
74 **I**: ah **is this to seye**: does this mean 76 **lordshipe**: protection, patronage
77 **Continuance**: continuation **biseke**: beseech 79 **quyk**: alive
80 **shame**: embarrassment 81 **sholde**: were to **smyten of**: cut off
82 **so**: how **sodeynliche**: suddenly 83 **wende konne**: thought he knew
84 **preyen**: entreat **wit**: mind **ironne**: run

Criseyde al this aspied wel ynough,   85
For she was wis, and loved hym nevere the lasse,
Al nere he malapert, or made it tough,
Or was to bold, to synge a fool a masse.
But whan his shame gan somwhat to passe,
His resons, as I may my rymes holde,   90
I yow wol telle, as techen bokes olde.

In chaunged vois, right for his verray drede,
Which vois ek quook, and therto his manere
Goodly abaist, and now his hewes rede,
Now pale, unto Criseyde, his lady dere,   95
With look down cast and humble iyolden chere,
Lo, the alderfirste word that hym asterte
Was, twyes, 'Mercy, mercy, swete herte!'

And stynte a while, and whan he myghte out
      brynge,
The nexte word was, 'God woot, for I have,   100
As ferforthly as I have had konnynge,
Ben youres al, God so my soule save,
And shal til that I, woful wight, be grave!
And though I dar, ne kan, unto yow pleyne,
Iwis, I suffre nought the lasse peyne.   105

'Thus muche as now, O wommanliche wif,
I may out brynge, and if this yow displese,
That shal I wreke upon myn owen lif

85 **aspied**: noticed   87 Even though he was not presumptuous (*malapert*),
nor too pressing (*made it tough*)   88 **Or**: nor   **synge a fool a masse**: use
flattery   89 **shame**: embarrassment   90 **resons**: words, remarks   **holde**: keep
up   91 **techen**: teach   92 **verray**: sheer   93 **quook**: trembled   **therto**: in
addition   94 **Goodly abaist**: becomingly abashed   **hewes**: complexion
rede: red   96 **iyolden**: submissive   97 **alderfirste**: very first   **asterte**: escaped
98 **twyes**: twice   99 **stynte**: paused   **out brynge**: utter anything   101 **As
ferforthly**: insofar   **konnynge**: ability   103 **grave**: buried   104 **dar, ne
kan**: neither dare nor can   106 **as now**: for the present   **wommanliche
wif**: (most) womanly woman   108 **wreke**: avenge

Right soone, I trowe, and do youre herte an ese,
110 If with my deth youre wreththe may apese.
But syn that ye han herd me somwhat seye,
Now recche I nevere how soone that I deye.'

Therwith his manly sorwe to biholde
It myghte han mad an herte of stoon to rewe;
115 And Pandare wep as he to water wolde,
And poked evere his nece new and newe,
And seyde, 'Wo bygon ben hertes trewe!
For love of God, make of this thing an ende,
Or sle us both at ones er ye wende.'

120 'I, what?' quod she, 'by God and by my trouthe,
I not nat what ye wilne that I seye.'
'I, what?' quod he, 'That ye han on hym routhe,
For Goddes love, and doth hym nought to deye!'
'Now thanne thus,' quod she, 'I wolde hym
                        preye
125 To telle me the fyn of his entente –
Yet wist I nevere wel what that he mente.'

'What that I mene, O swete herte deere?'
Quod Troilus, 'O goodly, fresshe free,
That with the stremes of youre eyen cleere
130 Ye wolde somtyme frendly on me see,
And thanne agreen that I may ben he,
Withouten braunche of vice on any wise,
In trouthe alwey to don yow my servise,

109 do . . . an ese: bring relief to, gratify 110 wreththe: wrath
apese: pacify 112 recche: care 114 rewe: feel pity 115 wep: wept
wolde: would (turn) 116 poked: nudged new and newe: again and again
117 And said, 'Loyal hearts are beset with sorrow!' 119 sle: kill at ones: at
the same time, together wende: leave 120 I: ah 121 not nat: do not know
wilne: wish 125 fyn of his entente: end he has in mind
128 goodly: excellent fresshe: lovely free: noble one 129 stremes: beams
cleere: bright 130 see: look 131 agreen: agree 132 braunche: any kind

'As to my lady right and chief resort,
With al my wit and al my diligence;   135
And I to han, right as yow list, comfort,
Under yowre yerde, egal to myn offence,
As deth, if that I breke youre defence;
And that ye deigne me so muche honoure
Me to comanden aught in any houre;   140

'And I to ben youre – verray, humble, trewe,
Secret, and in my paynes pacient,
And evere mo desiren fresshly newe
To serve, and ben ay ylike diligent,
And with good herte al holly youre talent   145
Receyven wel, how sore that me smerte;
Lo, this mene I, myn owen swete herte.'

Quod Pandarus, 'Lo, here an hard requeste,
And resonable, a lady for to werne!
Now, nece myn, by natal Joves feste,   150
Were I a god, ye sholden sterve as yerne,
That heren wel this man wol nothing yerne
But youre honour, and sen hym almost sterve,
And ben so loth to suffren hym yow serve.'

With that she gan hire eyen on hym caste   155
Ful esily and ful debonairly,
Avysyng hire, and hied nought to faste

134 **right**: true **resort**: resource, recourse   136 **han**: receive
comfort: consolation   137 **Under youre yerde**: subject to your authority
egal: appropriate   138 **As**: such as **breke**: disobey **defence**: prohibition
139 **deigne**: grant   141 **youre**: yours **verray**: loyal **trewe**: true servant
142 Discreet, and patient in my sufferings   143 **fresshly newe**: unfailingly
144 **ylike**: equally   145–6 And wholeheartedly accept your every wish
(*talent*), however severely it pains me   149 **werne**: refuse   150 **natal Joves
feste**: the feast of Jupiter (who presides over nativities)   151 **Were I**: if I were
sterve: die **as yerne**: very quickly   152 **yerne**: desire   153 **sen**: see
154 **loth**: reluctant **suffren**: allow   156 **esily**: gently **debonairly**: modestly
157 **Avysyng hire**: deliberating **hied**: hurried

With nevere a word, but seyde hym softely,
'Myn honour sauf, I wol wel trewely,
160   And in swich forme as he gan now devyse,
Receyven hym fully to my servyse,

'Bysechyng hym, for Goddes love, that he
Wolde, in honour of trouthe and gentilesse,
As I wel mene, ek menen wel to me,
165   And myn honour with wit and bisynesse
Ay kepe; and if I may don hym gladnesse,
From hennesforth, iwys, I nyl nought feyne.
Now beth al hool; no lenger ye ne pleyne.

'But natheles, this warne I yow,' quod she,
170   'A kynges sone although ye be, ywys,
Ye shal namore han sovereignete
Of me in love, than right in that cas is;
N'y nyl forbere, if that ye don amys,
To wratthe yow; and whil that ye me serve,
175   Chericen yow right after ye disserve.

'And shortly, deere herte and al my knyght,
Beth glad, and draweth yow to lustinesse,
And I shal trewely, with al my myght,
Youre bittre tornen al into swetenesse.
180   If I be she that may yow do gladnesse,
For every wo ye shal recovere a blisse –'
And hym in armes took, and gan hym kisse.

159 **Myn honour sauf**: without prejudice to my honour   160 **devyse**: set
forth   164 **mene**: intend   165 **with wit and bisynesse**: mindfully and
diligently   166 **Ay kepe**: always preserve   **don hym gladnesse**: make him
happy   167 **feyne**: hold back   168 **al hool**: completely cured
171 **sovereignete**: dominion, mastery   173 **N'y nyl forbere**: nor will I
refrain   174 **wratthe**: be angry with   175 Cherish you exactly as you
deserve   176 **shortly**: briefly   **al my**: my own   177 **draweth**: turn
lustinesse: pleasure   179 **bittre**: bitter suffering   181 **For**: in return for
recovere: get in return

Fil Pandarus on knees, and up his eyen
To heven threw, and held his hondes highe:
'Immortal god,' quod he, 'that mayst nought   185
    deyen,
Cupide I mene, of this mayst glorifie;
And Venus, thow mayst maken melodie!
Withouten hond, me semeth that in the towne,
For this merveille ich here ech belle sowne.

'But ho! namore as now of this matere,   190
For-whi this folk wol comen up anon,
That han the lettre red – lo, I hem here.
But I conjure the, Criseyde, anon,
And to, thow Troilus, whan thow mayst goon,
That at myn hous ye ben at my warnynge,   195
For I ful well shal shape youre comynge;

'And eseth there youre hertes right ynough;
And lat se which of yow shal bere the belle
To speke of love aright!' – therwith he lough –
'For ther have ye a leiser for to telle.'   200
Quod Troilus, 'How longe shal I dwelle,
Er this be don?' Quod he, 'Whan thow mayst ryse,
This thyng shal be right as I yow devyse.'

With that Eleyne and also Deiphebus
Tho comen upward, right at the steires ende;   205
And Lord, so thanne gan gronen Troilus,
His brother and his suster for to blende.
Quod Pandarus, 'It tyme is that we wende.

183 Fil: fell   186 mayst glorifie: (you) may boast   188 Withouten
hond: without (being rung by) hand   189 merveille: marvel, wonder ich
here: I hear   sowne: sound   190 ho: stop   as now: for the present
192 red: read   here: hear   193 conjure the: charge you   194 to: also   mayst
goon: are able to walk   195 at my warnynge: when I tell you
196 shape: contrive   197 eseth: comfort   198 bere the belle: take first
place   199 aright: well   therwith: at which   lough: laughed
200 leiser: opportunity   telle: talk   201 dwelle: wait   205 steires ende: top of
the stairs   207 blende: deceive   208 wende: depart

Tak, nece myn, youre leve at alle thre,
210   And lat hem speke, and cometh forth with me.'

She took hire leve at hem ful thriftily,
As she wel koude, and they hire reverence
Unto the fulle diden, hardyly,
And speken wonder wel, in hire absence,
215   Of hire in preysing of hire excellence –
Hire governaunce, hire wit, and hire manere
Comendeden, it joie was to here.

Now lat hire wende unto hire owen place,
And torne we to Troilus ayein,
220   That gan ful lightly of the lettre pace
That Deiphebus hadde in the gardyn seyn;
And of Eleyne and hym he wolde feyn
Delivered ben, and seyde that hym leste
To slepe, and after tales have reste.

225   Eleyne hym kiste, and took hire leve blyve,
Deiphebus ek, and hom wente every wight;
And Pandarus, as faste as he may dryve,
To Troilus tho com, as lyne right,
And on a paillet al that glade nyght
230   By Troilus he lay, with mery chere,
To tale, and wel was hem they were yfeere.

Whan every wight was voided but they two,
And alle the dores weren faste yshette,
To telle in short, withouten wordes mo,

---

209 at: of   211 thriftily: becomingly   212 koude: knew how   212–13 hire
reverence . . . diden: paid respect to her   213 Unto the fulle: without reserve
hardyly: certainly   214 wonder: marvellously   216 governaunce: conduct
wit: intelligence manere: bearing   217 Comendeden: (they) praised
220 lightly: quickly of . . . pace: glance over   221 seyn: seen
222 feyn: gladly   223 Delivered ben: be rid hym leste: he wished
224 tales: talking   227 dryve: go   228 as lyne right: as straight as a line,
directly   229 paillet: mattress   231 tale: talk wel was hem: they were
happy   232 voided: departed   233 faste yshette: shut tight

This Pandarus, withouten any lette,   235
Up roos, and on his beddes syde hym sette,
And gan to speken in a sobre wyse
To Troilus, as I shal yow devyse:

'Myn alderlevest lord, and brother deere,
God woot, and thow, that it sat me so soore,   240
When I the saugh so langwisshyng to-yere
For love, of which thi wo wax alwey moore,
That I, with al my myght and al my loore,
Have evere sithen don my bisynesse
To brynge the to joye out of distresse,   245

'And have it brought to swich plit as thow woost,
So that thorugh me thow stondest now in weye
To faren wel; I sey it for no bost,
And wostow whi? For shame it is to seye:
For the have I bigonne a gamen pleye   250
Which that I nevere do shal eft for other,
Although he were a thousand fold my brother.

'That is to seye, for the am I bicomen,
Bitwixen game and ernest, swich a meene
As maken wommen unto men to comen –   255
Al sey I nought, thow wost wel what I meene.
For the have I my nece, of vices cleene,
So fully maad thi gentilesse triste,
That al shal ben right as thiselven liste.

235 lette: delay   236 hym sette: sat down   237 sobre: grave
239 alderlevest: very dearest   240 sat: affected, pained soore: grievously
241 to-yere: this year   243 loore: knowledge   244 sithen: since don my
bisynesse: applied myself   246 plit: situation   247 stondest ... in weye: are
likely   248 faren wel: be successful bost: boast   249 And do you know
why? I am ashamed to say it   250 a gamen pleye: to pursue a course of
action   251 eft for other: again for anyone else   254 Bitwixen game and
ernest: half in jest, half seriously meene: go-between, intermediary   256 Al
sey I: even if I say   257 cleene: free   258 Made to trust so completely your
nobility of character   259 right: exactly thiselven liste: you wish

260   'But God, that al woot, take I to witnesse,
         That nevere I this for coveitise wroughte,
         But oonly for t'abregge that distresse
         For which wel neigh thow deidest, as me thoughte.
         But, goode brother, do now as the oughte,
265   For Goddes love, and kep hire out of blame,
         Syn thow art wys, and save alwey hire name.

         'For wel thow woost, the name as yet of here
         Among the peeple, as who seyth, halwed is;
         For that man is unbore, I dar wel swere,
270   That evere wiste that she dide amys.
         But wo is me, that I, that cause al this,
         May thynken that she is my nece deere,
         And I hire em, and traitour ek yfeere!

         'And were it wist that I, thorugh myn engyn,
275   Hadde in my nece yput this fantasie,
         To doon thi lust and holly to ben thyn,
         Whi, al the world upon it wolde crie,
         And seyn that I the werste trecherie
         Dide in this cas, that evere was bigonne,
280   And she forlost, and thow right nought ywonne.

         'Wherfore, er I wol ferther gon a pas,
         Yet eft I the biseche and fully seye,
         That privete go with us in this cas –

260 **al woot:** knows everything **to:** as my   261 That I never did this out of
desire of gain   262 **t'abregge:** to shorten   263 **deidest:** died **as me
thoughte:** as it seemed to me   264 **the oughte:** you ought
265 **blame:** disgrace   266 **save:** preserve **name:** reputation   267 **here:** her
268 **as who seyth:** as one might say **halwed is:** is revered   269 **unbore:** not
born   273 **traitour:** betrayer   274 **were it wist:** if it were known
engyn: contrivance   275 **yput:** put, implanted **fantasie:** inclination
276 **lust:** pleasure **holly:** wholly   277 **upon . . . crye:** cry out against,
condemn   280 **forlost:** utterly ruined **right nought ywonne:** in no way the
winner   281 **ferther gon a pas:** go a step further   283 **privete:** secrecy
cas: matter

That is to seyn, that thow us nevere wreye;
And be nought wroth, though I the ofte preye   285
To holden secree swich an heigh matere,
For skilfull is, thow woost wel, my praiere.

'And thynk what wo ther hath bitid er this,
For makyng of avantes, as men rede;
And what meschaunce in this world yet ther is,   290
Fro day to day, right for that wikked dede;
For which thise wise clerkes that ben dede
Han evere yet proverbed to us yonge,
That "firste vertu is to kepe tonge."

'And nere it that I wilne as now t'abregge   295
Diffusioun of speche, I koude almoost
A thousand olde stories the allegge
Of wommen lost through fals and foles bost.
Proverbes kanst thiself ynowe and woost
Ayeins that vice, for to ben a labbe,   300
Al seyde men soth as often as thei gabbe.

'O tonge, allas, so often here-byforn
Hath mad ful many a lady bright of hewe
Seyd "Weilaway, the day that I was born!"
And many a maydes sorwe for to newe;   305
And for the more part, al is untrewe

284 wreye: give away   285 wroth: angry   286 holden secree: keep secret
heigh: important   287 For you well know that my request is reasonable
(skilfull)   288 bitid: happened   289 avantes: boasts
290 meschaunce: misfortune   291 right for: precisely because of
292 dede: dead   293 proverbed to us yonge: taught us by means of proverbs
when young (n.)   294 kepe tonge: hold (one's) tongue   295 If it weren't that
at this time I wish to cut short   296 Diffusioun: prolixity   297 the
allege: cite to you   298 fals: falsehood   foles bost: fools' boasting
299 kanst: (you) know   ynowe: enough   300 labbe: tell-tale   301 Even if
people spoke the truth as often as they talk nonsense   302 O: one, a single
here-byforn: before this   303 bright of hewe: radiantly beautiful in
appearance   304 Seyd: (to have) said   Weilaway: alas   305 newe: renew
306 for the more part: mostly   untrewe: false

That men of yelpe, and it were brought to preve.
Of kynde non avauntour is to leve.

'Avauntour and a lyere, al is on;
310   As thus: I pose, a womman graunte me
Hire love, and seith that other wol she non,
And I am sworn to holden it secree,
And after I go telle it two or thre –
Iwis, I am avauntour at the leeste,
315   And lyere, for I breke my biheste.

'Now loke thanne, if they be nought to blame,
Swich manere folk – what shal I clepe hem, what? –
That hem avaunte of wommen, and by name,
That nevere yet bihyghte hem this ne that,
320   Ne knewe hem more than myn olde hat!
No wonder is, so God me sende hele,
Though wommen dreden with us men to dele.

'I sey nought this for no mistrust of yow,
Ne for no wis-man, but for foles nyce,
325   And for the harm that in the werld is now,
As wel for folie ofte as for malice;
For wel woot I, in wise folk that vice
No womman drat, if she be wel avised;
For wyse ben by foles harm chastised.

330   'But now to purpos, leve brother deere:
Have al this thyng that I have seyd in mynde,
And kep the clos, and be now of good cheere,

307 of yelpe: boast of and: if brought to preve: put to the test 308 Of
kynde: by nature avauntour: boaster to leve: to be believed 309 lyere: liar
on: the same 310 As thus: I pose: for example, suppose (for the sake of
argument) 311 wol: wants 315 biheste: promise 316 loke: consider
317 clepe: call 318 hem avaunte: boast 319 bihyghte: promised 321 me
sende hele: may grant me (good) health 322 dreden: fear dele: have
dealings 326 wel: much 328 drat (= dredeth): fears be wel avised: has
considered carefully 329 For the wise take warning from the harm that
befalls fools 330 purpos: the point leve: dear 332 kep the clos: keep it to

For at thi day thow shalt me trewe fynde.
I shal thi proces set in swych a kynde,
And God toforn, that it shal the suffise,   335
For it shal be right as thow wolt devyse.

'For wel I woot, thow menest wel, parde;
Therfore I dar this fully undertake.
Thow woost ek what thi lady graunted the,
And day is set the chartres up to make.   340
Have now good nyght, I may no lenger wake;
And bid for me, syn thow art now in blysse,
That God me sende deth or soone lisse.'

Who myghte tellen half the joie or feste
Which that the soule of Troilus tho felte,   345
Heryng th'effect of Pandarus byheste?
His olde wo, that made his herte swelte,
Gan tho for joie wasten and tomelte,
And al the richesse of his sikes sore
At ones fledde; he felte of hem namore.   350

But right so as thise holtes and thise hayis,
That han in wynter dede ben and dreye,
Revesten hem in grene when that May is,
Whan every lusty liketh best to pleye;
Right in that selve wise, soth to seye,   355
Wax sodeynliche his herte ful of joie,
That gladder was ther nevere man in Troie.

333 **at thi day**: on your (important) day   334 **proces**: proceedings
set: arrange **kynde**: manner   335 **the suffise**: be enough for you
338 **dar**: venture **fully undertake**: solemnly declare   340 **day is set**: a day is
fixed **the chartres up to make**: to draw up the documents (i.e. settle the
arrangements)   341 **wake**: remain awake   342 **bid**: pray **blysse**: heavenly
bliss   343 **lisse**: comfort   344 **feste**: rejoicing   346 **th'effect**: the essence
byheste: promise   347 **swelte**: grow faint   348 **wasten**: diminish
tomelte: melt away   349 **richesse**: abundance **sikes sore**: bitter sighs
351 **holtes**: woods **hayis**: hedges   352 **dede**: dead **dreye**: dry   353 **Revesten**
hem: clothe themselves anew   354 **lusty**: person full of the joys of life
pleye: sport, have fun   355 **selve**: selfsame

And gan his look on Pandarus up caste
Ful sobrely, and frendly for to se,
360   And seyde, 'Frend, in Aperil the laste –
As wel thow woost, if it remembre the –
How neigh the deth for wo thow fownde me,
And how thow dedest al thi bisynesse
To knowe of me the cause of my destresse.

365   'Thow woost how longe ich it forbar to seye
To the, that art the man that I best triste;
And peril non was it to the bywreye,
That wist I wel; but telle me, if the liste,
Sith I so loth was that thiself it wiste,
370   How dorst I mo tellen of this matere,
That quake now, and no wight may us here?

'But natheles, by that God I the swere,
That, as hym list, may al this world governe –
And, if I lye, Achilles with his spere
375   Myn herte cleve, al were my lif eterne,
As I am mortal, if I late or yerne
Wolde it bewreye, or dorst, or sholde konne,
For al the good that God made under sonne –

'That rather deye I wolde, and determyne,
380   As thynketh me, now stokked in prisoun,
In wrecchidnesse, in filthe, and in vermyne,
Caytif to cruel kyng Agamenoun;
And this in all the temples of this town

358 **up caste**: raise   359 **sobrely**: seriously   360 **Aperil the laste**: last April
361 **it remembre the**: you remember   363 **dedest al thi
bisynesse**: endeavoured   365 **ich it forbar to seye**: I refrained from telling it
367 And there was no danger in disclosing it to you   369 **loth**: reluctant
370 **dorst I**: would I dare **mo**: others   371 **quake**: am trembling   372 **the
swere**: swear to you   374–5 **Achilles . . . cleve**: may Achilles pierce
375 **al**: even if **eterne**: eternal   376 **late or yerne**: at any time
377 **bewreye**: reveal **dorst**: should dare **konne**: be able to
379 **determyne**: come to an end   380 **stokked**: put in the stocks   381 **in
vermyne**: among vermin   382 **Caytif to**: prisoner of
Agamenoun: Agamemnon (n.)

Upon the goddes alle, I wol the swere
To-morwe day, if that it liketh the here.   385

'And that thow hast so muche ido for me
That I ne may it nevere more disserve,
This know I wel, al myghte I now for the
A thousand tymes on a morwe sterve.
I kan namore, but that I wol the serve   390
Right as thi sclave, whider so thow wende,
For evere more, unto my lyves ende.

'But here, with al myn herte, I the biseche
That nevere in me thow deme swich folie
As I shal seyn: me thoughte by thi speche   395
That this which thow me dost for compaignie,
I sholde wene it were a bauderye –
I am nought wood, al if I lewed be!
It is nought so, that woot I wel, parde!

'But he that gooth for gold or for ricchesse   400
On swich message, calle hym what the list;
And this that thow doost, calle it gentilesse,
Compassioun, and felawship, and trist.
Departe it so, for wyde-wher is wist
How that ther is diversite requered   405
Bytwixen thynges like, as I have lered.

'And that thow knowe I thynke nought ne wene
That this servise a shame be or jape,
I have my faire suster Polixene,

385 Tomorrow morning, if you would care to hear   386 **ido**: done
388 **al**: even if   391 **sclave**: slave **whider so**: wherever   392 **lyves
ende**: death   394 **deme**: suppose **folie**: wrongdoing
396 **compaignie**: companionship   397 **bauderye**: act of procuring, pimping
398 **wood**: mad **al if**: even if **lewed**: ignorant   400 **ricchesse**: riches, wealth
401 **message**: errand   403 **Compassioun**: sympathy, fellow feeling
felawship: friendliness **trist**: trust   404 Make a distinction in this way, for it
is known far and wide   405 **diversite**: distinction **requered**: required
406 **like**: similar **lered**: learned   407 **that thow knowe**: so that you may
know   408 **a shame**: something dishonourable

410   Cassandre, Eleyne, or any of the frape –
      Be she nevere so fair or wel yshape,
      Tel me which thow wilt of everychone
      To han for thyn, and lat me thanne allone.

      'But, sith thow hast idon me this servyse
415   My lif to save and for non hope of mede,
      So for the love of God, this grete emprise
      Perfourme it out, for now is moste nede;
      For heigh and lough, withowten any drede,
      I wol alwey thyn hestes alle kepe.
420   Have now good nyght, and lat us bothe slepe.'

      Thus held hym ech of other wel apayed,
      That al the world ne myghte it bet amende;
      And on the morwe, whan they were arayed,
      Ech to his owen nedes gan entende.
425   But Troilus, though as the fir he brende
      For sharp desir of hope and of plesaunce,
      He nought forgat his goode governaunce,

      But in hymself with manhod gan restreyne
      Ech racle dede and ech unbridled cheere,
430   That alle tho that lyven, soth to seyne,
      Ne sholde han wist, by word or by manere,
      What that he mente, as touchyng this matere.
      From every wight as fer as is the cloude
      He was, so wel dissimilen he koude.

---

410 **frape:** company   411 **yshape:** formed   412 **everychone:** everyone,
each   413 **lat me thanne allone:** leave the rest to me   414 **idon:** done
415 **mede:** reward   416 **emprise:** enterprise   417 **Perfourme it out:** carry it
through to the end   418 **heigh and lough:** in all respects
419 **hestes:** commands   421 So each held himself well pleased with the
other   422 **amende:** improve   423 **arayed:** dressed   424 **nedes:** pressing
affairs **entende:** attend   425 **brende:** burned
427 **governaunce:** self-control   428 **with manhod:** manfully   429 Every
hasty (*racle*) action and uncontrolled expression   430 **tho that:** those who
432 **as touchyng:** with regard to   433 **fer:** distant   434 **dissimilen:** dissemble

And al the while which that I yow devyse,   435
This was his lif: with all his fulle myght,
By day, he was in Martes heigh servyse –
This is to seyn, in armes as a knyght;
And for the more part, the longe nyght
He lay and thoughte how that he myghte serve   440
His lady best, hire thonk for to deserve.

Nil I naught swere, although he lay ful softe,
That in his thought he nas somwhat disesed,
Ne that he torned on his pilwes ofte,
And wold of that hym missed han ben sesed.   445
But in swich cas men ben nought alwey plesed,
For aught I woot, namore than was he:
That kan I deme of possibilitee.

But certeyn is, to purpos for to go,
That in this while, as writen is in geeste,   450
He say his lady somtyme, and also
She with hym spak, whan that she dorst or leste;
And by hire bothe avys, as was the beste,
Apoynteden full warly in this nede,
So as they durste, how they wolde procede.   455

But it was spoken in so short a wise,
In swich await alwey, and in swich feere,
Lest any wight devynen or devyse
Wolde of hem two, or to it laye an ere,
That al this world so leef to hem ne were   460

435 yow devyse: tell you about   437 Martes: Mars's   439 more: greater
441 thonk: gratitude   442 Nil I naught: I will not   softe: comfortably
443 disesed: troubled   444 pilwes: pillows   445 And would have liked to
have been in possession (sesed, see n.) of what he lacked   446 men: one
447 For aught I woot: for all I know   448 deme of possibilitee: suppose to be
possible   449 purpos: the point   450 while: time   geeste: story, history
451 say: saw   452 dorst or leste: dared or pleased   453 hire bothe avys: the
judgement of them both   454 Apoynteden: decided   warly: prudently
457 await: watchfulness   458 devynen: suspect   devyse: conjecture
460 leef: dear

As that Cupide wolde hem grace sende
To maken of hire speche aright an ende.

But thilke litel that they spake or wroughte,
His wise goost took ay of al swych heede,
465   It semed hire he wiste what she thoughte
Withouten word, so that it was no nede
To bidde hym ought to doon, or ought forbeede;
For which she thought that love, al come it late,
Of alle joie hadde opned hire the yate.

470   And shortly of this proces for to pace,
So wel his werk and wordes he bisette,
That he so ful stood in his lady grace,
That twenty thousand tymes, er she lette,
She thonked God that evere she with hym mette.
475   So koude he hym governe in swich servyse,
That al the world ne myght it bet devyse.

For whi she fond hym so discret in al,
So secret, and of swich obëisaunce,
That wel she felte he was to hire a wal
480   Of stiel, and sheld from every displesaunce;
That to ben in his goode governaunce,
So wis he was, she was namore afered –
I mene, as fer as oughte ben requered.

462 To carry their conversation directly to a conclusion
463 **wroughte**: did   464 **goost**: spirit   465 **hire**: to her   466 **no
nede**: unnecessary   467 **bidde**: ask   **ought**: anything   **forbeede**: forbid
468 **al**: even if   469 **yate**: gate   470 **pace**: pass over   471 **bisette**: applied
472 **ful**: completely   **stood in . . . grace**: found favour with   473 **lette**: left
off   475 **hym governe**: conduct himself   476 **it bet devyse**: contrive it
better   477 **For whi**: because   **discret**: circumspect   **al**: everything
478 **secret**: discreet   **obëisaunce**: deference   480 **stiel**: steel   **sheld from**: shield
against   **displesaunce**: annoyance, disagreeableness   481 **in his goode
governaunce**: guided by him   482 **wis**: wise   **afered**: afraid

And Pandarus, to quike alwey the fir,
Was evere ylike prest and diligent;   485
To ese his frend was set al his desir.
He shof ay on, he to and fro was sent;
He lettres bar whan Troilus was absent;
That nevere man, as in his frendes nede,
Ne bar hym bet than he, withouten drede.   490

But now, paraunter, som man wayten wolde
That every word, or soonde, or look, or cheere
Of Troilus that I rehercen sholde,
In al this while unto his lady deere –
I trowe it were a long thyng for to here –   495
Or of what wight that stant in swich disjoynte,
His wordes alle, or every look, to poynte.

For sothe, I have naught herd it don er this
In story non, ne no man here, I wene;
And though I wolde, I koude nought, ywys;   500
For ther was som epistel hem bitwene,
That wolde, as seyth myn auctour, wel contene
Neigh half this book, of which hym liste nought write.
How sholde I thanne a lyne of it endite?

But to the grete effect: than sey I thus,   505
That stondyng in concord and in quiete,
Thise ilke two, Criseyde and Troilus,
As I have told, and in this tyme swete –
Save only often myghte they nought mete,

484 **quike**: keep alive   485 **ylike**: equally **prest**: prompt   486 **ese**: help,
benefit   487 **shof**: pressed   488 **bar**: carried   489 **as in**: in **nede**: time of
need   490 **bar hym**: conducted himself   491 **wayten**: expect
492 **soonde**: message   493 **rehercen**: recount   496–7 Or to describe in detail
(*poynte*) all the words or looks of anyone (*what wight*) who is (*stant*) in such
straits (*disjoynte*)   498 **For sothe**: in truth   500 **though I wolde**: even if I
wanted to   502 **contene**: fill   504 **endite**: write   505 **grete effect**: main
point   506 **concord**: harmony **quiete**: peace

510   Ne leiser have hire speches to fulfelle –
        That it bifel right as I shal yow telle:

        That Pandarus, that evere dide his myght
        Right for the fyn that I shal speke of here,
        As for to bryngen to his hows som nyght
515   His faire nece and Troilus yfere,
        Wheras at leiser al this heighe matere,
        Touchyng here love, were at the fulle up-bounde,
        Hadde out of doute a tyme to it founde.

        For he with gret deliberacioun
520   Hadde every thyng that herto myght availle
        Forncast and put in execucioun,
        And neither left for cost ne for travaille.
        Come if hem list, hem sholde no thyng faille;
        And for to ben in ought aspied there,
525   That, wiste he wel, an impossible were.

        Dredeles, it cler was in the wynd
        Of every pie and every lette-game;
        Now al is wel, for al the world is blynd
        In this matere, bothe fremde and tame.
530   This tymbur is al redy up to frame;
        Us lakketh nought but that we witen wolde
        A certeyn houre, in which she comen sholde.

510 **leiser**: opportunity **fulfelle**: carry to a conclusion 512 **dide his
myght**: exerted himself 514 **As**: namely 516 **Wheras**: where **at leiser**: at
leisure 517 **Touchyng**: concerning **were**: might be **at the fulle**: completely
up-bounde: brought to a conclusion 518 **out of doute**: certainly
520 **herto**: to this **availle**: be of use 521 **Forncast**: planned **put in
execucioun**: carried out 522 **left**: omitted, left anything undone
cost: expense **travaille**: effort 523 If they wished to come, they should lack
for nothing 524 **ought**: any way **aspied**: noticed
525 **impossible**: impossibility 526–7 Without doubt it was downwind from
(i.e. safe from notice by) every magpie (i.e. tell-tale) and every spoilsport
(*lette-game*) 529 **fremde and tame**: wild and tame (i.e. every creature)
530 **tymbur**: timber **up to frame**: to set up 531 **Us lakketh nought**: we lack
nothing **but**: except **witen**: know 532 **certeyn**: definite

And Troilus, that al this purveiaunce
Knew at the fulle, and waited on it ay,
Hadde hereupon ek mad gret ordinaunce,   535
And found his cause, and therto his aray,
If that he were missed, nyght or day,
Ther-while he was aboute this servyse,
That he was gon to don his sacrifise,

And moste at swich a temple allone wake,   540
Answered of Apollo for to be;
And first to sen the holy laurer quake,
Er that Apollo spak out of the tree,
To telle hym next whan Grekes sholde flee –
And forthy lette hym no man, God forbede,   545
But prey Apollo helpen in this nede.

Now is ther litel more for to doone,
But Pandare up and, shortly for to seyne,
Right sone upon the chaungynge of the moone,
Whan lightles is the world a nyght or tweyne,   550
And that the wolken shop hym for to reyne,
He streght o morwe unto his nece wente
Ye han wel herd the fyn of his entente.

Whan he was com, he gan anon to pleye
As he was wont, and of hymself to jape;   555
And finaly he swor and gan hire seye,
By this and that, she sholde hym nought escape,
Ne lenger don hym after hire to cape;

533 **purveiaunce**: preparation   534 **at the fulle**: completely **waited
on**: observed   535 **hereupon**: in this matter **ordinaunce**: preparation
536 **found**: devised **cause**: pretext **aray**: arrangements
538 **Ther-while**: whilst, during the time that   540 **moste**: must **wake**: keep
vigil   542 **laurer**: laurel (tree sacred to Apollo)   545 **lette hym no man**: may
no man hinder him   546 **nede**: hour of need   548 **up**: got up
549 **upon**: after   550 **lightles**: without any light   551 **wolken**: sky **shop
hym**: prepared itself **reyne**: rain   552 **streght o morwe**: first thing in the
morning   553 **fyn of his entente**: end he had in mind   555 **of hymself to
jape**: to tell jokes against himself   557 **escape**: evade   558 Nor make him
seek (*cape*) after her any longer

But certeynly she moste, by hire leve,
560   Come soupen in his hous with hym at eve.

At which she lough, and gan hire faste excuse,
And seyde, 'It reyneth; lo, how sholde I gon?'
'Lat be,' quod he, 'ne stant nought thus to muse.
This moot be don! Ye shal be ther anon.'
565   So at the laste herof they fille aton,
Or elles, softe he swor hire in hire ere,
He nolde nevere comen ther she were.

Soone after this, she to hym gan to rowne,
And axed hym if Troilus were there?
570   He swor hire nay, for he was out of towne,
And seyde, 'Nece, I pose that he were:
Yow thurste nevere han the more fere;
For rather than men myghte hym ther aspie,
Me were levere a thousand fold to dye.'

575   Nought list myn auctour fully to declare
What that she thoughte whan he seyde so,
That Troilus was out of towne yfare,
As if he seyde therof soth or no;
But that, withowten await, with hym to go,
580   She graunted hym, sith he hire that bisoughte,
And, as his nece, obeyed as hire oughte.

But natheles, yet gan she hym biseche,
Although with hym to gon it was no fere,
For to ben war of goosissh poeples speche,

---

559 **leve:** permission   560 **soupen:** dine **at eve:** in the evening
561 **lough:** laughed   563 Enough! Don't stand thinking things over like
this   565 **herof:** about this **fille aton:** agreed   566 **softe:** softly
568 **rowne:** whisper   571 **pose:** suppose for the sake of argument   572 **Yow**
thurste: you would need   574 **Me were levere:** I would rather   575 **Nought**
list: does not wish   577 **yfare:** gone   578 **As if:** whether **seyde therof**
soth: told the truth about that   579 **await:** delay   580 **hire that**
bisoughte: asked her (to do) that   583 **it was no fere:** there was nothing to
fear   584 **goosissh:** silly

That dremen thynges whiche as nevere were,   585
And wel avyse hym whom he broughte there;
And seyde hym, 'Em, syn I moste on yow triste,
Loke al be wel, and do now as yow liste.'

He swor hire yis, by stokkes and by stones,
And by the goddes that in hevene dwelle,   590
Or elles were hym levere, soule and bones,
With Pluto kyng as depe ben in helle
As Tantalus – what sholde I more telle?
Whan al was wel, he roos and took his leve,
And she to soper com, whan it was eve,   595

With a certein of hire owen men,
And with hire faire nece Antigone,
And other of hire wommen nyne or ten.
But who was glad now, who, as trowe ye,
But Troilus, that stood and myght it se   600
Thoroughout a litel wyndow in a stewe,
Ther he bishet syn mydnyght was in mewe,

Unwist of every wight but of Pandare?
But to the point: now whan that she was come,
With alle joie and alle frendes fare   605
Hire em anon in armes hath hire nome,
And after to the soper, alle and some,
Whan tyme was, ful softe they hem sette –
God woot, ther was no deynte for to fette!

585 **dremen**: dream up   586 **wel avyse hym**: consider carefully
587 **moste**: must (or, most) **on yow triste**: trust in you   588 **Loke**: make
sure   589 **stokkes . . . stones**: tree stumps . . . stones (i.e. pagan idols, made of
wood and stone)   591 **were hym levere**: he would rather   595 And when it
was evening she came to supper   596 **certein**: certain number
601 **Thoroughout**: through **stewe**: small (heated) room   602 Where he had
been shut up (*bishet*) in hiding (*in mewe*) since midnight   603 **Unwist**
of: unknown to **but of**: except to   605 **frendes fare**: friendliness
606 **nome**: taken   607 **alle and some**: one and all   608 **softe**: comfortably
hem sette: sat down   609 **deynte**: fine food and drink **for to fette**: lacking

610 And after soper gonnen they to rise,
At ese wel, with herte fresshe and glade;
And wel was hym that koude best devyse
To liken hire, or that hire laughen made:
He song; she pleyde; he tolde tale of Wade.
615 But at the laste, as every thyng hath ende,
She took hire leve, and nedes wolde wende.

But O Fortune, executrice of wyerdes,
O influences of thise hevenes hye!
Soth is, that under God ye ben oure hierdes,
620 Though to us bestes ben the causes wrie.
This mene I now: for she gan homward hye,
But execut was al bisyde hire leve
The goddes wil, for which she moste bleve.

The bente moone with hire hornes pale,
625 Saturne, and Jove, in Cancro joyned were,
That swych a reyn from heven gan avale
That every maner womman that was there
Hadde of that smoky reyn a verray feere;
At which Pandare tho lough, and seyde thenne,
630 'Now were it tyme a lady to gon henne!

'But goode nece, if I myghte evere plese
Yow any thyng, than prey ich yow,' quod he,
'To don myn herte as now so gret an ese

611 **At ese:** content **fresshe:** joyous   612 **wel was hym:** he was fortunate
devyse: contrive   613 **liken:** please   614 **Wade:** a legendary hero (n.)
616 **nedes:** necessarily   617 **executrice of wyerdes:** she who carries out (the
will of) the Fates (*wyerdes*)   618 **influences:** (astrological) influences,
powers   619 **Soth:** true **hierdes:** shepherds   620 **bestes:** creatures
wrie: hidden   621 **hye:** hasten   622–3 But the gods' will was carried out
(*execut*) quite without her consent   623 **moste bleve:** must remain
624 **bente moone:** crescent moon   625 (The planets) Saturn and Jupiter were
in conjunction in (the sign of) Cancer   626 **avale:** pour down
627 **maner:** sort of   628 **verray:** genuine   629 **tho lough:** then laughed
630 **tyme:** a fine time **henne:** from here   632 **any thyng:** at all   633 **don . . .**
ese: give pleasure

As for to dwelle here al this nyght with me,
For-whi this is youre owen hous, parde.   635
For by my trouthe, I sey it nought a-game,
To wende as now, it were to me a shame.'

Criseyde, which that koude as muche good
As half a world, took hede of his preiere;
And syn it ron, and al was on a flod,   640
She thoughte, 'As good chep may I dwellen here,
And graunte it gladly with a frendes chere,
And have a thonk, as grucche and thanne abide –
For hom to gon, it may nought wel bitide.'

'I wol,' quod she, 'myn uncle lief and deere;   645
Syn that yow list, it skile is to be so.
I am right glad with yow to dwellen here;
I seyde but a-game I wolde go.'
'Iwys, graunt mercy, nece,' quod he tho,
'Were it a game or no, soth for to telle,   650
Now am I glad, syn that yow list to dwelle.'

Thus al is wel; but tho bigan aright
The newe joie and al the feste agayn.
But Pandarus, if goodly hadde he myght,
He wolde han hyed hire to bedde fayn,   655
And seyde, 'Lord, this is an huge rayn!
This were a weder for to slepen inne –
And that I rede us soone to bygynne.

634 **dwelle**: stay   636 **a-game**: in jest   637 **as now**: now **shame**: source of
shame   638 **koude ... good**: had good sense   640 **ron**: rained **on a
flod**: flooded   641 **good chep**: profitably   642 **frendes chere**: friendly
manner   643 **have a thonk**: be thanked for it **grucche**: grumble
644 **bitide**: happen   645 **wol**: will (stay) **lief**: beloved   646 **skile is**: is
reasonable   648 **but a-game**: only in jest   649 **graunt mercy**: thank you
652 **aright**: directly   653 **feste**: party   654 **goodly hadde he myght**: he could
fittingly have done so   655 He would have liked to hurry her to bed
656 **huge rayn**: immense downpour   657 This is the sort of weather to sleep
through   658 **rede**: advise

'And nece, woot ye wher I wol yow leye,
660 For that we shul nat liggen far asonder,
And for ye neither shullen, dar I seye,
Heren noyse of reynes nor of thonder?
By God, right in my litel closet yonder.
And I wol in that outer hous allone
665 Be wardein of youre wommen everichone.

'And in this myddel chaumbre that ye se
Shal youre wommen slepen, wel and softe;
And there I seyde shal youreselven be;
And if ye liggen wel to-nyght, com ofte,
670 And careth nought what weder is alofte.
The wyn anon, and whan so that yow leste,
So go we slepe: I trowe it be the beste.'

Ther nys no more, but hereafter soone,
The voide dronke, and travers drawe anon,
675 Gan every wight that hadde nought to done
More in the place out of the chaumbre gon.
And evere mo so sterneliche it ron,
And blew therwith so wondirliche loude,
That wel neigh no man heren other koude.

680 Tho Pandarus, hire em, right as hym oughte,
With wommen swiche as were hire most aboute,
Ful glad unto hire beddes syde hire broughte,

659 **woot ye**: do you know **yow leye**: put you 660 **For**: so **liggen**: lie
asonder: apart 661 **for**: in order that **shullen**: shall 663 **closet**: small
private room **yonder**: over there 664 **hous**: room, area
665 **wardein**: guardian 669 **liggen wel**: sleep comfortably 670 **alofte**: in
the air 671 **The wyn anon**: let the wine be brought at once 672 **go we**: let
us 673 **hereafter soone**: soon after this 674 **voide**: nightcap of spiced wine
dronke: (having been) drunk **travers**: curtain, screen (dividing a room)
drawe: (having been) drawn 677 **evere mo**: continually
sterneliche: violently **ron**: rained 678 **wondirliche**: amazingly 681 **hire**
most aboute: closest to her

And took his leve, and gan ful lowe loute,
And seyde, 'Here at this closet dore withoute,
Right overthwart, youre wommen liggen alle,   685
That whom yow list of hem ye may here calle.'

So whan that she was in the closet leyd,
And alle hire wommen forth by ordinaunce
Abedde weren, ther as I have seyd,
There was nomore to skippen nor to traunce,   690
But boden go to bedde, with meschaunce,
If any wight was steryng anywhere,
And lat hem slepen that abedde were.

But Pandarus, that wel koude ech a deel
Th'olde daunce, and every point therinne,   695
Whan that he sey that alle thyng was wel,
He thought he wolde upon his werk bigynne,
And gan the stuwe doore al softe unpynne;
And stille as stoon, withouten lenger lette,
By Troilus adown right he hym sette,   700

And shortly to the point right for to gon,
Of al this werk he tolde hym word and ende,
And seyde, 'Make the redy right anon,
For thow shalt into hevene blisse wende.'
'Now, blisful Venus, thow me grace sende!'   705
Quod Troilus, 'For nevere yet no nede
Hadde ich er now, ne halvendel the drede.'

683 **gan ful lowe loute**: bowed very low   684 **at … withoute**: outside
685 **Right overthwart**: directly opposite   686 **whom yow list of
hem**: whichever of them you want   687 **leyd**: in bed   688 **by ordinaunce**: as
arranged   689 **Abedde**: in bed   690–92 There was to be no more skipping
or tramping about, but if anyone stirred anywhere he was ordered to go to
bed, with a curse   694 **koude**: knew **ech a deel**: in its entirety   695 **Th'olde
daunce**: all the old tricks **point**: detail **therinne**: in that   696 **sey**: saw
698 **stuwe doore**: door of the small room **softe**: quietly **unpynne**: unfasten
699 **lette**: delay   700 **hym sette**: sat down   702 **werk**: business **word and
ende**: beginning and end, all   703 **Make the redy**: get ready
704 **hevene**: heaven's   706–7 For I never had such need for it before now,
nor half the fear

Quod Pandarus, 'Ne drede the nevere a deel,
For it shal be right as thow wolt desire;
710   So thryve I, this nyght shal I make it weel,
Or casten al the gruwel in the fire.'
'Yet, blisful Venus, this nyght thow me enspire,'
Quod Troilus, 'As wys as I the serve,
And evere bet and bet shal, til I sterve.

715   'And if ich hadde, O Venus ful of myrthe,
Aspectes badde of Mars or of Saturne,
Or thow combust or let were in my birthe,
Thy fader prey al thilke harm disturne
Of grace, and that I glad ayein may turne,
720   For love of hym thow lovedest in the shawe –
I meene Adoun, that with the boor was slawe.

'O Jove ek, for the love of faire Europe,
The which in forme of bole awey thow fette,
Now help! O Mars, thow with thi blody cope,
725   For love of Cipris, thow me nought ne lette!
O Phebus, thynk whan Dane hireselven shette
Under the bark, and laurer wax for drede;
Yet for hire love, O help now at this nede!

'Mercurie, for the love of Hierse eke,
730   For which Pallas was with Aglawros wroth,
Now help! And ek Diane, I the biseke

708 Pandarus said, 'Don't be a bit afraid . . .'   710 **So thryve I**: as I may
prosper **weel**: as you wish   711 Or make a complete mess of everything
712 **thow me enspire**: may you inspire me   713 **wys**: surely
714 **bet**: better   715 **myrthe**: joy, gladness   716–18 (In my horoscope) at the
time of my birth, unfavourable dispositions of the planets Mars or Saturn, or
your influence was obscured (i.e. burned up, by proximity to the sun) or
hindered, pray your father (Jupiter) to turn aside all that harmful influence
719 **Of grace**: through (his) grace   720 **shawe**: wood   721 **Adoun**: Adonis
boor: boar **slawe**: slain   722 **Europe**: Europa   723 **bole**: bull
fette: abducted   724 **cope**: cloak   725 For love of Venus, don't hinder me
726 **Dane**: Daphne **shette**: shut   727 **laurer wax**: turned into a laurel tree
for drede: out of fear   729 **Hierse**: Herse   730 **Aglawros**: Aglauros
wroth: angry   731 **Diane**: Diana

That this viage be nought to the looth!
O fatal sustren which, er any cloth
Me shapen was, my destine me sponne,
So helpeth to this werk that is bygonne!'   735

Quod Pandarus, 'Thow wrecched mouses herte,
Artow agast so that she wol the bite?
Why! Don this furred cloke upon thy sherte,
And folwe me, for I wol have the wite.
But bid, and lat me gon biforn a lite.'   740
And with that word he gan undon a trappe,
And Troilus he brought in by the lappe.

The sterne wynd so loude gan to route
That no wight oother noise myghte heere;
And they that layen at the dore withoute,   745
Ful sikerly they slepten alle yfere;
And Pandarus, with a ful sobre cheere,
Goth to the dore anon, withouten lette,
There as they laye, and softely it shette.

And as he com ayeynward pryvely,   750
His nece awook, and axed, 'Who goth there?'
'My dere nece,' quod he, 'it am I.
Ne wondreth nought, ne have of it no fere.'
And ner he com and seyde hire in hire ere,
'No word, for love of God, I yow biseche!   755
Lat no wight risen and heren of oure speche.'

732 **viage**: undertaking **to the looth**: displeasing to you   733–4 O Fates
(*fatal sustren*) who, before any clothes were made for me (*me shapen was*),
spun for me (the threads of) my destiny   735 **werk**: business   737 **Artow
agast**: are you afraid   738 **Don**: put   739 **have the wite**: take the blame
740 **bid**: wait **lite**: little   741 **trappe**: trapdoor   742 **lappe**: hem or fold (of
his clothes)   743 **sterne**: violent **route**: roar   745 **at ... withoute**: outside
746 **sikerly**: soundly   747 **sobre**: grave   748 **lette**: delay
749 **shette**: closed   750 **ayeynward**: back again **pryvely**: stealthily   752 **it
am I**: it is I   753 Don't be surprised or frightened at it   756 **risen**: get up

'What, which wey be ye comen, benedicite?'
Quod she; 'And how, thus unwist of hem alle?'
'Here at this secre trappe-dore,' quod he.
760   Quod tho Criseyde, 'Lat me som wight calle!'
'I! God forbede that it sholde falle,'
Quod Pandarus, 'that ye swich folye wroughte!
They myghte demen thyng they nevere er thoughte.

'It is nought good a slepyng hound to wake,
765   Ne yeve a wight a cause to devyne:
Youre wommen slepen alle, I undertake,
So that, for hem, the hous men myghte myne,
And slepen wollen til the sonne shyne;
And whan my tale brought is to an ende,
770   Unwist, right as I com, so wol I wende.

'Now, nece myn, ye shul wel understonde,'
Quod he, 'so as ye wommen demen alle,
That for to holde in love a man in honde,
And hym hire lief and deere herte calle,
775   And maken hym an howve above a calle –
I meene, as love another in this while –
She doth hireself a shame and hym a gyle.

'Now, wherby that I telle yow al this:
Ye woot youreself, as wel as any wight,
780   How that youre love al fully graunted is
To Troilus, the worthieste knyght,
Oon of this world, and therto trouthe yplight,

---

757 **benedicite**: bless us!   758 **Unwist**: undetected   759 **secre**: secret
760 **tho**: then   761 **falle**: happen   762 **swich folye wroughte**: did such a
foolish thing   763 **demen**: suppose **er**: before   765 **cause**: reason
devyne: conjecture   767 **for hem**: as far as they are concerned
myne: undermine (as in a siege)   768 **wollen**: (they) will   773 **holde ... in
honde**: play along, lead on with false hopes   775 **howve above a calle**: hood
over a cap (i.e. engage in double-dealing, two-timing)   776 **in this while**: at
the same time   777 She dishonours herself and deceives him
778 **wherby**: why   781–2 **the worthieste knyght, Oon**: the most excellent
knight   782 **therto trouthe yplight**: your troth is plighted to him

That, but it were on hym along, ye nolde
Hym nevere falsen while ye lyven sholde.

'Now stant it thus, that sith I fro yow wente,   785
This Troilus, right platly for to seyn,
Is thorugh a goter, by a pryve wente,
Into my chaumbre come in al this reyn,
Unwist of every manere wight, certeyn,
Save of myself, as wisly have I joye,   790
And by that feith I shal Priam of Troie.

'And he is come in swich peyne and distresse
That, but he be al fully wood by this,
He sodeynly mot falle into wodnesse,
But if God helpe; and cause whi this is: 795
He seith hym told is of a frend of his
How that ye sholden love oon hatte Horaste,
For sorwe of which this nyght shal ben his laste.'

Criseyde, which that al this wonder herde,
Gan sodeynly aboute hire herte colde,   800
And with a sik she sorwfully answerde,
'Allas! I wende, whoso tales tolde,
My deere herte wolde me nought holde
So lightly fals! Allas, conceytes wronge,
What harm they don! For now lyve I to longe!   805

783 **That, but:** so that unless **on hym along:** through his fault
784 **falsen:** betray   785 **stant it:** the situation is   786 **platly:** bluntly
787 **thorugh:** via, by means of **goter:** gutter (?; see n.) **pryve wente:** secret
passage   790 **Save:** except **wisly have I:** surely as I hope to have
791 **shal:** owe   793 **but:** unless **wood:** mad **this:** this time
794 **wodnesse:** madness   795 **But if:** unless **cause whi this is:** this is the
reason why   796 **hym told is of:** he has been told by   797 How you are said
to love someone called Orestes   799 **wonder:** astonishing thing
800 **colde:** grow cold   801 **sik:** sigh   802 **wende:** supposed
whoso: whoever   803 **holde:** consider   804 **lightly:** easily **fals:** unfaithful
conceytes wronge: mistaken imaginings

'Horaste! Allas, and falsen Troilus?
I knowe hym nought, God helpe me so!' quod she.
'Allas, what wikked spirit tolde hym thus?
Now certes, em, tomorwe and I hym se,
810   I shal therof as ful excusen me,
As evere dide womman, if hym like.'
And with that word she gan ful soore sike.

'O God,' quod she, 'so worldly selynesse,
Which clerkes callen fals felicitee,
815   Imedled is with many a bitternesse!
Ful angwissous than is, God woot,' quod she,
'Condicioun of veyn prosperitee:
For either joies comen nought yfeere,
Or elles no wight hath hem alwey here.

820   'O brotel wele of mannes joie unstable!
With what wight so thow be, or how thow pleye,
Either he woot that thow, joie, art muable,
Or woot it nought; it mot ben oon of tweye.
Now if he woot it nought, how may he seye
825   That he hath verray joie and selynesse,
That is of ignoraunce ay in derknesse?

'Now if he woot that joie is transitorie,
As every joye of worldly thyng mot flee,
Than every tyme he that hath in memorie,

806 **falsen**: betray   808 **wikked**: malicious   809 **and**: if   810 I shall
exonerate myself of that as completely   812 **gan ful soore sike**: sighed very
deeply   813 **so**: how **selynesse**: happiness   814 **clerkes**: scholars
fals: spurious **felicitee**: happiness   815 **Imedled**: mingled
816 **angwissous**: painful **than**: then   817 **Condicioun**: state **veyn**: idle,
worthless **prosperitee**: good fortune   819 **alwey here**: continually in this
world   820 **brotel**: brittle, fragile **wele**: good fortune
unstable: impermanent   821 Whatever person you are with, or however you
play things   822 **muable**: mutable   823 **oon of tweye**: one of the two
825 **verray**: true   827 **transitorie**: transient   828 **flee**: pass away

The drede of lesyng maketh hym that he   830
May in no perfit selynesse be;
And if to lese his joie he sette a myte,
Than semeth it that joie is worth ful lite.

'Wherfore I wol diffyne in this matere,
That trewely, for aught I kan espie,   835
Ther is no verray weele in this world heere.
But O thow wikked serpent, jalousie,
Thow mysbyleved envyous folie,
Why hastow Troilus mad to me untriste,
That nevere yet agylte hym, that I wiste?'   840

Quod Pandarus, 'Thus fallen is this cas –'
'Why! Uncle myn,' quod she, 'who tolde hym this?
Why doth my deere herte thus, allas?'
'Ye woot, ye, nece myn,' quod he, 'what is.
I hope al shal be wel that is amys,   845
For ye may quenche al this, if that yow leste –
And doth right so, for I holde it the beste.'

'So shal I do to-morwe, ywys,' quod she,
'And God toforn, so that it shal suffise.'
'To-morwe? Allas, that were a fair!' quod he;   850
'Nay, nay, it may nat stonden in this wise,
For, nece myn, thus writen clerkes wise,
That peril is with drecchyng in ydrawe –
Nay, swiche abodes ben nought worth an hawe.

---

830 **drede of lesyng:** fear of loss   832 **lese:** lose **sette a myte:** values at a *mite*
(valueless small coin, n.)   833 **ful lite:** very little   834 **diffyne:** conclude
835 **for aught I kan espie:** for all I can see   836 **verray weele:** true happiness
838 **mysbyleved:** misbelieving **folie:** madness   839 Why have you made
Troilus distrustful of me   840 **agylte:** wronged **wiste:** knew of
841 Pandarus said, 'That is how matters stand'   844 **ye:** to be sure
846 **quenche:** put an end to   847 **holde:** consider   849 **suffise:** be enough
850 **were a fair:** would be a fine thing   851 **stonden:** remain   853 **with
drecchyng in ydrawe:** introduced by delaying   854 **abodes:** delays
hawe: hawthorn berry (i.e. a worthless thing)

855 'Nece, alle thyng hath tyme, I dar avowe;
For whan a chaumbre afire is or an halle,
Wel more nede is, it sodeynly rescowe
Than to dispute and axe amonges alle
How is this candel in the strawe ifalle.
860 A, benedicite! For al among that fare
The harm is don, and fare-wel feldefare!

'And nece myn – ne take it naught agrief –
If that ye suffre hym al nyght in this wo,
God help me so, ye hadde hym nevere lief!
865 That dar I seyn, now ther is but we two.
But wel I woot that ye wol nat do so;
Ye ben to wys to doon so gret folie,
To putte his lif al nyght in jupertie.'

'Hadde I hym nevere lief? By God, I weene
870 Ye hadde nevere thyng so lief!' quod she.
'Now by my thrift,' quod he, 'that shal be
        seene!
For syn ye make this ensaumple of me,
If ich al nyght wolde hym in sorwe se,
For al the tresour in the town of Troie,
875 I bidde God I nevere mote have joie.

'Now loke thanne, if ye that ben his love
Shul putte his lif al night in jupertie
For thyng of nought, now by that God above,

855 avowe: affirm, vow   856 afire is: is on fire   857–8 There is much more
need to save it promptly, than to argue and question all present
859 ifalle: fallen   860 Ah, bless us! For while that is going on . . .
861 fare-wel feldefare: goodbye, thrush (i.e. the bird has flown, all is over)
862 agrief: amiss   863 suffre hym: allow him to remain   864 hadde hym
nevere lief: never loved him   868 in jupertie: in jeopardy, at risk
869–70 I never loved him? By God, I believe (weene) you never loved
anything as much!   871 by my thrift: upon my word
872 ensaumple: example   873 If I would keep him in sorrow all night
874 tresour: treasure   875 bidde: pray mote: may   876 loke: consider
878 thyng of nought: nothing

Naught oonly this delay comth of folie,
But of malice, if that I shal naught lie.   880
What! Platly, and ye suffre hym in destresse,
Ye neyther bounte don ne gentilesse.'

Quod tho Criseyde, 'Wol ye don o thyng
And ye therwith shal stynte al his disese?
Have heere, and bereth hym this blewe ryng,   885
For ther is nothyng myghte hym bettre plese,
Save I myself, ne more hys herte apese;
And sey my deere herte that his sorwe
Is causeles; that shal be sene to-morwe.'

'A ryng?' quod he, 'Ye, haselwodes shaken!   890
Ye, nece myn, that ryng moste han a stoon
That myghte dede men alyve maken;
And swich a ryng trowe I that ye have non.
Discrecioun out of youre hed is gon –
That fele I now,' quod he, 'and that is routhe.   895
O tyme ilost, wel maistow corsen slouthe!

'Woot ye not wel that noble and heigh corage
Ne sorweth nought, ne stynteth ek, for lite?
But if a fool were in a jalous rage,
I nolde setten at his sorwe a myte,   900
But feffe hym with a fewe wordes white
Anothir day, whan that I myghte hym fynde;
But this thyng stant al in another kynde.

881 **and**: if   882 You behave neither kindly nor nobly   884 **therwith**: with
this **stynte**: cause to cease **disese**: distress   885 **Have heere**: take **bereth
hym**: carry to him **blewe**: blue   887 **apese**: assuage, soothe   889 **sey**: tell
890 **Ye, haselwodes shaken**: oh, fiddlesticks! (n.)   891 **stoon**: stone
894 **Discrecioun**: good sense   896 **maistow corsen slouthe**: may you curse
indolence   897 **heigh corage**: lofty spirit   898 Neither grieves, nor stops
grieving either, for a trivial reason   900 **setten at**: give for **myte**: jot (n.)
901 **feffe**: endow, present **white**: fair, specious   903 **stant al in another
kynde**: is of an entirely different nature

'This is so gentil and so tendre of herte
905   That with his deth he wol his sorwes wreke;
For trusteth wel, how sore that hym smerte,
He wol to yow no jalous wordes speke.
And forthi, nece, er that his herte breke,
So speke youreself to hym of this matere,
910   For with o word ye may his herte stere.

'Now have I told what peril he is inne,
And his comynge unwist is to every wight;
Ne, parde, harm may ther be non, ne synne:
I wol myself be with yow al this nyght.
915   Ye knowe ek how it is youre owen knyght,
And that bi right ye moste upon hym triste,
And I al prest to fecche hym whan yow liste.'

This accident so pitous was to here,
And ek so like a sooth at prime face,
920   And Troilus hire knyght to hir so deere,
His prive comyng, and the siker place,
That though that she did hym as thanne a grace,
Considered alle thynges as they stoode,
No wonder is, syn she did al for goode.

925   Criseyde answerde, 'As wisly God at reste
My soule brynge, as me is for hym wo!
And em, iwis, fayn wolde I don the beste,
If that ich hadde grace to do so;
But whether that ye dwelle or for hym go,

904 **This**: this man   905 **wreke**: make up for   906 For believe me, however painful it may be to him   910 **stere**: direct   913 **Ne**: nor   916 **bi right**: by rights **moste**: should   917 **prest**: ready   918 **accident**: occurrence **pitous**: pitiful   919 **sooth**: true thing **at prime face**: at first sight 921 **prive**: secret **siker**: safe   922 **though that**: although **as thanne**: at that time **grace**: favour   925 **wisly**: surely **at**: to   926 **me is . . . wo**: I am sorry 927 **fayn**: gladly **don the beste**: do what is best   929 **dwelle**: stay

I am, til God me bettre mynde sende,   930
At dulcarnoun, right at my wittes ende.'

Quod Pandarus, 'Yee, nece, wol ye here?
Dulcarnoun called is "flemyng of wrecches":
It semeth hard, for wrecches wol nought lere,
For verray slouthe or other wilfull tecches;   935
This seyd by hem that ben nought worth two
    fecches;
But ye ben wis, and that we han on honde
Nis neither hard, ne skilful to withstonde.'

'Than, em,' quod she, 'doth herof as yow list.
But er he com, I wil up first arise,   940
And for the love of God, syn al my trist
Is on yow two, and ye ben bothe wise,
So werketh now in so discret a wise
That I honour may have, and he plesaunce:
For I am here al in youre governaunce.'   945

'That is wel seyd,' quod he, 'my nece deere.
Ther good thrift on that wise gentil herte!
But liggeth stille, and taketh hym right here –
It nedeth nought no ferther for hym sterte.
And ech of yow ese otheres sorwes smerte,   950
For love of God! And Venus, I the herye;
For soone hope I we shul ben alle merye.'

930 **mynde:** mental state   931 **At dulcarnoun:** on the horns of a dilemma
(n.) **at my wittes ende:** at a loss   932 **Yee:** yes, indeed   933 **flemyng of
wrecches:** banishment of wretches (n. to 931)   934 **for:** since **lere:** learn
935 Because of sheer laziness or other self-willed faults   936 **This:** this is
by: about **fecches:** beans   937 **han on honde:** are concerned with
938 **skilful:** reasonable   939 **herof as yow list:** as you please about this
941 **trist:** trust, reliance   943 **werketh:** act   944 **plesaunce:** pleasure
945 **in:** under **governaunce:** guidance   947 **Ther good thrift on:** good luck
to   948 **liggeth:** lie **taketh:** receive   949 **sterte:** move   950 **ese:** ease,
soothe   951 **the herye:** praise you   952 **merye:** cheerful

This Troilus ful soone on knees hym sette
Ful sobrely, right be hyre beddes hed,
955   And in his beste wyse his lady grette.
But Lord, so she wex sodeynliche red!
Ne though men sholde smyten of hire hed,
She kouthe nought a word aright out brynge
So sodeynly, for his sodeyn comynge.

960   But Pandarus, that so wel koude feele
In every thyng, to pleye anon bigan,
And seyde, 'Nece, se how this lord kan knele!
Now for youre trouthe, se this gentil man!'
And with that word he for a quysshen ran,
965   And seyde, 'Kneleth now, while that yow leste;
There God youre hertes brynge soone at reste!'

Kan I naught seyn, for she bad hym nought rise,
If sorwe it putte out of hire remembraunce,
Or elles that she took it in the wise
970   Of dewete, as for his observaunce;
But wel fynde I she dede hym this plesaunce,
That she hym kiste, although she siked sore,
And bad hym sitte adown withouten more.

Quod Pandarus, 'Now wol ye wel bigynne.
975   Now doth hym sitte, goode nece deere,
Upon youre beddes syde al ther withinne,
That ech of yow the bet may other heere.'
And with that word he drow hym to the feere,

953 **on knees hym sette:** knelt   954 **sobrely:** gravely   955 **grette:** greeted
956 **wex:** became   957 Even if she were to have been beheaded
958 **aright:** properly   **out brynge:** utter   960 **feele:** be perceptive
961 **pleye:** be playful   963 **for youre trouthe:** for the sake of your pledged
word   964 **quysshen:** cushion   965 **while that yow leste:** as long as you
please   966 **There God . . . brynge:** may God set   967 **for:** since
bad: asked   968 If sorrow made her forget   969 **wise:** manner
970 **dewete:** due courtesy   **observaunce:** respectful attention   971 **dede . . .**
plesaunce: gave . . . pleasure   972 **siked:** sighed   973 **more:** more ado
974 **wel bigynne:** make a good start   975 **doth:** make   976 **withinne:** inside
the bedcurtains   978 **drow hym:** withdrew   **feere:** fire

And took a light, and fond his contenaunce,
As for to looke upon an old romaunce.   980

Criseyde, that was Troilus lady right,
And cler stood on a ground of sikernesse,
Al thoughte she hire servant and hire knyght
Ne sholde of right non untrouthe in hire gesse,
Yet natheles, considered his distresse,   985
And that love is in cause of swich folie,
Thus to hym spak she of his jalousie:

'Lo, herte myn, as wolde the excellence
Of love, ayeins the which that no man may –
Ne oughte ek – goodly make resistence,   990
And ek bycause I felte wel and say
Youre grete trouthe and servise every day,
And that youre herte al myn was, soth to seyne,
This drof me for to rewe upon youre peyne.

'And youre goodnesse have I founde alwey yit,   995
Of which, my deere herte and al my knyght,
I thonke it yow, as fer as I have wit,
Al kan I nought as muche as it were right;
And I, emforth my connyng and my might,
Have and ay shal, how sore that me smerte,   1000
Ben to yow trewe and hool with al myn herte,

979 **light**: lamp, candle **fond his contenaunce**: assumed an attitude
981 **Troilus lady right**: Troilus's own true lady   982 **cler**: unencumbered
ground of sikernesse: foundation of security, sure ground
983 **Al**: although   984 **of right**: rightfully **untrouthe**: faithlessness
gesse: suppose   985 **considered**: considering   986 **in cause of**: the cause of
988 **wolde**: would have it   990 **goodly**: properly   991 **say**: saw   993 **al myn
was**: was completely mine   994 **drof**: drove **rewe**: have pity   996 **al my**: my
own   997 **as fer as I have wit**: to the extent of my understanding
999 **emforth**: to the limit of **connyng**: ability   1000–1001 Have (been) and
shall . . . be   1000 **how sore that me smerte**: however painful to me it may
be   1001 **trewe and hool**: completely true

'And dredeles, that shal be founde at preve.
But, herte myn, what al this is to seyne
Shal wel be told, so that ye nought yow greve,
1005   Though I to yow right on youreself compleyne,
For therwith mene I fynaly the peyne
That halt youre herte and myn in hevynesse
Fully to slen, and every wrong redresse.

'My goode myn, noot I for-why ne how
1010   That jalousie, allas, that wikked wyvere,
Thus causeles is cropen into yow,
The harm of which I wolde fayn delyvere.
Allas, that he, al hool or of hym slyvere,
Shuld han his refut in so digne a place –
1015   Ther Jove hym sone out of youre herte arace!

'But O, thow Jove, O auctour of nature,
Is this an honour to thi deyte,
That folk ungiltif suffren hire injure,
And who that giltif is, al quyt goth he?
1020   O, were it lefull for to pleyn on the,
That undeserved suffrest jalousie,
Of that I wolde upon the pleyne and crie!

'Ek al my wo is this, that folk now usen
To seyn right thus, "Ye, jalousie is love!"
1025   And wolde a busshel venym al excusen,

1002 **founde at preve**: proved if put to the test   1004 **so that ye nought yow greve**: provided you don't take offence   1006 **therwith**: by that means **fynaly**: for good   1007 **halt** (= *holdeth*): holds **hevynesse**: sadness
1008 **slen**: put an end to   1009 **My goode myn**: my own good one   **noot I**: I do not know **for-why**: why   1010 **wyvere**: snake   1011 **cropen**: crept
1012 **delyvere**: be rid of   1013 **al hool**: completely **of hym slyvere**: a sliver of it   1014 **refut**: refuge **digne**: worthy   1015 **Ther Jove . . . arace**: may Jove uproot   1016 **auctour**: creator   1017 **deyte**: godhead
1018 **ungiltif**: guiltless **injure**: injury   1019 **giltif**: guilty **al quyt**: completely free   1020 **lefull**: legitimate **pleyn on**: make complaint against   1021 Who allow undeserved jealousy   1022 **upon the pleyne and crie**: complain about you   1023 **now usen**: are now accustomed   1024 **Ye**: to be sure
1025 **busshel venym**: bushel of venom **excusen**: make excuses for

For that o greyn of love is on it shove.
But that woot heighe God that sit above,
If it be likkere love, or hate, or grame –
And after that, it oughte bere his name.

'But certeyn is, som manere jalousie   1030
Is excusable more than som, iwys;
As whan cause is, and som swich fantasie
With piete so wel repressed is
That it unnethe doth or seyth amys,
But goodly drynketh up al his distresse –   1035
And that excuse I, for the gentilesse;

'And som so ful of furie is and despit
That it sourmounteth his repressioun.
But herte myn, ye be nat in that plit,
That thonke I God; for which youre passioun   1040
I wol nought calle it but illusioun
Of habundaunce of love and besy cure,
That doth youre herte this disese endure.

'Of which I am right sory but nought wroth;
But, for my devoir and youre hertes reste,   1045
Wherso yow list, by ordal or by oth,

1026 **For that**: because **o greyn**: one speck **shove**: laid 1027 **sit**: sits
1028 **likkere**: more like **grame**: anger, hatred 1029 **after**: according to
his: its (i.e. love's, hate's, anger's) 1030 **manere**: kind of
1031 **excusable**: pardonable **som**: some (others) 1032 **cause is**: there is a
cause **fantasie**: deluded imaginings 1033 **piete**: a sense of duty
1034 **unnethe**: scarcely 1035 **goodly**: gladly, willingly **drynketh
up**: swallows, i.e. endures (drains the cup of misery) 1036 **for the
gentilesse**: because of the nobility (of such behaviour) 1037 **som**: one
furie: rage **despit**: resentment 1038 **sourmounteth**: overcomes **his**: its
repressioun: power to repress it 1039 **herte myn**: my sweetheart
plit: position 1040 **passioun**: emotion 1041 **nought . . . but**: only
illusioun: delusion 1042 **Of**: out of **habundaunce**: abundance **besy
cure**: anxious care 1045 **devoir**: sake **hertes reste**: peace of mind
1046 **Wherso**: wherever **ordal**: trial by ordeal (n.) **oth**: oath

By sort, or in what wise so yow leste,
For love of God, lat preve it for the beste;
And if that I be giltif, do me deye!
1050   Allas, what myght I more don or seye?'

With that a fewe brighte teris newe
Owt of hire eighen fille, and thus she seyde,
'Now God, thow woost, in thought ne dede untrewe
To Troilus was nevere yet Criseyde.'
1055   With that here heed down in the bed she leyde,
And with the sheete it wreigh, and sighte soore,
And held hire pees; nought o word spak she more.

But now help God to quenchen al this sorwe!
So hope I that he shal, for he best may.
1060   For I have seyn of a ful misty morwe
Folowen ful ofte a myrie someris day;
And after wynter foloweth grene May;
Men sen alday, and reden ek in stories,
That after sharpe shoures ben victories.

1065   This Troilus, whan he hire wordes herde,
Have ye no care, hym liste nought to slepe;
For it thoughte hym no strokes of a yerde
To heere or seen Criseyde, his lady, wepe;
But wel he felt aboute his herte crepe,
1070   For everi tere which that Criseyde asterte,
The crampe of deth to streyne hym by the herte.

1047 **sort**: casting of lots, divination **wise**: way   1048 **lat preve it**: let it be
put to the test   1049 **do me deye**: put me to death   1052 **fille**: fell
1053 **untrewe**: unfaithful   1055 **heed**: head   1056 **wreigh**: covered **sighte
soore**: sighed bitterly   1057 **held hire pees**: kept quiet   1058 **quenchen**: put
an end to   1060 **of**: after   1061 **myrie**: pleasant **someris**: summer's
1063 **alday**: all the time   1064 **shoures**: assaults, battles   1066-7 Don't
worry, he didn't feel like sleeping; for it secmed to him like no strokes of a rod
(i.e. worse than being beaten)   1070 **Criseyde asterte**: escaped from
Criseyde   1071 **crampe**: spasm **streyne**: constrict, grip

And in his mynde he gan the tyme acorse
That he com there, and that, that he was born;
For now is wikke torned into worse,
And al that labour he hath don byforn,   1075
He wende it lost; he thoughte he nas but lorn.
'O Pandarus,' thoughte he, 'allas, thi wile
Serveth of nought, so weylaway the while!'

And therwithal he heng adown the heed,
And fil on knees, and sorwfully he sighte.   1080
What myghte he seyn? He felte he nas but deed,
For wroth was she that sholde his sorwes lighte.
But natheles, whan that he speken myghte,
Than seyde he thus, 'God woot that of this game,
Whan al is wist, than am I nought to blame.'   1085

Therwith the sorwe so his herte shette
That from his eyen fil there nought a tere,
And every spirit his vigour in knette,
So they astoned or oppressed were;
The felyng of his sorwe, or of his fere,   1090
Or of aught elles, fled was out of towne –
And down he fel al sodeynly a-swowne.

This was no litel sorwe for to se;
But al was hust, and Pandare up as faste:
'O nece, pes, or we be lost!' quod he,   1095

1072 **acorse**: curse   1073 **that, that**: the fact that   1074 **wikke**: bad
1076 **wende**: supposed **nas but lorn**: was as good as lost   1077 **wile**: guile
1078 **Serveth of nought**: is of no avail **weylaway the while**: alas the time!
1079 **therwithal**: thereupon **heng**: hung   1080 **fil**: fell   1081 **nas but
deed**: was as good as dead   1082 **lighte**: relieve   1085 **wist**: known
1086 **shette**: shut fast   1088 **every spirit**: i.e. the vital spirit (in the heart), the
natural spirit (in the liver), and the animal spirit (in the brain) **his vigour in
knette**: contracted its force   1089 **So**: as if **astoned**: stunned
oppressed: overcome   1090 **felyng of**: power to feel   1091 **out of
towne**: away   1092 **a-swowne**: in a swoon, unconscious
1094 **hust**: hushed **as faste**: very quickly   1095 **pes**: hush

'Beth naught agast!' But certeyn, at the laste,
For this or that, he into bed hym caste,
And seyde, 'O thef, is this a mannes herte?'
And of he rente al to his bare sherte,

1100   And seyde, 'Nece, but ye helpe us now,
Allas, youre owen Troilus is lorn!'
'Iwis, so wolde I, and I wiste how,
Ful fayn,' quod she. 'Allas, that I was born!'
'Yee, nece, wol ye pullen out the thorn
1105   That stiketh in his herte?' quod Pandare.
'Sey "Al for-yeve," and stynt is al this fare!'

'Ye, that to me,' quod she, 'ful levere were
Than al the good the sonne aboute gooth.'
And therwithal she swor hym in his ere,
1110   'Iwys, my deere herte, I am nought wroth,
Have here my trouthe!' – and many an other oth –
'Now speke to me, for it am I, Criseyde!'
But al for nought; yit myght he nought abreyde.

Therwith his pous and paumes of his hondes
1115   They gan to frote, and wete his temples tweyne;
And to deliveren hym fro bittre bondes
She ofte hym kiste; and shortly for to seyne,

1096 **agast:** afraid   1097 **For this or that:** one way or another **caste:** threw
1098 **thef:** wretch   1099 And he stripped off everything down to just his
shirt   1100 **but:** unless   1101 **lorn:** done for   1102 **and I wiste:** if I knew
1103 **Ful fayn:** very gladly   1105 **stiketh:** sticks   1106 **for-yeve:** forgiven
stynt: brought to an end **fare:** business   1107 **Ye:** indeed **ful levere
were:** would be much preferable   1108 **good:** goods, property **sonne:** sun
aboute gooth: revolves around   1109 **therwithal:** with that   1111 **Have here
my trouthe:** here is my pledge   1112 **am:** is   1113 But all in vain; he could
not yet come to   1114 **pous:** pulse **paumes:** palms   1115 **frote:** rub
wete: bathe   1116 **deliveren:** free **bittre bondes:** the grip of misery

Hym to revoken she did al hire peyne;
And at the laste, he gan his breth to drawe,
And of his swough sone after that adawe,   1120

And gan bet mynde and reson to hym take,
But wonder soore he was abayst, iwis;
And with a sik, whan he gan bet awake,
He seyde, 'O mercy, God, what thyng is this?'
'Why do ye with youreselven thus amys?'   1125
Quod tho Criseyde, 'Is this a mannes game?
What, Troilus, wol ye do thus, for shame?'

And therwithal hire arm over hym she leyde,
And al foryaf, and ofte tyme hym keste.
He thonked hire, and to hire spak, and seyde   1130
As fil to purpos for his hertes reste;
And she to that answerde hym as hire leste,
And with hire goodly wordes hym disporte
She gan, and ofte his sorwes to comforte.

Quod Pandarus, 'For aught I kan aspien,   1135
This light, nor I, ne serven here of nought.
Light is nought good for sike folkes yën!
But, for the love of God, syn ye ben brought
In thus good plit, lat now no hevy thought
Ben hangyng in the hertes of yow tweye –'   1140
And bar the candel to the chymeneye.

1118 **revoken**: revive **did al hire peyne**: devoted all her efforts
1120 **swough**: swoon **adawe**: awaken 1121 **bet**: better 1122 **wonder
soore**: amazingly intensely **abayst**: abashed 1123 **sik**: sigh 1125 Why are
you behaving so poorly? 1126 **a mannes game**: manly behaviour, the way
for a man to behave 1127 **for shame**: you should be ashamed 1129 **al
foryaf**: forgave everything **keste**: kissed 1131 **fil to purpos**: was pertinent
hertes reste: peace of mind 1133 **hym disporte**: to cheer him up
1135 Pandarus said, 'As far as I can see' 1136 **ne serven . . . of nought**: serve
no useful purpose 1137 **sike**: sick 1139 **plit**: state **hevy**: gloomy
1141 **bar**: carried **chymeneye**: fireplace

Soone after this, though it no nede were,
Whan she swiche othes as hire leste devyse
Hadde of hym take, hire thoughte tho no fere,
1145   Ne cause ek non to bidde hym thennes rise.
Yet lasse thyng than othes may suffise
In many a cas, for every wyght, I gesse,
That loveth wel, meneth but gentilesse.

But in effect she wolde wite anon
1150   Of what man, and ek wheer, and also why
He jalous was, syn ther was cause non;
And ek the sygne that he took it by,
She badde hym that to telle hire bisily,
Or elles, certeyn, she bar hym on honde
1155   That this was don of malice, hire to fonde.

Withouten more, shortly for to seyne,
He most obeye unto his lady heste;
And for the lasse harm, he moste feyne.
He seyde hire, whan she was at swich a feste,
1160   She myght on hym han loked at the leste –
Noot I nought what, al deere ynough a rysshe,
As he that nedes most a cause fisshe.

And she answerde, 'Swete, al were it so,
What harm was that, syn I non yvel mene?
1165   For, by that God that bought us bothe two,

1142 **no nede were**: was unnecessary   1143 **devyse**: think up   1144 **of hym take**: received from him **fere**: danger   1145 **bidde**: ask **thennes**: thence, from there   1146 **lasse**: a lesser   1148 **meneth but**: intends only   1149 **wolde wite**: wanted to know   1150 **wheer**: where   1152 **sygne**: evidence **took**: understood   1153 **badde**: requested **bisily**: earnestly   1154 **bar hym on honde**: accused him   1155 **fonde**: test   1157 **most**: must **lady heste**: lady's command   1158 **feyne**: pretend   1159 **swich a feste**: such and such a party   1160 **leste**: least   1161 **Noot I**: I do not know **al deere ynough a rysshe**: expensive enough at the cost of a rush (i.e. worthless)   1162 **nedes most**: necessarily must **a cause fisshe**: fish about for a reason (for being jealous)   1163 **al**: even if   1164 **non yvel mene**: intend nothing wrong   1165 **bought**: redeemed

In alle thyng is myn entente cleene.
Swiche argumentes ne ben naught worth a beene.
Wol ye the childissh jalous contrefete?
Now were it worthi that ye were ybete.'

Tho Troilus gan sorwfully to sike –   1170
Lest she be wroth, hym thoughte his herte deyde –
And seyde, 'Allas, upon my sorwes sike
Have mercy, swete herte myn, Criseyde!
And if that in tho wordes that I seyde
Be any wrong, I wol no more trespace.   1175
Doth what yow list: I am al in youre grace.'

And she answerde, 'Of gilt misericorde!
That is to seyn, that I foryeve al this;
And evere more on this nyght yow recorde,
And beth wel war ye do namore amys.'   1180
'Nay, dere herte myn,' quod he, 'iwys!'
'And now,' quod she, 'that I have don yow smerte,
Foryeve it me, myn owene swete herte.'

This Troilus, with blisse of that supprised,
Putte al in Goddes hand, as he that mente   1185
Nothing but wel; and sodeynly avysed,
He hire in armes faste to hym hente.
And Pandarus with a ful good entente
Leyde hym to slepe, and seyde, 'If ye be wise,
Swouneth nought now, lest more folk arise!'   1190

1166 entente: intention cleene: innocent   1167 argumentes: inferences,
assertions beene: bean   1168 jalous: jealous one contrefete: imitate
1169 were it worthi: it would be fitting ybete: beaten, spanked
1170 sike: sigh   1171 It seemed to him his heart was dying in case she were
angry   1172 sike: sickly   1175 trespace: transgress   1176 al in youre
grace: entirely dependent on your favour   1177 Of gilt misericorde: upon
guilt, mercy   1179 yow recorde: remember   1180 beth wel war: take good
care   1182 don yow smerte: caused you to feel pain
1184 supprised: overwhelmed   1186 avysed: resolved
1187 hente: clasped   1188 a ful good entente: the best of intentions
1189 Leyde hym: lay down   1190 Swouneth nought: don't swoon arise: get
up

What myghte or may the sely larke seye,
Whan that the sperhauk hath it in his foot?
I kan namore; but of thise ilke tweye –
To whom this tale sucre be or soot –
1195   Though that I tarie a yer, somtyme I moot,
After myn auctour, tellen hire gladnesse,
As wel as I have told hire hevynesse.

Criseyde, which that felte hire thus itake,
As writen clerkes in hire bokes olde,
1200   Right as an aspes leef she gan to quake,
Whan she hym felte hire in his armes folde.
But Troilus, al hool of cares colde,
Gan thanken tho the bryghte goddes sevene:
Thus sondry peynes bryngen folk in hevene.

1205   This Troilus in armes gan hire streyne,
And seyde, 'O swete, as evere mot I gon,
Now be ye kaught; now is ther but we tweyne!
Now yeldeth yow, for other bote is non!'
To that Criseyde answerde thus anon,
1210   'Ne hadde I er now, my swete herte deere,
Ben yolde, ywis, I were now nought heere!'

O, sooth is seyd, that heled for to be
As of a fevre or other gret siknesse,
Men moste drynke, as men may ofte se,

1191 **sely**: hapless   1192 **sperhauk**: sparrow hawk **foot**: talons   1193 **ilke tweye**: same two   1194 No matter to whom this tale be (like) sugar or soot (n.)   1195 **tarie**: delay   1197 **hevynesse**: sadness   1198 **itake**: seized
1200 **aspes leef**: aspen leaf   1202 **al hool of**: completely recovered from **cares colde**: chill miseries   1203 **goddes sevene**: seven planets
1204 **sondry**: various, different   1205 **streyne**: clasp tightly
1206 **swete**: sweetheart **mot I gon**: I may live   1208 **yeldeth yow**: surrender, submit **other bote is non**: there is no other remedy   1210–11 **Ne hadde I er now. . . Ben yolde**: if I had not surrendered before now   1211 **were now nought heere**: would not be here now   1212 **sooth is seyd**: it is truly said
1213 **fevre**: fever   1214 **moste**: must

Ful bittre drynke; and for to han gladnesse   1215
Men drynken ofte peyne and gret distresse –
I mene it here, as for this aventure,
That thorugh a peyne hath founden al his cure.

And now swetnesse semeth more swete,
That bitternesse assaied was byforn;   1220
For out of wo in blisse now they flete;
Non swich they felten syn that they were born.
Now is this bet than bothe two be lorn.
For love of God, take every womman heede
To werken thus, if it comth to the neede.   1225

Criseyde, al quyt from every drede and tene,
As she that juste cause hadde hym to triste,
Made hym swych feste it joye was to sene,
Whan she his trouthe and clene entente wiste;
And as aboute a tree, with many a twiste,   1230
Bytrent and writh the swote wodebynde,
Gan ech of hem in armes other wynde.

And as the newe abaysed nyghtyngale,
That stynteth first whan she bygynneth to synge,
Whan that she hereth any herde tale,   1235
Or in the hegges any wyght stirynge,
And after siker doth hire vois out rynge,
Right so Criseyde, whan hire drede stente,
Opned hire herte and tolde hym hire entente.

1215 drynke: potion   1216 drynken: swallow, i.e. endure   1218 his: its
1220 That: in that assaied: experienced   1221 flete: float   1223 lorn: lost
1224 take every womman: let every woman take   1225 werken: act comth
to the neede: becomes necessary   1226 quyt: free tene: trouble   1228 Made
hym swych feste: made such a fuss of him   1230 twiste: tendril
1231 Bytrent (= bitrendeth): encircles writh (= wrytheth): twines around
swote: sweet-smelling wodebynde: woodbine, honeysuckle
1232 wynde: clasp   1233 as: like newe: recently abaysed: startled
1234 stynteth first: stops just   1235 herde: shepherd tale: speak
1237 after: afterwards siker: confidently doth: makes   1238 drede
stente: fear ceased

1240   And right as he that seth his deth yshapen,
          And dyen mot, in ought that he may gesse,
          And sodeynly rescous doth hym escapen,
          And from his deth is brought in sykernesse,
          For al this world, in swych present gladnesse
1245   Was Troilus, and hath his lady swete.
          With worse hap God lat us nevere mete!

          Hire armes smale, hire streghte bak and softe,
          Hire sydes longe, flesshly, smothe, and white
          He gan to stroke, and good thrift bad ful ofte
1250   Hire snowissh throte, hire brestes rounde and lite.
          Thus in this hevene he gan hym to delite,
          And therwithal a thousand tyme hire kiste,
          That what to don, for joie unnethe he wiste.

          Than seyde he thus: 'O Love, O Charite!
1255   Thi moder ek, Citheria the swete,
          After thiself next heried be she –
          Venus mene I, the wel-willy planete!
          And next that, Imeneus, I the grete,
          For nevere man was to yow goddes holde
1260   As I, which ye han brought fro cares colde.

          'Benigne Love, thow holy bond of thynges,
          Whoso wol grace and list the nought honouren,
          Lo, his desir wol fle withouten wynges;

1240 **seth**: sees **yshapen**: ordained   1241 And must die, as far as he may
suppose   1242 **rescous**: rescue **doth hym escapen**: enables him to escape
1243 **in sykernesse**: to safety   1244 **For al this world**: exactly, in every
respect   1246 **hap**: luck   1247 **smale**: slender   1248 **flesshly**: shapely
smothe: smooth   1249 **good thrift bad**: called down blessings upon
1250 **snowissh**: snow-white **lite**: small   1252 **therwithal**: thereupon **hire
kiste**: (he) kissed her   1253 **unnethe**: scarcely   1255 **Citheria**: Venus
1256 **heried**: praised   1257 **wel-willy**: benevolent   1258 **next**: next to, after
Imeneus: Hymen (n.) **the grete**: salute you   1259 **holde**: beholden
1261 **Benigne**: gracious **bond**: binding force   1262 Whosoever wishes for
grace and does not care to honour you   1263 **fle**: (try to) fly

For noldestow of bownte hem socouren
That serven best and most alwey labouren,   1265
Yet were al lost, that dar I wel seyn, certes,
But if thi grace passed oure desertes.

'And for thow me, that koude leest disserve
Of hem that noumbred ben unto thi grace,
Hast holpen, ther I likly was to sterve,   1270
And me bistowed in so heigh a place
That thilke boundes may no blisse pace,
I kan namore; but laude and reverence
Be to thy bounte and thyn excellence!'

And therwithal Criseyde anon he kiste,   1275
Of which certein she felte no disese,
And thus seyde he: 'Now wolde God I wiste,
Myn herte swete, how I yow myght plese!
What man,' quod he, 'was evere thus at ese
As I, on which the faireste and the beste   1280
That evere I say deyneth hire herte reste?

'Here may men seen that mercy passeth right:
Th'experience of that is felt in me,
That am unworthi to so swete a wight.
But herte myn, of youre benignite,   1285
So thynketh, though that I unworthi be,

1264 **noldestow**: if you did not wish **of bownte**: out of goodness
socouren: to help   1265 **most alwey labouren**: always toil most   1266 **Yet were al**: everything would still be   1267 **But if**: unless **passed**: surpassed
oure desertes: what we deserve   1268–70 **for thow me . . . Hast holpen**: because you have helped me   1269 **noumbred ben unto thi grace**: are numbered among those enjoying your favour   1270 . . . when I was likely to die   1272 **boundes**: limits **pace**: surpass   1273 **laude**: praise
1274 **bounte**: goodness   1276 **disese**: distress   1277 **wolde God**: would that God would grant that   1279 **at ese**: content   1281 **say**: saw
deyneth: condescends **hire herte reste**: to settle her heart's affections
1282 **passeth**: surpasses **right**: justice   1284 **unworthi to**: undeserving of
1285 **benignite**: kindness

Yet mot I nede amenden in som wyse,
Right thorugh the vertu of youre heigh servyse.

'And for the love of God, my lady deere,
1290   Syn God hath wrought me for I shall yow serve –
As thus I mene: he wol ye be my steere,
To do me lyve, if that yow liste, or sterve –
So techeth me how that I may disserve
Youre thonk, so that I thorugh myn ignoraunce
1295   Ne do no thing that yow be displesaunce.

'For certes, fresshe wommanliche wif,
This dar I seye, that trouth and diligence,
That shal ye fynden in me al my lif;
N'y wol nat, certein, breken youre defence;
1300   And if I do, present or in absence,
For love of God, lat sle me with the dede,
If that it like unto youre wommanhede.'

'Iwys,' quod she, 'myn owen hertes list,
My ground of ese, and al myn herte deere,
1305   Gramercy, for on that is al my trist!
But lat us falle awey fro this matere,
For it suffiseth, this that seyd is heere,
And at o word, withouten repentaunce,
Welcome, my knyght, my pees, my suffisaunce!'

1287 **mot I nede:** I must necessarily **amenden:** improve   1288 Precisely
because of the value of nobly serving you   1290 **wrought:** created
1291 **wol:** wishes that **steere:** guide, helmsman   1292 To cause me to live, if
that is your pleasure, or to die   1294 **thonk:** thanks   1295 **yow be
displesaunce:** cause you displeasure   1296 **fresshe:** lovely **wommanliche
wif:** (most) womanly woman   1297 **trouth:** loyalty, faithfulness
1299 **N'y wol nat:** nor will I **breken youre defence:** disobey your
prohibition   1301 **lat sle me:** let me be killed **with the dede:** at once
1302 **wommanhede:** womanly nature   1303 **hertes list:** heart's delight
1304 **My ground of ese:** the foundation of my happiness
1305 **Gramercy:** thank you **trist:** trust, reliance   1306 **falle awey fro:** leave
1308 **at o word:** in brief **repentaunce:** regret, hesitation
1309 **suffisaunce:** fulfilment

Of hire delit or joies oon the leeste   1310
Were impossible to my wit to seye;
But juggeth ye that han ben at the feste
Of swich gladnesse, if that hem liste pleye!
I kan namore, but thus thise ilke tweye
That nyght, bitwixen drede and sikernesse,   1315
Felten in love the grete worthynesse.

O blisful nyght, of hem so longe isought,
How blithe unto hem bothe two thow weere!
Why nad I swich oon with my soule ybought,
Ye, or the leeste joie that was theere?   1320
Awey, thow foule daunger and thow feere,
And lat hem in this hevene blisse dwelle,
That is so heigh that al ne kan I telle!

But sooth is, though I kan nat tellen al,
As kan myn auctour, of his excellence,   1325
Yet have I seyd, and God toforn, and shal
In every thyng, al holly his sentence;
And if that ich, at Loves reverence,
Have any word in eched for the beste,
Doth therwithal right as youreselven leste.   1330

For myne wordes, heere and every part,
I speke hem alle under correccioun
Of yow that felyng han in loves art,

1310 **oon the leeste**: the very least   1311 **wit**: mind   1312 **juggeth**: judge
feste: celebration   1313 **hem liste pleye**: they wished to enjoy themselves
1314 **ilke tweye**: same two   1315 **sikernesse**: (a sense of) security
1316 Experienced the supreme excellence of love   1317 **isought**: sought for
1318 **blithe**: joyous   1319 **nad I**: had I not   **swich oon**: such a one (night)
ybought: purchased   1320 **Ye**: yes   **leeste**: smallest   1321 **Awey**: go away
foule: vile   **daunger**: reserve   1322 **hevene blisse**: heavenly happiness
1323 **heigh**: exalted   **al ne kan I telle**: I cannot recount the whole of it
1327 **al holly**: completely   **sentence**: purport   1328 **at Loves reverence**: out of
respect for Love   1329 **in eched**: added   1330 Do with that exactly as you
please   1333 **felyng**: understanding

And putte it al in youre discrecioun
1335   To encresse or maken dymynucioun
Of my langage, and that I yow biseche.
But now to purpos of my rather speche.

Thise ilke two, that ben in armes laft,
So loth to hem asonder gon it were,
1340   That ech from other wenden ben biraft,
Or elles – lo, this was hir mooste feere –
That al this thyng but nyce dremes were;
For which ful ofte ech of hem seyde, 'O swete,
Clippe ich yow thus, or elles I it meete?'

1345   And Lord! So he gan goodly on hire se
That nevere his look ne bleynte from hire face,
And seyde, 'O deere herte, may it be
That it be soth, that ye ben in this place?'
'Yee, herte myn, God thank I of his grace,'
1350   Quod tho Criseyde, and therwithal hym kiste,
That where his spirit was, for joie he nyste.

This Troilus ful ofte hire eyen two
Gan for to kisse, and seyde, 'O eyen clere,
It weren ye that wroughte me swich wo,
1355   Ye humble nettes of my lady deere!
Though ther be mercy writen in youre cheere,
God woot, the text ful hard is, soth, to fynde!
How koude ye withouten bond me bynde?'

1334 **discrecioun:** judgement   1335 **encresse:** amplify
dymynucioun: reduction   1337 **to purpos:** to the point **rather:** earlier
1338–40 To this same pair (whom the story left in each other's arms) it was
so hateful to separate that each thought they would be torn away from the
other   1341 **mooste:** greatest   1342 **nyce:** foolish   1343 **swete:** sweetheart
1344 **Clippe ich:** am I embracing **I it meete:** am I dreaming it   1345 **So:** how
goodly: intently **se:** look   1346 **bleynte:** turned away   1351 **That:** so that
nyste (= *ne wiste*): did not know   1353 **clere:** bright   1354 **wroughte** . . .
wo: caused misery   1355 **humble:** modest **nettes:** nets, snares
1356 **writen:** inscribed **cheere:** looks, expression   1357 **soth:** truly
1358 How could you bind me without a cord?

Therwith he gan hire faste in armes take,
And wel a thousand tymes gan he syke –   1360
Naught swiche sorwfull sikes as men make
For wo, or elles when that folk ben sike,
But esy sykes, swiche as ben to like,
That shewed his affeccioun withinne;
Of swiche sikes koude he nought bilynne.   1365

Soone after this they spake of sondry thynges,
As fel to purpos of this aventure,
And pleyinge entrechaungeden hire rynges,
Of whiche I kan nought tellen no scripture;
But wel I woot, a broche, gold and asure,   1370
In which a ruby set was lik an herte,
Criseyde hym yaf, and stak it on his sherte.

Lord, trowe ye a coveytous or a wrecche,
That blameth love and halt of it despit,
That of tho pens that he kan mokre and kecche   1375
Was evere yit yyeven hym swich delit
As is in love, in o poynt, in som plit?
Nay, douteles, for also God me save,
So perfit joie may no nygard have.

They wol seyn 'Yis,' but Lord, so that they lye,   1380
Tho besy wrecches, ful of wo and drede!
Thei callen love a woodnesse or folie,

1360 **wel**: fully **syke**: sigh   1362 **sike**: sick, ill   1363 **esy**: contented **to like**: pleasing   1364 **affeccioun withinne**: inner feeling
1365 **bilynne**: cease   1366 **sondry**: various   1367 **fel to purpos of**: were pertinent to   1368 **pleyinge**: in jest **entrechaungeden**: exchanged
1369 **tellen**: recount **scripture**: inscription, motto (on a ring)
1370 **broche**: brooch **asure**: lapis lazuli   1371 **ruby . . . lik an herte**: heart-shaped ruby   1372 **yaf**: gave **stak**: pinned   1373 **trowe ye**: do you think **coveytous**: covetous person   1374 **blameth**: censures **halt of it despit**: scorns it   1375 **pens**: pennies **mokre**: rake in, hoard **kecche**: catch
1376 **yyeven**: given   1377 **o poynt**: a single detail **som plit**: any situation
1378 **also God me save**: as God may save me   1379 **nygard**: miser
1380 **so**: how   1381 **Tho besy**: those anxious   1382 **woodnesse**: insanity **folie**: madness

But it shall falle hem as I shal yow rede:
They shal forgon the white and ek the rede,
1385   And lyve in wo, ther God yeve hem meschaunce,
And every lovere in his trouthe avaunce!

As wolde God tho wrecches that dispise
Servise of love hadde erys also longe
As hadde Mida, ful of coveytise,
1390   And therto dronken hadde as hoot and stronge
As Crassus dide for his affectis wronge,
To techen hem that they ben in the vice,
And loveres nought, although they holde hem
        nyce.

Thise ilke two of whom that I yow seye,
1395   Whan that hire hertes wel assured were,
Tho gonne they to speken and to pleye,
And ek rehercen how, and whan, and where
Thei knewe hem first, and every wo and feere
That passed was; but al swich hevynesse –
1400   I thank it God – was torned to gladnesse.

And evere mo, when that hem fel to speke
Of any wo of swich a tyme agoon,
With kissyng al that tale sholde breke
And fallen in a newe joye anoon;
1405   And diden al hire myght, syn they were oon,

1383 falle: befall rede: tell   1384 forgon: go without white . . . rede: silver
. . . gold   1385 ther God yeve: may God give meschaunce: misfortune
1386 avaunce: further   1387 As wolde: would to tho: those
1388 erys: ears also: as   1389 Mida: Midas (n.) coveytise: covetousness
1390 therto: also dronken: drunk   1391 affectis wronge: wrongful desires
1392 vice: wrong   1393 they holde hem nyce: they (the covetous) consider
them (lovers) foolish   1397 rehercen: go over   1398 hem: each other
1399 hevynesse: sadness   1401 hem fel: they happened   1402 agoon: past
1403 breke: be interrupted   1405 diden . . . hire myght: exerted themselves
oon: united

For to recoveren blisse and ben at eise,
And passed wo with joie contrepeise.

Resoun wol nought that I speke of slep,
For it acordeth nought to my matere:
God woot, they took of that ful litel kep!   1410
But lest this nyght, that was to hem so deere,
Ne sholde in veyn escape in no manere,
It was byset in joie and bisynesse
Of al that souneth into gentilesse.

But whan the cok, comune astrologer,   1415
Gan on his brest to bete and after crowe,
And Lucyfer, the dayes messager,
Gan for to rise and out hire bemes throwe,
And estward roos – to hym that koude it knowe –
Fortuna major, that anoon Criseyde,   1420
With herte soor, to Troilus thus seyde:

'Myn hertes lif, my trist, al my plesaunce,
That I was born, allas, what me is wo,
That day of us moot make disseveraunce!
For tyme it is to ryse and hennes go,   1425
Or ellis I am lost for evere mo!
O nyght, allas, why nyltow over us hove
As longe as whan Almena lay by Jove?

1406 **at eise:** happy   1407 **passed:** past **contrepeise:** to counterbalance
1408 **Resoun wol nought:** it is not reasonable (to expect)   1409 **acordeth . . .
to:** agrees with   1410 **kep:** notice   1412 **in veyn:** unprofitably **in no
manere:** in any way   1413 **byset:** employed **bisynesse:** eagerness
1414 **souneth into:** tends towards **gentilesse:** nobility
1415 **comune:** communal, public   1416 **bete:** beat **after:** then
1417 **Lucyfer:** the morning star, the planet Venus **dayes messager:** messenger
of day   1418 **out . . . throwe:** cast forth   1419–20 **estward roos . . .
Fortuna major:** in the east the constellation *Fortuna major* was rising (n.)
1419 **knowe:** recognize   1420 **that:** (it was then) that   1421 **soor:** grieving
1422 **my trist:** (the object of) my trust **plesaunce:** delight   1423 **what me is
wo:** how I grieve   1424 That day must separate us   1425 **hennes:** hence
1426 **lost:** ruined   1427 **nyltow:** will you not **hove:** hover
1428 **Almena:** Alcmena (n.) **lay by:** slept with

'O blake nyght, as folk in bokes rede,
1430 That shapen art by God this world to hide
At certeyn tymes wyth thi derke wede,
That under that men myghte in reste abide,
Wel oughten bestes pleyne and folk the chide,
That there as day wyth labour wolde us breste,
1435 That thow thus fleest, and deynest us nought reste.

'Thow doost, allas, to shortly thyn office,
Thow rakle nyght! Ther God, maker of kynde,
The, for thyn haste and thyn unkynde vice,
So faste ay to oure hemysperie bynde
1440 That nevere more under the ground thow wynde!
For now, for thow so hiest out of Troie,
Have I forgon thus hastili my joie!'

This Troilus, that with tho wordes felte,
As thoughte hym tho, for piëtous distresse
1445 The blody teris from his herte melte,
As he that nevere yet swich hevynesse
Assayed hadde, out of so gret gladnesse,
Gan therwithal Criseyde, his lady deere,
In armes streyne, and seyde in this manere:

1450 'O cruel day, accusour of the joie
That nyght and love han stole and faste iwryen,
Acorsed be thi comyng into Troye,

1430 **shapen**: created   1431 **wede**: cloak   1432 **abide**: remain   1433 Well
may beasts complain and people reproach you   1434 **there as**: where
breste: break   1435 **fleest**: flee away **deynest**: grant   1436 You perform
your role too quickly, alas   1437 **rakle**: hasty   1437–9 **Ther God, maker of
kynde . . . The . . . bynde**: may God, creator of Nature . . . tie you
1438 **unkynde**: unnatural   1439 **faste**: firmly **hemysperie**: hemisphere
1440 **wynde**: go, revolve   1441 **for**: because **hiest**: hasten
1442 **forgon**: lost   1444 **tho**: then **piëtous**: piteous
1447 **Assayed**: experienced   1449 **streyne**: clasp   1450 **day**: dawn
accusour: betrayer   1451 **stole**: stolen **faste**: closely **iwryen**: concealed
1452 **Acorsed**: accursed

For every bore hath oon of thi bryghte yën!
Envyous day, what list the so to spien?
What hastow lost? Why sekestow this place? –   1455
Ther God thi light so quenche, for his grace!

'Allas, what have thise loveris the agylt,
Dispitous day? Thyn be the peyne of helle!
For many a lovere hastow slayn, and wilt;
Thy pourynge in wol nowher lat hem dwelle.   1460
What profrestow thi light here for to selle?
Go selle it hem that smale selys grave;
We wol the nought; us nedeth no day have.'

And ek the sonne, Titan, gan he chide,
And seyde, 'O fool, wel may men the dispise,   1465
That hast the dawyng al nyght by thi syde,
And suffrest hire so soone up fro the rise
For to disese loveris in this wyse.
What, holde youre bed ther, thow, and ek thi Morwe!
I bidde God, so yeve yow bothe sorwe!'   1470

Therwith ful soore he syghte, and thus he seyde:
'My lady right, and of my wele or wo
The welle and roote, O goodly myn Criseyde,
And shal I rise, allas, and shal I so?
Now fele I that myn herte moot a-two,   1475
For how sholde I my lif an houre save,
Syn that with yow is al the lyf ich have?

1453 **bore:** chink   1454 **what list the:** why do you wish   1455 **sekestow:** do
you seek out   1456 **Ther God . . . quenche:** may God extinguish
1457 **what:** how **the agylt:** offended you   1458 **Dispitous:** cruel
1460 **pourynge:** peering   1461 **What profrestow:** why do you offer
1462 **smale selys grave:** engrave small seals   1463 **wol the nought:** do not
want you **day:** daylight   1464 **Titan:** i.e. the sun (but see n.)
chide: reproach   1466 **dawyng:** dawn, Aurora   1467 **suffrest:** permit **fro
the:** from beside you   1468 **disese:** distress   1469 **holde:** keep to
Morwe: dawn, Aurora   1470 **bidde:** pray **so yeve:** give
1471 **syghte:** sighed   1472 **lady right:** own true lady **wele:** happiness
1473 **welle:** source **goodly myn:** my excellent one   1475 **a-two:** (break) in
two

'What shal I don? For, certes, I not how,
Ne whan, allas, I shal the tyme see
1480   That in this plit I may ben eft with yow;
And of my lif, God woot how that shal be,
Syn that desir right now so streyneth me
That I am ded anon, but I retourne.
How sholde I longe, allas, fro yow sojourne?

1485   'But natheles, myn owen lady bright,
Yit were it so that I wiste outrely
That I, youre humble servant and youre knyght,
Were in youre herte iset so fermely
As ye in myn – the which thyng, trewely,
1490   Me levere were than thise worldes tweyne –
Yet sholde I bet enduren al my peyne.'

To that Criseyde answerde right anon,
And with a sik she seyde, 'O herte deere,
The game, ywys, so forforth now is gon
1495   That first shal Phebus fallen fro his speere,
And everich egle ben the dowves feere,
And everich roche out of his place sterte,
Er Troilus oute of Criseydes herte.

'Ye ben so depe in-with myn herte grave,
1500   That, though I wolde it torne out of my thought,
As wisly verray God my soule save,
To dyen in the peyne, I koude nought.
And, for the love of God that us hath wrought,

1478 **not**: do not know   1480 **plit**: situation   1482 **streyneth**: grips
1483 **but**: unless   1484 **fro yow sojourne**: remain away from you
1486 **were it**: if it were   **wiste**: knew   **outrely**: absolutely   1488 **iset**: fixed
1490 Were preferable to me than two worlds such as this   1492 **right
anon**: straightaway   1493 **sik**: sigh   1494 **game**: course of events
forforth: far   1495 **speere**: sphere, orbit   1496 **everich**: every   **egle**: eagle
dowves feere: dove's companion   1497 **roche**: rock   **sterte**: jump
1498 **oute**: go out   1499 **depe**: deeply   **in-with**: within   **grave**: engraved
1501 **wisly**: surely   **verray**: true   **save**: may save   1502 **To dyen in the
peyne**: even if I were to die under torture   1503 **wrought**: created

Lat in youre brayn non other fantasie
So crepe that it cause me to dye!   1505

'And that ye me wolde han as faste in mynde
As I have yow, that wolde I yow biseche;
And if I wiste sothly that to fynde,
God myghte nought a poynt my joies eche.
But herte myn, withouten more speche,   1510
Beth to me trewe, or ellis were it routhe,
For I am thyn, by God and by my trouthe!

'Beth glad, forthy, and lyve in sikernesse!
Thus seyde I nevere er this, ne shal to mo;
And if to yow it were a gret gladnesse   1515
To torne ayeyn soone after that ye go,
As fayn wolde I as ye that it were so,
As wisly God myn herte brynge at reste –'
And hym in armes tok, and ofte keste.

Agayns his wil, sith it mot nedes be,   1520
This Troilus up ros, and faste hym cledde,
And in his armes took his lady free
An hondred tyme, and on his wey hym spedde;
And with swich voys as though his herte bledde,
He seyde, 'Fare wel, dere herte swete –   1525
Ther God us graunte sownde and soone to mete!'

To which no word for sorwe she answerde,
So soore gan his partyng hire distreyne;
And Troilus unto his paleys ferde,

1504 **fantasie**: delusion   1506 **faste**: firmly   1508 And if I were sure of
finding that   1509 **a poynt**: one bit   **eche**: increase
1510 **speche**: discussion   1513 **forthy**: therefore   **sikernesse**: confidence
1514 **mo**: others in addition   1516 **torne ayeyn**: return   1518 **wisly**: surely
brynge at: may bring to   1519 **keste**: kissed   1520 **mot nedes be**: had to be
1521 **hym cledde**: got dressed   1522 **free**: noble   1523 **hym
spedde**: hastened   1526 **Ther**: may   **sownde**: in good health
1528 **distreyne**: afflict   1529 **ferde**: went

1530   As wo-bygon as she was, soth to seyne;
        So harde hym wrong of sharp desir the peyne
        For to ben eft there he was in plesaunce,
        That it may nevere out of his remembraunce.

        Retorned to his real paleys soone,
1535   He softe into his bed gan for to slynke,
        To slepe longe, as he was wont to doone;
        But al for nought – he may wel ligge and wynke,
        But slep ne may ther in his herte synke,
        Thynkyng how she for whom desir hym brende
1540   A thousand fold was worth more than he wende.

        And in his thought gan up and down to wynde
        Hire wordes alle, and every countenaunce,
        And fermely impressen in his mynde
        The leeste point that to him was plesaunce;
1545   And verraylich of thilke remembraunce
        Desir al newe hym brende, and lust to brede
        Gan more than erst, and yet took he non hede.

        Criseyde also, right in the same wyse,
        Of Troilus gan in hire herte shette
1550   His worthynesse, his lust, his dedes wise,
        His gentilesse, and how she with hym mette,
        Thonkyng Love he so wel hire bisette,
        Desiryng eft to han hire herte deere
        In swich a plit, she dorste make hym cheere.

1530 **wo-bygon**: miserable   1531 **wrong**: wrung, hurt   1533 That he could
never forget it   1534 **real**: royal   1535 **softe**: quietly **slynke**: creep
1536 **longe**: for a long time   1537 **for nought**: in vain **ligge**: lie **wynke**: close
his eyes   1538 But sleep is unable to penetrate his heart
1540 **wende**: imagined   1541 **up and down to wynde**: to turn over
1542 **countenaunce**: look   1543 **impressen**: imprint   1544 **leeste
point**: smallest detail **to him was plesaunce**: gave him pleasure
1545 **verraylich**: truly   1546 **al newe**: afresh **lust**: desire **brede**: arise, grow
1547 **erst**: before   1549 **shette**: store away   1550 His merit, his vigour and
his wise actions   1552 **bisette**: bestowed   1554 **plit**: situation **dorste make
hym cheere**: might receive him welcomingly

Pandare, o-morwe, which that comen was   1555
Unto his nece and gan hire faire grete,
Seyde, 'Al this nyght so reyned it, allas,
That al my drede is that ye, nece swete,
Han litel laiser had to slepe and mete.
Al nyght,' quod he, 'hath reyn so do me wake,   1560
That som of us, I trowe, hire hedes ake.'

And ner he com, and seyde, 'How stant it now
This mury morwe? Nece, how kan ye fare?'
Criseyde answerde, 'Nevere the bet for yow,
Fox that ye ben! God yeve youre herte kare!   1565
God help me so, ye caused al this fare,
Trowe I,' quod she, 'for al youre wordes white.
O, whoso seeth yow knoweth yow ful lite.'

With that she gan hire face for to wrye
With the shete, and wax for shame al reed;   1570
And Pandarus gan under for to prie,
And seyde, 'Nece, if that I shal be ded,
Have here a swerd and smyteth of myn hed!'
With that his arm al sodeynly he thriste
Under hire nekke, and at the laste hire kyste.   1575

I passe al that which chargeth nought to seye.
What! God foryaf his deth, and she also
Foryaf, and with here uncle gan to pleye,
For other cause was ther noon than so.
But of this thing right to the effect to go: 1580

1555 Pandarus, who in the morning had come   1556 **grete**: greet
1559 **laiser**: opportunity **mete**: dream   1560 **do me wake**: kept me awake
1561 **ake**: ache   1562 **stant it**: are you, are things   1563 **mury**: pleasant
fare: get on   1565 **God yeve**: may God give   1566 **fare**: business
1567 **for**: despite **white**: plausible   1568 **seeth**: (only) sees **lite**: little
1569 **wrye**: cover   1570 **wax**: became   1571 **prie**: peer   1572 **shal be
ded**: must die   1573 **smyteth of**: cut off   1574 **thriste**: thrust
1576 **passe**: pass over **chargeth nought**: is not important
1577 **foryaf**: forgave **his deth**: i.e. Christ's crucifixion   1579 **cause**: reason
1580 **effect**: point

Whan tyme was, hom til here hous she wente,
And Pandarus hath fully his entente.

Now torne we ayeyn to Troilus,
That resteles ful longe abedde lay,
1585   And pryvely sente after Pandarus,
To hym to com in al the haste he may.
He com anon – nought ones seyde he nay –
And Troilus ful sobrely he grette,
And down upon his beddes syde hym sette.

1590   This Troilus, with al th'affeccioun
Of frendes love that herte may devyse,
To Pandarus on knowes fil adown,
And er that he wolde of the place arise
He gan hym thonken in his beste wise
1595   An hondred sythe, and gan the tyme blesse
That he was born, to brynge hym fro destresse.

He seyde, 'O frend of frendes the alderbeste
That evere was, the sothe for to telle,
Thow hast in hevene ybrought my soule at reste
1600   Fro Flegitoun, the fery flood of helle,
That, though I myght a thousand tymes selle
Upon a day my lif in thi servise,
It myghte naught a moote in that suffise.

'The sonne, which that al the world may se,
1605   Saugh nevere yet my lif, that dar I leye,
So inly fair and goodly as is she

1581 til: to   1582 hath fully his entente: accomplished what he intended
1584 resteles: without finding rest   1585 pryvely: secretly   after: for
1587 ones: once   seyde he nay: did he refuse   1588 sobrely: gravely
grette: greeted   1589 hym sette: sat   1592 knowes: knees   fil adown: fell
down   1595 sythe: times   1597 alderbeste: best of all
1599 ybrought: brought   1600 Flegitoun: Phlegethon (n.)   fery: fiery
flood: river   1602 thi servise: serving you   1603 moote: particle, speck of
dust   suffise: be enough (to repay you)   1605 my lif: during my lifetime
leye: wager   1606 inly: superlatively

Whos I am al, and shal, tyl that I deye.
And that I thus am hires, dar I seye,
That thanked be the heighe worthynesse
Of Love, and ek thi kynde bysynesse.   1610

'Thus hastow me no litel thing yyive,
For which to the obliged be for ay
My lif. And whi? For thorugh thyn help I lyve,
Or elles ded hadde I ben many a day.'
And with that word down in his bed he lay,   1615
And Pandarus ful sobrely hym herde
Til al was seyd, and than he thus answerde:

'My deere frend, if I have don for the
In any cas, God wot, it is me lief,
And am as glad as man may of it be,   1620
God help me so; but tak now nat a-grief
That I shal seyn: be war of this meschief,
That, there as thow now brought art in thy blisse,
That thow thiself ne cause it nat to misse.

'For of fortunes sharpe adversitee   1625
The worste kynde of infortune is this:
A man to han ben in prosperitee,
And it remembren whan it passed is.
Th'art wis ynough; forthi do nat amys:
Be naught to rakel, theigh thow sitte warme,   1630
For if thow be, certeyn it wol the harme.

1607 **al**: entirely   1609 **That thanked be**: for that, thanks be to
1610 **bysynesse**: diligence   1611 **hastow**: you have **yyive**: given
1614 **elles**: otherwise   1619 **is me lief**: pleases me   1621 **tak . . . nat
a-grief**: do not be upset at   1622 **meschief**: misfortune   1624 **misse**: come to
grief   1626 **infortune**: misfortune   1627 **prosperitee**: good fortune
1629 **Th'art** (= *thow art*): you are   **do nat amys**: do not behave amiss
1630 **rakel**: rash, hasty   **theigh**: though   **sitte warme**: are sitting pretty
1631 **the harme**: do you harm

'Thow art at ese, and hold the wel therinne;
For also seur as reed is every fir,
As gret a craft is kepe wel as wynne.
1635 Bridle alwey wel thi speche and thi desir,
For worldly joie halt nought but by a wir.
That preveth wel, it brest al day so ofte;
Forthi nede is to werken with it softe.'

Quod Troilus, 'I hope, and God toforn,
1640 My deere frend, that I shal so me beere
That in my gylt ther shal nothyng be lorn,
N'y nyl nought rakle as for to greven heere.
It nedeth naught this matere ofte stere;
For wystestow myn herte wel, Pandare,
1645 God woot, of this thow woldest litel care.'

Tho gan he telle hym of his glade nyght,
And wherof first his herte dred, and how,
And seyde, 'Frend, as I am trewe knyght,
And by that feyth I shal to God and yow,
1650 I hadde it nevere half so hote as now;
And ay the more that desir me biteth
To love hire best, the more it me deliteth.

'I not myself naught wisly what it is,
But now I feele a newe qualitee –
1655 Yee, al another than I dide er this.'
Pandare answerd, and seyde thus, that 'he
That ones may in hevene blisse be,

1632 **at ese:** in contentment **hold the wel therinne:** keep yourself that way
1633 **also:** as **seur:** surely **reed:** red 1634 Keeping is as great a skill as
winning 1635 **Bridle:** control 1636 **halt** (= *holdeth*): holds on
wir: thread 1637 **preveth:** proves true **brest:** breaks **al day:** all the time
1638 **nede is:** it is necessary **werken with it softe:** treat it gently 1640 **me
beere:** conduct myself 1641 **in my gylt:** through my fault **lorn:** lost
1642 **N'y nyl nought rakle:** nor will I act rashly **as for:** so as **greven
heere:** cause her pain 1643 **stere:** bring up 1644 **wystestow:** if you knew
1645 **of . . . care:** worry about 1647 **wherof:** of what **dred:** was afraid
1649 **shal:** owe 1650 I never felt half so intensely as now 1653 **not:** do not
know **wisly:** certainly 1655 **Yee:** yes, indeed **al another:** quite different

He feleth other weyes, dar I leye,
Than thilke tyme he first herde of it seye.'

This is o word for al: this Troilus   1660
Was nevere ful to speke of this matere,
And for to preisen unto Pandarus
The bounte of his righte lady deere,
And Pandarus to thanke and maken cheere –
This tale ay was span-newe to bygynne,   1665
Til that the nyght departed hem atwynne.

Soon after this, for that Fortune it wolde,
Icomen was the blisful tyme swete
That Troilus was warned that he sholde,
There he was erst, Criseyde his lady mete,   1670
For which he felte his herte in joie flete
And feithfully gan alle the goddes herie –
And lat se now if that he kan be merie!

And holden was the forme and al the wise
Of hire commyng, and ek of his also,   1675
As it was erst, which nedeth nought devyse.
But pleynly to th'effect right for to go:
In joie and suerte Pandarus hem two
Abedde brought, whan that hem bothe leste,
And thus they ben in quyete and in reste.   1680

1658 **other weyes:** otherwise **leye:** wager   1660 **for al:** (to stand) for all
1661 **ful to speke:** sated with talking   1662 **preisen:** praise
1663 **bounte:** goodness **righte:** own true   1664 **maken cheere:** make much
of   1665 **span-newe:** brand new   1666 **departed hem atwynne:** separated
them   1667 **for that:** because **it wolde:** wished it   1668 **Icomen was:** came
1670 **There:** where **erst:** before **mete:** meet   1671 **flete:** float
1672 **feithfully:** devotedly **herie:** praise   1673 **lat se:** let us see
1674 **holden:** preserved **wise:** manner   1677 **pleynly:** simply **th'effect:** the
point   1678 **suerte:** safety   1679 **Abedde:** to bed **hem bothe leste:** they both
wished

Nought nedeth it to yow, syn they ben met,
To axe at me if that they blithe were;
For if it erst was wel, tho was it bet
A thousand fold; this nedeth nought enquere.

1685 Ago was every sorwe and every feere;
And bothe, ywys, they hadde, and so they
        wende,
As muche joie as herte may comprende.

This is no litel thyng of for to seye;
This passeth every wit for to devyse;
1690 For ech of hem gan otheres lust obeye.
Felicite, which that thise clerkes wise
Comenden so, ne may nought here suffise:
This joie may nought writen be with inke;
This passeth al that herte may bythynke.

1695 But cruel day – so wailaway the stounde! –
Gan for t'aproche, as they by sygnes knewe,
For which hem thoughte feelen dethis wownde;
So wo was hem that chaungen gan hire hewe,
And day they gonnen to despise al newe,
1700 Callyng it traitour, envyous, and worse,
And bitterly the dayes light thei corse.

Quod Troilus, 'Allas, now am I war
That Piros and tho swifte steedes thre,
Which that drawen forth the sonnes char,

1681 It is not necessary for you, since they have met   1682 axe at: consult,
ask of blithe: happy   1683 erst: before tho: then bet: better   1684 nedeth
nought: is not necessary enquere: to ask   1685 Ago: gone
1686 wende: thought   1687 comprende: contain   1689 passeth: surpasses
every wit: all intelligence devyse: describe   1690 otheres: the other's
lust: wish, desire   1691 Felicite: happiness   1692 Comenden: praise
suffise: suffice (to describe it)   1694 bythynke: think of
1695 wailaway: alas stounde: time   1697 dethis: death's   1698 So wo was
hem: they were so unhappy hewe: colour   1699 despise: speak ill of al
newe: afresh   1701 corse: curse   1702 am I war: I realize
1703 Piros: Pyroïs (n.)   1704 drawen forth: pull along sonnes char: chariot
of the sun

Han gon som bi-path in dispit of me;   1705
That maketh it so soone day to be;
And for the sonne hym hasteth thus to rise,
Ne shal I nevere don hire sacrifise.'

But nedes day departe hem moste soone,
And whan hire speche don was and hire cheere,   1710
They twynne anon, as they were wont to doone,
And setten tyme of metyng eft yfeere;
And many a nyght they wroughte in this manere,
And thus Fortune a tyme ledde in joie
Criseyde and ek this kynges sone of Troie.   1715

In suffisaunce, in blisse, and in singynges,
This Troilus gan al his lif to lede.
He spendeth, jousteth, maketh festeynges;
He yeveth frely ofte, and chaungeth wede,
And held aboute hym alwey, out of drede,   1720
A world of folk, as com hym wel of kynde,
The fresshest and the beste he koude fynde;

That swich a vois was of hym and a stevene,
Thorughout the world, of honour and largesse,
That it up rong unto the yate of hevene;   1725
And, as in love, he was in swich gladnesse
That in his herte he demed, as I gesse,

1705 **bi-path:** shortcut **in dispit of:** out of hostility towards   1708 **hire sacrifise:** sacrifice to them (the sun and its chariot horses)   1709 But necessarily day must soon separate them   1710 **speche:** talking **cheere:** endearments   1711 **twynne:** separate   1712 **setten:** fixed **metyng eft yfeere:** meeting together another time   1713 **wroughte:** acted   1714 **ledde:** led   1716 **suffisaunce:** fulfilment **singynges:** songs   1718 **spendeth:** spends money **maketh festeynges:** holds festivities, gives parties   1719 **yeveth:** gives **frely:** generously **wede:** clothes   1720 **held aboute:** kept around   1721 **world:** whole world **as com hym wel of kynde:** as well became him by nature   1722 **fresshest:** liveliest   1723 **vois:** (favourable) opinion **stevene:** talk, report   1724 **largesse:** generosity   1725 **rong:** resounded

That ther nys lovere in this world at ese
So wel as he; and thus gan love hym plese.

1730   The goodlihede or beaute which that kynde
In any other lady hadde yset
Kan nought the montance of a knotte unbynde
Aboute his herte of al Criseydes net;
He was so narwe ymasked and yknet,
1735   That it undon on any manere syde,
That nyl naught ben, for aught that may bitide.

And by the hond ful ofte he wolde take
This Pandarus, and into gardyn lede,
And swich a feste and swich a proces make
1740   Hym of Criseyde, and of hire womanhede,
And of hire beaute, that withouten drede
It was an hevene his wordes for to here;
And thanne he wolde synge in this manere:

Canticus Troili

'Love, that of erthe and se hath governaunce;
1745   Love, that his hestes hath in hevene hye;
Love, that with an holsom alliaunce
Halt peples joyned, as hym lest hem gye;
Love, that knetteth lawe of compaignie,
And couples doth in vertu for to dwelle:
1750   Bynd this acord, that I have told and telle.

1728–9 **at ese So wel**: in such contentment   1730 **goodlihede**: excellence
kynde: nature   1731 **yset**: put   732 **the montance of a knotte unbynde**: untie
the extent of (so much as) a (single) knot   734 **narwe**: closely
ymasked: enmeshed **yknet**: tied   1735–6 That to undo it on any side is not
to be, whatever may happen   1739–40 And to him so celebrated and talked
so much of Criseyde and her womanliness   1741 **drede**: doubt   1742 **an
hevene**: heavenly   1744 **of . . . governaunce**: controlling influence over
1745 **hestes**: commands   1746 **holsom**: beneficial **alliaunce**: association
1747 **Halt** (= *holdeth*): holds **hym lest hem gye**: it pleases him to guide them
1748 **knetteth**: weaves **compaignie**: companionship   1749 **doth**: causes
1750 **Bynd**: bind! (imperative)

'That, that the world with feith which that is stable
Diverseth so his stowndes concordynge;
That elementz that ben so discordable
Holden a bond perpetuely durynge;
That Phebus mote his rosy day forth brynge,   1755
And that the mone hath lordshipe over the nyghtes:
Al this doth Love, ay heried be his myghtes! –

'That, that the se, that gredy is to flowen,
Constreyneth to a certeyn ende so
His flodes that so fiersly they ne growen   1760
To drenchen erthe and al for evere mo;
And if that Love aught lete his bridel go,
Al that now loveth asondre sholde lepe,
And lost were al that Love halt now to-hepe.

'So wolde God, that auctour is of kynde,   1765
That with his bond Love of his vertu liste
To cerclen hertes alle and faste bynde,
That from his bond no wight the wey out wiste;
And hertes colde, hem wolde I that he twiste
To make hem love, and that hem liste ay rewe   1770
On hertes sore, and kepe hem that ben trewe!'

1751 **That, that**: the fact that (n.) **feith**: surety, regularity
stable: unchanging   1752 **Diverseth**: varies **stowndes**: times, seasons
concordynge: harmonious   1753 **elementz**: the four primary substances (n.)
discordable: inclined to discord   1754 **Holden**: maintain **perpetuely**
durynge: enduring forever   1755 **mote**: must   1756 **mone**: moon
lordshipe: dominion   1757 **heried**: praised **myghtes**: powers   1758 **That,**
that: and also that (referring back to 1757) **gredy**: eager **flowen**: overflow
1759 So confines within a fixed limit   1760 **flodes**: waters **fiersly**: violently
growen: increase   1761 **drenchen**: drown   1762 **aught**: at all **bridel**
go: bridle slip   1763 **asondre . . . lepe**: fly apart   1764 **to-hepe**: together
1765 **wolde God**: would that God would grant **auctour**: creator
kynde: nature   1766 **bond**: chain **of his vertu**: through its powers
1767–8 To encircle and bind tightly all hearts, so that no one might know the
way out from his (Love's) control   1769 **twiste**: would wring   1770 **hem**
liste: it please them   1771 **sore**: sorrowing **kepe**: sustain

In alle nedes for the townes werre
He was, and ay, the first in armes dyght;
And certeynly, but if that bokes erre,
1775   Save Ector, most ydred of any wight;
And this encrees of hardynesse and myght
Com hym of love, his ladies thank to wynne,
That altered his spirit so withinne.

In tyme of trewe, on haukyng wolde he ride,
1780   Or elles honte boor, beer, or lyoun;
The smale bestes leet he gon biside.
And whan that he com ridyng into town,
Ful ofte his lady from hire wyndow down,
As fressh as faukoun comen out of muwe,
1785   Ful redy was hym goodly to saluwe.

And moost of love and vertu was his speche,
And in despit hadde alle wrecchednesse;
And douteles, no nede was hym biseche
To honouren hem that hadde worthynesse,
1790   And esen hem that weren in destresse;
And glad was he if any wyght wel ferde,
That lovere was, whan he it wiste or herde.

For soth to seyne, he lost held every wyght,
But if he were in Loves heigh servise –
1795   I mene folk that oughte it ben of right.
And over al this, so wel koude he devyse
Of sentement and in so unkouth wise

1772 **nedes**: times of need, crises **werre**: war   1773 **dyght**: armed   1774 **but if**: unless **erre**: are mistaken   1775 **Save**: except **ydred**: feared
1776 **encrees**: increase **hardynesse**: boldness   1777 **Com hym of**: came to him out of **ladies thank**: lady's gratitude   1779 **trewe**: truce **on haukyng**: to hunt with a hawk   1780 **honte**: hunt **boor**: boar **beer**: bear   1781 **bestes**: animals **leet he gon biside**: he allowed to escape   1784 **faukoun**: falcon **muwe**: pen
1785 **goodly**: graciously **saluwe**: salute, greet   1787 **in despit hadde**: scorned **wrecchednesse**: meanness (of spirit or conduct)   1790 **esen**: relieve
1791 **ferde**: fared, got on   1793 **lost held**: considered lost   1794 **But if**: unless
1795 **it**: i.e. in Love's service **of right**: rightfully   1796 **over al this**: furthermore   1797 **Of sentement**: from personal feeling **unkouth**: striking

Al his array, that every lovere thoughte
That al was wel, what so he seyde or wroughte.

And though that he be come of blood roial,   1800
Hym liste of pride at no wight for to chace;
Benigne he was to ech in general,
For which he gat hym thank in every place.
Thus wolde Love – yheried be his grace! –
That Pride and Ire, Envye and Avarice   1805
He gan to fle, and everich other vice.

Thow lady bryght, the doughter to Dyone,
Thy blynde and wynged sone ek, daun Cupide,
Yee sustren nyne ek, that by Elicone
In hil Pernaso listen for t'abide,   1810
That ye thus fer han deyned me to gyde –
I kan namore, but syn that ye wol wende,
Ye heried ben for ay withouten ende!

Thorugh yow have I seyd fully in my song
Th'effect and joie of Troilus servise,   1815
Al be that ther was som disese among,
As to myn auctour listeth to devise.
My thridde bok now ende ich in this wyse,
And Troilus in lust and in quiete
Is with Criseyde, his owen herte swete.   1820

Explicit liber tercius.

1798 array: conduct   1799 **what so**: whatever **wroughte**: did   1801 **of**: out
of **chace**: harass   1802 **Benigne**: gracious **ech in general**: everyone
1803 **gat hym**: won for himself **thank**: gratitude   1804 **yheried**: praised
1805 **Ire**: wrath   1806 **fle**: shun   1807 **Dyone**: Dione (n.)
1808 **daun**: Lord   1809 **Yee sustren nyne**: you nine sisters (the Muses; n.)
Elicone: Helicon (n.)   1810 **hil Pernaso**: Mount Parnassus **listen**: are pleased
t'abide: to dwell   1811 **deyned**: deigned   1812 **kan**: can say
wende: depart   1813 **Ye heried ben**: may you be praised
1815 **Th'effect**: the essence **Troilus servise**: Troilus's service in love
1816 Although there was some distress intermingled   1819 **lust**: delight
Explicit, etc.: Here ends the third book

BOOK 4

Incipit prohemium quarti libri.

But al to litel, weylaway the whyle,
Lasteth swich joie, ythonked be Fortune,
That semeth trewest whan she wol bygyle
And kan to fooles so hire song entune
That she hem hent and blent, traitour comune!   5
And whan a wight is from hire whiel ythrowe,
Than laugheth she, and maketh hym the mowe.

From Troilus she gan hire brighte face
Awey to writhe, and tok of hym non heede,
But caste hym clene out of his lady grace,   10
And on hire whiel she sette up Diomede;
For which myn herte right now gynneth blede,
And now my penne, allas, with which I write,
Quaketh for drede of that I moste endite.

For how Criseyde Troilus forsook –   15
Or at the leeste, how that she was unkynde –
Moot hennesforth ben matere of my book,

As writen folk thorugh which it is in mynde.
Allas, that they sholde evere cause fynde
20   To speke hire harm! And if they on hire lye,
Iwis, hemself sholde han the vilanye.

O ye Herynes, Nyghtes doughtren thre,
That endeles compleignen evere in pyne,
Megera, Alete, and ek Thesiphone,
25   Thow cruel Mars ek, fader to Quyryne,
This ilke ferthe book me helpeth fyne,
So that the losse of lyf and love yfeere
Of Troilus be fully shewed heere.

Explicit prohemium quarti libri.

Incipit liber quartus.

Liggyng in oost, as I have seyd er this,
30   The Grekys stronge aboute Troie town,
Byfel that, whan that Phebus shynyng is
Upon the brest of Hercules lyoun,
That Ector, with ful many a bold baroun,
Caste on a day with Grekis for to fighte,
35   As he was wont, to greve hem what he myghte.

Not I how longe or short it was bitwene
This purpos and that day they fighten mente,
But on a day, wel armed, brighte, and shene,
Ector and many a worthi wight out wente,
40   With spere in honde and bigge bowes bente.

---

18 **thorough which:** by whom **in mynde:** recorded, remembered
21 **han:** bear **vilanye:** reproach   22 **Herynes:** Erinyes, Furies (n.)
doughtren: daughters   23 **endeles:** perpetually **pyne:** pain
25 **Quyryne:** Romulus (n.)   26 **ferthe:** fourth **fyne:** finish *Explicit, etc.*: Here
ends the proem of the fourth book *Incipit, etc.*: Here begins the fourth
book   29 **Liggyng in oost:** encamped   31 **Byfel:** it happened **Phebus:** the
sun   32 In the first part of the zodiacal sign of Leo (n.)   33 **bold:** brave
baroun: nobleman   34 **Caste:** decided   35 **wont:** accustomed **greve:** harm
what: as much as   36 **Not I:** I do not know   37 **purpos:** plan
38 **shene:** shining   40 **bigge:** strong

And in the berd, withouten lenger lette,
Hire fomen in the feld hem faste mette.

The longe day, with speres sharpe igrounde,
With arwes, dartes, swerdes, maces felle,
They fighte and bringen hors and man to   45
    grounde,
And with hire axes out the braynes quelle;
But in the laste shour, soth for to telle,
The folk of Troie hemselven so mysledden
That with the worse at nyght homward they
    fledden.

At which day was taken Antenore,   50
Maugre Polydamas or Monesteo,
Santippe, Sarpedoun, Polynestore,
Polite, or ek the Trojan daun Rupheo,
And other lasse folk as Phebuseo;
So that, for harm, that day the folk of Troie   55
Dredden to lese a gret part of hire joie.

Of Priamus was yeve, at Grek requeste,
A tyme of trewe, and tho they gonnen trete
Hire prisoners to chaungen, meste and leste,
And for the surplus yeven sommes grete.   60
This thing anon was couth in every strete,
Bothe in th'assege, in town, and everywhere,
And with the firste it com to Calkas ere.

41 **in the berd:** face to face **lette:** delay   42 **fomen:** enemies
43 **igrounde:** sharpened   44 **arwes:** arrows **dartes:** javelins **maces:** spiked
clubs **felle:** deadly   46 **quelle:** dash   47 **shour:** assault   48 **hemselven so
mysledden:** conducted themselves so badly   50 **At which:** on that same
taken: captured   51 **Maugre:** in spite of   53 **daun:** lord
54 **lasse:** lower-ranking   56 **Dredden to lese:** feared to lose   57 **Of:** by
yeve: granted   58 **trewe:** truce **trete:** negotiate   59 **chaungen:** exchange
meste and leste: great and small, everyone   60 And for the remainder
(*surplus*) give large sums (in ransom)   61 **couth:** known   62 **th'assege:** the
besieging army   63 **with the firste:** soon **Calkas ere:** Calchas's ear

Whan Calkas knew this tretis sholde holde,
65   In consistorie among the Grekes soone
He gan in thringe forth with lordes olde,
And sette hym there as he was wont to doone;
And with a chaunged face hem bad a boone,
For love of God, to don that reverence,
70   To stynte noyse and yeve hym audience.

Than seyde he thus: 'Lo, lordes myn, ich was
Troian, as it is knowen out of drede;
And, if that yow remembre, I am Calkas,
That alderfirst yaf comfort to youre nede,
75   And tolde wel how that ye shulden spede –
For dredeles, thorugh yow shal in a stownde
Ben Troie ybrend and beten down to grownde.

'And in what forme, or in what manere wise,
This town to shende, and al youre lust t'acheve,
80   Ye han er this wel herd me yow devyse;
This knowe ye, my lordes, as I leve.
And for the Grekis weren me so leeve,
I com myself, in my propre persone,
To teche in this how yow was best to doone.

85   'Havyng unto my tresor ne my rente
Right no resport, to respect of youre ese,
Thus al my good I lefte and to yow wente,
Wenyng in this my lordes yow to plese.
But al that los ne doth me no disese –

64 **tretis**: negotiation **holde**: be held   65 **consistorie**: council
66 **thringe**: press   68 **bad a boone**: requested   69 **don . . . reverence**: show
respect   70 **stynte**: cease **yeve . . . audience**: listen to   74 **alderfirst**: first of
all   75 **spede**: succeed   76 **stownde**: while   77 **ybrend**: burnt **beten**: razed
79 **shende**: destroy **lust**: wishes   81 **leve**: believe   82 **for**: because
leeve: dear   83 **com**: came **in my propre persone**: in person   84 To instruct
you how to act for the best in this matter   85 **tresor**: wealth, worldly goods
rente: income   86 **resport**: regard **to respect of**: in comparison with
ese: benefit   87 **good**: property   88 **Wenyng**: intending   89 **doth . . .
disese**: causes . . . distress

I vouchesauf, as wisly have I joie,   90
For yow to lese al that I have in Troie,

'Save of a doughter that I lefte, allas,
Slepyng at hom, whan out of Troie I sterte.
O sterne, O cruel fader that I was!
How myghte I have in that so hard an herte?   95
Allas, I ne hadde ibrought hire in hire sherte!
For sorwe of which I wol nought lyve to morwe,
But if ye lordes rewe upon my sorwe.

'For by that cause I say no tyme er now
Hire to delivere, ich holden have my pees;   100
But now or nevere, if that it like yow,
I may hire have right soone, douteles.
O help and grace amonges al this prees!
Rewe on this olde caytyf in destresse,
Syn I thorugh yow have al this hevynesse.   105

'Ye have now kaught and fetered in prisoun
Troians ynowe, and if youre willes be,
My child with oon may han redempcioun;
Now for the love of God and of bounte,
Oon of so fele, allas, so yive hym me!   110
What nede were it this preiere for to werne,
Syn ye shul bothe han folk and town as yerne?

---

90 **vouchesauf**: am willing **wisly**: certainly   91 **lese**: lose
93 **sterte**: departed   96 Alas that I did not bring her, even in her nightshirt
(i.e. not giving her time to dress)   97 **to morwe**: another day   98 **But
if**: unless **rewe**: have pity   99 **by that cause**: because **say**: saw   100 To
release her, I have held my peace   101 **if that it like yow**: if you please
103 **prees**: crowd   104 **caytyf**: wretch   105 **hevynesse**: sadness
106 **kaught**: captured **fetered**: shackled   107 **ynowe**: enough **youre willes
be**: you agree   108 My child may be ransomed in exchange for one (of
them)   109 **bounte**: goodness, kindness   110 **fele**: many **yive**: give
111 **werne**: refuse   112 **as yerne**: very soon

'On peril of my lif, I shal nat lye:
Appollo hath me told it feithfully;
115   I have ek founde it be astronomye,
By sort, and by augurye ek, trewely,
And dar wel say, the tyme is faste by
That fire and flaumbe on al the town shal sprede,
And thus shal Troie torne to asshen dede.

120   'For certein, Phebus and Neptunus bothe,
That makeden the walles of the town,
Ben with the folk of Troie alwey so wrothe
That they wol brynge it to confusioun,
Right in despit of kyng Lameadoun;
125   Bycause he nolde payen hem here hire,
The town of Troie shal ben set on-fire.'

Tellyng his tale alwey, this olde greye,
Humble in his speche and in his lokyng eke,
The salte teris from his eyen tweye
130   Ful faste ronnen down by either cheke.
So longe he gan of socour hem biseke
That, for to hele hym of his sorwes soore,
They yave hym Antenor, withouten moore.

But who was glad ynough but Calkas tho?
135   And of this thyng ful soone his nedes leyde
On hem that sholden for the tretis go,
And hem for Antenor ful ofte preyde
To bryngen hom kyng Toas and Criseyde;

---

114 **feithfully:** truthfully   115 **astronomye:** astrology   116 **sort:** casting of
lots **augurye:** divination through observation of the behaviour of birds
117 **faste by:** close at hand   118 **flaumbe:** flame   119 **asshen dede:** lifeless
ashes   120 **For certein:** certainly   **Neptunus:** Neptune   121 **makeden:** built
122 **wrothe:** angry   123 **confusioun:** destruction   124 **in despit of:** out of
hostility towards   **Lameadoun:** Laomedon   125 **hire:** payment, wages
127 **greye:** greybeard   128 **speche:** manner of speaking   **lokyng:** look
130 **ronnen:** ran   131 **socour:** help   **biseke:** beseech   133 **yave:** gave
moore: more ado   135 **his nedes leyde:** entrusted his requirements
136 **tretis:** negotiation   137 **hem . . . preyde:** begged them   138 **Toas:** Thoas
(n.)

And whan Priam his save-garde sente,
Th'embassadours to Troie streight they wente.   140

The cause itold of hire comyng, the olde
Priam, the kyng, ful soone in general
Let her-upon his parlement to holde,
Of which th'effect rehercen yow I shal:
Th'embassadours ben answerd for fynal;   145
Th'eschaunge of prisoners and al this nede
Hem liketh wel, and forth in they procede.

This Troilus was present in the place
Whan axed was for Antenor Criseyde,
For which ful soone chaungen gan his face,   150
As he that with tho wordes wel neigh deyde.
But natheles he no word to it seyde,
Lest men sholde his affeccioun espye;
With mannes herte he gan his sorwes drye,

And ful of angwissh and of grisly drede   155
Abod what lordes wolde unto it seye;
And if they wolde graunte – as God forbede! –
Th'eschaunge of hire, than thoughte he thynges tweye:
First, how to save hire honour, and what weye
He myghte best th'eschaunge of hire withstonde;   160
Ful faste he caste how al this myghte stonde.

Love hym made al prest to don hire byde,
And rather dyen than she sholde go;
But Resoun seyde hym, on that other syde,

139 **save-garde:** safe-conduct   140 **streight:** directly   141 **itold:** (having
been) told   142 **in general:** together, in one assembly   143 Then summoned
his parliament at once (*her-upon*)   144 **th'effect:** the outcome **rehercen
yow:** recount to you   145 **for fynal:** finally   146 **Th'eschaunge:** the
exchange **nede:** business   151 **As he that:** like one who
153 **affeccioun:** emotion **espye:** notice   154 **drye:** endure
155 **grisly:** terrible   156 **Abod:** awaited   160 **withstonde:** oppose
161 **faste:** intently **caste:** considered **stonde:** be   162 Love made him very
ready to cause her to stay

165 'Withouten assent of hire ne do nat so,
     Lest for thi werk she wolde be thy fo,
     And seyn that thorugh thy medlynge is iblowe
     Youre bother love, ther it was erst unknowe.'

     For which he gan deliberen, for the beste,
170 That though the lordes wolde that she wente,
     He wolde lat hem graunte what hem leste,
     And telle his lady first what that they mente;
     And whan that she hadde seyd hym hire entente,
     Therafter wolde he werken also blyve,
175 Theigh al the world ayeyn it wolde stryve.

     Ector, which that wel the Grekes herde,
     For Antenor how they wolde han Criseyde,
     Gan it withstonde, and sobrely answerde:
     'Syres, she nys no prisonere,' he seyde;
180 'I not on yow who that this charge leyde,
     But, on my part, ye may eftsone hem telle,
     We usen here no wommen for to selle.'

     The noyse of peple up stirte thanne at ones,
     As breme as blase of straw iset on-fire;
185 For infortune it wolde, for the nones,
     They sholden hire confusioun desire.
     'Ector,' quod they, 'what goost may yow enspyre
     This womman thus to shilde and don us leese
     Daun Antenor – a wrong wey now ye chese –

166 fo: enemy   167 seyn: say medlynge: interference iblowe: made known
168 Youre bother love: the love between you both erst: before   169 gan
deliberen: considered (it)   170 wolde: wished   173 seyd hym hire
entente: spoken her mind to him   174 Therafter: accordingly werken: act
also blyve: very quickly   175 Theigh: though ayeyn . . . stryve: oppose
178 withstonde: oppose sobrely: gravely   180 not: do not know
charge: responsibility   181 on: for eftsone: in reply   182 usen hcre no: are
not accustomed here selle: barter   183 noyse: clamour up stirte: sprang up
184 breme: fiercely blase: blaze   185 infortune: misfortune for the nones: at
that time   186 confusioun: (own) destruction   187 goost: spirit
enspyre: move   188 shilde: shield, protect don us leese: cause us to lose
189 Daun: Lord chese: choose

'That is so wys and ek so bold baroun?   190
And we han nede to folk, as men may se:
He is ek oon the grettest of this town.
O Ector, lat tho fantasies be!
O kyng Priam,' quod they, 'thus sygge we,
That al oure vois is to forgon Criseyde.'   195
And to deliveren Antenor they preyde.

O Juvenal, lord, trewe is thy sentence,
That litel wyten folk what is to yerne,
That they ne fynde in hire desir offence;
For cloude of errour lat hem nat discerne   200
What best is. And lo, here ensample as yerne:
This folk desiren now deliveraunce
Of Antenor, that brought hem to meschaunce,

For he was after traitour to the town
Of Troye. Allas, they quytte hym out to rathe!   205
O nyce world, lo, thy discrecioun!
Criseyde, which that nevere dide hem scathe,
Shal now no lenger in hire blisse bathe;
But Antenor, he shal com hom to towne,
And she shal out; thus seyden here and howne.   210

For which delibered was by parlement
For Antenor to yelden out Criseyde,
And it pronounced by the president,

190 **wys**: prudent **bold**: brave   191 **to**: of   192 **oon the grettest**: the very
greatest, most important   193 **lat tho fantasies be**: give up such delusions!
194 **sygge**: say   195 **vois**: vote **forgon**: give up   196 **deliveren**: release
preyde: beseeched   197 **sentence**: maxim   198 **wyten**: know **to yerne**: to be
desired   199 **offence**: harm   200 **errour**: confusion   201 **ensample as
yerne**: an example forthwith   202 **deliveraunce**: release
203 **meschaunce**: disaster   204 **after**: afterwards   205 **quytte hym out to
rathe**: ransomed him too soon   206 **nyce**: foolish **discrecioun**: judgement
207 **scathe**: harm   208 **bathe**: bask   210 **shal out**: must leave **here and
howne**: everyone (n.)   211 **delibered**: decided   212 **yelden**: surrender
213 **pronounced**: declared **president**: speaker

Altheigh that Ector 'nay' ful ofte preyde.
215 And fynaly, what wight that it withseyde,
It was for nought: it moste ben and sholde,
For substaunce of the parlement it wolde.

Departed out of parlement echone,
This Troilus, withouten wordes mo,
220 Unto his chambre spedde hym faste allone,
But if it were a man of his or two
The which he bad out faste for to go
Bycause he wolde slepen, as he seyde,
And hastily upon his bed hym leyde.

225 And as in wynter leves ben biraft,
Ech after other, til the tree be bare,
So that ther nys but bark and braunche ilaft,
Lith Troilus, byraft of ech welfare,
Ibounden in the blake bark of care,
230 Disposed wood out of his wit to breyde,
So sore hym sat the chaungynge of Criseyde.

He rist hym up, and every dore he shette,
And wyndow ek, and tho this sorwful man
Upon his beddes syde adown hym sette,
235 Ful lik a ded ymage, pale and wan;
And in his brest the heped wo bygan
Out breste, and he to werken in this wise
In his woodnesse, as I shal yow devyse.

214 'nay' . . . preyde: urged against it   215 what wight: whoever it
withseyde: spoke against it   216 for nought: unavailing moste: must
sholde: would have to be   217 substaunce: (the) majority   218 Departed . . .
echone: everyone (having) departed   220 spedde hym: hastened   221 But if
it were: except for   222 bad: told   225 leves: leaves biraft: removed
226 Ech: each one   227 ilaft: left   228 Lith: lies byraft: deprived
welfare: happiness   229 Ibounden in: confined inside bark: bark (of a tree)
230 Disposed: in a state wood: mad out of his wit to breyde: to go out of his
mind   231 sore: intensely sat: affected chaungynge: exchange   232 rist
hym: stands shette: shut   235 ded ymage: lifeless statue wan: pale, sickly
236 heped: accumulated   237 breste: burst werken: act
238 woodnesse: madness

Right as the wylde bole bygynneth sprynge,
Now her, now ther, idarted to the herte,   240
And of his deth roreth in compleynynge,
Right so gan he aboute the chaumbre sterte,
Smytyng his brest ay with his fistes smerte;
His hed to the wal, his body to the grounde
Ful ofte he swapte, hymselven to confounde.   245

His eyen two, for piete of herte,
Out stremeden as swifte welles tweye;
The heighe sobbes of his sorwes smerte
His speche hym refte; unnethes myghte he seye,
'O deth, allas, why nyltow do me deye?   250
Acorsed be that day which that Nature
Shop me to ben a lyves creature!'

But after, whan the furie and al the rage,
Which that his herte twiste and faste threste,
By lengthe of tyme somwhat gan aswage,   255
Upon his bed he leyde hym down to reste.
But tho bygonne his teeris more out breste,
That wonder is the body may suffise
To half this wo which that I yow devyse.

Than seyde he thus: 'Fortune, allas the while!   260
What have I don? What have I thus agylt?
How myghtestow for rowthe me bygile?
Is ther no grace, and shal I thus be spilt?
Shal thus Creiseyde awey, for that thow wilt?

239 **bole**: bull **sprynge**: leap   240 **idarted**: pierced   242 **sterte**: rush
243 **Smytyng**: striking **smerte**: sharply   245 **swapte**: dashed
confounde: destroy   246 **piete**: compassion   247 **stremeden**: gushed **as**: like
welles: springs   248 **heighe**: loud **smerte**: bitter   249 Deprived him of
speech; scarcely could he say   250 **nyltow**: won't you **do me deye**: cause me
to die   252 **Shop**: created **lyves**: living   254 **twiste**: wrung
threste: oppressed   255 **aswage**: diminish   258 **wonder is**: it is a marvel
suffise: be able to endure   260 **allas the while**: alas for the time (when it
happened)   261 **agylt**: offended   262 **myghtestow**: could you
rowthe: pity('s sake) **bygile**: deceive   263 **spilt**: killed, destroyed   264 **for
that**: because **wilt**: wish (it)

265   Allas, how maistow in thyn herte fynde
       To ben to me thus cruwel and unkynde?

       'Have I the nought honoured al my lyve,
       As thow wel woost, above the goddes alle?
       Whi wiltow me fro joie thus deprive?
270   O Troilus, what may men now the calle
       But wrecche of wrecches, out of honour falle
       Into miserie, in which I wol bewaille
       Criseyde – allas! – til that the breth me faille?

       'Allas, Fortune, if that my lif in joie
275   Displesed hadde unto thi foule envye,
       Why ne haddestow my fader, kyng of Troye,
       Byraft the lif, or don my bretheren dye,
       Or slayn myself, that thus compleyne and crye –
       I, combre-world, that may of nothyng serve,
280   But evere dye and nevere fulli sterve.

       'If that Criseyde allone were me laft,
       Nought roughte I whider thow woldest me steere;
       And hire, allas, than hastow me biraft.
       But everemore, lo, this is thi manere,
285   To reve a wight that most is to hym deere,
       To preve in that thi gerful violence:
       Thus am I lost; ther helpeth no diffence.

265 **maistow:** can you   267 **lyve:** life   269 **wiltow:** do you wish **fro:** of
271 **wrecche of wrecches:** most miserable of all wretches
272 **bewaille:** lament the loss of   273 **the breth me faille:** my breath gives
out   275 **foule:** vile   276 **ne haddestow:** haven't you   277 **Byraft:** deprived
of **don . . . dye:** caused to die, killed   279 I, an encumbrance to the world,
who may serve no useful purpose   280 **sterve:** die   281 **me laft:** left to me
282 **Nought roughte I:** I would not care **whider:** where
steere: steer   283 **hire:** her **hastow me biraft:** you have deprived me of
284 **everemore:** always **manere:** way   285 **reve:** take from **that:** that which
286 **preve:** demonstrate **gerful:** unpredictable   287 **diffence:** means of
defence

'O verrey lord, O Love! O god, allas!
That knowest best myn herte and al my thought,
What shal my sorwful lif don in this cas,   290
If I forgo that I so deere have bought?
Syn ye Criseyde and me han fully brought
Into youre grace, and bothe oure hertes seled,
How may ye suffre, allas, it be repeled?

'What shal I don? I shal, while I may dure   295
On lyve in torment and in cruwel peyne
This infortune or this disaventure,
Allone as I was born, iwys, compleyne;
Ne nevere wol I seen it shyne or reyne,
But ende I wol, as Edippe, in derknesse   300
My sorwful lif, and dyen in distresse.

'O wery goost, that errest to and fro,
Why nyltow fleen out of the wofulleste
Body that evere myghte on grounde go?
O soule, lurkynge in this wo, unneste,   305
Fle forth out of myn herte, and lat it breste,
And folowe alwey Criseyde, thi lady dere:
Thi righte place is now no lenger here.

'O woful eyen two, syn youre disport
Was al to sen Criseydes eyen brighte,   310
What shal ye don but, for my discomfort,
Stonden for naught, and wepen out youre sighte,
Syn she is queynt that wont was yow to lighte?

288 **verrey:** true   291 If I lose that for which I have paid so high a price
293 **seled:** sealed (like a legal document)   294 **suffre:** permit
repeled: revoked   295–8 I shal . . . **compleyne:** I shall lament
295 **dure:** remain   296 **On lyve:** alive   297 **infortune:** misfortune
disaventure: misadventure   300 **Edippe:** Oedipus (n.) **derknesse:** gloom,
despair   302 **wery:** weary **goost:** spirit, soul **that errest:** you who wander
303 **fleen:** fly **wofulleste:** most sorrowful   304 **on grounde go:** walk on
earth   305 **lurkynge:** hiding **unneste:** go out of the nest   306 **Fle:** fly
breste: break   308 **righte:** rightful   309 **disport:** delight
311 **discomfort:** distress   312 **Stonden for naught:** be of no use, count for
nought   313 **queynt:** extinguished **wont:** accustomed **lighte:** illuminate

In vayn fro this forth have ich eyen tweye
315   Ifourmed, syn youre vertu is aweye.

'O my Criseyde, O lady sovereigne
Of thilke woful soule that thus crieth,
Who shal now yeven comfort to the peyne?
Allas, no wight! But whan myn herte dieth,
320   My spirit, which that so unto yow hieth,
Receyve in gree, for that shal ay yow serve;
Forthi no fors is, though the body sterve.

'O ye loveris, that heigh upon the whiel
Ben set of Fortune, in good aventure,
325   God leve that ye fynde ay love of stiel,
And longe mote youre lif in joie endure!
But whan ye comen by my sepulture,
Remembreth that youre felawe resteth there –
For I loved ek, though ich unworthi were.

330   'O oold, unholsom, and myslyved man –
Calkas I mene – allas, what eiled the
To ben a Grek, syn thow art born Troian?
O Calkas, which that wolt my bane be,
In corsed tyme was thow born for me!
335   As wolde blisful Jove, for his joie,
That I the hadde wher I wolde, in Troie!'

A thousand sikes, hotter than the gleede,
Out of his brest ech after other wente,
Medled with pleyntes new, his wo to feede,

314 **this forth**: this time on   315 **Ifourmed**: been endowed with
vertu: power **aweye**: gone   318 **yeven**: give   320 **hieth**: hastens   321 **in
gree**: favourably   322 **no fors is**: it does not matter   324 **aventure**: fortune
325 **God leve**: may God grant **of stiel**: as true as steel   326 **mote**: may
327 **sepulture**: tomb   329 **ek**: too   330 **unholsom**: corrupt
myslyved: wicked   331 **eiled the**: was wrong with you   332 **ben**: i.e.
become **born**: by birth   333 **bane**: destroyer   335 **As wolde blisful
Jove**: would that blessed Jove would grant   337 **sikes**: sighs **gleede**: glowing
coal   339 **Medled**: mingled **pleyntes**: laments **feede**: nourish

For which his woful teris nevere stente;   340
And shortly, so his peynes hym torente,
And wex so mat, that joie nor penaunce
He feleth non, but lith forth in a traunce.

Pandare, which that in the parlement
Hadde herd what every lord and burgeys seyde,   345
And how ful graunted was by oon assent
For Antenor to yelden so Criseyde,
Gan wel neigh wood out of his wit to breyde,
So that for wo he nyste what he mente,
But in a rees to Troilus he wente.   350

A certeyn knyght that for the tyme kepte
The chambre door undide it hym anon;
And Pandare, that ful tendreliche wepte,
Into the derke chambre, as stille as ston,
Toward the bed gan softely to gon,   355
So confus that he nyste what to seye;
For verray wo his wit was neigh aweye.

And with his chiere and lokyng al totorn
For sorwe of this, and with his armes folden,
He stood this woful Troilus byforn,   360
And on his pitous face he gan byholden.
But Lord, so ofte gan his herte colden,
Seyng his frend in wo, whos hevynesse
His herte slough, as thoughte hym, for destresse.

340 stente: ceased   341 shortly: in brief hym torente: tore him apart
342 wex: (he) became mat: exhausted, dejected penaunce: misery 343 lith
forth: goes on lying traunce: daze   345 burgeys: burgess, citizen   346 by
oon assent: with one accord   347 yelden: hand over   348 wood: mad out of
his wit to breyde: to go out of his mind   349 mente: intended
350 rees: rush   351 kepte: guarded   352 hym: for him   355 gan softely to
gon: quietly went   356 confus: confused   357 verray: sheer aweye: gone
358 totorn: distraught   362 colden: grow cold   363 Seyng: seeing   364 His
herte slough: was killing his heart

365　This woful wight, this Troilus, that felte
　　　His frend Pandare ycomen hym to se,
　　　Gan as the snow ayeyn the sonne melte;
　　　For which this sorwful Pandare, of pitee,
　　　Gan for to wepe as tendreliche as he;
370　And specheles thus ben thise ilke tweye,
　　　That neither myghte o word for sorwe seye.

　　　But at the laste this woful Troilus,
　　　Neigh ded for smert, gan bresten out to rore,
　　　And with a sorwful noise he seyde thus,
375　Among hise sobbes and his sikes sore:
　　　'Lo, Pandare, I am ded, withouten more.
　　　Hastow nat herd at parlement,' he seyde,
　　　'For Antenor how lost is my Criseyde?'

　　　This Pandarus, ful ded and pale of hewe,
380　Ful pitously answerde and seyde, 'Yis!
　　　As wisly were it fals as it is trewe,
　　　That I have herd, and woot al how it is.
　　　O mercy, God, who wolde have trowed this?
　　　Who wolde have wend that in so litel a throwe
385　Fortune oure joie wold han overthrowe?

　　　'For in this world ther is no creature,
　　　As to my dom, that ever saugh ruyne
　　　Straunger than this, thorugh cas or aventure.
　　　But who may all eschue, or al devyne?
390　Swich is this world! Forthi I thus diffyne:

365 **felte**: sensed　367 **ayeyn the sonne**: in the sunshine　368 **of pitee**: out of
pity　371 **o**: one　373 **Neigh**: almost **smert**: pain **bresten**: burst **rore**: roar
374 **noise**: voice　375 **sikes sore**: deep sighs　376 **withouten**
more: forthwith, without more ado　379 **ded**: deathly **of hewe**: in colour
381 **As wisly were it**: would that it were surely as　382 **woot**: (I) know
383 **trowed**: believed　384 **wend**: imagined **litel a throwe**: short a space of
time　387 **As to my dom**: in my opinion **ruyne**: downfall
388 **Straunger**: more surprising **cas**: accident **aventure**: chance
389 **eschue**: avoid **devyne**: anticipate　390 **Forthi**: therefore
diffyne: conclude

Ne trust no wight to fynden in Fortune
Ay propretee; hire yiftes ben comune.

'But telle me this: whi thow art now so mad
To sorwen thus? Whi listow in this wise,
Syn thi desir al holly hastow had,   395
So that, by right, it oughte ynough suffise?
But I, that nevere felte in my servyse
A frendly cheere or lokyng of an eye,
Lat me thus wepe and wailen til I deye.

'And over al this, as thow wel woost thiselve,   400
This town is ful of ladys al aboute;
And, to my doom, fairer than swiche twelve
As evere she was, shal I fynde in som route
Yee, on or two, withouten any doute.
Forthi be glad, myn owen deere brother: 405
If she be lost, we shal recovere an other.

'What! God forbede alwey that ech plesaunce
In o thyng were and in non other wight!
If oon kan synge, an other kan wel daunce;
If this be goodly, she is glad and light;   410
And this is fair, and that kan good aright.
Ech for his vertu holden is for deere,
Both heroner and faucoun for ryvere.

391 **Ne trust no wight**: let no one trust   392 **propretee**: private property
yiftes: gifts **comune**: common to all   394 **sorwen**: sorrow **listow**: are you
lying down   395 **holly**: wholly   396 **by right**: justly   397 **servyse**: service in
love   398 **lokyng**: glance   400 **over**: in addition to   401 **aboute**: around
402 **to my doom**: in my opinion **swiche twelve**: twelve such
403 **route**: company   404 **Yee**: yes   406 **recovere**: get in return
410 **light**: lighthearted   411 **kan good aright**: well knows how to behave
412 Each is prized for its particular excellence   413 **heroner**: falcon for
hunting herons **faucoun for ryvere**: falcon for hunting waterfowl

'And ek, as writ Zanzis, that was ful wys,
415   "The newe love out chaceth ofte the olde";
And upon newe cas lith newe avys.
Thenk ek, thi lif to saven artow holde.
Swich fir, by proces, shal of kynde colde,
For syn it is but casuel plesaunce,
420   Som cas shal putte it out of remembraunce;

'For also seur as day comth after nyght,
The newe love, labour, or oother wo,
Or elles selde seynge of a wight,
Don olde affecciouns alle over-go.
425   And, for thi part, thow shalt have oon of tho
T'abregge with thi bittre peynes smerte;
Absence of hire shal dryve hire out of herte.'

Thise wordes seyde he for the nones alle,
To help his frend, lest he for sorwe deyde;
430   For douteles, to don his wo to falle,
He roughte nought what unthrift that he seyde.
But Troilus, that neigh for sorwe deyde,
Took litel heede of al that evere he mente –
Oon ere it herde, at tother out it wente –

435   But at the laste answerde, and seyde, 'Frend,
This lechecraft, or heeled thus to be,
Were wel sittyng, if that I were a fend –
To traysen a wight that trewe is unto me!
I pray God lat this conseil nevere ythe;

---

414 **writ**: writes **Zanzis**: Zeuxis (?; see n.)   415 **chaceth**: drives   416 A fresh
situation requires fresh consideration   417 **artow holde**: you are obliged
418 **by proces**: in course of time **of kynde**: by nature **colde**: grow cold
419 **casuel**: chance   420 **cas**: chance event   421 **also seur**: as surely
422 **labour**: work   423 **selde**: seldom **seynge**: seeing   424 **Don**: cause
over-go: to pass away   425 **tho**: those experiences (or, those women;
cf. 401)   426 **T'abregge with**: with which to shorten   428 **nones**: occasion,
purpose   430 **falle**: decrease   431 **unthrift**: nonsense   433 **mente**: said
434 **tother**: the other   436 **lechecraft**: remedy   437 **wel sittyng**: very
suitable **fend**: demon   438 **traysen**: betray   439 **conseil**: advice
ythe: succeed

But do me rather sterve anon-right here,   440
Er I thus do as thow me woldest leere!

'She that I serve, iwis, what so thow seye,
To whom myn herte enhabit is by right,
Shal han me holly hires til that I deye.
For Pandarus, syn I have trouthe hire hight,   445
I wol nat ben untrewe for no wight,
But as hire man I wol ay lyve and sterve,
And nevere other creature serve.

'And ther thow seist thow shalt as faire fynde
As she – lat be, make no comparisoun   450
To creature yformed here by kynde!
O leve Pandare, in conclusioun,
I wol nat ben of thyn opynyoun
Touchyng al this; for which I the biseche,
So hold thi pees; thow sleest me with thi speche!   455

'Thow biddest me I shulde love another
Al fresshly newe, and lat Criseyde go!
It lith nat in my power, leeve brother;
And though I myght, I wolde nat do so.
But kanstow playen raket, to and fro,   460
Nettle in, dok out, now this, now that, Pandare?
Now foule falle hire for thi wo that care!

'Thow farest ek by me, thow Pandarus,
As he that, whan a wight is wo bygon,
He cometh to hym a paas and seith right thus: 465

440 do me ... sterve: make me die   441 leere: teach   442 serve: i.e. in love
what so: whatever   443 enhabit: devoted by right: justly, with reason
444 holly: wholly   445 hight: promised   446 untrewe: unfaithful
451 kynde: nature   452 leve: dear   454 Touchyng: regarding   455 hold thi
pees: keep quiet sleest: kill   456 biddest: tell   457 Al fresshly newe: starting
all afresh   458 lith nat: does not lie leeve: dear   460 kanstow: can you
raket: rackets (a kind of tennis)   461 dok: dock (n.)   462 Now bad luck to
her who may care about your unhappiness   463 farest ... by: act towards
464 As: like wo bygon: in misery   465 a paas: apace, swiftly

"Thynk nat on smert, and thow shalt fele non."
Thow moost me first transmewen in a ston,
And reve me my passiones alle,
Er thow so lightly do my wo to falle.

470   'The deth may wel out of my brest departe
The lif, so longe may this sorwe myne,
But fro my soule shal Criseydes darte
Out nevere mo; but down with Proserpyne,
Whan I am ded, I wol go wone in pyne,
475   And ther I wol eternaly compleyne
My wo, and how that twynned be we tweyne.

'Thow hast here made an argument for fyn,
How that it sholde a lasse peyne be
Criseyde to forgon, for she was myn
480   And lyved in ese and in felicite.
Whi gabbestow, that seydest unto me
That "hym is wors that is fro wele ythrowe,
Than he hadde erst noon of that wele yknowe"?

'But tel me now, syn that the thynketh so light
485   To changen so in love ay to and fro,
Whi hastow nat don bisily thi myght
To chaungen hire that doth the al thi wo?
Why nyltow lete hire fro thyn herte go?
Whi nyltow love an other lady swete,
490   That may thyn herte setten in quiete?

466 smert: pain   467 transmewen in: transform into   468 reve: take from
passiones: feelings   469 lightly: easily do . . . falle: make . . . decrease
470 departe: remove   471 myne: undermine   472 darte: arrow
473 Out: go out Proserpyne: Proserpina   474 wone: dwell pyne: torment
476 twynned: separated   477 made an argument: reasoned for fyn: to this
end   478 lasse: lesser   479 forgon: lose for: because   481 gabbestow: do
you talk foolishly   482 fro wele ythrowe: deprived of good fortune
483 erst: before   484 the thynketh so light: it seems to you so easy   486 don
. . . thi myght: tried your utmost bisily: diligently   490 in quiete: at rest

'If thou hast had in love ay yet myschaunce
And kanst it not out of thyn herte dryve,
I, that levede in lust and in plesaunce
With hire, as muche as creature on lyve,
How sholde I that foryete, and that so blyve?   495
O, where hastow ben hid so longe in muwe,
That kanst so wel and formely arguwe?

'Nay, nay, God wot, nought worth is al thi red,
For which, for what that evere may byfalle,
Withouten wordes mo, I wol be ded.   500
O deth, that endere art of sorwes alle,
Com now, syn I so ofte after the calle;
For sely is that deth, soth for to seyne,
That, ofte ycleped, cometh and endeth peyne.

'Wel wot I, whil my lif was in quyete,   505
Er thow me slowe, I wolde have yeven hire;
But now thi comyng is to me so swete
That in this world I nothing so desire.
O deth, syn with this sorwe I am a-fyre,
Thow outher do me anon in teeris drenche,   510
Or with thi colde strok myn hete quenche.

'Syn that thow sleest so fele in sondry wyse
Ayeins hire wil, unpreyed, day and nyght,
Do me at my requeste this service:
Delyvere now the world – so dostow right –   515
Of me, that am the wofulleste wyght

491 ay yet: always until now   493 levede: lived lust: delight
495 blyve: quickly   496 hid . . . in muwe: cooped up, hidden away
497 formely: correctly   498 nought worth: worthless red: advice
499 Because of which, despite whatever may happen   501 that endere
art: who brings about the end   503 sely: blessed   504 ycleped: called
506 Before you slew me I would have paid a ransom   510 outher: either
drenche: be drowned   511 hete: heat (of passion), fever (of love)
512 fele: many sondry wyse: various ways   513 unpreyed: without being
asked   515 Delyvere: rid dostow right: you would be doing the right thing
516 wofulleste: most sorrowful

That evere was; for tyme is that I sterve,
Syn in this world of right nought may I serve.'

This Troilus in teris gan distille,
520   As licour out of a lambyc ful faste;
And Pandarus gan holde his tonge stille,
And to the ground his eyen down he caste;
But natheles, thus thought he at the laste:
'What! Parde, rather than my felawe deye,
525   Yet shal I somwhat more unto hym seye.'

And seyde, 'Frend, syn thow hast swich distresse,
And syn the list myn argumentz to blame,
Why nylt thiselven helpen don redresse
And with thy manhod letten al this grame?
530   Go ravysshe hire! Ne kanstow nat, for shame?
And outher lat hire out of towne fare,
Or hold hire stille, and leve thi nyce fare.

'Artow in Troie, and hast non hardyment
To take a womman which that loveth the
535   And wolde hireselven ben of thyn assent?
Now is nat this a nyce vanitee?
Ris up anon, and lat this wepyng be,
And kith thow art a man; for in this houre
I wol ben ded, or she shal bleven oure.'

517 **tyme is**: it is time   518 **serve**: be of use   519 **in teris gan distille**: wept
profusely   520 **licour**: liquor **lambyc**: alembic (retort used in distilling)
524 **felawe**: friend **deye**: should die   527 **the list**: you wish **blame**: find fault
with   528 **nylt thiselven**: will you not yourself **don redresse**: set matters
right   529 **with thy manhod**: manfully **letten**: prevent **grame**: grief
530 **ravysshe**: abduct **Ne kanstow nat**: can't you do it?   531 And either let
her leave town   532 **hold**: keep **nyce fare**: foolish behaviour
533 **Artow**: are you **hardyment**: daring   535 **of thyn assent**: in agreement
with you   536 **nyce vanitee**: folly   537 **lat . . . be**: give up   538 **kith**: show
in: within   539 **bleven oure**: remain ours

To this answerde hym Troilus ful softe,   540
And seyde, 'Parde, leve brother deere,
Al this have I myself yet thought ful ofte,
And more thyng than thow devysest here.
But whi this thyng is laft, thow shalt wel here;
And whan thow me hast yeve an audience,   545
Therafter maystow telle al thi sentence.

'First, syn thow woost this town hath al this
          werre
For ravysshyng of wommen so by myght,
It sholde nought be suffred me to erre,
As it stant now, ne don so gret unright.   550
I sholde han also blame of every wight,
My fadres graunt if that I so withstoode,
Syn she is chaunged for the townes goode.

'I have ek thought, so it were hire assent,
To axe hire at my fader, of his grace;   555
Than thynke I this were hire accusement,
Syn wel I woot I may hire nought purchace;
For syn my fader, in so heigh a place
As parlement hath hire eschaunge enseled,
He nyl for me his lettre be repeled.   560

'Yet drede I moost hire herte to perturbe
With violence, if I do swich a game;
For if I wolde it openly desturbe,

541 **leve . . . deere**: beloved . . . dear   543 **devysest**: speak of   544 **laft**: left
(undone)   545 **yeve an audience**: listened to   546 **Therafter**: afterwards
sentence: opinion   548 **ravysshyng**: abduction   **myght**: force   549 **suffred me
to erre**: permitted for me to transgress   550 **stant** (= *standeth*): stands
don: commit   **unright**: wrong   551 **han . . . blame of**: be blamed by
552 **graunt**: decree   **withstoode**: were to oppose   553 **chaunged**: exchanged
554 **so it were hire assent**: provided she agreed   555 To ask for her from my
father, out of his kindness   556 **were hire accusement**: would constitute an
accusation against her   557 **purchace**: obtain   559 **enseled**: ratified
560 **lettre**: decree   **repeled**: revoked   561 **drede I moost**: I fear most
perturbe: upset   562 **do**: perform   **game**: action   563 **it**: i.e. the exchange
openly: publicly   **desturbe**: impede

It mooste be disclaundre to hire name.

565   And me were levere ded than hire diffame –
As nolde God but if I sholde have
Hire honour levere than my lif to save!

'Thus am I lost, for aught that I kan see:
For certeyn is, syn that I am hire knyght,

570   I moste hire honour levere han than me
In every cas, as lovere ought of right.
Thus am I with desir and reson twight.
Desir for to destourben hire me redeth,
And reson nyl nat; so myn herte dredeth.'

575   Thus wepyng that he koude nevere cesse,
He seyde, 'Allas, how shal I, wrecche, fare?
For wel fele I alwey my love encresse,
And hope is lasse and lasse alway, Pandare.
Encressen ek the causes of my care.

580   So weilaway, whi nyl myn herte breste?
For, as in love, ther is but litel reste.'

Pandare answerde, 'Frend, thow maist, for me,
Don as the list; but hadde ich it so hoote,
And thyn estat, she sholde go with me,

585   Though al this town cride on this thyng by note:
I nolde sette at al that noys a grote!
For whan men han wel cryd, than wol they rowne;
Ek wonder last but nyne nyght nevere in towne.

564 **disclaundre**: slander   565–7 And I would rather be dead than bring dishonour upon her – God forbid that I should not hold her honour dearer than saving my own life   568 **for aught that**: as far as   570 **levere han**: value more highly   571 **of right**: rightfully   572 **twight**: torn, pulled   573 Desire advises me to prevent her departure   574 **dredeth**: is afraid   575 **that**: as if **cesse**: stop   576 **fare**: get on   578 **lasse**: less   581 **as in**: in   582 **for me**: as far as I'm concerned   583 Do as you please; but if I felt so intensely 584 **estat**: rank, status   585 **cride on**: cried out against **by note**: in unison 586 **sette at**: give for **grote**: groat (fourpenny piece)   587 **wel cryd**: shouted a lot **rowne**: whisper (i.e. quieten down)   588 **last but . . . nevere**: only ever lasts

'Devyne not in resoun ay so depe
Ne corteisly, but help thiself anon: 590
Bet is that othere than thiselven wepe,
And namely, syn ye two ben al on,
Ris up, for by myn hed, she shal not goon!
And rather be in blame a lite ifounde
Than sterve here as a gnat, withouten wounde.   595

'It is no shame unto yow, ne no vice,
Hire to witholden that ye love moost;
Peraunter she myghte holde the for nyce
To late hire go thus unto the Grekis oost.
Thenk ek Fortune, as wel thiselven woost,   600
Helpeth hardy man unto his enprise,
And weyveth wrecches for hire cowardise.

'And though thy lady wolde a lite hire greve,
Thow shalt thiself thi pees hereafter make;
But as for me, certeyn, I kan nat leve   605
That she wolde it as now for yvel take.
Whi sholde thanne of ferd thyn herte quake?
Thenk ek how Paris hath – that is thi brother –
A love; and whi shaltow nat have another?

'And Troilus, o thyng I dar the swere: 610
That if Criseyde, which that is thi lief,
Now loveth the as wel as thow dost here,
God help me so, she nyl nat take a-grief,
Theigh thow do boote anon in this meschief;

589 **Devyne:** speculate **resoun:** argument **depe:** profoundly   590 **corteisly:** in
a courtly manner   591 **Bet is:** it is better   592 **namely:** especially **al on:** as
one   593 **hed:** head   594 **in blame a lite ifounde:** found a little at fault
596 For you there is nothing dishonourable or wrong   597 **witholden:** keep
back   598 **holde the:** consider you **nyce:** foolish   599 **late:** let **oost:** army
601 **hardy:** bold **enprise:** enterprise   602 **weyveth:** abandons   603 **hire
greve:** take offence   605 **leve:** believe   606 **it . . . for yvel take:** take it amiss
as now: now   607 **of ferd:** because of being frightened   611 **lief:** beloved
612 **here:** her   613 **take a-grief:** be upset   614 **Theigh:** though **do
boote:** provide a remedy **meschief:** misfortune

615 And if she wilneth fro the for to passe,
 Thanne is she fals; so love hire wel the lasse.

 'Forthi tak herte, and thynk right as a knyght:
 Thorugh love is broken al day every lawe.
 Kith now somwhat thi corage and thi myght;
620 Have mercy on thiself for any awe.
 Lat nat this wrecched wo thyn herte gnawe,
 But manly sette the world on six and sevene –
 And if thow deye a martyr, go to hevene!

 'I wol myself ben with the at this dede,
625 Theigh ich and al my kyn upon a stownde
 Shulle in a strete as dogges liggen dede,
 Thorugh-girt with many a wid and blody wownde;
 In every cas I wol a frend be founde.
 And if the list here sterven as a wrecche,
630 Adieu, the devel spede hym that it recche!'

 This Troilus gan with tho wordes quyken,
 And seyde, 'Frend, graunt mercy, ich assente.
 But certeynly thow maist nat so me priken,
 Ne peyne non ne may me so tormente,
635 That, for no cas, it is nat myn entente,
 At shorte wordes, though I deyen sholde,
 To ravysshe hire, but if hireself it wolde.'

 'Whi, so mene I,' quod Pandare, 'al this day.
 But telle me thanne: hastow hire wil assayed,
640 That sorwest thus?' And he answerde hym, 'Nay.'

---

615 **wilneth**: desires 616 **fals**: unfaithful **wel the lasse**: much less 618 **al day**: continually 619 **Kith**: show **corage**: spirit 620 **for any awe**: despite any fear 622 But, like a man, stake the world on a throw of the dice 624 **dede**: action 625 **upon a stownde**: at one time 626 **Shulle**: shall 627 **Thorugh-girt**: pierced through **wid**: gaping 629 **as**: like 630 **spede**: assist **it recche**: may care about it 631 **quyken**: revive 632 **graunt mercy**: thank you 633 **priken**: incite, goad 634 **Ne peyne non ne may**: nor may any pain 635 **for no cas**: in no circumstances 636 **At shorte wordes**: briefly 637 **but if**: unless **it wolde**: wished it 639 **hire wil**

'Wherof artow,' quod Pandare, 'thanne amayed,
That nost nat that she wol ben yvele appayed
To ravysshe hire, syn thow hast nought ben there,
But if that Jove told it in thyn ere?

'Forthi ris up, as nought ne were, anon,   645
And wassh thi face, and to the kyng thow wende,
Or he may wondren whider thow art goon.
Thow most with wisdom hym and othere blende,
Or, upon cas, he may after the sende
Er thow be war; and shortly, brother deere,   650
Be glad, and lat me werke in this matere,

'For I shal shape it so, that sikerly
Thow shalt this nyght som tyme, in som manere,
Come speken with thi lady pryvely,
And by hire wordes ek, and by hire cheere,   655
Thow shalt ful sone aperceyve and wel here
Al hire entente, and in this cas the beste.
And fare now wel, for in this point I reste.'

The swifte Fame, which that false thynges
Egal reporteth lik the thynges trewe,   660
Was thorughout Troie yfled with preste wynges
Fro man to man, and made this tale al newe,
How Calkas doughter, with hire brighte hewe,
At parlement, withouten wordes more,
Ygraunted was in chaunge of Antenore.   665

641 **Wherof artow . . . amayed**: what are you upset about   642 **nost** (= *ne wost*): do not know   **yvele appayed**: displeased   643 **To ravysshe hire**: by your abducting her   644 **But if**: unless   645 **as nought ne were**: as if nothing were the matter   647 **wondren**: be curious   648 **most**: must   **othere**: other people   **blende**: deceive   649 **upon cas**: by chance   **after the**: for you   650 **war**: aware   652 **shape**: arrange   **sikerly**: certainly   654 **pryvely**: secretly   656 **aperceyve**: perceive   657 All she has in mind, and (what is) the best (thing to do) in this situation   659 **Fame**: fame, rumour   660 **Egal**: equally   **reporteth**: makes known   661 **yfled**: fled   **preste**: swift   662 **made this tale al newe**: kept retelling this story   663 **brighte hewe**: radiant looks   664 **wordes more**: more to be said   665 **chaunge of**: exchange for

The whiche tale anon-right as Criseyde
Hadde herd, she, which that of hire fader roughte,
As in this cas, right nought, ne whan he deyde,
Ful bisily to Jupiter bisoughte
670   Yeve hem meschaunce that this tretis broughte;
But shortly, lest thise tales sothe were,
She dorst at no wight asken it, for fere.

As she that hadde hire herte and al hire mynde
On Troilus iset so wonder faste
675   That al this world ne myghte hire love unbynde,
Ne Troilus out of hire herte caste,
She wol ben his, while that hire lif may laste.
And thus she brenneth both in love and drede,
So that she nyste what was best to reede.

680   But as men seen in towne and al aboute
That wommen usen frendes to visite,
So to Criseyde of wommen com a route,
For pitous joie, and wenden hire delite;
And with hire tales, deere ynough a myte,
685   Thise wommen, which that in the cite dwelle,
They sette hem down and seyde as I shall telle.

Quod first that oon, 'I am glad, trewely,
Bycause of yow, that shal youre fader see.'
Another seyde, 'Ywis, so nam nat I,
690   For al to litel hath she with us be.'
Quod tho the thridde, 'I hope, ywis, that she

666 **anon-right as:** as soon as   667 **roughte:** cared   668 **As in this cas:** now
669 **bisily:** earnestly   670 **meschaunce:** misfortune   **tretis:** treaty
671 **shortly:** in brief   **tales:** stories   674 **iset:** set, fixed   **wonder
faste:** amazingly firmly   675 **unbynde:** untie, undo   678 **brenneth:** burns
679 **best to reede:** the best plan to follow   681 **usen:** are accustomed
682 **route:** company   683 **pitous:** compassionate, tender-hearted   **wenden
hire delite:** thought to please her   684 **deere ynough a myte:** expensive
enough at the cost of a *myte*   688 **Bycause:** on account   **that:** who   690 **to
litel:** too short a time   691 **thridde:** third

Shal bryngen us the pees on every syde,
That, whan she goth, almyghty God hire gide!'

Tho wordes and tho wommanysshe thynges,
She herde hem right as though she thennes were,   695
For God it woot, hire herte on othir thyng is –
Although the body sat among hem there,
Hire advertence is alwey elleswhere,
For Troilus ful faste hire soule soughte;
Withouten word, on hym alwey she thoughte.   700

Thise wommen, that thus wenden hire to plese,
Aboute naught gonne alle hire tales spende:
Swich vanyte ne kan don hire non ese,
As she that al this mene while brende
Of other passioun than that they wende,   705
So that she felte almost hire herte dye
For wo and wery of that compaignie.

For which no lenger myghte she restreyne
Hir teeris, so they gonnen up to welle,
That yaven signes of the bittre peyne   710
In which hir spirit was, and moste dwelle,
Remembryng hir, fro heven into which helle
She fallen was, syn she forgoth the syghte
Of Troilus, and sorwfully she sighte.

And thilke fooles sittynge hire aboute   715
Wenden that she wepte and siked sore
Bycause that she sholde out of that route

693 **hire gide:** may guide her   694 **wommanysshe thynges:** women's talk
695 **thennes:** absent, somewhere else   698 **advertence:** attention
701 **wenden:** thought   702 **Aboute naught:** to no purpose **gonne ... tales
spende:** made conversation   703 **vanyte:** idle talk **don hire non ese:** bring her
no comfort   704 **brende:** was inflamed   707 **For wo and wery:** out of grief
and weariness (or, 'from grief, and [felt] weary')   709 **welle:** well up
710 **yaven:** gave   711 **moste dwelle:** must remain   713 **forgoth:** is losing
714 **sighte:** sighed   716 **siked sore:** sighed deeply   717–18 Because she was
to leave that company and never socialize with them again

        Departe, and nevere pleye with hem more.
        And they that hadde yknowen hire of yore
720   Seigh hire so wepe and thoughte it kyndenesse,
        And ech of hem wepte ek for hire destresse.

        And bisyly they gonnen hire comforten
        Of thyng, God woot, on which she litel thoughte;
        And with hire tales wenden hire disporten,
725   And to be glad they often hire bysoughte;
        But swich an ese therwith they hire wroughte,
        Right as a man is esed for to feele
        For ache of hed to clawen hym on his heele!

        But after al this nyce vanyte
730   They toke hire leve, and hom they wenten alle.
        Criseyde, ful of sorwful piete,
        Into hire chambre up went out of the halle,
        And on hire bed she gan for ded to falle,
        In purpos nevere thennes for to rise;
735   And thus she wroughte, as I shal yow devyse.

        Hire ownded heer, that sonnyssh was of hewe,
        She rente, and ek hire fyngeres longe and smale
        She wrong ful ofte, and bad God on hire rewe,
        And with the deth to doon boote on hire bale.
740   Hire hewe, whilom bright, that tho was pale,
        Bar witnesse of hire wo and hire constreynte;
        And thus she spak, sobbyng in hire compleynte:

---

719 **of yore**: for a long time   720 **Seigh**: saw   **kyndenesse**: natural affection
724 **wenden hire disporten**: thought to cheer her up   726–8 But by doing
that they gave her just such relief as one gets from a headache by being
scratched on the heel!   729 **nyce vanyte**: foolish and idle chatter
731 **sorwful piete**: pitiful sorrow   732 **Into . . . up went out of**: went up into
. . . from   733 **for ded**: as if dead   734 **In purpos**: intending
735 **wroughte**: did   **devyse**: tell   736 **ownded**: wavy   **heer**: hair
sonnyssh: sun-like, the colour of sunlight   **of hewe**: in appearance
737 **rente**: tore   **smale**: slender   738 **wrong**: wrung   **bad**: asked   **rewe**: to have
pity   739 **doon boote on**: provide a remedy for   **bale**: suffering
740 **hewe**: complexion   **whilom**: formerly   **bright**: radiant   741 **Bar**: bore
constreynte: distress   742 **in**: while making

'Allas,' quod she, 'out of this regioun
I, woful wrecche and infortuned wight,
And born in corsed constellacioun,   745
Moot goon and thus departen fro my knyght!
Wo worth, allas, that ilke dayes light
On which I saugh hym first with eyen tweyne,
That causeth me, and ich hym, al this peyne!'

Therwith the teris from hire eyen two   750
Down fille, as shour in Aperil ful swithe;
Hire white brest she bet, and for the wo
After the deth she cryed a thousand sithe,
Syn he that wont hire wo was for to lithe
She moot forgon; for which disaventure   755
She held hireself a forlost creature.

She seyde, 'How shal he don, and ich also?
How sholde I lyve if that I from hym twynne?
O deere herte eke, that I love so,
Who shal that sorwe slen that ye ben inne?   760
O Calkas, fader, thyn be al this synne!
O moder myn, that cleped were Argyve,
Wo worth that day that thow me bere on lyve!

'To what fyn sholde I lyve and sorwen thus?
How sholde a fissh withouten water dure?   765
What is Criseyde worth, from Troilus?
How sholde a plaunte or lyves creature
Lyve withoute his kynde noriture?

744 **infortuned**: ill-fated   745 **in corsed constellacioun**: under an
unfavourable disposition of the planets   747 **Wo worth**: a curse on
ilke: same   751 **fille**: fell **shour**: shower **swithe**: quickly   752 **bet**: beat **for
the wo**: because of her unhappiness   753 **After the deth**: for death
cryed: begged **sithe**: times   754–5 **Syn he ... She moot forgon**: since she
must give him up   754 **lithe**: soothe   755 **disaventure**: misfortune
756 **held**: considered **forlost**: utterly lost   758 **twynne**: separate
760 **slen**: put an end to   762 **moder**: mother **cleped**: called   763 **Wo
worth**: a curse on **me bere**: gave birth to me   765 **dure**: survive
766 **from**: separated from   767 **lyves**: living   768 **kynde noriture**: natural
nourishment

For which ful ofte a by-word here I seye,
770   That "rooteles moot grene soone deye."

'I shal doon thus – syn neither swerd ne darte
Dar I noon handle, for the crueltee –
That ilke day that I from yow departe,
If sorwe of that nyl nat my bane be,
775   Thanne shal no mete or drynke come in me
Til I my soule out of my breste unshethe,
And thus myselven wol I don to dethe.

'And, Troilus, my clothes everychon
Shul blake ben in tokenyng, herte swete,
780   That I am as out of this world agon,
That wont was yow to setten in quiete;
And of myn ordre, ay til deth me mete,
The observance evere, in youre absence,
Shal sorwe ben, compleynt, and abstinence.

785   'Myn herte and ek the woful goost therinne
Byquethe I with youre spirit to compleyne
Eternaly, for they shal nevere twynne;
For though in erthe ytwynned be we tweyne,
Yet in the feld of pite, out of peyne,
790   That highte Elisos, shal we ben yfeere,
As Orpheus and Erudice, his fere.

769 **by-word**: proverb   770 **rooteles moot grene**: without roots, foliage
must   771 **darte**: spear   772 **for the crueltee**: because of the suffering (they
would cause me)   774 **bane**: death   776 **unshethe**: unsheath, draw out
779 **in tokenyng**: as a sign   780 **as . . . agon**: as if withdrawn   781 **in
quiete**: at rest   782–4 And in your absence, till I meet with death, the
observances of my (religious) order will be sorrow, lamentation and
abstinence   785 **therinne**: within   787 **twynne**: part
788 **ytwynned**: separated   789 **feld of pite**: Elysian fields **out of
peyne**: beyond suffering   790 **highte**: is called **Elisos**: Elysium
yfeere: united   791 **Erudice**: Eurydice **fere**: companion

'Thus, herte myn, for Antenor, allas,
I soone shal be chaunged, as I wene.
But how shul ye don in this sorwful cas?
How shal youre tendre herte this sustene?   795
But, herte myn, foryete this sorwe and tene,
And me also – for sothly for to seye,
So ye wel fare, I recche naught to deye.'

How myghte it evere yred ben or ysonge,
The pleynte that she made in hire destresse?   800
I not; but, as for me, my litel tonge,
If I discryven wolde hire hevynesse,
It sholde make hire sorwe seme lesse
Than that it was, and childisshly deface
Hire heigh compleynte, and therfore ich it pace.   805

Pandare, which that sent from Troilus
Was to Criseyde – as ye han herd devyse
That for the beste it was acorded thus,
And he ful glad to doon hym that servyse –
Unto Criseyde, in a ful secree wise,   810
Ther as she lay in torment and in rage,
Com hire to telle al hoolly his message,

And fond that she hireselven gan to trete
Ful pitously, for with hire salte teris
Hire brest, hire face, ybathed was ful wete;   815
The myghty tresses of hire sonnysshe heeris
Unbroiden hangen al aboute hire eeris,

793 chaunged: exchanged wene: suppose   795 sustene: bear
796 tene: affliction   797 sothly: truly   798 Provided that you are all right, I
don't care if I die   799 yred: read ysonge: sung   800 pleynte: lamentation
801 not: do not know   802 discryven: describe hevynesse: sadness
804 childisshly: like a child deface: mar, spoil   805 heigh: lofty pace: pass
over   807 devyse: tell   808 acorded: settled   810 secree: secret
811 rage: frenzied grief   812 al hoolly: in full   813 fond: discovered
hireselven gan to trete: behaved   816 myghty: great heeris: hair
817 Unbroiden: unbraided, loose

Which yaf hym verray signal of martire
Of deth, which that hire herte gan desire.

820   Whan she hym saugh, she gan for sorwe anon
       Hire tery face atwixe hire armes hide;
       For which this Pandare is so wo-bygon
       That in the hous he myghte unnethe abyde,
       As he that pite felt on every syde;
825   For if Criseyde hadde erst compleyned soore,
       Tho gan she pleyne a thousand tymes more,

       And in hire aspre pleynte thus she seyde:
       'Pandare first of joies mo than two
       Was cause causyng unto me, Criseyde,
830   That now transmewed ben in cruel wo.
       Wher shal I seye to yow welcom or no,
       That alderfirst me broughte unto servyse
       Of love – allas! – that endeth in swich wise?

       'Endeth than love in wo? Ye, or men lieth,
835   And alle worldly blisse, as thynketh me.
       The ende of blisse ay sorwe it occupieth;
       And whoso troweth nat that it so be,
       Lat hym upon me, woful wrecche, ysee,
       That myself hate and ay my burthe acorse,
840   Felyng alwey fro wikke I go to worse.

       'Whoso me seeth, he seeth sorwe al atonys –
       Peyne, torment, pleynte, wo, distresse!
       Out of my woful body harm ther noon is,

818 signal: sign martire: martyrdom   821 tery: tear-stained
atwixe: between   823 myghte unnethe abyde: could scarcely bear to remain
825 erst: before   826 Tho: then   827 aspre: bitter   829 cause causyng: the
primary cause   830 transmewed ben: are transformed   831 Wher: whether
(introducing a question, but not translated)   832 alderfirst: first of all
834 men lieth: people are lying   836–7 Sorrow always takes possession of
the end of joy; and whoever does not believe that it is so   838 ysee: look
839 burthe: birth acorse: curse   840 Felyng alwey: suffering continually
wikke: bad   841 atonys: at the same time   843 No suffering is absent from
my sorrowful body

As angwissh, langour, cruel bitternesse,
Anoy, smert, drede, fury, and ek siknesse.   845
I trowe, ywys, from hevene teeris reyne
For pite of myn aspre and cruel peyne.'

'And thow, my suster, ful of discomfort,'
Quod Pandarus, 'What thynkestow to do?
Whi ne hastow to thyselven som resport?   850
Whi wiltow thus thiself, allas, fordo?
Leef al this werk, and tak now heede to
That I shal seyn; and herkne of good entente
This which by me thi Troilus the sente.'

Tornede hire tho Criseyde, a wo makynge   855
So gret that it a deth was for to see.
'Allas,' quod she, 'what wordes may ye brynge?
What wol my deere herte seyn to me,
Which that I drede nevere mo to see?
Wol he han pleynte or teris er I wende?   860
I have ynough, if he therafter sende!'

She was right swich to seen in hire visage
As is that wight that men on beere bynde;
Hire face, lik of Paradys the ymage,
Was al ychaunged in another kynde.   865
The pleye, the laughter, men was wont to fynde
In hire, and ek hire joies everichone,
Ben fled; and thus lith now Criseyde allone.

844 **As:** such as **langour:** suffering   845 **Anoy:** trouble   846 **teeris
reyne:** tears rain down   847 **aspre:** harsh   848 **discomfort:** distress
849 **thynkestow:** do you intend   850 **resport:** regard   851 **fordo:** destroy
852 **Leef:** leave off, cease **werk:** suffering   853 **herkne:** listen to, hear **of
good entente:** faithfully   855 **Tornede hire:** turned round **a wo
makynge:** lamenting   856 **a deth was:** was grievous   861 **therafter:** for any
862 **visage:** face   863 **beere:** bier **bynde:** tie   865 **al:** entirely
866 **pleye:** gaiety **men:** one **wont:** accustomed

Aboute hire eyen two a purpre ryng
870   Bytrent, in sothfast tokenyng of hire peyne,
That to biholde it was a dedly thyng;
For which Pandare myghte nat restreyne
The teeris from his eighen for to reyne;
But natheles, as he best myghte, he seyde
875   From Troilus thise wordes to Criseyde:

'Lo, nece, I trowe ye han herd al how
The kyng with othere lordes, for the beste,
Hath mad eschaunge of Antenor and yow,
That cause is of this sorwe and this unreste.
880   But how this cas dooth Troilus moleste,
That may non erthly mannes tonge seye –
For verray wo his wit is al aweye.

'For which we han so sorwed, he and I,
That into litel bothe it hadde us slawe;
885   But thorugh my conseyl this day finaly
He somwhat is fro wepynge now withdrawe,
And semeth me that he desireth fawe
With yow to ben al nyght, for to devyse
Remedie in this, if ther were any wyse.

890   'This, short and pleyn, th'effect of my message,
As ferforth as my wit kan comprehende,
For ye that ben of torment in swich rage
May to no long prologe as now entende.
And hereupon ye may answere hym sende;

869 purpre: purple   870 Bytrent: encircles sothfast: true tokenyng: sign
871 dedly: grievous   876 al: in full   879 unreste: emotional turmoil
880 dooth . . . moleste: distresses   882 For sheer misery he is at his wits'
end   884 into litel: nearly hadde us slawe: would have slain us
885 conseyl: advice   886 somwhat: to some extent is . . . withdrawe: has
refrained   887 fawe: eagerly   889 wyse: way   890 short and pleyn: briefly
and simply th'effect: the essence   891 As ferforth as: as far as
892 rage: violent grief   893 entende: attend   894 hereupon: concerning this
matter

And for the love of God, my nece deere,   895
So lef this wo er Troilus be here!'

'Gret is my wo,' quod she, and sighte soore
As she that feleth dedly sharp distresse;
'But yit to me his sorwe is muchel more,
That love hym bet than he hymself, I gesse.   900
Allas, for me hath he swich hevynesse?
Kan he for me so pitously compleyne?
Iwis, his sorwe doubleth al my peyne.

'Grevous to me, God woot, is for to twynne,'
Quod she, 'but yet it harder is to me   905
To sen that sorwe which that he is inne;
For wel I woot it wol my bane be,
And deye I wol in certeyn,' tho quod she;
'But bid hym come, er deth, that thus me threteth,
Dryve out that goost which in myn herte beteth.'   910

Thise wordes seyd, she on hire armes two
Fil gruf, and gan to wepen pitously.
Quod Pandarus, 'Allas, whi do ye so,
Syn wel ye woot the tyme is faste by
That he shal come? Aris up hastily,   915
That he yow nat bywopen thus ne fynde,
But ye wole have hym wood out of his mynde.

'For wiste he that ye ferde in this manere,
He wolde hymselven sle; and if I wende
To han this fare, he sholde nat come here   920
For al the good that Priam may dispende.
For to what fyn he wolde anon pretende,

896 So lef: leave off   898 dedly: agonizing   899 muchel: much
907 bane: death   908 in certeyn: certainly   909 threteth: threatens
910 beteth: beats   912 Fil gruf: fell face downwards   914 faste by: close at
hand   916 bywopen: in tears   917 But: unless   wole have hym wood: want
to have him go mad   918 wiste he: if he knew   ferde: behaved   919 sle: kill
920 fare: behaviour   921 good: wealth   dispende: spend   922 pretende: aim

That knowe ich wel; and forthi yet I seye:
So lef this sorwe, or platly he wol deye.

925 'And shapeth yow his sorwe for t'abregge,
And nought encresse, leeve nece swete!
Beth rather to hym cause of flat than egge,
And with som wisdom ye his sorwe bete.
What helpeth it to wepen ful a strete,
930 Or though ye bothe in salte teeris dreynte?
Bet is a tyme of cure ay than of pleynte.

'I mene thus: whan ich hym hider brynge,
Syn ye be wise and bothe of oon assent,
So shapeth how destourbe youre goynge,
935 Or come ayeyn soon after ye be went.
Women ben wise in short avysement;
And lat sen how youre wit shal now availle,
And what that I may helpe, it shal nat faille.'

'Go,' quod Criseyde, 'and uncle, trewely,
940 I shal don al my myght me to restreyne
From wepyng in his sighte, and bisily
Hym for to glade I shal don al my peyne,
And in myn herte seken every veyne.
If to his sore ther may be fonden salve,
945 It shal nat lakke, certeyn, on my halve.'

924 So lef: leave off platly: plainly   925 shapeth yow: find means
t'abregge: to curtail   926 leeve: dear   927 flat than egge: healing than hurt
(the flat of the sword-blade, not the cutting edge; n.)   928 bete: cure
929 ful a strete: a streetful   930 dreynte: drowned   931 Time is better spent
on a remedy than on complaining   932 hider: here   933 of oon assent: of
one mind   934 shapeth: plan destourbe: to prevent   935 ayeyn: back
went: gone   936 Women are shrewd at quick thinking   937 availle: be of
use   938 faille: be lacking   940 al my myght: all in my power
941 bisily: diligently   942 glade: make happy al my peyne: my utmost
943 seken every veyne: search every corner   944 to: for sore: wound
fonden: found salve: cure   945 lakke: be wanting halve: part

Goth Pandarus, and Troilus he soughte
Til in a temple he fond hym al allone,
As he that of his lif no lenger roughte;
But to the pitouse goddes everichone
Ful tendrely he preyde and made his mone,   950
To doon hym sone out of this world to pace,
For wel he thoughte ther was non other grace.

And shortly, al the sothe for to seye,
He was so fallen in despeir that day,
That outrely he shop hym for to deye.   955
For right thus was his argument alway:
He seyde he nas but lorn, so weylaway!
'For al that comth, comth by necessitee:
Thus to ben lorn, it is my destinee.

'For certeynly, this wot I wel,' he seyde,   960
'That forsight of divine purveyaunce
Hath seyn alwey me to forgon Criseyde,
Syn God seeth every thyng, out of doutaunce,
And hem disponyth, thorugh his ordinaunce,
In hire merites sothly for to be,   965
As they shul comen by predestyne.

'But natheles, allas, whom shal I leeve?
For ther ben grete clerkes many oon
That destyne thorugh argumentes preve;
And som men seyn that nedely ther is noon,   970
But that fre chois is yeven us everychon.

948 **roughte:** cared   949 **pitouse:** merciful   950 **Ful tendrely:** in a most
heartfelt way **made his mone:** complained   951 **doon:** cause **pace:** pass
952 **non other grace:** nothing else that could help him
955 **outrely:** absolutely **shop hym:** prepared   957 **nas but lorn:** was as good
as lost **weylaway:** alas   958 **comth:** happens   961 **forsight:** foreknowledge
purveyaunce: providence   962 Has always seen that I would lose Criseyde
963 **out of doutaunce:** without a doubt   964 **disponyth:** disposes
ordinaunce: decree   965 **In hire merites:** according to their merits
sothly: truly   966 **predestyne:** predestination   967 **leeve:** believe
968 **clerkes:** scholars **many oon:** many a one   969 **destyne:** predestination
preve: prove   970 **nedely:** of necessity **noon:** i.e. no predestination

O, welaway! So sleighe arn clerkes olde
That I not whos opynyoun I may holde.

'For som men seyn, if God seth al biforn –
975   Ne God may nat deceyved ben, parde –
Than moot it fallen, theigh men hadde it sworn,
That purveiance hath seyn byfore to be.
Wherfore I sey, that from eterne if he
Hath wist byforn oure thought ek as oure dede,
980   We han no fre chois, as thise clerkes rede.

'For other thought, nor other dede also,
Myghte nevere ben, but swich as purveyaunce,
Which may nat ben deceyved nevere mo,
Hath feled byforn, withouten ignoraunce.
985   For if ther myghte ben a variaunce
To writhen out fro Goddis purveyinge,
Ther nere no prescience of thyng comynge,

'But it were rather an opynyoun
Uncerteyn, and no stedfast forseynge;
990   And certes, that were an abusioun,
That God sholde han no parfit cler wytynge
More than we men that han doutous wenynge.
But swich an errour upon God to gesse
Were fals and foul, and wikked corsednesse.

972 **sleighe:** cunning   973 **not:** do not know   974 **seth al biforn:** sees
everything in advance   976 **fallen:** happen **theigh:** even though **it**
sworn: sworn the contrary   977 **That:** that which   978 **eterne:** eternity
979 **wist byforn:** foreknown   982 **ben:** exist   984 **feled:** perceived
withouten ignoraunce: infallibly   985 **variaunce:** variety of possible
alternatives   986 **writhen out:** wriggle out **Goddis purveyinge:** God's
providence   987 **nere no prescience:** would be no (certain) foreknowledge
988 **were:** would be   989 **stedfast:** stable **forseynge:** foresight
990 **abusioun:** absurdity   991 **parfit:** perfect **cler:** clear
wytynge: knowledge   992 **doutous:** doubtful **wenynge:** understanding
993 **errour:** mistake **upon:** in **gesse:** imagine   994 **corsednesse:** wickedness

'Ek this is an opynyoun of some   995
That han hire top ful heighe and smothe yshore:
They seyn right thus, that thyng is nat to come
For that the prescience hath seyn byfore
That it shal come; but they seyn that therfore
That it shal come, therfore the purveyaunce   1000
Woot it byforn, withouten ignoraunce;

'And in this manere this necessite
Retorneth in his part contrarie agayn.
For nedfully byhoveth it nat to bee
That thilke thynges fallen in certayn   1005
That ben purveyed; but nedly, as they sayn,
Byhoveth it that thynges whiche that falle,
That they in certayn ben purveyed alle.

'I mene as though I laboured me in this
To enqueren which thyng cause of which   1010
      thyng be:
As wheither that the prescience of God is
The certeyn cause of the necessite
Of thynges that to comen ben, parde,
Or if necessite of thyng comynge
Be cause certeyn of the purveyinge.   1015

'But now n'enforce I me nat in shewynge
How the ordre of causes stant; but wel woot I
That it byhoveth that the byfallynge

996 **top**: crown (of the head) **smothe yshore**: smoothly shaven (i.e. the
clerical tonsure)   998 **For that**: because **prescience**: (divine) foreknowledge
999 **therfore**: because   1001 **withouten ignoraunce**: infallibly   1003 Turns
back upon itself   1004–8 For it does not necessarily (*nedfully*) have to be
that those things that have been foreseen (*purveyed*) certainly happen; but,
necessarily (*nedly*), as they (clerks) say, it has to be that things that do happen
have certainly all been foreseen   1009 I intend, as if I were taking pains in
this matter (or, 'It is as if I strove . . .')   1013 **to comen ben**: are to come
1016 But I do not trouble myself now with showing   1017 **ordre**: sequence
stant: stands   1018 **it byhoveth**: it is necessary **byfallynge**: happening

Of thynges wist byfore certeynly
1020   Be necessarie, al seme it nat therby
That prescience put fallynge necessaire
To thyng to come, al falle it foule or faire.

'For if ther sitte a man yond on a see,
Than by necessite bihoveth it
1025   That, certes, thyn opynyoun sooth be
That wenest or conjectest that he sit.
And further over now ayeynward yit,
Lo, right so is it of the part contrarie,
As thus – now herkne, for I wol nat tarie:

1030   'I sey that if the opynyoun of the
Be soth, for that he sitte, than sey I this:
That he mot sitten by necessite;
And thus necessite in eyther is.
For in hym, nede of sittynge is, ywys,
1035   And in the, nede of soth; and thus, forsothe,
There mot necessite ben in yow bothe.

'But thow mayst seyn, the man sit nat therfore
That thyn opynyoun of his sittynge soth is,
But rather, for the man sit ther byfore,
1040   Therfore is thyn opynyoun soth, ywis.
And I seye, though the cause of soth of this
Comth of his sittyng, yet necessite
Is entrechaunged, both in hym and the.

1019 wist: known   1020 al seme it nat therby: even though it does not
appear from that   1021–2 That foreknowledge makes necessary the
occurrence of things to come, whether they turn out badly or well
1023 yond: over there   see: seat   1026 wenest: suppose
conjectest: conjecture   sit: sits   1027 further over: moreover   ayeynward: on
the other hand   1028 part contrarie: opposite side   1029 herkne: listen
tarie: delay   1030 the: you   1031 for that: because   1034–5 For he is
necessarily sitting, and your opinion is necessarily true   1035 in the: in you
1037 sit nat therfore: does not sit for the reason   1038 soth is: is true
1039 for: because   byfore: already   1043 entrechaunged: reciprocal

'Thus in this same wise, out of doutaunce,
I may wel maken, as it semeth me,   1045
My resonyng of Goddes purveyaunce
And of the thynges that to comen be;
By which resoun men may wel yse
That thilke thynges that in erthe falle,
That by necessite they comen alle.   1050

'For although that for thyng shal come, ywys,
Therfore is it purveyed, certeynly –
Nat that it comth for it purveyed is –
Yet natheles, bihoveth it nedfully
That thing to come be purveyd, trewely,   1055
Or elles, thynges that purveyed be,
That they bitiden by necessite.

'And this suffiseth right ynough, certeyn,
For to destruye oure fre chois every del.
But now is this abusioun, to seyn   1060
That fallyng of the thynges temporel
Is cause of Goddes prescience eternel.
Now trewely, that is a fals sentence,
That thyng to come sholde cause his prescience.

'What myght I wene, and I hadde swich a thought,   1065
But that God purveyeth thyng that is to come
For that it is to come, and ellis nought?
So myghte I wene that thynges alle and some
That whilom ben byfalle and overcome

1044 **out of doutaunce**: without a doubt   1048 **By which resoun**: from which
argument **yse**: see   1049 **falle**: happen   1051–3 For although because (*for*)
a thing shall happen indeed, it is therefore foreseen (*purveyed*), certainly – not
that it happens because it is foreseen   1054 **nedfully**: necessarily
1057 **bitiden**: happen   1058 And this is certainly enough
1059 **destruye**: destroy **every del**: completely   1060 **abusioun**: falsehood
1061 **fallyng**: occurrence **temporel**: transitory   1063 **sentence**: opinion
1065 **wene**: suppose **and**: if   1066 **purveyeth**: foresees   1067 **For
that**: because **ellis**: otherwise   1068 **alle and some**: one and all   1069 That
formerly have happened and occurred

1070   Ben cause of thilke sovereyne purveyaunce
        That forwoot al withouten ignoraunce.

        'And over al this, yet sey I more herto:
        That right as whan I wot ther is a thyng,
        Iwys, that thyng moot nedfully be so;
1075   Ek right so, whan I woot a thyng comyng,
        So mot it come; and thus the bifallyng
        Of thynges that ben wist bifore the tyde,
        They mowe nat ben eschued on no syde.'

        Thanne seyde he thus: 'Almyghty Jove in trone,
1080   That woost of al thys thyng the sothfastnesse,
        Rewe on my sorwe: or do me deyen sone,
        Or bryng Criseyde and me fro this destresse!'
        And whil he was in al this hevynesse,
        Disputyng with hymself in this matere,
1085   Com Pandare in, and seyde as ye may here:

        'O myghty God,' quod Pandarus, 'in trone,
        I! Who say evere a wis man faren so?
        Whi, Troilus, what thinkestow to doone?
        Hastow swich lust to ben thyn owen fo?
1090   What, parde, yet is nat Criseyde ago!
        Whi list the so thiself fordoon for drede
        That in thyn hed thyne eyen semen dede?

1070 **sovereyne:** supreme   1071 **forwoot:** foreknows   1072 **over al this:** furthermore   **herto:** to this   1073 **right:** just
1074 **nedfully:** necessarily   1075 **right so:** in just the same way   **comyng:** (to be) coming   1076 **bifallyng:** occurrence   1077 **tyde:** time (of their happening)   1078 **mowe:** may   **eschued:** evaded   **on no syde:** in any way
1079 **trone:** throne   1080 **sothfastnesse:** truth   1081 **Rewe:** have pity   **do:** let   1083 **hevynesse:** despondency   1084 **Disputyng:** debating   **in this matere:** on this subject   1085 **here:** hear   1087 **I:** ah   **say:** saw   **wis:** wise   **faren:** behave   1088 **thinkestow:** do you think   1089 **lust:** desire   **fo:** foe   1090 **What!** By God, Criseyde hasn't gone yet   1091 **fordoon:** destroy   **for drede:** through fear   1092 **semen:** appear   **dede:** dead

'Hastow nat lyved many a yer byforn
Withouten hire, and ferd ful wel at ese?
Artow for hire and for noon other born?   1095
Hath Kynde the wrought al only hire to plese?
Lat be, and thynk right thus in thi disese:
That, in the dees right as ther fallen chaunces,
Right so in love ther come and gon plesaunces.

'And yet this is my wonder most of alle,   1100
Whi thow thus sorwest, syn thow nost nat yit,
Touchyng hire goyng, how that it shal falle,
Ne yif she kan hireself destourben it:
Thow hast nat yet assayed al hire wit.
A man may al bytyme his nekke beede   1105
Whan it shal of, and sorwen at the nede.

'Forthi tak hede of that I shal the seye:
I have with hire yspoke and longe ybe,
So as acorded was bitwixe us tweye;
And evere mor me thynketh thus, that she   1110
Hath somwhat in hire hertes privete
Wherwith she kan, if I shal right arede,
Destourbe al this of which thow art in drede.

'For which my counseil is, whan it is nyght
Thow to hire go and make of this an ende;   1115
And blisful Juno thorugh hire grete myght

1094 **ferd ful wel at ese**: got on perfectly contentedly   1096 Has Nature
created you solely to please her?   1097 **disese**: distress   1098 That just as at
dice there occur winning throws (*chaunces*)   1099 **plesaunces**: pleasures
1100 **wonder**: marvel   1101 **nost nat yit**: still do not know
1102 **Touchyng**: concerning   **falle**: turn out   1103 **destourben**: impede
1104 **assayed**: ascertained   **wit**: intent   1105 A man may offer (*beede*) his
neck (to the executioner) soon enough   1106 **it shal of**: his head must (be
cut) off   **at the nede**: when it becomes necessary   1108 **longe**: for a time
ybe: been   1109 **acorded**: agreed   1110 **evere mor**: continually
1111 **somwhat**: something   **hertes privete**: heart's inmost thoughts
1112 **Wherwith**: through which   **right**: correctly   **arede**: form an opinion
1113 **of which thow art in drede**: which you fear   1115 **make of this an
ende**: come to a conclusion about this   1116 **blisful**: blessed

Shal, as I hope, hire grace unto us sende.
Myn herte seyth, "Certeyn, she shal nat wende."
And forthi put thyn herte a while in reste,
1120   And hold this purpos, for it is the beste.'

This Troilus answerd, and sighte soore:
'Thow seist right wel, and I wol don right so.'
And what hym liste, he seyde unto it more.
And whan that it was tyme for to go,
1125   Ful pryvely hymself, withouten mo,
Unto hire com, as he was wont to doone;
And how they wroughte, I shal yow tellen soone.

Soth is, that whan they gonnen first to mete,
So gan the peyne hire hertes for to twiste
1130   That neyther of hem other myghte grete,
But hem in armes toke, and after kiste.
The lasse woful of hem bothe nyste
Wher that he was, ne myghte o word out brynge,
As I seyde erst, for wo and for sobbynge.

1135   The woful teeris that they leten falle
As bittre weren, out of teris kynde,
For peyne, as is ligne aloes or galle –
So bittre teeris weep nought, as I fynde,
The woful Mirra thorugh the bark and rynde –
1140   That in this world ther nys so hard an herte
That nolde han rewed on hire peynes smerte.

1117 grace: divine favour, grace   1120 hold: keep to   1121 sighte
soore: sighed bitterly   1125 withouten mo: and nobody else
1127 wroughte: acted   1128 Soth is: the truth is   1129 twiste: wring
1130 grete: greet   1131 hem in armes toke: embraced each other
1132 Even the less unhappy one of the pair did not know   1133 out
brynge: utter   1134 erst: before   1136 out of teris kynde: beyond the nature
of tears   1137 ligne aloes: aloe galle: gall   1138 weep: wept
1139 Mirra: Myrrha (n.) rynde: bark   1141 nolde han rewed: would not
have had pity

But whan hire woful weri goostes tweyne
Retourned ben ther as hem oughte dwelle,
And that somwhat to wayken gan the peyne
By lengthe of pleynte, and ebben gan the welle   1145
Of hire teeris, and the herte unswelle,
With broken vois, al hoors forshright, Criseyde
To Troilus thise ilke wordes seyde:

'O Jove, I deye, and mercy I beseche!
Help, Troilus . . . !' And therwithal hire face   1150
Upon his brest she leyde and loste speche –
Hire woful spirit from his propre place,
Right with the word, alwey o poynt to pace.
And thus she lith with hewes pale and grene,
That whilom fressh and fairest was to sene.   1155

This Troilus, that on hire gan biholde,
Clepyng hire name – and she lay as for ded –
Withoute answere, and felte hire lymes colde,
Hire eyen throwen upward to hire hed,
This sorwful man kan now noon other red,   1160
But ofte tyme hire colde mowth he kiste.
Wher hym was wo, God and hymself it wiste!

He rist hym up, and long streght he hire leyde;
For signe of lif, for aught he kan or may,
Kan he non fynde in nothyng on Criseyde,   1165
For which his song ful ofte is 'weylaway!'
But whan he saugh that specheles she lay,

1142 **hire**: their **weri**: weary   1144 **wayken**: lessen   1145 **ebben**: to ebb,
decrease **welle**: spring   1146 **unswelle**: become less full (of emotion)
1147 **hoors**: hoarse **forshright**: worn out from shrieking
1150 **therwithal**: thereupon   1151 **speche**: (the power of) speech
1152 **his**: its **propre**: usual   1153 **o poynt to pace**: on the point of
departing   1154 **lith**: lies **hewes**: complexion **grene**: sickly
1155 **whilom**: formerly   1157 **Clepyng**: calling   1158 **lymes**: limbs
1159 **throwen**: rolled **to**: in   1160 **kan**: knows **red**: course of action
1162 **Wher**: whether   1163 **rist hym up**: gets up **long streght**: stretched out
at full length   1164 **for aught**: so far as   1165 **in nothyng**: at all

With sorweful vois and herte of blisse al bare,
He seyde how she was fro this world yfare.

1170   So after that he longe hadde hire compleyned,
His hondes wrong, and seyd that was to seye,
And with his teeris salt hire brest byreyned,
He gan tho teeris wypen of ful dreye,
And pitously gan for the soule preye,
1175   And seyde, 'O Lord, that set art in thi trone,
Rewe ek on me, for I shal folwe hire sone!'

She cold was, and withouten sentement
For aught he woot, for breth ne felte he non,
And this was hym a pregnant argument
1180   That she was forth out of this world agon.
And whan he say ther was non other woon,
He gan hire lymes dresse in swich manere
As men don hem that shal ben layd on beere.

And after this, with sterne and cruel herte,
1185   His swerd anon out of his shethe he twighte
Hymself to slen, how sore that hym smerte,
So that his soule hire soule folwen myghte
Ther as the doom of Mynos wolde it dighte,
Syn Love and cruel Fortune it ne wolde
1190   That in this world he lenger lyven sholde.

1168 **bare:** deprived   1169 **yfare:** departed   1170 **hire**
compleyned: mourned her   1171 **wrong:** wrung **that:** what
1172 **byreyned:** showered   1173 **of:** off **dreye:** dry   1175 **set art:** are
seated   1177 **sentement:** feeling, sensation   1178 **aught he woot:** all he
knew   1179 **pregnant:** compelling   1180 **forth ... agon:** departed
1181 **say:** saw **woon:** course   1182 **lymes:** limbs **dresse:** arrange
1183 **beere:** bier   1185 **shethe:** sheath **twighte:** pulled   1186 **how**
sore: however grievously **hym smerte:** hurt him   1188 **Ther as:** to where
doom: judgement **Mynos:** Minos (n.) **dighte:** assign   1189 **it ne**
wolde: would not have it

Than seyde he thus, fulfild of heigh desdayn:
'O cruel Jove, and thow, Fortune adverse,
This al and som: that falsly have ye slayn
Criseyde, and syn ye may do me no werse,
Fy on youre myght and werkes so dyverse!   1195
Thus cowardly ye shul me nevere wynne;
Ther shal no deth me fro my lady twynne.

'For I this world, syn ye have slayn hire thus,
Wol lete and folwe hire spirit low or hye.
Shal nevere lovere seyn that Troilus   1200
Dar nat for fere with his lady dye;
For certeyn I wol beere hire compaignie.
But syn ye wol nat suffre us lyven here,
Yet suffreth that oure soules ben yfere.

'And thow, cite, which that I leve in wo,   1205
And thow, Priam, and bretheren alle yfeere,
And thow, my moder, farwel, for I go;
And Atropos, make redy thow my beere;
And thow, Criseyde, o swete herte deere,
Receyve now my spirit –' wolde he seye,   1210
With swerd at herte, al redy for to deye.

But as God wolde, of swough therwith
      sh'abreyde,
And gan to sike, and 'Troilus!' she cride;
And he answerde, 'Lady myn, Criseyde,
Lyve ye yet?' – and leet his swerd down glide.   1215
'Ye, herte myn, that thonked be Cipride!'

1191 fulfild: full desdayn: indignation 192 adverse: unfavourable
1193 al and som: is the whole of the matter falsly: treacherously
1195 Fy on: I scorn dyverse: unfavourable, hostile
1196 wynne: overcome 1199 lete: leave 1201 Dar: dare
1202 beere: keep 1203 suffre: permit 1204 yfere: together
1205 leve: leave 1208 beere: bier 1212 swough: swoon therwith: with
that sh'abreyde: she revived 1213 sike: sigh 1215 down glide: drop
1216 that thonked be Cipride: may Venus be thanked for it

Quod she; and therwithal she soore syghte,
And he bigan to glade hire as he myghte,

Took hire in armes two, and kiste hire ofte,
1220 And hire to glade he did al his entente;
For which hire goost, that flikered ay o-lofte,
Into hire woful herte ayeyn it wente.
But at the laste, as that hire eye glente
Asyde, anon she gan his swerd espie,
1225 As it lay bare, and gan for fere crye,

And asked hym, whi he it hadde out drawe?
And Troilus anon the cause hire tolde,
And how hymself therwith he wolde han slawe;
For which Criseyde upon hym gan biholde,
1230 And gan hym in hire armes faste folde,
And seyde, 'O mercy, God! Lo, which a dede!
Allas, how neigh we weren bothe dede!

'Than if I nadde spoken, as grace was,
Ye wolde han slayn youreself anon?' quod she.
1235 'Yee, douteles.' – And she answerde, 'Allas,
For by that ilke Lord that made me,
I nolde a forlong wey on lyve have be
After youre deth, to han ben crowned queene
Of al that lond the sonne on shyneth sheene.

1240 'But with this selve swerd, which that here is,
Myselve I wolde han slawe,' quod she tho.
'But hoo, for we han right ynough of this,

1217 therwithal: thereupon soore syghte: sighed deeply 1218 glade: cheer,
comfort 1220 al his entente: his utmost 1221 flikered: fluttered ay: all the
time o-lofte: above 1222 ayeyn it wente: it returned
1223 glente: glanced 1224 espie: notice 1225 bare: unsheathed
1226 drawe: drawn 1228 therwith: with it slawe: slain 1230 faste: tightly
folde: embraced 1231 which a dede: what a dreadful act
1232 neigh: nearly dede: dead 1233 nadde (= ne hadde): had not
1236 ilke: same, very 1237 I would not have remained alive a few minutes
(n.) 1238 to han: not even to have 1239 on shyneth sheene: shines brightly

And lat us rise, and streght to bedde go,
And there lat us speken of oure wo;
For, by the morter which that I se brenne,   1245
Knowe I ful wel that day is nat far henne.'

Whan they were in hire bed, in armes folde,
Naught was it lik tho nyghtes here-byforn.
For pitously ech other gan byholde,
As they that hadden al hire blisse ylorn,   1250
Bywaylinge ay the day that thcy were born;
Til at the laste this sorwful wight, Criseyde,
To Troilus thise ilke wordes seyde:

'Lo, herte myn, wel woot ye this,' quod she,
'That if a wight alwey his wo compleyne   1255
And seketh nought how holpen for to be,
It nys but folie and encrees of peyne;
And syn that here assembled be we tweyne
To fynde boote of wo that we ben inne,
It were al tyme soone to bygynne.   1260

'I am a womman, as ful wel ye woot,
And as I am avysed sodcynly,
So wol I telle yow, whil it is hoot.
Me thynketh thus: that nouther ye nor I
Ought half this wo to maken, skilfully;   1265
For ther is art ynough for to redresse
That yet is mys, and slen this hevynesse.

1245 **morter:** night-light, float-wick lamp   1246 **henne:** from now   1247 **in
armes folde:** embraced in each other's arms   1248 **here-byforn:** before this
1250 **ylorn:** lost   1251 **Bywaylinge ay:** always lamenting   1254 **wel woot
ye:** you well know   1256 **holpen:** helped   1257 **folie:** foolishness
encrees: increase   1258 **assembled be we tweyne:** we two have met
1259 **boote of:** remedy for (the)   1260 **al tyme:** high time   1262 **am avysed
sodeynly:** have suddenly made up my mind   1263 **hoot:** fresh in my mind
1264 **nouther:** neither   1265 **skilfully:** reasonably, with reason   1266 **is
art:** are ways **redresse:** set right   1267 **mys:** amiss **slen:** put an end to

'Soth is, the wo, the which that we ben inne,
For aught I woot, for nothyng ellis is
1270   But for the cause that we sholden twynne:
Considered al, ther nys namore amys.
But what is thanne a remede unto this,
But that we shape us soone for to meete?
This al and som, my deere herte sweete.

1275   'Now, that I shal wel bryngen it aboute
To come ayeyn, soone after that I go,
Therof am I no manere thyng in doute;
For, dredeles, withinne a wowke or two
I shal ben here; and that it may be so
1280   By alle right and in a wordes fewe,
I shal yow wel an heep of weyes shewe.

'For which I wol nat make long sermoun –
For tyme ylost may nought recovered be –
But I wol gon to my conclusioun,
1285   And to the beste, in aught that I kan see.
And for the love of God, foryeve it me
If I speke aught ayeyns youre hertes reste;
For trewely, I speke it for the beste,

'Makyng alwey a protestacioun
1290   That now thise wordes which that I shal seye
Nis but to shewen yow my mocioun
To fynde unto oure help the beste weye;
And taketh it non other wise, I preye,

1269 **for nothyng ellis is**: is for no other reason   1270 **for the
cause**: because   1271 Taking everything into account, there is nothing else
amiss   1272 **remede**: solution   1273 **shape us**: set ourselves, contrive
1274 **This al and som**: this is the whole of the matter   1275–7 I am not at all
in doubt . . . that I shall contrive to come back   1277 **Therof**: about that
1278 **wowke**: week   1281 **heep**: heap, host   1282 **sermoun**: speech
1285 **to**: for **in aught that**: as far as   1286 **foryeve**: forgive   1287 If I say
anything contrary to your peace of mind   1289 **protestacioun**: declaration,
avowal   1291 **Nis but**: is only **mocioun**: desire   1293 **wise**: way

For in effect, what so ye me comaunde,
That wol I don, for that is no demaunde.   1295

'Now herkneth this: ye han wel understonde
My goyng graunted is by parlement
So ferforth that it may nat be withstonde
For al this world, as by my jugement.
And syn ther helpeth non avisement   1300
To letten it, lat it passe out of mynde,
And lat us shape a bettre wey to fynde.

'The soth is this: the twynnyng of us tweyne
Wol us disese and cruelich anoye,
But hym byhoveth somtyme han a peyne   1305
That serveth Love, if that he wol have joye.
And syn I shal no ferther out of Troie
Than I may ride ayeyn on half a morwe,
It oughte lesse causen us to sorwe;

'So as I shal not so ben hid in muwe,   1310
That day by day, myn owne herte deere –
Syn wel ye woot that it is now a trewe –
Ye shal ful wel al myn estat yheere.
And er that trewe is doon, I shal ben heere;
And thanne have ye both Antenore ywonne   1315
And me also. Beth glad now, if ye konne,

1294 **in effect**: actually, in fact **what so**: whatever   1295 **for that is no
demaunde**: of that there is no question   1298 **So ferforth**: to such an extent
withstonde: opposed   1299 **al this world**: anything **jugement**: opinion
1300–1301 And since no deliberation will help prevent it
1302 **shape**: contrive   1303 **soth**: truth **twynnyng**: separation
1304 **disese**: distress **cruelich**: cruelly **anoye**: disturb   1305 **hym
byhoveth**: he must   1307 **shal**: shall go   1308 **morwe**: morning   1310 **So
as**: as **hid in muwe**: cooped up   1312 **trewe**: truce   1313 **myn estat
yheere**: hear of how I am getting on   1314 **doon**: over
1315 **ywonne**: gained   1316 **konne**: are able

'And thenk right thus: "Criseyde is now agon.
But what, she shal come hastiliche ayeyn!"
And whanne, allas? By God, lo, right anon,
1320   Er dayes ten, this dar I saufly seyn.
And than at erste shal we be so feyn,
So as we shal togideres evere dwelle,
That al this world ne myghte oure blisse telle.

'I se that oft-tyme, there as we ben now,
1325   That for the beste, oure counseyl for to hide,
Ye speke nat with me, nor I with yow
In fourtenyght, ne se yow go ne ride.
May ye naught ten dayes thanne abide,
For myn honour, in swich an aventure?
1330   Iwys, ye mowen ellis lite endure!

'Ye knowe ek how that al my kyn is heere,
But if that onliche it my fader be,
And ek myn othere thynges alle yfeere,
And nameliche, my deere herte, ye,
1335   Whom that I nolde leven for to se
For al this world, as wyd as it hath space –
Or ellis se ich nevere Joves face!

'Whi trowe ye my fader in this wise
Coveyteth so to se me, but for drede
1340   Lest in this town that folkes me despise
Bycause of hym, for his unhappy dede?
What woot my fader what lif that I lede?

1317 **agon:** gone   1318 **hastiliche:** soon   1320 **saufly:** safely   1321 **than at
erste:** then at last **feyn:** glad   1322 **So as:** as **togideres:** together   1324 **there
as we ben now:** in our present situation   1325 **counseyl:** secret
1327 **fourtenyght:** a fortnight **se:** do I see   1328 **abide:** await, be patient
1329 **For:** for the sake of **aventure:** circumstance   1330 **mowen:** can
lite: little   1331 **kyn:** family   1332 Except for my father
1333 **yfeere:** together   1334 **nameliche:** especially   1335 **nolde leven for to
se:** would not stop seeing   1336 For this whole wide world   1337 **se
ich:** may I see   1338 **trowe ye:** do you suppose **wise:** way
1339 **Coveyteth:** desires   1340 **despise:** regard with contempt
1341 **unhappy:** ill-fated

For if he wiste in Troie how wel I fare,
Us neded for my wendyng nought to care.

'Ye sen that every day ek, more and more,   1345
Men trete of pees, and it supposid is
That men the queene Eleyne shal restore,
And Grekis us restoren that is mys;
So, though ther nere comfort non but this,
That men purposen pees on every syde,   1350
Ye may the bettre at ese of herte abyde.

'For if that it be pees, myn herte deere,
The nature of the pees moot nedes dryve
That men moost entrecomunen yfeere,
And to and fro ek ride and gon as blyve   1355
Alday as thikke as been fleen from an hyve,
And every wight han liberte to bleve
Whereas hym liste the bet, withouten leve.

'And though so be that pees ther may be non,
Yet hider, though ther nevere pees ne were,   1360
I moste come; for whider sholde I gon,
Or how, meschaunce, sholde I dwelle there
Among tho men of armes evere in feere?
For which, as wisly God my soule rede,
I kan nat sen wherof ye sholden drede.   ·   1365

1343 **fare**: get on   1344 We should not need to worry about my departure
1345 **sen**: see   1346 **trete of**: discuss   1347 **restore**: give back
1348 **mys**: amiss   1349 **nere**: were not   1350 **purposen**: propose   1351 **at
ese of herte**: with peace of mind   **abyde**: remain   1353 **dryve**: compel,
require   1354 **entrecomunen yfeere**: have dealings with one another
1355 **gon**: walk   **blyve**: readily   1356 **Alday**: continually   **been**: bees
fleen: fly   1357 **bleve**: remain   1358 Wherever he prefers, without
permission   1359 **though so be**: even if it should happen   1360 **hider**: here
1361 **whider**: where   1362 **meschaunce**: confound it!   1363 **men of
armes**: armed men   1364 **wisly**: surely   as **rede**: may guide
1365 **wherof**: why

'Have here another wey, if it so be
That al this thyng ne may yow nat suffise:
My fader, as ye knowen wel, parde,
Is old, and elde is ful of coveytise,
1370   And I right now have founden al the gise,
Withouten net, wherwith I shal hym hente.
And herkeneth how, if that ye wol assente:

'Lo, Troilus, men seyn that hard it is
The wolf ful and the wether hool to have;
1375   This is to seyn, that men ful ofte, iwys,
Mote spenden part the remenant for to save;
For ay with gold men may the herte grave
Of hym that set is upon coveytise;
And how I mene, I shal it yow devyse:

1380   'The moeble which that I have in this town
Unto my fader shal I take, and seye
That right for trust and for savacioun
It sent is from a frend of his or tweye,
The whiche frendes ferventliche hym preye
1385   To senden after more, and that in hie,
Whil that this town stant thus in jupartie.

'And that shal ben an huge quantite –
Thus shal I seyn – but lest it folk espide,
This may be sent by no wight but by me.
1390   I shal ek shewen hym, yf pees bitide,
What frendes that I have on every side

1366 wey: way, course   1367 ne may yow nat suffise: may not be enough for
you   1369 elde: old age   coveytise: avarice   1370 gise: way
1371 wherwith: with which   hente: catch   1374 To have the wolf full and the
sheep (*wether*) unharmed   1376 remenant: remainder   1377 grave: make an
impression on   1380 moeble: personal possessions   1382 trust: confidence
(in him)   savacioun: safe-keeping   1384 ferventliche: earnestly
1385 after: for   in hie: speedily   1386 stant: stands, is   jupartie: danger
1388 espide: should notice   1390 bitide: come about   1391 on every
side: on all sides

Toward the court, to don the wrathe pace
Of Priamus and don hym stonde in grace.

'So what for o thing and for other, swete,
I shal hym so enchaunten with my sawes   1395
That right in hevene his soule is, shal he mete;
For al Appollo, or his clerkes lawes,
Or calkullynge, avayleth nought thre hawes;
Desir of gold shal so his soule blende
That, as me list, I shal wel make an ende.   1400

'And if he wolde aught by his sort it preve
If that I lye, in certayn I shal fonde
Distourben hym and plukke hym by the sleve,
Makynge his sort, and beren hym on honde
He hath not wel the goddes understonde;   1405
For goddes speken in amphibologies,
And for o soth they tellen twenty lyes.

'Ek, "Drede fond first goddes, I suppose" –
Thus shal I seyn – and that his coward herte
Made hym amys the goddes text to glose,   1410
Whan he for fered out of Delphos sterte.
And but I make hym soone to converte
And don my red withinne a day or tweye,
I wol to yow oblige me to deye.'

1392 Toward: at don the wrathe pace: cause the anger to pass 1393 don
hym stonde in grace: cause him to be in favour 1394 swete: sweetheart
1395 sawes: speeches 1396 shal he mete: he will dream 1397 For
al: notwithstanding clerkes lawes: scholarly precepts
1398 calkullynge: calculation, divination hawes: hawthorn berries
1399 blende: blind, deceive 1400 me list: I please make an ende: bring to
fulfilment 1401 aught: at all sort: casting of lots preve: test 1402 in
certayn: certainly fonde: try 1403 Distourben: to impede plukke: tug
1404 While he is making his divination, and deceive him into thinking
1406 amphibologies: ambiguities 1407 o: one 1408 Also, 'Fear first
invented gods, I believe' 1410 amys: wrongly glose: interpret
1411 fered: fear Delphos: Delphi sterte: hurried 1412 but: unless
converte: change his mind 1413 don my red: do what I advise 1414 oblige
me: pledge myself

1415 And treweliche, as writen wel I fynde
That al this thyng was seyd of good entente,
And that hire herte trewe was and kynde
Towardes hym, and spak right as she mente,
And that she starf for wo neigh whan she wente,
1420 And was in purpos evere to be trewe:
Thus writen they that of hire werkes knewe.

This Troilus, with herte and erys spradde,
Herde al this thyng devysen to and fro,
And verrayliche hym semed that he hadde
1425 The selve wit; but yet to late hire go
His herte mysforyaf hym evere mo;
But fynaly, he gan his herte wreste
To trusten hire, and took it for the beste.

For which the grete furie of his penaunce
1430 Was queynt with hope, and therwith hem bitwene
Bigan for joie th'amorouse daunce;
And as the briddes, whanne the sonne is shene,
Deliten in hire song in leves grene,
Right so the wordes that they spake yfeere
1435 Delited hem, and made hire hertes clere.

But natheles, the wendyng of Criseyde,
For al this world, may nat out of his mynde,
For which ful ofte he pitously hire preyde
That of hire heste he myghte hire trewe fynde,
1440 And seyde hire, 'Certes, if ye be unkynde,

1416 of good entente: in good faith   1419 starf . . . neigh: nearly died
1420 was in purpos: intended   1421 werkes: actions   1422 erys: ears
spradde: spread open wide, receptive   1423 devysen: discussed   to and
fro: back and forth   1424 verrayliche: truly   hym semed: it seemed to him
1425 selve: same   wit: mind, opinion   late: let   1426 mysforyaf: misgave
evere mo: continually   1427 wreste: constrain   1429 For which: as a result
of which   penaunce: suffering   1430 queynt: quenched
therwith: thereupon   1431 th'amourouse daunce: love-making
1432 briddes: birds   shene: bright   1435 made . . . clere: brightened
1436 wendyng: departure   1437 may nat out: is unable to go out

And but ye come at day set into Troye,
Ne shal I nevere have hele, honour, ne joye.

'For also soth as sonne uprist o-morwe –
And God so wisly thow me, woful wrecche,
To reste brynge out of this cruel sorwe! –   1445
I wol myselven sle if that ye drecche.
But of my deth though litel be to recche,
Yet, er that ye me causen so to smerte,
Dwelle rather here, myn owen swete herte.

'For trewely, myn owne lady deere,   1450
Tho sleghtes yet that I have herd yow stere
Ful shaply ben to faylen alle yfeere.
For thus men seyth: "That on thenketh the beere,
But al another thenketh his ledere."
Youre syre is wys; and seyd is, out of drede,   1455
"Men may the wise atrenne, and naught atrede."

'It is ful hard to halten unespied
Byfore a crepel, for he kan the craft;
Youre fader is in sleght as Argus eyed;
For al be that his moeble is hym biraft,   1460
His olde sleighte is yet so with hym laft
Ye shal nat blende hym for youre wommanhede,
Ne feyne aright; and that is al my drede.

1441 but: unless day set: the appointed day 1442 hele: well-being
1443–5 For as truly as the sun rises in the morning – and God, may you as
surely bring me, unhappy wretch, out of this cruel sorrow to rest!
1446 sle: kill drecche: delay 1447 litel be to recche: there may be little to
care about 1448 smerte: feel pain 1451 Tho sleghtes: those stratagems
stere: propose 1452 Ful shaply: very likely faylen: prove unsuccessful
1453–4 . . . 'The bear thinks one thing, but his master (ledere) thinks quite
another.' 1455 syre: father seyd is: it is said 1456 One may outrun
(atrenne) the wise, but not outwit them 1457 halten: (pretend to) limp
unespied: undetected 1458 crepel: cripple kan: knows craft: knack
1459 sleght: cunning as Argus eyed: with as many eyes as Argus (who had
one hundred) 1460 al be that: although hym biraft: taken from him
1461 sleighte: cunning laft: left 1462 for youre wommanhede: despite your
woman's ways 1463 feyne: dissemble aright: successfully

'I not if pees shal evere mo bitide;
1465   But pees or no, for ernest ne for game,
I woot, syn Calkas on the Grekis syde
Hath ones ben and lost so foule his name,
He dar nomore come here ayeyn for shame:
For which that wey, for aught I kan espie,
1470   To trusten on nys but a fantasie.

'Ye shal ek sen, youre fader shal yow glose
To ben a wif; and as he kan wel preche,
He shal som Grek so preyse and wel alose
That ravysshen he shal yow with his speche,
1475   Or do yow don by force as he shal teche;
And Troilus, of whom ye nyl han routhe,
Shal causeles so sterven in his trouthe!

'And over al this, youre fader shal despise
Us alle, and seyn this cite nys but lorn,
1480   And that th'assege nevere shal aryse,
For-whi the Grekis han it alle sworn,
Til we be slayn and down oure walles torn.
And thus he shal yow with his wordes fere,
That ay drede I that ye wol bleven there.

1485   'Ye shal ek seen so many a lusty knyght
Among the Grekis, ful of worthynesse,
And ech of hem with herte, wit, and myght
To plesen yow don al his bisynesse,
That ye shul dullen of the rudenesse

1464 not: do not know   1465 for ernest ne for game: in any event
1467 ones: once foule: shamefully name: good name   1469–70 Therefore
to rely on that course of action, as far as I can see, is nothing but a delusion
1471 sen: see glose: cajole   1473 alose: commend   1474 ravysshen . . .
yow: carry you away   1475 do yow don: make you do teche: instruct
1477 causeles: without cause trouthe: faithfulness   1478 over al
this: furthermore despise: speak ill of   1479 nys but lorn: is as good as lost
1480 th'assege: the siege aryse: be raised   1483 fere: frighten
1484 bleven: remain   1485 lusty: dashing   1488 bisynesse: utmost
1489 dullen of: grow bored with rudenesse: lack of refinement

Of us sely Troians, but if routhe   1490
Remorde yow, or vertu of youre trouthe.

'And this to me so grevous is to thynke
That fro my brest it wol my soule rende;
Ne dredeles, in me ther may nat synke
A good opynyoun, if that ye wende,   1495
For whi youre fadres sleghte wol us shende.
And if ye gon, as I have told yow yore,
So thenk I n'am but ded, withoute more.

'For which, with humble, trewe, and pitous herte,
A thousand tymes mercy I yow preye;   1500
So rueth on myn aspre peynes smerte,
And doth somwhat as that I shal yow seye.
And lat us stele awey bitwixe us tweye;
And thynk that folie is, whan man may chese,
For accident his substaunce ay to lese.   1505

'I mene thus: that syn we mowe er day
Wel stele awey and ben togidere so,
What wit were it to putten in assay,
In cas ye sholden to youre fader go,
If that ye myghten come ayeyn or no?   1510
Thus mene I: that it were a gret folie
To putte that sikernesse in jupertie.

1490 **sely**: simple **but if**: unless **routhe**: compassion 1491 **Remorde yow**: cause you remorse **vertu**: power **trouthe**: pledged word
1492 **grevous**: painful 1493 **rende**: tear 1494–5 And undoubtedly, a favourable expectation cannot enter my thoughts if you depart
1496 **sleghte**: cunning **shende**: destroy 1497 **yore**: before
1498 **thenk**: consider **n'am but ded**: am as good as dead 1501 **rueth**: have pity **aspre**: sharp **smerte**: bitter 1503 **stele**: steal 1504 **folie is**: it is foolishness **chese**: choose 1505 To lose forever the essential quality (*substaunce*) for the sake of an inessential attribute (*accident*) 1506 **mowe er day**: can before daybreak 1507 **so**: thus 1508 **What wit were it**: what sense would it make **in assay**: to the test 1509 **In cas**: in the event that, if
1512 **that sikernesse**: what is assured

           'And vulgarly to speken of substaunce
           Of tresour, may we bothe with us lede
1515   Inough to lyve in honour and plesaunce
           Til into tyme that we shal ben dede;
           And thus we may eschuen al this drede.
           For everich other wey ye kan recorde,
           Myn herte, ywys, may therwith naught acorde.

1520   'And hardily, ne dredeth no poverte,
           For I have kyn and frendes elleswhere
           That, though we comen in oure bare sherte,
           Us sholde neyther lakken gold ne gere,
           But ben honured while we dwelten there.
1525   And go we anon – for as in myn entente,
           This is the beste, if that ye wole assente.'

           Criseyde, with a sik, right in this wise
           Answerde, 'Ywys, my deere herte trewe,
           We may wel stele awey, as ye devyse,
1530   And fynden swich unthrifty weyes newe,
           But afterward ful soore it wol us rewe.
           And helpe me God so at my mooste nede,
           As causeles ye suffren al this drede!

           'For thilke day that I for cherisynge
1535   Or drede of fader, or for other wight,
           Or for estat, delit, or for weddynge,
           Be fals to yow, my Troilus, my knyght,
           Saturnes doughter, Juno, thorugh hire myght,

1513 **vulgarly**: in the ordinary sense **substaunce**: means, money (i.e. not the philosophical sense of 1505 above)   1514 **lede**: carry   1516 **Til into tyme**: until the time **dede**: dead   1517 **eschuen**: avoid **drede**: anxiety 1518 **recorde**: call to mind   1519 **acorde**: agree   1520 **hardily**: assuredly 1522 **in oure bare sherte**: wearing only a shirt   1523 **gere**: possessions 1525 **go we**: let us go **entente**: opinion   1527 **sik**: sigh   1529 **stele**: steal 1530 **unthrifty**: profitless **weyes**: courses, directions   1531 **soore**: bitterly **us rewe**: cause us to repent   1532 And as God may help me in my hour of greatest need   1533 **causeles**: without cause   1534 **cherisynge**: love 1536 **estat**: status **delit**: pleasure   1537 **fals**: unfaithful   1538–9 **Juno ... do**

As wood as Athamante do me dwelle
Eternalich in Stix, the put of helle!   1540

'And this on every god celestial
I swere it yow, and ek on ech goddesse,
On every nymphe and deite infernal,
On satiry and fawny more and lesse,
That halve goddes ben of wildernesse;   1545
And Attropos my thred of lif tobreste
If I be fals! Now trowe me if yow leste!

'And thow, Symois, that as an arwe clere
Thorugh Troie ay rennest downward to the se,
Ber witnesse of this word that seyd is here: 1550
That thilke day that ich untrewe be
To Troilus, myn owene herte fre,
That thow retourne bakward to thi welle,
And I with body and soule synke in helle!

'But that ye speke, awey thus for to go   1555
And leten alle youre frendes, God forbede
For any womman that ye sholden so,
And namely syn Troie hath now swich nede
Of help. And ek of o thyng taketh hede:
If this were wist, my lif lay in balaunce,   1560
And youre honour – God shilde us fro meschaunce!

'And if so be that pees heere-after take,
As alday happeth after anger game,
Whi, Lord, the sorwe and wo ye wolden make,

1539 wood: mad Athamante: Athamas (n.)   1540 Stix: Styx put: pit
1541 celestial: of heaven   1543 deite: deity infernal: of the lower regions
1544 satiry: satyrs fawny: fauns   1545 halve goddes: demigods
1546 tobreste: break in pieces   1547 trowe: believe   1548 Symois: Simois
(n.) arwe clere: bright arrow   1550 word: vow seyd: uttered
1551 thilke: that very same   1552 fre: noble   1553 welle: source
1556 leten: leave   1558 namely: especially   1560 lay: would lie in
balaunce: at risk   1561 shilde: protect   1562 take: come to pass   1563 As
joy constantly comes about after anger

1565   That ye ne dorste come ayeyn for shame!
        And er that ye juparten so youre name,
        Beth naught to hastif in this hoote fare,
        For hastif man ne wanteth nevere care.

        'What trowe ye the peple ek al aboute
1570   Wolde of it seye? It is ful light t'arede:
        They wolden seye, and swere it out of doute,
        That love ne drof yow naught to don this dede,
        But lust voluptuous and coward drede.
        Thus were al lost, ywys, myn herte deere,
1575   Youre honour, which that now shyneth so clere.

        'And also thynketh on myn honeste,
        That floureth yet, how foule I sholde it shende,
        And with what filthe it spotted sholde be,
        If in this forme I sholde with yow wende.
1580   Ne though I lyved unto the werldes ende,
        My name sholde I nevere ayeynward wynne;
        Thus were I lost, and that were routhe and synne.

        'And forthi sle with resoun al this hete!
        Men seyn, "The suffrant overcomith," parde;
1585   Ek "Whoso wol han lief, he lief moot lete."'

1565 ne dorste: would not dare ayeyn: back   1566 juparten: endanger
1567 to: too hastif: hasty hoote: fiery fare: behaviour   1568 wanteth: lacks
care: sorrow   1570 light t'arede: easy to guess   1571 out of
doute: certainly   1572 drof: impelled   1573 lust voluptuous: desire for
sensual gratification coward: cowardly   1574 were al: would be entirely
1575 clere: brightly   1576 And give some thought too to my good name
1577 floureth: flourishes foule: shamefully shende: defile
1578 filthe: infamy spotted: stained   1579 forme: manner   1580 Ne
though: even if   1581 name: good name ayeynward wynne: get back again
1582 lost: ruined   1583 sle . . . this hete: put an end to this passion
1584 suffrant: patient one   1585-6 Also, 'Whoever will have something he
wants, must give up something he wants (lief = something desired).' In this
way make the best of what must be

Thus maketh vertu of necessite
By pacience, and thynk that lord is he
Of Fortune ay that naught wole of hire recche,
And she ne daunteth no wight but a wrecche.

'And trusteth this: that certes, herte swete,   1590
Er Phebus suster, Lucina the sheene,
The Leoun passe out of this Ariete,
I wol ben here, withouten any wene.
I mene, as helpe me Juno, hevenes quene,
The tenthe day, but if that deth m'assaile,   1595
I wol yow sen withouten any faille.'

'And now, so this be soth,' quod Troilus,
'I shal wel suffre unto the tenthe day,
Syn that I se that nede it mot be thus.
But for the love of God, if it be may,   1600
So late us stelen priveliche away;
For evere in oon, as for to lyve in reste,
Myn herte seyth that it wol be the beste.'

'O mercy, God, what lif is this?' quod she.
'Allas, ye sle me thus for verray tene!   1605
I se wel now that ye mystrusten me,
For by youre wordes it is wel yseene.
Now for the love of Cinthia the sheene,
Mistrust me nought thus causeles, for routhe,
Syn to be trewe I have yow plight my trouthe.   1610

1587 lord: master   1588 recche: care   1589 daunteth: overcomes
1591–2 Before the sun's sister, the bright moon, having left this (present) sign
of Aries, passes the sign of Leo (and the intervening signs of Taurus, Gemini
and Cancer; n.)   1593 wene: doubt   1595 but if that: unless
m'assaile: assails me   1596 withouten any faille: for certain
1597 so: provided that   1598 suffre: endure   1599 nede: necessarily
1601 priveliche: secretly   1602 evere in oon: always   1605 sle: slay   verray
tene: sheer vexation   1608 Cinthia: the moon (n.)   1609 causeles: without
cause   for routhe: for pity's sake   1610 plight: pledged   trouthe: loyalty

'And thynketh wel that somtyme it is wit
To spende a tyme, a tyme for to wynne;
Ne, parde, lorn am I naught fro yow yit,
Though that we ben a day or two atwynne.
1615   Drif out the fantasies yow withinne,
And trusteth me, and leveth ek youre sorwe,
Or here my trouthe: I wol naught lyve tyl morwe.

'For if ye wiste how soore it doth me smerte,
Ye wolde cesse of this; for, God, thow wost,
1620   The pure spirit wepeth in myn herte
To se yow wepen that I love most,
And that I mot gon to the Grekis oost.
Ye, nere it that I wiste remedie
To come ayeyn, right here I wolde dye!

1625   'But certes, I am naught so nyce a wight
That I ne kan ymaginen a wey
To come ayeyn that day that I have hight,
For who may holde a thing that wol awey?
My fader naught, for al his queynte pley!
1630   And by my thrift, my wendyng out of Troie
Another day shal torne us alle to joie.

'Forthi with al myn herte I yow biseke,
If that yow list don ought for my preyere,
And for that love which that I love yow eke,
1635   That er that I departe fro yow here,
That of so good a confort and a cheere

1611 **is wit**: makes good sense   1612 **wynne**: gain   1613 **lorn**: lost
1614 **atwynne**: apart   1615 **fantasies**: delusions   **yow withinne**: within you
1616 **leveth**: leave   1617 **here my trouthe**: take my word for it   **tyl
morwe**: another day   1618 **doth me smerte**: pains me   1619 **cesse of**: cease
from   1620 **pure spirit**: very spirit   1623 **nere it**: were it not
remedie: means   1625 **nyce**: foolish   1626 **ymaginen**: devise
1627 **ayeyn**: back   **hight**: promised   1628 **holde**: retain   **wol** (go)
1629 **naught**: i.e. cannot   **queynte pley**: ingenious contrivance   1630 **by my
thrift**: if I succeed   1633 **ought**: anything   **for my preyere**: at my request

I may yow sen that ye may brynge at reste
Myn herte, which that is o poynt to breste.

'And over al this I prey yow,' quod she tho,
'Myn owene hertes sothfast suffisaunce,   1640
Syn I am thyn al hol, withouten mo,
That whil that I am absent, no plesaunce
Of oother do me fro youre remembraunce;
For I am evere agast, for-why men rede
That love is thyng ay ful of bisy drede.   1645

'For in this world ther lyveth lady non,
If that ye were untrewe – as God defende! –
That so bitraised were or wo-bigon
As I, that alle trouthe in yow entende.
And douteles, if that ich other wende,   1650
I ner but ded; and er ye cause fynde,
For Goddes love, so beth me naught unkynde!'

To this answerde Troilus and seyde,
'Now God, to whom ther nys no cause ywrye,
Me glade, as wys I nevere unto Criseyde,   1655
Syn thilke day I saugh hire first with yĕ,
Was fals, ne nevere shal til that I dye.
At shorte wordes, wel ye may me leve.
I kan na more; it shal be founde at preve.'

1638 o poynt to: about to   1639 over al this: in addition   1640 sothfast
suffisaunce: true fulfilment   1641 al hol: completely withouten mo: without
any others, alone   1642–3 . . . no delight in another make you forget me
1644 agast: afraid   1645 bisy: anxious   1647 defende: forbid
1648 bitraised: betrayed were: would be wo-bigon: overwhelmed with
sorrow   1649 entende: hope for, expect   1650 ich other wende: I thought
otherwise   1651 ner but ded: would be as good as dead er ye cause
fynde: until you have reason to be   1652 so beth . . . naught: don't be
unkynde: cruel   1654 ywrye: hidden   1655 Me glade: make me happy
wys: certainly as   1657 fals: unfaithful shal: shall be   1658 At shorte
wordes: briefly leve: believe   1659 founde at preve: proved by trial

1660   'Grant mercy, goode myn, iwys!' quod she,
        'And blisful Venus lat me nevere sterve
        Er I may stonde of plesaunce in degree
        To quyte hym wel that so wel kan deserve;
        And while that God my wit wol me conserve,
1665   I shal so don, so trewe I have yow founde,
        That ay honour to me-ward shal rebounde.

        'For trusteth wel that youre estat roial,
        Ne veyn delit, nor only worthinesse
        Of yow in werre or torney marcial,
1670   Ne pompe, array, nobleye, or ek richesse
        Ne made me to rewe on youre destresse,
        But moral vertu, grounded upon trouthe –
        That was the cause I first hadde on yow routhe!

        'Eke gentil herte and manhod that ye hadde,
1675   And that ye hadde, as me thoughte, in despit
        Every thyng that souned into badde,
        As rudenesse and poeplissh appetit,
        And that youre resoun bridlede youre delit:
        This made, aboven every creature,
1680   That I was youre, and shal while I may dure.

1660 **Grant mercy:** thank you **goode myn:** my treasure
1661 **blisful:** blessed   1662 **of plesaunce in degree:** in so happy a situation
1663 **quyte:** repay   1664 **wit:** mind, reason **me conserve:** preserve for me
1665 **don:** act   1666 **to me-ward:** towards me **rebounde:** return
1667 **estat:** rank, status   1668 **veyn delit:** empty pleasure
worthinesse: distinction, preeminence   1669 **torney marcial:** tournament
1670 **pompe:** grandeur **array:** splendour **nobleye:** nobility **richesse:** riches
1672 **grounded:** founded   1674 **gentil:** nobly courteous **manhod:** manly
qualities   1675 **hadde . . . in despit:** disdained   1676 **souned into:** tended
towards   1677 **rudenesse:** crudeness, boorishness **poeplissh appetit:** vulgar
desires   1678 **bridlede:** reined in **delit:** gratification of desire
1679 **made:** caused it to be   1680 **youre:** yours **dure:** live

'And this may lengthe of yeres naught fordo,
Ne remuable Fortune deface.
But Juppiter, that of his myght may do
The sorwful to be glad, so yeve us grace
Or nyghtes ten to meten in this place,   1685
So that it may youre herte and myn suffise!
And fareth now wel, for tyme is that ye rise.'

And after that they longe ypleyned hadde,
And ofte ykist, and streite in armes folde,
The day gan rise, and Troilus hym cladde,   1690
And rewfullich his lady gan byholde,
As he that felte dethes cares colde,
And to hire grace he gan hym recomaunde –
Wher hym was wo, this holde I no demaunde.

For mannes hed ymagynen ne kan,   1695
N'entendement considere, ne tonge telle
The cruele peynes of this sorwful man,
That passen every torment down in helle.
For whan he saugh that she ne myghte dwelle,
Which that his soule out of his herte rente,   1700
Withouten more out of the chaumbre he wente.

Explicit liber quartus.

1681 **fordo:** destroy   1682 **remuable:** changeable **deface:** obliterate
1683 **do:** cause   1685 **Or nyghtes ten:** before (the passing of) ten nights
1687 **fareth now wel:** now farewell   1688 **ypleyned:** lamented
1689 **ykist:** kissed **streite:** tightly **in armes folde:** embraced   1690 **hym
cladde:** dressed   1691 **rewfullich:** ruefully, sorrowfully   1693 **hym
recomaunde:** commend himself   1694 There is no question (*demaunde*)
about whether (*wher*) he was unhappy   1696 **entendement:** understanding
considere: think about   1698 **passen:** surpass   1700 **rente:** tore
1701 **Withouten more:** without more ado *Explicit, etc.*: Here ends the fourth
book

BOOK 5

Incipit liber quintus.

Aprochen gan the fatal destyne
That Joves hath in disposicioun,
And to yow, angry Parcas, sustren thre,
Committeth to don execucioun;
For which Criseyde moste out of the town,   5
And Troilus shal dwellen forth in pyne
Til Lachesis his thred no lenger twyne.

The golde-tressed Phebus heighe on-lofte
Thries hadde alle with his bemes cleene
The snowes molte, and Zepherus as ofte   10
Ibrought ayeyn the tendre leves grene,
Syn that the sone of Ecuba the queene
Bigan to love hire first for whom his sorwe
Was al, that she departe sholde a-morwe.

Incipit, etc.: Here begins the fifth book   1 **fatal:** fated **destyne:** destiny
2 **disposicioun:** (his) power to control   3 **Parcas:** Fates
4 **Committeth:** entrusts **don execucioun:** carry out   5 **moste out:** must go
out   6 **dwellen:** remain **forth:** afterwards **pyne:** suffering
7 **Lachesis:** second of the Fates **his thred:** the thread of his life **twyne:** twist,
spin   8–11 The sun on high above (*on-lofte*), adorned with golden tresses,
three times had melted the snows with his pure (*cleene*) beams, and the west
wind (*Zepherus*) as often had brought back the tender green foliage   12 **Syn
that:** since **Ecuba:** Hecuba (Troilus's mother)   14 **sholde:** was to
a-morwe: in the morning

15 Ful redy was at prime Diomede
    Criseyde unto the Grekis oost to lede,
    For sorwe of which she felt hire herte blede,
    As she that nyste what was best to rede.
    And trewely, as men in bokes rede,
20 Men wiste nevere womman han the care,
    Ne was so loth out of a town to fare.

    This Troilus, withouten reed or loore,
    As man that hath his joies ek forlore,
    Was waytyng on his lady evere more
25 As she that was the sothfast crop and more
    Of al his lust or joies heretofore.
    But Troilus, now far-wel al thi joie,
    For shaltow nevere sen hire eft in Troie!

    Soth is that while he bood in this manere,
30 He gan his wo ful manly for to hide,
    That wel unnethe it sene was in his chere;
    But at the yate ther she sholde out ride,
    With certeyn folk he hoved hire t'abide,
    So wo-bigon, al wolde he naught hym pleyne,
35 That on his hors unnethe he sat for peyne.

    For ire he quook, so gan his herte gnawe,
    Whan Diomede on horse gan hym dresse,
    And seyde to hymself this ilke sawe:

15–16 Diomede was all prepared at 9.00 a.m. to conduct Criseyde to the Greek army 18 **to rede**: as a plan, to do 20 **care**: sorrow 21 **loth**: unwilling **fare**: depart 22 **reed**: plan **loore**: instructions 23 **forlore**: lost 24 **waytyng on**: waiting for **evere more**: continually 25 **sothfast**: true **crop and more**: growing tip and root (i.e. beginning and end) 26 **lust**: pleasure **heretofore**: before this 28 **shaltow**: you shall **sen**: see **eft**: again 29 **Soth is**: true it is **bood**: waited 31 That it was scarcely visible in his expression 32 **sholde**: was to 33 **hoved**: lingered **hire t'abide**: to wait for her 34 **al**: although **hym pleyne**: complain 35 **unnethe**: with difficulty **for peyne**: because of his suffering 36 **ire**: rage **quook**: shook **gnawe**: to feel a gnawing pain 37 **gan hym dresse**: mounted 38 **sawe**: speech

'Allas,' quod he, 'thus foul a wrecchednesse,
Whi suffre ich it? Whi nyl ich it redresse?   40
Were it nat bet atones for to dye
Than evere more in langour thus to drye?

'Whi nyl I make atones riche and pore
To have inough to doone er that she go?
Why nyl I brynge al Troie upon a roore?   45
Whi nyl I slen this Diomede also?
Why nyl I rather with a man or two
Stele hire away? Whi wol I this endure?
Whi nyl I helpen to myn owen cure?'

But why he nolde don so fel a dede,   50
That shal I seyn, and whi hym liste it spare:
He hadde in herte alweyes a manere drede
Lest that Criseyde, in rumour of this fare,
Sholde han ben slayn – lo, this was al his care.
And ellis, certeyn, as I seyde yore,   55
He hadde it don, withouten wordes more.

Criseyde, whan she redy was to ride,
Ful sorwfully she sighte, and seyde 'Allas!'
But forth she moot, for aught that may bitide;
Ther is non other remedie in this cas.   60
And forth she rit ful sorwfully a pas.
What wonder is, though that hire sore smerte,
Whan she forgoth hire owen swete herte?

39 **foul**: despicable **wrecchednesse**: misery   40 **suffre ich**: do I endure **nyl ich**: won't I **redresse**: set right   41 **atones**: at once   42 **langour**: suffering **drye**: endure   43 **riche and pore**: one and all   45 **roore**: uproar 46 **slen**: kill   49 **cure**: remedy   50 **fel**: violent **dede**: deed, act   51 **hym liste it spare**: he chose to refrain from it   52 **a manere drede**: a kind of fear 53 **rumour**: the uproar **fare**: action, conduct   54 **care**: concern 55 **ellis**: otherwise **yore**: previously   58 **sighte**: sighed   59 But she must leave, whatever may happen   60 **cas**: situation   61 **rit** (= *rideth*): rides **a pas**: at walking pace   62 **hire sore smerte**: it pained her grievously 63 **forgoth**: gives up

This Troilus, in wise of curteysie,
65   With hauk on honde and with an huge route
Of knyghtes, rood and did hire companye,
Passyng al the valeye fer withoute,
And ferther wolde han riden, out of doute,
Ful fayn, and wo was hym to gon so sone;
70   But torne he moste, and it was ek to done.

And right with that was Antenor ycome
Out of the Grekis oost, and every wight
Was of it glad, and seyde he was welcome.
And Troilus, al nere his herte light,
75   He peyned hym with al his fulle myght
Hym to withholde of wepyng atte leeste,
And Antenor he kiste and made feste.

And therwithal he moste his leve take,
And caste his eye upon hire pitously,
80   And neer he rood, his cause for to make,
To take hire by the honde al sobrely.
And Lord, so she gan wepen tendrely!
And he ful softe and sleighly gan hire seye,
'Now holde youre day, and do me nat to deye.'

85   With that his courser torned he aboute
With face pale, and unto Diomede
No word he spak, ne non of al his route;
Of which the sone of Tideus took hede,
As he that koude more than the crede

64 **in wise of curteysie**: by way of courtesy   65 **hauk on honde**: hawk on his wrist   **route**: company   66 **rood**: rode   **did**: kept   68 **out of doute**: certainly   69 **fayn**: gladly   **wo was hym**: he was miserable   70 But turn back he must, and it had to be done   72 **oost**: army   74 And Troilus, although his heart was not cheerful   75 **peyned hym**: strove   76 **withholde of**: restrain from **leeste**: least   77 **made feste**: made much of him   78 **therwithal**: thereupon **moste**: must   79 **caste his eye**: looked   80 **neer**: closer   **make**: plead   81 **sobrely**: gravely   83 **softe**: softly   **sleighly**: stealthily   84 **holde youre day**: keep to your appointed day   **do**: cause   85 **courser**: warhorse   **torned he aboute**: he turned back   88 **hede**: note   89 **koude**: knew   **crede**: rudiments

In swich a craft, and by the reyne hire hente;   90
And Troilus to Troie homward he wente.

This Diomede, that ledde hire by the bridel,
Whan that he saugh the folk of Troie aweye,
Thoughte, 'Al my labour shal nat ben on ydel,
If that I may, for somwhat shal I seye,   95
For at the werste it may yet shorte oure weye.
I have herd seyd ek tymes twyes twelve,
"He is a fool that wol foryete hymselve."'

But natheles, this thoughte he wel ynough,
That 'Certeynlich I am aboute nought,   100
If that I speke of love or make it tough;
For douteles, if she have in hire thought
Hym that I gesse, he may nat ben ybrought
So soon awey; but I shal fynde a meene
That she naught wite as yet shal what I mene.'   105

This Diomede, as he that koude his good,
Whan tyme was, gan fallen forth in speche
Of this and that, and axed whi she stood
In swich disese, and gan hire ek biseche
That if that he encresse myghte or eche   110
With any thyng hire ese, that she sholde
Comaunde it hym, and seyde he don it wolde.

90 **craft:** art **reyne:** rein **hente:** took   93 **aweye:** were gone
94 **labour:** effort **on ydel:** in vain   96 **shorte:** shorten **weye:** journey
97 **twyes:** twice   98 **foryete:** forget   100 **aboute nought:** wasting my time
101 **make it tough:** am too pressing   103–4 **ybrought . . . awey:** put out of
her mind   104 **meene:** means   105 **wite:** know **mene:** intend   106 **koude**
his good: knew what was to his advantage   107 **tyme was:** it seemed
opportune **fallen forth in speche:** engage in conversation   108 **stood:** was
109 **disese:** distress   110 **encresse:** increase **eche:** add to   111 **ese:** comfort
112 **seyde he don it wolde:** (he) said he would do it

For treweliche he swor hire as a knyght
That ther nas thyng with which he myghte hire
    plese,
115   That he nolde don his peyne and al his myght
To don it, for to don hire herte an ese;
And preyede hire she wolde hire sorwe apese,
And seyde, 'Iwis, we Grekis kan have joie
To honouren yow as wel as folk of Troie.'

120   He seyde ek thus: 'I woot yow thynketh straunge –
Ne wonder is, for it is to yow newe –
Th'aquayntaunce of thise Troianis to chaunge
For folk of Grece, that ye nevere knewe.
But wolde nevere God but if as trewe
125   A Grek ye sholde among us alle fynde
As any Troian is, and ek as kynde.

'And by the cause I swor yow right, lo, now,
To ben youre frend, and helply, to my myght,
And for that more aquayntaunce ek of yow
130   Have ich had than another straunger wight,
So fro this forth, I pray yow, day and nyght
Comaundeth me, how soore that me smerte,
To don al that may like unto youre herte;

'And that ye me wolde as youre brother trete,
135   And taketh naught my frendshipe in despit;
And though youre sorwes be for thynges grete –

114–16 That there was nothing by which he might please her that he would
not take trouble (*don his peyne*) and do his utmost (*al his myght*) to perform
in order to gratify her   117 **apese:** calm   120 **yow thynketh straunge:** it
seems to you strange   121 **Ne wonder is:** it is no wonder
122 **aquayntaunce:** companionship   124–5 But God forbid that you should
not find as faithful a Greek among us all   127 **by the cause:** because
128 **helply:** helpful **to my myght:** to the best of my ability   129 **for
that:** because   130 **straunger wight:** stranger   131 **fro this forth:** from now
on   132 **how soore that me smerte:** however grievously it may pain me
133 **like:** be pleasing   134 **trete:** treat   135 **taketh ... in despit:** scorn

Not I nat whi – but out of more respit
Myn herte hath for t'amende it gret delit;
And if I may youre harmes nat redresse,
I am right sory for youre hevynesse,   140

'For though ye Troians with us Grekes wrothe
Han many a day ben, alwey yet, parde,
O god of Love in soth we serven bothe.
And for the love of God, my lady fre,
Whomso ye hate, as beth nat wroth with me,   145
For trewely, ther kan no wyght yow serve
That half so loth youre wratthe wold disserve.

'And nere it that we ben so neigh the tente
Of Calcas, which that sen us bothe may,
I wolde of this yow telle al myn entente –   150
But this enseled til anothir day.
Yeve me youre hond; I am, and shal ben ay,
God helpe me so, while that my lyf may dure,
Youre owene aboven every creature.

'Thus seyde I nevere er now to womman born,   155
For God myn herte as wisly glade so,
I loved never womman here-biforn
As paramours, ne nevere shal no mo.
And for the love of God, beth nat my fo,
Al kan I naught to yow, my lady deere,   160
Compleyne aright, for I am yet to leere.

137 I do not know why – but without further delay 138 amende: relieve
it: i.e. Criseyde's sorrowful state delit: pleasure 139 harmes: sorrows
redresse: set right 140 hevynesse: sadness 141 wrothe: angry 143 O: one
in soth: truly 144 fre: noble 145 Whomso: whomsoever as beth nat: do
not be 147 loth: reluctantly wratthe: anger disserve: deserve 148 nere
it: were it not 149 Of Calchas, who can see us both 150 myn
entente: what I have in mind 151 this: this is enseled: sealed up
153 dure: last 155 womman born: living woman 156 For as certainly as
God may make my heart happy 157 here-biforn: before this 158 As
paramours: in the manner of a lover mo: more 159 fo: enemy
160 Al: although 161 aright: correctly leere: be taught

'And wondreth nought, myn owen lady bright,
Though that I speke of love to yow thus blyve;
For I have herd er this of many a wight,
165   Hath loved thyng he nevere saigh his lyve.
Ek I am nat of power for to stryve
Ayeyns the god of Love, but hym obeye
I wole alwey; and mercy I yow preye.

'Ther ben so worthi knyghtes in this place,
170   And ye so fayr, that everich of hem alle
Wol peynen hym to stonden in youre grace.
But myghte me so faire a grace falle,
That ye me for youre servant wolde calle,
So lowely ne so trewely yow serve
175   Nil non of hem as I shal til I sterve.'

Criseyde unto that purpos lite answerde,
As she that was with sorwe oppressed so
That, in effect, she naught his tales herde
But here and ther, now here a word or two.
180   Hire thoughte hire sorwful herte brast a-two,
For whan she gan hire fader fer espie
Wel neigh down of hire hors she gan to sye.

But natheles she thonketh Diomede
Of al his travaile and his goode cheere,
185   And that hym list his frendshipe hire to bede;

162 **wondreth nought**: do not be amazed   163 **blyve**: quickly
165 **thyng**: something **saigh**: saw **his lyve**: in his life   166 **nat of
power**: unable **stryve**: contend   169 **so**: such   170 **everich**: every one
171 **peynen hym**: endeavour **stonden**: be **grace**: favour   172–5 But might
such good fortune befall me, that you would call me your servant, none of
them will serve you as humbly or loyally as I shall till I die
176 **purpos**: argument **lite answerde**: made little response   177 **As she
that**: for she **oppressed**: overcome   178 **tales**: conversation   180 **Hire
thoughte**: it seemed to her **brast a-two**: broke in two   181 **fer**: in the
distance **espie**: make out   182 **Wel neigh**: very nearly **sye**: sink   184–5 For
all his trouble and kind welcome, and that he wished to offer her his
friendship

And she accepteth it in good manere,
And wol do fayn that is hym lief and dere,
And tristen hym she wolde, and wel she myghte,
As seyde she; and from hire hors sh'alighte.

Hire fader hath hire in his armes nome,   190
And twenty tyme he kiste his doughter sweete,
And seyde, 'O deere doughter myn, welcome!'
She seyde ek she was fayn with hym to mete,
And stood forth muwet, milde, and mansuete.
But here I leve hire with hire fader dwelle.   195
And forth I wol of Troilus yow telle.

To Troie is come this woful Troilus,
In sorwe aboven alle sorwes smerte,
With feloun look and face dispitous.
Tho sodeynly doun from his hors he sterte,   200
And thorugh his paleis, with a swollen herte,
To chaumbre he wente; of nothyng took he hede,
Ne non to hym dar speke a word for drede.

And ther his sorwes that he spared hadde
He yaf an issue large, and 'Deth!' he criede;   205
And in his throwes frenetik and madde
He corseth Jove, Appollo, and ek Cupide;
He corseth Ceres, Bacus, and Cipride,
His burthe, hymself, his fate, and ek nature,
And, save his lady, every creature.   210

186 in good manere: civilly   187 that: whatever lief: pleasing
188 tristen: trust   189 sh'alighte: she dismounted   190 nome: taken
193 mete: meet   194 stood forth: stood there muwet: mute
milde: mild-mannered mansuete: meek   196 forth: further
198 aboven: beyond smerte: painful   199 feloun: sullen dispitous: pitiless
200 Tho: then sterte: sprang   201 paleis: palace swollen: full
202 hede: notice   203 Ne non: nor did anyone dar: dare drede: fear
204 spared: held back   205 yaf an issue large: gave full vent to
206 throwes: throes frenetik: frantic   207 corseth: curses
208 Bacus: Bacchus Cipride: Venus   209 burthe: birth   210 save: except

To bedde he goth, and walwith ther and torneth
In furie, as doth he Ixion in helle,
And in this wise he neigh til day sojorneth.
But tho bigan his herte a lite unswelle
215   Thorugh teris, which that gonnen up to welle,
And pitously he cryde upon Criseyde,
And to hymself right thus he spak, and seyde,

'Wher is myn owene lady, lief and deere?
Wher is hire white brest? Wher is it, where?
220   Wher ben hire armes and hire eyen cleere
That yesternyght this tyme with me were?
Now may I wepe allone many a teere,
And graspe aboute I may, but in this place,
Save a pilowe, I fynde naught t'enbrace.

225   'How shal I do? Whan shal she come ayeyn?
I not, allas, whi lete ich hire to go;
As wolde God ich hadde as tho ben sleyn!
O herte myn, Criseyde, O swete fo!
O lady myn, that I love and na mo,
230   To whom for evermo myn herte I dowe,
Se how I dey – ye nyl me nat rescowe!

'Who seth yow now, my righte lode-sterre?
Who sit right now or stant in youre presence?
Who kan conforten now youre hertes werre?
235   Now I am gon, whom yeve ye audience?
Who speketh for me right now in myn absence?

211 **walwith**: writhes **torneth**: turns about   213 **wise**: manner **neigh til**: till
nearly **sojorneth**: remains   214 **tho**: then **lite**: little **unswelle**: become less
swollen   215 **up to welle**: to well up   216 **cryde**: called   220 **cleere**: bright
221 **yesternyght**: last night **this tyme**: at this time   223 **graspe**: feel
224 Except for a pillow, I find nothing to embrace   226 **not**: do not know
lete ich: I let   227 **As wolde God**: would to God **as tho**: then **sleyn**: slain
228 **fo**: foe   229 **na mo**: no others   230 **dowe**: dedicate   231 **dey**: am dying
ye nyl: if you will not **rescowe**: rescue   232 **seth**: sees **righte**: true
lode-sterre: guiding star   233 **sit** (= *sitteth*): sits **stant** (= *standeth*): stands
234 **youre hertes werre**: the conflict in your heart   235 **yeve ye audience**: do

Allas, no wight; and that is al my care,
For wel woot I, as yvele as I ye fare.

'How sholde I thus ten dayes ful endure,
Whan I the firste nyght have al this tene?   240
How shal she don ek, sorwful creature?
For tendernesse, how shal she ek sustene
Swich wo for me? O pitous, pale and grene
Shal ben youre fresshe, wommanliche face
For langour, er ye torne unto this place.'   245

And whan he fil in any slomberynges,
Anon bygynne he sholde for to grone
And dremen of the dredefulleste thynges
That myghte ben; as mete he were allone
In place horrible makyng ay his mone,   250
Or meten that he was amonges alle
His enemys, and in hire hondes falle.

And therwithal his body sholde sterte,
And with the stert al sodeynliche awake,
And swich a tremour fele aboute his herte   255
That of the fere his body sholde quake;
And therwithal he sholde a noyse make,
And seme as though he sholde falle depe
From heighe o-lofte; and thanne he wolde wepe,

237 **no wight**: no one **care**: sorrow   238 For I well know, you suffer as much
as I (do)   239 **ten dayes ful**: a full ten days   240 **tene**: affliction
241 **don**: get on   242 **For tendernesse**: because of her sensitive nature
sustene: bear   243 **pitous**: pitiful **grene**: sickly   245 **langour**: distress
torne: return   246 **fil**: fell **slomberynges**: slumber   247 **Anon**: at once
sholde: would **grone**: groan   248 **dredefulleste**: most frightening
249 **as**: such as **mete**: dream   250 **horrible**: appalling **mone**: lamentation
252 **in hire hondes falle**: fallen into their hands   253 **therwithal**: with that
sholde: would **sterte**: give a start   254 **stert**: start **awake**: would he
awaken   255 **tremour**: palpitation   256 **fere**: fear **sholde**: would
quake: tremble, shake   259 **o-lofte**: above

260 And rewen on hymself so pitously
     That wonder was to here his fantasie.
     Another tyme he sholde myghtyly
     Conforte hymself, and sein it was folie
     So causeles swich drede for to drye;
265 And eft bygynne his aspre sorwes newe,
     That every man myght on his sorwes rewe.

     Who koude telle aright or ful discryve
     His wo, his pleynt, his langour, and his pyne?
     Naught alle the men that han or ben on lyve.
270 Thow, redere, maist thiself ful wel devyne
     That swich a wo my wit kan nat diffyne;
     On ydel for to write it sholde I swynke,
     Whan that my wit is wery it to thynke.

     On hevene yet the sterres weren seene,
275 Although ful pale ywoxen was the moone,
     And whiten gan the orisonte shene
     Al estward, as it wont is for to doone;
     And Phebus with his rosy carte soone
     Gan after that to dresse hym up to fare
280 Whan Troilus hath sent after Pandare.

     This Pandare, that of al the day biforn
     Ne myghte han comen Troilus to se,
     Although he on his hed it hadde sworn

260 **rewen on**: feel sorry for **pitously**: piteously   261 **wonder was**: it was
astonishing **here**: hear **fantasie**: imaginings   262 **sholde**: would
myghtyly: greatly   263 **sein**: say   264 **causeles**: without cause **drede**: fear
drye: endure   265 **aspre**: bitter   267 **aright**: truly **ful discryve**: fully
describe   268 **pleynt**: lament **langour**: distress **pyne**: suffering   269 **han or
ben**: have (been) or are **on lyve**: alive   270 **redere**: reader **devyne**: guess
271 **wit**: mind **diffyne**: describe   272 **On ydel**: in vain **swynke**: labour, toil
273 **wit**: mind **wery**: weary   274 The stars were still visible in the sky
275 **ywoxen**: grown   276 **whiten**: become white **orisonte**: horizon
shene: bright   277 **estward**: towards the east **wont**: accustomed
278 **rosy**: rose-coloured **carte**: chariot   279 **dresse hym**: prepare **up to
fare**: to travel upwards   280 **after**: for   281 **of**: during   282 **Ne myghte han
comen**: was not able to come   283 **hed**: head

For with the kyng Priam al day was he,
So that it lay nought in his libertee   285
Nowher to gon – but on the morwe he wente
To Troilus, whan that he for hym sente.

For in his herte he koude wel devyne
That Troilus al nyght for sorwe wook;
And that he wolde telle hym of his pyne,   290
This knew he wel ynough, withoute book.
For which to chaumbre streght the wey he took,
And Troilus tho sobrelich he grette,
And on the bed ful sone he gan hym sette.

'My Pandarus,' quod Troilus, 'the sorwe   295
Which that I drye I may nat longe endure –
I trowe I shal nat lyven til to-morwe –
For which I wolde alweys, on aventure,
To the devysen of my sepulture
The forme; and of my moeble thow dispone   300
Right as the semeth best is for to done.

'But of the fir and flaumbe funeral
In which my body brennen shal to glede,
And of the feste and pleyes palestral
At my vigile, I prey the, tak good hede   305
That that be wel; and offre Mars my steede,
My swerd, myn helm; and, leve brother deere,
My sheld to Pallas yef, that shyneth cleere.

---

285 **it lay nought in his libertee**: he was not at liberty   286 **on the morwe**: the
next day   288 **devyne**: guess   289 **for**: because of **wook**: remained awake
291 **withoute book**: i.e. he did not need a book to tell him this
292 **streght**: directly   293 **tho**: then **sobrelich**: gravely **grette**: greeted
294 **ful sone**: very soon **hym sette**: sit down   298 **alweys**: in any event **on
aventure**: in case (I should die)   299–300 To describe to you the form of my
tomb; and dispose of my personal possessions   301 **the semeth best**: seems
best to you   302 **fir and flaumbe**: fire and flame   303 **brennen**: burn
glede: glowing embers   304 **feste**: ceremony **pleyes palestral**: athletic
games   305 **vigile**: wake   306 **wel**: well done **steede**: horse
307 **helm**: helmet **leve**: dear   308 **sheld**: shield **yef**: give **cleere**: brightly

'The poudre in which myn herte ybrend shal torne,
310   That preye I the thow take and it conserve
In a vessell that men clepeth an urne,
Of gold, and to my lady that I serve,
For love of whom thus pitouslich I sterve,
So yeve it hire, and do me this plesaunce,
315   To preye hire kepe it for a remembraunce.

'For wel I fele, by my maladie
And by my dremes now and yore ago,
Al certeynly that I mot nedes dye.
The owle ek, which that hette Escaphilo,
320   Hath after me shright al thise nyghtes two.
And god Mercurye, of me now, woful wrecche,
The soule gyde, and whan the liste, it fecche!'

Pandare answerde and seyde, 'Troilus,
My deere frend, as I have told the yore,
325   That it is folye for to sorwen thus,
And causeles, for which I kan namore.
But whoso wil nought trowen reed ne loore,
I kan nat sen in hym no remedie,
But lat hym worthen with his fantasie.

330   'But, Troilus, I prey the, tel me now
If that thow trowe er this that any wight
Hath loved paramours as wel as thow?
Ye, God woot, and fro many a worthi knyght
Hath his lady gon a fourtenyght,

309 **poudre:** ashes **ybrend:** burnt   310 **take:** collect **conserve:** preserve
311 **clepeth:** call   313 **pitouslich:** piteously **sterve:** die
314 **plesaunce:** favour   315 **for:** as **remembraunce:** memento
316 **maladie:** illness   317 **yore:** long   318 **nedes:** necessarily   319 **hette:** is
called **Escaphilo:** Ascalaphus (n.)   320 **shright:** shrieked **nyghtes two:** past
two nights   321–2 **of me . . . The soule gyde:** guide my soul (n.)   322 **the
liste:** it pleases you **fecche:** fetch away   324 **yore:** formerly
325 **sorwen:** sorrow   326 **kan namore:** cannot say or do any more
327 **reed:** advice **loore:** instruction   328 I can see no cure for him
329 **worthen:** remain **fantasie:** delusion   332 **paramours:** passionately
God knows   334 **fourtenyght:** fortnight

And he nat yet made halvendel the fare.   335
What nede is the to maken al this care?

'Syn day by day thow maist thiselven se
That from his love, or ellis from his wif,
A man mot twynnen of necessite –
Ye, though he love hire as his owene lif   340
Yet nyl he with hymself thus maken strif.
For wel thou woost, my leve brother deere,
That alwey frendes may nat ben yfeere.

'How don this folk that seen hire loves wedded
By frendes myght, as it bitit ful ofte,   345
And sen hem in hire spouses bed ybedded?
God woot, they take it wisly, faire, and softe,
For-whi good hope halt up hire herte o-lofte.
And for they kan a tyme of sorwe endure,
As tyme hem hurt, a tyme doth hem cure.   350

'So shuldestow endure, and laten slide
The tyme, and fonde to ben glad and light;
Ten dayes nys so longe nought t'abide.
And syn she the to comen hath bihyght,
She nyl hire heste breken for no wight.   355
For dred the nat that she nyl fynden weye
To come ayein; my lif that dorste I leye.

---

335 **halvendel the fare**: half the fuss   336 What need is there for you to
lament so much?   339 **twynnen**: separate   341 **nyl he**: he will not **maken
strif**: quarrel   342 **woost**: know **leve**: dear   343 **yfeere**: together   344 **don
this folk**: do these people behave   345 By **frendes myght**: through the
powerful influence of friends **bitit** (= *bitideth*): happens   346 **ybedded**: put to
bed   347 **wisly**: sensibly **faire**: quietly **softe**: without objection   348 **halt** (=
holdeth): holds **o-lofte**: high   349 **for**: because   350 **hurt** (= *hurteth*): hurts
doth hem cure: heals them   351 **shuldestow**: should you **laten slide**: let pass
by   352 **fonde**: try **light**: cheerful   353 **abide**: wait   354 **the**: you
bihyght: promised   355 **heste**: promise **wight**: person   356 **dred the nat**: do
not doubt   357 To come back; I dare wager my life on that

'Thi swevnes ek and al swich fantasie
Drif out and lat hem faren to meschaunce,
360   For they procede of thi malencolie
That doth the fele in slep al this penaunce.
A straw for alle swevenes signifiaunce!
God helpe me so, I counte hem nought a bene!
Ther woot no man aright what dremes mene.

365   'For prestes of the temple tellen this,
That dremes ben the revelaciouns
Of goddes, and as wel they telle, ywis,
That they ben infernals illusiouns;
And leches seyn that of complexiouns
370   Proceden they, or fast, or glotonye –
Who woot in soth thus what thei signifie?

'Ek oother seyn that thorugh impressiouns,
As if a wight hath faste a thyng in mynde,
That therof cometh swiche avysiouns;
375   And other seyn, as they in bokes fynde,
That after tymes of the yer, by kynde,
Men dreme, and that th'effect goth by the moone –
But leve no drem, for it is nought to doone.

358–9 Banish your dreams (*swevnes*) and all such imaginings (*fantasie*), and
let them go (*faren*) to the devil (*meschaunce*)!   360 **procede of**: originate
from **malencolie**: melancholy   361 **doth the**: makes you
penaunce: suffering   362 **A straw for**: i.e. an expression of contempt
swevenes: dreams'   363 **counte**: value **nought a bene**: not worth a bean
364 **Ther woot no man**: no man knows **aright**: correctly
365 **prestes**: priests   368 **infernals illusiouns**: delusions from hell
369 **leches**: physicians **complexiouns**: temperaments, the balance of the
'humours'   370 **fast**: fasting **glotonye**: over-indulgence   371 **woot in
soth**: knows in truth   372 **oother**: others   373 **faste**: firmly
374 **therof**: through that **avysiouns**: dreams   375 **other seyn**: other people
say   376–7 That people dream according to the season of the year, by
nature, and that the outcome (*effect*) is governed (*goth*) by the moon
378 **leve**: believe **to doone**: to be done

'Wel worthe of dremes ay thise olde wives,
And treweliche ek augurye of thise fowles,   380
For fere of which men wenen lese here lyves,
As ravenes qualm, or shrichyng of thise owles.
To trowen on it bothe fals and foul is.
Allas, allas, so noble a creature
As is a man shal dreden swich ordure!   385

'For which with al myn herte I the biseche,
Unto thiself that al this thow foryyve;
And ris now up withowten more speche,
And lat us caste how forth may best be dryve
This tyme, and ek how fresshly we may lyve   390
Whan that she comth, the which shal be right
        soone.
God helpe me so the beste is thus to doone

'Ris, lat us speke of lusty lif in Troie
That we han led, and forth the tyme dryve;
And ek of tyme comyng us rejoie,   395
That bryngen shal oure blisse now so blyve;
And langour of thise twyes dayes fyve
We shal therwith so foryete or oppresse
That wel unneth it don shal us duresse.

379 May it always be well with these old woman, regarding dreams (i.e. let old women believe in dreams), and truly, also, divination (*augurye*) by means of these birds   381 **fere:** fear **wenen lese:** think to lose   382 Such as ravens' croaking (*qualm*) or these owls' screeching   383 **trowen on:** believe in **fals:** wrong **foul:** shameful   385 **dreden:** fear **ordure:** rubbish   387 That you spare yourself (for believing) all this   388 **ris:** rise   389 **caste:** consider **forth . . . dryve:** spent   390 **fresshly:** joyously   393 **lusty:** cheerful   394 **forth . . . dryve:** pass   395 **us rejoie:** let us rejoice   396 **blyve:** soon   397 **langour:** suffering **twyes dayes fyve:** twice five (i.e. ten) days   398 **foryete:** forget **oppresse:** repress   399 **unneth:** scarcely **don:** cause **duresse:** hardship

400 'This town is ful of lordes al aboute,
    And trewes lasten al this mene while.
    Go we pleye us in som lusty route
    To Sarpedoun, nat hennes but a myle;
    And thus thow shalt the tyme wel bygile,
405 And dryve it forth unto that blisful morwe
    That thow hire se, that cause is of thi sorwe.

    'Now ris, my deere brother Troilus,
    For certes it non honour is to the
    To wepe and in thi bedde to jouken thus;
410 For trewelich, of o thyng trust to me:
    If thow thus ligge a day, or two, or thre,
    The folk wol wene that thow for cowardise
    The feynest sik, and that thow darst nat rise!'

    This Troilus answerde, 'O brother deere,
415 This knowen folk that han ysuffred peyne,
    That though he wepe and make sorwful cheere
    That feleth harm and smert in every veyne,
    No wonder is; and though ich evere pleyne,
    Or alwey wepe, I am no thyng to blame,
420 Syn I have lost the cause of al my game.

    'But syn of fyne force I mot arise,
    I shal arise as soone as evere I may;
    And God, to whom myn herte I sacrifice,

---

401 **trewes:** truces, times of truce **mene while:** meanwhile   402 **pleye us:** amuse ourselves **lusty route:** lively company   403 **nat hennes but a myle:** only a mile from here   404 **bygile:** wile away   405 **dryve . . . forth:** pass   409 **jouken:** roost (as a falcon), lie at rest   410 For truly, believe me about one thing   411 **ligge:** lie   412 **wene:** suppose   413 **The feynest sik:** pretend to be ill **darst:** dare   415 **ysuffred:** suffered   416–18 It is no wonder if someone who feels pain (*harm*) and anguish (*smert*) in every part (*veyne*) of his body should weep and behave sorrowfully (*make sorwful cheere*), and although I always lament . . .   419 **no thyng:** in no way   420 **game:** happiness   421 **syn of fyne force:** since of sheer necessity

So sende us hastely the tenthe day!
For was ther nevere fowel so fayn of May   425
As I shal ben whan that she comth in Troie
That cause is of my torment and my joie.

'But whider is thi reed,' quod Troilus,
'That we may pleye us best in al this town?'
'By God, my conseil is,' quod Pandarus,   430
'To ride and pleye us with kyng Sarpedoun.'
So longe of this they speken up and down
Til Troilus gan at the laste assente
To rise, and forth to Sarpedoun they wente.

This Sarpedoun, as he that honourable   435
Was evere his lyve, and ful of heigh largesse,
With al that myghte yserved ben on table
That deynte was, al coste it gret richesse,
He fedde hem day by day, that swich noblesse,
As seyden bothe the mooste and ek the leeste,   440
Was nevere er that day wist at any feste.

Nor in this world ther is non instrument
Delicious, thorugh wynd or touche of corde,
As fer as any wight hath evere ywent,
That tonge telle or herte may recorde,   445
That at that feste it nas wel herd acorde;
Ne of ladys ek so fair a compaignie
On daunce, er tho, was nevere iseye with ie.

---

424 **hastely:** soon   425 **fowel:** bird   426 **comth:** comes   428 **whider is thi
reed:** where do you advise (us to go)   429 **pleye us:** amuse ourselves
430 **conseil:** advice   432 **up and down:** back and forth   433 **at the
laste:** finally   436 **his lyve:** during his life **largesse:** generosity
438 **deynte:** choice, delicious **al coste it gret richesse:** even if it cost a fortune
439 **noblesse:** magnificence   440 **mooste and ek the leeste:** greatest and also
the least (i.e. everyone)   441 **wist:** known **feste:** festivity   442–3
. . . delightful-sounding wind or string instrument   444 **fer:** far
wight: person **ywent:** supposed   445 **recorde:** remember   446 **wel herd
acorde:** heard played harmoniously   448 **On daunce:** in the dance **er
tho:** before that time **iseye:** seen **ie:** eye

But what availeth this to Troilus,
450   That for his sorwe nothyng of it roughte?
For evere in oon his herte pietous
Ful bisyly Criseyde, his lady, soughte.
On hire was evere al that his herte thoughte,
Now this, now that, so faste ymagenynge
455   That glade, iwis, kan hym no festeyinge.

Thise ladies ek that at this feste ben,
Syn that he saugh his lady was aweye,
It was his sorwe upon hem for to sen,
Or for to here on instrumentes so pleye.
460   For she that of his herte berth the keye
Was absent, lo, this was his fantasie –
That no wight sholde maken melodie.

Nor ther nas houre in al the day or nyght,
Whan he was there as no wight myghte hym heere,
465   That he ne seyde, 'O lufsom lady bryght,
How have ye faren syn that ye were here?
Welcome, ywis, myn owne lady deere!'
But weylaway, al this nas but a maze.
Fortune his howve entended bet to glaze!

470   The lettres ek that she of olde tyme
Hadde hym ysent, he wolde allone rede
An hondred sithe atwixen noon and prime,

449 **availeth this:** use was this   450 **for:** because of **nothyng of it
roughte:** cared nothing about it   451 **evere in oon:** continually
pietous: pitiful   452 **bisyly:** intently   455 **glade:** make happy
festeyinge: festivity   458 **sen:** look   460 **For:** because **berth** (= *bereth*):
holds   461 **fantasie:** caprice   462 **melodie:** music   463 **Nor ther nas:** nor
was there   464 **there as:** where **heere:** hear   465 **lufsom:** lovely
466 **faren:** fared, got on   468 **weylaway:** alas **nas but a maze:** was only a
delusion   469 Fortune intended to hoodwink him further (n.)   470 **of olde
tyme:** formerly   472 **sithe:** times **atwixen noon and prime:** between the
periods of noon (12.00–15.00) and prime (6.00–9.00), i.e. all afternoon and
night, until next morning

Refiguryng hire shap, hire wommanhede,
Withinne his herte, and every word or dede
That passed was; and thus he drof t'an ende   475
The ferthe day, and seyde he wolde wende.

And seyde, 'Leve brother Pandarus,
Intendestow that we shal here bleve
Til Sarpedoun wol forth congeyen us?
Yet were it fairer that we toke oure leve.   480
For Goddes love, lat us now soone at eve
Oure leve take, and homward lat us torne,
For treweliche, I nyl nat thus sojourne.'

Pandare answerde, 'Be we comen hider
To fecchen fir and rennen hom ayein?   485
God help me so, I kan nat tellen whider
We myghte gon, if I shal sothly seyn,
Ther any wight is of us more feyn
Than Sarpedoun; and if we hennes hye
Thus sodeynly, I holde it vilanye.   490

'Syn that we seyden that we wolde bleve
With hym a wowke, and now, thus sodeynly,
The ferthe day to take of hym owre leve –
He wolde wondren on it, trewely!
Lat us holden forth oure purpos fermely;   495
And syn that ye bihighten hym to bide,
Holde forward now, and after lat us ride.'

---

473 **Refiguryng**: picturing to himself **shap**: figure
wommanhede: womanliness   475 **drof t'an ende**: passed   476 **ferthe**: fourth
wende: go   477 **Leve**: dear   478 **Intendestow**: do you intend **bleve**: remain
479 **congeyen us**: bid us goodbye (i.e. invite us to go)   480 **were it fairer**: it
would be more seemly   481 **soone at eve**: this very evening   482 **torne**: go
483 **sojourne**: stay   484 **hider**: here   485 **fecchen fir**: borrow a light
rennen: run   486 **whider**: where   487 **sothly**: truly   488 **Ther**: where
feyn: glad   489 **hennes hye**: hurry away from here   490 **holde**: consider
vilanye: bad manners   492 **wowke**: week   494 **wondren on**: be very
surprised at   495 **holden**: keep to **purpos**: plan   496 **bihighten**: promised
bide: stay   497 **Holde forward**: keep your promise **after**: afterwards

Thus Pandarus, with alle peyne and wo,
Made hym to dwelle; and at the wikes ende
500 Of Sarpedoun they toke hire leve tho,
And on hire wey they spedden hem to wende.
Quod Troilus, 'Now Lord me grace sende,
That I may fynden at myn hom-comynge
Criseyde comen –' and therwith gan he synge.

505 'Ye, haselwode!' thoughte this Pandare,
And to hymself ful softeliche he seyde,
'God woot, refreyden may this hote fare,
Er Calkas sende Troilus Criseyde!'
But natheles, he japed thus, and pleyde,
510 And swor, ywys, his herte hym wel bihighte
She wolde come as soone as evere she myghte.

Whan they unto the paleys were ycomen
Of Troilus, they doun of hors alighte,
And to the chambre hire wey than han they nomen;
515 And into tyme that it gan to nyghte
They spaken of Criseÿde the brighte;
And after this, whan that hem bothe leste,
They spedde hem fro the soper unto reste.

On morwe, as soone as day bygan to clere,
520 This Troilus gan of his slep t'abrayde,
And to Pandare, his owen brother deere,
'For love of God,' ful pitously he sayde,
'As go we sen the palais of Criseyde;

498 **peyne**: effort   499 **wikes**: week's   500 **tho**: then   501 **spedden hem**: hastened **wende**: go   502 **me grace sende**: send me the grace
504 **comen**: returned   505 **Ye, haselwode**: a likely story! (n.)
506 **softeliche**: softly   507 God knows, this ardent behaviour may cool off (*refreyden*)   509 **japed**: joked **pleyde**: was playful   510 **bihighte**: promised, assured   513 **of hors alighte**: dismounted from their horses
514 **nomen**: taken   515 **into tyme**: until the time **nyghte**: become night
516 **spaken**: spoke   517 **hem bothe leste**: it pleased them both   519 **On morwe**: the next morning **clere**: dawn   520 **t'abrayde**: to wake up   523 **As go we sen**: let us go and see

For syn we yet may have namore feste,
So lat us sen hire paleys atte leeste.'   525

And therwithal, his meyne for to blende,
A cause he fond in towne for to go,
And to Criseydes hous they gonnen wende.
But Lord, this sely Troilus was wo!
Hym thoughte his sorwful herte braste a-two.   530
For whan he saugh hire dores spered alle,
Wel neigh for sorwe adoun he gan to falle.

Therwith, whan he was war and gan biholde
How shet was every wyndow of the place,
As frost, hym thoughte, his herte gan to colde;   535
For which with chaunged dedlich pale face,
Withouten word, he forthby gan to pace,
And as God wolde, he gan so faste ride
That no wight of his contenance espide.

Than seide he thus: 'O paleys desolat,   540
O hous of houses whilom best ihight,
O paleys empty and disconsolat,
O thow lanterne of which queynt is the light,
O paleys, whilom day, that now art nyght,
Wel oughtestow to falle, and I to dye,   545
Syn she is went that wont was us to gye!

---

524 **namore feste**: any greater pleasure   526 **his meyne**: the members of his
household **blende**: deceive   527 **cause**: pretext **fond**: invented   528 **gonnen
wende**: went   529 **sely**: poor   530 **Hym thoughte**: it seemed to him
braste: would burst **a-two**: in two   531 **spered**: barred   533 **Therwith**: at
the same time **war**: aware   534 **shet**: shut   535 **hym thoughte**: it seemed to
him **colde**: grow cold   536 **dedlich**: deathly   537 **forthby . . . pace**: pass by
538 **wolde**: would have it   539 **of his contenance espide**: noticed his
expression   540 **desolat**: deserted   541 **whilom best ihight**: formerly called
the best   542 **disconsolat**: cheerless   543 **queynt**: quenched, put out
545 **oughtestow** (= *oughtest thow*): ought you **falle**: fall in ruins   546 Since
she, who was accustomed to guide us, has gone

'O paleis, whilom crowne of houses alle,
Enlumyned with sonne of alle blisse!
O ryng, fro which the ruby is out falle,
550   O cause of wo, that cause hast ben of lisse!
Yet, syn I may no bet, fayn wolde I kisse
Thy colde dores, dorste I for this route;
And farwel shryne, of which the seynt is oute!'

Therwith he caste on Pandarus his yë,
555   With chaunged face, and pitous to biholde;
And whan he myghte his tyme aright aspie,
Ay as he rood to Pandarus he tolde
His newe sorwe and ek his joies olde,
So pitously and with so ded an hewe
560   That every wight myghte on his sorwe rewe.

Fro thennesforth he rideth up and down,
And every thyng com hym to remembraunce
As he rood forby places of the town
In which he whilom hadde al his plesaunce.
565   'Lo, yonder saugh ich last my lady daunce;
And in that temple, with hire eyen clere,
Me kaughte first my righte lady dere.

'And yonder have I herd ful lustyly
My dere herte laugh; and yonder pleye
570   Saugh ich hire ones ek ful blisfully;

547 **crowne**: crowning example   548 **Enlumyned**: illuminated **sonne**: sun
blisse: joy   549 **out falle**: fallen out   550 **lisse**: joy   551 Yet since I can't do
better, I'd gladly kiss   552 **dorste I**: if I dared **for this route**: because of this
crowd   553 **farwel**: farewell **seynt is out**: saint is absent   554 **caste ... his
yë**: looked   556 **his tyme aright aspie**: see an opportune moment   557 **Ay as
he rood**: continually as he rode along   559 **ded**: deathly pale
560 **wight**: person   561 **Fro thennesforth**: after that   562 **com hym to
remembraunce**: brought back memories to him   563 **forby**: past
564 **whilom**: formerly **plesaunce**: delight   565 **yonder**: over there **saugh
ich**: saw I   566 **clere**: bright   567 My own true, beloved lady first captured
me   568 **lustyly**: cheerfully   569 **pleye**: enjoy herself   570 **ones**: once
blisfully: happily

And yonder ones to me gan she seye,
"Now goode swete, love me wel, I preye";
And yond so goodly gan she me biholde
That to the deth myn herte is to hire holde.

'And at that corner, in the yonder hous,   575
Herde I myn alderlevest lady deere
So wommanly, with vois melodious,
Syngen so wel, so goodly, and so cleere
That in my soule yet me thynketh ich here
The blisful sown; and in that yonder place   580
My lady first me took unto hire grace.'

Thanne thoughte he thus: 'O blisful lord Cupide,
Whan I the proces have in my memorie
How thow me hast wereyed on every syde,
Men myght a book make of it, lik a storie.   585
What nede is the to seke on me victorie,
Syn I am thyn and holly at thi wille?
What joie hastow thyn owen folk to spille?

'Wel hastow, lord, ywroke on me thyn ire,
Thow myghty god, and dredful for to greve!   590
Now mercy, lord! Thow woost wel I desire
Thi grace moost of alle lustes leeve,
And lyve and dye I wol in thy byleve;

572 **goode swete**: my excellent sweetheart   573 And over there she looked at
me so graciously   574 **holde**: bound, obliged   576 **alderlevest**: most
beloved   577 **So wommanly**: in so womanly a way   578 **goodly**: beautifully
cleere: clearly   579 **me thynketh**: it seems to me   **ich here**: I hear
580 **sown**: sound   581 **grace**: favour   582 **blisful**: blessed
583 **proces**: course of events   584 **me hast wereyed**: have made war upon
me   585 **storie**: story, history   586 **nede is the**: need is there for you
seke: seek   587 **thyn**: yours (i.e. thine)   **holly at thi wille**: completely in your
power   588 **hastow** (= *hast thow*): do you have   **spille**: destroy   589 **Wel
hastow**: you have well   **ywroke**: avenged   **ire**: anger   590 **dredful**: terrible
greve: offend   591 **woost**: know   592 **of**: above   **lustes leeve**: dear
pleasures   593 **byleve**: faith

For which I n'axe in guerdoun but o bone –
595   That thow Criseyde ayein me sende sone.

'Destreyne hire herte as faste to retorne
As thow doost myn to longen hire to see;
Than woot I wel that she nyl naught sojorne.
Now blisful lord, so cruel thow ne be
600   Unto the blood of Troie, I preye the,
As Juno was unto the blood Thebane,
For which the folk of Thebes caughte hire bane.'

And after this he to the yates wente
Ther as Criseyde out rood a ful good paas,
605   And up and down ther made he many a wente,
And to hymself ful ofte he seyde, 'Allas,
Fro hennes rood my blisse and my solas!
As wolde blisful God now, for his joie,
I myghte hire sen ayein come into Troie!

610   'And to the yonder hille I gan hire gyde,
Allas, and ther I took of hire my leve!
And yond I saugh hire to hire fader ride,
For sorwe of which myn herte shal tocleve;
And hider hom I com whan it was eve,
615   And here I dwelle out cast from alle joie,
And shal, til I may sen hire eft in Troie.'

594 For which I ask only one favour in reward   595 **ayein**: again
sone: soon   596 **Destreyne**: constrain **faste**: firmly   597 **longen**: long
598 **Than**: then **woot**: know **sojorne**: remain   599 Now blessed lord, do not
be so cruel   600 **blood**: lineage, blood royal   602 **caughte**: came by
bane: destruction   604 **Ther as**: where **a ful good paas**: briskly   605 **made
. . . many a wente**: took many a turn   607 **Fro hennes**: from here **rood**: rode
solas: joy   608 **As wolde . . . God**: would that God would grant that
610 **gyde**: guide   613 **tocleve**: split in two   614 **hider hom I com**: I came
home here

And of hymself ymagened he ofte
To ben defet, and pale, and waxen lesse
Than he was wont, and that men seyden softe,
'What may it be? Who kan the sothe gesse   620
Whi Troilus hath al this hevynesse?'
And al this nas but his malencolie,
That he hadde of hymself swich fantasie.

Another tyme ymaginen he wolde
That every wight that wente by the weye   625
Hadde of hym routhe, and that they seyen sholde,
'I am right sory Troilus wol deye.'
And thus he drof a day yet forth or tweye,
As ye have herd; swich lif right gan he lede
As he that stood bitwixen hope and drede.   630

For which hym likede in his songes shewe
Th'enchesoun of his wo, as he best myghte;
And made a song of wordes but a fewe,
Somwhat his woful herte for to lighte;
And whan he was from every mannes syghte,   635
With softe vois he of his lady deere,
That absent was, gan synge as ye may heere:

Canticus Troili

'O sterre, of which I lost have al the light,
With herte soor wel oughte I to biwaille
That evere derk in torment, nyght by nyght,   640

---

618 **defet**: disfigured **waxen lesse**: grown thinner   619 **was wont**: used to be
softe: quietly   620 **may it be**: can the matter be **sothe**: truth
621 **hevynesse**: sadness   622 **nas but**: was only   623 **fantasie**: imaginings
625 **wente by the weye**: passed by   626 **routhe**: pity **seyen**: say   628 **drof
. . . forth**: passed **tweye**: two   630 **drede**: fear   631 **hym likede**: it pleased
him **shewe**: to reveal   632 **Th'enchesoun of**: the reason for   633 **but**: only
634 **lighte**: cheer   635 **from**: out of   638 **sterre**: star   639 **soor**: grieving
biwaille: lament   640 **derk**: dark

Toward my deth with wynd in steere I saille;
For which the tenthe nyght, if that I faille
The gydyng of thi bemes bright an houre,
My ship and me Caribdis wol devoure.'

645   This song whan he thus songen hadde, soone
He fil ayeyn into his sikes olde;
And every nyght, as was his wone to doone,
He stood the brighte moone to byholde,
And al his sorwe he to the moone tolde,
650   And seyde, 'Ywis, whan thow art horned newe,
I shal be glad, if al the world be trewe!

'I saugh thyn hornes olde ek by the morwe
Whan hennes rood my righte lady dere
That cause is of my torment and my sorwe;
655   For which, O brighte Latona the clere,
For love of God, ren faste aboute thy spere!
For whan thyne hornes newe gynnen sprynge,
Than shal she come that may my blisse brynge.'

The dayes moore and lenger every nyght
660   Than they ben wont to be, hym thoughte tho,
And that the sonne went his cours unright
By lenger weye than it was wont to do;
And seyde, 'Ywis, me dredeth evere mo
The sonnes sone, Pheton, be on lyve,
665   And that his fader carte amys he dryve.'

641 **in steere**: astern, at my back   642 **faille**: lack   643 **gydyng**: guidance
bemes: beams **an houre**: for an hour   644 **Caribdis**: Charybdis (see n.)
devoure: swallow up   645 **songen**: sung   646 **fil ayeyn**: fell back **sikes**
olde: former sighs   647 **wone**: custom   650 **art horned newe**: have your new
horns (i.e. the new, crescent moon)   651 **trewe**: faithful   652 **hornes**
olde: i.e. the last quarter of the old moon **by the morwe**: in the morning
653 **hennes**: from here **righte**: true   655 **Latona**: the moon (see n.)
clere: bright   656 **ren**: run **spere**: orbit   657 **sprynge**: appear
659 **moore**: greater (i.e. longer)   660 **wont**: accustomed **hym thoughte tho**: it
seemed to him then   661 **went his cours**: travelled his course
unright: wrongly   663 **me dredeth**: I fear **evere mo**: constantly   664 The
s̲o̲n̲n̲e̲s̲ s̲o̲n̲e̲,̲ P̲h̲e̲t̲o̲n̲,̲ is alive   665 **fader**: father's **carte**: chariot **amys**: awry

Upon the walles faste ek wolde he walke,
And on the Grekis oost he wolde se;
And to hymself right thus he wolde talke:
'Lo, yonder is myn owene lady free,
Or ellis yonder, ther tho tentes be;   670
And thennes comth this eyr, that is so soote
That in my soule I fele it doth me boote.

'And hardily, this wynd that more and moore
Thus stoundemele encresseth in my face
Is of my ladys depe sikes soore.   675
I preve it thus: for in noon other place
Of al this town, save onliche in this space,
Fele I no wynd that sowneth so lik peyne;
It seyth, "Allas! Whi twynned be we tweyne?"'

This longe tyme he dryveth forth right thus   680
Til fully passed was the nynthe nyght;
And ay bisyde hym was this Pandarus,
That bisily did al his fulle myght
Hym to conforte and make his herte light,
Yevyng hym hope alwey the tenthe morwe   685
That she shal come and stynten al his sorwe.

Upon that other syde ek was Criseyde,
With wommen fewe, among the Grekis stronge,
For which ful ofte a day 'Allas,' she seyde,
'That I was born! Wel may myn herte longe   690
After my deth, for now lyve I to longe.

667 se: look   669 free: noble   670 tho: those   671 thennes: from there
eyr: breeze soote: sweet   672 doth me boote: does me good
673 hardily: certainly   674 stoundemele: hour by hour   675 sikes: sighs
soore: sad   676 preve: prove   677 save: except onliche: only
678 sowneth: sounds   679 twynned: separated tweyne: two   680 dryveth
forth: passes   681 passed: gone by   682 ay bisyde hym: always at his side
683 Who solicitously did his utmost   684 light: cheerful
685 Yevyng: giving   686 stynten: bring to an end   688 stronge: powerful
689 ful ofte a day: many times a day   690–91 longe After: long for
691 to: too

Allas, and I ne may it nat amende,
For now is wors than evere yet I wende!

'My fader nyl for nothyng do me grace
695   To gon ayeyn, for naught I kan hym queme;
And if so be that I my terme pace,
My Troilus shal in his herte deme
That I am fals, and so it may wel seme:
Thus shal ich have unthonk on every side –
700   That I was born so weilaway the tide!

'And if that I me putte in jupartie
To stele awey by nyght, and it bifalle
That I be kaught, I shal be holde a spie;
Or elles – lo, this drede I moost of alle –
705   If in the hondes of som wrecche I falle,
I nam but lost, al be myn herte trewe.
Now, myghty God, thow on my sorwe rewe!'

Ful pale ywoxen was hire brighte face,
Hire lymes lene, as she that al the day
710   Stood, whan she dorste, and loked on the place
Ther she was born, and ther she dwelt hadde ay;
And al the nyght wepyng, allas, she lay.
And thus despeired, out of alle cure,
She ladde hire lif, this woful creature.

692 **amende:** put right   693 **wende:** imagined   694–5 My father will not
allow me (*do me grace*) to go back at any price (*for nothyng*), whatever I do
to please (*queme*) him   696 **terme:** appointed time (of ten days) **pace:** go
beyond   697 **deme:** suppose   698 **fals:** unfaithful   699 **unthonk:** reproach
on every side: on all sides   700 **weilaway the tide:** alas the time!
702 **stele:** steal **bifalle:** happen   703 **kaught:** captured **holde:** considered
704 **drede:** fear   705 **wrecche:** ruffian   706 I am as good as lost, although
my heart may be faithful   707 **thow . . . rewe:** may you have pity
708 **ywoxen:** grown **brighte:** lovely   709 **lymes:** limbs **lene:** thin
710 **dorste:** dared   711 **Ther:** where **dwelt hadde ay:** had always lived
713 **despeired:** in despair **out of:** beyond **cure:** help, remedy   714 **ladde:** led

Ful ofte a day she sighte ek for destresse,   715
And in hireself she wente ay purtraynge
Of Troilus the grete worthynesse,
And al his goodly wordes recordynge
Syn first that day hire love bigan to springe.
And thus she sette hire woful herte afire   720
Thorough remembraunce of that she gan desire.

In al this world ther nys so cruel herte
That hire hadde herd compleynen in hire sorwe
That nolde han wepen for hire peynes smerte,
So tendrely she weep, bothe eve and morwe.   725
Hire nedede no teris for to borwe!
And this was yet the werste of al hire peyne:
Ther was no wight to whom she dorste hire
           pleyne.

Ful rewfully she loked upon Troie,
Biheld the toures heigh and ek the halles;   730
'Allas,' quod she, 'the plesance and the joie,
The which that now al torned into galle is,
Have ich had ofte withinne the yonder walles!
O Troilus, what dostow now?' she seyde.
'Lord, wheyther thow yet thenke upon Criseyde?   735

'Allas, I ne hadde trowed on youre loore
And went with yow, as ye me redde er this!
Than hadde I now nat siked half so soore.

716 in hireself . . . purtraynge: picturing to herself   718 goodly: gracious
recordynge: remembering   719 springe: grow   720 afire: on fire
721 remembraunce: memory   722 so cruel herte: so cruel-hearted a person
723 That hire hadde herd: if he had heard her   724 nolde han wepen: would
not have wept smerte: painful, bitter   725 weep: wept bothe eve and
morwe: all day long   726 Hire nedede: she needed borwe: borrow
727 werste: worst   728 dorste: dared hire pleyne: confide her sorrow
729 rewfully: sorrowfully   730 toures: towers   731 plesance: delight
732 galle: bitter sorrow   734 dostow: do you do   735 wheyther thow
yet: do you still   736 Alas that I did not trust in your advice
737 redde: advised   738 Than: then siked: sighed soore: bitterly

Who myghte han seyd that I hadde don amys
740   To stele awey with swich oon as he ys?
But al to late comth the letuarie
Whan men the cors unto the grave carie.

'To late is now to speke of that matere.
Prudence, allas, oon of thyne eyen thre
745   Me lakked alwey, er that I come here!
On tyme ypassed wel remembred me,
And present tyme ek koud ich wel ise,
But future tyme, er I was in the snare,
Koude I nat sen; that causeth now my care.

750   'But natheles, bityde what bityde,
I shal to-morwe at nyght, by est or west,
Out of this oost stele in som manere syde,
And gon with Troilus where as hym lest.
This purpos wol ich holde, and this is best.
755   No fors of wikked tonges janglerie,
For evere on love han wrecches had envye.

'For whoso wol of every word take hede,
Or reulen hym by every wightes wit,
Ne shal he nevere thryven, out of drede;
760   For that that som men blamen evere yit,
Lo, other manere folk comenden it.

739 **myghte**: could **don amys**: acted wrongly   740 **stele**: steal **swich oon**: such a person   741 **to**: too **comth**: comes **letuarie**: medicine
742 **cors**: corpse   743 **To late is**: it is too late   744 **eyen thre**: three eyes (n.)   745 **Me lakked**: I lacked   746 I remembered past time clearly
747 **koud ich**: I could **ise**: see   749 **care**: sorrow   750 **bityde what bityde**: come what may   751 **est**: east   752 **stele**: steal away **in som manere syde**: on one side or the other   753 **where as**: where **hym lest**: it pleases him   755–6 It does not matter about the gossip (*janglerie*) of malicious tongues, for wretches have always been envious of love
757 **whoso**: whosoever **hede**: notice   758 **reulen hym**: conduct himself by: according to **wit**: opinion   759 **thryven**: prosper   760 **that that**: that which **blamen**: censure   761 **manere**: kind of **comenden**: praise

And as for me, for al swich variaunce,
Felicite clepe I my suffisaunce.

'For which, withouten any wordes mo,
To Troie I wole, as for conclusioun.'   765
But God it wot, er fully monthes two,
She was ful fer fro that entencioun!
For bothe Troilus and Troie town
Shal knotteles thorughout hire herte slide;
For she wol take a purpos for t'abide.   770

This Diomede, of whom yow telle I gan,
Goth now withinne hymself ay arguynge,
With al the sleghte and al that evere he kan,
How he may best, with shortest taryinge,
Into his net Criseydes herte brynge.   775
To this entent he koude nevere fyne;
To fisshen hire he leyde out hook and lyne.

But natheles, wel in his herte he thoughte
That she nas nat withoute a love in Troie,
For nevere sythen he hire thennes broughte   780
Ne koude he sen hire laughe or maken joie.
He nyst how best hire herte for t'acoye;
'But for t'asay,' he seyde, 'it naught ne greveth,
For he that naught n'asaieth naught n'acheveth.'

762 **for al**: despite, notwithstanding **variaunce**: diversity of opinion
763 I call happiness enough for me   764 **For which**: because of which
765 **wole**: mean to go **as for conclusioun**: definitely   766 But God knows,
before two months were completely over . . .   767 **fer fro**: far from
769 **knotteles**: i.e. without impediment, like a thread without knots
slide: slip   770 **take a purpos**: decide **abide**: stay   772 **ay arguynge**: always
debating   773 **sleghte**: cunning **al that evere he kan**: everything that he
knows how to do   774 **taryinge**: delay   776 **entent**: purpose, end
fyne: desist   777 **fisshen**: fish for   780 **sythen**: since **thennes**: from there
781 **maken joie**: be happy   782 **t'acoye**: to soothe   783–4 'But to try
(**t'asay**),' he said, 'does no harm, for he who does not try anything (*naught
n'asaieth*), does not achieve anything.'

785   Yet seyde he to hymself upon a nyght,
       'Now am I nat a fool, that woot wel how
       Hire wo for love is of another wight,
       And hereupon to gon assaye hire now?
       I may wel wite it nyl nat ben my prow,
790   For wise folk in bookes it expresse,
       "Men shal nat wowe a wight in hevynesse."

       'But whoso myghte wynnen swich a flour
       From hym for whom she morneth nyght and day,
       He myghte seyn he were a conquerour.'
795   And right anon, as he that bold was ay,
       Thoughte in his herte, 'Happe how happe may,
       Al sholde I dye, I wol hire herte seche!
       I shal namore lesen but my speche.'

       This Diomede, as bokes us declare,
800   Was in his nedes prest and corageous,
       With sterne vois and myghty lymes square,
       Hardy, testif, strong, and chivalrous
       Of dedes, lik his fader Tideus;
       And som men seyn he was of tonge large;
805   And heir he was of Calydoigne and Arge.

       Criseyde mene was of hire stature;
       Therto of shap, of face, and ek of cheere,
       Ther myghte ben no fairer creature.

788 **hereupon**: concerning this **assaye hire**: address myself to her
789 **wite**: know **my prow**: to my advantage   791 **wowe**: woo **wight**: person
hevynesse: sadness   792 **flour**: flower   793 **morneth**: longs   794 **seyn**: say
conquerour: conqueror, winner   795 **right anon**: at once   796 **Happe how
happe may**: come what may   797 **Al sholde I dye**: even if I should die
seche: seek   798 **lesen**: lose   799 **declare**: tell   800 **nedes**: affairs
prest: prompt   801 **myghty**: powerful **lymes**: limbs **square**: thick-set
802 **Hardy**: bold **testif**: headstrong **chivalrous**: knightly   804 **of tonge
large**: free with his tongue   805 **Calydoigne**: Calydon **Arge**: Argos
806 Criseyde was of average height   807 **Therto of shap**: in addition, in
figure

And ofte tymes this was hire manere:
To gon ytressed with hire heres clere   810
Doun by hire coler at hire bak byhynde,
Which with a thred of gold she wolde bynde;

And, save hire browes joyneden yfeere,
Ther nas no lak, in aught I kan espien;
But for to speken of hire eyen cleere,   815
Lo, trewely, they writen that hire syen
That Paradis stood formed in hire yën;
And with hire riche beaute evere more
Strof love in hire ay, which of hem was more.

She sobre was, ek symple, and wys withal,   820
The best ynorisshed ek that myghte be,
And goodly of hire speche in general,
Charitable, estatlich, lusty, fre;
Ne nevere mo ne lakked hire pite;
Tendre-herted, slydynge of corage –   825
But trewely, I kan nat telle hire age.

And Troilus wel woxen was in highte,
And complet formed by proporcioun
So wel that kynde it nought amenden myghte;
Yong, fressh, strong, and hardy as lyoun;   830

810–11 To go about with her bright hair braided and hanging down over her
collar behind   812 **bynde:** tie   813 **save:** except that **browes:** eyebrows
joyneden yfeere: were joined together in the middle   814 **lak:** flaw
aught: anything **espien:** observe   815 **cleere:** bright   816 **that hire syen:** who
saw her   817 **formed:** modelled, mirrored   818 **evere more:** continually
819 Love ever contended in her as to which of them was greater
820 **sobre:** demure **symple:** unaffected **wys:** discreet **withal:** as well
821 **best ynorisshed:** most well-bred   822 **goodly:** gracious **in general:** in all
respects   823 **Charitable:** kindly **estatlich:** dignified **lusty:** vivacious
fre: generous   824 **ne lakked hire pite:** she did not lack compassion
825 **Tendre-herted:** soft-hearted **slydynge of corage:** irresolute (n.)
827 **woxen:** grown   828 **complet:** perfectly **by:** in   829 **kynde:** nature
amenden: improve upon   830 **fressh:** tireless **hardy:** brave

Trewe as stiel in ech condicioun;
Oon of the beste entecched creature
That is or shal whil that the world may dure.

And certeynly in storye it is yfounde
835   That Troilus was nevere unto no wight,
As in his tyme, in no degree secounde
In durryng don that longeth to a knyght.
Al myghte a geant passen hym of myght,
His herte ay with the first and with the beste
840   Stood paregal, to durre don that hym leste.

But for to tellen forth of Diomede:
It fel that after, on the tenthe day
Syn that Criseyde out of the citee yede,
This Diomede, as fressh as braunche in May,
845   Com to the tente ther as Calkas lay,
And feyned hym with Calkas han to doone;
But what he mente, I shal yow tellen soone.

Criseyde, at shorte wordes for to telle,
Welcomed hym and down hym by hire sette –
850   And he was ethe ynough to maken dwelle!
And after this, withouten longe lette,
The spices and the wyn men forth hem fette;
And forth they speke of this and that yfeere,
As frendes don, of which som shal ye heere.

831 **stiel**: steel **ech**: every **condicioun**: quality (or situation)
832 **entecched**: endowed, imbued (with good qualities)   833 **shal**: shall be
dure: last   835 **wight**: man   836 **in no degree**: in no way   837–40 In daring
to do (*durryng don*) that which befits (*longeth to*) a knight. Although a giant
might surpass him in strength (*myght*), his heart was always fully equal
(*paregal*) to the first and best in daring to do what he wished
842 **fel**: happened **after**: afterwards   843 **yede**: went   845 **ther as**: where
lay: stayed   846 And he pretended to have business to do with Calchas
847 **soone**: at once   848 **at shorte wordes**: briefly   849 Welcomed him and
had him sit beside her   850 **ethe**: easy **dwelle**: stay   851 **lette**: delay
852 **spices**: spiced cakes **fette**: fetched   853 **forth**: further

He gan first fallen of the werre in speche   855
Bitwixe hem and the folk of Troie town;
And of th'assege he gan hire ek biseche
To telle hym what was hire opynyoun;
Fro that demaunde he so descendeth down
To axen hire if that hire straunge thoughte   860
The Grekis gise and werkes that they wroughte;

And whi hire fader tarieth so longe
To wedden hire unto som worthy wight.
Criseyde, that was in hire peynes stronge
For love of Troilus, hire owen knyght,   865
As ferforth as she konnyng hadde or myght
Answerde hym tho; but as of his entente,
It semed nat she wiste what he mente.

But natheles, this ilke Diomede
Gan in hymself assure, and thus he seyde: 870
'If ich aright have taken of yow hede,
Me thynketh thus, O lady myn, Criseyde,
That syn I first hond on youre bridel leyde,
Whan ye out come of Troie by the morwe,
Ne koude I nevere sen yow but in sorwe.   875

'Kan I nat seyn what may the cause be,
But if for love of som Troian it were,
The which right sore wolde athynken me
That ye for any wight that dwelleth there
Sholden spille a quarter of a tere   880

855 **fallen . . . in speche**: to talk   857 **assege**: siege   859 **demaunde**: request
descendeth down: proceeds   860 **hire . . . thoughte**: seemed to her
861 **gise**: ways, manners **werkes**: deeds **wroughte**: did   862 **tarieth**: delays
864 **stronge**: severe   866 **ferforth**: far **konnyng**: ability **myght**: power
867 **as of**: as for   869 **ilke**: same   870 **assure**: grow confident   871 If I have
observed you correctly   873 **hond . . . leyde**: laid hand   874 **by the
morwe**: in the morning   875 I have only ever been able to see you in
sorrow   877 **But if**: unless   878 **sore**: deeply **athynken**: grieve
880 **tere**: tear

Or pitously youreselven so bigile –
For dredeles, it is nought worth the while.

'The folk of Troie, as who seyth, alle and some
In prisoun ben, as ye youreselven se;
885   For thennes shal nat oon on-lyve come
For al the gold atwixen sonne and se.
Trusteth wel, and understondeth me,
Ther shal nat oon to mercy gon on-lyve,
Al were he lord of worldes twiës fyve!

890   'Swich wreche on hem for fecchynge of Eleyne
Ther shal ben take, er that we hennes wende,
That Manes, which that goddes ben of peyne,
Shal ben agast that Grekes wol hem shende,
And men shul drede, unto the worldes ende,
895   From hennesforth to ravysshen any queene,
So cruel shal oure wreche on hem be seene.

'And but if Calkas lede us with ambages –
That is to seyn, with double wordes slye,
Swiche as men clepe a word with two visages –
900   Ye shal wel knowen that I naught ne lie,
And al this thyng right sen it with youre yë,
And that anon, ye nyl nat trowe how sone;
Now taketh hede, for it is for to doone.

---

881 **pitously**: pitifully **bigile**: delude   882 **dredeles**: without a doubt   883 **as who seyth**: as one might say **alle and some**: one and all   885 **thennes**: from there **oon**: one **on-lyve come**: escape alive   886 **atwixen**: between **sonne**: sun **se**: sea   888 Not one shall survive to receive mercy   889 **Al were he**: even if he were **twiës**: twice   890 **wreche**: vengeance **fecchynge**: abduction   891 **take**: taken **hennes wende**: leave here   893 **agast**: afraid **shende**: ruin   894 **shul drede**: shall fear   895 **hennesforth**: from now on **ravysshen**: abduct   897 **but if**: unless **lede us**: is leading us on **ambages**: ambiguities   898 **double**: duplicitous **slye**: wily, tricky   899 **clepe**: call **with two visages**: double-faced, equivocating   900 **naught ne lie**: am not lying   901 **sen**: (you shall) see   902 **trowe**: believe **sone**: soon   903 **is for to doone**: has to happen

'What! Wene ye youre wise fader wolde
Han yeven Antenor for yow anon, 905
If he ne wiste that the cite sholde
Destroied ben? Whi, nay, so mote I gon!
He knew ful wel ther shal nat scapen oon
That Troian is; and for the grete feere
He dorste nat ye dwelte lenger there. 910

'What wol ye more, lufsom lady deere?
Lat Troie and Troian fro youre herte pace!
Drif out that bittre hope, and make good cheere,
And clepe ayeyn the beaute of youre face
That ye with salte teris so deface, 915
For Troie is brought in swich a jupartie
That it to save is now no remedie.

'And thenketh wel, ye shal in Grekis fynde
A moore parfit love, er it be nyght,
Than any Troian is, and more kynde, 920
And bet to serven yow wol don his myght.
And if ye vouchesauf, my lady bright,
I wol ben he to serven yow myselve,
Yee, levere than be lord of Greces twelve!'

And with that word he gan to waxen red, 925
And in his speche a litel wight he quok,
And caste asyde a litel wight his hed,
And stynte a while; and afterward he wok,
And sobreliche on hire he threw his lok,

904 **Wene ye:** do you think   905 **yeven:** exchanged   907 **so mote I gon:** as I
may live   908 **scapen:** escape **oon:** one   910 **dorste nat ye dwelte:** dared not
let you remain   911 **wol ye more:** more do you want **lufsom:** lovely
912 **pace:** pass   913 **Drif out:** banish **make good cheere:** be in good spirits
914 **clepe ayeyn:** summon back   915 **deface:** disfigure
916 **jupartie:** danger   917 That no remedy can save it now   918 **in
Grekis:** among the Greeks   919 **parfit:** perfect   921 and (one who), to serve
you better, will do his utmost   922 **vouchesauf:** permit   923 **he:** the one
924 **Yee:** yes, indeed **levere:** rather   925 **waxen:** grow   926 **a litel wight:** a
little bit **quok:** trembled   927 **caste:** turned   928 **stynte:** paused
wok: roused himself   929 **sobreliche**

930 And seyde, 'I am, al be it yow no joie
     As gentil man as any wight in Troie.

     'For if my fader Tideus,' he seyde,
     'Ilyved hadde, ich hadde ben er this
     Of Calydoyne and Arge a kyng, Criseyde!
935 And so hope I that I shal yet, iwis.
     But he was slayn – allas, the more harm is! –
     Unhappily at Thebes al to rathe,
     Polymytes and many a man to scathe.

     'But herte myn, syn that I am youre man –
940 And ben the first of whom I seche grace –
     To serve yow as hertely as I kan,
     And evere shal whil I to lyve have space,
     So, er that I departe out of this place,
     Ye wol me graunte that I may to-morwe,
945 At bettre leyser, telle yow my sorwe.'

     What sholde I telle his wordes that he seyde?
     He spak inough for o day at the meeste.
     It preveth wel; he spak so that Criseyde
     Graunted on the morwe, at his requeste,
950 For to speken with hym at the leeste –
     So that he nolde speke of swich matere.
     And thus to hym she seyde, as ye may here,

930 **al be it yow:** although it be to you   931 **gentil:** nobly born   933 Had
lived, I would have been before now   935 **shal:** shall be   936 **the more harm
is:** the more's the pity   937 **Unhappily:** unluckily **al to rathe:** all too soon
938 To the detriment of Polynices (n.) and many a man   939 **man:** servant,
vassal (in love)   940 **ben:** (since you) are **seche grace:** seek favour
941 **hertely:** sincerely   942 **space:** space of time   943 **So:** as long as
944 **graunte:** permit   945 **At bettre leyser:** at greater length
946 **What:** why   947 **o:** one **meeste:** most   948 **preveth wel:** proves
successful   950 **at the leeste:** at least   951 **So that he nolde:** as long as he
would not   952 **here:** hear

As she that hadde hire herte on Troilus
So faste that ther may it non arace;
And strangely she spak, and seyde thus: 955
'O Diomede, I love that ilke place
Ther I was born; and Joves, for his grace,
Delyvere it soone of al that doth it care!
God, for thy myght, so leve it wel to fare!

'That Grekis wolde hire wrath on Troie wreke,   960
If that they myght, I knowe it wel, iwis;
But it shal naught byfallen as ye speke,
And God toforn! And forther over this,
I woot my fader wys and redy is,
And that he me hath bought, as ye me tolde,   965
So deere, I am the more unto hym holde.

'That Grekis ben of heigh condicioun
I woot ek wel; but certeyn, men shal fynde
As worthi folk withinne Troie town,
As konnyng, and as parfit, and as kynde,   970
As ben bitwixen Orkades and Inde;
And that ye koude wel yowre lady serve,
I trowe ek wel, hire thank for to deserve.

'But as to speke of love, ywis,' she seyde,
'I hadde a lord, to whom I wedded was,   975
The whos myn herte al was, til that he deyde;

954 **faste:** firmly **arace:** uproot   955 **strangely:** distantly   956 **ilke:** same
957 **Ther:** where   958 **Delyvere . . . of:** free . . . from **doth:** causes
care: sorrow (or, as verb, to feel anxiety)   959 **leve:** grant **wel to fare:** to
prosper   960 **wrath:** anger **wreke:** avenge   962 **byfallen:** happen
speke: say   963 **forther over this:** furthermore   964 **wys:** prudent
redy: resourceful   965–6 **bought . . . So deere:** paid so dearly for
966 **holde:** obliged, beholden   967 **condicioun:** character
970 **konnyng:** knowledgeable **parfit:** perfect   971 As are between the
Orkneys and India (n.)   973 **trowe:** believe   974 **as to speke of:** speaking
of   976–8 To whom my heart entirely belonged, until he died; and there is
no other love in my heart, nor ever was, as Pallas may help me now

And other love, as help me now Pallas,
Ther in myn herte nys, ne nevere was.
And that ye ben of noble and heigh kynrede,
980   I have wel herd it tellen, out of drede.

'And that doth me to han so gret a wonder
That ye wol scornen any womman so.
Ek, God woot, love and I ben fer ysonder!
I am disposed bet, so mot I go,
985   Unto my deth, to pleyne and maken wo.
What I shal after don I kan nat seye;
But trewelich, as yet me list nat pleye.

'Myn herte is now in tribulacioun,
And ye in armes bisy day by day.
990   Herafter, whan ye wonnen han the town,
Peraunter thanne so it happen may,
That whan I se that nevere yit I say,
Than wol I werke that I nevere wroughte!
This word to yow ynough suffisen oughte.

995   'To-morwe ek wol I speken with yow fayn,
So that ye touchen naught of this matere.
And whan yow list, ye may come here ayayn;
And er ye gon, thus muche I sey yow here:
As help me Pallas with hire heres clere,

979 **heigh**: exalted **kynrede**: lineage   981 **doth**: makes **han . . . wonder**: be
amazed   982 **scornen**: mock **so**: like this   983 **fer**: far **ysonder**: apart
984 **disposed bet**: more inclined **so mot I go**: as I may live   985 **Unto**: until
pleyne: complain **maken wo**: lament   986 **after**: afterwards, in the future
987 **me list nat pleye**: I have no thought of enjoyment   988 **in**
tribulacioun: suffering anguish   989 **ye in armes bisy**: you (are) engaged in
fighting   990 **Herafter**: after this **wonnen**: conquered   991–3 Perhaps it
may so happen then, that when I see what I never saw before, then will I do
(*werke*) what I have never done before   994 **suffisen oughte**: ought to
suffice   996 **So that**: provided that **of**: upon **matere**: subject   997 **yow**
list: you please   998 **sey**: say to   999 **heres clere**: brightly shining hair

If that I sholde of any Grek han routhe,   1000
It sholde be youreselven, by my trouthe!

'I say nat therfore that I wol yow love,
N'y say nat nay; but in conclusioun,
I mene wel, by God that sit above!'
And therwithal she caste hire eyen down,   1005
And gan to sike, and seyde, 'O Troie town,
Yet bidde I God in quiete and in reste
I may yow sen, or do myn herte breste.'

But in effect, and shortly for to seye,
This Diomede al fresshly newe aycyn   1010
Gan pressen on, and faste hire mercy preye;
And after this, the sothe for to seyn,
Hire glove he took, of which he was ful feyn;
And finaly, whan it was woxen eve
And al was wel, he roos and tok his leve.   1015

The brighte Venus folwede and ay taughte
The wey ther brode Phebus down alighte;
And Cynthea hire char-hors overraughte
To whirle out of the Leoun, if she myghte;
And Signifer his candels sheweth brighte   1020
Whan that Criseyde unto hire bedde wente
Inwith hire fadres faire brighte tente,

1000 **han routhe**: take pity   1001 **by my trouthe**: upon my word   1003 **N'y
say nat nay**: nor do I say 'no'   1004 **sit** (= *sitteth*): sits   1007 **bidde**: pray
1008 **do**: make   **breste**: break   1009 **in effect**: actually   **shortly**: briefly
1010 **fresshly newe**: afresh   1011 **pressen on**: push forward   **faste**: intently
preye: beg, ask   1013 **feyn**: glad   1014 **was woxen**: had become
eve: evening   1015 **roos**: got up   1016 **folwede**: followed
taughte: indicated   1017 **ther**: where   **brode**: spreading   **alighte**: descended
1018 And Cynthia (the moon) reached over her chariot horses (to urge them
on)   1019 **the Leoun**: the sign of Leo   1020 **Signifer**: the zodiac
candels: candles (i.e. the stars)   **sheweth**: displays   1022 **Inwith**: within

Retornyng in hire soule ay up and down
The wordes of this sodeyn Diomede,
His grete estat, and perel of the town,
And that she was allone and hadde nede
Of frendes help; and thus bygan to brede
The cause whi, the sothe for to telle,
That she took fully purpos for to dwelle.

The morwen com, and gostly for to speke,
This Diomede is come unto Criseyde;
And shortly, lest that ye my tale breke,
So wel he for hymselven spak and seyde
That alle hire sikes soore adown he leyde;
And finaly, the sothe for to seyne,
He refte hire of the grete of al hire peyne.

And after this the storie telleth us
That she hym yaf the faire baye stede
The which he ones wan of Troilus;
And ek a broche – and that was litel nede –
That Troilus was, she yaf this Diomede;
And ek, the bet from sorwe hym to releve,
She made hym were a pencel of hire sleve.

I fynde ek in the stories elleswhere,
Whan thorugh the body hurt was Diomede
Of Troilus, tho wep she many a teere

1025

1030

1035

1040

1045

1023 **Retornyng**: turning over   1024 **sodeyn**: impetuous   1025 His high
rank, and the danger Troy was in   1027 **brede**: grow   1029 **took . . .
purpos**: decided **fully**: completely **dwelle**: stay   1030 **gostly**: truthfully
1032 **breke**: interrupt   1033 **spak**: spoke   1034 **sikes soore**: bitter sighs
adown he leyde: he allayed   1036 **refte**: relieved **grete**: chief part
1038 **yaf**: gave **baye stede**: bay horse   1039 **ones**: once **wan of**: won from
(in battle)   1040 **broche**: brooch **that was litel nede**: there was little need for
that   1041 **That Troilus was**: that was Troilus's   1042 **bet**: better
releve: relieve   1043 **were**: wear **a pencel of hire sleve**: her sleeve as a lover's
token   1044 **stories**: sources   1045–6 When Diomede was wounded by
Troilus, then she wept . . .

Whan that she saugh his wyde wowndes blede,
And that she took, to kepen hym, good hede;
And for to hele hym of his sorwes smerte,
Men seyn – I not – that she yaf hym hire herte.   1050

But trewely, the storie telleth us,
Ther made nevere womman moore wo
Than she, whan that she falsed Troilus.
She seyde, 'Allas, for now is clene ago
My name of trouthe in love for everemo,   1055
For I have falsed oon the gentileste
That evere was, and oon the worthieste!

'Allas, of me, unto the worldes ende,
Shal neyther ben ywriten nor ysonge
No good word, for thise bokes wol me shende.   1060
O, rolled shal I ben on many a tonge!
Thorughout the world my belle shal be ronge!
And wommen moost wol haten me of alle –
Allas, that swich a cas me sholde falle!

'Thei wol seyn, in as muche as in me is,   1065
I have hem don dishonour, weylaway!
Al be I nat the first that dide amys,
What helpeth that to don my blame awey?
But syn I se ther is no bettre way,
And that to late is now for me to rewe,   1070
To Diomede algate I wol be trewe.

1048 And that she took good care to look after him   1049 **hele**: heal
smerte: painful   1050 **not**: don't know   1053 **falsed**: betrayed   1054 **clene**
ago: completely gone   1055 **name of trouthe**: reputation for fidelity
1056 **oon the gentileste**: the noblest   1057 **oon the worthieste**: the most
excellent   1059 **ywriten**: written **ysonge**: sung   1060 **shende**: ruin
1061 **I**: my name, Criseyde   1062 **my belle shal be ronge**: my story shall be
told   1064 **cas**: occurrence **falle**: befall   1065 They will say, inasmuch as it
is my doing   1067 **Al be I nat**: even if I am not **dide**: acted   1068 **don . . .**
awey: remove **blame**: guilt   1069 **syn I se**: since I see   1070 **to**: too **rewe**: be
sorry   1071 **algate**: at any rate

'But, Troilus, syn I no bettre may,
And syn that thus departen ye and I,
Yet prey I God, so yeve yow right good day,
1075   As for the gentileste, trewely,
That evere I say, to serven feythfully,
And best kan ay his lady honour kepe –'
And with that word she brast anon to wepe.

'And certes yow ne haten shal I nevere;
1080   And frendes love, that shal ye han of me,
And my good word, al sholde I lyven evere.
And trewely I wolde sory be
For to seen yow in adversitee;
And gilteles, I woot wel, I yow leve.
1085   But al shal passe; and thus take I my leve.'

But trewely, how longe it was bytwene
That she forsok hym for this Diomede,
Ther is non auctour telleth it, I wene.
Take every man now to his bokes heede:
1090   He shal no terme fynden, out of drede;
For though that he bigan to wowe hire soone,
Er he hire wan, yet was ther more to doone.

Ne me ne list this sely womman chyde
Forther than the storye wol devyse.
1095   Hire name, allas, is punysshed so wide

1072 But Troilus, since I am able (to do) no better   1073 **departen:** separate
1074 I still pray God, may he grant you very good fortune   1076 **say:** saw
feythfully: loyally   1077 **lady:** lady's **kepe:** protect   1078 **brast anon to
wepe:** at once burst out crying   1079 And to be sure, I shall never hate you
1081 **good word:** approval **al:** although **evere:** for ever
1084 **gilteles:** blameless **leve:** believe   1086 **bytwene:** in the meanwhile
(before)   1087 **forsok:** abandoned   1088 **auctour:** author, writer   1089 Let
every man now consult his books   1090 **terme:** specified period of time
1091 **wowe:** woo   1092 **wan:** won   1093 I do not want to reproach this
poor woman   1094 **Forther:** further **devyse:** set forth
1095 **name:** reputation **punysshed:** punished (with ill repute) **wide:** widely

That for hire gilt it oughte ynough suffise.
And if I myghte excuse hire any wise,
For she so sory was for hire untrouthe,
Iwis, I wolde excuse hire yet for routhe.

This Troilus, as I byfore have told,   1100
Thus driveth forth, as wel as he hath myght;
But often was his herte hoot and cold,
And namely that ilke nynthe nyght,
Which on the morwe she hadde hym bihight
To com ayeyn. God woot, ful litel reste   1105
Hadde he that nyght – nothyng to slepe hym leste.

The laurer-crowned Phebus with his heete
Gan, in his cours ay upward as he wente,
To warmen of the est se the wawes weete,
And Nysus doughter song with fressh entente,   1110
Whan Troilus his Pandare after sente;
And on the walles of the town they pleyde,
To loke if they kan sen aught of Criseyde.

Tyl it was noon they stoden for to se
Who that ther come, and every maner wight   1115
That com fro fer, they seyden it was she –
Til that thei koude knowen hym aright.
Now was his herte dul, now was it light;
And thus byjaped stonden for to stare
Aboute naught this Troilus and Pandare.   1120

1096 **suffise:** be sufficient   1097 **excuse:** exonerate **any wise:** in any way
1098 **untrouthe:** faithlessness   1099 **for routhe:** out of compassion
1101 Endures in this way as best he can   1103 **namely:** especially **ilke:** very
1104 **morwe:** next morning **bihight:** promised   1106 **nothyng to slepe hym
leste:** he had no wish at all to sleep   1107 **laurer:** laurel **heete:** heat
1108 **cours:** course   1109 **est se:** east sea (n.) **wawes:** waves **weete:** wet
1110 **Nysus doughter:** i.e. Scylla (n.) **song:** sang **entente:** endeavour
1111 **after sente:** sent for   1112 **pleyde:** amused themselves   1113 **sen
aught:** see anything   1114 **stoden:** stood   1115 **maner wight:** sort of
person   1116 **fer:** far   1117 **knowen:** recognize **aright:** properly
1118 **dul:** heavy **light:** cheerful   1119 **byjaped:** deluded   1120 **Aboute
naught:** to no purpose

To Pandarus this Troilus tho seyde,
'For aught I woot, byfor noon, sikirly,
Into this town ne comth nat here Criseyde.
She hath ynough to doone, hardyly,
1125 To wynnen from hire fader, so trowe I.
Hire olde fader wol yet make hire dyne
Er that she go – God yeve hys herte pyne!'

Pandare answerede, 'It may wel be, certeyn,
And forthi lat us dyne, I the byseche,
1130 And after noon than maystow come ayeyn.'
And hom they go, withoute more speche,
And comen ayeyn – but longe may they seche
Er that they fynde that they after cape:
Fortune hem bothe thenketh for to jape!

1135 Quod Troilus, 'I se wel now that she
Is taried with hire olde fader so,
That er she come, it wol neigh even be.
Com forth; I wol unto the yate go.
Thise porters ben unkonnyng evere mo,
1140 And I wol don hem holden up the yate
As naught ne were, although she come late.'

The day goth faste, and after that com eve,
And yet com nought to Troilus Criseyde.
He loketh forth by hegge, by tre, by greve,
1145 And fer his hed over the wal he leyde;
And at the laste he torned hym and seyde,

1121 tho: then   1122 aught I woot: all I know sikirly: certainly
1123–4 Criseyde is not coming here into this town. She has difficulty,
certainly   1125 wynnen: get away   1127 yeve: give pyne: pain, suffering
1128 certeyn: certainly   1129 forthi: therefore   1130 maystow (= *mayest
thow*): you can   1132 seche: seek   1133 cape: gape   1134 jape: deceive
1136 taried: delayed   1137 neigh even: nearly evening   1138 Com
forth: come on   1139 porters: gate-keepers unkonnyng: ignorant evere
mo: always   1140 don: make holden up: keep open yate: portcullis
1141 As naught ne were: as if there were nothing in it   1144 hegge: hedge
1145 fer: far leyde: craned

'By God, I woot hire menyng now, Pandare!
Almoost, ywys, al newe was my care.

'Now douteles, this lady kan hire good;
I woot she meneth riden pryvely.   1150
I comende hire wisdom, by myn hood!
She wol nat maken peple nycely
Gaure on hire whan she comth, but softely
By nyghte into the town she thenketh ride.
And, deere brother, thynk nat longe t'abide.   1155

'We han naught elles for to don, ywis.
And Pandarus, now woltow trowen me?
Have here my trouthe, I se hire! Yond she is!
Heve up thyn eyen, man! Maistow nat se?'
Pandare answerede, 'Nay, so mote I the!   1160
Al wrong, by God! What saistow, man? Where
    arte?
That I se yond nys but a fare-carte.'

'Allas, thow seyst right soth,' quod Troilus.
'But, hardily, it is naught al for nought
That in myn herte I now rejoysse thus;   1165
It is ayeyns som good I have a thought.
Not I nat how, but syn that I was wrought
Ne felte I swich a comfort, dar I seye;
She comth to-nyght, my lif that dorste I leye!'

1148 Indeed, my sorrow was very nearly renewed   1149 **kan hire
good**: knows what is her best course   1150 **meneth**: intends
pryvely: secretly   1152 **nycely**: foolishly   1153 **Gaure on**: gawp at
softely: quietly   1154 **thenketh ride**: intends to ride   1155 And, dear
brother, don't expect to have to wait very long   1157 **woltow trowen**: will
you believe   1158 **Have here my trouthe**: take my word for it   **Yond**: over
there   1159 **Heve**: lift, raise   **Maistow**: can you   1160 **mote I the**: may I
prosper   1161 **saistow**: do you say   **arte** (= *art thow*): are you   1162 **nys
but**: is only   **fare-carte**: cart (for carrying merchandise)   1163 **seyst right
soth**: speak very truly   1164 **hardily**: certainly   **for nought**: in vain
1165 **rejoysse**: rejoice   1166 I believe it forebodes some good   1167 **Not I
nat**: I do not know   **wrought**: created   1169 **dorste I leye**: I would dare wager

1170 Pandare answerde, 'It may be, wel ynough,'
And held with hym of al that evere he seyde;
But in his herte he thoughte, and softe lough,
And to hymself ful sobreliche he seyde,
'From haselwode, there joly Robyn pleyde,
1175 Shal come al that that thow abidest heere.
Ye, fare wel al the snow of ferne yere!'

The warden of the yates gan to calle
The folk which that withoute the yates were,
And bad hem dryven in hire bestes alle,
1180 Or all the nyght they moste bleven there.
And fer withinne the nyght, with many a teere,
This Troilus gan homward for to ride,
For wel he seth it helpeth naught t'abide.

But natheles, he gladed hym in this:
1185 He thought he misacounted hadde his day,
And seyde, 'I understonde have al amys.
For thilke nyght I last Criseyde say,
She seyde, "I shal ben here, if that I may,
Er that the moone, O deere herte swete,
1190 The Leoun passe, out of this Ariete."

'For which she may yet holde al hire byheste.'
And on the morwe unto the yate he wente,
And up and down, by west and ek by este,

1171 **held with hym of**: agreed with him in   1172 **softe**: softly
lough: laughed   1173 **sobreliche**: seriously   1174 **haselwode**: hazel wood
joly: merry **Robyn**: traditional name for a shepherd or rustic character (n.)
pleyde: sported   1175 **abidest**: await   1176 **ferne yere**: yesteryear
1177 **warden**: guard   1178 **withoute**: outside   1179 **bestes**: animals
1180 **moste**: must **bleven**: remain   1181 **fer**: far **withinne**: into
1183 **helpeth naught**: is of no use   1184 **gladed hym**: took comfort
1185 **misacounted**: miscalculated   1186 **al amys**: entirely wrongly
1187 **say**: saw   1190 Having left this (present) sign of Aries, pass the sign of
Leo   1191 **holde**: keep **byheste**: promise   1193 **este**: east

Upon the walles made he many a wente.
But al for nought; his hope alwey hym blente.   1195
For which at nyght, in sorwe and sikes sore,
He wente hym hom withouten any more.

His hope al clene out of his herte fledde;
He nath wheron now lenger for to honge;
But for the peyne hym thoughte his herte bledde,   1200
So were his throwes sharpe and wonder stronge;
For whan he saugh that she abood so longe,
He nyste what he juggen of it myghte,
Syn she hath broken that she hym bihighte.

The thridde, ferthe, fifte, sexte day   1205
After tho dayes ten of which I tolde,
Bitwixen hope and drede his herte lay,
Yet somwhat trustyng on hire hestes olde.
But whan he saugh she nolde hire terme holde,
He kan now sen non other remedie   1210
But for to shape hym soone for to dye.

Therwith the wikked spirit – God us blesse –
Which that men clepeth woode jalousie,
Gan in hym crepe, in al this hevynesse;
For which, by cause he wolde soone dye,   1215
He ne et ne drank, for his malencolye,
And ek from every compaignye he fledde:
This was the lif that al the tyme he ledde.

1194 **made he many a wente**: he turned many times (while walking)
1195 **blente**: deceived   1197 **withouten any more**: without more ado
1198 **clene**: completely   1199 He doesn't have (*nath*) anything to hang on to
anymore   1201 **throwes**: sufferings **wonder stronge**: amazingly severe
1202 **abood**: remained   1203 **juggen**: think   1204 **that**: that which
bihighte: promised   1205 **sexte**: sixth   1208 **hestes**: promises   1209 **hire
terme holde**: keep to her appointed time   1211 **shape hym**: prepare
1212 **Therwith**: thereupon **God us blesse**: (from which) God protect us
1213 **men clepeth**: one calls **woode**: mad   1215 **wolde soone dye**: wished to
die soon   1216 **et**: ate **for**: because of **malencolye**: depression

He so defet was, that no manere man
1220   Unneth hym myghte knowen ther he wente;
So was he lene, and therto pale and wan,
And feble, that he walketh by potente;
And with his ire he thus hymselve shente.
But whoso axed hym wherof hym smerte,
1225   He seyde his harm was al aboute his herte.

Priam ful ofte, and ek his moder deere,
His bretheren and his sustren gonne hym freyne
Whi he so sorwful was in al his cheere,
And what thyng was the cause of al his peyne –
1230   But al for naught. He nolde his cause pleyne,
But seyde he felte a grevous maladie
Aboute his herte, and fayn he wolde dye.

So on a day he leyde hym down to slepe,
And so byfel that in his slep hym thoughte
1235   That in a forest faste he welk to wepe
For love of hire that hym these peynes wroughte;
And up and down as he the forest soughte,
He mette he saugh a bor with tuskes grete,
That slepte ayeyn the bryghte sonnes hete.

1240   And by this bor, faste in his armes folde,
Lay, kyssyng ay, his lady bright, Criseyde.
For sorwe of which, whan he it gan biholde,
And for despit, out of his slep he breyde,
And loude he cride on Pandarus, and seyde:

1219 **defet**: disfigured   1220 **Unneth**: with difficulty **knowen**: recognize
1221 **lene**: thin **therto**: also   1222 **feble**: enfeebled **by potente**: with a
crutch   1223 **shente**: destroyed   1224 **wherof hym smerte**: what he was
suffering from   1225 **harm**: pain **aboute**: around   1227 **gonne hym
freyne**: asked him   1230 **for naught**: in vain **his cause pleyne**: lament (i.e.
divulge) the cause of his trouble   1231 **grevous**: grave   1234 **byfel**: it
happened   1235 **faste**: dense **welk**: walked   1236 **wroughte**: caused
1237 **soughte**: explored   1238 **mette**: dreamed **bor**: boar   1239 **ayeyn**: in
sonnes hete: sun's heat   1240 **faste**: tightly **folde**: embraced
1243 **despit**: resentment **breyde**: started

'O Pandarus, now know I crop and roote.   1245
I n'am but ded; ther nys noon other bote.

'My lady bright, Criseyde, hath me bytrayed,
In whom I trusted most of any wight.
She elliswhere hath now hire herte apayed.
The blisful goddes thorugh hire grete myght   1250
Han in my drem yshewed it ful right.
Thus in my drem Criseyde have I biholde –'
And al this thing to Pandarus he tolde.

'O my Criseyde, allas, what subtilte,
What newe lust, what beaute, what science,   1255
What wratthe of juste cause have ye to me?
What gilt of me, what fel experience
Hath fro me raft, allas, thyn advertence?
O trust, O feyth, O depe asseuraunce!
Who hath me reft Criseyde, al my plesaunce?   1260

'Allas, whi leet I you from hennes go,
For which wel neigh out of my wit I breyde?
Who shal now trowe on any othes mo?
God wot, I wende, O lady bright, Criseyde,
That every word was gospel that ye seyde!   1265
But who may bet bigile, if hym liste,
Than he on whom men weneth best to triste?

1245 **crop and roote:** growing tip and root (of a plant), i.e. everything
1246 **n'am but ded:** am as good as dead **bote:** remedy   1249 Her heart has
now found pleasure elsewhere   1251 **yshewed:** revealed **right:** exactly
1254 **subtilte:** guile   1255 **lust:** pleasure **science:** knowledge   1256 **juste
cause:** good reason **to:** against   1257 **gilt of me:** fault of mine **fel:** dreadful
1258 **raft:** diverted **advertence:** attention, concern   1259 **feyth:** faithfulness
asseuraunce: confidence   1260 **me reft:** deprived me of   1261 **leet:** let
hennes: hence   1262 Because of which I'm very nearly going out of my
mind   1263 **othes:** oaths **mo:** again, any longer   1264 **wende:** believed
1265 **gospel:** absolute truth   1266 **may bet bigile:** is better able to deceive
1267 **men weneth:** one thinks

'What shal I don, my Pandarus, allas?
I fele now so sharp a newe peyne,
1270   Syn that ther lith no remedye in this cas,
That bet were it I with myn hondes tweyne
Myselven slowh, alwey than thus to pleyne;
For thorugh my deth my wo sholde han an ende,
Ther every day with lyf myself I shende.'

1275   Pandare answerde and seyde, 'Allas the while
That I was born! Have I nat seyd er this,
That dremes many a maner man bigile?
And whi? For folk expounden hem amys.
How darstow seyn that fals thy lady ys
1280   For any drem, right for thyn owene drede?
Lat be this thought; thow kanst no dremes rede.

'Peraunter, ther thow dremest of this boor,
It may so be that it may signifie
Hire fader, which that old is and ek hoor,
1285   Ayeyn the sonne lith o poynt to dye,
And she for sorwe gynneth wepe and crie,
And kisseth hym, ther he lith on the grounde:
Thus sholdestow thi drem aright expounde!'

'How myghte I than don,' quod Troilus,
1290   'To knowe of this, yee, were it nevere so lite?'
'Now seystow wisly,' quod this Pandarus;

1270 **lith**: lies, is   1271 **bet were it**: it would be better if   1272 Slew myself
than continually to be lamenting like this   1274 **shende**: reproach
1275 **Allas the while**: alas for the time   1277 That dreams deceive many
kinds of people   1278 **expounden**: interpret **amys**: wrongly
1279 **darstow**: dare you **fals**: unfaithful   1280 **For**: because of **right for**: just
because of   1281 Forget this idea; you don't know how to interpret any
dreams   1282 **Peraunter**: perhaps **ther**: where   1284 **hoor**: white-haired
1285 **Ayeyn**: in **o poynt to dye**: on the point of death   1288 **sholdestow**: you
should **aright**: correctly   1290 To know the correct interpretation of this,
indeed, even if it were ever so trifling   1291 **seystow**: you are talking

'My red is this: syn thow kanst wel endite,
That hastily a lettre thow hire write,
Thorugh which thow shalt wel bryngyn it aboute
To know a soth of that thow art in doute.   1295

'And se now whi: for this I dar wel seyn,
That if so is that she untrewe be,
I kan nat trowen that she wol write ayeyn.
And if she write, thow shalt ful sone yse
As wheither she hath any liberte   1300
To come ayeyn; or ellis in som clause,
If she be let, she wol assigne a cause.

'Thow hast nat writen hire syn that she wente,
Nor she to the; and this I dorste laye,
Ther may swich cause ben in hire entente   1305
That hardily thow wolt thiselven saye
That hire abod the best is for yow twaye.
Now write hire thanne, and thow shalt feele sone
A soth of al. Ther is namore to done.'

Acorded ben to this conclusioun,   1310
And that anon, thise ilke lordes two;
And hastily sit Troilus adown,
And rolleth in his herte to and fro
How he may best discryven hire his wo;
And to Criseyde, his owen lady deere,   1315
He wrot right thus, and seyde as ye may here:

1292 **red**: advice **endite**: compose   1295 **a soth**: the truth   1297 **so is**: it is
so   1298 **ayeyn**: in reply   1299 **yse**: see   1302 **let**: prevented (from coming)
assigne: offer **cause**: reason   1304 **dorste laye**: would dare to bet
1305 **entente**: purpose   1306 **hardily**: certainly   1307 **abod**: delay
twaye: two   1308 **feele**: perceive   1309 **A soth of al**: the truth about
everything   1310 **Acorded**: agreed **conclusioun**: decision   1312 **sit** (=
sittith): sits   1313 **rolleth**: turns over   1314 **discryven hire**: describe to her

Litera Troili

'Right fresshe flour, whos I ben have and shal,
Withouten part of elleswhere servyse,
With herte, body, lif, lust, thought, and al,
1320   I, woful wyght, in everich humble wise
That tonge telle or herte may devyse,
As ofte as matere occupieth place,
Me recomaunde unto youre noble grace.

'Liketh yow to witen, swete herte,
1325   As ye wel knowe, how longe tyme agon
That ye me lefte in aspre peynes smerte,
Whan that ye wente, of which yet boote non
Have I non had, but evere wors bigon
Fro day to day am I, and so mot dwelle,
1330   While it yow list, of wele and wo my welle.

'For which to yow, with dredful herte trewe,
I write, as he that sorwe drifth to write,
My wo, that everich houre encresseth newe,
Compleynyng, as I dar or kan endite;
1335   And that defaced is, that may ye wite
The teris which that fro myn eyen reyne,
That wolden speke, if that they koude, and pleyne.

Litera Troili: Troilus's letter   1317 **Right fresshe flour:** freshest of flowers
1318 Without any share of my love-service bestowed elsewhere
1320 **wise:** way   1321 **devyse:** imagine   1322 As long as matter takes up
space   1323 **Me recomaunde:** commend myself   1324 **Liketh yow to
witen:** may it please you to recall   1325 **agon:** ago   1326 **aspre peynes
smerte:** sharp and bitter pains   1327 **boote:** remedy   1328 **wors bigon:** in a
worse state   1329 **mot dwelle:** must remain   1330 For as long as it pleases
you, the source of my joy and sorrow   1331–3 Because of which, with
fearful, faithful heart, as one whom sorrow compels to write, I am writing to
you of my unhappiness that grows anew by the hour   1335 **that defaced
is:** the fact that my letter is smudged **wite:** blame upon

'Yow first biseche I, that youre eyen clere
To loke on this defouled ye nat holde;
And over al this, that ye, my lady deere,   1340
Wol vouchesauf this lettre to byholde;
And by the cause ek of my cares colde
That sleth my wit, if aught amys m'asterte,
Foryeve it me, myn owen swete herte!

'If any servant dorste or oughte of right   1345
Upon his lady pitously compleyne,
Thanne wene I that ich oughte be that wight,
Considered this, that ye thise monthes tweyne
Han taried, ther ye seyden, soth to seyne,
But dayes ten ye nolde in oost sojourne –   1350
But in two monthes yet ye nat retourne.

'But for as muche as me moot nedes like
Al that yow liste, I dar nat pleyne moore,
But humblely, with sorwful sikes sike,
Yow write ich myn unresty sorwes soore,   1355
Fro day to day desiryng evere moore
To knowen fully, if youre wille it weere,
How ye han ferd and don whil ye be theere;

'The whos welfare and hele ek God encresse
In honour swich that upward in degree   1360
It growe alwey, so that it nevere cesse.

1338–9 First I beg you that you do not consider (*holde*) your bright eyes
defiled by looking at this (letter)   1340 **over al this**: furthermore
1341 **vouchesauf**: agree   1342 **by the cause**: because   1343 That overcomes
my understanding, if anything amiss escape me   1345 **dorste**: dared **of**
right: justifiably   1348 **Considered**: taking into account
1349 **taried**: delayed **ther**: whereas   1350 **oost**: (the besieging Greek) army
sojourne: stay   1352–3 **me moot nedes like Al that yow liste**: all that pleases
you must necessarily please me   1354 **with sorwful sikes sike**: with
sorrowful, sickly sighs (or, sick from sorrowful sighs)   1355 **Yow write ich**: I
write to you of **unresty**: upsetting   1357 **youre wille it weere**: it were your
will   1358 **ferd**: fared, got on   1359–61 The whose (i.e. Criseyde's)
happiness and well-being too, may God increase in honour such that it may
grow ever higher unceasingly

Right as youre herte ay kan, my lady free,
Devyse, I prey to God so moot it be,
And graunte it that ye soone upon me rewe,
1365   As wisly as in al I am yow trewe.

'And if yow liketh knowen of the fare
Of me, whos wo ther may no wit discryve,
I kan namore but, chiste of every care,
At wrytyng of this lettre I was on-lyve,
1370   Al redy out my woful gost to dryve,
Which I delaye, and holde hym yet in honde,
Upon the sighte of matere of youre sonde.

'Myn eyen two, in veyn with which I se,
Of sorwful teris salte arn waxen welles;
1375   My song, in pleynte of myn adversitee;
My good, in harm; myn ese ek woxen helle is;
My joie, in wo; I kan sey yow naught ellis,
But torned is – for which my lif I warie –
Everich joie or ese in his contrarie;

1380   'Which with youre comyng hom ayeyn to Troie
Ye may redresse, and more a thousand sithe
Than evere ich hadde encressen in me joie.
For was ther nevere herte yet so blithe
To han his lif as I shal ben as swithe
1385   As I yow se; and though no manere routhe
Commeve yow, yet thynketh on youre trouthe.

1363 **Devyse**: imagine   1365 **wisly**: certainly **al**: everything   1366–7 **the
fare Of me**: my condition   1368 **kan namore**: can say no more
chiste: receptacle **care**: sorrow   1369 **At**: at (the time of) **on-lyve**: alive
1370 **gost**: spirit   1371 **holde hym yet in honde**: keep it in suspense
1372 Until I see the content of your message (*sonde*)   1374 **arn waxen**: have
become **welles**: springs   1375 **in**: (has turned) into **pleynte**: lamentation
1376 **ese**: comfort **woxen helle is**: has become hell   1378 **warie**: curse
1381 **redresse**: set right **sithe**: times   1383 **blithe**: happy   1384 **as swithe**: as
soon   1385 **though**: even if **manere**: kind of   1386 **Commeve**: move
trouthe: pledged word

'And if so be my gilt hath deth deserved,
Or if yow list namore upon me se,
In guerdoun yet of that I have yow served,
Byseche I yow, myn owen lady free,   1390
That hereupon ye wolden write me,
For love of God, my righte lode-sterre,
That deth may make an ende of al my werre;

'If other cause aught doth yow for to dwelle,
That with youre lettre ye me recomforte;   1395
For though to me youre absence is an helle,
With pacience I wol my wo comporte,
And with youre lettre of hope I wol desporte.
Now writeth, swete, and lat me thus nat pleyne;
With hope, or deth, delivereth me fro peyne.   1400

'Iwis, myne owene deere herte trewe,
I woot that whan ye next upon me se,
So lost have I myn hele and ek myn hewe,
Criseyde shal nought konne knowen me.
Iwys, myn hertes day, my lady free,   1405
So thursteth ay myn herte to byholde
Youre beute, that my lif unnethe I holde.

'I say namore, al have I for to seye
To yow wel more than I telle may;
But wheither that ye do me lyve or deye,   1410
Yet praye I God, so yeve yow right good day!
And fareth wel, goodly, faire, fresshe may,

1387 **so be**: it be the case that   1389 **guerdoun**: reward
1391 **hereupon**: concerning this   1392 **righte**: true **lode-sterre**: guiding star
1393 **werre**: inward strife   1394 **aught**: at all **doth**: causes **dwelle**: delay
1395 **That**: (I beseech you) that **recomforte**: comfort
1397 **comporte**: endure   1398 **desporte**: take comfort
1400 **delivereth**: release   1403 **hele**: health **hewe**: colour   1404 **konne**
knowen: be able to recognize   1405 **myn hertes day**: sun of my life
1406 **thursteth**: longs   1407 **beute**: beauty **unnethe**: with difficulty
holde: sustain   1408 **al have I**: although I have   1411 I still pray God to
bless you   1412 **fareth wel**: farewell **may**: girl

As she that lif or deth may me comande!
And to youre trouthe ay I me recomande,

1415   'With hele swich that, but ye yeven me
The same hele, I shal non hele have.
In yow lith, whan yow liste that it so be,
The day in which me clothen shal my grave;
In yow my lif, in yow myght for to save
1420   Me fro disese of alle peynes smerte;
And far now wel, myn owen swete herte!
                              Le vostre T.'

This lettre forth was sent unto Criseyde,
Of which hire answere in effect was this:
Ful pitously she wroot ayeyn, and seyde,
1425   That also sone as that she myghte, ywys,
She wolde come, and mende al that was mys;
And fynaly she wroot and seyde hym thenne,
She wolde come, ye, but she nyste whenne.

But in hire lettre made she swich festes
1430   That wonder was, and swerth she loveth hym best,
Of which he fond but botmeles bihestes.
But Troilus, thow maist now, est or west,
Pipe in an ivy lef, if that the lest!

1414 **trouthe:** faithfulness **me recomande:** commend myself
1415 **hele:** health **but:** unless **yeven:** give   1417 **In yow lith:** in your power
lies   1418 The day on which my grave shall clothe me   1419 **In yow:** in
your power lies (*lith* understood from 1417)   1420 **disese:** distress
1421 **Le vostre T.:** Your T   1423 **in effect:** essentially
1424 **pitously:** compassionately **ayeyn:** in reply   1425 **also:** as
1426 **mende:** put right **mys:** amiss   1428 **ye:** indeed **nyste whenne:** did not
know when   1429 **made she swich festes:** she paid such compliments
1430 **wonder was:** it was very surprising **swerth:** swears   1431 **botmeles
bihestes:** groundless promises   1432 **est or west:** in any direction, anywhere
1433 **Pipe in an ivy lef:** go whistle (vainly) **the lest:** you wish

Thus goth the world. God shilde us fro
   meschaunce,
And every wight that meneth trouthe avaunce!   1435

Encressen gan the wo fro day to nyght
Of Troilus, for tarying of Criseyde;
And lessen gan his hope and ek his myght,
For which al down he in his bed hym leyde;
He ne eet, ne dronk, ne slep, ne no word seyde,   1440
Ymagynyng ay that she was unkynde,
For which wel neigh he wex out of his mynde.

This drem, of which I told have ek byforn,
May nevere come out of his remembraunce:
He thought ay wel he hadde his lady lorn,   1445
And that Joves of his purveyaunce
Hym shewed hadde in slep the signifiaunce
Of hire untrouthe and his disaventure,
And that the boor was shewed hym in figure.

For which he for Sibille his suster sente,   1450
That called was Cassandre ek al aboute,
And al his drem he tolde hire er he stente,
And hire bisoughte assoilen hym the doute
Of the stronge boor with tuskes stoute;
And fynaly, withinne a litel stounde,   1455
Cassandre hym gan right thus his drem expounde:

1434 **shilde**: protect   1435 And promote every person who intends to be
faithful   1436 **Encressen gan the wo**: the misery increased **fro day to
nyght**: all day long   1437 **for tarying of Criseyde**: because of Criseyde's
delaying   1438 **lessen**: decrease **myght**: strength   1440 **eet**: ate
dronk: drank **slep**: slept   1441 **unkynde**: cruel   1442 **wex**: went
1445 **lorn**: lost   1446 **purveyaunce**: providence   1447 **signifiaunce**: sign,
portent   1448 **untrouthe**: faithlessness **disaventure**: misfortune   1449 **in
figure**: as a symbol or prefigurement   1450 **Sibille**: prophetess (n.)
1452 **stente**: stopped   1453 And begged her to resolve his uncertainty
1454 **stronge**: powerful **stoute**: mighty   1455 **stounde**: while

She gan first smyle, and seyde, 'O brother deere,
If thow a soth of this desirest knowe,
Thow most a fewe of olde stories heere,
1460   To purpos how that Fortune overthrowe
Hath lordes olde, thorugh which, withinne a throwe,
Thow wel this boor shalt knowe, and of what kynde
He comen is, as men in bokes fynde.

'Diane, which that wroth was and in ire
1465   For Grekis nolde don hire sacrifice,
Ne encens upon hire auter sette afire,
She, for that Grekis gonne hire so despise,
Wrak hire in a wonder cruel wise;
For with a boor as gret as ox in stalle
1470   She made up frete hire corn and vynes alle.

'To sle this boor was al the contre raysed,
Amonges which ther com, this boor to se,
A mayde, oon of this world the beste ypreysed;
And Meleagre, lord of that contree,
1475   He loved so this fresshe mayden free
That with his manhod, er he wolde stente,
This boor he slough, and hire the hed he sente;

'Of which, as olde bokes tellen us,
Ther ros a contek and a gret envye;
1480   And of this lord descended Tideus
By ligne, or ellis olde bookes lye.
But how this Meleagre gan to dye

1458 **soth**: true thing   1459 **most**: must   1460 **To purpos**: pertinent to the
subject   1461 **throwe**: short time   1462 **knowe**: recognize **kynde**: family
1464 **Diane**: Diana **wroth**: angry   1466 **encens**: incense **auter**: altar
afire: on fire   1467 **gonne . . . despise**: neglected   1468 **Wrak hire**: avenged
herself **wonder**: amazingly   1469 **with**: by **stalle**: (its) stall   1470 **made up**
frete: caused to be consumed   1471 **raysed**: up in arms   1473 **A mayde**: i.c.
Atalanta **beste**: most **ypreysed**: praised   1474 **Meleagre**: Meleager
1476 **with his manhod**: boldly, manfully **stente**: cease   1477 **slough**: slew
1479 **contek**: strife **envye**: enmity   1481 **By ligne**: lineally

Thorugh his moder, wol I yow naught telle,
For al to longe it were for to dwelle.'

She tolde ek how Tideus, er she stente,   1485
Unto the stronge citee of Thebes,
To cleymen kyngdom of the citee, wente,
For his felawe, daun Polymytes,
Of which the brother, daun Ethiocles,
Ful wrongfully of Thebes held the strengthe;   1490
This tolde she by proccs, al by lengthe.

She tolde ek how Hemonydes asterte,
Whan Tideus slough fifty knyghtes stoute.
She tolde ek alle the prophecyes by herte,
And how that seven kynges with hire route   1495
Bysegeden the citee al aboute;
And of the holy serpent, and the welle,
And of the furies, al she gan hym telle;

Associat profugum Tideo primus Polymytem;
Tidea legatum docet insidiasque secundus;
Tercius Hemoduden canit et vates latitantes;
Quartus habet reges ineuntes prelia septem;
Mox furie Lenne quinto narratur et anguis;
Archymory bustum sexto ludique leguntur;
Dat Grayos Thebes et vatem septimus umbris;

1483 **Thorugh his moder**: through his mother's doing   1484 **dwelle**: delay
1487 **cleymen**: claim **kyngdom**: kingship   1488 **felawe**: friend **daun**: Lord
Polymytes: Polynices   1489 **Ethiocles**: Eteocles   1490 **strengthe**: power
1491 **by proces**: in due course **by lengthe**: at length
1492 **Hemonydes**: Maeon (n.) **asterte**: escaped   1493 **stoute**: bold
1495 **route**: company
(The first [book] connects exiled Polynices with Tydeus; the second tells of
Tydeus as ambassador and of the ambush [by Eteocles]; the third sings of the
son of Haemon [Maeon] and the secretive seers; the fourth has the Seven
Kings going into battle; then in the fifth the Furies of Lemnos are told of,
together with the serpent; and in the sixth the cremation of Archemorus and
the games are read about; the seventh takes the Greeks to Thebes and the seer
[Amphiaraus]

Octavo cecidit Tideus, spes, vita Pelasgis;
Ypomedon nono moritur cum Parthenopea;
Fulmine percussus, decimo Capaneus superatur;
Undecimo sese perimunt per vulnera fratres;
Argiva flentem narrat duodenus et ignem;

Of Archymoris brennynge and the pleyes,
1500   And how Amphiorax fil thorugh the grounde,
How Tideus was sleyn, lord of Argeyes,
And how Ypomedoun in litel stounde
Was dreynt, and ded Parthonope of wownde;
And also how Capaneus the proude
1505   With thonder-dynt was slayn, that cride loude.

She gan ek telle hym how that eyther brother,
Ethiocles and Polymyte also,
At a scarmuche ech of hem slough other,
And of Argyves wepynge and hire wo;
1510   And how the town was brent, she tolde ek tho;
And so descendeth down from gestes olde
To Diomede, and thus she spak and tolde:

'This ilke boor bitokneth Diomede,
Tideus sone, that down descended is
1515   Fro Meleagre, that made the boor to blede;

to the shades; in the eighth Tydeus fell, hope [and] life of the Pelasgians; in the ninth Hippomedon dies together with Parthenopaeus; in the tenth Capaneus – struck by lightning – is overcome; in the eleventh the brothers [Eteocles and Polynices] destroy each other with wounds; the twelfth tells of the weeping Argia [Argiva] and the fire.)

1499 **Archymoris brennynge**: Archemorus's cremation (n.) **pleyes**: funeral games   1500 **Amphiorax**: Amphiaraus (n.) **fil**: fell   1501 **Argeyes**: Argives (people of Argos)   1502 **Ypomedoun**: Hippomedon (n.) **stounde**: while 1503 **Was drowned, and Parthenopaeus was dead from his wounds** (n.) 1505 **thonder-dynt**: thunderbolt **cride**: boasted **loude**: loudly 1508 **scarmuche**: skirmish **slough other**: slew the other   1509 **Argyves wepynge**: the weeping of Argia (n.)   1510 **brent**: burnt   1511 **descendeth down**: proceeded **gestes olde**: ancient histories   1513 **ilke**: same **bitokneth**: symbolizes

And thy lady, wherso she be, ywis,
This Diomede hire herte hath, and she his –
Wep if thow wolt, or lef, for out of doute,
This Diomede is inne, and thow art oute.'

'Thow seyst nat soth,' quod he, 'thow sorceresse,   1520
With al thy false goost of prophecye!
Thow wenest ben a gret devyneresse!
Now sestow nat this fool of fantasie
Peyneth hire on ladys for to lye?
Awey!' quod he. 'Ther Joves yeve the sorwe!   1525
Thow shalt be fals, peraunter, yet tomorwe!

'As wel thow myghtest lien on Alceste,
That was of creatures, but men lye,
That evere weren, kyndest and the beste!
For whan hire housbonde was in jupertye   1530
To dye hymself but if she wolde dye,
She ches for hym to dye and gon to helle,
And starf anon, as us the bokes telle.'

Cassandre goth, and he with cruel herte
Foryat his wo, for angre of hire speche;   1535
And from his bed al sodeynly he sterte,
As though al hool hym hadde ymad a leche.
And day by day he gan enquere and seche
A sooth of this with al his fulle cure;
And thus he drieth forth his aventure.   1540

1516 **wherso**: wherever   1518 **lef**: refrain   1520 **seyst nat soth**: are not
speaking the truth   1521 **goost**: spirit   1522 You imagine yourself to be a
great prophetess   1523 **sestow**: do you not see (a rhetorical question, not
addressed to Cassandra)   **fool of fantasie**: victim of delusions
1524–5 'Takes pains to tell lies about ladies? Away with you!' said he. 'May
Jove give you sorrow!'   1526 **fals**: (proved) wrong   1527 You might as well
lie about Alcestis   1528 **but**: unless   1531 **but if**: unless   1532 **ches**: chose
533 **starf**: died   1535 **Foryat**: forgot **for angre of**: out of anger at
1536 **sterte**: leaped   1537 As though a doctor had made him completely
well   1538 **enquere**: enquire **seche**: seek   1539 **A sooth**: the truth
cure: attention   1540 **drieth forth**: endures **aventure**: lot

Fortune, which that permutacioun
Of thynges hath, as it is hire comitted
Thorugh purveyaunce and disposicioun
Of heighe Jove, as regnes shal be flitted
1545 Fro folk in folk, or when they shal be smytted,
Gan pulle awey the fetheres brighte of Troie
Fro day to day, til they ben bare of joie.

Among al this, the fyn of the parodie
Of Ector gan aprochen wonder blyve.
1550 The fate wolde his soule sholde unbodye,
And shapen hadde a mene it out to dryve,
Ayeyns which fate hym helpeth nat to stryve;
But on a day to fighten gan he wende,
At which, allas, he caughte his lyves ende!

1555 For which me thynketh every manere wight
That haunteth armes oughte to biwaille
The deth of hym that was so noble a knyght;
For as he drough a kyng by th'aventaille,
Unwar of this, Achilles thorugh the maille
1560 And thorugh the body gan hym for to ryve;
And thus this worthi knyght was brought of lyve.

For whom, as olde bokes tellen us,
Was mad swich wo that tonge it may nat telle,
And namely, the sorwe of Troilus,

1541 **permutacioun**: alteration 1543 **purveyaunce**: foresight
disposicioun: arrangement 1544 **regnes**: kingdoms, dominion
flitted: transferred 1545 **folk in folk**: people to people **smytted**: disgraced
1547 **bare**: deprived 1548 **Among**: amidst **fyn**: end **parodie**: lifetime,
period (of life) 1549 **wonder blyve**: marvellously swiftly
1550 **unbodye**: leave the body 1551 **shapen**: devised **mene**: means
1552 **hym helpeth nat**: it does not help him **stryve**: struggle
1553 **wende**: go 1554 **caughte**: met **lyves ende**: death
1556 **haunteth**: makes a practice of **armes**: deeds of arms
1558 **drough**: dragged **th'aventaille**: the chain-mail neck-guard (of a
helmet) 1559 **Unwar**: unaware, unsuspecting **maille**: mail-armour
1560 **ryve**: stab 1561 **worthi**: brave **brought of lyve**: killed

That next hym was of worthynesse welle;   1565
And in this wo gan Troilus to dwelle
That, what for sorwe, and love, and for unreste,
Ful ofte a day he bad his herte breste.

But natheles, though he gan hym dispaire,
And dradde ay that his lady was untrewe,   1570
Yet ay on hire his herte gan repaire,
And as thise lovers don, he soughte ay newe
To gete ayeyn Criseyde, brighte of hewe;
And in his herte he wente hire excusynge,
That Calkas caused al hire tariynge.   1575

And ofte tyme he was in purpos grete
Hymselven lik a pilgrym to desgise
To seen hire; but he may nat contrefete
To ben unknowen of folk that weren wise,
Ne fynde excuse aright that may suffise   1580
If he among the Grekis knowen were;
For which he wep ful ofte and many a tere.

To hire he wroot yet ofte tyme al newe
Ful pitously – he lefte it nought for slouthe –
Bisechyng hire that syn that he was trewe,   1585
That she wol come ayeyn and holde hire trouthe.
For which Criseyde upon a day, for routhe –
I take it so – touchyng al this matere,
Wrot hym ayeyn, and seyde as ye may here:

1565 **next**: next to **welle**: fount   1566 **dwelle**: remain
1567 **unreste**: emotional turmoil   1568 **bad**: begged **breste**: to break
1570 **dradde**: feared **untrewe**: unfaithful   1571 Yet his heart always resorted
to her   1572 **ay newe**: constantly   1573 **gete ayeyn**: win back **brighte of**
hewe: radiantly beautiful in appearance   1574 **hire excusynge**: exonerating
her   1575 **tariynge**: delaying   1576 **was in purpos grete**: fully intended
1577 To disguise himself like a pilgrim   1578 **contrefete**: pass himself off
1579 **unknowen**: unrecognized   1580 Nor devise an adequate excuse
1581 **knowen**: recognized   1583 **al newe**: afresh   1584 **lefte**: neglected **for**
slouthe: out of laziness   1586 **holde**: keep **trouthe**: pledge   1587 **for**
routhe: out of pity   1588 **touchyng**: concerning   1589 **ayeyn**: in reply

Litera Criseydis

1590   'Cupides sone, ensample of goodlyheede,
        O swerd of knyghthod, sours of gentilesse,
        How myght a wight in torment and in drede
        And heleles, yow sende as yet gladnesse?
        I herteles, I sik, I in destresse!
1595   Syn ye with me, nor I with yow, may dele,
        Yow neyther sende ich herte may nor hele.

        'Youre lettres ful, the papir al ypleynted,
        Conceyved hath myn hertes pietee;
        I have ek seyn with teris al depeynted
1600   Youre lettre, and how that ye requeren me
        To come ayeyn, which yet ne may nat be;
        But whi, lest that this lettre founden were,
        No mencioun ne make I now, for feere.

        'Grevous to me, God woot, is youre unreste,
1605   Youre haste, and that the goddes ordinaunce
        It semeth nat ye take it for the beste;
        Nor other thyng nys in youre remembraunce,
        As thynketh me, but only youre plesaunce.
        But beth nat wroth, and that I yow biseche;
1610   For that I tarie is al for wikked speche.

Litera Criseydis: Criseyde's letter   1590 **ensample**: model, pattern
goodlyheede: excellence   1591 **swerd**: sword **sours**: fount
1593 **heleles**: devoid of well-being   1594 **herteles**: disheartened **sik**: sick, ill
1595 **dele**: have dealings   1596 I can send you neither heart nor health
1597–8 My heart's compassion (*pietee*) has comprehended (*conceyved*) your
copious letters, the paper all filled with lamentations (*ypleynted*)
1599 **depeynted**: stained   1600 **requeren**: request   1601 **ayeyn**: back
1602–3 I won't mention why now . . .   1604 **Grevous**: painful
unreste: distress   1605 **haste**: impatience **ordinaunce**: decree
1607 **remembraunce**: memory, recollection   1608 **plesaunce**: pleasure
1609 **wroth**: angry   1610 The reason I delay is all because of malicious talk

'For I have herd wel moore than I wende,
Touchyng us two, how thynges han ystonde,
Which I shal with dissymelyng amende.
And beth nat wroth, I have ek understonde
How ye ne do but holden me in honde.   1615
But now no force. I kan nat in yow gesse
But alle trouthe and alle gentilesse.

'Comen I wol; but yet in swich disjoynte
I stonde as now that what yer or what day
That this shal be, that kan I naught apoynte.   1620
But in effect I pray yow, as I may,
Of youre good word and of youre frendship ay;
For trewely, while that my lif may dure,
As for a frend ye may in me assure.

'Yet preye ich yow, on yvel ye ne take   1625
That it is short which that I to yow write;
I dar nat, ther I am, wel lettres make,
Ne nevere yet ne koude I wel endite.
Ek gret effect men write in place lite;
Th'entente is al, and nat the lettres space.   1630
And fareth now wel. God have yow in his grace!
                                    La vostre C.'

This Troilus this lettre thoughte al straunge
Whan he it saugh, and sorwfullich he sighte;
Hym thoughte it lik a kalendes of chaunge.

1611 **wende:** expected   1612 **Touchyng:** regarding **ystonde:** stood
1613 **with dissymelyng amende:** put right by dissembling   1614 **beth nat
wroth:** do not be angry   1615 How you are only deceiving me   1616 **no
force:** it does not matter **gesse:** imagine   1618 **disjoynte:** difficult situation
1619 **stonde:** am placed **as now:** now   1620 **apoynte:** specify   1621 **in
effect:** essentially **pray:** beseech   1622 **good word:** approval
1623 **dure:** last   1624 **in me assure:** count on me   1625 **on yvel ye ne
take:** that you don't take it amiss   1627 **make:** write
1628 **endite:** compose   1629 Also, people write matters of great consequence
in little space   1630 **entente:** meaning, import **the lettres space:** the length of
the letter **La vostre C.:** Your C   1632 **straunge:** distant
1633 **sorwfullich:** sorrowfully   1634 **kalendes:** bo͞vi͞ni͞n…

1635   But fynaly, he ful ne trowen myghte
        That she ne wolde hym holden that she hyghte;
        For with ful yvel wille list hym to leve
        That loveth wel, in swich cas, though hym greve.

        But natheles men seyn that at the laste,
1640   For any thyng, men shal the soothe se;
        And swich a cas bitidde, and that as faste,
        That Troilus wel understod that she
        Nas nought so kynde as that hire oughte be.
        And fynaly, he woot now out of doute
1645   That al is lost that he hath ben aboute.

        Stood on a day in his malencolie
        This Troilus, and in suspecioun
        Of hire for whom he wende for to dye.
        And so bifel that thoroughout Troye town,
1650   As was the gise, iborn was up and down
        A manere cote-armure, as seith the storie,
        Byforn Deiphebe, in signe of his victorie;

        The whiche cote, as telleth Lollius,
        Deiphebe it hadde rent fro Diomede
1655   The same day. And whan this Troilus
        It saugh, he gan to taken of it hede,
        Avysyng of the lengthe and of the brede,
        And al the werk; but as he gan byholde,
        Ful sodeynly his herte gan to colde,

1635 **ful**: completely   1636–8 That she would not keep her promise to him;
for he who is very much in love is very reluctant to believe in such a case,
although it may trouble him   1640 **For**: despite **soothe**: truth
1641 **bitidde**: happened **as faste**: very quickly   1645 **aboute**: engaged in
1646 **malencolie**: depression   1647 **suspecioun**: suspicion   1648 **wende for
to dye**: thought he would die   1649 **bifel**: it happened   1650 **gise**: custom
1650–51 **iborn . . . cote-armure**: a kind of tunic (embroidered with a heraldic
device) was borne   1652 **Byforn**: in front of **Deiphebe**: Deiphebus
signe: token   1654 **rent**: torn   1656 **taken of it hede**: pay attention to it
1657 **Avysyng of**: studying **brede**: breadth   1658 **werk**: workmanship
1659 **colde**: grow cold

As he that on the coler fond withinne   1660
A broch that he Criseyde yaf that morwe
That she from Troie moste nedes twynne,
In remembraunce of hym and of his sorwe.
And she hym leyde ayeyn hire feith to borwe
To kepe it ay! But now ful wel he wiste,   1665
His lady nas no lenger on to triste.

He goth hym hom and gan ful soone sende
For Pandarus, and al this newe chaunce,
And of this broche, he tolde hym word and ende,
Compleynyng of hire hertes variaunce,   1670
His longe love, his trouthe, and his penaunce;
And after deth, withouten wordes moore,
Ful faste he cride, his reste hym to restore.

Than spak he thus, 'O lady myn, Criseyde,
Where is youre feith, and where is youre biheste?   1675
Where is youre love? Where is youre trouthe?' he
     seyde.
'Of Diomede have ye now al this feeste?
Allas, I wolde han trowed atte leeste
That syn ye nolde in trouthe to me stonde,
That ye thus nolde han holden me in honde.   1680

'Who shal now trowe on any othes mo?
Allas, I nevere wolde han wend, er this,
That ye, Criseyde, koude han chaunged so;

1660 **coler**: collar **withinne**: inside   1661 **broch**: brooch   1662 **moste nedes twynne**: must necessarily depart   1664 And in return (*ayeyn*) she gave him her word as a pledge (*to borwe*)   1666 **on to triste**: to be trusted
1668 **chaunce**: occurrence   1669 **word and ende**: beginning and end, everything   1670 **variaunce**: changeability, fickleness
1671 **penaunce**: suffering   1672–3 **after deth . . . he cride**: he called upon death   1675 **feith**: pledged word **biheste**: promise   1677 **feeste**: enjoyment
1679 **in trouthe to me stonde**: to remain faithful to me   1680 **holden me in honde**: deceived me, played me along   1681 **trowe**: believe **othes**: oaths
1682 **wend**: imagined

Ne, but I hadde agilt and don amys,
1685   So cruel wende I nought youre herte, ywis,
To sle me thus! Allas, youre name of trouthe
Is now fordon, and that is al my routhe.

'Was ther non other broch yow liste lete
To feffe with youre newe love,' quod he,
1690   'But thilke broch that I, with teris wete,
Yow yaf as for a remembraunce of me?
Non other cause, allas, ne hadde ye
But for despit, and ek for that ye mente
Al outrely to shewen youre entente.

1695   'Thorugh which I se that clene out of youre mynde
Ye han me cast – and I ne kan nor may,
For al this world, withinne myn herte fynde
To unloven yow a quarter of a day!
In corsed tyme I born was, weilaway,
1700   That yow, that doon me al this wo endure,
Yet love I best of any creature!

'Now God,' quod he, 'me sende yet the grace
That I may meten with this Diomede!
And trewely, if I have myght and space,
1705   Yet shal I make, I hope, his sydes blede.
O God,' quod he, 'that oughtest taken heede
To fortheren trouthe, and wronges to punyce,
Whi nyltow don a vengeaunce of this vice?

1684 **Ne:** nor **but:** unless **agilt:** offended   1686 **sle:** kill **name of trouthe:** reputation for loyalty   1687 **fordon:** destroyed **routhe:** sorrow
1688 **yow liste lete:** you were willing to give up   1689 **To feffe with:** with which to endow   1690 **wete:** wet   1691 **Yow yaf:** gave you **as for:** for **remembraunce:** memento   1693 **for despit:** as an insult   1694 **Al outrely:** quite openly   1695 **clene:** completely, clean   1697 **For al this world:** for anything   1698 **unloven:** cease to love   1699 **corsed:** accursed **weilaway:** alas   1700 **doon:** make   1701 **Yet:** still
1704 **space:** opportunity   1705 **sydes:** sides (of his body)   1706 **taken heede:** to take care   1707 **fortheren:** promote **punyce:** punish
1708 **vice:** wrong

'O Pandare, that in dremes for to triste
Me blamed hast, and wont art oft upbreyde,   1710
Now maistow sen thiself, if that the liste,
How trewe is now thi nece, bright Criseyde!
In sondry formes, God it woot,' he seyde,
'The goddes shewen bothe joie and tene
In slep, and by my drem it is now sene.   1715

'And certeynly, withouten moore speche,
From hennesforth, as ferforth as I may,
Myn owen deth in armes wol I seche;
I recche nat how soone be the day!
But trewely, Criscyde, swete may,   1720
Whom I have ay with al my myght yserved,
That ye thus doon, I have it nat deserved.'

This Pandarus, that al thise thynges herde,
And wiste wel he seyde a soth of this,
He nought a word ayeyn to hym answerde;   1725
For sory of his frendes sorwe he is,
And shamed for his nece hath don amys,
And stant, astoned of thise causes tweye,
As stille as ston; a word ne kowde he seye.

But at the laste thus he spak, and seyde: 1730
'My brother deer, I may do the namore.
What sholde I seyen? I hate, ywys, Criseyde;
And, God woot, I wol hate hire evermore!
And that thow me bisoughtest don of yoore,
Havyng unto myn honour ne my reste   1735
Right no reward, I dide al that the leste.

1710 **wont art**: are accustomed **upbreyde**: to reproach   1711 **maistow
sen**: you can see   1713 **sondry**: differing   1714 **shewen**: reveal
tene: affliction   1717 **ferforth**: far   1718 **armes**: deeds of arms **seche**: seek
1719 **recche**: care   1720 **may**: girl   1724 **seyde a soth of**: spoke the truth
about   1725 **ayeyn**: in reply   1727 **shamed**: ashamed **don amys**: acted
wrongly   1728 **stant**: remains **astoned**: dumbfounded   1734 **that**: what
bisoughtest: implored **of yoore**: formerly   1736 **reward**: regard **the
leste**: you wished

'If I dide aught that myghte liken the,
It is me lief; and of this tresoun now,
God woot that it a sorwe is unto me!
1740   And dredeles, for hertes ese of yow,
Right fayn I wolde amende it, wiste I how.
And fro this world, almyghty God I preye
Delivere hire soon! I kan namore seye.'

Gret was the sorwe and pleynte of Troilus,
1745   But forth hire cours Fortune ay gan to holde.
Criseyde loveth the sone of Tideüs,
And Troilus moot wepe in cares colde.
Swich is this world, whoso it kan byholde;
In ech estat is litel hertes reste –
1750   God leve us for to take it for the beste!

In many cruel bataille, out of drede,
Of Troilus, this ilke noble knyght,
As men may in thise olde bokes rede,
Was seen his knyghthod and his grete myght,
1755   And dredeles, his ire, day and nyght,
Ful cruwely the Grekis ay aboughte;
And alwey moost this Diomede he soughte.

And ofte tyme, I fynde that they mette
With blody strokes and with wordes grete,
1760   Assayinge how hire speres weren whette;
And, God it woot, with many a cruel hete
Gan Troilus upon his helm to bete!

1737 aught: anything liken the: please you   1738 It is me lief: I am glad of it
tresoun: treachery   1740 for hertes ese of yow: to comfort you
1741 amende: set right wiste I: if I knew   1744 pleynte: lamentation
1745 cours: course holde: keep to   1748 byholde: perceive
1749 estat: condition, state   1750 leve: grant   1752–4 The knighthood and
the great strength of this noble knight Troilus was seen, as can be read about
in old books   1756 aboughte: paid for   1760 Assayinge: testing
speres: spears whette: sharpened   1761 hete: onslaught of rage
1762 helm: helmet bete: strike

But natheles, Fortune it naught ne wolde
Of oothers hond that eyther deyen sholde.

And if I hadde ytaken for to write   1765
The armes of this ilke worthi man,
Than wolde ich of his batailles endite;
But for that I to writen first bigan
Of his love, I have seyd as I kan –
His worthi dedes, whoso list hem heere,   1770
Rede Dares, he kan telle hem alle ifeere –

Bysechyng every lady bright of hewe,
And every gentil womman, what she be,
That al be that Criseyde was untrewe,
That for that gilt she be nat wroth with me.   1775
Ye may hire gilt in other bokes se;
And gladlier I wol write, if yow leste,
Penelopeës trouthe and good Alceste.

N'y sey nat this al oonly for thise men,
But moost for wommen that bitraised be   1780
Thorugh false folk – God yeve hem sorwe, amen! –
That with hire grete wit and subtilte
Bytraise yow. And this commeveth me
To speke, and in effect yow alle I preye,
Beth war of men, and herkneth what I seye!   1785

1763 **it naught ne wolde**: would not have it   1764 **oothers**: the other's
1765 **ytaken**: undertaken   1766 **armes**: feats of arms   1767 **endite**: write
1770 Whoever wishes to hear of his brave deeds   1771 **Rede Dares**: read
Dares Phrygius (n.) **ifeere**: together   1772 **bright of hewe**: radiantly beautiful
in appearance   1773 **what**: whoever   1774 **al be that**: although
untrewe: unfaithful   1775 **gilt**: offence **wroth**: angry   1777 **gladlier**: more
willingly **write**: write about   1778 **Penelopeës trouthe**: the faithfulness of
Penelope (n.)   1779 **N'y sey nat**: nor do I say **al oonly**: solely
1780 **moost**: chiefly **bitraised**: betrayed   1781 **false**: treacherous
1782 **wit**: cunning **subtilte**: craftiness   1783 **Bytraise**: betray
commeveth: moves   1784 **in effect**: essentially   1785 **Beth war**: beware

Go, litel bok, go, litel myn tragedye,
Ther God thi makere yet, er that he dye,
So sende myght to make in som comedye!
But litel book, no makyng thow n'envie,
1790   But subgit be to alle poesye;
And kis the steppes where as thow seest pace
Virgile, Ovide, Omer, Lucan, and Stace.

And for ther is so gret diversite
In Englissh and in writyng of oure tonge,
1795   So prey I God that non myswrite the,
Ne the mysmetre for defaute of tonge;
And red wherso thow be, or elles songe,
That thow be understonde, God I biseche! –
But yet to purpos of my rather speche:

1800   The wrath, as I bigan yow for to seye,
Of Troilus the Grekis boughten deere,
For thousandes his hondes maden deye,
As he that was withouten any peere,
Save Ector, in his tyme, as I kan heere.
1805   But weilawey, save only Goddes wille,
Despitously hym slough the fierse Achille.

And whan that he was slayn in this manere,
His lighte goost ful blisfully is went
Up to the holughnesse of the eighthe spere,

1787–8 **Ther God . . . sende**: may God . . . send **makere**: author **he**: i.e. the
author **mygt**: (the) power **make in**: compose   1789 **no makyng thow
n'envie**: do not vie with other compositions   1790 **subgit be to**: be humble,
deferential, towards **poesye**: poetry   1791 **steppes**: footprints **pace**: pass
by   1792 **Omer**: Homer **Stace**: Statius   1793 **diversite**: variety
1794 **tonge**: language   1795 **myswrite**: mistranscribe, miscopy   1796 Nor
spoil your metre (*mysmetre*) on account of deficient command of language
(see n. to 1793–6)   1797 **red**: read **wherso**: wherever **be**: may be
songe: sung   1799 **purpos**: the subject, the point **rather**: former
1801 **boughten deere**: paid for dearly   1803 **peere**: equal   1805 But alas –
except that it was God's will   1806 **Despitously**: cruelly **fierse**: ferocious
Achille: Achilles   1808 **lighte**: weightless **goost**: spirit **blisfully**: happily **is
~~~~ ~~~ ~~~~**   1809 **holughnesse**: concave inner side **spere**: sphere

In convers letyng everich element;   1810
And ther he saugh with ful avysement
The erratik sterres, herkenyng armonye
With sownes ful of hevenyssh melodie.

And down from thennes faste he gan avyse
This litel spot of erthe that with the se   1815
Embraced is, and fully gan despise
This wrecched world, and held al vanite
To respect of the pleyn felicite
That is in hevene above; and at the laste,
Ther he was slayn his lokyng down he caste,   1820

And in hymself he lough right at the wo
Of hem that wepten for his deth so faste,
And dampned al oure werk that foloweth so
The blynde lust, the which that may nat laste,
And sholden al oure herte on heven caste;   1825
And forth he wente, shortly for to telle,
Ther as Mercurye sorted hym to dwelle.

Swich fyn hath, lo, this Troilus for love!
Swich fyn hath al his grete worthynesse!
Swich fyn hath his estat real above!   1830
Swich fyn his lust, swich fyn hath his noblesse!
Swych fyn hath false worldes brotelnesse!

1810 Leaving behind every element (the planetary spheres, or the four
elements) on the reverse (convex) side (*In convers*)   1811 **ful
avysement**: unimpeded vision   1812 **erratik sterres**: wandering stars (the
seven planets) **herkenyng**: hearing **armonye**: the music of the spheres
1813 **sownes**: sounds **hevenyssh**: celestial   1814 **faste**: intently
avyse: contemplate   1815 **spot**: speck **se**: sea   1817 **held al**: considered
everything   1818 In comparison with the complete happiness
1820 **Ther**: to where **lokyng**: gaze **caste**: directed   1821 **lough**: laughed
1823 **dampned**: condemned **werk**: actions **foloweth so**: are so much in
pursuit of   1825 **sholden**: (we) should **caste**: direct   1827 **Ther as**: to where
sorted: assigned   1828 **Swich fyn**: such an end   1830 **estat real**: royal
station   1831 **noblesse**: nobility   1832 **false**: untrustworthy, deceptive
brotelnesse: fickleness, fragility

And thus bigan his lovyng of Criseyde,
As I have told, and in this wise he deyde.

1835 O yonge, fresshe folkes, he or she,
In which that love up groweth with youre age,
Repeyreth hom fro worldly vanyte,
And of youre herte up casteth the visage
To thilke God that after his ymage
1840 Yow made, and thynketh al nys but a faire,
This world that passeth soone as floures faire.

And loveth hym the which that right for love
Upon a crois, oure soules for to beye,
First starf, and roos, and sit in hevene above;
1845 For he nyl falsen no wight, dar I seye,
That wol his herte al holly on hym leye.
And syn he best to love is, and most meke,
What nedeth feynede loves for to seke?

Lo here, of payens corsed olde rites!
1850 Lo here, what alle hire goddes may availle!
Lo here, thise wrecched worldes appetites!
Lo here, the fyn and guerdoun for travaille
Of Jove, Appollo, of Mars, of swich rascaille!
Lo here, the forme of olde clerkis speche
1855 In poetrie, if ye hire bokes seche.

1834 deyde: died   1836 In whom love grows as you yourselves grow up
1837 Repeyreth hom: return home vanyte: vain pursuits, pleasures
1838 And turn your heart's face up   1839 thilke: that same   1840 nys
but: is only faire: fair (i.e. a temporary entertainment)   1841 floures
faire: lovely flowers   1843 crois: cross beye: redeem   1844 starf: died
roos: rose sit: sits   1845 falsen: betray   1846 holly: wholly leye: commit
1847 meke: meek   1848 nedeth: need is there feynede: pretended, not real
seke: seek   1849 payens: pagans' corsed: accursed rites: rites, practices
1850 See what use all their gods can be!   1851 appetites: hungers, cravings
1852 travaille: effort   1853 rascaille: rabble   1854 forme: essence
1855 seche: examine

O moral Gower, this book I directe
To the and to the, philosophical Strode,
To vouchen sauf, ther nede is, to correcte,
Of youre benignites and zeles goode.
And to that sothfast Crist, that starf on rode,   1860
With al myn herte of mercy evere I preye,
And to the Lord right thus I speke and seye:

Thow oon, and two, and thre, eterne on lyve,
That regnest ay in thre, and two, and oon,
Uncircumscript, and al maist circumscrive,   1865
Us from visible and invisible foon
Defende, and to thy mercy, everichon,
So make us, Jesus, for thi mercy, digne,
For love of mayde and moder thyn benigne.
                                        Amen.

Explicit liber Troili et Criseydis.

1856 **Gower:** John Gower (n.)   **directe:** dedicate (or send)
1857 **Strode:** Ralph Strode (n.)   1858 **vouchen sauf:** agree **ther nede
is:** where needed   1859 **Of:** out of **benignites:** kindness **zeles:** zeal
1860 **sothfast:** true **starf:** died **rode:** cross   1861 **of mercy evere I preye:** I
beg for mercy continually   1863 **oon, and two, and thre:** Trinity of Father,
Son, and Holy Ghost **eterne on lyve:** living everlastingly   1864 **That
regnest:** who reign   1865 **Uncircumscript:** boundless **al maist
circumscrive:** may encompass everything   1866 **foon:** foes
1868 **digne:** worthy   1869 **mayde:** virgin **benigne:** gracious *Explicit,
etc.:* Here ends the book of Troilus and Criseyde

A Table of Parallels: *Troilus and Criseyde* and *Il Filostrato*

The following table sets out the main parallels between the two poems, referring to line numbers in *Troilus and Criseyde* and to stanzas in *Il Filostrato* (with some line-numbers, where provided, after an oblique). Some parallels are more fully described in the following Notes.

Troilus, Book 1	Filostrato
21–30	1.5–6
57–140	7–16
148–231	17–25
267–73	26
281–329	27–32/6
354–92	32/7–37
421–546	38–57
547–53	2.1
568–630	2–10
646–7	11/1
666–7	13/7–8
673–86	11/7–8; 12
701–3, 708–14	13
722–4	15/1–2
856–65; 874–89	16–17; 20–22
967–94	24; 27–8
1009–64	29–34

Troilus, Book 2	Filostrato
148–52	2.35
274–91	35–6; 44
316–20	46
393–9	54–5
407–20	47–8
501–9, 519–22	55–7
540–41	61/1–2
554–78	62–4
584–8	43
596–604	68
659–65; 704–7	72
733–5	70
746–63; 768–812	69; 73; 75–8
960–81	79–81; 89
995–1009	90–91
1044–64	93–5
1065–92	97; 105; 107
1093–1104	108–9
1120–58	109–13
1173–8	114
1195–1200	118
1205–9	119
1212–26	120–28; 134
1321–51	128–31

Troilus, Book 3	Filostrato
1–38	3.74–9
239–87	5–10

330–36	9–10	1331–48	131–4
344–441	11–20	1359–72	132/2; 134/2;
1310–23	31–3		135–6
1338–65	34–7	1422–46	137–40
1373–86	38–9	1464–1542	141–6
1394–1426	40–43	1555–1659	147–63
1443–52	44	1667–1701	164–7
1471–93	44–8		
1499–1555	49–56/1		

Troilus, Book 5 *Filostrato*

15–90	5.1–6; 10–13
190–261	14–21; 24–8
280–95	22–3
323–36;	29–32
353–64	
386–686	33–8; 40–61;
	67–71

1588–1624	56–60		
1639–80	61–5		
1695–1701	70		
1709–43	71–3		
1772–1806	90–93		

Troilus, Book 4 *Filostrato*

1–10	3.94	687–93;	6.1–6
29–35	4.1	708–43	
47–112	2–11	750–55	7
127–68	12–16	766–805	8; 10–11; 33;
211–322	17; 22; 26–36		24
330–57	38–43	841–7	9
365–85	44–6	855–942	12–25
393–406	47–8	953–8	26–7
415	49	967–91	28–31
439–51	50	1100–1354	7.1–32; 40–41;
452–628	52; 54–8;		48–55
	60–75	1373–1421	60; 62; 72; 75
631–7	76	1422–39	76; 105; 77
645–795	77–92	1513–22	27; 89–90
799–821	95–6	1523–37	100–102; 104
841–926	97–107	1562–86	8.1–5
939–48	108–9	1632–1764	6–26
1083–95	109–10	1800–1806	27
1108–1253	110; 112–27	1828–36	28–9
1303–6;	133		
1324–7			

Notes

References in these notes to works of Chaucer other than *Troilus and Criseyde* are to *The Riverside Chaucer*, general editor Larry D. Benson (Boston, 1987; Oxford, 1988). References to Boccaccio's works are to *Tutte le opere di Giovanni Boccaccio*, general editor V. Branca (Verona, 1964– ; *Il Filocolo* in vol. 1, *Il Filostrato* and *Il Teseida* in vol. 2), and to his *De genealogia deorum*, editor V. Romano (Bari, 1951). References to classical authors are to the relevant volume in the Loeb Classical Library. Biblical references are to the Vulgate Bible and Apocrypha unless otherwise stated.

References to the following works are by author name and/or title:

Andreas Capellanus *De Amore*, in Walsh 1982

Benoît, *Troie* Benoît de Sainte-Maure, *Le Roman de Troie*, in Constans 1904–12

CT The Canterbury Tales

Dante *La divina commedia*, in Singleton 1970–75; other works, in Moore and Toynbee 1924

Gower *Complete Works of John Gower*, in Macaulay 1899–1902

Guido, *Historia* Guido de Columnis, *Historia destructionis Troiae*, in Griffin 1936

Hassell J. W. Hassell, *Middle French Proverbs, Sentences, and Proverbial Phrases* (Toronto, 1982)

Machaut *Oeuvres de Guillaume de Machaut*, in Hoepffner 1908–21

MED Middle English Dictionary, ed. H. Kurath, S. M. Kuhn and Robert E. Lewis (Ann Arbor, 1954–2001)

PL Patrologia Latina in Migne 1844–

Roman de la Rose in Langlois 1914–24

Roman de Thèbes in Constans 1890

Romaunt Romaunt of the Rose, in *The Riverside Chaucer*

TC Troilus and Criseyde

Vatican Mythographers *Scriptores rerum mythicarum Latini tres*, in Bode 1834

Walther H. Walther, *Proverbia Sententiaeque Latinitatis Medii Aevi* (9 vols.; Göttingen, 1963–9)

Whiting B. J. and H. W. Whiting, *Proverbs, Sentences, and Proverbial Phrases from English Writings Mainly Before 1500* (Cambridge, Mass., 1968)

Ylias Joseph of Exeter, *Frigii Daretis Ylias*, in Gompf 1970

Other references are in short form by modern author/editor name and date of publication (e.g. Windeatt 1984) to items in the Bibliography.

Citations from texts in languages other than English are usually confined to English translations by the present editor, except where inclusion of the original text also may be germane. Wherever possible, the *Roman de la Rose* is cited from the Middle English version in the *Romaunt of the Rose*; Boethius, *De consolatione philosophiae*, is generally cited from Chaucer's translation, the *Boece*.

For Cp+, Ph+ and R+, and a discussion of divergencies, see A Note on the Text. The identity of the manuscripts forming the Ph+ and R+ groups does not remain constant throughout the poem (for a table, see Windeatt 1992: 23). For the extant manuscripts of *TC*, and their abbreviations, see the List of Manuscripts.

The following conventions are used in any notes below on textual variants. The wording before the lemma (]) is the reading adopted in the text and usually represents the reading of all manuscripts not containing the variants listed after the lemma. In some cases, where relatively few manuscripts contain the adopted reading, those manuscripts may be listed immediately after the lemma (e.g. *herte*] Cp J).

BOOK 1

1–56 Not set off as a proem by a Latin incipit and explicit like the proems of Books 2, 3 and 4, but 1.52–6 signals a boundary between preface and narrative. *Filostrato*'s prose prologue tells how the author, during his lady's absence from Naples, decides to send her, in the story of Troiolo and Criseida, a likeness of his own love for her and sorrow in her absence. The author's account in this prologue of his sorrow at places he associates with their love is then echoed in *Filostrato* Part 5 and adapted into *TC* (see 5.561–81 and n.).

1–5   In the announcement of subject, in a syntactical structure of complement preceding verb, of lofty inversion and delay ('The double sorwe . . . to tellen . . . My purpos is') are contained echoes of how the epic poems of Virgil, Lucan and Statius begin, although Chaucer may have also known from Ovid's *Amores* the mock-epic use of such epic announcements of subject in order to begin a poem of love.

1   *double sorwe*: perhaps recalling Dante's reference to Statius, author (in his *Thebaid*) of 'the double sorrow of Jocasta' (*Purgatorio*, 22.56); cf. Troiolo's 'double sorrow' over the fainted Criseida (*Filostrato*, 4.118), and Orpheus's 'love that doublide his sorwe' (*Boece*, 3.m.12.26).

3–4   *TC* is later termed a tragedy (see 5.1786n.), and movement through 'wele' and 'wo' (a common collocation) recalls the definition of tragedy in Chaucer's translation of Boethius: 'a dite [literary work] of a prosperite for a tyme, that endeth in wrecchidnesse' (*Boece*, 2.pr.2.71–2).

5–7   For the stance of addressing a present audience (5) and of being in the act of composing a written text (7), see Introduction, p. xxx.

5   *fro ye*: The only instance in Chaucer's works where *ye* takes the place of the normal objective form *yow*; possibly a weakened form appropriate to informal spoken use (Mustanoja 1960: 125; Davis 1974: 70). For the rhyming of two words with one (*Troye*/*fro ye*), known as 'broken rhyme', see Metre and Versification.

6–9   *Thesiphone*: In the opening of *Filostrato* (1.2) Boccaccio addresses his lady as his muse (see *TC* 2.9), but *TC* instead addresses Tisiphone, one of the Furies (invoked by Oedipus in Statius, *Thebaid*, 1.56–9, 85–7). For the Furies as both tormenting and suffering (cf. *TC* 4.22–4), see *Boece*, 3.m.12.33–7 ('And the thre goddesses, furiis and vengeresses of felonyes, that tormenten and agasten the soules by anoy, woxen sorweful and sory, and wepyn teeris for pite'), and also Ovid, *Metamorphoses*, 10.45–6; Virgil, *Aeneid*, 2.337, 7.324.

7   *vers, that wepen*: Cf. *Filostrato*, 1.6 ('my tearful verses'), and *Boece*, 1.m.1.1–2 ('Allas! I wepynge, am constreyned to bygynnen vers of sorwful matere').

11   *to pleyne*: Boethius defines the function of tragedy as complaint and lamentation: 'What other thynge bywaylen the cryinges of tragedyes but oonly the dedes of Fortune . . . ?' (*Boece*, 2.pr.2.67–8).

14   A rhetorical commonplace; see *Squire's Tale*, V.103 ('Accordant to his wordes was his cheere') and Whiting W254.

15   Alluding to the papal title 'servus servorum Dei' ('The Pope calleth
      hymself servant of the servantz of God', *Parson's Tale*, X.773).
      Language of love-as-service and of lovers as servants will be
      pervasive in *TC*, as also the stance of writing as an outsider to the
      experience of love. For the convention of the 'religion of love' (cf.
      1.15–49), see also 1.36–42, 2.530–32 (the sin of despair); 1.336–
      40, 4.778–84 (love as a form of religious order); 1.932–45,
      2.523–41 (confession and repentance); 1.995–1008, 2.1503
      (conversion, heresy, salvation); 3.704, 1656–9 (heavenly bliss);
      3.1267, 1282 (grace and mercy).

22   *ye loveres*: With the address to lovers, cf. *Filostrato*, 1.6 ('I beg
      those of you who are lovers . . . to pray for me to Love, who
      afflicts me as he did Troiolo').

29–46 These exhortations to prayer imitate the form of the 'bidding
      prayer' in which the priest requests prayers for particular cate-
      gories of people, as in *The Lay Folks' Mass Book* (Simmons 1879:
      61–80, 315–46; especially p. 74: 'And in generall for all men
      & women of relygyon . . . And for all the lordys gentylles &
      comynerrys . . . And specially for all thos s[ou]llys that has moste
      nyde to be prayed for').

36   *despeired*: Cf. the sin of despairing of the mercy of God, which is
      to sin against the Holy Ghost (see *Parson's Tale*, X.693–705).

39   *wikked tonges*: Fear of gossips is a motif of medieval courtly
      literature; cf. the role of Male Bouche ('Wikked Tunge') in the
      Roman de la Rose, and see *TC* 2.785; 5.1610. On the lovers'
      concern for secrecy in *TC*, see 1.322n., 743–6; 2.785–6; 3.281ff.

56   *er she deyde*: Chaucer's sources included no account of the death
      of Criseyde, and neither does *TC* (see 5.1058–60n.).

58–60 For the thousand ships and the ten-year war, see Virgil, *Aeneid*,
      2.198, and Ovid, *Heroides*, 13.97. Benoît de Sainte-Maure
      numbers the ships at 1130 (*Troie*, 5701–2), and Guido de Col-
      umnis corrects Homer's 1186 ships to 1222 (*Historia*, p. 90).

62   *Eleyne*: Wife of Menelaus (younger brother of Agamemnon), king
      of Sparta; Helen's abduction by Paris led to the Siege of Troy.

66   *Calkas*: In Homer a Greek (*Iliad*, 1.69); in medieval tradition a
      Trojan, taking the place of Homer's Chryses, priest of Apollo (see
      Lumiansky 1954; Greenfield 1967; Rigg 1998); in *Filostrato* an
      astrologer, Calchas's status as 'a lord of gret auctoritee' is
      increased by Chaucer.

70   *Delphicus*: Apollo has this epithet in Ovid, *Metamorphoses*,
      2.543, and *Fasti*, 3.856. For Calchas's visit to the oracle of Apollo
      at Delphi (not in *Filostrato*) Chaucer returns to Benoît (*Troie*,

5817–920) and Guido (*Historia*, p. 98). Warned by the oracle, Calchas defects to the Greeks, having met Achilles at Delphi. See also 4.1409–11.

71–7 Calchas's astrological calculations and divination by casting of lots allow word-play on 'Calchas/calculation', as too on 'Troy/destroyed'.

83   *In trust that he hath*: The Ph+ variant here ('Hopyng in hym') is closer to *Filostrato*, 1.9: 'Da lui sperando' (from him hoping for).

85   *The noise up ros*: The Ph+ variant 'Gret rumour gan' translates *Filostrato*, 1.10: 'Fu'l romor grande'.

87–91 *Filostrato* tells how Calchas had acted like a traitor (1.10), but Chaucer's version suggests an awareness of the English law of treason: *TC* emphasizes the breach of faith (1.87), twice terms it treason (1.107, 117), and the popular judgement is to burn not his house (as in *Filostrato*) but Calchas himself, and to extend the punishment to his family. Although *De legibus et consuetudinibus angliae*, the medieval English legal treatise attributed to Henry de Bracton, held that a convicted traitor should be punished with death and loss of his goods and that his heirs should be disinherited in perpetuity and 'hardly permitted their lives', in practice the punishment extended only to the perpetrator (Bellamy 1970: 138–76; Hornsby 1988: 121–31). See also 4.203–5n.

96   *As she that*: Possibly a calque (loan-translation) on the Old French 'com cil qui', meaning 'for she' (Kerkhof 1982: 278), but in some contexts it may also be understood to mean 'like a person who' (Yager 1994); cf. 2.841; 3.1162; 5.18, 177, 953, 1413.

97–8 *allone Of any frend*: Emphasis on Criseyde's isolation is added to *Filostrato* (1.11), despite her uncle Pandarus, three nieces and other company mentioned later.

99   *Criseyde*: Boccaccio altered to 'Criseida' ('Griseida' in some *Filostrato* MSS) the name 'Briseida' that he found in Benoît's *Troie* and Guido's *Historia*. In *Remedia Amoris* (467–75) Ovid describes how the Trojan priest Chryses appeals to the Greeks to ransom back his captured daughter Chryseis, and they do so at the intervention of a Greek soothsayer named Calchas. Boccaccio may have misunderstood Ovid to be referring to 'Chryseida' in the *Remedia* as the daughter of Calchas.

104–5 Boccaccio's Criseida too is so angelic in appearance that she does not seem mortal (1.11), but Criseyde's heavenly perfection seems to defy nature itself. For Nature's role under God, cf. *Physician's Tale*, VI.19–22, and for traditional references in descriptions of feminine beauty to Nature's role and pleasure in her handiwork, cf. *Book of the Duchess*, 870–73; *Anelida and Arcite*, 78–80; *Parliament of Fowls*, 372–8.

110 *Ector*: The eldest son of Priam and Hecuba, brother of Troilus, and greatest and bravest of Trojan warriors. Chaucer later adds Hector's principled opposition to Criseyde's exchange (4.176–82; not in *Filostrato*); his death in battle at the hands of Achilles is lamented (*TC* 5.1548–65).

111 The Ph+ variant form of this line ('With chere and voys ful pytous and wepynge') is closer to *Filostrato*, 1.12: 'E con voce e con vista assai pietosa' (And with voice and look most piteous).

132–3 Actually, *Filostrato* (1.15) plainly says she had not been able to have children, and in Benoît's *Troie* she is an unmarried girl ('pucele': 13111). For the fiction of omissions or lacking information in the source, see also *TC* 3.501–4; 5.826, 1088; for references to a source, when Chaucer is actually working independently of *Filostrato*, cf. *TC* 2.14, 18, 49, 699–700; 3.575, 1196, 1325, 1817; 4.1415; 5.799n.

138–40 For the commonplace of Fortune's wheel (not in *Filostrato* here), see *TC* 4.1–11 and *Boece*, 2.pr.2.51–4 ('I torne the whirlynge wheel with the turnynge sercle; I am glad to chaungen the loweste to the heyeste, and the heyeste to the loweste'); cf. Whiting F506, Hassell F123, R85.

139 *And under eft*] *Now up now down* Cp; *And wonder ofte* Cl A D Dg S2; *Right wondir ofte* H4; *And eyther oft* Gg.

143 *here*] J Gg H3 Cx; *right* R; other MSS omit.

146 *Omer ... Dares ... Dite*: Boccaccio does not refer to these authorities here in *Filostrato*. The *De excidio Troiae historia* (The Fall of Troy, A History) by Dares Phrygius and the *Ephemeridos belli Troiani libri* (A Journal of the Trojan War) by Dictys Cretensis both purport to be eyewitness accounts by participants in the Trojan War, but the extant Latin versions date from the sixth and fourth centuries AD respectively, and both probably derive from first-century Greek originals (see Introduction, p. xvi; cf. Eisenhut 1958, Frazer 1966, Meister 1873). Homer's *Iliad* would not have been known directly to Chaucer, and Dares was more widely read than Dictys in the medieval west (cf. *TC* 5.1771), which regarded Homer as unreliably partial to the Greeks. Chaucer probably relied on the twelfth-century Anglo-Latin expansion of Dares by Joseph of Exeter (see 5.799–840). Dares and Dictys (spelled 'Tytus') are listed among authorities on the Trojan story in the *House of Fame*, 1466–74; both Benoît and Guido spell Dictys without the 'c'. Benoît claims to follow

Dares (*Troie*, 45ff.); Guido claims to follow Dares and Dictys (*Historia*, p. 4).

153 *Palladion*: The Palladium, a sacred image of Pallas, upon which Troy's safety depended, until betrayed by Antenor (4.204–5); Chaucer follows a common French spelling of the classical name (cf. 2.105, 5.1500). For Chaucer's spelling of classical proper names, see 4.1411, 5.3, and for his Italianate spellings, see 2.435–6n.

156 *Aperil*: References to time and season in *TC* are generally added to *Filostrato*: Troilus first sees Criseyde in April; Book 2 opens on 3 May and continues in early May; consummation occurs at some time thereafter (3.624–5n.), but after Book 3 a break in time evidently intervenes, for at Criseyde's exchange the snows are said to have melted three times since Troilus and Criseyde first loved (5.8–13). In *Filostrato* the action lasts from one spring (1.18) until the next (7.78). The action of *TC* Book 2 apparently begins in May of the same year as the April mentioned here (see 2.54–5; 3.360), although the duration of Troilus's languishing is unspecified (1.442, 482, 487). For the time-scheme of Book 5, see 5.687n., 1086–92n. (On the *TC* time-scheme, see Sams 1941; Longo 1961; Bessent 1969; Bie 1976; Windeatt 1992: 198–204.) Working from the association of the planetary conjunction described in *TC* 3.624–5 with an actual occurrence of such a conjunction in May–June 1385, it has been suggested (North 1988) that the action of Books 1–3 occurs as if in April–June 1385 and that the action of Books 4–5, occurring three years later (5.8–13), may be synchronized with, and read in the light of, the actual state of the heavens in 1388 (see also 3.624–5; 4.32, 1591–2; 5.652–8, 1016–20, 1348–51).

162–70 First sight of the beloved in church or temple is a convention: Dante first saw Beatrice in church at Florence; Petrarch first saw Laura in church at Avignon; Boccaccio first saw 'Fiammetta' in church at Naples, at Easter (Griffin and Myrick 1929: 12ff.). Cf. especially Benoît's account (*Troie*, 17489ff.) of how Achilles fell in love with Polyxena (on whom, see *TC* 1.455n.). For parallels in accounts of the hero's falling in love between *Filostrato* and Boccaccio's own *Filocolo*, see Young 1908: 40–44, 167–70.

169 *Among thise othere folk*] *Among the which(e* Ph+. Cf. *Filostrato*, 1.19: 'Tra li qua' fu' (among whom was).

171 *oure firste lettre is now an A*: Perhaps a compliment to Anne of Bohemia, married to Richard II in January 1382. Cf. Henryson's *Testament of Cresseid*, 78–9: 'O fair Cresseid, the flour and *A*

per se [outstanding person] | Of Troy and Grece' (Fox 1981: 113).

175 *so bright a sterre*: For Criseyde as Troilus's star, see 5.232, 638,
1392. On Criseyde's association with light, see 4.313; 5.543–4,
1405; and with the traditional epithet 'bright' (fair, radiant) for
a lady, see 3.1485; 4.663, 740; 5.162n. Her fair hair is said to be
the colour of sunlight (4.736, 816).

182 'Assured Maner' is one of the lady's personified attributes in
Chaucer's *Complaint unto Pity* (40), and Machaut includes assur-
ance with humility as attributes of courtly women: in *Jugement
dou Roy de Behaingne* (394–5), 'she was graced with a modest
and confident manner' ('manière humble et asseüree'), and
Remède de Fortune (185–91, 197–200) praises first the lady's
humility but then 'sa manière asseüree . . .' (Anderson 1991).

183 *This Troilus*: The demonstrative 'this' with the name Troilus is
used some forty-two times, eleven times with Pandarus, sixteen
with Diomede, never with Criseyde.

184 *His yonge knyghtes*: Virgil (*Aeneid*, 1.475), Dares (*De excidio*,
ch. 12), Dictys (*Ephemeridos*, 4.11) and Joseph of Exeter (*Ylias*,
4.62; see below, 5.827–40n.) all refer to Troilus's youth, as do
Benoît (*Troie*, 5437–40), Guido (*Historia*, p. 44) and Boccaccio
(*Filostrato* proem: 'the valiant young Troiolo'); the First Vatican
Mythographer reports the tradition (cf. Plautus, *Bacchides*, 953–
5) that if Troilus attained the age of twenty Troy could not be
overthrown (Bode 1834: 210, 66). Since the love affair between
Troilus and Criseyde is later said to have lasted three years (*TC*
5.9), and if there is an indeterminate period before Criseyde
abandons Troilus for Diomede (5.1086–92n.) and before
Troilus's death in battle while still under twenty, this might make
Troilus sixteen or less in the present scene. But while the youth
of Troilus is noted (see *TC* 2.636; 5.830), the ages of Chaucer's
Criseyde and Pandarus are more uncertain (cf. 2.752; 3.293, 468;
5.826).

192 *his eighen baiten*: Cf. Love's advice to the Lover in the *Roman de
la Rose* upon catching sight of the lady: 'But with that sight thyne
eyen fede' (*Romaunt*, 2460).

203 *war by other*: Proverbial (Whiting F449). See also 1.630, 635,
3.329n.

210 'As proud as a peacock' is proverbial (Whiting P280). For the
plucked feathers of doomed Troy, see 5.1546.

211 *blynde*: Cf. *Filostrato*, 1.25 ('O blindness of worldly minds!') and
Dante's references to the 'blind world' (*Inferno*, 27.25, *Purgato-
rio*, 16.66). See *Boece*, 5.m.3.27–9; and also 4.pr.2.49–51 for

'the entencioun of the wil of mankynde, whiche that . . . hasteth to comen to blisfulnesse'. The ensuing excursus on love is added; Chaucer returns to following *Filostrato* at 1.267. On blindness, see also *TC* 1.628; 2.21; 3.528, 1808; 4.300, 312; 5.1824.

214–16 Cf. the proverb 'Pride will have a fall' (Whiting P393); the passage may suggest Troilus has stepped on to Fortune's wheel.

217 Proverbial: cf. Whiting F448, and John Barbour, *The Bruce*, 1.582, 11.21: 'But oft failyeis the fulis thocht' (Duncan 1997).

218 *proude Bayard*: Traditionally the bay steed given by Charlemagne to Renaud, but the name became associated with rashness (see *Canon's Yeoman's Tale*, VIII.1413–4: 'Ye been as boold as is Bayard the blynde, | That blondreth forth and peril casteth noon'). Horses were proverbially proud (Whiting H521; Walther 16856, 19031a), and traditionally an emblem of fleshly lusts, as also of lack of reason (Burnley 1976).

229 *a-fere*: For other such Kentish forms in rhyme, see 1.330; 3.510, 978, 1129.

233–5 In the *Roman de la Rose* the God of Love can 'maken folkis pride fallen; | And he can wel these lordis thrallen' (*Romaunt*, 881–2).

237 *alle thing may bynde*: See Troilus's song (3.1744–71); cf. also *Boece*, 3.m.12.53–5 ('Love is a grettere lawe and a strengere to hymself thanne any lawe that men mai yyven'), and *Knight's Tale*, I.1163–8. For the recurrent theme of binding and constraint in *TC*, see Barney 1972.

241–3 Cf. *Romaunt*, 4757–64 and Whiting M224. For Solomon, Virgil and Aristotle as love's 'wise' victims in medieval tradition, see Gower, *Confessio amantis*, 6.78–99. For Samson and Hercules, love's 'strong' victims, see *Wife of Bath's Prologue*, III.721–6.

245 Echoing the *Gloria Patri* ('as it was in the beginning, is now, and ever shall be').

250–52 The morally improving effects of love are emphasized later at 1.1076–85, 3.24–6, 1786–1806; cf. also Dante, *Vita Nuova*, 11, and Ovid, *Amores*, 1.9.46.

256 *bynde*: Cf. Love in the *Roman de la Rose*: 'For thee so sore I wole now bynde | That thou away ne shalt not wynde' (*Romaunt*, 2055–6).

257–8 Proverbial (Whiting B484).

264 *cares colde*: 'Cold' care (a common collocation) is recurrently associated with Troilus's misery, see 1.612; 3.1202, 1260; 4.1692; 5.1342, 1747.

274–80 This stanza, and also 295–301, on Troilus's inward reactions
to the sight of Criseyde, are added to *Filostrato*.

281   *nat with the leste*: This conforms with Joseph of Exeter's report
that Briseis was of average height (*Ylias*, 4.156; see *TC* 5.806n.);
Filostrato here (1.27) describes Criseida as tall.

295–8   The lady's appearance imprinted in the lover's heart is a
commonplace; on how 'alle figures most first comen fro thinges
fro withoute into soules, and ben emprientid into soules', see
Boece, 5.m.4.6–20. Imagery of impression for inward processes
recurs in *TC* (see 1.325; 3.1499–1502, 1541–4). Cf. Machaut,
Jugement dou Roy de Behaingne, 411–13 ('The sweet image of
her face was so imprinted within my heart that it remains there
still').

300   *his hornes in to shrinke*: Proverbial (Whiting H491). Cf. the
preachers' handbook, *Fasciculus Morum*, where the humble,
patient man 'can be compared to the turtle which, when you
touch it, at once draws in its horns and hides. When . . . touched
by his superior with fatherly correction, he will bow his head and
withdraw and hide his horns of pride and impatience' (Wenzel
1976: 148).

305   *subtile stremes*: As medieval physiology had it, an effluence passed
from Criseyde's eyes through Troilus's eyes into his heart. Cf.
Knight's Tale, I.1096–7.

307   *spirit in his herte*: The rays from Criseyde's eyes affect the 'vital'
spirit in his heart, which controlled pulse and breathing. (The
other two 'spirits' in medieval physiology were the 'natural' spirit
in the liver, and the 'animal' in the brain.) See Bartholomaeus
Anglicus, *De Proprietatibus Rerum* (trans. Trevisa), 3.14 (Sey-
mour 1975: i.103). See also *TC* 3.1088, 4.1142; and for the
context in medieval physiology, see Metlitzki 1977: 64–73.

321–2   For the concern with secrecy, see Introduction, pp. xxxiii–
xxxiv and Windeatt 1979b.

330–50   Although Boccaccio's Troiolo is reported as scorning lovers
(1.32), Chaucer adds this mocking direct speech for his Troilus.

336   *youre ordre is ruled*: Alluding to lovers as if members of a religious
order, with its observances and devotions. See also 1.998–1008,
4.782–4.

353   *lyme*: Birds were caught by liming the twigs of trees, and in the
Roman de la Rose Love is seen as a bird-catcher, trapping 'These
damoysels and bachelers. | Love will noon other briddes cacche'
(*Romaunt*, 1622–3). See also Ovid, *Ars amatoria*, 1.391 ('Once
its wings are limed, the bird cannot escape'). For other bird

references in *TC*, see 1.671; 2.925–31; 3.1191–2, 1233–7, 1496, 1784; 4.1432–3; 5.1546.

363 *a-temple*] Cl; *and temple* Cp A Gg H1 H3 J S1 Th W; *in the tempill* Dg H2 H5 Ph S2; *in temple* H4; *at temple* R.

365 *mirour of his mynde*: Cf. *Boece*, 5.m.4.6–20 (the belief that the soul, like a mirror or parchment, is imprinted with images it receives); *Romaunt*, 2804–8 (thought makes the lover's mind a mirror in which he sees his lady's person).

384–5 Cf. Andreas Capellanus, *De amore*, 2.8, rule 13: 'When made public, love rarely endures' (Walsh 1982). For bitter-sweet contrasts throughout the poem, see also 1.638–9; 3.179, 813–15, 1116–17, 1212–21; 5.731–2.

392 *nought repente*: The lover's resolution to love without repentance is a commonplace; cf. the lover in *Romaunt*, 1974–6 ('I wole been hool at youre devis ... And repente for nothyng'), and Machaut, *Fonteinne Amoreuse*, 2231 ('Et ameray sans repentir').

394 *Lollius*: Despite actually following Boccaccio's *Filostrato*, and shortly (1.400–420) borrowing from Petrarch, Chaucer claims (and again at 5.1653) a certain 'Lollius' as his authority, perhaps based on a misunderstanding of lines in one of the *Epistles* of Horace (1.2.1–2), in which he addresses his friend Maximus Lollius: 'Troiani belli scriptorem, Maxime Lolli, | dum tu declamas Romae, Praeneste relegi' (whilst you, Maximus Lollius, are engaged in oratory at Rome, I have been rereading at Praeneste the writer of the Trojan War [i.e. Homer]). This epistle (like Horace's *Ode*, 4.9) refers to Trojan matters, and if 'Maxime' were misread as 'greatest' instead of as part of the proper name, and if 'scriptorem' were read as 'scriptorum', then Lollius might be construed as 'the greatest writer about Troy'. The lines are quoted in John of Salisbury's *Policraticus* (Webb 1909: 7.9), which Chaucer knew, and a late twelfth-century *Policraticus* manuscript (Bodleian Library, MS Lat. misc. c.16) contains the line thus miscopied ('Troiani belli scriptorum maxime lolli ...'); moreover, in his French translation of *Policraticus*, made in 1372, Denis Foullechat declares of Horace: 'il dit que Lolli fu principal escrivain de la bataille de Troye ...' (he says that Lollius was the principal writer about the Trojan War; Pratt 1950). Lamenting that brave men lived, uncelebrated by poets, before the heroes of the Trojan War and are now forgotten, Horace's *Ode*, 4.9, aims to immortalize Lollius the Roman public figure and soldier ('O Lollius, I shall not let your efforts fade into oblivion'). Chaucer also mentions Lollius, among those whose works support the

fame of Troy, in *The House of Fame* (1465–72), a poem usually thought to pre-date *TC*. For the fiction of a Latin source, see 2.14 and n.

400–420 *Canticus Troili*: The apparatus of Latin rubrics or headings in *TC*, signalling the beginnings and ends of proems and books, and introducing songs and letters, is consistently present in good early manuscripts and is assumed to derive from Chaucer (the authorial origin of division into books is signalled within the text: see 3.1818; 4.26). Such an apparatus in a vernacular English poem was probably unknown hitherto, although some fifteenth-century scribes of *TC* manuscripts extended and elaborated an apparatus of headings and marginal glosses (see Benson and Windeatt 1990; Boffey 1995; Butterfield 1996).

Boccaccio simply reports that Troiolo sings (*Filostrato*, 1.37), without including the words of his song; Chaucer inserts his adaptation of Petrarch's sonnet 132 (here cited from Contini and Ponchiroli 1964: 184), the first extant use of a Petrarch sonnet in English before Wyatt. Among Chaucer's added motifs are the quenchless thirst (406), the strange illness (411) and the sensation of dying (420):

> S'amor non è, che dunque è quel ch'io sento?
> ma s'egli è amor, perdio, che cosa et quale?
> se bona, onde l'effecto aspro mortale?
> se ria, onde sí dolce ogni tormento?
>
> S'a mia voglia ardo, onde 'l pianto e lamento?
> S'a mal mio grado, il lamentar che vale?
> O viva morte, o dilectoso male,
> come puoi tanto in me s'io nol consento?
>
> Et s'io 'l consento, a gran torto mi doglio.
> Fra sí contrari venti in frale barca
> mi trovo in alto mar senza governo,
>
> sí lieve di saver, d'error sí carca
> ch'i' medesmo non so quel ch'io mi voglio,
> e tremo a mezza state, ardendo il verno.

(If this is not love, what is it that I feel then? But if it is love, by God, what kind of thing is it? If it is good, whence comes this bitter mortal effect? If it is evil, why is every torment so sweet? If

I am burning by my own will, whence comes the weeping and lamentation? If against my will, what use is there in lamenting? O living death! O delightful harm! How can you have so much power over me if I do not consent to it? And if I do consent to it, I complain very wrongly. Amid such contrary winds I find myself at sea in a fragile boat, so light of wisdom, so laden with error, that I myself do not know what I want; and I shiver in midsummer, burning in winter.)

400–403 Petrarch asks whether his incomprehensible feeling is love or not, and whether it is good or bad. Troilus poses a more general question: does love exist, and is the general nature of love good or bad? For the phrasing of 402–3, cf. *Boece*, 1.pr.4.198– 201: 'Yif God is, whennes comen wikkide thyngis? And yif God ne is, whennes comen gode thynges?' (Kaylor 1993).

400 Cf. the common Latin distich beginning: 'Nescio quid sit amor' (I do not know what love may be; Walther 16532).

406 For proverbial analogues, see Whiting D403; for imagery of drinking in *TC*, see 2.651, 784; 3.1214–16.

409 *If harme agree me*: Possibly mistranslating 'S'a mal mio grado' (if against my will), but Chaucer's manuscript may have read 'Se mal mi agrada' (if evil gives me pleasure).

411 *quike deth . . . swete harm*: Cf. Reason's critique of love in the *Roman de la Rose*, 4293–334, itself derived from Alanus de Insulis, *De planctu Naturae*, 9, especially: 'It is sike hele and hool seknesse, | A thurst drowned in dronknesse, | And helthe full of maladie' (*Romaunt*, 4721–3).

415 *possed*: Cf. *Roman de la Rose*: 'Thus am I possed up and doun | With dool, thought, and confusioun' (*Romaunt*, 4479–80).

416 *sterelees*: The rudderless boat is proverbial (Whiting S247; Hassell N9). For further navigational imagery in *TC*, see 1.526 and 606n. Petrarch's lines 12–13 are omitted here in *TC*.

420 Resembling Petrarch, *Rima* 182.5: 'Trem'al più caldo, ard'al più freddo cielo' (I shiver when it's hottest, burn when it's coldest). Cf. *Roman de la Rose* on the hot and cold of love: 'Thou shalt no whyle be in o stat, | But whylom cold and whilom hat' (*Romaunt*, 2397–8).

425 *goddesse or womman*: Troiolo has the same uncertainty in *Filostrato*, 1.38; cf. *Knight's Tale*, I.1101 (Palamon is uncertain whether Emelye is goddess or woman).

427 *as hire man*: Here and in 1.432–4 Troilus seems to allude to the language and gestures of the feudal homage ceremony with its pledge to become the lord's man, made by the vassal while

kneeling before the lord with hands enclosed within the lord's clasped hands, in symbolic resignation to the lord (see also 3.131–3n.).

435–6 On love's power, cf. 'Love is so mekyll of myghte, | That it will daunte bothe kyng and knyght' in the romance of *Ipomadon A*, 7346–7 (Purdie 2001).

449 Proverbial (Whiting F193); cf. *Romaunt*, 2478 ('Who is next fyr, he brenneth moost').

455 *Polixene*: The daughter of Priam and Hecuba, sister of Troilus. In early tradition Polyxena was sacrificed to the ghost of Achilles, prompting later stories that Achilles fell in love with her; Benoît's *Troie* includes a full account of their love affair.

458 *Good*] Cl J S1; *Goode* H1; *God* other MSS. *and*] Cl A Gg H5 R Th W; *in* Dg S2; other MSS omit. (For the reading 'Good goodly, whom to serven I laboure', see Brewer 1981.)

465 *fownes*] *fewnes* Cp; *foules* D; *fode no(r* Dg S2; *fantasie* H2 Ph; *sownes* H4; H5 omits.

484–7 For these typical symptoms of love sickness, cf. Andreas Capellanus, *De amore*, rules 23 and 15: 'He whom the thought of love vexes eats and sleeps very little', 'Every lover regularly turns pale in the presence of his love' (Walsh 1982); see also *Knight's Tale*, I.1355–76.

488–9 For the device of the feigned illness, see also 2.1512n.

502 For the bleeding heart of sorrow, see also 4.12, 5.17.

507 For love as a snare, see 1.663, 5.748 and *Romaunt*, 1647–8.

517 *daunce*: Cf. the Wife of Bath: 'Of remedies of love she knew per chaunce, | For she koude of that art the olde daunce' (*CT*, *General Prologue*, I.475–6). See also *TC* 2.1106, 3.695.

524–5 Proverbial comparisons (Whiting F679, S433).

532 *that fol*: Unidentified.

535–9 Chaucer omits the following *Filostrato* stanza (1.56), where Troiolo declares that, if Criseida told him to kill himself, he would do it to please her. See 1.608–9n.

543 *in salte teres dreynte*: To drown in tears is a courtly commonplace; see 4.510, 930, and also Chaucer's *Complaint of Mars*, 89, and *Envoy to Scogan*, 12.

547ff. Pandaro's entrance here begins the second Part of *Filostrato*, the opening scene of which Chaucer turns into the second half of his Book 1, which thus ends later, with Pandarus's agreement to help Troilus in his suit. Cf. Boccaccio, *Filocolo*, 1.214–22, where Duke Feramonte extracts a confession of love from Florio. Confession to a confidant of the hero's or heroine's being in love, and the confidant's plan to gain the beloved, is a type-scene of the romance genre, with a number of parallels in extant Middle English romance (Windeatt 1988: 138–40).

548 *Pandare*: Although the name may derive from 'Pandarus de Sezile' in Benoît's *Troie* (6667) – itself going back ultimately to Homer's Lydian archer Pandarus (*Iliad*, 4.125–6, 5.95ff.), mentioned in Plato's *Republic* (379E) as a violator of oaths – it is Boccaccio who in *Filostrato* creates the prototype of Chaucer's character of Pandarus (perhaps taking the name's etymology to mean 'He who gives all') in the romance tradition of confidants and go-betweens. Possible models include the various go-betweens in Boccaccio's *Filocolo*; Galehout in the thirteenth-century French prose romance *Lancelot du Lac*; Ami (Friend), Raison (Reason), La Vieille (the Old Woman) and Faus Semblant (False Seeming) in the *Roman de la Rose*; perhaps the old woman go-between in *Pampilus de Amore* in its Latin or French versions (Garbáty 1967; Micszkowski 1985); the biblical Jonadab (see 2.1512n. below); or, even more distantly, the figure of Davus in Roman comedy and satire (Levine 1991). Other parallels may be noted with the figure of Philosophy in Boethius, *De consolatione philosophiae* (see *TC* 1.730–31, 841–54, 857–8), and Esperance (Hope) in Machaut, *Remède de Fortune* (see *TC* 1.813–19, 897–900). That Pandarus is Criseyde's uncle (revealed later, at 1.975), rather than her cousin as in *Filostrato*, where he is expressly a young man of noble birth (2.1), may suggest that he is older than Criseyde and Troilus, but the text includes no firm indication (see 3.293n.), nor any description of his appearance. For Pandarus in the context of the substantial medieval literature on friendship (cf. 1.584–95), see Cook 1970. The earliest attested instance of the noun 'pandar' (i.e. procurer) dates from *c.* 1440 (*MED*, s.v. *pandar*); see also *TC* 3.396–7. For metrical reasons the form of the name in *TC* varies between 'Pandarus' and 'Pandare' (used 113 and 78 times respectively). Boccaccio's Pandaro lacks the humour and exceptional verbal facility of Chaucer's Pandarus, and does not need his strategic inventiveness.

552 *O mercy, God!*: Of more than two hundred oaths in *TC*, Pandarus swears over eighty, Criseyde over sixty, and Troilus about forty (see Elliott 1974: 251). As emerges later (cf. 2.505–53), Pandarus already suspects Troilus is in love.

554–67 These stanzas have no equivalent in *Filostrato*.

561 *for the nones*: Cf. 4.428.

603–7   From *Filostrato*, 2.7, itself echoing Francesca da Rimini on the power of love in Dante, *Inferno*, 5.100–105.

606   *sailleth*: For nautical imagery, not in *Filostrato*, see also *TC* 1.969; 2.1–6, 1104; 3.1291; 4.282; 5.641–4.

608–9   In *Filostrato* (2.7) Troiolo scarcely restrains himself from suicide a thousand times. On suicide, see also *TC* 1.535–9, 820–26; 4.417; 5.1274n.

623   *How devel*: Probably 'How the devil . . . ?', but possibly addressing Pandarus ('How, devil . . .').

625   *Though I be nyce*: Cf. Ovid, *Ars amatoria*, 2.547–8 ('I confess I am not perfect in this art – what am I to do? I am less than my own counsels').

630   Proverbial (Whiting F404).

631–2   Proverbial (Whiting W217); cf. Horace, *Ars poetica*, 304–5 ('so I shall play a whetstone's role, which makes steel sharp, but of itself cannot cut'), referring to his role in teaching the poet's office and duty. Pandarus's speech (631–65) is added to *Filostrato*, with echoes of the *Roman de la Rose*, Boethius and Ovid. Cf. the quoting of exempla by the go-between Duke Feramonte in Boccaccio, *Filocolo*, 1.219 (Young 1908: 162).

635   Not recorded as a proverb before Chaucer (cf. Whiting M340). See also 3.329.

637   Proverbial (Whiting C415, T110); see also *Boece*, 3.m.1, 4.pr.2.10–12 ('And of thise thinges, certes, everiche of hem is declared and schewed by other'), and *Roman de la Rose*, 21573–82 ('things go by contraries; one is the gloss of the other'). Cf. *TC* 1.946–52.

638–9   Proverbial (Whiting S943); cf. *Roman de la Rose*, 21559–72, and *Boece*, 3.m.1.5–6 ('Hony is the more swete, if mouthes han first tasted savours that ben wykke'). See also *TC* 3.1212–20.

640–41   Proverbial (cf. Whiting M236).

642–3   'White seems more by black' is proverbial (Whiting W231).

645   *of two contraries is o lore*: Proverbial (Whiting C415).

653–8   Alluding to the letter to Paris from Oenone, a nymph of Mount Ida (Ovid, *Heroides*, 5), after he deserted her for Helen of Troy. Criseyde will later echo Paris's vow of loyalty to Oenone (4.1548–53). At 658 S2 has the marginal gloss 'Littera Oenone' (letter of Oenone); at 659 S1 has the gloss 'Cantus Oenonee' (song of Oenone).

659–65   In *Heroides*, 5.145ff., Oenone laments that her own medical knowledge cannot cure her of love; Chaucer may have drawn on lines in *Heroides* texts now considered spurious, and also on the

Italian translation attributed to Filippo Ceffi (Meech 1930: 112–13). For Phoebus Apollo as the inventor of medicine who cannot cure himself of his love for Daphne, see Ovid, *Metamorphoses*, 1.521–4. In love with the daughter of 'kyng Amete' (Admetus, husband of Alcestis), Apollo served him as a shepherd for seven years (as recalled in Boccaccio, *Teseida*, 3.25, 4.46). For the physician who cannot cure himself, see Luke 4:23 and Ovid, *Remedia amoris*, 313–14; also proverbial (Whiting L171).

666–7 On Pandarus as an unsuccessful lover, see also 2.57–63, 96–8; 4.397–9, 484–97.

670–71 For allusions to hawks and hawking, see 3.1192, 1779–85; 4.413; 5.65; on medieval hawking, see Cummins 1988.

676–8 Such a union with 'thi brother wif' would be considered incestuous under canon law (Kelly 1991: 127–8, citing the *Decretals of Gregory IX*).

681–2 *now*] H3 H4 J R Cx; other MSS omit. *final*] *finally* Cp A Cl D Gg H1 H3 J S1.

687–8 *bothe two ben vices*: Cf. Seneca, *Epistles*, 3.4 ('Either is a fault, to trust everyone or to trust no one'); also proverbial (Walther 32756c), and quoted in a gloss to Boethius, 3.m.8 (Robinson 1957: 816). The two stanzas, *TC* 1.687–700, have no equivalent in *Filostrato*.

694–5 *Wo hym that is allone*: Cf. Ecclesiastes 4:10, attributed to the 'wise man', Solomon (as in R's marginal gloss), and cited in such medieval treatises on friendship as Aelred of Rievaulx, *De spirituali amicitia* (PL 195: 671A) and Peter of Blois, *De amicitia christiana* (Davy 1932: 116).

699–700 *Nyobe*: The wife of Amphion, king of Thebes, and daughter of Tantalus (cf. *TC* 3.593); Niobe was turned to stone as she wept for her seven sons and seven daughters, slain in punishment for her offending of Latona, mother of Apollo and Diana, 'and even to this day tears trickle from the marble' (Ovid, *Metamorphoses*, 6.312). R has a marginal gloss 'Require in methamorphosios' (look in *Metamorphoses*).

704 *in wo thi wo to seche*: Cf. Ovid, *Metamorphoses*, 7.720 ('I am set on seeking out something I may grieve over'), and Seneca, *Epistles*, 99.26 ('For what is worse than to chase after pleasure in grief itself, indeed from grief, and even to seek out what gives pleasure amid tears').

708–9 Proverbial (Whiting W715; Hassell S111; Walther 29943; R and S1 cite the Latin proverb in marginal glosses); cf. *Canon's Yeoman's Tale*, VIII.746–7.

713–14 *namore harde grace . . . no space*: Cf. Ovid, *Ex Ponto*, 2.7.41–
2 ('so wounded am I by the continual blows of Fortune that there
is scarcely room upon me for a new wound'), and 4.16.51–2
('What pleasure is there for you, Malice, to drive the steel into
limbs already dead? There is no space in me now for a new
wound'). R has another marginal gloss 'Require in Ouidio' (look
in Ovid).

722–5 Here Troiolo blushingly confesses that he loves a relative of
Pandaro (2.15), but Chaucer now stops following Boccaccio
closely, inventing a longer scene of Troilus's more reluctant con-
fession and Pandarus's fuller arguments, before picking up again
with *Filostrato*, 2.16, at *TC* 1.855.

730 *litargie*: Cf. *Boece*, 1.pr.2.19–21, where Philosophy comes to
Boethius in his despair ('he is fallen into a litargye, whiche that is
a comune seknesse to hertes that been desceyved').

731 *lik an asse to the harpe*: Proverbial since ancient times (Whiting
A227; Hassell A137; Walther 27969); cf. *Boece*, 1.pr.4.2–3 (Phil-
osophy asks Boethius: ' "Felistow," quod sche, "thise thynges,
and entren thei aughte in thy corage? Artow like an asse to the
harpe?" '). Cf. *Le Donnei des amanz*, 1149–50: 'Whoever teaches
an ass to play the harp uselessly wastes his effort' (Burnley 1998:
89). R has a marginal gloss: 'Baicius de consolacione philosophie'.

733–5 See the commentary on Boethius, 1.pr.4, by Nicholas Trevet
(*c.* 1258–after 1334), English Dominican friar and commentator
on classical texts: 'Unde asinis similes sunt homines qui audientes
sermones racionabilis tantum prebent aures ad audiendum non
animum ad percipiendum intellectum' (similar to asses are men
who, when they hear meaningful utterances, only use their ears
in order to listen, but not their mind in order to understand the
meaning; Minnis 1981: 342). Contemporary preaching also used
the example of the ass lifting his head to listen while feeding, but
once the music stops: 'he putteth down [h]is hed ageyn to [h]is
mete and thenketh no more thereof. Forsothe ryght so itt fareth
by a synnefull man, thow he listen never so well Goddes worde'
(Rowland 1971: 32).

740–42 'To make a rod for one's own back' is proverbial (Whiting
S652).

744 *love that oughte ben secree*: Cf. the Lover in *Roman de la Rose*:
'For thurgh me never discovred was | Yit thyng that oughte be
secree' (*Romaunt*, 4402–3). See also 1.321–2n.

747–8 *a craft to seme fle*: Cf. *Roman de la Rose*, 7557–8; *Romaunt*,

4783–4. For allusions to hunting, see *TC* 2.964, 1535; 3.1779–85; 4.413; 5.65, 1471–7.

760   *Lat be . . . ensaumples*: Cf. Ovid, *Remedia amoris*, 461 ('Why do I dwell on examples, the number of which wearies me?').

773   *brother*: The first of many occasions when Troilus and Pandarus so address each other (Ph+ reads: 'Why no, parde, sir . . .'). In *Roman de la Rose* Love advises the Lover to have a friend who keeps his counsel: 'yee, every other | Shall helpen as his owne brother' (*Romaunt*, 2883–4).

786–8   *Ticius*: Chaucer's only other reference to the eternal torments of Tityus in Hades is when translating Boethius, where the vulture that preys ceaselessly on his liver is overcome by the music of Orpheus (*Boece*, 3.m.12.41–5). The torments of Tityus were usually interpreted as the pains of lust, constantly renewed (cf. Servius, *ad Aen.* 6.596; Lucretius 3.992–4), although Macrobius, in his *Commentary on the Dream of Scipio*, explains them as incessant pangs of conscience (Stahl 1952: 1.10.12). In his commentary on Boethius, Trevet interprets Tityus as a philosopher who, intent on searching into future things, practised the art of divination and was punished for trying to rape the mother of Apollo, god of divination (Fox 1981: 389–90, 422). For associations of the lovers' experience with hell, see also *TC* 1.872; 3.1600; 4.712, 1698; 5.212, 1376, 1396.

809   *Unknowe, unkist*: Gower's *Confessio amantis*, 2.467 ('And for men sein "unknowe, unkest"'), confirms this was proverbial, although unrecorded before Chaucer (cf. Whiting U5).

810–12   For the theme of the lover who never kissed, cf. *Roman de la Rose*, 20889–92 (Pygmalion remarks: 'Many lovers in many countries have loved many ladies and served them as much as they could, without a single kiss from them').

813–19   Resembling the speech of Esperance to the Lover in Machaut, *Remède de Fortune*, 1636–51, 1662 ('You must not pity yourself if you love her well, nor be dismayed that she doesn't pay you a thousand times more than you deserve for loving and serving her . . . for the very least reward she is able to give you . . . is worth five hundred times more than you could deserve, were you to love and serve her . . . as long as this world endures . . . You must not despair'). While instructing the Lover how to rise above Fortune's adversity on the model of Boethius's Lady Philosophy, Machaut's Esperance identifies true happiness not, like Boethius, beyond this world but in virtuous possession of the loved lady.

837 *Fortune is my fo*: A commonplace (Whiting F529), as in *Piers Plowman*, B 11.61 ('And thanne was Fortune my foo').

838–40 Cf. *Boece*: 'She, cruel Fortune, casteth adoun kynges that whilom weren ydradd . . . Thus sche pleyeth, and thus sche proeveth hir strengthes' (2.m.1.7–15).

841–54 Pandarus's speech on Fortune echoes Philosophy's account to Boethius of Fortune's character in *De consolatione philosophiae*, 2.pr.1, 2, 3; cf. Reason's discourse against Fortune in *Roman de la Rose*, 5842–93. For Pandarus's views on Fortune, see also 3.1625–8; 4.383–92, 600–602.

843–4 Cf. *Boece*: 'thow that art put in the comune realme of alle, desire nat to lyven by thyn oonly propre ryght' (2.pr.2.84–6).

845–7 Cf. *Boece*: 'For yif thou therfore wenest thiself nat weleful, for thynges that tho semeden joyeful ben passed, ther nys nat why thow sholdest wene thiself a wrecche; for thynges that semen now sory passen also' (2.pr.3.75–9).

848–50 Cf. *Boece*: 'Enforcestow the to aresten or withholden the swyftnesse and the sweighe of hir turnynge wheel? O thow fool of alle mortel foolis! Yif Fortune bygan to duelle stable, she cessede thanne to ben Fortune' (2.pr.1.110–14). Cf. also Esperance to the Lover about Fortune in Machaut, *Remède de Fortune*, 2531–8 ('If she were constant and behaved reasonably, so that she was just and true to everyone, she would not be Fortune'), and for the *torne/sojourne* rhyme, cf. *Remède*, 912–14 ('Quant elle tourne | . . . qu'elle ne sejourne').

851–3 Cf. Fortune's words: 'What eek yif my mutabilite yeveth the ryghtful cause of hope to han yit bettere thynges?' (*Boece*, 2.pr.2.81–3).

858 *unwre his wounde*: Cf. *Boece*, 1.pr.4.4–6; Ovid, *Remedia amoris*, 125–6; also proverbial (Whiting L173).

859 *Cerberus*: Three-headed canine porter of hell (cf. *Boece*, 3.m.12.31–2); also thought to devour the dead (Servius, *ad Aen.* 6.395).

860–61 With Pandarus's willingness here, cf. Troilus's later offer of his sisters (3.407–13).

875 For near deaths from fear, pity, sorrow, see also 2.449, 1356, 1530; 3.263; 4.151.

888–9 Criseyde's disposition towards honour, like her virtuousness (897–900), is a recommendation and not, as in *Filostrato* (2.23), something inconvenient to Troiolo's sexual aspirations.

891–3 Cf. Seneca, *Epistles*, 2.1 ('The primary indication, to my thinking, of a well-ordered mind is a man's ability to remain in one

place and linger in his own company'), and *Boece*, 2.pr.4.131–8:
'I schal schewe the schortly the poynt of soverayn blisfulnesse . . .
yif it so be that thow art myghty over thyself (*that is to seyn, by
tranquillite of thi soule*), than hastow thyng in thi powere that
thow noldest nevere leesen, ne Fortune may nat bynymen it the
[take it away from you].' This stanza (890–96) is extant only in
the Ph+ MSS (here H2, H4, Ph). Something of an interpolation
into the argument, it may represent the survival of an authentic
but draft stanza (cf. 2.1750n.). For an argument that 1.890–96
was meant to follow rather than precede 1.897–903, see DiMarco
1998.

892 *ordeyné*: Cf. *Boece*, 1.m.4.1–5, 'Whoso it be that is cleer of
vertue, sad and wel ordynat of lyvynge, that hath put under
fote the proude wierdes [fates], and loketh upryght upon either
fortune, he may holden his chere undesconfited.' With Chaucer's
'ordeyne', cf. Jean de Meun's translation of Boethius here: 'de
aage bien ordené' (Dedeck-Héry 1952: 176).

894–5 Cf. Dante, *Purgatorio*, 17.97–9 ('while [love] is directed on
the primal good and on the secondary keeps right measure, it
cannot be the cause of sinful pleasure').

897–900 Cf. Machaut, *Remède de Fortune*, 1671–83, where Esper-
ance encourages the Lover that, since his lady is virtuous, she
must have pity ('And also you must believe . . . if you wish to find
joy and peace once more . . . that since she possesses perfectly all
the qualities one may possibly imagine, tell or think of . . . and
since she is endowed with virtues and free from all vices, she must
of necessity have sincerity and pity, humility and charity'). See
TC 3.1282; cf. Machaut, *Jugement dou Roy de Behaingne*, 459–
62 ('Sweet Hope softly and loyally assured me that never could
there be such great beauty without pity . . .'), *Dit dou Vergier*,
751–2, and the poem of Charles d'Orléans, 'A ladies hert forto
want pite | Hit is to fowle ageyne nature . . .' (Steele and Day
1970: 132). For the ready compassion of the 'gentil' heart, see
also *Knight's Tale*, I.1761; *Man of Law's Tale*, II.660; *Squire's
Tale*, V.479.

906–66 This part of Pandarus's speech has no equivalent in *Filostrato*,
2.23–4.

910 *Seynt Idiot*: Chaucer's Trojans refer to saints (2.118, 894; 5.553),
and R+ and Ph+ read 'Seynt Venus' for 'blisful Venus' at 3.705
and 712 respectively, but 'saint' could be applied in Middle
English in non-Christian contexts (cf. *Legend of Good Women*,
1870–73, and see *MED*, s.v. *seint(e* n. 3(a)).

916 *blaunche fevere*: I.e. 'white sickness', a form of love sickness that turns its victims pale; Gower's *Confessio amantis* (6.239–40) says 'blanche fievere' brings chills and shivering.

927–8 Cf. *Roman de la Rose*, 21551–2 ('It's good to try everything in order to take greater pleasure in one's good fortune').

932 *bet thi brest*: Like a priest, Pandarus invites Troilus to confess and repent. See also 2.525, 540–41, and cf. 1.995–1008.

939 *Pandare*] Pandarus Cp A Cl Dg Gg H1 J S2.

946–52 Cf. Ovid, *Remedia amoris*, 43–6 (the former teacher of love now offers to heal its wounds: 'the same earth fosters healing herbs and noxious, the nettle is often nearest the rose'). For comparable series of antitheses, see Whiting G478, N108, Walther 22030; also Alan of Lille, *Liber Parabolarum* (*PL*, 210: 582–3). In line 949 Ph+ reads: 'The lilie wexith white, smothe and soft'.

953 *bridel*: See also 3.1635, 1762; 4.1678, and *Boece*, 5.m.1.18–23.

956 Proverbial (Whiting H171); cf. Chaucer's *Tale of Melibee*, *CT* VII.1054.

960–61 *he that parted is . . . Is nowher hol*: Cf. *Roman de la Rose*, 2245–6; *Romaunt*, 2367–8 ('To many his herte that wole depart, | Everich shal have but litel part'); Seneca, *Epistles*, 2.2; *Boece*, 3.pr.11.62–9.

964–6 Proverbial (Whiting T474; Walther 17403a); cf. Seneca, *Epistles*, 2.3 ('a plant that is often moved can never flourish').

975 *my nece*: This is the first reference to the kinship between Pandarus and Criseyde. In *Filostrato* (2.15) Troiolo, reluctant to reveal his lady's identity, refers earlier to loving a relative ('parente') of Pandaro; in *TC* this is omitted at the equivalent point (1.722). Granted Pandarus's easy relations with the Trojan ruling family and King Priam (2.1402–4; 5.284), he is presumably Criseyde's deceased mother's brother, rather than the brother of her traitor father, Calchas.

976 *wyse lered*: Unidentified, but cf. Dante, *Purgatorio*, 17.91–3 ('Neither Creator nor creature . . . was ever without love, either natural or of the spirit'), although the contrast between 'celestial' love and earthly, natural love 'of kynde' was a commonplace. Boccaccio's Pandaro here expresses the view that Criseida, like all women, is amorous (*Filostrato*, 2.27). Cf. *TC* 1.236–45. Chaucer also omits Pandarus's acknowledgement (2.25–6) that passionate affairs accord ill with a lady's honour, and to become the subject of common gossip would bring disgrace.

995–1008 This 'conceyte' of Troilus as the zealous convert has no equivalent in *Filostrato*.

1000 *beste post*: Cf. the innuendo in *General Prologue*, *CT* I.214 ('Unto his ordre he [the Friar] was a noble post').

1014 The prayer to Venus is not in *Filostrato*, 2.29. Apart from 2.972, other references to Venus in *TC* represent Chaucer's changes to *Filostrato*, but see especially 3.1–49n.

1021–2 Cf. Troiolo's fears that Criseida will not listen to Pandaro 'in order to show you how respectable she is' (*Filostrato*, 2.30). But in *TC* an alternative meaning may be: 'because of the behaviour of you (*manere Of the*), her uncle, she won't hear of any such thing'.

1024 *out of the moone*: For a Middle English lyric in which the Man in the Moon fears he will fall, see Brown 1932: 160; also Whiting M138.

1038 *borugh*: A 'borwe' (cf. also 2.134–5) functioned either as a surety for the undertaking of an obligation (forcing the debtor to pay his debt or fulfilling the obligation himself), or as a mainpernor who ensured a defendant's appearance in court (Hornsby 1988: 76–7).

1053 Cf. the Lover to Love in the *Roman de la Rose*: 'My lyf, my deth is in youre hond; I I may not laste out of youre bond' (*Romaunt*, 1955–6).

1065–71 Not in *Filostrato*, but from the rhetorical handbook, Geoffrey of Vinsauf's *Poetria nova* (43–5), describing the necessary premeditation before the poet begins his work: 'Si quis habet fundare domum, non currit ad actum I Impetuosa manus: intrinseca linea cordis I Praemetitur opus' (If anyone has a house to build, his impetuous hand does not rush into action; the inward measuring line of his heart measures out [*praemetitur*] the work beforehand). (Chaucer's text perhaps read 'praemittitur' or 'praemittetur', i.e. 'will be sent out'.) See Faral 1924: 198; but this passage circulated excerpted in various compilations: e.g. in the Dominican encyclopaedist, Vincent of Beauvais (d. after 1264), *Speculum doctrinale*, 4.93, 'De maturitate' (Norton-Smith 1974: 2), and in the late fourteenth-century John de Briggis, *Compilatio de arte dictandi* (Camargo 1995: 98–9; Murphy 1964: 1–20). Cf. also Luke 14: 28–30; Walther 29021; and *Boece*, 4.pr.6.82–93 (where the distinction between a workman's seeing in his mind's eye beforehand the artefact he is to make and the extended process of bringing it forth in time is used to distinguish between

God's all-seeing providence and the workings of destiny over the course of time).

1072–92 This account of Troilus is not in *Filostrato* here (cf. *TC* 3.1772–1806), which moves on to Pandaro's visit to Criseida, a scene much revised in *TC*, Book 2.

1074 *pleyde the leoun*: Cf. 5.830 and *Filostrato*, 7.80 ('As when the famished lion rises up . . . so was Troiolo's spirit roused [by renewal of the war]').

1078 The same is said of Constance (*Man of Law's Tale*, II.532) and Griselda (*Clerk's Tale*, IV.413).

1081 *oon the beste*: I.e. 'the very best', not 'one of the best'. For the usage, see Mustanoja 1960: 297–9. See also, for example, *TC* 2.746–7; 3.781–2, 1310; 5.1056–7.

1092 This line is echoed at 5.1540.

BOOK 2

1–4 From *Purgatorio*, 1.1–3 ('To course over better waters the little boat of my wit now hoists her sails, leaving behind her so cruel a sea . . .'), although the figure of a voyage for poetic composition was a commonplace (see Curtius 1953: 128–30); cf. Chaucer's *Anelida and Arcite*, 20; and also *Filostrato*, 9.3–4; *Teseida*, 11.12; Ovid, *Ars amatoria*, 1.772, 3.26, 748; *Remedia amoris*, 811–12.

7 *kalendes*: Used again later when Criseyde's letter seems 'a kalendes of chaunge' to Troilus (5.1634).

8 *Cleo*: Clio, the muse of history (H4 glosses 'domina eloquentie', mistress of eloquence); i.e. the writer's purported role is confined to versifying historical report, and he needs no other inspiration or art. Cf. Statius, *Thebaid*, 1.41 ('Which of the heroes, Clio, shall rank first?'); also *Purgatorio*, 22.58, and 1.8–9 (which invokes the Muses in general, but particularly Calliope; cf. *TC* 3.45). Chaucer and Gower (see *TC* 5.1856) are the earliest English writers known to have spoken of their muse.

13 *of no sentement*: To compose 'de sentement' is the claim of Machaut (*Remède de Fortune*, 407–8: 'For he who does not compose from personal feeling falsifies his work and his song'), and Froissart (*Paradys d'amours*, 1604–6; *L'Espinette amoreuse*, 919–21, 3925–30). See also *TC* 1.15–18; 3.43, 1331–3.

14 *out of Latyn*: I.e. continuing the fiction of a classical source (cf. 1.394; 2.22–5). Boccaccio's *Filostrato*, principal source of *TC*, is written in Italian verse, and in his early fifteenth-century *Fall of*

Princes (Prologue, 283–7: Bergen 1924–7) John Lydgate already knew that *TC* derived not from a Latin but a 'Lombard', i.e. Italian, source (see Introduction, p. xxviii). Claims to ancient authority and a source written in Latin are recurrent fictions of romance. Boccaccio in his proem to *Filostrato* pretends to have drawn the poem from ancient legends ('l'antiche storie') rather than from Benoît and Guido; his preface to *Teseida* claims 'I discovered a most ancient story which was unknown to most people'. In opening his *Knight's Tale*, drawn from *Teseida*, Chaucer makes no mention of his Italian source but has a Latin epigraph from Statius's *Thebaid*, and in translating part of *Teseida* from Italian for his *Anelida and Arcite* Chaucer elaborates Boccaccio's stress on an ancient source by claiming 'in Englyssh to endyte | This olde storie, in Latyn which I fynde' (*Anelida*, 9–10).

18   See 2.49, below, and cf. Benoît in opening his *Roman de Troie* (139–44): 'I shall follow the Latin closely, I shall put in nothing but as I find it written. Nor do I say or add any good word, even had I skill, but I shall follow my matter.'

21   Cf. Dante, *De vulgari eloquentia*, 2.6.24–7 ('Let the ignorant be ashamed of their audacity in rushing headlong into composition ... we scorn them as we would a blind man making distinctions between colours'), but also proverbial (Whiting M50; Walther 2208a, 2214a).

22   *in forme of speche is chaunge*: Cf. Dante, *Convivio*, 1.5.55–66: 'Hence in the cities of Italy, if we will look attentively back over some fifty years, we see that many words have become extinct and have come into existence and been altered; wherefore, if a short time so changes the language, a longer time changes it much more. Thus I say that if those who died a thousand years ago were to return to their cities, they would believe that these had been occupied by some foreign people, because the language would be at variance with their own.' See also Dante's *De vulgari eloquentia*, 1.9.85–93 ('the language of one people varies gradually over the years and can in no way remain stable ... just as manners and customs vary'), and ultimately Horace, *Ars poetica*, 70–72 ('Many terms that have fallen out of use shall be born again, and those shall fall that are now in repute, if usage so wills it, in whose hands lies the judgement, the right and the rule of speech'), cited in *Convivio*, 2.14.83–9, and John of Salisbury's *Metalogicon* (Webb 1929: 1.16; 3.3); also circulated independently (Walther 15417).

28   Proverbial (Whiting T63).

36–7   Cf. Alanus de Insulis, *Liber parabolarum* (*PL* 210: 591): 'A
thousand ways lead men through the centuries to Rome', and
also another proverb 'A mind of lovers seeks a thousand roads
and a thousand ways' (Walther 14873, 14873a; see also Whiting
P52, T63); cf. Chaucer's *Treatise on the Astrolabe*: 'right as
diverse pathes leden diverse folk the righte way to Rome' (Pro-
logue 39–40).

41   If punctuated '*In visityng, in forme*', then *forme* would be 'formal
etiquette'. It would be possible to translate *seyde* as a gerund
'saying' (Elliott 1974: 72).

42   *Ecch contree hath his lawes*: Proverbial; see 2.28 and Walther
22657, 23133, 4176, 33849; cf. also *Boece*, 2.pr.7.72–7.

50–56   Cf. Boccaccio, *Teseida*, 3.5–7 ('Phoebus, ascending with his
steeds, was in the sign of that humble beast [Taurus, the bull]
which carried off Europa ... From this propitious state of the
heavens the earth enjoyed benign effects and was reclothed with
fresh new grass and lovely flowers ... And spirited youths, dis-
posed to loving, felt love grow more ardent than ever within their
hearts'). For the conventional May opening, see *Roman de la
Rose*, 45–66 (*Romaunt*, 49–70).

55   *the white Bole*: Either that white bull in whose shape Jupiter
ravished Europa (Ovid, *Metamorphoses*, 2.852: cf. *TC* 3.722–
3), and taken by medieval commentators as the origin of the
zodiacal sign Taurus (Bode 1834: 253; Pauly–Wissowa 1894–
1972: s.v. *Tauros*; Chaucer, *Complaint of Mars*, 86), or a recollec-
tion of Virgil's 'candidus ... Taurus' (*Georgics*, 1.217–18; Clay-
ton 1979), cited in Macrobius's *Commentary on the Dream of
Scipio* (Stahl 1952: 1.18.15). In the *Nun's Priest's Tale* on 3 May
the sun 'in the signe of Taurus hadde yronne | Twenty degrees
and oon, and somwhat moore' (VII.3194–5), confirmed by the
contemporary *Kalendarium* of Nicholas of Lynn (Eisner 1980:
32).

56   *Mayes day the thrydde*: Also the date of Chauntecleer's capture
by the fox (*Nun's Priest's Tale*, VII.3188–90) and of Palamon's
escape from prison (*Knight's Tale*, I.1462–3); considered one of
the 'Egyptian' or 'dismal' (i.e. unlucky) days. This is presumably
the month of May in the same year as that April in which Troilus
first sees Criseyde (see 1.156n.).

64   *Proigne*: The wife of Tereus; Procne was metamorphosed into a
swallow, and her sister Philomela into a nightingale, after they
avenged Tereus's rape of Philomela by killing the son of Tereus

and Procne and feeding Tereus a meal of the child's flesh. Ovid tells the tale in *Metamorphoses*, 6.412–674, retold by Chaucer in his *Legend of Good Women*, 2228–2393 (R glosses 'Require in Methamorphosios'). Chaucer's allusion probably recalls Dante's in *Purgatorio*, 9.13–15: 'Nell'ora che comincia i tristi lai | la rondinella presso alla mattina, | forse a memoria de' suo' primi guai . . .' (At the hour near morning when the swallow begins her plaintive songs, in remembrance, perhaps, of her ancient woes). Cf. also *Teseida*, 4.73 ('Then hearing Philomela sing as she made merry over dead Tereus . . .'), and Petrarch, Sonnet 42, In morte, 'Zefiro torna'. At the close of the day here beginning with Pandarus's awakening, Criseyde will fall asleep to the song of the nightingale (2.918–24).

74   *And caste*: This may suggest that Pandarus checked the day of the lunar month in a *lunarium* or moon-book to see if it was propitious. It is now 4 May (cf. 2.56). The third day of the month 'ys noght fortunat to begynne ony werke upon' but the fourth day 'is gode to begynne every worldly occupacioun' according to John Metham's moon-book *Days of the Moon* (see Craig 1916: 149; also North 1988: 383–5). In his *Liber judiciis astrorum* Albohazen Haly discusses elections to determine the best time for beginning a journey: 'In order to elicit or secure love and friendship it is agreed that Luna should be favourable' (Curry 1960: 254–5).

76   The home of Chaucer's Criseyde is termed a palace (see also 2.1094; 5.523), unlike the house of Boccaccio's Criseida. Medieval London houses were increasingly well-appointed, with 'glass in domestic windows from the fourteenth century . . . tiled floors and, even more frequently, chimneys of stone and brick' (Schofield 1994: 133).

77   *Janus*: Roman god of thresholds and doorways, represented with two faces, looking in opposite directions. See Ovid, *Fasti*, 1.125–7, 139. (R has a Latin marginal gloss: 'Look in Ovid's book *Fasti* concerning Janus etc.')

78–595   The first interview between Pandarus and Criseyde grows from 32 stanzas or 256 lines (*Filostrato*, 2.35–67) to 74 stanzas or 518 lines in *TC*.

78–80   Medieval London houses 'were so arranged that at a crucial single point . . . the visitor decided, or was directed, which way to go: left, into the hall (or parlour [see 82n. below] as it was then being called) and thereafter the garden or stairs to the upper chambers' (Schofield 1994: 92).

81–4 In this scene of reading aloud as a domestic pastime is a picture
      of how *TC* may well have been enjoyed by its early audiences (see
      below, 2.1347n.). The story – Middle English 'geste' (2.83) – of
      Thebes is then specified as 'This romaunce is of Thebes' (2.100),
      which may suggest Criseyde is listening to a version of the twelfth-
      century French *Roman de Thèbes*, itself based on the 12-book
      Latin *Thebaid* of Statius, to which Pandarus (2.108) apparently
      refers. (A contrast may be intended with the ladies' vernacular
      romance reading matter.) The *Roman de Thèbes* was sometimes
      bound in the same volume with the *Roman de Troie* which
      contained Criseyde's own story. An outline summary or *argu-
      mentum* of the *Thebaid* in Latin is included in most manuscripts
      of *TC* after 5.1498. For other references by Chaucer's Trojans to
      the earlier fated city of Thebes, see 5.601–2, 937, 1485–1509.

82   *parlour*: A smaller room apart from the main hall, affording some
      privacy for private conversation; usually on the ground floor,
      often overlooking a garden, and 'an intentionally comfortable
      room . . . References to paving and to paving tiles in London
      buildings suggest that tiles were a valued commodity. A tenement
      in the parish of St Bartholomew the Less was dignified by the
      name *le Pavedhalle* in 1348' (Schofield 1994: 66–7, 113). This
      room is one of the comforts of the substantial household that
      Chaucer's Criseyde maintains (see 2.813–23, 1228–9).

101–2 How Laius died at the hands of his son Oedipus is narrated in
      Roman de Thèbes, 175–224, more fully than in *Thebaid*, 1.57ff.
      (R has a marginal Latin gloss: 'Look in Statius's *Thebaid*'.)

103   *lettres rede*: I.e. the rubrication or headings (often beginning
      'How . . .'; cf. 2.101, 104) used to set off titles, chapters or sec-
      tions of works in the page layout of medieval manuscripts, with
      which Criseyde here shows herself familiar.

104–5 *the bisshop . . . Amphiorax*: Amphiaraus was betrayed by his
      wife into joining the war against Thebes, the fatal outcome of
      which he foretold (cf. *Wife of Bath's Tale*, III.740–46); his death
      is narrated at the close of Statius, *Thebaid*, Book 7, in *Roman de
      Thèbes*, 4711–4842, and recalled later in Cassandra's summary
      to Troilus (*TC* 5.1500). Amphiaraus is termed *vates* (seer) in
      Thebaid (7.815) and *evesque* (bishop) or *arcevesques* (arch-
      bishop) in *Thèbes* (4791, 5053); the Middle English word 'bishop'
      could also be applied to non-Christian chief priests (*MED*, s.v.
      bishop 3). In his spelling *Amphiorax*, Chaucer follows the French
      spelling of the classical name (cf. 1.153 and n.).

110   *barbe*: Some manuscripts read 'wimpel'. Worn by nuns, and by

widows as a sign of mourning, the 'barbe' was a piece of pleated white linen worn over or under the chin and reaching to the breast. (For a barbe worn by Alianore de Bohun, Duchess of Gloucester, on her funeral brass of 1399, see Houston 1965: 117, fig. 216.)

112 For the custom of doing honour to the month of May, see *Knight's Tale*, I.1500–1512; *Legend of Good Women*, Prologue F 36–9.

114 *a widewes lif*: On widowhood as a pious life, see I Timothy 5:5–6. Boccaccio's widowed Criseida claims to Pandaro that she is still grief-stricken over her husband's death and will remain so for the rest of her life (*Filostrato*, 2.49). (On medieval widows and widowhood, see Barron and Sutton 1994; Mirrer 1992; Walker 1993.)

117–18 Criseyde pictures herself like some penitent saint in her cave; cf. 'Who fedde the Egipcien Marie in the cave, | Or in desert?' (*Man of Law's Tale*, II.500–501, referring to St Mary of Egypt). See the later reference to saints (*TC* 2.894–5), but the word could be applied to pagan figures (*MED*, s.v. *seint(e*, 3(a), (b)); cf. also the earlier 'Seynt Idiot' (1.910).

157–61 For Troilus's qualities and as second only to Hector, cf. Benoît, *Troie*, 3991–2, 5393–6.

158 *Ector the secounde*: On Troilus as second only to Hector, see also 2.644, 740; 3.1775; 5.1565, 1804. Benoît (*Troie*, 5439–40) describes Troilus as 'li plus proz, fors que sis frere | Hector' (the most valiant, except for his brother Hector); Guido (*Historia*, p. 86) calls him 'alius Hector uel secundus ab ipso' (another Hector or the second to him).

167–8 Deriving from Lucan, *Pharsalia*, 8.494–5 (which S2's gloss 'Lucanus' recognizes), as cited in *Roman de la Rose*, 5660–62 (concluding the story of Appius and Virginia). Cf. Whiting E148; Walther 33667.

170 *sones tweye*: In classical tradition (cf. Homer, *Iliad*, 24.496) Priam had fifty sons, nineteen by Queen Hecuba. In Dares (*De excidio*, ch. 4) and medieval traditions of the legend of Troy, Priam and Hecuba have five sons: Hector, Paris, Deiphebus, Helenus and Troilus (the youngest); and three daughters: Cassandra, Andromache and Polyxena.

180 *wis and worthi*: A common collocation (cf. *General Prologue*, *CT* I.68: 'And though that he were worthy, he was wys'). On the topos of 'fortitudo et sapientia' (bravery and wisdom), see Curtius 1953: 176–80, and cf. *Knight's Tale*, I.865.

193–4 *swarm of been*: A traditional figure (Whiting B167). See also

TC 4.1356; *Summoner's Prologue*, III.1693; *Roman de la Rose*, 8721–2.

197–203 The martial dimension to Troilus's life, generally absent from *Filostrato*, is restored in *TC* on the general model of his battle exploits in Benoît's *Troie* and Guido's *Historia*, which however lack this incident. Cf. Boccaccio, *Teseida*, 8.81: '[Arcita] carved a path for himself with his sword ... turning here and there, he felled this one and struck that other. As he fought he displayed the great prowess that love created in his heart. And he spared no one, but moved like lightning, terrifying everyone.'

202 For the negative construction with *ther*, see also 2.1050, 3.1538, 4.1197, 5.146.

215–17 *TC* is represented as taking place in the circumstances of a medieval household, where privacy is the exception and must be deliberately sought. Pandarus has to find opportunities for private conversation with Criseyde and Troilus, who are shown leading their lives in households which allow less privacy than is assumed in *Filostrato*; see also 2.939–66, 1100ff., 1163–9, 1172–6, 1193–4, and cf. Windeatt 1979b.

220 *tyme is that*] Dg S1 S2 Th; *is tyme* Cp A Cl D H1 J Cx; *is tyme that* H4 Ph; *is it tyme* Gg H2 H3; *is it tyme that* H5.

232 *Mynerve*: Roman goddess of wisdom, often identified with Pallas. Troilus later invokes Minerva when about to compose his letter to Criseyde (2.1062).

236 *Withouten paramours*: Cf. the ambiguity of *General Prologue*, *CT* I.460–61: 'Housbondes at chirche dore she hadde fyve, | Withouten oother compaignye in youthe –'

248 *fremde*] A D Th (*fremed* Th); *frende* Cp H1; *frend* H2 H4 Ph; *frendly* Cl; *friende* J; *fryend* S1; *fraynyd* H5; *fy(e)ned(e* Dg S2.

260 *th'ende is every tales strengthe*: A traditional commonplace ('The end crowns the work', 'The last word binds the tale'); see Whiting E75, E78, E81, W598; Hassell F89; Walther 9536.

262 *peynte*] *poynte* Cp Cl H1. Cf. 3.497.

268 *proces*: In contemporary preaching there was a specific technical sense of 'proces' as the ordered development of a sermon or of its parts after the division of the theme (Wenzel 1976: 154). For other references to the language of preaching, see 2.367n., 729n.

271–2 Cf. *Squire's Tale*, V.221–4 ('As lewed peple demeth comunly | Of thynges that been maad moore subtilly | Than they kan in hir lewednesse comprehende; | They demen gladly to the badder ende') ; also Whiting W411.

281–2 Cf. Pandarus's later comments on time: 2.989, 3.855.

286   *slouthe*: First of a series (not in *Filostrato*) of urgings against sloth
      in Book 2 (see 959, 1008, 1136, 1500), to which 'sin' in love
      Gower devotes Book 4 of his *Confessio amantis*.

320–22 *it wol his bane be*: That the lover may die for love is a
      commonplace of courtly rhetoric; cf. Hoccleve's *Letter of Cupid*
      (26–8): 'they sey, so importable [unbearable] ys her penaunce, |
      That but her lady lust to schew hem grace | They ryght anoone
      mote sterven in the place' (Furnivall and Gollancz 1892: 73), and
      Charles d'Orléans: 'But many suche as ye in wordis dy | That
      passyng hard ther graffis [graves] ar to spy' (Steele and Day 1941:
      177). Among Chaucer's other works, see especially *Franklin's
      Tale*, V.974–5, 978; *Merchant's Tale*, IV.1987–94; *Miller's Tale*,
      I.3280–81. For Pandarus's further references to the risk of
      Troilus's dying, see 2.333–43, 362, 385, 575, 1152, 1279–80,
      1736; 3.904–5.

328   See also 3.35 and 5.777 for other references to fishing.

331   *That trewe man*: The faithfulness of Troilus was perhaps already
      proverbial: see Whiting T483 ('Troilus the true'), citing instances
      from *c.* 1400 onwards; also Benson 1989. The idea of his living
      death will return: see *TC* 4.279–80, 295–301.

343   Proverbial (Whiting A62).

344   *gemme vertulees*: Powers, particularly of healing, were attributed
      to gems (cf. Evans 1922), and reference in *House of Fame* (line
      1352) to the *Lapidaire* suggests Chaucer knew a French transla-
      tion of the well-known 'lapidary' (treatise on precious stones,
      their properties and virtues), the *De lapidibus* of Marbodus of
      Rennes. For references to jewels and jewellery in *TC* (and not in
      Filostrato) see 3.885, 890–92, 1368–72; 5.549, 1040.

349   *If ... ther be no routhe*: Cf. Pandarus's earlier argument to
      Troilus (1.897–900) that Criseyde's virtuousness must include
      pity.
      ther] *ne* J Gg Th; Cp H2 H4 Ph Cx omit.

351–7 In this stanza Pandarus switches to using the familiar second
      person singular to address Criseyde, having previously (except at
      2.319) used the polite plural (for other lapses, see 2.395–6; 3.193;
      4.848–54). After 1.553 Pandarus usually addresses Troilus as
      'thou' (but note 4.596–7; 5.496). Troilus and Criseyde address
      each other in the polite second person plural form, with a few
      exceptions (e.g. 4.1209, 1641; 5.734–5, 1258). See Schmidt 1975
      and Walcutt 1935.

353   *baude*: See also 3.253–63, 395–7.

367   *sette*: See 2.729 ('sette a caas') and 3.310, 571 ('I pose'). These

are English equivalents of Latin terms introducing examples, hypotheses or concessions in fourteenth-century sermons and preachers' handbooks (Wenzel 1976: 155).

371 *love of frendshipe*: Cf. *Romaunt*, 5201, where 'love of freendshipp' translates 'amitiés' in Reason's discussion of friendship, drawn from Cicero, *De amicitia*, chs. 5, 6, 13, 17. The genitive 'of frendshipe' is used as an adjective (for 'the genitive of description or quality', see Mustanoja 1960: 80–81). See also below, 2.962.

384 *daunger*: In the *Roman de la Rose* (see *Romaunt*, 3018), Daunger is the personification of the lady's reserve, disdain and standoffishness. For the lady's moderating of her disdain and daunger, see also *TC* 2.1217, 1376.

393–405 *elde wasteth*: Cf. *Filostrato*, 2.54, and Ovid, *Ars amatoria*, 2.113–18 ('Beauty is a fragile advantage, that grows less as time goes on and is devoured by its own years . . . To you, handsome youth, will soon come grey hairs, and wrinkles to furrow your body').

398 'Too late aware' is proverbial (Whiting B155); cf. Gower, *Confessio amantis*: 'Bot now, allas, too late war | That I ne hadde him loved ar [before]' (4.1421–2).

400–405 On court fools, see Welsford 1935: 113–27, and Southworth 1998: 8, who comments, 'the clever fool . . . contrives to hold a mirror to the king in which his patron can see a magnified image of his own attitudes and decisions, and recognize for himself the folly in them'.

406 *I*] *Nece I* Cp+.

424 *paynted proces*: Cf. *Piers Plowman*, B 20.115: 'And with pryvee speche and peyntede wordes'; also Barclay's *Ship of Fools*, 2.40 (cited in Whiting: W611): 'So paynted wordes hydeth a fals entent'. Painting suggests the 'colours' of rhetoric, deceptively applied: cf. *Clerk's Prologue*, IV.16; *Squire's Tale*, V.38–9; *Franklin's Tale*, V.723–6; *House of Fame*, 859. On 'proces', see 2.268n

425 *Pallas*: A virgin goddess, Pallas is defender of Troy. Troilus first sees Criseyde during a festival of Pallas (1.153, 159–64). Cf. 5.977, 999.

432 *wel*] *ful wel* Cp+.

435–6 Cf. Boccaccio, *Teseida*, 1.58: 'O fiero Marte, o dispettoso iddio' (O cruel Mars, O vengeful god), and 3.1: 'Marte nella sua fredda regione | con le sue Furie insieme s'è tornato' (Mars returned to his cold domain, together with his Furies); Mars and the Furies are again linked later in *TC* (4.22–5). With the Italian form 'Marte', cf. 2.988 and 3.437 (deriving from *Filostrato*, 3.20). Italianate spelling of classical proper names (which recurs more widely in Chaucer's works) occurs in *TC* independently of *Filostrato*: cf. 'Mida' (3.1389), 'Flegitoun' (3.1600), 'Pernaso' (3.1810), 'Alete' (4.24), 'Phebuseo' (4.54), 'Athamante' (4.1539), 'Escaphilo' (5.319); for instances from *Filostrato*, cf. 'Monesteo' and 'Santippe' (4.51–2).

438 *that*] H2 H4 Ph S1 omit. *vilenye*] *any vilenye* Cp A Cl H1 H2 Ph S1 S2.

450 *the ferfulleste wight*: Twentieth-century criticism often explained Criseyde's character in terms of fear, influenced by this celebrated analysis: 'Fortunately Chaucer has so emphasized the ruling passion of his heroine, that we cannot mistake it. It is Fear – fear of loneliness, of old age, of death, of love, and of hostility; of everything, indeed, that can be feared ... Such is Chaucer's Cryseide; a tragic figure in the strictest Aristotelian sense, for she is neither very good nor execrably wicked ... But there is a flaw in her, and Chaucer has told us what it is: "she was the ferfulleste wight | That myghte be"' (Lewis 1936: 185–90). Cf. also Criseyde's later comments on fear as the motive behind pagan religion (4.1408–11).

465 *in*] *in a* Cp H1 H2 H3 H4 J R Th.

470 Proverbial (Whiting E193).

477 See also 3.773 and Whiting H75. Chaucer's *Book of the Duchess* recalls approvingly how 'Hyr lust to holde no wyght in honde' (1019); cf. also *House of Fame*, 692.

483 Proverbial (Whiting C121; Hassell C17).

507 *This other day*: In *Filostrato* Pandaro specifies (2.61–2) that this episode occurred before he came across Troiolo lamenting alone in his room (cf. 1.549). Chaucer leaves open the possibility that it is all Pandarus's invention. For the device of the noble lover's overheard complaint or soliloquy, see Machaut, *Jugement dou Roy de Behaingne*, 33–55, and *Dit de la Fonteinne Amoureuse*, 69–234; also *Filostrato*, 7.77–8 (Deiphebus overhears Troiolo), and *Knight's Tale*, I.1497–1576 (Palamon overhears Arcite).

508 *gardyn, by a welle*: A typical setting; in *Roman de la Rose* the Lover rests 'Besydes a wel, under a tree' (*Romaunt*, 1456). Machaut's *Dit de la Fonteinne Amoureuse* (1313–1424) describes an Amorous Fountain in a delightful park, haunt of Cupid, carved with depictions of Venus, the affair of Paris and Helen, and 'Troilus, too, was depicted, suffering greatly for his Briseyda, the daughter of Calchas of Troy'.

516 *afer*] J R; *aftir* A D Gg H3 H4 H5 Cx Th; *a fere* H2 Ph; *ther after*
Cp Cl Dg H1 S1 S2.

525 *mea culpa*: from the *Confiteor*, or form of confession; see also
TC 2.540–41, which suggests the posture and murmur of the
penitent in the confessional (Hutson 1954).

526–7 With Troilus's prayer, cf. Boethius's discussion of providence
(*Boece*, 4.pr.6.60–107).

530 *disesperaunce*: Alluding to despair as the Christian sin against the
Holy Ghost; see the first two proems (1.36–42; 2.6).

533–5 See 1.295–308; beams from the lady's eyes strike through the
lover's eyes into his heart. Cf. *Roman de la Rose*, where Love
shoots his arrow through the Lover's eye into his heart (*Romaunt*,
1727–9); *Knight's Tale*, I.1567 ('Ye sleen me with youre eyen,
Emelye!'), and two poems doubtfully attributed to Chaucer,
Complaynt d'Amours, 41–2 ('Yet alwey two thinges doon me
dye, | That is to seyn, hir beautee and myn yë'), and *Merciles
Beaute*, 1–3 ('Your yen two wol slee me sodenly; | I may the
beautee of hem not sustene, | So woundeth hit thourghout my
herte kene').

538–9 With the covered embers, cf. Ovid, *Metamorphoses*, 4.64, in
the story of Pyramus and Thisbe, which Chaucer renders 'As wry
the glede and hotter is the fyr' (*Legend of Good Women*, 735);
also proverbial (Whiting G154; Walther 26157).

545–50 Playing on the convention of lovers' sleeplessness; see 1.484,
and also Troilus's earlier mockery of lovers, 1.195–6, 920–21.

583 *ykaught withouten net*: Cf. 4.1370–71; on binding without a
cord, see 3.1358, and also 1.237n.

585 From *Filostrato*, 2.43. See 2.1087; 3.1371; 5.549. Rubies, accord-
ing to the lapidaries, had powers to cure the body, soothe the
mind, ward off illness and trouble, bring joy to the possessor, and
confer love between men and women (Jennings 1976).

588 *yet graunte us*] Cl A D Gg R S1 S2 Th; *g. us* Cp Dg J; *g. us that*
H1; *us g. to* H2 H3 H4 Ph.

589 *ha, ha!*: Probably representing the sound of laughter (as in the
Cook's Prologue, I.4327), although it is also used to express
indignant reproach or abhorrence in the sense 'get out, away
with you!' (Mustanoja 1960: 624–5), or to represent a shout to
frighten away a marauding animal ('Ha, ha! The fox!', *Nun's
Priest's Tale*, VII.3381).

593 Mars was traditionally associated with hasty, angry conduct;
cf. Third Vatican Mythographer, 6.8; Boccaccio, *De genealogia
deorum*, 9.3; *Teseida*, 7.30–37.

599 *closet*: From this room (which has a window to the street through which she will see Troilus) Criseyde later descends down a staircase into her garden (2.813–14). She will again retreat into her 'closet' in order to write to Troilus (2.1215), and when staying overnight at her uncle's house she sleeps in his closet (3.663n., 684) which is provided with a fireplace (3.1141). Chaucer uses the term 'closet' nowhere else in his works except *TC*.

600 *as stylle as any ston*: A stock phrase (Whiting S772); see also 2.1494; 3.699; 4.354; 5.1729.

603 *wex*] Gg H2 H4 H5 Ph Th; *was* other MSS.

610 Boccaccio's Criseida here debates with herself whether to love (2.69–78), then gazes at Troiolo and Pandaro from her window as they walk by (2.82). Chaucer inserts Troilus's first ride past (2.619ff.) before Criseyde's monologue (2.687ff.), perhaps recalling Hector's triumphant return from battle (*Troie*, 10201–18) and Lavinia's sight of Aeneas in the *Roman d'Eneas* (c. 1155–60; Salverda de Grave 1925–9: 8047–8126, 8381–98).

617–18 *the yate ... Of Dardanus*: In Guido the first of Troy's six gates (*Historia*, p. 47), in Benoît the second (*Troie*, 3148); Dardanus was the ancestor, possibly grandfather, of Priam. Barrier chains were used to close off gates and streets to horsemen.

622–3 Proverbial (Whiting N160). Cf. *Boece*, 5.pr.6.164–5 ('... thilke thing that ne mai nat unbytide, it mot bytiden by necessite').

634–6 *To don that thing ... so weldy*: 'The verb *weelden* has, inevitably, a common sexual sense in Middle English, and "that thing" seems a probable euphemism' (Donaldson 1970: 66n.).

637 Cf. *Squire's Tale*, V.558 ('His manere was an hevene for to see'); see also *TC* 1.1078; 2.826; 3.1742.

649 *his chere aspien*: Cf. the exchange of looks between Troiolo and Criseida: 'Then he went with Pandaro alone to gaze at leisure on Criseida's beauty – looking hard to see if he might discover any change in her because of what Pandaro had told her. She was standing at one of her windows and perhaps was expecting this to happen. And she did not behave cruelly or severely towards Troiolo as he looked at her, but turning round gazed modestly at him over her right shoulder. At this Troiolo went away contented ...' (*Filostrato*, 2.81–2).

651 *Who yaf me drynke?*: Possibly referring to a love-potion (as in the legend of Tristan and Iseult), but perhaps simply any intoxicating drink. On 'love-drunkenness', see Gower's *Confessio amantis*, 6.76–529.

652 Cf. *Shipman's Tale*, VII.111 ('And of his owene thought he wax al reed').

666–7 With this imagined objection, cf. *Filostrato*, which actually declares of Criseida: 'And so suddenly was she overcome' (2.83).

671 Proverbial (Whiting E164).

677 *herte*] Dg H2 H3 Ph S2 Cx; *inwardly* R; other MSS omit.
myne: see also 3.767; 4.471.

681 *seventhe hous*: A 'house' is one of the twelve divisions of the celestial sphere, formed by great circles passing through the north and south points of the horizon; the seventh house (just above the western horizon; see Chaucer's *Treatise on the Astrolabe*, 2.37.3–4) is especially associated with questions of love and marriage (for a diagram, see Curry 1960: 173). As an evening star in the seventh house, with Jupiter and Mercury standing in favourable aspect to her ('with aspectes payed': 682), the benefic planet Venus is here auspiciously placed, as she also was in Troilus's horoscope at the time of his birth. The aspect is the relative position, described in angular distance, of one planet or sign to another, and hence the good or bad influence of such a position. This stanza (680–86) has no equivalent in *Filostrato*.

698 For the alternation of heat and cold, see 2.811.

700 *myn auctour*: Chaucer is working very freely with *Filostrato* here (2.69–78).

715 'Moderation in all things' is proverbial (Whiting M464).

716–18 Cf. *Roman de la Rose*, 5744–5 ('Because I forbid drunkenness, I don't wish to forbid drinking'); also proverbial (Whiting D423).

724 *avantour*: On the evils of lovers' boasting, see Pandarus's argument (3.295–322); cf. Helen of Troy in Ovid, *Heroides*, 17.17–18: 'My good name is clear, and thus far I have lived without reproach, and no false lover makes his boast of me.'

729 *sette a caas*: Postulate a case; English equivalent of the Latin 'pono casum', a standard verbal marker which introduces an example, a hypothesis, or a concession in fourteenth-century sermons and preachers' handbooks (Wenzel 1976: 155). See also 2.367; 3.310, 571.

746 *oon the faireste*: Cf. Helen of Troy in Ovid, *Heroides*, 17.37–8: 'Not that I lack grounds for confidence, or that my beauty is not well known to me.'

752 *Right yong*: Information on Criseyde's age is later declared to be unavailable (5.826). As a widow she has distanced herself from 'yonge wyves' (2.119), and later welcomes love while feeling it has come late (3.468), but both these passages, like the present

one, express a view of herself at a particular moment, rather than her actual age. Some references in *Filostrato* to Criseida as young do not survive into *TC* (see 5.872n., 1317n.), but Pandarus refers to Criseyde's youth (1.982). Although medieval women might marry very young, Criseyde's status and bearing as a widow and the mistress of an independent household have suggested to some readers that she is (at least a little) older than Troilus, who must be under twenty (see 1.184n.), yet the ages of all the characters remain a matter of inference (see 3.293n.; 5.826n.).

754   *Chek mat!*: Use of the chess figure was a commonplace (Whiting C169; Hassell E15); cf. *Book of the Duchess*, 659.

756   *novelrie*: Cf. 'Men loven of propre kynde newefangelnesse ... | And loven novelries of propre kynde' (*Squire's Tale*, V.610, 619).

759   *I am naught religious*: Cf. 1.983–4; 2.117–18.

764–70 For other references to clouds, see 1.175; 2.781; 3.433; 4.200; cf. also the cloud and sky imagery in Boethius (e.g. 1.m.1).

776   *dredfull joye*: Cf. 'The dredful joye alwey that slit so yerne [slips by so quickly]: | Al this mene I by Love' (*Parliament of Fowls*, 3–4).

777   *why*] A Gg; *wex* J; *wey(e, way* other MSS.

784   For the notion of drinking up unhappy experience, see 3.1035, 1214–16; and *House of Fame*, 1879–80 ('For what I drye, or what I thynke, | I wil myselven al hyt drynke'); see also *MED*, s.v. *drinken* v. 2(b).

789   *harm ydoon is doon*: Proverbial (Whiting H134).

791   Proverbial (cf. Whiting B200, 201; Hassell A48; Walther 18425). S1 has the gloss 'Acriores in principi[o] franguntur in fine' (Those very keen in the beginning are broken in the end), which also occurs twice in preaching material in British Library MSS Harley 7322 and 4894, labelled 'istud verbum antiquum' and 'illud vulgare proverbium' (Wenzel 1976: 147).

798   See *Boece*, 5.pr.1.43–4 ('no thing hath his beynge of naught'); also proverbial (Whiting N151; Walther 8299).

804–5 Proverbial-sounding, but no other recorded instance (Whiting T399).

807–8 'nothing ventured, nothing gained': proverbial (Whiting N146; Hassell A17, A218, E53); Diomede later cites the same proverb (5.784).

811   The God of Love warns the Lover he will feel now hot, now cold (*Roman de la Rose*, 2278; *Romaunt*, 2398).

813–931 This scene in Criseyde's garden, and Antigone's song, are not from Boccaccio, although later in *Filostrato* (3.73–89)

Troiolo sings a song to Pandaro in a garden (cf. *TC* 3.1737–71).

816   *Flexippe . . . Tharbe . . . Antigone*: Chaucer would have known
the name Antigone, the sister of Polynices and Eteocles (5.1485–
90, 1506–8) from the story of Thebes (cf. also Ovid, *Metamor-
phoses*, 6.93–7), but the origin of the other two names is doubtful:
Plexippus (spelled Flexippus in some manuscripts) is one of the
uncles slain by Meleager (Ovid, *Metamorphoses*, 8.440; cf. Boc-
caccio, *Teseida*, 8.43) in the quarrel Cassandra will later recall to
Troilus (*TC* 5.1478–9), and a 'rex Thabor' appears in Guido,
Historia, p. 115 (Hamilton 1903: 94–6; McKinley 1992).

820–22   Criseyde's garden has the features of a typical medieval
English garden, with sanded paths railed by palings (generally
painted), and with benches (made of earth, with wooden or walled
sides, topped with turf; cf. *Legend of Good Women*, Prologue G
97–9). See McLean 1981: 103–19, 160–61, which also describes
'a little staircase down from the Queen's apartments to her
garden' at Guildford Palace, 'a popular device also used at the
royal palace at Kennington, and in many noble houses' (pp. 102–
3). See *TC* 2.1705, and cf. Howes 1997. From accounts of medi-
eval London houses and their gardens 'within the city, the parlour,
when on the ground floor . . . was nearly always to be found
overlooking the garden, and it is clear that the two went together;
only occasionally is a parlour found without an adjacent garden'
(Schofield 1994: 90). Apart from the garden mentioned at 3.1738
(from *Filostrato*, 3.73) the garden settings in *TC* (see also 2.508,
1114–17, 1705) have no equivalent in *Filostrato*.

827–75   *Cantus Antigone . . .* : Cp, Cl, H1 and J lack this Latin rubric,
but D, H4, H5 and S1 contain it, S2 and Ph have 'Cantus Antigone
de amore' (Antigone's song about love), and R has 'The songe of
Antigonee'. The song has general similarities to Machaut's lay *Le
Paradis d'amours*, and to various of his lyrics, especially the
Mireoir amoureux, in which ladies sing in praise of love and their
lovers (Wimsatt 1976). Antigone's song may be seen (Borthwick
1961) as responding point for point as follows to Criseyde's
earlier hesitations about love: 2.862–4 (cf. 2.781), 865 (cf.
2.782–3), 866 (cf. 2.784), 867–8 (cf. 2.785–6), 869–73 (cf.
2.786–9), 874–5 (cf. 2.790–91).

831–2   With love's grace, cf. a Machaut *balade* in his *La Louange des
dames*: 'I don't believe that to any creature Love dispenses his
blessings so generously and with so much favour as to me'
(Wilkins 1972: 78).

841–7   With these epithets for the lover, cf. Chaucer's *Complaint of*

Venus, 1–24 ('. . . In him is bounte, wysdom, governaunce . . .'), and *Mireoir amoureux*, 15–20, 122–6, 85–7 (Wimsatt 1976).

843 *Apollo*: 'god of science and of lyght' (*House of Fame*, 1091); cf. *Mireoir amoureux* (122–6): 'It is the sapphire that makes all hearts rejoice, and it is the true sun that with its beams makes all that is good to flourish' (Wimsatt 1976).

851–4 For love's improving effects, see also 1.1079–85; 3.1800–1806.

861 Cf. the proverb 'Many men speak of Robin Hood and shot never in his bow' (Whiting R156), perhaps here echoed in the allusion to the God of Love, Cupid the archer, and his arrows. H4 and Ph read 'speken of Robyn Hood'.

867–8 The proverb 'People who live in glass houses shouldn't throw stones' is unrecorded in English before Chaucer (Whiting H218), but for the notion of a glass helmet as delusive protection, see 5.469 and n.

872–3 Cf. the grafting image in Machaut's short lyric 'Moult sui de bonne heure née' (26–9): 'One desire, one thought, one heart, one soul is grafted in us, and also we are united in will.'

884 *sike*: The rhyme with *endite/white* (2.886, 887) is a very rare case in *TC* of an imperfect rhyme. Skeat (1894: 2.471) conjectured that 'sike' was a corruption of the rare Northern 'site' (be anxious), although it is doubtful that Chaucer would have used this; cf. also the conjectural reading 'to sike a lite' in place of 'therwith to sike' (DiMarco 1999).

905 *al this clepe I the sonne*: Cf. *Franklin's Tale*, V.1017–18 ('For th'orisonte hath reft the sonne his lyght – | This is as muche to seye as it was nyght – '). For traditional parody of such periphrases, see Curtius 1953: 275–6.

918 *A nyghtyngale*: Cf. the earlier allusion to the Procne story, 2.64–70.

925–31 Criseyde's dream of the white eagle is not in *Filostrato*, but may be influenced by Troiolo's later dream (7.23–4) of the boar (Diomede) tearing out Criseida's heart with his tusks, to her apparent pleasure (cf. 5.1233–42). The eagle, king of birds, suggests the prince Troilus; 'white as bone' is a traditional comparison (Whiting B443). For visions of eagles, cf. Dante, *Purgatorio*, 9.19–20 (lines that closely follow some already echoed at *TC* 2.64–70); see also *House of Fame*, 496ff., and *Purgatorio*, 29.108.

930 *she nought agroos*: 'Freud points out that "In a dream I may be in a horrible, dangerous and disgusting situation without feeling any fear or repulsion"' (Spearing 1972: 145).

931   The exchange of hearts is a conventional conceit of courtly poetry; cf. 2.872–3 above.

939–66   Expanded from *Filostrato*, 2.79, where Pandaro is able to come directly to Troiolo. Chaucer adds a sense of Troilus's household: he must send messengers and wait through a meal before a private conversation with Pandarus. The dialogue between Troilus and Pandarus develops from 10 stanzas (*Filostrato*, 2.86–95) to 18 stanzas (2.939–1064) in *TC*.

954   *don thyn hood*: A phrase of uncertain meaning; perhaps 'call it a day', 'get ready to sleep', 'relax' ('keep your shirt on'), with 'hood' as a nightcap, or hood for a falcon (Cassidy 1958). Other suggestions have included: 'be at ease (said to someone who has courteously doffed his hat)' (Baugh 1963) or, taking 'hood' as a battle-helmet, 'prepare for action' (Sadlek 1982).

957   *Sire*: The only occasion when Pandarus so addresses Troilus; cf. 2.1416, 1459 (Pandarus addressing Deiphebus).

962   *love of frendshipe*: See above, 2.371 and n.

964   *hameled*: Apparently conceiving of Troilus's sorrow as a hound that is pursuing him but now hambled or lamed; less probably referring to Criseyde as prey, now half captured.

965   *lenger sermoun*: With the concern for brevity, cf. 2.1071, 1219, 1264, 1299, 1595; 3.1576; 5.1032.

967–71   From *Filostrato*, 2.80, itself following *Inferno*, 2.127–32.

968   *stalke*] D Gg H3 H4 H5; *stalk* Cp Cl H1; *stalkes* other MSS.

985–7   For references to execution, see also 3.1240–45; 4.1105–6.

989   *every thing hath tyme*: Proverbial (Whiting T88), deriving from Ecclesiastes 3:1. Cf. *TC* 2.281–2; 3.855. It is still the evening of 4 May.

992   *pryme*: The first division of the day, from 6.00 to 9.00 a.m.

1003   *A thousand fold*: Pandaro only thinks Troiolo six times more far-seeing than himself (*Filostrato*, 2.91).

1005   *Right*] Cp A Cl D H1 J S2 omit.

1013   *ryd forth by the place*: This second, contrived ride past is not in *Filostrato*.

1022   *don thyn eris glowe*: A traditional notion (cf. Whiting E12).

1023   *Towchyng thi lettre*: Recalling the advice in Ovid, *Ars amatoria*, 1.455–68 (e.g. the lover should address his lady with coaxing words; he is not to address her as he would the senate or a judge; only a fool would declaim at his lady: 463–5). Pandarus's advice on letter-writing (*TC* 1023–43) is not in *Filostrato*.

1027   *Biblotte it*: Cf. Ovid, *Heroides*, 3.3 ('Whatever blots you see, tears have made').

1033 *Touche ay o stryng*: Horace advises against this (*Ars poetica*, 355–6: 'a harpist is laughed at who always blunders on the same string'); also proverbial (Whiting S839).

1041–3 *if a peyntour*: Cf. the opening five lines of Horace, *Ars poetica*: 'If a painter chose to join a human head to the neck of a horse, and to spread feathers of many a colour over limbs picked up now here, now there, so that what at the top is a beautiful woman ends up below in a black and ugly fish, could you . . . refrain from laughing?' (partly quoted in John of Salisbury, *Policraticus*, Webb 1929: 2.18).

1044 *to] unto* Cp Cl D H1 H3 S2 Th; J H5 Cx omit.

1055 *Right*] Cp A Cl D H1 H3 S2 omit.

1064 *wrot right in this wyse*: The following summary (1065–85) replaces Boccaccio's verbatim presentation of Troiolo's 11-stanza letter (2.96–106).

1086–7 For the wetting of the seal with tears, see Boccaccio, *Filocolo*, 1.274. Rubies were believed to burn more brightly if wetted (Jennings 1976).

1093 *Pandare tok the lettre*: His role in conveying letters (see 3.488) recalls that of the 'fedelissimo servidore' (most faithful servant) in *Filocolo*, 1.267–75. It is now the morning of 5 May (see *TC* 2.74n.). The dialogue between Pandarus and Criseyde is expanded from 9 stanzas (*Filostrato*, 2.108–13, 118–20) to some 30 stanzas (2.1093–1302) in *TC*.

1094 *his neces paleis*: Chaucer adds to *Filostrato* the description of Criseyde's house as a palace.

1099 *a joly wo, a lusty sorwe*: I.e. the traditional oxymorons of the language of love (cf. Troilus's song, 1.400–420).

1104 Proverbial (Whiting W343).

1106 *loves daunce*: The expression 'old daunce' is unrecorded in English before Chaucer, who always associates it with questions of love and sex (*General Prologue, CT* I.476; *Physician's Tale*, VI.79). In French the phrase suggested artfulness and shrewdness, not originally confined to sexual matters. See also *TC* 1.517–18.

1109–10 Although to find 'Game in myn hood' may mean to 'find me amusing' or 'find a joke at my expense', there may also be some sense of hoodwinking, of playing a trick on the unwary (Smith 1983). For other references to headgear, with overtones of hood-winking and trickery, see 2.1181–2; 3.773–7; 5.469.

1111ff. To gain a moment of privacy Pandarus must invent this excuse of secret matters concerning the Trojan War, whereas (*Filostrato*, 2.109) Pandaro replies immediately with the equivalent of what

Pandarus can only say privately at 2.1121ff. Criseyde again descends to her garden (cf. 2.813–14), from where she returns to the hall (2.1170), retiring from there into her 'chambre' (2.1173) to read Troilus's letter, presumably returning into the hall (2.1179) in order to dine, retreating again into her 'closet' (2.1215) to write to Troilus, and apparently returning again into the hall where Pandarus is sitting in a streetside window-seat (2.1226–9).

1130–34 With Criseyde's scruples, cf. the late fourteenth-century *Le Menagier de Paris*: the husband advises his young wife to read any intimate and confidential letters from her husband alone in private and to reply to him in private by her own hand if she knows how or by the hand of some discreet person (cf. *TC* 2.1172–9, 1213–32), and not to receive or read any other letters except in public, nor write letters to others except by another's hand (Brereton and Ferrier 1981: 56; Stanbury 1994).

1145 *smyten . . . with thondre*: The fate of Capaneus; see *TC* 5.1504–5, and Statius, *Thebaid*, 10.888–939.

1154–5 Cf. *Filostrato*, 2.112–13: ' "I've told you a great deal about this business, so you shouldn't start turning bashful on me. I beg you now not to refuse me this." Criseida smiled when she heard him, and took the letter and placed it in her bosom. "When I've the time," she said to him, "I'll read it as best I can. If I'm acting less than prudently now, it's because I can't do less than please you – may God look down from heaven upon this and protect my innocence!" '

1204 *sowe and plite*: When sent, a letter 'was folded to form a small packet and secured by stitching with string or by passing narrow paper tape through the slits and sealing the ends with wax' (Davis 1971: xxxiv).

1213–14 Criseyde is not illiterate (cf. 2.103, 118); she reads Troilus's letter alone (2.1175–6), and Troilus later reads through the letters she has sent to him during their affair (5.470–72). Helen of Troy also claims to be a novice at letter-writing in Ovid, *Heroides*, 17.143–4. Cf. Caxton's *The Book of the Knight of the Tower*: 'as for wrytyng it is no force [matter] / yf a woman can nought of hit but as for redynge I saye that good and prouffytable is to al wymen / For a woman that can rede may better knowe the peryls of the sowle' (Offord 1971: 122).

1217 *desdaynes prison*: The lady's reserve or standoffishness (her 'daunger') is a traditional aspect of the lover's difficulties in courtly literature; cf. *Merciles Beaute*: 'For Daunger halt [holds] your mercy in his cheyne' (16).

1219 *to telle in short*: Boccaccio's verbatim account of the letter (2.121–7) is again replaced with a summary here, but Chaucer will draw on the Italian letters for his lovers' letters in 5.1317–1421, 1590–1631.

1224 *as his suster*: Boccaccio's Criseida later says to Pandaro: 'under no circumstances do I mean to yield him the crown of my honour. But I shall always love him most honourably like a brother because of his great goodness' (*Filostrato*, 2.134).

1228–9 The stone seat is fashioned from jasper, the medieval term for a kind of bright-coloured chalcedony or quartz, often green in colour, rather than the modern jasper. In *Pearl* jasper is green, and a wall of jasper glistens like glass (Andrew and Waldron 1978: lines 999–1001, 1017–18). In the furnishing of later medieval London houses 'cushions are frequently mentioned in wills and inventories, and must therefore have been of some value and opulence' (Schofield 1994: 132, 251, n.295, citing references in 1356, 1391, and later, which specify sets of cushions, some richly embroidered). Cf. 3.964. Criseyde's palace is richly appointed (cf. 2.82n., 820–22n.).

1234–5 Unrecorded elsewhere (cf. Whiting T150), Pandarus's proverb modifies the common proverb 'An evil beginning has a foul ending' (Whiting B199; Hassell F90).

1238–9 *Impressiounes lighte . . . flighte*: unrecorded elsewhere as an English proverb (Whiting I26); H4 glosses: 'Levis impressio, levis recessio' (light impression, light recession). All MSS except H4 and S2 read 'impressiouns'.

1240 *played the tirant*] *played tirant* Cp+.
      That the lady's powers over her lover resemble those of an absolute ruler was a courtly commonplace, as also was the conventional plea to her not to be as merciless as a tyrant. In the Prologue to the *Legend of Good Women* Alcestis urges the wrathful God of Love not to be as pitiless as some late-medieval Italian despots ('And not ben lyk tyraunts of Lumbardye . . .', G.354–64), and the *Merchant's Tale* compares May's concessiveness to Damian with the cruelty of a tyrant-mistress ('Som tyrant is, as ther be many oon . . . |Which wolde han lat hym sterven in the place | Wel rather than han graunted hym hire grace', IV.1989–92).

1257–8 With Troilus's behaviour, cf. Love's advice to the Lover in *Roman de la Rose* on haunting the lady's house: 'And if so be it happe thee | That thou thi love there maist see, | In siker wise thou hir salewe, | Wherewith thi colour wole transmewe, | And eke thy

blod shal al toquake, | Thyn hewe eke chaungen for hir sake'
(*Romaunt*, 2523–8)

1272–3 *a thorn*: Cf. 3.1104–5 and II Corinthians 12:7.

1276 Cf. 'Strike while the iron is hot' (Whiting I60), and Chaucer's
Tale of Melibee, CT VII.1036–7.

1298 *yeres two*: This may have been considered an appropriate period
of widowhood before remarriage. Cf. Andreas Capellanus, *De
amore*, rule 7: 'When one lover dies, a widowhood of two years
is required of the survivor' (Walsh 1982); and also: 'A woman
who is left a widow by the death of her lover may seek a new love
after two years have elapsed' (2.7.14). Three MSS (A D S1) read
'monthes' for 'yeres'.

1332 From *Filostrato* (2.85), but also proverbial (Whiting W560).

1335 Proverbial: Whiting O7, G418, K12; Walther 5105; Alanus de
Insulis, *Liber parabolarum* (*PL* 210: 583).

1347 *thise dees*: Dicing might be used for divination in love affairs; it
is among the lovers' pastimes in Gower, *Confessio amantis*, along
with debating questions about love or listening to romances about
lovers like Troilus: 'Bot on the dees to caste chaunce, | Or axe of
love som demaunde, | Or elles that hir list comaunde | To rede
and here of Troilus' (4.2792–5). Cf. also the Middle English
poem *The Chance of the Dice*, which has numbered 'fortunes'
and character portraits, including one of Criseyde ('Ye leve youre
olde and taken newe and newe', 383), to be read after players
have thrown the dice (Hammond 1925).

1349 *gistes*: If this means stopping or resting places (*MED*, s.v. *giste*),
the sense is perhaps of pacing the stages of a journey; cf. also
'flowed with the tide of events' (Barney 1987: 1036). The sug-
gested meaning of 'throws of the dice' for *gistes* (Root 1926: 454)
is unattested elsewhere; another suggestion is to read as *gestes*
(deeds, accomplishments) with the sense 'And regulated his pace
according to his achievements' (Baugh 1963: 119). The MSS
point to scribal confusion: *gistes*] J Cl H4; *giftis* A D Ph S1 Cx;
gostes Cp; *gestes* other MSS.

1374–6 *Kynde wolde ... Seyth Daunger*: Criseyde's reactions are
personified as an inner conflict between nature and reserve; for
'daunger', see 2.384, 399.

1380 *the stordy ook*: Cf. the proverbs 'An oak falls all at once' and
'The oak is feeble that falls at the first stroke' (Whiting O8, T471);
also 'For no man at the firste strok | Ne may nat felle down an
ok' (*Romaunt*, 3687–8).

1387–9 Proverbial (Whiting R71); cf. 1.257.

1398 *Deiphebus*: The third of the five sons of Priam and Hecuba (*Troie*, 2939); Virgil alludes to the tradition that he married Helen after the death of Paris (*Aeneid*, 6.511–12). In Dares and Benoît, Deiphebus dies before Paris, but Dictys treats the marriage.

1401ff. The whole episode of the family visit to the sick Troilus here in *TC* may have been prompted in part by the much later family visit to the sick Troiolo organized by Deiphebus in *Filostrato* (7.77–102), an episode rewritten in *TC* as Cassandra's visit to interpret Troilus's dream (5.1450–1534).

1408 Deiphebus uses the familiar second person singular 'thow' form to address Pandarus, politely but as a social inferior.

1466 *wher*] Gg H5 J Ph S1; *wheither* other MSS.

1467 *Poliphete*: Chaucer may derive the name from a Trojan priest (Polyphoetes or Polyboetes), seen by Aeneas in the underworld (*Aeneid*, 6.484) shortly before he meets Deiphebus, who tells how Helen betrayed him at the fall of Troy.

1474 In one tradition, Antenor and Aeneas were the betrayers of Troy (see 4.203–5).

1495 *word and ende*: A common corruption of an older expression 'ord and ende' (beginning and end).

1503 *saved by thi feyth*: Cf. Luke 8:48, 18:42.

1512 *sleyghte*: The device of the feigned illness may derive (Muscatine 1948) from the story of Amnon and Tamar (II Samuel 13: 1–20), itself cited in medieval treatises on friendship as an example of what one friend ought *not* to do for another; cf. Aelred of Rievaulx, *De spirituali amicitia* (*PL* 195: 675A); Peter of Blois, *De amicitia christiana* (Davy 1932: 154–6). In the story of how Amnon's friend Jonadab advises him to pretend to be ill so that Tamar may come to visit him, there are the following parallels with *TC*: a similar group of characters, comprising the lover, his trusted friend (characterized by certain intellectual powers), the beautiful woman and the innocent visitors; the lover is the king's son, so desperately in love that he becomes ill and changed in appearance but unable to help himself; the friend, noticing the lover's changed appearance, asks the cause and receives the lover's confidence.

1533 Unrecorded elsewhere as a proverb (cf. Whiting H553).

1534–5 Pandarus will drive the prey towards where the hunter waits with bow and arrow. For other hunting imagery, see 1.747–8n.

1554 *a wood man for to renne*: That mad men run wild was a commonplace.

1556 *the faire queene Eleyne*: For the mythographers, Helen of Troy was largely a figure of treachery and disaster; in the iconography of the histories of Troy, she is generally depicted as beautiful, gracious and charming (Baswell and Taylor 1988). Chaucer knew Ovid's *Heroides*, 17 – Helen's letter to Paris before she has given herself to him – which offers parallels with Criseyde's uncertainties and (ironic) concern for her reputation (see *TC* 2.724, 746; 5.1058–60, 1067–71). For allusions to Paris's affair with Oenone, see *TC* 1.652–65 and 4.1553. See also 4.608–9: Pandarus offers another parallel between the loves of Troilus and Criseyde, and Paris and Helen.

1557 *an houre after the prime*: 10.00 a.m. was the hour of dinner; see earlier, 2.1095, 1163.

1564 *prolixitee*: See *Roman de la Rose*, 18298: 'Bon fait prolixité foïr' (It is a good thing to flee prolixity); cf. *Squire's Tale*, V.404–5; Whiting P408.

1610 *alle folk be trewe*: Cf. 5.651.

1615 Cf. the Pardoner's delivery: 'And rynge it out as round as gooth a belle' (*Pardoner's Prologue*, VI.331); also Whiting B234.

1638 *beere*: I.e. funeral bier (cf. 4.863, 1183), here with the bawdy innuendo of something Troilus will lie on, as also with a possible pun on 'bere' (pillow-case), as in *Book of the Duchess*, 254–5 ('And many a pilowe, and every ber | Of cloth of Reynes [Rennes], to slepe softe – ').

1646 *the chaumbre is but lite*: The party is taking place in 'the grete chaumbre' (2.1712) of Deiphebus's house: those assembled there will see Criseyde with Pandarus go into Troilus's small sick-room off the great chamber, which they have already seen Deiphebus and Helen enter, but without knowing that the latter pair will exit from the sick-room by a door on the other side and go down a staircase into a garden where they will remain for an hour (2.1705–7), possibly a hint at their subsequent relationship (Sundwall 1975).

1663 *yow*] me Cp Cl Dg H1 S2; *it* Gg H4 R Th.

1665 *his*] this Cp Cl D Dg H1 S1 S2 Cx.

1699 Perhaps an allusion to the Greek prisoner of war, King Thoas, later exchanged, together with Criseyde, for Antenor (see 4.138n.). In Guido's *Historia* (pp. 155–6) Priam and his council debate whether Thoas should be put to death (Benson 1979).

1732 The line may continue the direct speech of previous lines: 'And thus let us begin (to go) in very softly'.

1735 *corones tweyne*: Now obscure and unexplained (for discussion, see Doob 1972; Malarky 1963; Thundy 1985), but the two crowns may refer to pity and bounty, or justice and mercy. Cf. Chaucer's *Complaint unto Pity*, 58, 72–7 (where pity is 'coroune of vertues alle', 'annexed ever unto Bounte ... | Ye be also the corowne of Beaute'), and *An ABC*, 137–44 (addressing the Virgin: 'Soth is that God ne granteth no pitee | Withoute thee ... | ... and he represseth his justise | After thi wil; and therfore in witnesse | He hath thee corowned in so rial wise'). Boccaccio's Criseida refers to 'la corona dell'onestà mea' (the crown of my honour: see above, 2.1224n.), to which Pandaro retorts: 'That crown is what priests praise when they can't deprive the wearer of it' (*Filostrato*, 2.134–5).

1750 Between lines 1750 and 1751 R includes a unique penultimate stanza here (possibly surviving from Chaucer's work in progress), which makes explicit the concerns with mercy and bounty perhaps reflected in the above allusion to 'corones tweyne':

> For ye must outher chaungen your face
> That is so ful of mercy and bountee
> Or elles must ye do this man sum grace
> For this thyng folweth of necessytee
> As sothe as god ys in his magestee
> That crueltee with so benigne a chier
> Ne may not last in o persone yfere.

This stanza may be compared with 1.890–96, surviving in only three MSS. Both seem to be not quite integrated, even interruptions in their present contexts, as if Chaucer may have not settled where or whether to fit them in. Two earlier lines (2.1576–7) are confusedly repeated before the unique R stanza, and marked 'vacat' (to be cancelled, or perhaps, material is lacking) in the margin, which suggests how material to be added from extra sheets or slips might be labelled for the copyist and signalled for inclusion by an indication in the margin. Another hypothesis is that the stanza was actually intended to follow 2.1736 (Root 1926: 458).

1752 *kankedort*: 'Predicament, quandary'; a translation, inferred from the context, of this unexplained word. For a review of suggested etymologies and meanings, see Gillmeister 1978.

BOOK 3

1–49   The third proem is brought forward from *Filostrato*, 3.74–9,
       part of Troiolo's song, itself derived in part from Boethius, *De
       consolatione*, 2.m.8, and perhaps Dante, *Paradiso*, 8.1–15. (At
       the close of his third book, Chaucer substitutes for his Troilus a
       song adapted directly from *Boece*, 2.m.8; see 3.1744–71.)
       Troiolo's song to Venus after his union with Criseida thus
       becomes the proem to Book 3 of *TC*; Venus is invoked both as
       planet, with benefic astrological influence, and as pagan goddess
       of love, while love is invoked both as sexual attraction and
       as that cosmic love which binds together the universe. For the
       mythographers the two Venuses represent the dual potential of
       human love, virtuous or wanton; cf. Bernardus Silvestris in his
       Commentum super sex libros Eneidos Virgilii (Riedel 1924: 9):

> We read that there are indeed two Venuses, one lawful, and the
> other the goddess of wantonness. The lawful Venus is the harmony
> of the world, that is, the even proportion of worldly things, which
> some call Astraea, and others call natural justice. This subsists in
> the elements, in the stars, in the seasons, in living beings. The
> shameless Venus, however, the goddess of wantonness, is carnal
> concupiscence since that is the mother of all fornications.

   Cf. also Third Vatican Mythographer 11.18, and Boccaccio, *De
       genealogia deorum*, 3.22–3. Apart from 2.972, other references
       to Venus in *TC* are Chaucer's additions to *Filostrato*. For further
       background, see Tinkle 1996.

1–3   Venus is addressed both astrologically and mythologically: as
       planet of the third sphere (reckoned outwards from the earth,
       after the moon and Mercury); as Jove's daughter; and as beloved
       of the sun, because Venus accompanies the sun through the
       heavens both as morning and evening star (cf. Dante, *Paradiso*,
       8.11–12).

5   Closer than the corresponding line in *Filostrato* – 'Benigna donna
       d'ogni gentil core' (Gracious mistress of every noble heart: 3.74)
       – is Guido Guinizelli's line 'Al cor gentil rempaira sempre Amore'
       (Love always repairs to noble hearts; Contini 1960: 2.460), cited
       by Dante in *Convivio*, 4.20. See also Dante, *Inferno*, 5.100:
       'Amor, ch'al cor gentil ratto s'apprende' (Love, which is quickly
       kindled in the gentle heart).

11   *vapour*: From *Filostrato*, 3.75, but cf. Dante, *Purgatorio*, 11.6
      ('tuo dolce vapore') and Wisdom of Solomon 7:25 (wisdom 'is a
      breath of the power of God and a clear emanation from the glory
      of the Almighty').

15–21 In *Filostrato* (3.76) Venus's influence moves Jove to mercy on
      mankind's offences against him; the 'thousand formes' recalls
      Jove's amorous escapades, e.g. with Europa (see *TC* 3.722).

15–38 The shift to the polite plural *ye* form of address alters *Filostrato*,
      which uses the familiar *tu* form throughout.

17   *him*: Conjectural reading; all MSS read *hem*.

22   *Ye fierse Mars apaisen*: In astrology Venus offsets Mars's malefic
      influence, and in mythology Mars, god of wrath and contention,
      becomes lover of the goddess of love, as Troilus later recalls
      (3.725).

25   *shame, and vices*: One of recurrent references to the morally
      improving and ennobling effects of love (e.g. 1.250–52, 1076–
      85; 3.1786–1806).

39–40 *benignite*: Recalling epithets used in addressing the Virgin
      Mary; cf. *Prioress's Prologue*, *CT* VII.478, and Dante, *Paradiso*,
      33.16.

43–4 For an earlier disclaimer to be writing 'of sentement', see 2.13.

45   *Caliope*: Muse of epic poetry; perhaps recalled (like the opening
      lines of Book 2) from the opening of Dante's *Purgatorio* (1.7–9);
      cf. also Statius, *Thebaid*, 4.34–5, and *Boece*, 3.m.12.24 (where
      Calliope is interpreted as 'eloquence' in Nicholas Trevet's com-
      mentary). Medieval commentators interpreted Calliope as the
      'best voice' among the Muses (e.g. Fulgentius, *Mitologie*, 1.15;
      Third Vatican Mythographer, 8.18; Boccaccio, *De genealogia
      deorum*, 11.2).

50   After a two-stanza proem Part 3 of *Filostrato* takes just 29 stanzas
      (232 lines) to narrate how one night Troiolo comes by prior
      arrangement to Criseida's house and the lovers go to bed together,
      a point only reached in *TC* at 3.1310–16, 180 stanzas (1260
      lines) after the Book 3 narrative begins.

51   *Recordying his lesson*: Cf. the lover's confusion in his lady's pres-
      ence in Machaut, *Jugement dou Roy de Behaingne*, 465–76 ('I
      resolved to speak to her of my love. All alone I went over this with
      myself, but when I was about to tell her of my troubles, my heart
      was so fearful, feeble, exhausted, anguished, discomfited, trem-
      bling, embarrassed, and so overcome by lovesickness, that there
      was no sense, manner or wit in it; rather, it was overwhelmed').

81   Cf. 3.957.

83   *sire*: This 'solitary reference in *TC* to a single lord suggests the king himself, or a great lord, in an actual audience' (Brewer 1973: 212).

91   *as techen bokes olde*: The following scene of the lovers' meeting is actually invented by Chaucer.

101 *ferforthly*] *feythfully* Cp+ (and H3 Th).

110 *wreththe*] *herte* Cp+ (and H2 H3 S1 Cx).

114 *an herte of stoon to rewe*: Cf. *Legend of Good Women*, 1841–2, and Whiting H277; see also *TC* 5.266, 560.

115 *as he to water wolde*: Proverbial phrase; cf. *Squire's Tale*, V.496, and Whiting W81.

129 With the lover's request for his lady's friendly look, cf. Machaut, *Remède de Fortune*, 1319–20.

131–3 Troilus seems to echo the terms of a vassal's pledge of fealty to his lord, while Criseyde's response (3.160–61, 176–82) echoes the lord's accepting the vassal as a knight into his service and then sealing the pact with a kiss: 'The vows Troilus and Criseyde exchange explicitly mimic those exchanged by vassal and lord when they enter into a feudal contract' (Hornsby 1988: 137–8).

150 *natal Joves feste*: Probably 'the feast of Jupiter who presides over nativities' (Robinson 1957) rather than 'the festival of Jove's birth' (Root 1926). In St Jerome's *Epistola adversus Jovinianum* (1.48) a wise man is advised to take a mate and not go against 'Jovem Gamelium & Genethlium', i.e. Jove, god of betrothals and of procreation (Pratt 1962). (For the suggestion that Juno, goddess of childbearing, rather than Jove, may have been Chaucer's intention, see Barney 1987.)

169–75 Cf. 1.432–9.

184 *held his hondes highe*: A gesture of prayer.

188 *Withouten hond*: Instances of bells ringing 'without hand' recur at especially joyful or solemn moments in ballads, romances and saints' lives. For ballads, see Child 1882–98: i.173, 231; iii.235, 244 ('And a' the bells a merry Lincoln | Without men's hands were rung'), 519–20; for romance, see Tatlock 1914: 98; for saints' lives, see Barry 1915: 28–9, who suggests that the origin of many such stories is a tale told about the monks of Fulda by the eighth-century St Willibrord in the *Vita S. Bonifatii*.

189 *merveille*] Cp+; *miracle* other MSS.

198 *bere the belle*: This may mean 'take the prize' or 'lead the flock' (as a bellwether); see Whiting B230; *MED*, s.v. *bell* 9(a); or perhaps derives from falconry, where an esteemed falcon might bear a bell (Breeze 1992).

232 Chaucer here resumes following *Filostrato* with Pandaro's speech
on confidentiality (3.4–10), but changes the setting from the
temple where Pandaro finds Troiolo lost in thought, which
Chaucer will use later for his Troilus's added soliloquy on free
will (*TC* 4.953–1078).

241 *to-yere*: Troilus first saw Criseyde in April (1.156; 3.360); Pand-
arus visited Criseyde in early May (2.50).

273 *traitour*: Chaucer mistranslates Boccaccio's 'trattator' (procurer,
go-between: 3.8).

282 The R+ variant line reads: 'The preie ich eft, althogh thow shuldest
deye'.

293 *to us yonge*: This may mean 'to us young folk' or, alternatively,
'to us when young'. The former would be the only reference to
Pandarus's age: his role as Criseyde's uncle and Troilus's adviser
may suggest that he is older, but he is also – unsuccessfully – a
lover (2.57–63, 96–8) and presents himself as joining Troilus in
exercise (2.512–13). In *Filostrato* (2.1) Pandaro is introduced as a
young Trojan of noble lineage. See also 1.184n.; 2.752n.; 5.826n.
(and cf. Brewer 1982; Slocum 1979). The R+ variant line reads:
'Han writen or this as men yit teche us yonge'.

294 Proverbial, from the Pseudo-Cato, *Disticha*, 1.3, a popular medi-
eval school-book of moral maxims (cf. Walther 33716; also
Whiting V41; Dg and S2 have a marginal gloss 'Cato' here). Cf.
Manciple's Tale, IX.332–3, and *Roman de la Rose*, 7037, 7041–
5, 7055–7.

303 *Hath*] *Hastow* Cp+ (and Gg H3 H5 S1 Th).

309 Proverbial (Whiting A244).

316–20 With Pandarus's argument, cf. the Friend's warning to the
Lover against ruining women's reputations through false boast-
ing, in *Roman de la Rose*, 9853–68.

320 Although this line sounds proverbial, there is no other recorded
instance (Whiting H176).

323–4 As Pandarus is alone with Troilus, any fools must be among
the audience.

329 Proverbial (cf. Whiting F449, W47, W391, W400, C161; Hassell
C101; Walther 8952, 8927) and see *TC* 1.203, 630, 635. See also
Roman de la Rose, 8003–4: 'Mout a beneüree vie | Cis qui par
autrui se chastie' (He who corrects himself by another's example
has a very happy life), and *Wife of Bath's Prologue*, III.180–83.

330 *to purpos*: For marked attention in Book 3 to the narrative's
'purpos', 'point' and 'effect', see also 3.449, 505, 604, 701, 1337,
1580, 1677.

340 *chartres*: Although a 'chartre' might be any formal document which is signed and sealed, the term most specifically refers to a deed conveying title to a tract of land (*MED*, s.v. *chartre* n. 2(b)), perhaps associating 'Criseyde's grant of her love to Troilus with a property conveyance' and suggesting 'that once the charters are drawn up the property will vest in Troilus' (Hornsby 1988: 90–91). For other allusions to the legal language of conveyance, see also 3.445, 901; 5.1689.

342 *bid for me*: Like a Christian saint in heaven, Troilus will be able to intercede for Pandarus. For Troilus as in heaven, see also 3.704, 1204, 1251, 1322, 1599.

351–7 Drawn from *Filostrato*, 3.12; but cf. also the May opening in *Roman de la Rose*, 47–54, 78–80 (*Romaunt*, 49–56, 82–4).

360 *in Aperil the laste*: Reference to 'to-yere' (this year: 3.241) suggests Troilus means the April of the current year. Events in Book 2 take place in May (2.56n., 1093n.). Unless one whole year is understood to have elapsed between the temple scene in Book 1 and Troilus's confession of his love to Pandarus, Troilus thus refers here to the April one or more months earlier.

374–5 Troilus is indeed to be killed by Achilles (5.1806).

379–81 In the *Roman de la Rose* Love tells how lovers' hopes make them endure like a prisoner who 'lyeth in vermyn and in ordure' (*Romaunt*, 2758).

382 *Agamenoun*: King of Mycenae, Agamemnon was the leader of the Greek forces besieging Troy.

404 *Departe it so*: Cf. Thomas Aquinas, *Summa theologica*, 1–1.31.2: 'Diversitas requirit distinctionem' (diversity requires a distinction).

407–13 With Troilus's offer here (derived from *Filostrato*, 3.18), cf. Pandarus's offer, 1.860–61.

414 *sith*] *sith that* Cp A Cl H1 Th. *idon*] J H2 Ph R S1; *don* other MSS.

435 *al the while*: Between the day of Deiphebus's party and the day that Pandarus visits Criseyde (3.549–52) an indeterminate period of time intervenes (see 3.450, 494, 508).

437 *Martes*: Perhaps an anglicization of the Italian 'Marte' (from *Filostrato*, 3.20) which Chaucer has already used (*TC* 2.435, 988), possibly influenced by Latin usage (cf. *TC* 4.1411; 5.3, and also *Squire's Tale*, V.50).

445 *sesed*: A Middle English legal term associated with the conveyance of property, where it means to be put in legal possession ('seisin') of a tract of land (Hornsby 1988: 91; *MED*, s.v. *seisin* v. 2b).

450 *as writen is in geeste*: Again, the pretension to a source precisely where one is not being followed.

468–9 *love, al come it late*: Cf. Criseyde's later remark to Diomede about her late husband (5.974–8).

497 *poynte*: For a discussion of 'pointing', especially characteristic of the scale and detail of narrative in *TC*, *Sir Gawain and the Green Knight* and *Ipomadon A* amongst Middle English texts, see Burrow 1971: 69–78, and cf. *Sir Gawain*, 1008–9, and *Monk's Tale*, VII.2458–62.

500–504 As Chaucer is not following *Filostrato*, this account of omissions in his sources is invented; the R+ MSS (here J, H4, R, Cx) read 'an hundred vers' instead of 'neigh half this book'. Troilus and Criseyde send each other more letters than are quoted in the text: e.g. 2.1342–4; 5.470–71, 1422–30, 1583

511 *it bifel*: Chaucer's account of how Troilus and Criseyde meet secretly is independent of *Filostrato* until the lovers are in bed together (3.1310), and has points in common with the lovers' meeting in Boccaccio's *Filocolo* (2.165–83), including the role of the go-between, the concealment of the lover, the incidence of jealousy, the exchange of vows and rings (see Young 1908: 139–61). In the twelfth century Latin *Pamphilus* (the opening line of which is quoted in *Franklin's Tale*, V.1109–10), the lady is invited to a meal at the house of the go-between, where she is surprised by the entry of the lover who calls on her to yield; the lover's jealousy has been aroused by the go-between's invented tales of a rival (Garbáty 1967).

526–7 For the chattering magpie, see *Parliament of Fowls*, 345 ('the janglynge pye'), and *House of Fame*, 703–4 ('Though that Fame had alle the pies | In al a realme, and alle the spies').

529 *fremde*] H5; *wild(e)* R+ (and H3 S1); *frend(e)* Gg H2 Ph; *fremed* other MSS.

530 Referring to the construction of a medieval timber-frame house (on which, see Schofield 1994: 143–6); cf. the earlier parallel between the love affair and building a house (1.1065–71).

542 *the holy laurer*: When Daphne is metamorphosed into the laurel as he pursues her, Apollo declares: 'Since you cannot be my bride, you shall at least be my tree' (Ovid, *Metamorphoses*, 1.557–9).

550 *lightles*: I.e. an especially dark night, both moonless and cloudy.

570 In *Filostrato* (3.21–2) Troiolo has indeed gone out of town on military business, as Pandaro truthfully reports to Criseida before sending a messenger to bring him back.

575 *myn auctour*: The reticent source here is another of Chaucer's invented references to an author.

587 *moste*: Probably to be taken as 'must' rather than the adverb 'most', but the construction in the original is – perhaps designedly – ambiguous. Cf. 3.916

589 *by stokkes and by stones*: A phrase applied contemptuously to pagan idols, i.e. gods of wood and stone. 'A powerful way of swearing "yes" – but "yes" what? It is not clear whether Pandarus is swearing yes, he will "loke al be wel" (and again, it is unclear what that would mean), or yes, he will do as he pleases' (Spearing 1976: 15).

592 *Pluto kyng*: God of the underworld.

593 *Tantalus*: Doomed in Hades to stand up to his chin in water that receded whenever he tried to quench his thirst (see Ovid, *Metamorphoses*, 4.458–9); like Tityus (*TC* 1.786) and Ixion (5.212), affected by the music of Orpheus (*Boece*, 3.m.12.38–40).

601 *stewe*: A small room, usually with a fireplace. Troilus has been hiding here since the previous night. Cf. Boccaccio's *Filocolo*, 2.172, where the lover watches secretly through a 'piccolo pertugio' (small aperture) as his lady enters unawares (Young 1908: 144–5), and also the Ph+ variant line: 'Thurghout an hole withyn a litil stewe'.

614 *He . . . she . . . he*: Probably referring to members of the company, retinue, or hired entertainers.
Wade: There are various references in medieval literature to Wade as a celebrated hero (e.g. *Alliterative Morte Arthure* (Benson 1986: line 964) pairs him with Gawain; see too *Sir Beves of Hamtoun* (Kölbing 1973: line 2605)), but his story is now lost and this allusion remains unexplained; Chaucer also refers to Wade's boat in *Merchant's Tale*, IV.1424.

615 *every thyng hath ende*: Proverbial (Whiting T87).

617 *executrice of wyerdes*: For Fortune as the agency which, under God, puts into effect in human lives the decrees of fate, cf. *Boece*, 4.pr.6.42–107; 5.m.1.18–23, and also Dante, *Inferno*, 7.78–80 (echoed at *TC* 5.1541–5).

624–5 Occurring in the year 1385, for the first time since AD 769, the rare conjunction of Saturn and Jupiter in the sign of Cancer, with the crescent moon appearing in the evening, may be dated to 9 or 10 June, although in his *Historia Anglicana* the contemporary chronicler Thomas Walsingham reports the conjunction of Saturn and Jupiter in Cancer as occurring in May 1385, and followed by a great disturbance of kingdoms (Windeatt 1992: 6, 10). While differing over the precise date – including 9 June (North 1988: 369–78), 12 May (Olson and Laird 1990) and 13 May (Root and Russell 1924) – modern commentators agree that May or June 1385 is meant. Conjunctions of Saturn and Jupiter were held to be portents of great events (including Noah's Flood) and associated with heavy rain. The lovers' union during a rainstorm (in *Filostrato* the night is simply dark and cloudy: 3.24) may be an echo of that of Dido and Aeneas (cf. Virgil, *Aeneid*, 4.160–62).

663   *closet*: A small room perhaps adjoining, at the dais end, the hall where they have been dining; a 'travers' (curtain, or partitioning screen) might be drawn or placed across the hall (cf. *Merchant's Tale*, IV.1817), forming for Criseyde's women a 'middle' chamber nearest the room where she is to sleep, and an outer room where Pandarus is to sleep (Smyser 1956). However, there is also evidence that a closet might be a small chamber off a bedroom where the occupant could retire for privacy and rest, and that 'the closet was not associated with the hall' and 'was never heated' (Schofield 1994: 81), although Pandarus's closet does have a fireplace (3.978, 1141). Pandarus may simply be indicating a sequence of connecting chambers. How Pandarus moves through the house, the location of Troilus's hiding place, and if or when Pandarus leaves Criseyde's room (cf. *TC* 3.914, 1189, 1555), remain unexplained.

671   *The wyn anon*: Wine was drunk as a nightcap; cf. *General Prologue*, *CT* I.819–20.

695   *olde daunce*: Cf. 2.1106. There may be a play here on 'point' as a note in music or as a short snatch of melody (Harvey 1968).

697   *his werk bigynne*: In *Filostrato* Troiolo has already entered Criseida's house by a secret entry and waits in hiding until Criseida (having hurried everyone to bed) comes to lead him upstairs, apologizing for keeping him cooped up there (3.24–8).

711   Proverbial (Whiting G484).

715–19   Troilus prays to Venus as goddess of love (and a benefic planet in astrology) to intercede with her father Jupiter (also astrologically benefic) to avert any harm if at his birth the malefic planets, Mars and Saturn (see *Knight's Tale*, I.1995–2038, 2456–69), were in unfavourable 'aspect' (the angle between two planets as seen from the earth). If 'combust', i.e. too near and hence obscured by the sun, Venus lost influence. (On the planets, see North 1988: 194–208; Seymour 1975: 479–83.)

721 *Adoun*: Beloved of Venus, Adonis was killed by a boar; see Ovid, *Metamorphoses*, 10.503–739. In marginal glosses H4 cites this *Metamorphoses* passage and the three mentioned below in notes to lines 722, 726–7 and 729–30 (see Windeatt 1992: 43). Cf. Boccaccio, *Teseida*, 7.43 and *Knight's Tale*, I.2221–5 ('O lady myn, Venus . . . | For thilke love thow haddest to Adoon, | Have pitee of my bittre teeris smerte').

722–32 Excluding the malefic Saturn, Troilus now prays to the gods in the descending order of their distance from the earth as planets in medieval cosmology: Jupiter, Mars, Phoebus (the sun), Mercury, Diana (the moon). Venus, positioned between the sun and Mercury, has already been invoked.

722 *Europe*: For Jove's abduction of Europa in the form of a bull, see Ovid, *Metamorphoses*, 2.833–75; cf. *Legend of Good Women*, Prologue F 113–14 and *TC* 2.55.

724 *blody cope*: Cf. Statius, *Thebaid*, 7.69–71 ('Mars . . . glorious | In Caspian gore, his ghastly spattering | Transforming the wide fields'), and the scholiast glosses on Statius (Clogan 1964: 607–8).

725 *Cipris*: I.e. the goddess Venus, associated with Cyprus; cf. the form 'Cipride' (4.1216, 5.208). For prayer to Mars by his love for Venus, see *Knight's Tale*, I.2383–92.

726–7 *Dane*: Fleeing from Phoebus Apollo, Daphne was metamorphosed into the laurel; see Ovid, *Metamorphoses*, 1.452–567, and *TC* 3.542

729–30 *for the love of Hierse*: Aglauros incurred the enmity of Pallas, who caused her to envy her sister, the Athenian princess Herse, for which Mercury (enamoured of Herse) turned Aglauros to stone when she attempted to prevent his entering Herse's chamber; see Ovid, *Metamorphoses*, 2.708–832. But Chaucer is mistaken in suggesting that Pallas's enmity towards Aglauros was caused by Mercury's love for Herse.

731 *Diane*: Diana, the moon (cf. 2.74–5), and goddess of chastity.

733 *fatal sustren*: I.e. the three Fates, Clotho, Atropos and Lachesis. For other references to the Fates in *TC* (none derived from *Filostrato*), see also 4.1208, 1546; 5.7. Clotho spins the thread of life (as glosses in H4 and J note), and it was a commonplace that a child's fate was spun before his first clothes were made (cf. Whiting D106); also *Knight's Tale*, I.1566; *Legend of Good Women*, 2629–30. The H4 and J glosses show some similarity to Lactantius's gloss on Statius, *Thebaid*, 2.249 (Clogan 1964: 608).

741 *trappe*: A trapdoor in floor or ceiling, apparently connecting the

room, where Criseyde is in bed, with the 'stewe' where Troilus has waited.

742 *by the lappe*: Just as Pandarus had led Criseyde by a fold of clothing to Troilus's bedside (3.59).

764 Proverbial (Whiting H569).

787 *thorugh a goter*: 'Via a secret route, by a gutter'; 'goter' may here mean a window leading to the gutter or eaves trough (*MED*, s.v. *goter* 4), and Hypermnestra's husband escapes from their bedroom 'Out at this goter . . . | And at a wyndow lep he fro the lofte' (*Legend of Good Women*, 2705–9); but it could mean a sewer (*MED*, s.v. *goter* 2.(a)) – with some play on 'pryve wente' – which might have been situated nearer to the 'outer hous' (*TC* 3.664), if that is 'my chaumbre' to which Pandarus refers (Brody 1998). Troilus's entry by any such a route is, of course, Pandarus's fiction.

797 *Horaste*: Chaucer invents this character, apparently adapting the name from Orestes (spelled 'Horrestes' in Guido, *Historia*, pp. 249, 253, and 'Horeste' in Gower, *Confessio amantis*, 3.2176); the motif of the lover's jealousy may be borrowed from Boccaccio's *Filocolo*, 1.247–89.

808 *wikked spirit*: Boccaccio uses the phrase 'wicked spirit of jealousy' (*Filostrato*, 7.18; *Filocolo*, 1.259–60).

813–40 Criseyde's monologue, particularly in its first three stanzas, echoes lines in Boethius, 2.pr.4 (Philosophy argues that worldly happiness is not true happiness), although the sentiments were commonplaces.

813–15 Cf. *Boece*, 2.pr.4.118–19: 'The swetnesse of mannes weleful-nesse is sprayned with many bitternesses'; cf. *Man of Law's Tale*, II.422, and also, for proverbial instances later than Chaucer, Whiting J59, S516.

816–19 Cf. *Boece*, 2.pr.4.75–8: 'Forwhy ful anguysschous thing is the condicioun of mannes goodes; for eyther it cometh nat altogi-dre to a wyght, or elles it ne last nat perpetuel.'

820–26 Cf. *Boece*, 2.pr.4.150–55: 'what man that this towmblynge welefulnesse ledeth, eyther he woot that it is chaungeable, or elles he woot it nat. And yif he woot it nat, what blisful fortune may ther ben in the blyndnesse of ignoraunce?'

827–33 Cf. *Boece*, 2.pr.4.155–62: 'And yif he woot that it is chaunge-able, he mot alwey ben adrad that he ne lese that thyng that he ne douteth nat but that he may leesen it . . . for whiche the contynuel drede that he hath ne suffreth hym nat to ben weleful'.

832 *myte*: A small Flemish coin, often mentioned in expressions of

worthlessness (cf. *Legend of Good Women*, 741; Whiting M596–611). See also *TC* 4.684.

836 Cf. *Boece*, 2.pr.4.180–81: 'how myghte thanne this present lif make men blissful . . . ?'

837 For jealousy as a snake, see 3.1010; Ovid has Envy eating snake flesh, her proper food in *Metamorphoses*, 2.768–9, the story of Aglauros (see *TC* 3.729–30).

853 Proverbial (Whiting P145; Walther 31436–8); H1 and H4 gloss 'Mora trahit periculum' (delay draws danger).

854 *an hawe*: A hawthorn berry, proverbially worthless (Whiting H193); for the negative comparison ('nought worth . . .') in expressions of worthlessness, see also *TC* 3.936, 1167.

855 *alle thyng hath tyme*: Proverbial (Whiting T88; Hassell C198), deriving from Ecclesiastes 3:1. Cf. *TC* 2.989.

861 *fare-wel feldefare*: A proverbial expression for 'All is over' (Whiting F130); the 'frosty feldefare' (*Parliament of Fowls*, 364) is a species of thrush which migrates northwards at the end of winter.

885 *blewe ryng*: Blue is proverbially the colour of constancy; cf. Whiting B384 ('Blue is true'), Hassell B112; also *Squire's Tale*, V.643–5, and the poem, doubtfully attributed to Chaucer, *Against Women Unconstant*, 7, 14, 21.

890 *Ye, haselwodes shaken!*: Pandarus's three references to hazelwood (see also 5.505, 1174) have perplexed successive commentators. Here, 'haselwodes shaken' has usually been conjectured from the context to denote doing something foolish or futile (*MED*, s.v. *hasel* n. 2(b)), and hence ('Yea, hazel bushes shake!') to be an expression of incredulity or derision, since it is no news that hazel trees shake. Cf. another gloss on this phrase, 'My! You hazel bushes shake! (what an earth-shattering suggestion!)' (Pearsall 1999a: 53). There is also some ambiguity as to whether 'Ye' is to be taken as the personal pronoun (you) or as the interjection (yes, indeed), which may express either vague assent or opposition or objection. If a pronoun, Pandarus could be saying 'You're shaking hazel[tree]s!' and hence 'You're going a-nutting' which, since 'nut' can denote something of little value (*MED*, s.v. *note* 1(b)), may imply 'You're trifling' (Barney 1987: 1041). (Cf. the modern colloquial gloss 'nuts!' offered by Fisher 1977: 467, who also assumes 'shaken' is a variant of the normal Chaucerian imperative form ending in -*eth*: 'Yes, shake the hazelnut trees'.) If the aim of shaking hazel trees is to harvest the hazelnuts (R reads 'haselnotes' instead of 'haselwodes'), and granted some literary evidence that the hazelwood, the hazelnut

and going nutting were all associated with love and love-making, Pandarus may be saying 'Indeed, hazel trees are shaking (i.e. being shaken for nuts)' or 'You (Criseyde) are shaking hazel trees (for the nuts)' with some erotic insinuation (Wentersdorf 1992); some MSS read 'haselwode is shaken' for 'haselwodes shaken'. There seems no convincing reference in the present context to the traditional use of hazel for divining rods (Gnerro 1962).

891   *a stoon*: Cf. Pandarus's earlier reference to the power of gems (2.344). In romance there are rings with magic stones that protect against all harm (*Ywain and Gawain*, Braswell 1995: 1532–44), against venom and witchcraft (*William of Palerne*, Bunt 1985: 4424–8), and even against death (*Sir Perceval of Galles*, Braswell 1995: 1857–63).

896   *tyme ilost*: Cf. the proverb 'Lost time cannot be recovered' (Whiting T307); and Ovid, *Ars Amatoria*, 3.64 ('Nor can the hour that has passed return'); also *TC* 4.1283, *Roman de la Rose*, 4623–4 (*Romaunt*, 5123–4: 'For tyme lost, as men may see, | For nothyng may recured be'), *Man of Law's Tale*, II.19–28, *House of Fame*, 1257–8. John Bromyard's manual for preachers twice cites the Latin proverb (Walther 4893): 'I weep for the loss of things, but I weep more for the loss of time' (Wenzel 1976: 146).

901   *wordes white*: See 3.1567. Cf. Whiting W627 and Hassell P61; also *Boece*, 2.pr.3.64–5: 'tho feffedestow Fortune with glosynge wordes and desceyvedest hir'.

     feffe: The verb 'feffen' (cf. 'sesed': 3.445 and n.) is a legal term, meaning to put someone in possession of a tract of land or to endow a person with something by way of gift (*MED*, s.v. *feffen* v. 1, 2). 'To be seised of an estate in land is to be enfeoffed of that land' (Hornsby 1988: 92). See also *TC* 5.1689.

907   *no jalous wordes*: Because Troilus is not privy to Pandarus's invention of his jealousy of Horaste.

914   It is unclear how long Pandarus remains in the bedroom, but outside the lovers' curtained bed (see 3.1189, 1555–6).

920–45   This exchange may recall material in the conversation between Pandaro and Criseida (*Filostrato*, 2.133, 139, 121), left unused in Chaucer's reformulation of the end of his second book.

925–6   Hope for rest of heart and spirit is a recurrent motif in Book 3: see also 966, 1045, 1131, 1279–81, 1309, 1518, 1599, 1680, 1819–20.

931   *At dulcarnoun*: 'On the horns of a dilemma'. Derived from the Arabic term for 'two-horned' (referring to the shape of the diagram), 'Dulcarnoun' was a name for the 47th proposition of the

first book of Euclid's geometry, and hence a term for a puzzle or perplexing difficulty. In reply, Pandarus evidently confuses 'Dulcarnoun' with the 5th proposition of Euclid's first book, known as the 'Fuga Miserorum', which he translates as 'flemyng of wrecches' (*TC* 3.933), i.e. the banishment or putting to flight of weak students.

at my wittes ende: See Whiting W412.

936 *fecches*: I.e. vetch-seeds, proverbially worthless (cf. Whiting V27).

956 *sodeynliche red*: Cf. the blushing, tongue-tied Troilus, when visited by Criseyde (3.82–4).

1016–19 Cf. *Boece*, 1.m.5.31–49; *Knight's Tale*, I.1313–14: 'What governaunce is in this prescience, | That giltelees tormenteth innocence?'

1024 *jalousie is love*: Not recorded as a proverb before Chaucer (cf. Whiting J22).

1035 For experience as a bitter drink, see 2.784; 3.1214–16.

1046 *by ordal or by oth*: Criseyde offers to put the truth of her denial of Troilus's charges of infidelity to the test of ordeal or compurgation (Hornsby 1988: 144). In trial by ordeal claimants or defendants would hold or walk on hot iron, or immerse a hand in boiling water, and if they were innocent God would prevent their being harmed. Trial by ordeal was abolished in England in 1219, although literary and pictorial allusions (such as the depiction of legendary ordeals) kept the custom alive in the imagination (Bartlett 1986). By means of compurgation – used as a mode of proof in English courts until the late Middle Ages – defendants could prove the truth of their oath denying charges against them by producing neighbours who would swear to their credibility (Bellamy 1973: 142–4). See also Pollock and Maitland 1898: 2.598–601.

1047 *By sort*: I.e. by sortilege, the use of divination to reveal the truth of a testimony.

1060–64 *misty morwe ... victories*: Proverbial lore (cf. Whiting M693, W372, S277, S278).

1088 *spirit*: For the three spirits in medieval physiology, see 1.307n. Cf. the Lover's similar faint in Machaut, *Remède de Fortune*, 1490–95 ('I'd fallen into a trance, like someone who sees and senses his death fast upon him').

1092 *a-swowne*: The swoon is partly modelled on Troiolo's later swoon in *Filostrato*, 4.18–19, when the Trojan council agrees to Criseida's exchange (Chaucer omits the swoon from the corresponding scene: see *TC* 4.218).

1103 For Criseyde's regret that she was ever born, see also 3.1423; 4.763; 5.689–90, 700; for such regret expressed by Troilus and Pandarus, see 4.251–2; 5.1275–6, 1699. Cf. Job 3:3.

1104 *pullen out the thorn*: See the earlier references to thorns in the flesh (2.1272–4).

1114–18 Cf. *Filostrato*, 4.19: after Troiolo's faint his father and brothers rub his wrists, bathe his face, and try to recall him to consciousness.

1137 Proverbial (Whiting L260).

1141 *chymeneye*: There is evidence for increasing numbers of wall fireplaces and chimneys in London houses from the fourteenth century onwards, allowing more rooms to be heated (Schofield 1994: 113–17).

1165 *bought*: 'Redeemed' (the Cp+ reading; other MSS read *wrought*, i.e. created, avoiding the Christian reference).

1177 H4 has the marginal gloss 'Beati misericord' (Matthew 5:7: 'Blessed are the merciful') and at 1183 'petite et actipites' ('ask and ye shall receive'; cf. Matthew 7:7). For other references to mercy and grace, see 3.1266–7, 1282, 1356.

1189 *Leyde hym to slepe*: Whether in the 'outer hous' mentioned earlier (3.664), or in the same room as the lovers but outside their curtained bed, remains unclear.

1191–2 'To flee as the lark does the sparhawk' is proverbial; cf. Whiting L84, and Boccaccio's *Filocolo*, 2.165–6 ('come ... la columba sotto il rapace sparviere'); cf. Criseida's later words to Troiolo: 'Love is a rapacious spirit, and when he seizes anything he grasps it so hard and fast with his talons that it is in vain to seek ways to release it' (*Filostrato*, 3.48). R has the marginal note here: 'How bace phisik come in honde betwene Creysseyde & Troylys'.

1194 Soot is proverbially bitter; cf. Whiting S480, Hassell S123; *Roman de la Rose*, 10633–4: 'amer | Plus que n'est suie' (more bitter than soot).

1200 *aspes leef*: Cf. *Legend of Good Women*, 2648 ('And quok as doth the lef of aspe grene'), and *Summoner's Prologue*, III.1667 ('That lyk an aspen leef he quook for ire'); and for later instances, Whiting A216.

1203 *the bryghte goddes sevene*: Cf. Chaucer's *Envoy to Scogan* (3): 'I see the bryghte goddis sevene'. *bryghte*] *blisful* Cp+.

1210–11 'We see that this must be true; but when exactly was the moment of yielding? We cannot tell: it seems to have happened in one of the gaps between scenes (perhaps after Criseyde awoke

from her dream in Book II?) rather than in any specific scene'
(Spearing 1976: 19).

1212–16 Cf. the proverb 'A bitter drink heals a fever' (Whiting D393);
for the notion of drinking misery, see 2.784n.

1219–20   Proverbial (Whiting S944; Walther 6407); cf. *Boece*,
3.m.1.5–6 ('Hony is the more swete, if mouthes han first tasted
savours that ben wykke').

1222   *syn that*] R Cl D H3 H4 H5 S1 (*sith* Cl H3; *set* H5); *syn* Cp H1
J S2; *sithe* Gg; *sethen* H2; *or that* A.

1231   *wodebynde*: Tree and vine, tree and creeper, are commonplace
similes for lovers (e.g. Ovid, *Metamorphoses*, 4.365); Tristan and
Iseult 'resembled the honeysuckle that clings to the hazel branch:
when it has wound itself all round and attached itself to the tree'
(in the late twelfth-century Marie de France, *Chevrefoil*, Ewert
1944: 68–73). Queen Philippa had a corset of black cloth
embroidered with a ribbon of plate gold bearing the motto 'Ich
wyndemuth' (? I twine myself around), while Edward III had a
motto 'syker as ye wodebynd', which, together with a spray of
woodbine was embroidered in letters of gold and silk on a 'cote'
and hood of black satin (see Newton 1980: 56–7).

1255   *Citheria*: I.e. Venus, named after Cythera, where she arose from
the sea; cf. Dante, *Purgatorio*, 27.95, and *Knight's Tale*, I.2215–
16 ('Unto the blisful Citherea benigne –|I mene Venus, honurable
and digne').

1257   *wel-willy planete*: The benevolence of Venus – 'the fair planet
that prompts to love' (*Purgatorio*, 1.19) – was a commonplace.

1258   *Imeneus*: Hymen, god of marriage. Cf. Criseida's reference to
'Le nuove spose' (the newly married) as she offers to disrobe just
before the lovers' union in *Filostrato* (3.31); and for some perhaps
quasi-matrimonial aspects of this *TC* scene, see 3.1368n below.

1261–7   Recalled from St Bernard's prayer to the Virgin Mary in
Dante's *Paradiso*, 33.14–18:

> . . . che qual vuol grazia ed a te non ricorre,
>   sua disïanza vuol volar sanz'ali.
>   La tua benignità non pur soccorre
>   a chi domanda, ma molte fïate
>   liberamente al dimandar precorre.

(. . . whoso would have grace and does not turn to you, his desire
would fly without wings. Your loving-kindness not only succours
him that asks, but many times it freely anticipates the asking.)

For the 'holy bond of thynges' (*TC* 3.1261) and its Boethian associations, see Troilus's song (3.1744–71), and also *Knight's Tale*, I.2987–3089. For a series of borrowings from, or resemblances to, Dante from here into Book 4, see especially *TC* 3.1387–93, 1419–20, 1625–8, 1807–8; 4.22–4, 225–7, 239–41, 1188, 1538–40.

1263 *fle withouten wynges*: Proverbial (Walther 29675; Hassell V143).

1266–7 Cf. 3.1282.

1271 *so heigh a place*: Troilus's idea of himself at this high point comes at the mid-point, the 4120th of the poem's 8239 lines.

1282 *mercy passeth right*: Proverbial (Whiting M508); cf. Psalms 84:11 (AV 85:10); Machaut, *Remède de Fortune*, 1686 ('Pitez est dessus droiture'); *Knight's Tale*, I.3089 ('For gentil mercy oghte to passen right'); *Legend of Good Women*, Prologue F 160–62 ('Al founde they Daunger for a tyme a lord, | Yet Pitee, thurgh his stronge gentil myght, | Forgaf, and made Mercy passen Ryght').

1293–5 Cf. the knight's words after the lady has accepted him in Machaut's *Jugement dou Roy de Behaingne*: 'If I do anything contrary to your pleasure, or at which your heart be angry or aggrieved, please to know in truth that this will be through ignorance' (665–7).

1309 On 'suffisaunce', see *Boece*, 3.pr.9. Perhaps (Devereux 1965) faintly echoing the wording of 'levation prayers' uttered by the faithful during elevation of the host at mass: extant prayers mostly open with 'Welcome' or 'Hail', and some invoke Christ with 'Heil Knight' and 'Hayle Pese'.

1316 Translating *Filostrato*, 3.32: 'D'amor sentiron l'ultimo valore' (they felt the ultimate value of love).

1317–20 Cf. *Filostrato*, 2.88 ('If I might spend one winter night with you, I'd then spend a hundred and fifty in hell!').

1317 *O blisful nyght*: Perhaps (Dronke 1964) echoing the 'O vere beata nox' (O true blessed night) of the Easter-night liturgy.

1324–37 In R+ (here H3, J, R, S1, Cx) these stanzas come after 3.1414, but line 1337 (reverting to a former topic) does not sit well before 1415 (introducing a new one). Lines 1324–37 are interpolated between two *TC* stanzas based on consecutive *Filostrato* stanzas (3.33–4) just after Chaucer has resumed working from *Filostrato* for the first time since earlier in Book 3. Perhaps lines 1324–37 were written on a separate slip and copied in different positions by some scribes (H4 has lines 1324–37 twice, after 1323 *and* 1414).

1331–7   The request for correction was a convention; see 5.1856–9 and n.

1360   *a thousand*] R+; *an hondred* other MSS. Cf. *Filostrato*, 3.37: 'mille sospiri'.

1365   *nought bilynne*] H1; *nothyng blynne* R; *never blynne* A H5; *n. blynne* other MSS.

1368   This 'pleyinge' exchange of rings (not in *Filostrato*) is unlikely to represent a form of clandestine marriage as this was known in Chaucer's England, i.e. legitimate under canon law, albeit discouraged by the church: Richard II's mother, Joan of Kent, had been involved in a famous case of clandestine marriage. (For discussion and background, see Kelly 1975: 49–67, 163–242; Maguire 1974; Wentersdorf 1980.) In Boccaccio's *Filocolo*, Florio espouses himself to Biancifiore with a ring (2.181), but, following *Filostrato* (4.69), Troilus later speaks of asking for Criseyde from his father, presumably in marriage (*TC* 4.554–5), suggesting that for the lovers this exchange of rings does not constitute clandestine marriage. In two later English redactions of Guido's *Historia*, the *Laud Troy Book* (13555) and the *Gest Hystoriale of the Destruction of Troy* (9952–3), Criseyde remarks that she cannot marry Troilus (Mieszkowski 1971: 113–14). A clandestine marriage might be formed by exchanging vows indicating a present or future consent to become man and wife, the vow then followed by sexual intercourse. At issue is whether the promissory language, vows, pledges and plighting of troth between Troilus and Criseyde – especially just before and after the consummation (e.g. 3.1296–9, 1510–12) – represent an intention to contract marriage. From extant evidence of matrimonial disputes in medieval English church courts, clear matrimonial intent had to be expressed in the words exchanged between parties, usually corroborated by two witnesses, in order for a contested clandestine marriage to be held valid (Helmholz 1974: 40–47, 195–9). A church court would not have judged Troilus and Criseyde married on the evidence presented in *TC* (Hornsby 1988: 56–66), yet the pagan lovers' promissory language, reference to Hymen (3.1258) and gamesome exchange of rings serve to affirm the earnest of their intent.

1369   *scripture*: For inscriptions on medieval rings, see Evans 1931.

1370–72   *a broche . . . Criseyde hym yaf*: Not in *Filostrato*; perhaps the same brooch that Troilus is later reported to have given Criseyde at her departure from Troy (*TC* 5.1040–41, 1661–5). Heart-shaped pins were evidently fashionable in late-medieval

England: in his will of 1383 Hugh, Earl of Stafford, left a heart-shaped brooch to his daughter Joan, and a surviving brooch from Fishpool in Nottinghamshire bears the inscription on its back 'Ie suy vostre sans de partier' (Cherry 1974). On the powers attributed to gems, see 2.344n., 585n. The inference (Anderson 1982: 126–8) that this is the fateful Brooch of Thebes (Statius, *Thebaid*, 2.265–305) that brought misfortune to all who coveted it – described in Chaucer's *Complaint of Mars*, 255, as bringing 'double wo' – is linked to the inference that Criseyde's mother shared not simply the name but the identity of the Theban Argia (see *TC* 4.762; 5.1509); neither inference has won general acceptance.

1375 *kecche*] Cl J Cx Th; *crache* Gg; *cretche* H5; *te(c)ch(e* Cp A H3 H4; *the(c)che* H1 Ph R S1 S2.

1384 *white and ... rede*: Evidently (white) silver and (red) gold; (*MED*, s.v. *whit* n.8). Cf. *Filostrato*, 3.39 ('they will lose their money').

1389–91 *Mida ... Crassus*: Stock examples of covetousness, associated together in Dante, *Purgatorio*, 20.106–8, 116–17, and added by Chaucer to the censure of avarice in *Filostrato* here (3.39). Midas, first granted his wish that all he touched should turn to gold, was later punished with long ass's ears for his folly in preferring Pan's music to Apollo's (see Ovid, *Metamorphoses*, 11.100–193); Crassus, notorious for love of gold, was killed on an expedition against the Parthians (53 BC), who poured molten gold into his mouth. Cf. Andreas Capellanus, *De amore*, rule 10: 'Love is always a stranger in the house of avarice' (Walsh 1982), and also the scorn for misers in *Romaunt*, 5769–5810.

1392–3 R+ (here J, H4, R, Cx) reads instead: 'To techen hem that covetise is vice | And love is vertu thogh men halde it nyce.'

1402 *wo*] *thing* Cp+ (*woo* A; *thing* Th).

1415 *comune astrologer*: The epithet ('vulgaris astrologus') is from Alanus de Insulis, *De planctu naturae* (Häring 1979: 2.163–4), which six *TC* MSS cite in Latin as a gloss, and H4 attributes to Alanus.

1417 *Lucyfer*: I.e. Venus as morning star; five *TC* MSS gloss 'stella matutinal' (morning star). This differs from the actual sky in 1385, where until at least September Venus was an evening star (North 1988: 381). For references to 'Lucifer', see Ovid, *Amores*, 1.6.65–6; 2.11.55–6; *Heroides*, 18.112; also *Boece*, 3.m.1.8–12; 4.m.6.17–18.

1420 *Fortuna major*: A figure in the occult art of geomancy, associated with the sun and with Aquarius, having the form of a four of diamonds placed above a two of diamonds (a figure also corresponding to a group of six stars in the constellations of Aquarius and Pisces, which would have been rising in the east at dawn in mid-May 1385). Cf. *Purgatorio*, 19.4–5 ('when the geomancers see in the east before dawn their *Fortuna Major*'), where Dante, like Chaucer here, may refer either to the group of stars or the sun rising. (See Root and Russell 1924: 56–8; and North 1988: 238–43, who suggests the Pleiades.)

1427 *O nyght, allas*: The lovers' laments at dawn (3.1429–42, 1450–70, 1695–1708) are much expanded from *Filostrato* in the tradition of the lyric dawn-song (the French 'aube' or 'aubade', the Provençal 'alba'), which goes back to Ovid, *Amores*, 1.13. Criseyde's lament at night's departure is not in *Filostrato* here (3.43).

1428 *Almena*: When Jupiter lay with Alcmena, and Hercules was conceived, the night was miraculously lengthened; see Ovid, *Amores*, 1.13.45–6; Statius, *Thebaid*, 6.288–9, 12.300–301; *Roman de Thèbes*, 2.88; Boccaccio, *Teseida*, 4.14, *De genealogia deorum*, 13.1; and also the second-century AD handbook of mythology, Hyginus, *Fabulae*, 29.

1433 *Wel oughten bestes pleyne*: Cf. Ovid, *Amores*, 1.13.15–34.

1438–41 R+ (here J, H3, H4, R, Cx) reads instead: 'For thow so downward hastest of malice | The corse and to oure emysperye bynde | That never mo under the grownde thow wynde | For thorugh thy rakel hying out of Troye'.

1450–84 The address to the day is a recurrent dawn-song motif, but usually voiced by the lady; grief at parting and desire that the lover return soon (1475–84) are more commonly assigned to the lady: 'Chaucer seems to have bestowed on Troilus several speeches usually assigned to the lady in an aube, and on Criseyde certain speeches usually assigned to the lover' (Kaske 1961: 170–73).

1462 Those employed in close work, such as engraving seals, would gladly buy more light; cf. Ecclesiasticus 38:27.

1464 *Titan*: Frequently confused with Tithonus, the mortal lover of Aurora (the dawn); see Ovid, *Heroides*, 18.111–14.

1482 *streyneth*] *biteth* Cp+ (*brenneth* Cl). Cf. *Filostrato*, 3.46: 'sì mi stringe il disio' (desire presses upon me so).

1490 *thise worldes tweyne*: *Filostrato* has 'dearer to me than the Trojan realm' (3.47), and Chaucer possibly meant 'the realms of both Greece and Troy'.

1492–1518 The promise of fidelity is a dawn-song convention, although often given by the lover, rather than, as here, by the lady (Kaske 1961: 173).

1495–8 See Criseyde's later list of 'impossibles' (4.1534–54); for the tradition of such 'impossibilia', see Curtius 1953: 95–8; Brookhouse 1965. The impossibilia cited by Criseyde to avow her constancy may have reminded a medieval audience of the popular anti-feminist 'lying songs' in which such formulae were deployed to affirm the impossibility of a trustworthy woman (Schibanoff 1977).

1496 Cf. Ovid, *Fasti*, 2.90: 'et accipitri iuncta columba fuit' (and the dove has been neighbour to the hawk). R+ reads 'hawkes' for 'dowves'.

1499 *grave*: See 1.295–8 and n.

1502 Cf. 1.674, and the Lover's rebuff to Reason in the *Roman de la Rose*: 'Me were lever dye in the peyne, | Than Love to me-ward shulde arette [attribute] | Falsheed, or tresoun on me sette' (*Romaunt*, 3326–8).

1510–12 Such a pledge of faith – although here uttered by an ancient pagan – could have both moral and legal force in Chaucer's own society: 'When someone made a promise upon a pledge of faith, he symbolically gave his faith, his hope of salvation, into the hands of another as security to bind that promise. By extension, when someone swore upon God, God became his surety … Criseyde secures her promise with a formula … that created a moral, and according to canon law, a legal obligation … a promise vested with the formal trappings of an agreement recognized as binding by fourteenth-century English church courts' (Hornsby 1988: 41–4).

1517 *that*] Cp A Cl D Gg H1 J S2 omit.

1524 *voys as though*] *wordes as* Cp+.

1555 *Pandare, o-morwe*: In *Filostrato*, where the consummation occurs at Criseida's house, there is no morning visit by Pandaro. In *Pamphilus* the go-between returns in the morning with mock-innocent enquiries and is roundly accused of duplicity by the lady (see *TC* 3.511n.).

1565 *Fox that ye ben!*: Proverbially wily and resourceful, the fox is the arch-trickster in the medieval tradition of beast fable and epic that informs the *Nun's Priest's Tale*. For associations of cunning with foxes, see also *Legend of Good Women*, 1389–93, 2447–8; *Canon's Yeoman's Tale*, VIII.1079–81.

1577 *God foryaf his deth*: Cf. Luke 23:34; also proverbial (Hassell D80).

1600 *Flegitoun*: The infernal river of fire; named in Virgil, *Aeneid*, 6.551, and Dante, *Inferno*, 14.116, 131; Chaucer perhaps follows the Italianate spelling. (Some R+ MSS – H3 H4 R Cx; J corrected over erasure – have, variously corrupted, the variant reading 'Cocytus', the classical river of lamentation.) For medieval commentators, Phlegethon represented the fiery passion of anger and cupidity: see Third Vatican Mythographer, 6.4; Macrobius, *Commentary* (Stahl 1952: 1.10.11); Boccaccio, *De genealogia deorum*, 1.14; 3.16

1625–8 For the particular misery of remembering lost happiness, cf. *Boece*, 2.pr.4.5–9; Aquinas, *Summa*, 2–2.36.1; Dante, *Inferno*, 5.121–3; *Romaunt*, 4138–40; also proverbial (Walther 6534, 31586).

1634 Proverbial (Whiting C518; Walther 16215); cf. Ovid, *Ars amatoria*, 2.11–14 ('nor is there less skill in keeping what is won than in seeking; in that there is chance, but this task demands skill'); see also *Roman de la Rose*, 8261–4.

1636–7 Proverbial (cf. Whiting W671).

1642 *rakle*: Probably an adjective with (be) understood, but *MED* (s.v. *rakelen* v) takes this as a unique instance of a verb derived from the adjective.

1643 *stere*] R H3 S1 Cx; *tere* other MSS.

1670 *There he was erst*: I.e. they meet again at Pandarus's house. By the time of their last meeting, three years later, the lovers are spending the night at Criseyde's house (4.1125–6), as in *Filostrato*.

1674–87 TC omits here Criseida's speech (*Filostrato*, 3.66–8) expressing her desire for Troiolo: 'I could never express the happiness and the burning desire that you have kindled in my breast ... I desire and long for you day and night'.

1691–2 Cf. *Boece*, 3.pr.2.8–13: 'And blisfulnesse is swiche a good, that whoso that hath geten it, he ne may over that nothyng more desire. And this thyng forsothe is the soverayn good that conteneth in hymself alle maner goodes'.

1694–5 Cf. Dante, *Paradiso*, 19.7–9; 24.25–7 ('What I have now to tell, tongue never conveyed nor ink wrote'; 'Therefore my pen jumps and I do not write of it').

1703 *Piros*: Pyroïs; The sun's other three horses were Eoüs, Aethon and Phlegon (see Ovid, *Metamorphoses*, 2.153–4).

1718–19 While following *Filostrato*, 3.72, these lines also recall an earlier description of Troiolo in 2.84: 'Troiolo sings and is amazingly happy – jousting, giving presents, and spending freely; and he often renews and changes his attire, all the time growing more ardently in love'.

1718 *festeynges*] S1; *festeynynges* Cl H1; *festynges* other MSS.

1744–71 *Canticus Troili*: Two Ph+ MSS (H2 and Ph) omit Troilus's song, although the text has been inset in Ph on a separate leaf during correction (see Windeatt 1992: 25), and the song is contained normally in the other two Ph+ MSS (Gg and H5) at this point. All extant MSS read 'And thanne he wolde synge in this manere' at 3.1743, so that the song's absence from some MSS – 3.1743 being the last line at the foot of a page in H2 – presumably stems from scribal mistranscription (see A Note on the Text). Having already borrowed part of Troiolo's song at this point (*Filostrato*, 3.74–9) for the third proem (*TC* 3.1–49), Chaucer substitutes a song adapted from Boethius, 2.m.8, the closing poem of the second book of *De Consolatione* and a pivotal transition in that work's argument for transcendence of fortune and of earthly values and pursuits. For the *TC* stanzas Chaucer draws on his own prose translation in the *Boece*, somewhat reorganizing material so that the hailing of love comes first in Troilus's song:

That the world with stable feyth varieth accordable chaungynges; that the contrarious qualites of elementz holden among hemself allyaunce perdurable; that Phebus, the sonne, with his goldene chariet bryngeth forth the rosene day; that the moone hath comaundement over the nyghtes, whiche nyghtes Esperus, the eve-sterre, hath brought; that the see, gredy to flowen, constreyneth with a certein eende his floodes, so that it is nat leveful to strecche his brode termes or bowndes uppon the erthes (that is to seyn, to coveren al the erthe) – al this accordaunce [and] ordenaunce of thynges is bounde with love, that governeth erthe and see, and hath also comandement to the hevene. And yif this love slakede the bridelis, alle thynges that now loven hem togidres wolden make batayle contynuely, and stryven to fordo the fassoun of this world, the which they now leden in accordable feith by fayre moevynges. This love halt togidres peples joyned with an holy boond, and knytteth sacrement of mariages of chaste loves; and love enditeth lawes to trewe felawes. O weleful were mankynde, yif thilke love that governeth hevene governede yowr corages!

The *Boece* in turn had drawn on Jean de Meun's French prose version of *De Consolatione* (Dedeck-Héry 1952); Chaucer also refers back to the Latin metrum for Troilus's song, and uses the commentary on Boethius by Nicholas Trevet (Gleason 1987).

1748 *lawe of compaignie*: Emended from *Boece* 2.m.8, which itself reads 'sacrement of mariages of chaste loves'.

1751 *That, that*: The first 'that' is a demonstrative pronoun used as a noun, the second is a conjunction, and they may be paraphrased 'this, namely that' (De Vries 1971: 503). The first 'that' hence anticipates 'this' in line 1757, and the stanza's movement embodies 'the power of the syntax that itself seems to enact the binding force of the divine love' (Brewer and Brewer 1969: 122).

1751–4 Cf. *Boece*, 3.m.9.18–24, and *Parliament of Fowls*, 380–81.

1753–4 *elementz*: Earth, water, air, fire; cf. *Knight's Tale*, I.2991–3 ('For with that faire cheyne of love he bond | The fyr, the eyr, the water, and the lond | In certeyn boundes, that they may nat flee').

1766 For the bond or chain of love, see 3.1261.

1775 For Troilus as second to Hector, see 2.158–61.

1784 *fressh as faukoun*: A traditional comparison (Whiting F25). In *Filostrato*, 3.91 (itself from Dante, *Paradiso*, 19.34), it is Troiolo who is compared to a falcon as seen by Criseida; for Troilus's riding past Criseyde's house, cf. *TC* 2.610ff., 1247ff.

1807–20 These stanzas have no equivalent in *Filostrato*.

1807–8 For Dione, mother of Venus, see Virgil, *Aeneid*, 3.19; Ovid, *Ars amatoria*, 2.593, 3.3, 3.769; *Amores*, 1.14.33. On the tradition of Cupid's blindness, see Whiting C634 and Panofsky 1939: ch. 4; also *Knight's Tale*, I.1963–5, and *House of Fame*, 137–8. Cf. *Paradiso*, 8.7–8: 'ma Dïone onoravano e Cupido, | questa per madre sua, questo per figlio' (but they honoured Dione and Cupid, her as his mother, him as her son); Dante here describes the ancients' worship of Venus who 'wheeling in the third epicycle, rayed forth mad love' (8.2–3), perhaps recalled in the proem to *TC*, Book 3 (39–48), which, in these closing invocations of Venus and the Muses, Chaucer seems to echo.

1809–10 *Yee sustren nyne*: The invocation of the Muses may mingle recollections of Boccaccio's *Teseida*, 1.1: 'O sorelle castalie, che nel monte | Elicona contente dimorate, | dintorno al sacro gorgoneo fonte' (O Castalian sisters, who dwell in bliss upon Mount Helicon beside the sacred Gorgonian spring), and 11.63: 'Sopra Parnaso, presso a l'Elicone | fonte seder con le nove amorose | Muse . . .' (Upon Parnassus, near the Helicon spring, seated with the nine loving Muses . . .).

Elicone: Actually a mountain rather than a spring (as Chaucer erroneously takes it here and in *House of Fame*, 521–2) and not near Mount Parnassus ('hil Pernaso'); but confusion was common, and Boccaccio takes Helicon first as a mountain but later as a spring in *Teseida* (1.1; 11.63). Both Dante (*Purgatorio*, 29.40) and Guido (*Historia*, p. 15) suggest Helicon is a spring.

1811–16 Cf. *Filostrato*, 4.24: 'I have up until this point been celebrating the happiness that Troiolo experienced in love, although this was mingled with sighs'.

BOOK 4

1–10 Adapted from the final stanza (3.94) of the third part of *Filostrato*; the remainder of the fourth proem is Chaucer's invention. Chaucer postpones the ominous note so that it opens his fourth book rather than ending his third, but some Cp+ MSS (Cp, Cl, D, H1) apparently preserve the division as in *Filostrato* by having a rubric *Explicit liber tercius* (Here ends the third book) *after* 4.28. This confusion may derive from Chaucer's working copy of *TC*. For Fortune as short lasting, cf. *Man of Law's Tale*, II.1132–3, 1140–41; as most deceptive when seeming truest, see *Boece*, 2.pr.1, m.1; as blinding her victims and as traitor, see *Book of the Duchess*, 620, 647, 813; as 'comune', see *TC* 1.843, 4.392, *House of Fame*, 1547–8; for Fortune's bright face, see *Monk's Tale*, VII.2765–6. For commonplaces on Fortune, see also Machaut, *Remède de Fortune*, 1049–62, and *Jugement dou Roy de Behaingne*, 684–91.

3–5 Cf. *Boece*, 2.pr.1.17–21: '[Fortune] useth ful flaterynge famylarite with hem that sche enforceth to bygyle, so longe, til that sche confounde with unsuffrable sorwe hem that sche hath left in despeer unpurveied'; also proverbial (Whiting F535).

6–7 Cf. *Boece*, 2.m.1.12–14: 'she is so hard that sche leygheth and scorneth the wepynges of hem, the whiche sche hath maked wepe with hir free wille.'

7 For the grimace, cf. *Roman de la Rose*, 8039–41: 'Et me firent tretuit la moe | Quant il me virent sous la roe | De Fortune' (they made fun of me when they saw me at the bottom of Fortune's wheel).

9 Cf. *Romaunt*, 4353ff.: 'It is of Love, as of Fortune, | That chaungeth ofte, and nyl contune [continue] . . . | She can writhe hir heed awey'.

13–14 Cf. Dante, *Paradiso*, 24.25, where the pen jumps from the page for joy at the subject.

22 *Herynes*: Cf. Chaucer's *Complaint unto Pity* (92), where Pity is termed 'Herenus quene', and Dante, *Inferno*, 9.43–51, where the 'fierce Erinyes' (Megaera, Alecto and Tisiphone) are the hand-maids of Proserpina, 'the queen of everlasting lamentation'. (Chaucer's form 'Alete' for Alecto may derive from Dante's 'Aletto' in *Inferno*, 9.47). For the Furies both as tormenting and as suffering pain, see *TC* 1.6–9n.; as daughters of Night, see Ovid, *Metamorphoses*, 4.451–2; Virgil, *Aeneid*, 12.845–7; Boccaccio, *De genealogia deorum*, 3.6–9. For invocations of the Furies, cf. *Metamorphoses*, 8.481ff. (where Meleager's mother avenges her brothers on her son; see *TC* 5.1482–4); Ovid, *Heroides*, 11.103; Statius, *Thebaid*, 11.57ff., 344ff. H4 has a marginal gloss here erroneously citing Lucan, *Pharsalia*, 8.90.

25 *cruel Mars ... fader to Quyryne*: For 'cruel Mars', cf. Statius, *Thebaid*, 7.703 ('saevi'); Pandarus has already linked Mars and the Furies (2.435–6; cf. Boccaccio, *Teseida*, 3.1); Troilus has mentioned the malefic Mars of astrology (3.716). Quirinus, i.e. Romulus, was the mythical founder of Rome (see Ovid, *Fasti*, 2.475–80); as son of Mars, cf. Ovid, *Fasti*, 2.419, *Metamorphoses*, 15.863; Virgil, *Aeneid*, 1.274–6; Dante, *Paradiso*, 8.131–2.

26–8 These lines may indicate that *TC* was once planned in four books; two MSS have 'feerde & laste' (H4) and 'fyfte and laste' (H3) instead of 'ferthe'.

32 The zodiacal sign Leo is linked with Hercules (cf. Ovid, *Ars amatoria*, 1.68), who, as one of his labours, killed the Nemean lion and is traditionally represented bearing or clad in a lion skin. The sun being in Leo from around 12 July to early August, the 'breast' of the lion may suggest the earlier part of this period; Boccaccio gives no date for the episode. (However, the allusion may be to the star Regulus in the constellation of Leo, known as 'cor Leonis' and – as part of an argument that the poem's time-scheme is synchronized with the actual state of the heavens in 1385 and 1388 – a date of April 1388 has been suggested; see North 1988: 387–91.) For the sun in the 'brest' of the sign Taurus, the bull, see *Legend of Good Women*, Prologue F 112–14.

37 *fighten*] *fouhten* H4; *issen* J; *issu* Ph. Cf. *Filostrato*, 4.1: 'uscì' (went out).

38–42 This battle, in which Antenor is captured, corresponds to the fifth battle in Benoît's *Troie*, 11995–12006. With the alliteration, cf. the battle-descriptions in *Knight's Tale*, I.2601–16 and *Legend of Good Women*, 635–49.

50–53 In *Filostrato* (4.3) all those mentioned here are taken captive; with his 'in spite of' ('Maugre', *TC* 4.51) Chaucer follows the account in Benoît and Guido (*Troie*, 12551–65; *Historia*, p. 159), where only Antenor is captured. By omitting 'Maugre' H3 may retain from Chaucer's drafts a detail closer to *Filostrato*. The Italianate name 'Phebuseo' is apparently Chaucer's invention, derived from 'Phoebus'. 'Santippe' (from 'Santippo' in *Filostrato*, 4.3) is Antiphus, king of Frisia; 'Polynestore' is Polimestor, king of Thrace; for Sarpedon, see *TC* 5.403 and n. 'Polite' (Polites, *Aeneid*, 2.526), 'Monesteo' (Mnestheus, *Aeneid*, 5.116) and 'Rupheo' (Ripheus, 'foremost in justice among Trojans and most zealous for the right', *Aeneid*, 2.426–7; cf. Dante, *Paradiso*, 20.67–72) are Chaucer's versions of names in *Filostrato*, 4.3, probably derived from the *Aeneid*, or possibly the *Roman de Troie*, 12647–9.

57 *at Grek requeste*: In *Filostrato* (4.4) Priam requests the truce, but in Benoît and Guido the Greeks send Ulysses and Diomede as envoys to seek a truce (*Troie*, 12822–13120; *Historia*, p. 160). The variants in H3 ('To Pryamus whas yeven at his requeste') and, with variations, in R+ ('But natheles a trewe was ther take | At Grekys requeste') are closer to *Filostrato* and may retain traces of Chaucer's work on the text.

88 *my lordes yow*] *yow lordes for* Cp Cl H1 S2 Th.

114–19 The prediction of Troy's destruction that Calchas received from the oracle at Delphi (see 1.70n.) has been confirmed by his own predictive arts as a soothsayer.

120–26 For the story (unmentioned in *Filostrato* here) of how 'Lameadoun' (Laomedon) withheld the wages of 'Phebus' (Apollo) and Neptune, see Ovid, *Metamorphoses*, 11.194–206; Servius, *Comm. in Aeneida*, 2.610; Boccaccio, *De genealogia deorum*, 6.6; Vatican Mythographers, 1.43–4, 138, 174. Benoît's *Troie* (25920–23) mentions that Neptune built and Apollo consecrated Troy's walls, but passes over the withheld wages.

138 *Toas*: In *Filostrato* Antenor is exchanged for Criseida, without mention of Thoas, but in Benoît and Guido Thoas is exchanged for Antenor, and Priam also agrees that Briseida be sent to her father (*Troie*, 13079–120; *Historia*, pp. 160–61).

143 *parlement*: The sources depict a council or parley; Chaucer presents a parliament more in the English sense.

151 For some added references to death (not in *Filostrato*), cf. *TC*

4.163, 429, 432, 444, 447, 524, 623, 856, 1419, 1477, 1595, 1661.

166   R+ reads: 'Yif thow debate it lest she be thy foo'.

176–217   With this parliament scene Chaucer expands on the brief report of the decision to exchange Criseida in *Filostrato*, 4.17, possibly recalling Hector's opposition in Priam's council to the truce during which Antenor and Thoas are exchanged (*Troie*, 12965–98; *Historia*, pp. 160–61); cf. also, in Dictys Cretensis (2.25), Hector's opposition in a parley to the forced repatriation of Helen (Hoy 1990).

183–4   *noyse of peple . . . blase of straw*: Possibly referring ironically to the traditional phrase 'Vox populi, vox Dei' (the voice of the people is the voice of God; cf. Whiting V54, Hassell V140; H4 glosses 'Vox populi in oppositum'); perhaps with a pun on the name of Jack Straw, a leader of the Peasants' Revolt of 1381, just as Gower puns on Straw's name in his *Vox clamantis*, 1.652, 655. Cf. also *Clerk's Tale*, IV.995–1001, and *Boece*, 4.m.5.31–3.

197–201   From Juvenal, *Satires*, 10.2–4 ('there are few who can distinguish true blessings from their opposite, putting aside the mists of error'); cf. Walther 20873, and also *Boece*, 3.m.11.10 ('the blake cloude of errour').

203–5   For Antenor's betrayal of Troy, in removing the Palladium, upon which Troy's safety depended (cf. *TC* 1.153–4), see Benoît, *Troie*, 24397–5713, and Guido, *Historia*, pp. 228–9. This is one of a series of allusions to Antenor not present in *Filostrato*: see *TC* 4.212, 347, 378, 792, 878, 1315.

210   *here and howne*: Literally 'master and servant alike' (i.e. one and all, everyone). See *MED*, s.v. *houne* n (2). However, 'here' has also been translated as 'army' (Brennan 1979), and Henry Knighton's *Chronicle* (c. 1379–96) recounts an incident in Anglo-Saxon history found in earlier chroniclers when the English, led by a certain Huna, avenge abuse of their womenfolk by the Danes: 'They assembled a great army which was called "Howneher" [Howne's army], after a certain Howne, who first advised the army's formation and became its leader' (Hanning 1997, conjecturing that this army and its leader may have generated a colloquial expression signifying unanimity).

218   In *Filostrato* at this point (4.18–21) Troiolo faints at the parley which agrees to Criseida's exchange.

225–7   From Dante, *Inferno*, 3.112–14 (itself derived from *Aeneid*, 6.309–12): 'As in autumn the leaves drop off one after another until the branch sees all its spoils on the ground'.

229 In his misery Troilus is as if pent up and enclosed within the bark
     of a tree; cf. the metamorphosis into trees of Daphne and Myrrha,
     cited in *TC* (see 3.726–7; 4.1138–9); also Virgil, *Aeneid*, 3.22–
     48, Ovid, *Metamorphoses*, 2.358–66, Dante, *Inferno*, 13. Refer-
     ence to blackness may allude to the 'black bile' of melancholy,
     one of the four 'humours' in medieval physiology.

239–41 From *Filostrato*, 4.27, itself borrowing from Dante, *Inferno*,
     12.22–4, which in turn derives from Virgil, *Aeneid*, 2.222–4.

246–7 From *Filostrato*, 4.28, itself recalled from Dante, *Vita Nuova*,
     31: 'Li occhi dolenti per pietà del core . . .' (the sorrowful eyes in
     sympathy with the heart). The Ph+ MSS (Gg, II5, Ph) have a
     variant form of line 247 ('So wepyn that they semen wellys
     tweye') which is closer to *Filostrato*: 'forte piangean, e parean
     due fontane' (wept copiously and resembled two fountains).

251–2 For regret at having been born, see 3.1103n., and cf. *Clerk's
     Tale*, IV.902–3.

258 *wonder is*] *wel onethe* Ph+. Cf. *Filostrato*, 4.29: 'appena' (hardly).

271–2 Cf. the Monk's definition of a tragic victim as 'hym that stood
     in greet prosperitee, | And is yfallen out of heigh degree | Into
     myserie, and endeth wrecchedly' (*Monk's Prologue*, VII. 1975–
     7). See also 1.3–4n. and 5.1786n.

279 Cf. Oedipus in Statius, *Thebaid*, 11.698: 'patriae quantum miser
     incubo terrae' (how wretchedly I encumber my native earth).

290 *What*] *How* Ph+. Cf. *Filostrato*, 4.33: 'Come' (How).

293 *oure hertes seled*: Cf. the Lover's idea that Love 'holdith myn
     hertc undir his sel' (*Romaunt*, 5145); also Gower mentions 'that
     writ | Which Love with his hond enseleth, | Fro whom non erthly
     man appeleth' (*Confessio amantis*, 8.2698–700).

298 *Allone as I was born*: Cf. *Knight's Tale*, I.1633; *Wife of Bath's
     Tale*, III.885.

300 *Edippe*: The living death of Oedipus, who blinded himself on
     discovering that he had unwittingly killed his father Laius and
     married his mother Jocasta, would have been known to Chaucer
     from Statius's *Thebaid*, 1.46–8, 11.580–82, the *Roman de
     Thèbes*, 497–500, and Boccaccio, *Teseida*, 5.58, 10.97.
     Chaucer's Troilus and Criseyde foresee death and hell peopled
     with a sequence of classical figures not mentioned in *Filostrato*:
     for example, *TC* 4.473, 791, 1188.

312 *Stonden for naught*: Possibly a pun on 'naught' as zero, the shape
     of an eye, playing on the idea that the word 'omo' (man) was
     reflected in the human facial features of eyes, brows and nose; cf.
     Dante, *Purgatorio*, 23.32 (Kornbluth 1959).

313 *queynt*: 'Quenched, extinguished', perhaps with a pun (see 5.543).

316 *O lady sovereigne*: Cf. *Legend of Good Women*, Prologue F 94, 275 ('Be ye my gide and lady sovereyne!', 'So passeth al my lady sovereyne').

318 *the*] *my* A D Gg H2 H5 Ph; *thy* S1 Th; *youre* H3. Cf. *Filostrato*, 4.36: 'mie pene' (my pains).

323–9 Not in *Filostrato*; cf. Ovid's epitaph in *Tristia*, 3.3.73–6 ('I, who lie here, with tender loves once played . . . Do not begrudge a prayer, O lover, as you pass by'), echoed in Boccaccio's *Teseida*, 11.91 ('As you are now, I once was . . .'); also the lover's epitaph in Boccaccio's *Filocolo*, 1.266; but the sense of unworthiness is Chaucer's addition.

357 Cf. 1.108, 4.882, 5.1262; also *Man of Law's Tale*, II.609.

359 *with his armes folden*: A traditional gesture of melancholy.

390–92 *Swich is this world*: Cf. 5.1434 (Whiting W665; Hassell M163). On the 'common' nature of Fortune's gifts, see Pandarus (*TC* 1.843–4), and *Boece*, 2.pr.2.9–14, 84–6.

407–13 Not in *Filostrato*; cf. Ovid, *Amores*, 2.4.9–48 ('There's no one fixed beauty that arouses my passion . . . Whether it's some beauty with modest downcast eyes or another that's pertly forward, I'm aflame . . . Because this one sings sweetly, I long to snatch a kiss . . . another attracts me by her sense of movement and rhythm').

414 *Zanzis*: Unexplained; perhaps referring to Zeuxis, the ancient Greek painter (apparently named 'Zanzis' in *Physician's Tale*, VI.16), described as valuing different qualities in different ladies (Cicero, *De inventione*, 2.1; *Roman de la Rose*, 16155ff.; cf. also Fry 1971), although possibly he is the wise man Zeuxis in the story of Alexander (Kittredge 1917: 70). In *Filostrato* (4.49/2) Pandaro cites the equivalent of line 415 as something he has often heard said, rather than referring it to any particular source. (*TC* MSS include variant spellings *Zansis*, *Zauzis*, *Zauzius*, *Zenes*.)

415 Cf. *Filostrato*, 4.49: 'The new love always chases out the old', and Andreas Capellanus, *De amore*, Rule 17 ('a new love compels the old to leave': Walsh 1982). Cf. also Ovid, *Remedia amoris*, 462, 484 ('every love is vanquished by a new successor'; 'his passion was allayed, for the new drove out the old') where it is Agamemnon's readiness to replace Chryseis with Briseis as his concubine which exemplifies, and is sandwiched between, these two maxims; the former became proverbial (Whiting L547; Walther 30604).

416 Cf. Chaucer's *Tale of Melibee*, *CT* VII.1223–5: 'For the lawe seith that "upon thynges that newely bityden bihoveth newe conseil."'

423–4 Cf. the proverb 'Seldom seen, soon forgotten' (Whiting S130; also S307).

428–34 This stanza is not in *Filostrato*; cf. *TC* 1.561–4.

434 Cf. the Lover's indifference to Reason's speeches in the *Roman de la Rose* ('For al yede [went] out at oon ere | That in that other she dyd lere [teach]', *Romaunt*, 5151–2). Probably already proverbial, but Whiting (E4) records no earlier English instance. *at tother*] H1; *at the other* Cl Gg H5 Th; *at that other* D H4 Cx; *atte other* S2; *at(te another* R A H3; *at oothir* other MSS.

451 For Criseyde as surpassing Nature, see 1.105.

461 *Nettle in, dok out*: Part of a charm to be repeated while applying dock-leaves, traditional cure for nettle-stings (cf. Whiting D288): 'Nettle in, dock out, dock rub nettle out.' Cf. Troiolo in *Filostrato*, 2.132: 'If only the nettle of love which thus stings and weakens me were to prick her just a little'.

466 A commonplace; cf. Seneca, *Epistles*, 78.13, and *Boece*, 2.pr.4.109–13.

468 *passiones*] Gg H4 S1; *passions* other MSS.

473–4 *Proserpyne ... pyne*: Cf. 'That quene ys of the derke pyne' (*House of Fame*, 1512); Proserpina, queen of the underworld, wife of Pluto; cf. *Merchant's Tale*, IV.2038–41.

481–3 See Pandarus's earlier advice (3.1625–8).

491–532 Cp omits. Text based on J and Cl.

498 *Nay, nay, God wot*] R+ (and S1); *Nay God wot* Cl+; *Nay Pandarus* Ph+.

499 Ph+ reads: 'But doutelees for aught that may befalle'.

503–4 Cf. *Boece*, 1.m.1.18–20: 'Thilke deth of men is weleful that ne comyth noght in yeeris that ben swete, but cometh to wrecches often yclepid.'

519–20 Cf. in *Roman de la Rose* (6382–3) Reason's encouragement of the Lover to spurn love and its misery: 'Many times I see you crying as an alembic does into an aludel'.

548 *ravysshyng of wommen*: Telamon abducted Hesione, Priam's sister; in reprisal, Paris abducted Helen (Benoît, *Troie*, 2793–804, 3187–650, 4059–68; Guido, *Historia*, pp. 42, 74–5).

555 *To axe hire at my fader*: presumably in marriage (see 3.1368n.); Boccaccio's Troiolo knows his father would object to Criseida's low birth (*Filostrato*, 4.69).

588 *wonder last but nyne nyght*: Proverbial (Whiting W555).

590 *corteisly*: Cf. *Filostrato*, 4.72: 'Non guarda amor cotanto sottil-

mente' (Love does not make such subtle distinctions). The Ph+ reading 'preciously' retains Chaucer's translation of Boccaccio's 'sottilmente'. See also 4.596, 750–56 and 820 for traces of Chaucer's composition of this section.

596 Cf. *Filostrato*, 4.73: 'Tu non hai a rapir donna che sia | dal tuo voler lontana' (You don't have to carry off a woman whose wishes are far from your own), which is closer to the Ph+ reading for this line: 'It is no rape in my dom ne no vice'.

600–601 *Fortune . . . Helpeth hardy man*: Proverbial (Whiting F519; Hassell F120; Walther 1687–8, cited in Latin in the margins of H4 and J). Cf. Virgil, *Aeneid*, 10.284, and Seneca, *Epistles*, 94.28.

608–9 Cf. Pandaro in *Filostrato*, 4.74: 'Let her do without reputation, as Helen does, so long as she does everything you wish.'

618 Cf. *Boece*, 3.m.12.52–5: 'But what is he that may yeven a lawe to loverys? Love is a grettere lawe and a strengere to hymself thanne any lawe that men mai yyven'; and *Knight's Tale*, I.1163–8; also proverbial (Whiting L579; Walther 25383).

622 *on six and sevene*: Unexplained phrase, presumably from the dicing game of hazard (cf. *Pardoner's Tale*, VI.653); recorded as a proverbial phrase after Chaucer (Whiting S359). The sense is apparently 'Stake everything' (Isaacs 1967).

623 A martyr's death was believed to ensure entry to heaven. That lovers' sufferings constitute a form of martyrdom was a commonplace; cf. 4.818; *Romaunt*, 1875.

626 *as dogges liggen dede*: Proverbial (Whiting D329). Pandaro offers to be present (*Filostrato*, 4.75), but most of this stanza is Chaucer's invention.

638–44 This stanza has no equivalent in *Filostrato*. Ph+ line 638 reads: 'Pandare answerde of that be as be may'.

659–61 *swifte Fame . . . with preste wynges*: From *Filostrato*, 4.78, in turn deriving from Virgil, *Aeneid*, 4.174, 180, 188 ('Rumour, of all evils the most swift . . . fleet of wing . . . clinging to the false and wrong, yet heralding truth').

708–14 Cp omits. Text from J.

712–14 Cf. the Lover's sorrow in the *Roman de la Rose* when he can no longer approach the Rose: 'For I am fallen into helle | From paradys' (*Romaunt*, 4136–7).

724 *tales*] *wordes* Ph+. Cf. *Filostrato*, 4.85: 'parole' (words).

728 *ache*: *Filostrato* (4.85) has 'itch' in the head instead of ache. Gg reads 'eche'.

745 *born in cursed constellacioun*: I.e. her 'nativity', the state of the

planets at her birth, which was believed to influence subsequent life, character and fortune; for Troilus's 'nativity', see 2.684–6.

750–56 This stanza, and lines 736–42, derive from *Filostrato*, 4.87, while lines 743–9 and 757–63 derive from *Filostrato*, 4.88–9. In Ph+ (here Gg, H3, J, Ph) this stanza follows 735, thus corresponding more closely to the sequence of stanzas in *Filostrato*, and possibly deriving from the processes of the poem's composition and early transcription.

762 *Argyve*: The name of Criseyde's mother is not mentioned by Benoît, Guido or Boccaccio; Chaucer may derive the name from that of Polynices' wife, mentioned by Cassandra (*TC* 5.1509), and deriving from 'Argia' in Statius, *Thebaid*, 2.297.

765 Proverbial (Whiting F233).

766–70 These lines have no counterpart in *Filostrato*.

767–8 Cf. *Boece*, 3.pr.11.96–109.

770 Proverbial (Whiting G453).

776 *unshethe*: Perhaps recalling Apollo's flaying of Marsyas 'out of the sheath of his limbs' (Dante, *Paradiso*, 1.20–21; cf. *House of Fame*, 1229–32).

782–4 *of myn ordre ... abstinence*: In Troilus's absence Criseyde imagines herself dressed in the habit and observing the duties of a nun (a role she earlier disclaimed: 2.759). Boccaccio's Criseida will wear black simply as a widow (*Filostrato*, 4.90). For an earlier reference to love as a form of religious order, see *TC* 1.336–40.

785–7 For the lover's testament, see *Romaunt*, 4610–11 ('And make in haste my testament, | As lovers doon that feelen smert'); *Knight's Tale*, I.2768–9 ('But I biquethe the servyce of my goost | To yow ...'); cf. also *TC* 4.470–76, and Troilus's testament (5.298–322).

789–90 *the feld of pite ... Elisos*: Not from *Filostrato* and possibly deriving from 'arva piorum' (fields of the pious) in Ovid's allusion to how Orpheus went there to rescue his wife Eurydice from the underworld (*Metamorphoses*, 11.61–6: lines 61–4 appear as a gloss in H4; Ph+ reads 'Ther Pluto regneth' for 'That highte Elisos'). Chaucer possibly knew an etymology connecting Elysium with the 'Kyrie eleison' (Lord have mercy upon us) of the liturgy (R reads 'eleisos' for 'Elisos'). A Latin gloss on Lucan, *Pharsalia*, 3.12, by Arnulf of Orleans reads: '*Elysian*: "Eleison," that is, "to pity," hence "Elysian Fields," as it were "fields of pity" where the pious rest; or *Elysian*: placed "beyond injury [*extra lesionem*]"' (Marti 1958: 156); Chaucer's 'out of peyne' may be linked to a gloss by Lactantius on Statius, *Thebaid*, 3.108–11, interpreting Elysium as 'extra lesionem' (see Steadman 1972: 41, and Clogan 1964: 609–10). Another suggested source is the *Ovide moralisé* (c. 1316–28) – an allegorization providing moral interpretations of Ovid's tales – where those who have not deserved pain repose in the Elysian fields (14827–30), and where Orpheus finds Eurydice 'En la piteuse compaignie' (11167–8; see Witlieb 1969). Dante, *Inferno*, 4, may have had a more general influence.

791 How Orpheus went to hell and won, through his music, the release of his wife Eurydice is recounted in *Boece*, 3.m.12. All the infernal inhabitants affected by Orpheus's music in this metrum are mentioned somewhere in *TC* but not in *Filostrato*: Cerberus (see *TC* 1.859); the Furies (1.6–9; 4.22–4); Ixion (5.212); Tantalus (3.593); Tityus (1.786); and also Orpheus's mother, Calliope (3.45).

799 *yred ben or ysonge*: A formula, also used by Criseyde (5.1059) and near the poem's close (5.1797); this is not evidence that *TC* was sung in performance.

813–19 From *Filostrato*, 4.96, but perhaps also recalling Briseida's grief upon hearing of her exchange, in Guido, *Historia*, p. 163 ('and her golden hair, released from the restraint of bands, she tore'), and also *Filocolo*, 1.188.

818 *martire*] H2 H4; *matire* Cp D J R S1; *matere* other MSS.

820 *for sorwe*: Ph+ instead reads 'for shame', which more closely translates Criseida's hiding her face 'per vergogna' (for shame) in *Filostrato*, 4.96. See *TC* 4.596: 'It is no shame unto yow'.

827–47 Criseyde's complaint here has no equivalent in *Filostrato*.

829 *cause causyng*: I.e. the 'causa causans' or primary cause in logic. H4 has a gloss 'causa causans'.

834 *than*] *thanne* Cp A Cl H1 H2 J.

836 Cf. Proverbs 14:13 (partly cited in a Latin gloss in H4 here) and *Man of Law's Tale*, II.424 ('Wo occupieth the fyn of oure gladnesse'); also proverbial (Whiting E80, J58, J61).

841–7 In *Filostrato* the corresponding stanza (4.97) is uttered by Pandaro.

882 Ph+ and R+ read: 'As he that shortly shapith hym to deye'. Cf. *Filostrato*, 4.102 (variant reading): 'che cerca disperato di morire' (who seeks desperately to die).

906 Ph+ reads: 'To sen hym in that wo that he is inne'. Cf. *Filostrato*, 4.105: 'di veder Troiolo afflitto' (to see Troiolo suffering).

910 *beteth*] Gg H3 H4 R Cx Th; *that betith* Ph; *he beteth* other MSS.

918–19   From *Filostrato*, 4.107, but cf. also Boccaccio, *Filocolo*,
1.117–18.

927   *cause of flat than egge*: Perhaps alluding to the sword with which
Achilles wounded Telephus, which had the power to heal the
wound it inflicted (see Ovid, *Metamorphoses*, 12.112, 13.171–
2; *Tristia*, 5.2, 15; *Remedia amoris*, 44–8; also Dante, *Inferno*,
31.4–6; and *Squire's Tale*, V.156–65, 239–40). The ceremonial
conferring of knighthood involved the candidate's being touched
with the flat of the sword.

935   This is the course of action later proposed to Troilus by Criseyde
(4.1307–20).

936   Found as a proverb after Chaucer (cf. Whiting W531); see also
4.1261–3.

946–52   Pandaro finds Troiolo at home looking pensive and downcast
(*Filostrato*, 4.109); the temple setting and despairing prayer for
death are only in *TC* here (but see above, 3.232n.). H3 and Ph
have a variant form of lines 950–52: 'He fast made his compleynt
and his mone | Bysekyng hem to sende hym othir grace | Or from
this world to done hym sone to pace.'

953–1078   This passage – not in *Filostrato* and absent from some *TC*
MSS – derives closely from Chaucer's translation of Boethius, *De
consolatione philosophiae* (5.pr.3), but has been given a more
predestinarian slant (Huber 1965). In its original context the
speech is answered by Philosophia's explanation of how God's
foreknowledge does not preclude man's free will. Chaucer's two
stanzas before and after the passage (*TC* 4.946–52, 1086–92)
derive from a single *Filostrato* stanza (4.109). Lines 953–1078
are omitted by some Ph+ MSS (Gg, H3, Ph), and by one MS from
outside the Ph+ group here (H4), which elsewhere shows signs of
conflation (see 3.1324–37n.). However, the passage has been
added on an inset leaf in Ph. H3 and H4 also omit lines 1079–
85, contained by Ph on its inset leaf, and contained by Gg. Lines
1079–85, unlike the the rest of the passage, are not derived from
Boethius but refer to Troilus 'Disputyng with hymself in this
matere' as only the soliloquy shows him doing. Similarly, the H3
and Ph variant form of lines 950–52 implies a 'compleynt' by
Troilus, although H3 and Ph do not include the soliloquy. J
(which agrees with the Ph+ group from early in Book 4) contains
the passage but, between the main soliloquy and that final stanza
which Gg also contains, there is a blank page, a cancelled leaf
and another blank space, while at the foot of the last written
page, *after* the main body of the soliloquy, is a scribal note: 'her

faileth thing that is nat yet made' (Windeatt 1992: 29). This note in a MS copied decades after the poem's composition is less likely to derive from an early scribe waiting for Chaucer to provide the soliloquy text than from a scribal guess at rationalizing a gap in his exemplar after the soliloquy which there was no way of filling. It is unlikely to be authentic in suggesting that Chaucer was intending to translate *more* of the Boethius than he actually does (see A Note on the Text).

958   Resembling 'omnia que eveniunt de necessitate eveniunt' (all things that come about come about from necessity) in John Wyclif's *Responsiones ad argumenta Radulfi Strode*, his rejoinder to Chaucer's philosopher friend Ralph Strode, to whom *TC* was submitted for correction (see 5.1857n.). This deterministic opinion may be found repeated almost verbatim at least eight times in Wyclif's works (Utz 1996).

968   *grete clerkes*: Cf. the reference to Augustine, Boethius and Archbishop Thomas Bradwardine (d. 1349) on predestination in *Nun's Priest's Tale*, VII.3243–4 ('Wheither that Goddes worthy forwityng [foreknowledge] | Streyneth me nedely for to doon a thyng').

974–80   Cf. *Boece*, 5.pr.3.8–16: 'For yif so be that God loketh alle thinges byforn, ne God ne mai nat ben desceyved in no manere, thanne moot it nedes ben that alle thinges betyden the whiche that the purveaunce of God hath seyn byforn to comen. For whiche, yif that God knoweth byforn nat oonly the werkes of men, but also hir conseilles and hir willes, thanne ne schal ther be no liberte of arbitrie'.

981–7   Cf. *Boece*, 5.pr.3.16–23: 'ne certes ther ne may be noon othir dede, ne no wil, but thilke whiche that the devyne purveaunce, that ne mai nat ben disseyved, hath felid byforn. For yif that thei myghten writhen awey in othere manere than thei ben purveyed, thanne ne sholde ther be no stedefast prescience of thing to comen'.

988–94   Cf. *Boece*, 5.pr.3.23–5: 'but rather an uncerteyn opynioun; the whiche thing to trowen of God, I deme it felonye and unleveful.'

995–1001   Cf. *Boece*, 5.pr.3.26–36: 'Ne I ne proeve nat thilke same resoun (as who seith, I ne allowe nat, or I ne preyse nat, thilke same resoun) by whiche that som men wenen that thei mowe assoilen and unknytten the knotte of this questioun. For certes thei seyn that thing nis nat to comen for that the purveaunce of God hath seyn byforn that it is to comen, but rathir the contrarie;

and that is this: that, for that the thing is to comen, that therfore
ne mai it nat ben hidd fro the purveaunce of God'.

1002–8 Cf. *Boece*, 5.pr.3.36–40: 'and in this manere this necessite
slideth ayein into the contrarie partie: ne it ne byhoveth nat nedes
that thinges betiden that ben ipurveied, but it byhoveth nedes that
thinges that ben to comen ben ipurveied –'

1009–15 Cf. *Boece*, 5.pr.3.40–47: 'but as it were Y travailed (*as
who seith, that thilke answere procedith ryght as though men
travaileden or weren besy*) to enqueren the whiche thing is cause
of the whiche thing, as whethir the prescience is cause of the
necessite of thinges to comen, or elles that the necessite of thinges
to comen is cause of the purveaunce.'

1016–22 Cf. *Boece*, 5.pr.3.47–53: 'But I ne enforce me nat now to
schewen it, that the bytidynge of thingis iwyst byforn is necessarie,
how so or in what manere that the ordre of causes hath itself;
although that it ne seme naught that the prescience bringe in
necessite of bytydinge to thinges to comen.'

1019 *byfore*] *byfor* Cp H1 Ph; *byforn* Cl J.

1023–9 Cf. *Boece*, 5.pr.3.54–7: 'For certes yif that any wyght sitteth,
it byhoveth by necessite that the opynioun be soth of hym that
conjecteth that he sitteth; and ayeinward also is it of the contrarie'.

1025 *thyn opynyoun*: Although alone in the temple, Troilus speaks as
if responding to an interlocutor, recalling Boethius's dialogue
form in the *Consolation*.

1030–36 Cf. *Boece*, 5.pr.3.57–63: 'yif the opinioun be soth of any
wyght for that he sitteth, it byhoveth by necessite that he sitte.
Thanne is here necessite in the toon and in the tothir; for in the
toon is necessite of syttynge, and certes in the tothir is necessite
of soth.'

1037–43 Cf. *Boece*, 5.pr.3.63–71: 'But therfore ne sitteth nat a wyght
for that the opynioun of the sittynge is soth, but the opinioun is
rather soth for that a wyght sitteth byforn. And thus, althoughe
that the cause of the soth cometh of that other side (*as who seith,
that althoughe the cause of soth cometh of the sittynge, and nat
of the trewe opinioun*), algatis yit is ther comune necessite in that
oon and in that othir.'

1044–50 Cf. *Boece*, 5.pr.3.71–3: 'Thus scheweth it that Y may make
semblable skiles of the purveaunce of God and of thingis to
comen.'

1051–7 Cf. *Boece*, 5.pr.3.73–9: 'For althoughe that for that thingis
ben to comen therfore ben thei purveied, and nat certes for thei
be purveied therfore ne bytide thei nat; yit natheles byhoveth it

by necessite that eyther the thinges to comen ben ipurveied of
God, or elles that the thinges that ben ipurveyed of God betyden.'

1058–64 Cf. *Boece*, 5.pr.3.79–86: 'And this thing oonly suffiseth
inow to destroien the fredom of oure arbitre (that is to seyn, of
our fre wil). But certes now schewith it wel how fer fro the sothe
and how up-so-doun is this thing that we seyn, that the betydynge
of temporel thingis is cause of the eterne prescience.'

1065–71 Cf. *Boece*, 5.pr.3.86–91: 'But for to wenen that God purvei-
eth the thinges to comen for thei ben to comen – what oothir
thing is it but for to wene that thilke thinges that bytidden whilom
ben cause of thilke soverein purveaunce that is in God?'

1072–8 Cf. *Boece*, 5.pr.3.91–9: 'And herto I adde yit this thing: that
ryght as whanne that I woot that a thing is, it byhoveth by
necessite that thilke selve thing be; and eek whan I have knowen
that any thing schal betyden; so byhovith it by necessite that
thilke same thing betide; so folweth it thanne that the betydynge
of the thing iwyste byforn ne may nat ben eschued.'

1078 Troilus's soliloquy ceases to follow Boethius before the response
by Philosophy; cf. Dante, *Paradiso*, 17.37–40 ('Contingency,
which does not extend beyond the volume of your material world,
is all depicted in the Eternal Vision, yet does not thence derive
necessity').

1098 For references to dicing, see 2.1347 and 4.622.

1105 Proverbial (cf. Whiting M157).

1107 *of that I shal the*] R H2 H4 Cx; *of that I shal* Cp; *of that that I
shal* Cl A; *of al that I shall* D H1 S2 Th; *of that I shall yow* S1;
what that I shal the J Gg H3 Ph (*that* Gg H3 omit; *the* Ph omits.).

1116 *Juno*: Roman goddess, wife of Jupiter. This invocation of her –
like those at 4.1538, 1594; 5.601 – is not in *Filostrato* (cf. 4.111–
12).

1137 *ligne aloes*: The aloe, used medicinally, was proverbially bitter,
like gall (cf. Whiting G8; Walther 33629).

1139 *Mirra*: Myrrha, daughter of Cinyras, king of Cyprus, who was
metamorphosed into a myrrh tree, and whose continuing tears
exude through the bark as aromatic gum (see Ovid, *Metamor-
phoses*, 10.298–502; H4 has lines 500–501 as a marginal gloss).

1140–41 A commonplace; cf. the depiction of Sorrow in the *Roman
de la Rose*: 'In world nys wight so hard of herte | That hadde sen
her sorowes smerte, | That nolde have had of her pyte' (*Romaunt*,
333–5).

1142 *goostes*: From 'spiriti' (*Filostrato*, 4.116), but Boccaccio meant
the physiological spirits, not the lovers' souls.

1149ff. For this scene of Criseyde's swoon, Troilus's grief over her body (1163–5), and narrowly averted suicide (1184ff.), Chaucer works from the model in *Filostrato*, which itself draws on Boccaccio's *Filocolo* (Young 1908: 66–103).

1154 Cf. 5.243–5, and *Book of the Duchess*, 488–99.

1159 *throwen upward*: Although *Filostrato*, 4.117, describes Criseida's eyes as 'velati' (veiled, closed), Chaucer's copy perhaps read 'levati' (cast up).

1166–8 'To sing "weylawey"' is a proverbial expression (cf. Whiting S469) and, like 'of blisse al bare', recurs in the expression of distress in English romances (Windeatt 1988: 140) .

1188 *Mynos*: The ancient judge of the dead (cf. Virgil, *Aeneid*, 6.431–3), Minos sits at the entrance of Dante's second circle, of carnal sinners (*Inferno*, 5.4–6), and later judges the suicides (13.94–6).

1208 *Atropos*: The third of the three Fates, who cuts the thread of life spun by the second Fate, Lachesis (see 5.7). Criseyde calls on Atropos to break the thread of her life (4.1546).

1216 *Cipride*: I.e. the Cyprian Venus (see 3.725, 1255). See also 5.208. *Cipride*] J R H2 Ph S1; *enpride* A; *Cupide* other MSS.

1218 *to glade*] *comfort* Ph+. Cf. *Filostrato*, 4.124: 'la confortò' (he comforted her).

1237 *a forlong wey*: I.e. the time it takes, reckoned at two and a half minutes, to walk a furlong (an eighth of a mile).

1241 *slawe*] R Gg; *slayn(e* other MSS.

1262 *avysed sodeynly*: Cf. Pandarus earlier on women's quick thinking (4.936).

1283 Proverbial (Whiting T307); see 3.896n.

1303 *this the*] R H2 H4 S1; *that the* Cl D H3; *this that* J Ph; *this is that* Gg; *the* Cp A H1 S2 Th.

1305–6 Cf. *Roman de la Rose*, 2601–2; *Romaunt*, 2741–2 ('In thank that thyng is taken more, | For which a man hath suffred sore').

1320 For the promise to return on the tenth day, see 4.1595n.

1324 *oft-tyme*] H1 S1 S2 Th; *ofte tyme(s* Cp A Cl D; *ofte(n* other MSS.

1356 A commonplace figure (cf. Whiting B167, and see 2.193).

1369 *elde is ful of coveytise*: Proverbial (Whiting C490). Criseyde's plans to deceive her father (1368–1414) are elaborated from one stanza in *Filostrato* (4.136): Criseida will tell her avaricious father he had better let her return to Troy to protect his interests.

1370–71 On catching without net, cf. 2.583.

1373–4 'It's hard to have the wolf full and the sheep unharmed': i.e. you cannot have your cake and eat it; but unrecorded as a proverb elsewhere (cf. Whiting W444).

1388–1409 Cp omits. Text based on J and Cl.

1397–1411 Not in the corresponding section of *Filostrato* (4.136), and recalling Briseida's reproaches to Calchas in Benoît and Guido (omitted in *Filostrato* and *TC* 5.193–4) when she arrives in the Greek camp and claims Apollo has deceived him (*Troie*, 13768–73; *Historia*, pp. 165–6). With Criseyde's scepticism, cf. Capaneus's defiance of the gods (*TC* 5.1504–5 and n.); Gower cites him as an example of presumption: 'That to the goddes him ne liste | In no querele to beseche, | Bot seide it was an ydel speche, | Which caused was of pure drede' (*Confessio amantis*, 1.1984–7).

1398 *avayleth nought thre hawes*: A proverbial expression of worthlessness (Whiting H189); cf. 3.854.

1404 *beren hym on honde*: For the idiom, cf. *Wife of Bath's Prologue*, III.232, and *MED*, s.v. *beren* v. 13.(i). Criseyde will convince Calchas by false asseveration.

1408 *Drede fond first goddes*: Proverbial in Latin (cf. Walther 22405), but unrecorded in English before Chaucer (Whiting D385); a version in Petronius (Fragment 27) – 'Primus in orbe deos fecit timor' (fear first made gods in the world) – is quoted in Statius, *Thebaid*, 3.661 (a speech by Capaneus), and thence by Servius, *Comm. in Aeneida*, 2.715, and is variously quoted by medieval commentators, e.g. Third Vatican Mythographer (Bode 1834: 152). 'Timor invenit deos' occurs as a marginal gloss on Criseyde's words in H4.

1411 *Delphos*: I.e. Delphi (from the Latin accusative form), site of the oracle of Apollo; on Calchas's defection, see 1.64–84. Chaucer elsewhere uses Latin oblique forms (cf. 'Parcas', 5.3).

1415–21 This stanza has no equivalent in *Filostrato* here (4.136, 137); for Criseyde's sorrow at departing, see *Filostrato*, 5.7, and *TC* 5.19–21; cf. Benoît, *Troie*, 13495–7 ('The girl thinks she will die when she must part from him she loves so much and holds so dear'), and Guido, *Historia*, p. 163.

1422 Perhaps some echo of Boethius's rapt attention to Lady Philosophy at the opening of *De consolatione*, 3.pr.1.

1453–4 Proverbial (Whiting B101). Troilus's quoting of proverbs (1453–63) is not in *Filostrato*.

1456 Proverbial (Whiting O29); cf. also *Knight's Tale*, I.2449.

1457–8 Proverbial (Whiting H50; Hassell B127).

1459 *Argus*: A mythical monster with one hundred eyes, of proverbial cunning (cf. Ovid, *Ars Amatoria*, 3.616–18; Whiting A180; Walther 1374). For women's capacity to outwit Argus, see *Wife of Bath's Prologue*, III.358–61, and *Merchant's Tale*, IV.2111–14. In mythographical tradition Argus represented cupidity and avarice, calculating cunning, worldly wisdom (Hoffman 1965; Schibanoff 1976).

1478–82 Here *Filostrato*, 4.142, may be supplemented from Calchas's response to Briseida's reproaches in Benoît, *Troie*, 13803–9, and Guido, *Historia*, p. 166 ('I know for certain through the promises of the infallible gods that . . . the city of Troy will be destroyed and ruined within a short time, with all its nobles destroyed and its whole populace cut down by the edge of the sword').

1505 For the philosophical distinction between the essential quality ('substaunce') and an inessential attribute ('accident'), see also *Pardoner's Tale*, VI.538–9. 'It is not good to lose the substance for an accident' is H4's marginal gloss in Latin on Troilus's argument, which is developed (*TC* 4.1512–13) with a further play on 'accident' as 'uncertainty', the opposite of 'sikernesse', and on 'substaunce' as 'means, wealth, possessions'.

1538–40 For 'Athamante', see Ovid, *Metamorphoses*, 4.416–562, where 'Saturnian Juno', enemy of Thebes, crosses the Stix to request the fury Tisiphone (see *TC* 1.6) to drive Athamas, king of Thebes, to madness; cf. also *Inferno*, 30, which opens with Juno's enmity to both Thebes and Troy, as exemplified in the fates of Athamas and Hecuba, and includes among the 'falsifiers' Myrra (see *TC* 4.1139) and Sinon, betrayer of Troy. The Stix is one of the rivers of hell, but the pit of hell is a medieval commonplace.

1543–5 Cf. Ovid, *Metamorphoses*, 1.192–3: 'I have demigods, rustic divinities, nymphs, fauns and satyrs, and forest deities upon the mountain slopes.'

1548 *Symois*: Cf. Ovid, *Amores*, 1.15.10: 'As long as Simois will roll its swift waters to the sea'; but Simois, a tributary of the ancient Scamander, does not flow through Troy.

1553 *retourne bakward to thi welle*: Cf. Ovid, *Metamorphoses*, 13.324 ('sooner will Simois flow backwards . . . than . . .'), and Oenone's letter to Paris: 'If Paris can go on breathing, having abandoned Oenone, the water of the Xanthus shall run backwards to its source' (Ovid, *Heroides*, 5.29–30, also cited in *Roman de la Rose*, 13225–8; cf. *TC* 1.652–65). Cf. the earlier 'impossibilia', *TC* 3.1495–8

1560–61 Cf. 2.468–9.

1568 Proverbial (Whiting M97, R32, H157–68); cf. 1.956.

1584 *The suffrant overcomith*: Proverbial (Whiting S865; Walther

24454); cf. also *Franklin's Tale*, V.773–8, and *Parson's Tale*,
X.661

1585 Proverbial (Whiting L233).

1586 *maketh vertu of necessite*: Proverbial in French (Hassell V79),
but unrecorded in English before Chaucer (Whiting V43); cf.
Knight's Tale, I.3041–2 ('Thanne is it wysdom . . . | To maken
vertu of necessitee'), and also *Squire's Tale*, V.593.

1591–2 I.e. before the moon ('Lucina'), sister of the sun ('Phebus'),
passes from its present position in the zodiacal sign of Aries ('this
Ariete'), through Taurus, Gemini and Cancer, and beyond Leo
('The Leoun'). See also 5.650–58, 1018–19. (For an attempt to
date Criseyde's promise to 5–7 April or 2–4 May 1388, see North
1988: 391.)

1594 *Juno, hevenes quene*: Applying to Juno the title of the Virgin
Mary.

1595 The promise to return on the tenth day derives from *Filostrato*
(4.154) – and is not present in Benoît or Guido – but Criseida
does not link her return with the moon.

1608 *Cinthia*: The moon (cf. 5.1018), emblem of change, with whose
movements Criseyde has linked her return (4.1591–3). Cf.
Albumasar's *Introductorium in astronomiam* (3.1): 'The motion
of the moon is swifter than that of any other planet; it has,
accordingly, more to do than any other in regulating mundane
affairs' (Curry 1960: 247), and was hence an emblem of change-
ableness and inconstancy.

1628 Proverbial (Whiting H413).

1645 Cf. Ovid, *Heroides*, 1.12 ('Love is something always full of
anxious fear'); also proverbial (Whiting L517; Walther 26666).

1660–66 This stanza is not in *Filostrato*.

1667–87 In the equivalent speech in *Filostrato* (4.164–6), it is Troiolo
who explains to Criseida why he loves *her*.

1667–73 Re-expressing Troiolo's argument in *Filostrato*, 4.164 ('It
was not your beauty . . . or breeding . . . or adornments or
wealth').

1674–80 Cf. *Filostrato*, 4.165: Troiolo praises Criseida's noble
actions, worthiness, courtly speech, noble manners and her
charming womanly pride, which makes her scorn every common
('popolesco') desire and deed.

1695–6 For this common formula, see 5.445, 1321, and *Romaunt*,
3181–4; cf. I Corinthians 2:9.

BOOK 5

1–14 Not demarcated as a proem in the *TC* MSS (except the late S1), these stanzas have no equivalent in *Filostrato*, which Chaucer begins to follow at line 15.

1   Cf. Boccaccio, *Teseida*, 9.1: 'Già s'appressava il doloroso fato' (Now approached the dolorous fate).

3   *Parcas*: Either an anglicization or the accusative form (cf. 4.1411) of the Latin 'Parcae', the Fates, i.e. Clotho who spins, Lachesis (5.7) who apportions, and Atropos (4.1208) who cuts the thread of life; but the roles were often confused, and here Lachesis spins. (Cf. *Roman de la Rose*, 19768–75; Dante, *Purgatorio*, 21.25–7.) On the Fates as instruments in the execution of Jove's decrees, see Statius, *Thebaid*, 1.212–13; *Boece*, 4.pr.5.88–93; *Knight's Tale*, I.1663–5. For other references to the Fates in *TC*, see 3.733–4; 4.1208, 1546.

7   *Lachesis*: Spelling from Cx and Th; all MSS read 'Lathesis'. Cf. Dante, *Purgatorio*, 25.79: 'When Lachesis has no more more flax [to spin]'.

8 11 Cf. Boccaccio, *Teseida*, 2.1:

> Il sole avea due volte dissolute
> le nevi en gli alti poggi, e altrettante
> Zeffiro aveva le frondi rendute
> e i be' fiori alle spogliate piante,
> poi che . . .

(The sun had twice melted the snows upon the high peaks, and Zephyrus had as many times restored leaves and fair flowers to the denuded plants since . . .) See also Statius, *Thebaid*, 4.1–3 ('Three times had Phoebus brought the zephyrs' balm to free the frozen year'), and Petrarch's sonnet 310, 'Zefiro torna' (Zephyrus returns and leads back the fine weather).

8   *golde-tressed*] D H3 Th; *golde dressed* A; *goldtressed* other MSS. Perhaps deriving from the Latin epithet 'auricomus', used of the sun in Valerius Flaccus, *Argonauticon*, 4.92, and Martianus Capella, *De nuptiis Philologiae et Mercurii*, 1.12, and repeated in Latin glosses in H2 and H4. Cf. also Walther 20109.

9   *Thries*: Three springs have passed since Troilus fell in love with Criseyde; on the time-scheme in *TC*, see 1.156n.
       cleene] J Ph; *shene* H2 H4 R S1; *clere* other MSS.

12   *sone of Ecuba the queene*: I.e. Troilus, son of Hecuba, queen of Troy.

27–8 Cf. Benoît's anticipations at the lovers' parting of Briseida's change of heart (*Troie*, 13425–7, 13436–7).

37   *horse*] Gg H2 S1 Th; *his hors* J; *hors* other MSS.

67   *valeye*: Mistranslating 'vallo' (ramparts) in *Filostrato*, 5.10.

88   *sone of Tideus*: I.e. Diomede; for Tydeus, see notes to 5.932–8, 1485–1510, 1501.

89   *koude more than the crede*: Knowledge of the creed represents elementary knowledge.

90   *by the reyne hire hente*: Perhaps mistranslating *Filostrato*, 5.13, where Diomede 'sé di colei piglia' (is taken with love for Criseida), or following Benoît's *Troie*, 13529: 'E li fiz Tydeüs l'en meine' (And the son of Tydeus leads her). For the taking of reins, cf. *Troie*, 4815–16, 4845–8 (Paris, then Priam, lead Helen into Troy), 13425 (Troilus leads Briseida from Troy), 15562–3 (Priam leads Hector back to Troy). See also Chaucer's *Anelida and Arcite*, 183–4.

98   *He is a fool ... hymselve*: Not recorded as a proverb before Chaucer (cf. Whiting F437).

107   *tyme was*] *this was don* Cp+. Boccaccio does not record a conversation here between Criseida and Diomede, whose courtship begins when he visits her four days later. Chaucer adapts Benoît's account (*Troie*, 13529–712) of how Diomede immediately declares his love as they ride from Troy, somewhat altering the sequence of points in Diomede's speech in *Troie*, and anticipating some of Diomede's later courtship in *Filostrato*, 6.10–25. Guido gives only a brief summary of the episode in Benoît: that Diomede is taken with love of Briseida, rides alongside her, reveals his heart and tries to tempt her (*Historia*, p. 164).

108–12 Cf. Benoît's Diomede, who comes immediately to the point: although he can see Briseida is distressed, he urges her to receive him as a lover (*Troie*, 13539–43).

113–16 Benoît's Diomede will submit himself to great pain if he can through his embraces and kisses relieve Briseida of the sorrow with which he sees her oppressed (*Troie*, 13596–610).

120–23 Benoît's Diomede fears Briseida hates the Greeks, and she cannot be blamed for inclining to her own people (*Troie*, 13546–51).

122   *Troianis*] D H2 H4 R S1; *Troians* other MSS.

124–6 Cf. Diomede's later insistence to Criseida in *Filostrato*, 6.22:

'Do not believe that there is not among the Greeks love higher and more perfect than among the Trojans.'

135 Cf. Benoît's Diomede to Briseida: 'Ne refusez le mien homage' (Do not refuse my devotion; *Troie*, 13585).

152 *Yeve me youre hond*: At this point Benoît's Diomede takes Briseida's glove (*Troie*, 13709–12), which Chaucer delays to a later meeting (*TC* 5.1013).

155–8 Diomede (whose wife Aigale is mentioned by Benoît) insists he has never loved (*Troie*, 13557–8); he has never asked any woman for love, and Briseida is the first and will be the last (13591–8).

162 For the association with Criseyde in this final book of 'bright' (fair, radiant), the conventional epithet for ladies, see also: 5.465, 516, 708, 922, 1241, 1247, 1264, 1573, 1712.

164–5 Benoît's Diomede has often heard of people who have loved without ever having met (*Troie*, 13552–5); this is a romance motif, as in the love of Alexander and Candace in the English romance *Kyng Alisaunder*, 6652–5.

166–8 Brought forward from Diomede's brief response after Briseida's reply in *Troie* (see *TC* 5.183–9); he gives himself to serve love without resistance (*Troie*, 13691–4).

169–75 Benoît's Diomede warns Briseida that the richest, handsomest, best men in the world are in the Greek camp and will seek her love, but, if she will make him her love, he is ready to honour and serve her for the rest of his life (*Troie*, 13575–90).

176–89 Chaucer summarizes selectively Briseida's reply in *Troie* (13619–80), omitting the most encouraging part, the conclusion, which is recalled later (see *TC* 5.1000–1003), and adding his Criseyde's distraction. Benoît's Briseida replies composedly that it is not time to promise love; many women are deceived in love; she has just left her friends and home; it would be unfitting to embark on a love affair in an armed camp; but she knows Diomede's qualities; no lady could refuse him, if inclined to love, and nor is she refusing him; but she does not intend or desire to love anyone at present, although if she decided to do so, she would prefer no one over him. Chaucer omits Diomede's insight here in *Troie* that Briseida is not unfavourable, and his further speech (cf. *TC* 5.166–8). The inclusion of Diomede's speech from *Troie*, along with Criseyde's response, gives attention to her experience without defining or explaining her state of mind.

207–8 Apollo is the god responsible for Calchas's flight to the Greeks (1.64–84); Ceres and Bacchus, gods of food and wine, are associated with Venus in *Parliament of Fowls*, 275–7 (from Boccaccio, *Teseida*, 7.66), but the association was a commonplace (cf. Terence, *Eunuchus*, 4.5.732, and Whiting C125, W359).

211 *walwith*] Gg H4 Cx; *waltryth* R; *whieleth* J; *swellith* Ph; *waileth* other MSS.

212 *Ixion*: He was tied to an ever-turning wheel in hell (sometimes associated with Fortune's wheel) for attempting to lie with Juno (cf. *Boece*, 3.m.12.37–8). In Nicholas Trevet's commentary on Boethius, Ixion is the man devoted to worldly matters, ever raised up in prosperity and cast down in adversity, for the wheel stops turning when a wise man condemns earthly things (Fox 1981: 389).

223–4 *Save a pilowe*: Cf. *Filostrato*, 5.20 ('Now I find myself embracing my pillow'), and also Ariadne feeling in her bed for Theseus, who has abandoned her (Ovid, *Heroides*, 10.12; cf. *Legend of Good Women*, 2186). The lover's embracing his pillow in place of his absent lady is a motif in some other romance, such as *William of Palerne* (Windeatt 1988: 141).

260–80 These three stanzas have no equivalent in *Filostrato*.

270 *Thow, redere*: This unique reference to a reader in *TC* does not derive from *Filostrato*, and may recall a device in Dante; cf. *Inferno*, 8.94 ('Judge, reader, if'), 25.46 ('If, reader, you are now slow to believe'), 34.23 ('do not ask, reader, for I do not write it'), *Paradiso*, 5.109 ('Think, reader, if'), 10.7 ('Look up, reader').

274–8 From a stanza of 'chronographia' (time-description) in Boccaccio, *Teseida*, 7.94:

> Il ciel tutte le stelle ancor mostrava,
> ben che Febea già palida fosse,
> e l'orizonte tutto biancheggiava
> nell'oriente, e eransi già mosse
> l'ore, e col carro in cui la luce stava
> giungevano i cavai, vedendo rosse
> le membra del celeste bue levato,
> dall'amica Titonia accompagnato ...

(The sky still showed all the stars, although Phoebe [the moon] was already pale, and the entire horizon was growing white in the east, and the hours were already in motion, and were yoking the horses to the chariot in which stood the light, beholding the ruddy-coloured limbs of the celestial bull [Taurus] accompanied

by his beloved, Titonia [Aurora] . . .) Cf. also *Boece*, 2.m.3.1–5:
'Whan Phebus, the sonne, bygynneth to spreden his clernesse
with rosene chariettes, thanne the sterre, ydymmed, paleth hir
white cheeres by the flambes of the sonne that overcometh the
sterre lyght'; and *Thebaid*, 12.1–4.

295–315 For the motif of the lover's testament, see also 4.327, 785–
7; R and S2 have at 295 (and H4 at 306) a marginal gloss
'The testament of Troilus', and S1 has 'Here maketh Troilus his
testament'.

299–315 Troilus's instructions for his tomb and funeral are added to
Filostrato (4.327), recalling details of the death and pagan funeral
of Arcita in Boccaccio's *Teseida*, 10–11 (cf. *Knight's Tale*,
I.2853–2966), especially the funeral games (11.59–68), the
horses and arms brought to the pyre (11.35), and the cremated
ashes collected in a golden urn (11.58). Cf. also the cremation
and funeral games of Archemorus in Statius, *Thebaid*, 6 (see *TC*
5.1499).

304 *pleyes palestral*: Cf. Boccaccio's *Teseida*, 7.4, 27: 'palestral gioco'
(athletic contest).

308 *My sheld to Pallas yef*: The divine protectress of Troy was often
represented as armed and warlike, which may be why Troilus
bequeaths her his shield. In classical tradition (cf. Apollodorus,
Epitome, 3.12.3) the Palladium, the miraculous guardian statue
of Pallas at Troy, showed her holding aloft a spear in her right
hand, and in her left a distaff and spindle (see *TC*, 1.153n.).

309–15 A dying lover orders that his heart be sent to his lady as a
token in the romance *The Knight of Curtesy* (Windeatt 1988:
135).

319 For the owl as a bird of foreboding, see *Parliament of Fowls*, 343;
Legend of Good Women, 2253–4 (from Ovid, *Metamorphoses*,
6.432); also Alanus de Insulis, *De planctu naturae* (Häring 1979:
2.167–8), and Bartholomaeus Anglicus, trans. Trevisa (Seymour
1975: 1.614). *Escaphilo*: Ascalaphus, metamorphosed into an
owl for revealing that Proserpina had eaten a pomegranate in the
underworld, and so could not return to her home (*Meta-
morphoses*, 5.539–50; a marginal gloss in H4 mistakenly refers
to *Metamorphoses*, 2). For Chaucer's Italianate spelling of the
classical name, see 2.435–6n.

321 *Mercurye . . . soule gyde*: Mercury, guide of souls ('psychopomp'),
who will indeed guide Troilus's soul after death (see 5.1827, from
Boccaccio, *Teseida*, 11.3).

343 Proverbial (Whiting F639).

346 For the custom of blessing the wedding chamber and bed, see *Merchant's Tale*, IV.1818–19.

350 Perhaps proverbial (cf. Whiting T300).

358–85 Expanding on *Filostrato*, 5.32, where Pandaro attributes Troiolo's dreams to melancholy. Much dream lore was common knowledge, and Pandarus's comments derive ultimately from the summary list of causes of dreams given in Gregory the Great's *Dialogues*, Book 4, which was quoted in school commentaries on Cato's *Distichs*, 2.31: 'sompnia ne cures' (pay no attention to dreams; Hazelton 1960: 357–80). Discouragement of belief in dreams was proverbial (Whiting D387; Hassell S106; Walther 30025b, 30026–8a). See *Nun's Priest's Tale*, VII.2941; *Piers Plowman*, A 8.135–6, C 10.302–3.

360 *thi malencolie*: Troilus's dream is a 'somnium naturale', caused by physiological disturbance through the melancholic humour and of no prophetic value. See *Nun's Priest's Tale*, VII.2922–39. Medieval dream classification also included the 'somnium animale' (a dream of mental origin, prompted by the waking mind's preoccupations) and the 'somniun coeleste' (a dream from outside the mind, deriving from God, or diabolical or planetary influence). On medieval dream lore, echoed by Pandarus in what follows, see Curry 1960: 195–232.

365–8 A sceptical view of the 'somnium coeleste' (dream with a supernatural cause); the *Roman de la Rose* is non-committal on 'whether God sends revelations through such visions or the malign spirits do so' (18509–12).

372 On 'impressiouns', see *Squire's Tale*, V.371–2, and *House of Fame*, 36–40: 'Or that the cruel lyf unsofte | Which these ilke lovers leden | That hopen over-muche or dreden, | That purely her impressions | Causeth hem avisions'. Cf. also *Parliament of Fowls*, 99–105.

376 *tymes of the yer*: On variation of dreams with the seasons, see Vincent of Beauvais, *Speculum naturale*, 26.63: 'Dreams are diversified by the position of the body and in accordance with the seasons; in spring and autumn they are particularly confused, disordered and false' (Curry 1960: 211).

380 *augurye of thise fowles*: Cf. the condemnation in the *Parson's Tale*: 'What seye we of hem that bileeven on divynailes [divinations], as by flight or by noyse of briddes ... or by sort, by nigromancie, by dremes ... Certes, al this thyng is deffended [forbidden] by God and by hooly chirche. For which they been acursed' (X.605–6).

398 *or*] H3 H4 Ph R; *oure* other MSS.

403 *Sarpedoun*: King of Licia, kinsman of Priam (cf. *Troie*, 6685–90); Sarpedon took part in the fatal battle when Antenor was captured (*TC* 4.52).

412 *wene*] Cp+; *seyn* other MSS. Cf. *Filostrato*, 5.35: 'diria l'uom' (people will say).

425 *nevere fowel so fayn of May*: A commonplace; cf. Whiting B292, F561, F566; *Romaunt*, 71–7; and also *Knight's Tale*, I.2437, *Shipman's Tale*, VII.51, *Canon's Yeoman's Tale*, VIII.1342–3.

436 *largesse*] *prowesse* Cp+ (and S1 Th).

445 Cf. 4.1695–6.

460 From *Filostrato*, 5.43, but a courtly commonplace; in the *Roman de la Rose* Love tells the Lover: ' "With this keye heere | Thyn herte to me now wole I shette" ' (*Romaunt*, 2090–91). Cf. also Chaucer's *Anelida and Arcite*, 323–4.

462 *melodie*: Arcite, in his lover's melancholy, cannot hear music without tears (*Knight's Tale*, I.1367–8).

469 *his howve . . . to glaze*: To make him a better hood or helmet of glass, i.e. to delude by offering delusive protection. Cf. Antigone's reference to a head of glass (2.867–8); also Whiting H624.

485 Proverbial (Whiting F201).

504–5 Troilus's bursting into song here is not in *Filostrato* (5.48). With *Ye, haselwode!*, cf. *TC* 3.890, 5.1174; Pandarus expresses exasperation. There are several references in English lyric and romance which associate love, the singing of birds and the hazel tree; cf. 'Somer is comen with love to toune, | With blostme [blossom] and with brides roune [bird-song], | The note [nut] of hasel springeth' (Brown 1932: 101). The political poem *Friar Daw's Reply*, rebutting Wycliffite attacks on the mendicant orders, contains the rejoinder that, as far as paradise or the bliss of heaven are concerned, 'thou maist of hasilwode singe', which may suggest activity both futile and to do with love (Wentersdorf 1992: 305–6).

507 For the association of cold and unhappiness in this final book, see 5.535, 552, 1102, 1342, 1659, 1747.

509 *pleyde*] H2 H3 H4 Cx; *seyde* other MSS.

523 *palais*: Boccaccio calls Criseida's home a 'casa' (house: 5.50). See also *TC* 2.76, 1094.

540–53 O *paleys desolat . . .*: Troilus's address to the beloved's house expands on *Filostrato* (5.53) in the tradition of the 'paraclausithy-ron' (apostrophe at the door), of which there are many classical examples (Bloomfield 1972). In Robert Holcot's *Commentary on*

Wisdom, Lectio 17, a poet addresses a deserted palace, lamenting its present emptiness as a token of the transitoriness of human life (Smalley 1960: 169–70).

543 *queynt*: Past participle of 'quenchen', which (Adams 1963) may be a bawdy pun (cf. *Miller's Tale*, I.3276: 'And prively he caughte hire by the queynte').

545 *oughtestow to falle*: Cf. the destruction of Sheen Palace by Richard II after the death of his wife, Anne of Bohemia (Mathew 1968: 34; Saul 1997: 456).

549 Possibly with sexual innuendo; cf. Pandarus's remark 'Wel in the ryng than is the ruby set' (2.585).

551–3 These lines are not in *Filostrato*. Cf. Love's account of the lover's life, including watching outside the lady's house and 'Loke if the gate be unspered' (*Romaunt*, 2656); the lover should also 'for the love of that high sanctuary . . . kiss the door' (*Roman de la Rose*, 2536–8), making sure that no one sees him.

561–81 From *Filostrato*, 5.54–5, itself recalling Boccaccio's proem ('How often have my eyes, to ease their pain, turned aside from gazing at the temples, arcades, squares and other places where they eagerly sought, and sometimes joyfully found, your likeness'), and perhaps Petrarch's Sonnet 112. See also *Filocolo*, 1.120, 263, and cf. Song of Songs 3:2; Lamentations 1:1 (cited in the *Filostrato* proem); Virgil, *Aeneid*, 4.68–9; *Roman d'Eneas*, 1393ff. (Salverda de Grave 1925–9). Ovid's *Remedia Amoris* (725–58) warns: 'Avoid places that know the secret of your unions; they hold the seeds of sorrow. "Here was she, here she lay; in that chamber did we sleep; here did she grant me wanton joys at night." Love recalled to mind is stung to life, and the wound is torn anew . . . Beware of spots that once were all too pleasant!' (Besserman 1990).

565 *last my lady*] *myn owen(e lady* Cp+ (and S1 Th).

565–81 The remembered haughtiness and changeable moods of Boccaccio's Criseida (*Filostrato*, 5.55) are replaced by memories of Criseyde's dancing and singing.

591–3 Cf. the Lover's declared intent to die and live in Love's law (*Roman de la Rose*, 10367–8).

601 Perhaps recalling Dante, *Inferno*, 30.1–2: 'Nel tempo che Iunone era crucciata | per Semelè contra'l sangue tebano' (In the time when, because of Semele, Juno was enraged against the blood of Thebes). Juno's enmity to Thebes arose from the affairs of Jove, her husband, with the Theban women Semele and Alcmena (cf.

Statius, *Thebaid*, 1.250–82; *Knight's Tale*, I.1329–31; *Anelida and Arcite*, 50–54; *TC* 3.1428 and 4.1538–40).

638–44 *Canticus Troili*: replacing Troiolo's five-stanza song (*Filostrato*, 5.62–6), itself derived from a canzone by Cino da Pistoia. Perhaps Chaucer misread 'disii porto di morte' (I carry desires of death) in *Filostrato*, 5.62, or recalled Troiolo addressing Criseida as 'bright star that shows me the way to a haven of bliss' (4.143), but imagery of navigation and of light and darkness is recurrent in *TC* (see notes to 1.175, 400–420, 606; and for a general resemblance to Petrarch's Sonnet 189, see Stillinger 1992: 165–89).

644 *Caribdis*: A whirlpool opposite Scylla's rock; Scylla and Charybdis lie between Italy and Sicily (see Virgil, *Aeneid*, 3.420; Ovid, *Metamorphoses*, 14.75). Cf. Reason's attack on love in the *Roman de la Rose*: 'It is Karibdous perilous' (*Romaunt*, 4713).

652–8 Cf. 4.1590–96. Criseyde left Troy when the moon was in Aries, and the sun in Leo (4.32). The moon was thus in its last quarter phase; when passed beyond Leo, the 'hornes newe' of its crescent would appear.

655 *Latona*: Mother of Diana (and perhaps here confused by Chaucer with the moon). For the moon as 'Latonia', see Virgil, *Aeneid*, 9.405, 11.534; Ovid, *Metamorphoses*, 1.696, 8.394. Cx and Th emend to 'Lucyna'.

659–62 Troilus imagines that days and nights have been lengthened by a change in the sun's orbit of the earth.

664 *Phethon*: Allowed by his father, the sun, to drive his chariot for a day, Phaeton lost control and was killed by Jove's thunderbolt (see Chaucer's account in *House of Fame*, 940–56, following Ovid, *Metamorphoses*, 2.31–328, to which H4's marginal gloss refers: 'pheton / filius solis methamorphoseos .2.o').

671 *this eyr*: For the motif of feeling the wind softer from where the beloved is, cf. *Filostrato*, 5.70, and proem; also Boccaccio's *Filocolo*, 1.120, and *Teseida*, 4.32.

681 *the nynthe nyght*: The time structure of *TC* Book 5 is altered from *Filostrato*: the first ten days of Troilus's waiting have been adapted from Part 5 of *Filostrato*; but Chaucer moves Diomede's visit to Criseyde from the fourth to the tenth day (842–3), and then anticipates the process of Criseyde's future change of heart (1023–99) while denying certain knowledge of its duration (1086–92), before returning to Troilus on the ninth night (1103). After the tenth day, time is passed over more summarily (1205–6, 1233) until two months have passed (1348–51); thereafter

unspecified periods of time pass (1538, 1576, 1758; cf. 1619–20), and events occur on unspecified days (1553, 1587, 1646).

687 *Upon that other syde* . . .: With this transition Boccaccio opens Part 6 of *Filostrato*, but Chaucer, making no division, here begins to fashion a single fifth book from Parts 5–8 of *Filostrato*, and much expands his narrative of events in *Filostrato*, Part 6 (Criseyde in the Greek camp). Gg has large capitals at 5.687, 1100 and 1541 (as well as at other points), and these three instances correspond to the openings of Parts 6, 7 and 8 in *Filostrato*. This is only part of a much larger pattern of correspondences (probably more than may be explained as coincidental) between occurrences of the summary prose 'arguments' which subdivide the narrative in *Filostrato* and the various division markers, marginal annotations, large capitals and spacings found in some *TC* MSS (see A Table of Parallels and Hardman 1995).

689–707 This speech is expanded from *Filostrato*, 6.1, allowing Criseyde to admit her mistaken judgement and express her fears.

701–6 Cf. Ovid, *Heroides*, 3.17–20 (Briseis writing to Achilles): 'I've often wished to elude my guards and return to you; but the enemy was there, to seize upon a timid girl. If I'd gone far, I feared I'd be taken captive in the night and handed over as a gift to one of Priam's daughters-in-law.'

726 *nedede*] Cl; *nedith* H3; *nede* S2; *neded* other MSS. *no*] *none* Cp A Gg; *non* J H1; *nat no* R. Cf. Chaucer's *Complaint to his Lady*: 'Ther nedeth me no care for to borwe' (10).

732 *galle*: Proverbially bitter; see 4.1137, and cf. 1.384–5n.

741–2 Proverbial (Whiting L168 and C51; Hassell M105); cf. *Knight's Tale*, I.2759–60.

744 *Prudence*: Cf. *Purgatorio*, 29.130–32, interpreted by early commentators on Dante as the three-eyed Prudence that regards past, present and future, and represented with three eyes in Ambrogio Lorenzetti's frescoes in the Palazzo Pubblico in Siena. (On illustrations of the three-eyed Prudence in Dante manuscripts, see Matthews 1976, 1981.) For the tripartite nature of Prudence, see Cicero, *De inventione*, 2.53; Aquinas, *Summa theologica*, 1–2.57.6; Dante, *Convivio*, 4.27.5.

748 *future*: Cf. *Boece*, 5.pr.6.19–20, where Chaucer is apparently first in using the word in English (*MED*, s.v. *futur(e* adj., (a)).

757–9 Proverbial (Whiting W629).

763 On 'suffisaunce', see *Boece*, 3.pr.2.90–94, pr.3.41–55, 96–100, pr.9.6–9. Cf. also *TC* 3.1309.

766   *er fully monthes two*: The time span is not specified here in *Filostrato*, (6.8), but said to be 'soon . . . in short time'.

777   *To fisshen hire*: The association of love with fishing is traditional in both religious (Matthew 4:19) and amatory contexts: see Ovid, *Ars Amatoria*, 1.393–4 ('Let the fish be held that is wounded from seizing the hook; once you assail her, press the attack . . .'), and Andreas Capellanus, *De amore*, 1.3 ('Love gets its name, *amor*, from the word for hook, *amus*, which means "to capture" or "to be captured", for he who is in love is captured in the chains of desire and wishes to capture someone else with his hook. Just as a skilful fisherman tries to attract fishes by his bait, and to capture them on his crooked hook, so a man who is a captive of love tries to attract another person by his allurements and exerts all his efforts': Walsh 1982). Cf. Isidore of Seville, *Etymologiae* (Lindsay 1911: vol.1, x.i.5). See also Chaucer's *Complaint of Mars*, 236–44.

784   'Nothing ventured, nothing gained': proverbial (Whiting N146); Criseyde has already used the same proverb (2.807–8).

790   *wise folk in bookes*: Not identified, but cf. Ovid, *Ars amatoria*, 1.361–2 ('When hearts are glad and not bound fast with grief, they lie open – then Love steals in with alluring art').

799–840 Although Dares, Benoît and Guido all provide a series of descriptions of the chief figures of the Trojan War, including Diomede, Briseis and Troilus, Chaucer's 'portraits' here (which thus conform to a convention of the main Troy narratives) are based on *Ylias* (itself based on Dares); Joseph's descriptions were excerpted and circulated separately, and some MSS of Guido's *Historia* contain illustrations of the characters (Buchthal 1971: plates 46–7; Gompf 1970: 51–5; Root 1917). Lines from *Ylias* occur as glosses in Gg and J, possibly deriving from the poem's composition process.

799–805 For the portrait of Diomede, see *Ylias*, 4.124–7: 'Voce ferox, animo preceps, fervente cerebro | Audentique ira validos quadratur in artus | Titides plenisque meretur Tidea factis, | Sic animo, sic ore fero, sic fulminat armis' (His voice was fierce, his temper violent. His brains boiled and his rage was daring; his limbs were massive and he stood four-square. His mighty deeds made him the worthy son of his father, Tydeus – such were the lightning bolts leaping from his spirit, his savage voice, and his arms; Roberts 1970: 43).

799   *as bokes us declare*: Frequent references to unnamed sources mark Chaucer's borrowings in Book 5 from the medieval traditional

account of the Trojan War, including Joseph of Exeter and Benoît's *Troie*; see *TC* 5.834, 1037, 1044, 1051, 1088–9, 1094, 1562, 1753. Cf. also 5.1459, 1478, 1533.

804 *of tonge large*: Boccaccio calls Diomede eloquent (*Filostrato*, 6.33); cf. Virgil's description of Drances in *Aeneid*, 11.338: 'largus opum et lingua melior' (lavish of wealth and even more of tongue; Frost 1979).

805 *heir ... of Calydoigne and Arge*: See 5.932–4 (from *Filostrato*, 6.24). In *Ylias* (4.349) Diomede is 'Calidonius heros' (hero of Calidon), but the marginal gloss in J has 'heres' (heir), and the *TC* line may derive from such a misreading.

806–26 For Criseyde's portrait, cf. *Troie*, 5275–88; *Historia*, p. 85; and *Ylias*, 4.156–62:

> In medium librata statum Briseis heriles
> Promit in affectum vultus. Nodatur in equos
> Flavicies crinita sinus, umbreque minoris
> Delicias oculus iunctos suspendit in arcus.
> Diviciis forme certant insignia morum,
> Sobria simplicitas, comis pudor, arida numquam
> Poscenti pietas et fandi gracia lenis.

(Briseis was of medium height, and displayed a noble countenance. Her golden hair was plaited into coils of equal length. Her eye suspends in a joined arch the delights of a lesser shade. The riches of her beauty were rivalled only by the excellence of her character – sober simplicity, courteous modesty, never-failing compassion, and a kindly and gentle manner of speech; Roberts 1970: 43.)

806 *mene ... of hire stature*: This accords with Dares (*De excidio*, ch. 13), Benoît, 'Ne fu petite ne trop grant' (neither short nor tall; *Troie*, 5276) and Guido, 'nec longa nec brevis' (neither tall nor short; *Historia*, p. 85), although Boccaccio, as followed by Chaucer earlier, implied Criseida was tall (*TC* 1.281; cf. *Filostrato*, 1.27).

809–12 Cf. the earlier description of the widowed Criseyde with her 'barbe' (2.110).

813 *browes joyneden yfeere*: Joined eyebrows are considered a blemish by Benoît and Guido (*Troie*, 5279–80; *Historia*, p. 85), although a sign of beauty in the ancient world. Medieval physiognomic treatises held joined brows to signify a range of undesirable characteristics, including vanity, cruelty, envy (Hanson 1971:

285–6); they are a sign of femininity and fickleness in Albertus Magnus, *Quaestiones super De Animalibus*, I.qu.26: 'And if [the brows] are linear, over their extent joining into a line, they are signs of humidity, because the humid easily receives all impression, and consequently they are signs of womanliness and instability (*flexibilitatis*)' (Burnley 1982b: 38; 1998: 91–2).

817 Cf. Beatrice's remark in Dante, *Paradiso*, 18.21: 'For not only in my eyes is Paradise'.

819 *Strof love in hire*: Probably deriving from a misreading of 'morum' (of good character) as 'amorum' (of loves) in *Ylias* (a misreading found in J's gloss).

825 *slydynge of corage*: Cf. Benoît: 'mais sis corages li chanjot' (but her purpose wavered in her; 5286), and Guido: 'animi constantiam non servasset' (she had not maintained constancy of mind; *Historia*, p. 85); see also *Boece*, 1.m.5.34–5: 'Why suffrestow that slydynge Fortune turneth so grete enterchaungynges of thynges?'

826 *hire age*: According to Dictys Cretensis, Briseida was twenty-one when the abduction of Helen occurred (Griffin 1907: 43), but Dares and his Latin successors do not mention her age.

827–40 For Troilus's portrait, cf. Benoît, *Troie*, 5393–446; Guido, *Historia*, p. 86; and *Ylias*, 4.61–4: 'Troilus in spacium surgentes explicat artus, | Mente Gigas, etate puer nullique secundus | Audendo virtutis opus, mixtoque vigore | Gratior illustres insignit gloria vultus' (Troilus was broad and tall. In spirit he was a giant, but in age he was a boy. He was second to none in venturing upon brave deeds. Pride graced his noble features, more pleasing because it was blended with manly vigour; Roberts 1970: 41).

830 *hardy as lyoun*: Proverbial (Whiting L314; cf. *TC* 1.1074).

831 *Trewe as stiel*: Proverbial (Whiting S709).

842 *tenthe day*: This meeting occurs on the fourth day in *Filostrato* (6.9); at *TC* 5.1103 Chaucer's narrative returns to the ninth night.

852 Spices were taken with wine, but 'spices' could also mean 'spiced cakes', as apparently in the *Squire's Tale*, V.291–4.

872 *O lady myn*: Omitting Diomede's address to Criseida as 'young lady' (*Filostrato*, 6.14).

892 *Manes*: Gods of the underworld; in antiquity, sometimes also meaning punishments inflicted in the lower world, perhaps reflected here in 'that goddes ben of peyne', and possibly influenced by scholiasts' glosses to Statius, *Thebaid* (Clogan 1964: 610–11). Gower describes Manes as gods of the dead (*Confessio amantis*, 5.1361–4). In *Filostrato*, 6.16, Greek revenge will be an

example to the living and the dead in hell; in *TC* that revenge will frighten even the deities of hell.

924   *lord*] Cp+ (and S1 Th); *kyng* other MSS. Cf. *Filostrato*, 6.22: 're' (king).

932   *Tideus*: King of Calydon; see 5.1485–1510n., 1501n., and *Thebaid*, 7.538–59.

938   *Polymytes*: For Polynices, see 5.1488.

971   *Orkades and Inde*: The western and eastern limits of the known world, i.e. the furthest points.

974–8   Cf. 2.468–9.

977   *Pallas*: Protectress of Troy; Criseyde invoked her before (2.425).

991–2   *thanne*] Cl Gg H4 R S2; *thenne* A; *than* other MSS; Cp Ph omit. *nevere yit I*] H4 Ph Cx; *I nevere yit* J; *nevere yit ne* Gg; *I nevere* R; *I nevere er(e* Cp+; *never ere I* S1.

994   Cf. the proverb 'sapienti pauca' (a few words to the wise suffice), of which all recorded English instances postdate Chaucer (Whiting W588). Criseyde's concluding lines (995–1008) have no equivalent in *Filostrato*.

1000–1004   Cf. Benoît, *Troie*, 13674–8 ('I have no intention nor desire to love you or anyone else at present, but be assured that if I decided to do so, I should hold no one dearer than you'), and Guido, *Historia*, p. 164 ('the offers of your love I at present neither repudiate nor admit').

1009–99   Chaucer replaces the conclusion of *Filostrato*, Part 6, in which Diomede is encouraged by Criseida's reply (32), Diomede's person is described (33), and Criseida's devotion to Troiolo is said to cool (34). Chaucer makes selective use of Benoît's *Troie* before returning to follow *Filostrato* at 5.1100.

1010–11   Perhaps recalling the urgent pleas of Benoît's Diomede at the end of the ride from Troy; cf. *Troie*, 13706–8, 15053–6.

1013   *Hire glove he took*: In Benoît, *Troie* (13709–11), and Guido, *Historia* (p. 165), Diomede takes the glove at the end of the ride escorting Briseida from Troy.

1016–20   Venus as an evening star follows the sun in setting, so showing where the sun has gone down. As moon and sun are both in Leo (4.31–2), the moon is not visible, and the stars of the zodiac (*Signifer*) would show more brightly. Criseyde promised (4.1590–94) to return before the moon passed out of Leo. (If Criseyde's promise to return in ten days may be dated as if made on 3 May 1388 – see 4.1591–2n., 5.652–8n. – it may be noted that the moon left Leo at about 6.00 p.m. on 13 May 1388, when the exaltation of Venus would have been found precisely at lower mid-heaven; North 1988: 394.)

1023-9 Cf. *Filostrato*, 6.33-4, where Criseida is chiefly interested by Diomede's personal attractions ('He was tall and handsome … and spoke well').

1026-7 In Benoît's *Troie* (20287-8) Briseida excused to herself the transfer of her affections to Diomede on the grounds that she was without friends.

1037-43 Chaucer here refers to some incidents in the *Roman de Troie*, omitted from *Filostrato*: after Diomede has been unhorsed Briseida returns to him the horse he had earlier won from Troilus and presented to her (15079-186); and Briseida gives Diomede her silk sleeve as a pennon (15176-9). The lady's sleeve as a love-token recurs in romance (e.g. *Octavian*, 1027-32: Mills 1973), and the heroes of such romances as *William of Palerne* and *Ipomadon* send to their ladies presents of the horses captured in their various battles (Windeatt 1988: 134). Note the frequent acknowledgement of the 'storie(s)' in this passage: 5.1044, 1051, 1094.

1040-41 This is the brooch later seen by Troilus on a garment snatched from Diomede in battle in both *Filostrato* (8.8-10) and *TC* (5.1661); possibly the brooch presented at *TC* 3.1370-72.

1044-50 Cf. Benoît's *Troie*, 20202-28: Briseida weeps over Diomede's serious wound, visits him often, and henceforth her heart is wholly inclined towards him. Guido only briefly reports her change, omitting her tears (*Historia*, p. 198).

1051-7 Benoît represents Briseida as knowing that she is doing wrong in deserting Troilus (*Troie*, 20229-36), and regretting her betrayal of the best lover a woman might have (20242-4, 20264-6).

1054-85 Criseyde's soliloquy (not present in *Filostrato* or Guido's *Historia*) is drawn selectively from Briseida's long soliloquy of regret when she forsakes Troilus for Diomede (*Troie*, 20238-340).

1058-60 Cf. Benoît's Briseida: 'Nothing good will ever be written or sung about me' (*Troie*, 20238-9); also Helen of Troy's concern for her reputation in Ovid, *Heroides*, 17.207ff. By trying to preserve her good name, Criseyde has not only lost that name but will become a by-word for shame. Chaucer's compassionate interpretation of Criseyde stands apart from a tradition of anti-feminist critique of her character already present in Benoît, but especially in Guido, and subsequently compounded in England by the early printing (from Thynne's edition of 1532 onwards) of *TC*, followed by Henryson's *Testament of Cresseid*, in editions of Chaucer's works (Rollins 1917; Mieszkowski 1971; Donaldson 1979; Benson 1989; Windeatt 1992: 360–82).

1062 *my belle shal be ronge*: Proverbial (Whiting B233).

1063–6 Benoît's Briseida foresees that the women of Troy will talk of the shame she has brought them (*Troie*, 20257–60) and later finds herself hated by women (20678–82).

1067–71 Cf. Benoît's Briseida: 'What good would it do me to repent? I shall never be able to make amends by such means. Let me then be true to this man who is a most valiant and excellent knight' (*Troie*, 20275–8). Cf. also Helen of Troy in Ovid, *Heroides*, 17.41–2, 47.

1072–85 Expanded from Briseida's parting tribute and farewell to Troilus: 'May God grant Troilus happiness! Since I may no longer cherish him, nor he me, I shall submit and surrender myself to Diomede' (*Troie*, 20317–20). Chaucer omits Briseida's self-extenuation, in which she says she would never have wavered if she had not been so isolated in the Greek camp, and could have held out even to death, if only she had had some comfort from Troy. If she had not taken mercy on herself, she would now be dead (20283–96).

1078 *she brast anon to wepe*: In her soliloquy Briseida declares that her eyes have often been filled with tears (*Troie*, 20316–17).

1085 *al shal passe*: Proverbial (Whiting T99).

1086–92 *But trewely ... non auctour telleth it ...* : Actually, in Benoît's account of events, the period between Briseida's arrival in the camp and her acceptance of Diomede can hardly be less than two years. Briseida arrives before the eighth battle, which lasts a month (14516), followed by a truce of six months (15187) until the ninth battle, which is followed by one month's truce (15221). The eleventh battle occurs a year after Hector's death in the tenth (17489). There is a truce of two months between the thirteenth and fourteenth battles (19384), and of one week between the fourteenth and fifteenth (20060), after which Briseida succumbs.

1095 *punysshed*] *publysshed* R H2 Ph Cx Th.

1100 Chaucer here returns to drawing upon *Filostrato* (at 7.1). Boccaccio's Part 7 (Troiolo waiting on the tenth day and later) is over three times as long as his Part 6 (Criseida in the Greek camp), but Chaucer so expands his equivalent of Part 6 (*TC* 5.687–1099) and so reduces his equivalent of Part 7 (*TC* 1100–1540) as to divide the narrative more equally between his Criseyde and Troilus.

1107 *laurer-crowned Phebus*: Cf. Ovid, *Ars amatoria*, 3.389: 'laurigero ... Phoebo' (laurel-adorned Phoebus). H4 has a marginal gloss: 'laurigerus: laurer'.

1109 *the est se*: Chaucer may have thought the sea lay to the east of Troy, as in *Legend of Good Women*, 1425–6, itself deriving from Guido's *Historia*, p. 7.

1110 *Nysus doughter*: Scylla (gazing out from her city's walls) fell in love with its besieger Minos, to whom she betrayed the city, but was then betrayed by him. See Ovid, *Metamorphoses*, 8.6–151, and *Legend of Good Women*, 1902–21. She was changed into the bird 'ciris', which Chaucer perhaps found explained as 'lark' in a gloss, or in the *Ovide moralisé* (Meech 1931: 189).

1162 *fare-carte*: I.e. a cart for sending outside the manor, a rustic vehicle inappropriate for Criseyde to travel in, as the reading 'soory cart' in H2 and H4 evidently registers. Th has 'farre carte'.

1174 *haselwode ... joly Robyn*: In *Filostrato*, 7.10, Pandaro declares: 'This poor young fellow is waiting for a (cool) breeze from Etna!' (i.e. waiting in vain). On hazel wood, its possible erotic associations, and as an expression of a sense of futility, see 3.890n., 5.504–5; some French love lyrics and pastourelles are set in hazel woods (Wentersdorf 1992: 301–3). The term 'joly Robyn' was a generic name for a shepherd or rustic, as in pastoral plays or poems where Robin is an amorous, sportive figure, but often cuckolded in his love for the pretty shepherdess Marion: the pastourelle is a genre in which the joy of lovers seldom endures. However, 'joly Robyn' may refer here to Robin Hood (cf. 2.861n.). Perhaps Pandarus means something like: 'From (the) never-never land (of pastoral) will come all you're waiting for', or even: 'From the green wood of Robin Hood and his merry men ...'

1176 *snow of ferne yere*: With Pandarus's farewell, cf. the refrain 'Mais ou sont les neiges d'antan?' (But where are the snows of yesteryear?) in François Villon's 'Ballade des dames du temps jadis' (Mary 1970: 31–2). Cf. also *TC* 5.8–11.

1189–90 For the moon to pass beyond the sign of Leo would give Criseyde an extra day, see 4.1591–2n.

1233–74 Cp omits. Text based on J and Cl.

1238–41 In *Filostrato* Troiolo dreams that the boar tears out Criseida's heart with its tusks, to her apparent pleasure (7.23–4). Cf. Criseyde's dream (*TC* 2.925–31).

1240 *his*] Cl H4; *in armes* H2 H3 Ph Cx; *in hire armes* other MSS. In *Filostrato* Criseida is beneath the boar's feet ('sotto a' suoi pie': 7.24).

1244–54 In *Filostrato* here (7.27–8) Troiolo himself interprets the boar as signifying Diomede.

1266–7 Cf. *Boece*, 3.pr.5.68–70 ('And what pestilence is more myghty for to anoye a wyght than a famylier enemy?'); *Romaunt*, 3931–2 ('For he may best, in every cost, | Disceyve, that men tristen most'); for the proverb 'A familiar enemy is the worst', see Whiting E97.

1274 *myself I shende*: Troiolo's attempted suicide with a knife, frustrated by Pandaro, is here omitted (cf. *Filostrato*, 7.33–9).

1276–81 See Pandarus's earlier arguments against attributing significance to dreams (5.358–85 and n.). The deceptiveness of dreams was proverbial (Whiting D387); cf. a gloss to Pseudo-Cato: 'nam fallunt sompnia plures' (for dreams deceive most people; Hazelton 1960: 368).

1317–1421 *Litera Troili*: Much rewritten from the letter in *Filostrato* (7.52–75) – which is closely followed only in *TC* 5.1345–58 – and using some standard epistolary formulas found in French and fifteenth-century English letters (see Davis 1965), including: the respectful opening address (cf. 5.1317); a humble commendation of the writer to the recipient (1320–23); an expression of desire to hear of the recipient's welfare (1356–8), with a prayer for the continuation and increase of that welfare (1359–63); a deferential offer of news of the writer's welfare (1366–7) and of the writer's good health at the time of writing (1369). 'Chaucer's polite, graceful and conventional style [in 5.1317–1421 and 1590–1631] ... sets the tone for the vast number of amatory verse epistles which was to be written in England in the fifteenth century ... Chaucer's letter style closely resembles that of two verse epistles written by Deschamps to ladies of his acquaintance, *Balades* 1244 and 1245' (Norton-Smith 1974: 214–15).

1317 *Right fresshe flour*: This form of address, commonly beginning with 'right', an adjective of respect and appropriate noun, is standard in English letter-writing, here replacing Troiolo's address to Criseida as 'Giovane donna' (Youthful lady) in *Filostrato*.

1320–21 Cf. a letter of 1419 to the Duke of Clarence (cited in Davis 1965): 'in as humble wyse as any poure man best can or may ymagine and devise'. See also *TC* 4.1695–6.

1323–4 Common formulas in English letter-writing.

1335 *defaced*: Cf. Briseis writing to Achilles, in Ovid, *Heroides*, 3.3–4 ('whatever blots you see, her tears have made').

1345–6 *If any servant dorste ... compleyne*: From *Filostrato*, 7.54, possibly recalling Ovid, *Heroides*, 3.5–6 ('if it is right for me to utter brief complaint about my master and my beloved, of you I will utter brief complaint').

1348 *monthes tweyne*: In *Filostrato* (7.54) Criseida has stayed away forty days. (Assuming a date of 3 May for Criseyde's departure – 4.1590–96; 5.650–58 – Troilus's letter might be dated around 3 July 1388, according to North 1988: 396.)

1356–63 With Troilus's polite epistolary formulas, cf. Elizabeth Poynyngs, in *The Paston Letters*, writing to her mother, Agnes Paston, on 3 January 1459, 'evermore desiryng to here of your welfare and prosperite, the which I pray God to contynw and encresce to your hertes desyre' (Davis 1965: 236).

1366–8 Elizabeth Poynyngs continues to her mother: 'And yf it lyked youre gode moderhede to here of me and how I do . . .', while 'I kan namore' is another epistolary commonplace, occurring in an English letter of 1402 (Davis 1965: 236).

1369 *I was on-lyve*: Possibly playing on the conventional proffer of news about the writer's good health: cf. Margery Brews writing to John Paston III in 1477: 'I am not in good heele of body ner of herte, nor schall be tyll I here from yowe' (Davis 1965: 237), and a poem attributed to the Duke of Suffolk: 'And yf ye lyst have knowlech of my qwert [health], I am in hele – God thankyd mot he be – I As of body, but treuly not in hert, I Nor nought shal be to tyme I may you se' (Robbins 1955: 190).

1373–9 For the contraries and antitheses of love, see *Book of the Duchess*, 599–616, and *Romaunt*, 4703ff. (Reason speaks against love).

1413 *she*] J Gg H2 H3 H4 Ph R; *ye* other MSS.

1415–16 Cf. Ovid, *Heroides*, 4.1 ('with wishes for the well-being which she herself, unless you give it her, will ever lack').

1421 *Le vostre T.*: Troilus's signature reflects the strong influence of French epistolary conventions on English letter-writing, but is absent from all MSS except Cp, J and S1.

1424 *she wroot ayeyn*: Criseida does not reply immediately (*Filostrato*, 7.76); Chaucer invents the summary (*TC* 5.1424–28) of her reply.

1433 *Pipe in an ivy lef*: Also used of futile activity in *Knight's Tale*, I.1838, and proverbial after Chaucer (Whiting I72).

1434 *Thus goth the world*: Proverbial (Whiting W665; Hassell M163); see also *TC* 4.390, 5.1748.

1440 *no*] Gg H4 R Cx; other MSS omit.

1443 Chaucer here ceases to follow Boccaccio's Part 7, not drawing directly on *Filostrato* until the opening of its Part 8 (see *TC* 5.1541).

1450 *Sibille*: Like some other medieval writers, Chaucer evidently takes 'Sibille' (i.e. sibyl, prophetess) as another proper name for Cassandra, one of Priam's three daughters and traditionally the prophetess of disaster (cf. Ovid, *Heroides*, 5.113–25, 16.121–6; Benoît, *Troie*, 4143ff., 4881ff., 10417ff., 27183ff.). In *Filostrato* Troiolo has already interpreted his dream for himself and is overheard lamenting by Deiphebus, who sends his sisters and other ladies to console his brother for his unhappy love affair; Cassandra taunts Troiolo with Criseida's low birth, and an altercation ensues (7.77–106).

1459–84 *a fewe of olde stories* . . . : For the story of Meleager, see Ovid, *Metamorphoses*, 8.270–525. The maiden Atalanta (1473) comes to join the boar hunt, and as soon as he sees her Meleager is inflamed with love. See Boccaccio, *De genealogia deorum*, 9.15, 19; cf. also the *Ovide moralisé* (Witlieb 1970).

1480–81 *descended Tideus By ligne*: Boccaccio's *De genealogia deorum* (9.21) correctly states classical tradition that Tydeus was a half-brother of Meleager, but in *Filostrato* (7.27) Meleager is described as Diomede's grandfather. The mythographers' testimony was confusing: Meleager is described as ancestor of Tydeus in Lactantius Placidus's commentary on Statius, *Thebaid*, 1.463, while the First Vatican Mythographer describes Meleager as having been killed by his brother Tydeus, perhaps on the basis of *Thebaid*, 1.402–3 (Wetherbee 1984: 130).

1483 *Thorugh his moder*: Meleager's presentation of the boar's head to Atalanta starts a quarrel among the huntsmen and Meleager slays his two uncles, who have taken the head from Atalanta. His mother avenges her brothers on her son by burning the piece of wood, given her by the Fates, upon which Meleager's life depends.

1485–1510 Cassandra here summarizes the events of Statius's *Thebaid*; (H4 has the marginal gloss 'Stacius Thebaydos'). Polynices and Eteocles, sons of Oedipus, were to rule alternately over Thebes, but Eteocles expelled Polynices. King Adrastus of Argos came to the aid of Polynices, and with Tydeus, Amphiaraus, Capaneus, Hippomedon and Parthenopaeus, fought the war of the Seven against Thebes. All except Adrastus perished, and Creon, who took power in Thebes, refused burial of their bodies (see Chaucer's *Anelida and Arcite*, 50–70; *Knight's Tale*, I.931–

47). After 5.1498 all *TC* MSS except two (H4 and R) include a 12-line Latin 'argument' summarizing the 12-book *Thebaid*; for Cassandra's English summary, Chaucer draws on both this Latin argument and a series of fuller 12-line Latin arguments for each *Thebaid* book (Magoun 1955: 409–20), and on the *Thebaid* itself (Clogan 1967). As with the glosses from *Ylias* in some *TC* MSS (see 5.799–840n.), this Latin argument's inclusion in the text may derive from the poem's composition process rather than subsequent scribal commentary.

1492   *Hemonydes*: Maeon, son of Haemon; one of fifty warriors sent by Eteocles to waylay Tydeus, who single-handedly slew all except Maeon (*Thebaid*, 3).

1494   *prophecyes*: Possibly those of Maeon, Amphiaraus or Laius (*Thebaid*, 3.71–7; 3.640–45; 4.637–44). Cf. the 'praesagia' mentioned in line 8 of the Latin metrical argument to *Thebaid*, Book 3 (Magoun 1955: 413).

1497   *holy serpent*: Sent by Jove, it stings to death Archemorus, infant son of King Lycurgus, while his nurse Hypsipyle guides the Argive army to the river Langia (termed a 'welle' by Chaucer: *TC* 5.1497). Cf. *Thebaid*, 5.505–40; 'holy' may derive from 'sacro serpente' in the Latin argument to 5.10 (Magoun 1955: 414).

1498   *furies*: They incited the women of Lemnos to kill every male on the island except one.

1499   *Archymoris brennynge*: The cremation of Archemorus is described, along with the interment of the ashes and the funeral games, in *Thebaid*, 6; the *Roman de Thèbes* (2621–30) tells only of burying not cremation, and all but two *TC* MSS (D and Gg) read *burying* for *brennynge*.

1500   *Amphiorax*: For Amphiaraus's death, previously mentioned by Criseyde (2.104–5), see *Thebaid*, 6.794–823.

1501   *How Tideus was sleyn*: See Statius, *Thebaid*, 8.716ff. Tydeus's savage end, gloating over the severed head of the foe who had fatally wounded him, repels even Mars, god of war.

1502–3   *Ypomedoun*: For the drowning of Hippomedon, see Statius, *Thebaid*, 9.526ff.; for the death of Parthenopaeus, see *Thebaid*, 9.841ff. Hippomedon's drowning is unmentioned in the 12-line Latin argument to the *Thebaid*, but H2 contains the extra line 'Fervidus ypomedon timidique [i.e. tumidoque] in gurgite mersus' (raging Hippomedon immersed in the swollen torrent), taken from the 12-line argument to *Thebaid*, 9.

1504–5   *Capaneus*: Defiantly contemptuous of the gods and scornful of priests, oracles and prophecy, he is struck dead for his blasphemy by Jove's thunderbolt (see Statius, *Thebaid*, 3.611–18, 648–69; 9.550; 10.907–36). Gower includes him as an example of presumption (*Confessio amantis*, 1.1984–7).

1506–8 *eyther brother . . . slough other*: See Statius, *Thebaid*, 11.389–573.

1509 *Argyves*: Argia was the wife of Polynices; Chaucer apparently borrows the name for Criseyde's mother (see 4.762n.).

1510 *the town was brent*: The burning of Thebes is not described in Statius's *Thebaid*; Chaucer may recall the *Roman de Thèbes*, 10131–9, Boccaccio's *Teseida*, 2.81, or perhaps the reference to fire (actually the cremation of the dead) in the 12-line argument's last line.

1513–19 Chaucer's recasting of *Filostrato* here (see *TC* 5.1450n.) has omitted the occasion by which Deiphebus, and hence Troiolo's family, have already learned that his languishing is for love of Criseida.

1527 *Alceste*: The wife of Admetus, king of Pherae in Thessaly (see 1.664), Alcestis chose to die so that her husband might live. For her story, see Hyginus, *Fabulae*, 51; Boccaccio, *De genealogia deorum*, 13.1; Gower, *Confessio amantis*, 7.1917–43; *Legend of Good Women*, Prologue F 510ff. For the mythographers, Admetus is the human mind or spirit, subject to fear, and Alcestis is the spiritual courage to which he aspires (Wetherbee 1984: 142, citing Fulgentius, *Mitologiae*, 1.22, and the Vatican Mythographers, 1.92, 2.154, 3.13.3).

1541–5 Cf. *TC* 3.617–20, *Boece*, 4.pr.6.60–107, and Dante, *Inferno*, 7.78–82 ('He ordained a general minister and guide who should in due time change vain wealth from race to race and from one to another blood, beyond the prevention of human wits, so that one race rules and another languishes'). For the concept of 'translatio imperii' (transfer of empire) and its biblical and classical antecedents, see Curtius 1953: 28–9. With Hector's death, Part 8 of *Filostrato* begins.

1558 *aventaille*: A chainmail strip forming the lower part of the helmet and serving to protect the neck and upper chest (Blair 1958: 52–3).

1559 *Unwar of this*: Cf. Guido, *Historia*: '[Achilles] took a very strong lance, which Hector did not observe (*non aduertente Hectore*), and rushed upon him and wounded him mortally' (p. 175).

1577 *lik a pilgrym*: In Boccaccio's *Filocolo* (4.16) Florio also describes himself as a pilgrim, a not infrequent wartime disguise in both medieval literary and historical texts (for instances, see Magoun 1944, Whiting 1945).

1590–1631 *Litera Criseydis*: Boccaccio gives only a summary here of Criseida's replies: 'From her he had only fine words and large but unfulfilled promises' (*Filostrato*, 8.5). Chaucer invents Criseyde's letter, making some use of earlier letters between Troiolo and Criseida (2.96, 122, 126), omitted from *TC*, Book 2. Except for its closing line, Criseyde's letter is without the letter-writing formulas used in Troilus's letter (*TC* 5.1317–1421), although it conforms to the five-part structure outlined in the *artes dictandi* (medieval guides to composition): a combined *salutatio* and *benevolentiae captatio* (i.e. an attempt to gain the recipient's sympathy: *TC* 5.1590–96); a *narratio*, relating her attitudes (5.1597–1620); a *peticio*, asking Troilus for friendship and not to be displeased by brevity (5.1621–6); a second *benevolentiae captatio* using *sententiae* (proverbs) (5.1627–30); and a simple *conclusio* (5.1631). On the *artes dictandi*, see Camargo 1995, and for a medieval treatise on letter-writing, see Murphy 1971: 1–25; cf. also McKinnell 1979.

1592–6 Cf. the opening of Troiolo's first letter to Criseida: 'How can he who is placed in torment, in heavy sorrow, and in dreadful state, as I am for you, O lady, give salutation to anyone?' (*Filostrato*, 2.96).

1597–1600 Cf. Criseida's reply to Troiolo's first letter: 'I have received those pages covered with your writing in which I have read of your life in misery; and, as I hope for joy, I was not unmoved. And although they are adorned with tears, I have pondered them carefully' (*Filostrato*, 2.122).

1625–8 Cf. *Filostrato*, 2.126: 'of little value, as you can see, is the writing and art in this letter, which I would wish might give you more pleasure'.

1625 *on*] *an* Cp Cl H1; *in* D H4; *to* S2.

1631 *La vostre C.*: Only D H1 S1 S2 Th contain; other MSS omit.

1634 *kalendes of chaunge*: Possibly a word-play on a commercial term, since the first day of the month was the due date for payment of debts and interest (see *MED*, s.v. *calende(s* n. 2., and *Oxford English Dictionary* s.v. *calends* 3).

1640 *men shal the soothe se*: Proverbial, 'truth shall be seen', i.e. truth will reveal itself (Whiting S491).

1651 *cote-armure*: A garment embroidered with a heraldic device, often worn over armour; see *Knight's Tale*, I.1016–19, where heralds recognize Palamon and Arcite from their 'cote-armures'.

1653 *as telleth Lollius*: Chaucer is actually adapting *Filostrato* here; for Lollius, see *TC* 1.394n.

1661 *broch*: Unmentioned at the lovers' parting, but perhaps the brooch Criseyde had given Troilus (3.1370–72); her gift of the brooch to Diomede was recorded earlier (5.1040–41).

1705 *sydes blede*: For the bleeding sides (unmentioned in *Filostrato*, 8.16), cf. Diomede's wounding through the sides in Benoît's *Troie*, 20071–5; cf. also the duelling of Palamon and Arcite in *Knight's Tale*, I.2635: 'Out renneth blood on bothe hir sydes rede.'

1731–43 Pandarus's hatred of Criseyde, sorrow at her 'tresoun' (see 1.87–91n.), and prayer for her death, rewrite Pandaro's less vehement disapproval (*Filostrato*, 8.23–4): 'I shall not try to excuse this great wickedness of hers . . . Leave it to God . . . whom I earnestly pray to punish her in such a way that she will not be able again to commit a crime of this sort.'

1748 *Swich is this world*: Proverbial, 'thus goes the world' (Whiting W665); cf. 4.390; 5.1434.

1751–7 From *Filostrato*, 8.25 ('And Troiolo continually took part in battles, looking above all others for Diomede'), but in the 'olde bokes' of Benoît's *Troie* (19281–21189) and Guido's *Historia* (pp. 197–203) full accounts of these battles might be found.

1758–64 From *Filostrato*, 8.26; but an extended account of Troilus's exploits was available in *Troie*, 19955–21189. Little further use is made of *Filostrato*, although lines *TC* 1800–1806 correspond to Boccaccio's 8.27, and *TC* 1828–41 to 8.28–9. The final stanzas, 8.30–33, comment on young women ('forever fickle like a leaf in the wind') and advise: 'take pity on both Troiolo and yourselves . . . and pray to Love to set [Troiolo] in peace in that region where he dwells'. In the last ninth part of *Filostrato*, an envoy, Boccaccio sends the poem on its way to his lady.

1765–6 Recalling the opening line of Virgil's *Aeneid*: 'Arma virumque cano . . .' (cf. *House of Fame*, 143–4: 'I wol now synge, yif I kan, | The armes and also the man').

1771 *Dares*: Chaucer probably means Joseph of Exeter's *Frigii Daretis Ylias*, itself often referred to in the Middle Ages as 'Dares' (see 1.146; 5.799–840).

1777–8 *gladlier I wol write . . . good Alceste*: Perhaps foreshadowing Chaucer's *Legend of Good Women* in which, in its Prologue (F 332–40, 466–97), Chaucer represents himself as commanded to write by Alcestis in recompense to Love for translating the *Roman de la Rose* and writing *TC*. Penelope (who rejected suitors during

the long absence of her husband, Ulysses), together with Alcestis,
are traditional instances of womanly constancy; see *TC* 5.1527–
33; *Man of Law's Tale*, II.75; *Franklin's Tale*, V.1442–4; *Book
of the Duchess*, 1080–81; *Anelida and Arcite*, 79–82.

1786 *Go, litel bok*: A formula since classical times; cf. Ovid, *Tristia*,
1.1.1 ('Little book, you will go without me into the city'); also
Boccaccio's address to 'my little book' in the envoy to *Filocolo*,
2.376–8, and his description of *Filostrato* as a little book ('picci-
olo libro') in the proem.

tragedye: Greek tragedy was unknown in the medieval west, and
Aristotle's *Poetics* was available only through Hermann
Alemannus's translation of the version by Averroes (see Minnis
and Scott 1991: 277–307), but the Roman tragedies of Seneca
were studied. Uses of the term 'tragedy' by other late medieval
English writers (*MED*, s.v. *tragedi(e* n.) show widespread mis-
understanding; however, Chaucer had translated the definition
of tragedy as an abrupt change of fortune which Philosophy
represents Fortune as giving to Boethius in *De consolatione*:
'What other thynge bywaylen the cryinges of tragedyes but oonly
the dedes of Fortune, that with an unwar strook overturneth the
realmes of greet nobleye? (*Glose. Tragedye is to seyn a dite of a
prosperite for a tyme, that endeth in wrecchidnesse)*' (*Boece*,
2.pr.2.67–72). Chaucer's gloss here omits the connection made
in some medieval commentary on Boethius between tragic misfor-
tune and punishment of moral failing in the unfortunate person:
Pseudo-Aquinas (a fourteenth-century commentary on Boethius,
misattributed to Thomas Aquinas) glosses tragedy as 'a poem
that reprehends vices, which begins in prosperity and ends in
adversity', and Trevet glosses as 'a poem about great crimes or
iniquities, beginning in prosperity and ending in adversity' (Kelly
1993: 128–9). Implicit in Chaucer's translated definition is the
notion that tragedy is an unexpected change of fortune suffered
by protagonists (like Boethius) whose high social or political
estate is part of their prosperity. Chaucer also knew the 'Fall of
Princes' tradition from the examples in the *Roman de la Rose* and
Boccaccio's *De casibus virorum illustrium* (The Falls of Illustrious
Men) and *De claris mulieribus* (Concerning Famous Women).
These influenced his *Monk's Tale* with its definition of tragedy
as a fall (*Monk's Prologue*, VII.1973–7), but also its closing
implication of a link between Fortune's overthrow and pride:
'Tragediës noon oother maner thyng | Ne kan in syngyng crie ne
biwaille | But that Fortune alwey wole assaille | With unwar

strook the regnes that been proude' (VII.2761–4). Yet tragedy was also associated with love, and given the limited medieval understanding of ancient tragedy as theatre and drama, tragedy could be understood as a narrative form. In *Inferno* (20.113) Dante has Virgil refer to his *Aeneid* as a tragedy, and in *De vulgari eloquentia* (2.4) the most fitting subjects for tragic style are the highest: the security of nations, love and virtue. In his *Tristia* (2.381–4, 407–8) Ovid had explicitly made a link between the genre of tragedy and the topic of love ('Every kind of writing is surpassed in seriousness by tragedy, but this also constantly deals with the theme of love'; cf. Walther 19819a), as too in the stories of unfortunate love in his *Heroides* and *Metamorphoses*. Romances and reworkings of classical stories witness to the medieval popularity of various tales of unfortunate love: a group of unfortunate lovers – including Paris and Helen, Tristan and Iseult, and Troilus – is depicted together in *The Parliament of Fowls* (288–94), and in the *Decameron* the fourth day, devoted to tales of love that end unhappily, is under the governance of the character Filostrato ('the one overwhelmed by love'), whose name Boccaccio uses as the epithet of his Troiolo and hence the title of *Filostrato*, Chaucer's main source for *TC*. (See Kelly 1993, 1997.)

1788 *comedye*: Chaucer may have known definitions of comedy as the opposite of tragedy: Vincent of Beauvais declares 'Comedy is poetry changing a sad beginning to a joyful end; but tragedy is poetry with a joyful beginning that comes to a sad end', and defines comedy as dealing with private persons and joyful matters, where tragedy deals with public affairs, histories of kings, and sorrowful matters (*Speculum doctrinale*, 3.109–10); cf. also Osbern of Gloucester's dictionary: 'Tragedy is a mournful poem, because it begins in joy and ends in sadness; comedy is its contrary, because it begins in sadness and ends in joy' (see Kelly 1997: 81–2).

1789 *no makyng thow n'envie*: Prologues and epilogues deprecating envy are a conventional device; see Chaucer's *Treatise on the Astrolabe*, Prologue, 64 ('And with this swerd shal I sleen envie').

1791 *kis the steppes*: For the kissing of footprints, see the close of Statius's *Thebaid*, 12.816–17 ('nor try to match the divine *Aeneid*, but follow from afar and evermore worship its footprints [vestigia]').

      pace] Cl H4 Ph Th (Cl corrected); *space* other MSS.

1792 For the list of poets, cf. Boccaccio's envoy to *Filocolo* (2.376–8) which mentions Virgil, Lucan, Statius, Ovid and Dante; see also *Inferno*, 4.88–90 (Dante, guided by Virgil, meets Homer, Horace, Ovid and Lucan), and *House of Fame*, 1456–1512. In his commentary (*c.* 1314–17) on Seneca's tragedies, Trevet notes: 'So, Virgil in his *Aeneid*, Lucan, and Ovid in the *Metamorphoses* can be called tragic poets, because their subject-matter was that of tragedy: the misfortunes of kings and great men, and affairs of state. But yet this description does not exactly fit their work' (Minnis and Scott 1991: 344).

1793–6 As sources of manuscript corruption Chaucer probably refers to dialectical variation in English and to neglect of the final *-e* upon which the metre of many *TC* lines depends. Criticism of scribes was conventional; see Chaucer's little poem *Chaucers Wordes unto Adam, His Owne Scriveyn*:

> Adam scriveyn, if ever it thee bifalle
> *Boece* or *Troylus* for to wryten newe,
> Under thy long lokkes thou most have the scalle [scaly
>   scalp disease],
> But [unless] after my makyng thow wryte more trewe;
> So ofte adaye I mot thy werk renewe,
> It to correcte and eke to rubbe and scrape [erase],
> And al is thorugh thy negligence and rape [haste].

1795 I] *I to* Cp H1 H2 H4 S2 Th; *thi* A; *to* J H3 Ph Cx.
1797 *red . . . or elles songe*: A formula; see 4.799; 5.1059.
1798 *God I*] *god* Cp A Cl J; *I god* R; *god I the* H2.
1800–1801 *The wrath . . . Of Troilus*: Possibly echoing the opening of Homer's *Iliad* ('Achilles' wrath . . . O heavenly goddess, sing!'), which Chaucer perhaps knew from Latin *florilegia* (Boitani 1989: 209).
1807–27 The absence of these stanzas from certain *TC* MSS (see A Note on the Text) may reflect scribal editing and conflation. Only one of the Ph+ MSS here (Ph) omits the passage, although it has been included on an inset leaf. In this omission Ph is joined by H2 and H4, which at this point in the text normally agree with the R+ group. Not in *Filostrato*, the *TC* stanzas have been borrowed from Boccaccio's description of the ascent of Arcita's soul in *Teseida*, 11.1–3 (an episode omitted from the *Knight's Tale*):

Finito Arcita colei nominando
la qual nel mondo più che altro amava,
l'anima leve se ne gì volando
ver la concavità del cielo ottava,
degli elementi i convessi lasciando;
quivi le stelle ratiche ammirava,
l'ordine loro e la somma bellezza,
suoni ascoltando pien d'ogni dolcezza.

Quindi si volse in giù a rimirare
le cose abandonate, e vide il poco
globo terreno, a cui intorno il mare
girava e l'aere e di sopra il foco,
e ogni cosa da nulla stimare
a rispetto del ciel; ma poi al loco
là dove aveva il suo corpo lasciato
gli occhi fermò alquanto rivoltato;

e seco rise de' pianti dolenti
della turba lernea, la vanitate
forte dannando dell'umane genti,
li quai, da tenebrosa cechitate
mattamente oscurati nelle menti,
seguon del mondo la falsa biltate,
lasciando il cielo; e quindi se ne gio
nel loco che Mercurio li sortio.

(When Arcita had finished naming her whom he loved more than
any other in the world, his weightless spirit went soaring up
towards the concavity of the eighth sphere, leaving behind the
convexes of the elements. There he gazed in wonder at the wander-
ing stars, their order and supreme beauty, hearing sounds full of
all sweetness. Then he turned to look back down at the things he
had left behind, and he saw the little globe of earth, which the sea
and air encircled, and the fire above, and everything of no account
in comparison with heaven. But then, having turned back, he
fixed his gaze on the place where he had left his body. And he
laughed to himself at the sad laments of the Greeks, strongly
condemning the futile conduct of humankind, who, insanely
befogged in mind by dark blindness, pursue the false beauty of
the world, and turn aside from heaven. Then he departed to the
place that Mercury allotted him.)

Principal sources for this *Teseida* passage are Lucan, *Pharsalia*, 9.1–14 (the ascent of Pompey's soul); the *Somnium Scipionis*; Dante, *Paradiso*, 22; and Boethius, 2.pr.7, 152–7 and 4.m.1, where, in a typical pattern, the ascending soul first leaves behind the material elements (earth, air, watery clouds, fire), then passes the spheres of the planets (Phoebus, Saturn), the stars and the 'primum mobile' (firmament), until it attains the 'clerenesse of God' (see Courcelle 1967: 197–9 and Appendix 2, on medieval depictions of a winged Boethius):

> I have, forthi, swifte fetheris that surmountcn the heighte of the hevene. Whanne the swift thoght hath clothid itself in tho fetheris, it despiseth the hateful erthes, and surmounteth the rowndenesse of the gret ayr; and it seth the clowdes byhynde his bak, and passeth the heighte of the regioun of the fir, that eschaufeth [grows hot] by the swifte moevynge of the firmament, til that he areyseth hym into the houses that beren the sterres, and joyneth his weies with the sonne, Phebus, and felawschipeth the weie of the olde colde Saturnus; and he, imaked a knyght of the clere sterre (*that is to seyn, whan the thought is makid Godis knyght by the sekynge of trouthe to comen to the verray knowleche of God*) – and thilke soule renneth by the cercle of the sterres ... And whan that he hath gon there inoghe, he schal forleten [leave] the laste point of the hevene, and he schal pressen and wenden on the bak of the swifte firmament, and he schal be makid parfit of the worschipful lyght or dredefulle clerenesse of God.
>
> (*Boece*, 4.m.1.1–28)

For other instances of the ascended soul's contemning of the world, see Statius, *Silvae*, 2.7, and Seneca, *De Consolatione ad Marciam*, 25; and on the literary tradition of apotheosis, see Kellogg 1960; Steadman 1972.

1809 *eighthe spere*: Although all but two TC MSS (J and R) read 'seventh', Boccaccio's *Teseida*, 11.1, reads 'cielo ottava' (eighth sphere), which is therefore probably what Chaucer wrote, although what he (or Boccaccio) meant by this remains disputed. The context does not make clear whether Chaucer is here numbering the spheres outwards from the earth (as in *TC* 3.2), or from the outside towards the earth (as in his *Complaint of Mars*, 29, and *Envoy to Scogan*, 9) and, in the latter case, with which sphere the numbering would begin (whether with Saturn, the fixed stars or the 'primum mobile'). To number outwards suggests Troilus's destination is the sphere of the fixed stars, as in Cicero's *Somnium Scipionis* or Dante's *Paradiso*, 22.100–154 (and in Chaucer's *Treatise on the Astrolabe*, 1.17.37–40, 21.78, and in *The Equatorie of the Planetis*, C/34 – possibly written by Chaucer – the eighth sphere is that of the fixed stars, as also in the *Franklin's Tale*, V.1280). To number inwards suggests the sphere of the moon (as in Lucan's *Pharsalia*). If Troilus leaves behind the planetary spheres in his ascent (see next note) he may reach the fixed stars; if he leaves behind the four elements he may reach the moon. In either sphere his soul has risen above the realm of sublunary change, but (as *TC* 5.1826–7 suggests) his location is only a temporary vantage-point. (For discussion, see Bloomfield 1958; Clark 1951; Conlee 1972; Cope 1952; Drake 1975; Scott 1956; Steadman 1972: 1–20; Wood 1970: 180–91.)

1810 *element*: This is likely to mean 'planetary sphere', as is probably also denoted in Boccaccio's *Teseida*, 11.1, where the soul ascends 'leaving behind the convex [i.e. outer] surfaces of the *elementi*', although the four elements (earth, water, air, and fire) may be meant. Roger Bacon, writing *c*. 1270, used 'in convexitate' (meaning 'as viewed from the outside') in the description of a sphere (Manzalaoui 1964).

1812 *erratik sterres*: Wandering stars, i.e. the planets. On the harmony of the spheres, see *Parliament of Fowls*, 59–63, and also Macrobius, *Commentary on the Dream of Scipio* (Stahl 1952: 2.1–4).

1815 *This litel spot*: Cf. Dante, *Paradiso*, 22.133–5 ('with my sight I returned through every one of the seven spheres, and I saw this globe such that I smiled at its paltry semblance').

1820–22 Cf. Lucan, *Pharsalia*, 9.1–18, where Pompey's spirit, ascended to the moon's orbit, looks down amused on the mistreatment of his body. Cf. also Statius, *Silvae*, 2.7.107–10.

1821 Cf. *Boece*, 2.pr.7.152–7: 'And yif the soule, whiche that hath in itself science of gode werkes, unbownden fro the prysone of the erthe, weendeth frely to the hevene, despiseth it nat thanne al erthly ocupacioun; and usynge [enjoying] hevene rejoyseth that it is exempt fro alle erthly thynges?'

1824 *blynde lust*: Cf. 1.211, and Dante, *Inferno*, 12.49: 'cieca cupidigia' (blind cupidity).

1826–7 This has been interpreted to signify that Troilus's soul did indeed ascend first (cf. 1809n.) to the *seventh* sphere – of Saturn (cf. *Boece*, 4.m.1ff.; cited above in 5.1807–27n.) – and was led thence by Mercury to the eighth (North 1988: 31–2). The posthumous fate and reward of those virtuous and meritorious pagans who happened to live before Christ was a subject of keen medieval interest and debate (see Vitto 1989). The final destination of Troilus's soul is left unspecified.

1833 Cf. 1.55–6.

1835 *he or she*: *Filostrato* addresses only young men (8.29).

1840 *faire*: Cf. the proverb 'all is nothing but a fair' (Whiting W662), and Gower, *Confessio amantis*, Prologue, 454–5: 'For al is bot a chirie feire | This worldes good, so as thei telle.' Contemporary preaching likened 'the feire of this world' to a deceptive market-place (Wenzel 1976: 151).

1841 'Passes as soon as fairest flowers': proverbial (Whiting F326); cf. Isaiah 40:6–8.

1849 *payens corsed olde rites*: Cf. the disowning of paganism at the close of Boccaccio, *De genealogia deorum*; *Teseida*, 11.42; Benoît, *Troie*, 21715–40; Guido, *Historia*, pp. 93–7.

1856 *Gower*: John Gower (c. 1330–1408), author of the Anglo-Norman moral poem *Mirour de l'omme* (c. 1374–8) and of the Latin poem *Vox clamantis* (c. 1385), a denunciation of contemporary society. In his English poem *Confessio amantis* (begun c. 1386) Gower salutes Chaucer (8.2941–57), a passage later excised (cf. Macaulay 1900–1901: xxvi–xxviii). On the friendship of Gower and Chaucer, see Fisher 1964: 27–36.

1857 *Strode*: The Ralph Strode recorded as a Fellow of Merton College, Oxford, before 1360, is thought to be the same Ralph Strode (d. 1387) recorded as Common Sergeant of the City of London (1373–85) and Standing Counsel for the City from 1386, although 'if the one Ralph Strode did all these things he was a very remarkable man' (Tout 1929: 388). The London Strode evidently maintained his Oxford connections. As late as 1378–9 Strode engaged in amicable controversy with John Wyclif, although Strode's position is now known only through Wyclif's rejoinders, *Responsio ad decem questiones magistri R. Strode* and *Responsiones ad argumenta Radulfi Strode*, in which Wyclif calls Strode a dear friend whom he had known at the university. (Strode and Wyclif are recorded as mainpernors or sureties for a former Oxford acquaintance in 1374, and as late as 1377 Strode is mainpernor in a document involving Merton College.) Strode's chief work on logic is now lost, but fragments of his logical system survive in his treatises *Consequentiae* and *Obligationes* (Bodleian Library, MS Canon. Misc. 219; printed at Venice, 1493; Strode's work was still in the curriculum at Pavia in the later fifteenth century). Strode contested Wyclif's doctrine of predestination as depriving man of hope and denying free will. In 1382 Strode and Chaucer were both sureties for the peaceful behaviour of John Hende, a well-to-do London draper; they pursued careers in the civil service in London concurrently, and both occupied residences over nearby city gates (Chaucer at Aldgate from 1374, Strode at Aldersgate from 1375). A Latin colophon in Cambridge University Library MS Dd.3.53 of Chaucer's *Treatise on the Astrolabe*, claiming that Strode tutored Chaucer's son Lewis, is probably unreliable, but the dedication of *TC* witnesses to Chaucer's friendship with this eminent contemporary philosopher. A 1422 Latin Catalogue of Fellows of Merton declares of Strode: 'he was a noble poet, and he composed a book in elegiac meter called "Ralph's Vision" '. See the article by Sir Israel Gollancz in the *Dictionary of National Biography*; cf. also Emden 1957–9:3.1807–8 and Delasanta 1991.

1858 *correcte*: The request for correction was a convention; in his *Ameto*, *De genealogia deorum*, *Vita di Dante* and *De casibus*, Boccaccio variously requests correction.

1863–5 From the song of the spirits in Dante, *Paradiso*, 14.28–30: 'Quell'uno e due e tre che sempre vive | e regna sempre in tre e 'n due e 'n uno, | non circunscritto, e tutto circunscrive . . .' (That One and Two and Three who ever lives and ever reigns in Three and Two and One and, uncircumscribed, circumscribes all . . .).

1869 *Explicit*: Half the manuscripts that contain the poem's ending (including Cl, H1, J) have some form of 'Here ends the Book of Troilus and Criseyde' in Latin or English. Cp has 'Explicit liber Troily' (Here ends the Book of Troilus); Ph has 'Explicit Troylus' (Here ends Troilus), and Cx has 'Here endeth Troylus / as touchyng Creseyde'. On the poem's title, see Introduction, n. 18.

This stanza follows in S1 after the colophon and arms of Henry Sinclair (see Robbins and Cutler 1965: item 524):

> Blak be thy bandis and thy wede also
> Thou soroufull book of mater disesparit
> In tokenyng of thyn inward mortall wo
> Quhiche is so bad that may not ben enparit
> Thou oughtest neuer outward ben enfarit
> That hast within so many a soroufull clause
> Suich be thyne habyte as thou hast thy cause.

The following stanzas are found after the text in Wynkyn de Worde's 1517 edition of what he entitles *The noble and amerous auncyent hystory of Troylus and Cresyde in the tyme of the syege of Troye. Compyled by Geffraye Chaucer*:

The auctour.

And here an ende / of Troylus heuynesse
As touchynge Cresyde / to hym ryght vnkynde
Falsly forsworn / deflouryng his worthynes
For his treue loue / she hath hym made blynde
Of feminine gendre / ye woman most vnkynde
Dyomede on her whele / she hathe set on hye
The faythe of a woman / by her now maye you se

Was not Arystotle / for all his clergye
Vyrgyll the cunnynge / deceyued also
By women inestymable / for to here or se
Sampson the stronge / with many a .M. mo
Brought in to ruyne / by woman mannes fo
There is no woman / I thynke heuen vnder
That can be trewe / and that is wondre

O parfyte Troylus / good god be thy guyde
The moste treuest louer / that euer lady hadde
Now arte thou forsake / of Cresyde at this tyde
Neuer to retourne / who shall make the gladde
He that for vs dyed / and soules frome hell ladde
And borne of the vyrgyne / to heuen thy soule brynge
And all that ben present / at theyr latre endynge.

A M E N.

Thus endeth the treatyse / of Troylus the heuy
By Geffraye Chaucer / compyled and done
He prayenge the reders / this mater not deny
Newly correcked / in the cyte of London
In flete strete / at the sygne of the sonne
Inprynted by me / Wynkyn de worde
The .M.CCCCC. and. xvii. yere of our lorde.

Bibliography

Adams, John F., 'Irony in Troilus' Apostrophe to the Vacant House of Criseyde', *Modern Language Quarterly*, 24 (1963), 61–5.

Anderson, D., 'Theban History in Chaucer's *Troilus*', *Studies in the Age of Chaucer*, 4 (1982), 109–33.

Anderson, J. J., 'Criseyde's Assured Manner', *Notes and Queries*, 38 (1991), 160–61.

Andrew, Malcolm and Waldron, Ronald (eds.), *The Poems of the Pearl Manuscript* (London, 1978).

Barney, Stephen A., 'Troilus Bound', *Speculum*, 47 (1972), 445–58.

— (ed.), *Troilus and Criseyde*, in L. D. Benson 1987.

Barron, Caroline M. and Sutton, Anne F. (eds.), *Medieval London Widows, 1300–1500* (London, 1994).

Barry, P., 'Bells Ringing Without Hands', *Modern Language Notes*, 30 (1915), 28–9.

Bartlett, Robert, *Trial by Fire and Water: The Medieval Judicial Ordeal* (Oxford, 1986).

Baswell, Christopher C. and Taylor, Paul Beekman, 'The *Faire Queene Eleyne* in Chaucer's *Troilus*', *Speculum*, 63 (1988), 293–311.

Baugh, A. C. (ed.), *Chaucer's Major Poetry* (New York, 1963).

Beadle, Richard and Griffiths, Jeremy (eds.), *St John's College, Cambridge, Manuscript L.1: A Facsimile* (Norman, OK, 1983).

Beecher, Donald A. and Ciavolella, Massimo (eds. and trans.), *A Treatise on Lovesickness: Jacques Ferrand* (Syracuse, NY, 1990).

Bellamy, J. G., *The Law of Treason in England in the Later Middle Ages*, ed. D. E. C. Yale (Cambridge, 1970).

—, *Crime and Public Order in England in the Later Middle Ages* (London, 1973).

Benson, C. David, 'King Thoas and the Ominous Letter in Chaucer's *Troilus*', *Philological Quarterly*, 58 (1979), 264–7.

—, *The History of Troy in Middle English Literature* (Cambridge, 1980).

—, 'True Troilus and False Cresseid: The Descent from Tragedy', in Piero Boitani (ed.), *The European Tragedy of Troilus* (Oxford, 1989), 153–70.

Benson, C. David and Windeatt, Barry, 'The Manuscript Glosses to Chaucer's *Troilus and Criseyde*', *Chaucer Review*, 25 (1990), 33–53.

Benson, Larry D. (ed.), *King Arthur's Death* (Exeter, 1986).

— (ed.), *The Riverside Chaucer* (3rd edn, Boston 1987; Oxford 1988).

Bergen, H. (ed.), *Lydgate's Fall of Princes*, EETS, e.s. 121–4 (London, 1924–7).

Bessent, Benjamin R., 'The Puzzling Chronology of Chaucer's *Troilus*', *Studia neophilologica*, 41 (1969), 99–111.

Besserman, Lawrence, 'A Note on the Sources of Chaucer's *Troilus* V, 540–613', *Chaucer Review*, 24 (1990), 306–8.

Bie, Wendy A., 'Dramatic Chronology in *Troilus and Criseyde*', *English Language Notes*, 14 (1976), 9–13.

Blair, C., *European Armour, circa 1066 to circa 1700* (London, 1958).

Bloomfield, Morton W., 'The Eighth Sphere: A Note on Chaucer's *Troilus and Criseyde*, V, 1809', *Modern Language Review*, 53 (1958), 408–10.

—, 'Troilus' Paraclausithyron and its Setting: *Troilus and Criseyde*, V, 519–602', *Neuphilologische Mitteilungen*, 73 (1972), 15–24.

Bode, G. H. (ed.), *Scriptores rerum mythicarum Latini tres* (Celle, 1834).

Boffey, Julia, 'Annotation of Some Manuscripts of *Troilus and Criseyde*', *English Manuscript Studies*, 1100–1700, 5 (1995), 1–17.

Boffey, Julia and Edwards, A. S. G. (eds.), *The Works of Geoffrey Chaucer and 'The Kingis Quair': A Facsimile of Bodleian Library, Oxford, MS Arch. Selden. B.24* (Woodbridge, 1997).

Boitani, Piero (ed.), *Chaucer and the Italian Trecento* (Cambridge, 1983).

—, *The Tragic and the Sublime in Medieval Literature* (Cambridge, 1989).

Borthwick, Sister Mary Charlotte, 'Antigone's Song as "Mirour" in Chaucer's *Troilus and Criseyde*', *Modern Language Quarterly*, 22 (1961), 227–35.

Branca V. (ed.), *Tutte le opere di Giovanni Boccaccio* (Verona, 1964–).

Braswell, Mary F. (ed.), *Sir Perceval of Galles and Ywain and Gawain* (Kalamazoo, MI, 1995).

Breeze, A., '"Bear the Bell" in Dafydd ap Gwilym and *Troilus and Criseyde*', *Notes and Queries*, 39 (1992), 441–3.

Brennan, J. P., '*Troilus and Criseyde*, IV, 209–10', *English Language Notes*, 17 (1979), 15–18.

Brereton, G. E. and Ferrier, J. M. (eds.), *Le Menagier de Paris* (Oxford, 1981).

Brewer, Derek, *Chaucer* (3rd edn, London, 1973).

— (ed.), *Chaucer: The Critical Heritage* (2 vols.; London, 1978).

—, 'Observations on the Text of *Troilus*', in P. L. Heyworth (ed.), *Medieval Studies for J. A. W. Bennett* (Oxford, 1981), 121–38.

—, 'The Ages of Troilus, Criseyde and Pandarus', in his *Tradition and Innovation in Chaucer* (London, 1982), 80–88.

Brewer, Derek and Brewer, L. E. (eds.), *Troilus and Criseyde (abridged)* (London, 1969).

Brody, Saul N., 'Making a Play for Criseyde: The Staging of Pandarus's House in Chaucer's *Troilus and Criseyde*', *Speculum*, 73 (1998), 115–40.

Brookhouse, C., 'Chaucer's *Impossibilia*', *Medium Aevum*, 34 (1965), 40–42.

Brown, Carleton (ed.), *English Lyrics of the XIIIth Century* (Oxford, 1932).

Brown, William H., jun., 'A Separate Peace: Chaucer and the Troilus of Tradition', *Journal of English and Germanic Philology*, 83 (1984), 492–508.

Buchthal, H., *Historia Troiana* (London, 1971).

Bunt, G. H. V. (ed.), '*William of Palerne*': *An Alliterative Romance* (Groningen, 1985).

Burnley, J. D., 'Proude Bayard: *Troilus and Criseyde*, I. 218', *Notes and Queries*, 23 (1976), 148–52.

—, 'Inflexion in Chaucer's Adjectives', *Neuphilologische Mitteilungen*, 83 (1982a), 169–77.

—, 'Criseyde's Heart and the Weakness of Women: An Essay in Lexical Interpretation', *Studia neophilologica*, 54 (1982b), 25–38.

—, *Courtliness and Literature in Medieval England* (Harlow, 1998).

Burrow, J. A., *Ricardian Poetry* (London, 1971).

— (ed.), *Thomas Hoccleve's 'Complaint' and 'Dialogue'*, EETS, o.s. 313 (Oxford, 1999).

Butterfield, Ardis, '*Mise-en-page* in the *Troilus* Manuscripts: Chaucer and French Manuscript Culture', in S. Lerer (ed.), *Reading from the Margins: Textual Studies, Chaucer, and Medieval Literature* (San Marino, CA, 1996), 49–80.

Camargo, Martin (ed.), *Medieval Rhetorics of Prose Composition: Five English Artes Dictandi and Their Tradition* (Binghamton, NY, 1995).

Campbell, J. J., 'A New *Troilus* Fragment', *PMLA*, 73 (1958), 305–8.

Cassidy, F. G., ' "Don Thyn Hood" in Chaucer's *Troilus*', *Journal of English and Germanic Philology*, 57 (1958), 739–42.

Cherry, J., 'The Medieval Jewellery from the Fishpool, Nottinghamshire, Hoard', *Archaeologia*, 104 (1974), 307–21.

Child, Francis J. (ed.), *The English and Scottish Popular Ballads* (5 vols.; London, 1882–98).

Clark, John, 'Trinovantum – The Evolution of a Legend', *Journal of Medieval History*, 7 (1981), 135–51.

Clark, John W., 'Dante and the Epilogue of the *Troilus*', *Journal of English and Germanic Philology*, 50 (1951), 1–10.

Clayton, M., 'A Virgilian Source for Chaucer's "White Bole" ', *Notes and Queries*, 26 (1979), 103–4.

Clogan, Paul M., 'Chaucer and the *Thebaid* Scholia', *Studies in Philology*, 61 (1964), 599–615.

—, 'Chaucer's Use of the *Thebaid*', *English Miscellany*, 18 (1967), 9–31.

Conlee, John W., 'The Meaning of Troilus' Ascension to the Eighth Sphere', *Chaucer Review*, 7 (1972), 27–36.

Constans, L. (ed.), *Le Roman de Thèbes*, Société d'anciens textes français (2 vols.; Paris, 1890).

— (ed.), *Le Roman de Troie*, Société d'anciens textes français (6 vols.; Paris, 1904–12).

Contini, G. (ed.), *Poeti del Duecento* (Milan, 1960).

Contini, G. and Ponchiroli, D. (eds.), *Canzoniere* (Turin, 1964).

Cook, Robert G., 'Chaucer's Pandarus and the Medieval Idea of Friendship', *Journal of English and Germanic Philology*, 69 (1970), 407–24.

Cope, Jackson I., 'Chaucer, Venus and the "Seventhe Spere" ', *Modern Language Notes*, 67 (1952), 245–6.

Courcelle, P., *La Consolation de philosophie dans la tradition littéraire: antécédents et postérité de Boèce* (Paris, 1967).

Cowen, Janet and Kane, George (eds.), *Geoffrey Chaucer: 'The Legend of Good Women'* (East Lansing, MI, 1995).

Craig, H. (ed.), *Works of John Metham*, EETS, o.s. 132 (London, 1916).

Crescini, V., 'Azalais d'Altier', *Zeitschrift für Romanische Philologie*, 14 (1890), 128–32.

Crow, Martin M. and Olson, Clair C. (eds.), *Chaucer Life-Records* (Oxford, 1966).

Cummins, J., *The Hound and the Hawk: The Art of Medieval Hunting* (London, 1988).

Curry, Walter Clyde, *Chaucer and the Mediaeval Sciences* (2nd edn, Oxford, 1960).

Curtius, Ernst Robert, *European Literature and the Latin Middle Ages*, trans. W. R. Trask (London, 1953).

Davis, Norman, 'The Litera Troili and English Letters', *Review of English Studies*, 16 (1965), 233–44.

— (ed.), *Paston Letters and Papers of the Fifteenth Century*, vol. 1 (Oxford, 1971).

—, 'Chaucer and Fourteenth-Century English', in D. Brewer (ed.), *Geoffrey Chaucer: Writers and their Background* (London, 1974), 58–84.

Davy, M. M. (ed.), *Un Traité de l'Amour du XIIe Siècle* (Paris, 1932).

Dedeck-Héry, V. L., 'Boethius' *De Consolatione* by Jean de Meun', *Mediaeval Studies*, 14 (1952), 165–275.

Delasanta, Rodney, 'Chaucer and Strode', *Chaucer Review*, 26 (1991), 205–18.

Devereux, James A., 'A Note on *Troilus and Criseyde*, Book III, Line 1309', *Philological Quarterly*, 44 (1965), 550–52.

De Vries, F. C., '*Troilus and Criseyde*, Book III, Stanza 251, and Boethius', *English Studies*, 52 (1971), 502–7.

DiMarco, Vincent, '"Renewing" *Troilus*, 1.890–96: *Si Erravit Scriptor, Debes Corrigere, Lector*', *Chaucer Yearbook*, 5 (1998), 61–78.

—, '*Troilus and Criseyde* 2.884 and 933–36: Two Conjectural Emendations', *Chaucer Review*, 33 (1999), 252–63.

Donaldson, E. Talbot, *Speaking of Chaucer* (London, 1970).

—, 'Briseis, Briseida, Criseyde, Cresseid, Cressid: Progress of a Heroine', in E. Vasta and Z. P. Thundy (eds.), *Chaucerian Problems and Perspectives* (Notre Dame, IN, 1979), 3–12.

Doob, Penelope B. R., 'Chaucer's "Corones Tweyne" and the Lapidaries', *Chaucer Review*, 7 (1972), 85–96.

Doyle, A. I. and Parkes, M. B., 'The Production of Copies of *The Canterbury Tales* and *Confessio Amantis* in the early fifteenth century', in M. B. Parkes and A. G. Watson (eds.), *Medieval Scribes, Manuscripts and Libraries: Essays Presented to N. R. Ker* (London, 1978), 163–210.

Drake, Gertrude C., 'The Moon and Venus: Troilus's Havens in Eternity', *Papers on Language and Literature*, 11 (1975), 3–17.

Dronke, Peter, 'The Conclusion of *Troilus and Criseyde*', *Medium Aevum*, 33 (1964), 47–52.

—, *Medieval Latin and the Rise of the European Love Lyric* (2nd edn, Oxford, 1968).

Duffell, Martin J., 'Chaucer, Gower and the history of the hendecasyllable', in C. B. McCully and J. J. Anderson (eds.), *English Historical Metrics* (Cambridge, 1996), 210–18.

Duncan, A. A. M. (ed.), *John Barbour: The Bruce* (Edinburgh, 1997).

Edwards, Robert E., *Chaucer and Boccaccio: Antiquity and Modernity* (Basingstoke, 2002).

Eisenhut, W. (ed.), *Dictys Cretensis ephemeridos belli Troiani libri* (Leipzig, 1958).

Eisner, S. (ed.), *The Kalendarium of Nicholas of Lynn*, Chaucer Library, 2 (Athens, GA, 1980).

Elliott, R. W. V., *Chaucer's English* (London, 1974).

Emden, A. B., *A Biographical Register of the University of Oxford to A.D. 1500* (3 vols.; Oxford, 1957–9).

Evans, Joan, *Magical Jewels of the Middle Ages and the Renaissance* (Oxford, 1922).

—, *English Posies and Posy Rings* (London, 1931).

Ewert, A. (ed.), *Marie de France: Lais* (Oxford, 1944).

Faral, E. A. (ed.), *Les arts poétiques du XIIe et du XIIIe siècle* (Paris, 1924).

Fisher, John H., *John Gower, Moral Philosopher and Friend of Chaucer* (London, 1964).

— (ed.), *The Complete Poetry and Prose of Geoffrey Chaucer* (New York, 1977).

Fox, Denton (ed.), *The Poems of Robert Henryson* (Oxford, 1981).

Frazer, R. M., jun. (trans.), *The Trojan War: The Chronicles of Dictys of Crete and Dares the Phrygian* (Bloomington, IN, 1966).

Frost, William, 'A Chaucer–Virgil Link in *Aeneid* XI and *Troilus and Criseyde* V', *Notes and Queries*, 26 (1979), 104–5.

Fry, Donald K., 'Chaucer's Zanzis and a Possible Source for *Troilus and Criseyde*, IV, 407–413', *English Language Notes*, 9 (1971), 81–5.

Furnivall, F. J. and Gollancz, I. (eds.), *Hoccleve's Works: The Minor Poems* (revised by J. Mitchell and A. I. Doyle), EETS, e.s. 61, 73 (London, 1892; repr. 1970).

Garbáty, Thomas, 'The *Pamphilus* Tradition in Ruiz and Chaucer', *Philological Quarterly*, 46 (1967), 457–70.

Gillmeister, Heiner, 'Chaucer's *Kan Ke Dort* (*Troilus*, II, 1752), and the "Sleeping Dogs" of the Trouvères', *English Studies*, 59 (1978), 310–23.

Gleason, Mark J., 'Nicholas Trevet, Boethius, Boccaccio: Contexts of Cosmic Love in *Troilus*, Book III', *Medievalia et Humanistica*, 15 (1987), 161–88.

Gnerro, Mark L., '"Ye, Haselwodes Shaken!" – Pandarus and Divination', *Notes and Queries*, 9 (1962), 164–5.

Gompf, Ludwig (ed.), *Joseph Iscanus: Werke und Briefe* (Leiden, 1970).

Gordon, R. K. (ed. and trans.), *The Story of Troilus* (London, 1934; repr. Toronto, 1978).

Green, Richard F., 'Troilus and the Game of Love', *Chaucer Review*, 13 (1979), 201–20.

Greenfield, Stanley B., 'The Role of Calkas in *Troilus and Criseyde*', *Medium Aevum*, 36 (1967), 141–51.

Griffin, N. E., 'Un-Homeric Elements in the Story of Troy', *Journal of English and Germanic Philology*, 7 (1907), 32–52.

— (ed.), *Historia destructionis Troiae* (Cambridge, Mass., 1936).

Griffin, N. E. and Myrick, A. B., *The Filostrato of Giovanni Boccaccio: A Translation with Parallel Text* (Philadelphia, PA, 1929; repr. New York, 1967).

Hamilton, G. L., *The Indebtedness of Chaucer's 'Troilus and Criseyde' to Guido delle Colonne's 'Historia Trojana'* (New York, 1903).

Hammond, E. P., 'A Burgundian Copy of Chaucer's *Troilus*', *Modern Language Notes*, 26 (1911), 32.

—, 'The Chance of the Dice', *Englische Studien*, 59 (1925), 1–16.

Hanly, Michael G., *Boccaccio, Beauvau, Chaucer: 'Troilus and Criseyde': Four Perspectives on Influence* (Norman, OK, 1990).

Hanna, Ralph, III, 'Robert K. Root', in Paul G. Ruggiers (ed.), *Editing Chaucer: The Great Tradition* (Norman, OK, 1984), 191–205.

—, 'The Scribe of Huntington HM 114', *Studies in Bibliography*, 42 (1989), 120–33.

—, 'The Manuscripts and Transmission of Chaucer's *Troilus*', in J. M. Dean and C. K. Zacher (eds.), *The Idea of Medieval Literature* (Cranbury, NJ, 1992), 173–88.

Hanning, Robert W., '*Troilus and Criseyde*, 4.210: A New Conjecture', *Chaucer Yearbook*, 4 (1997), 79–83.

Hanson, Thomas B., 'Criseyde's Brows Once Again', *Notes and Queries*, 18 (1971), 285–6.

Häring, N. (ed.), '*De planctu naturae*', *Studi medievali*, 19 (1979).

Hardman, Phillipa, 'Chaucer's Articulation of the Narrative in *Troilus*: The Manuscript Evidence', *Chaucer Review*, 30 (1995), 111–33.

—, 'Interpreting the Incomplete Scheme of Illustration in Cambridge, Corpus Christi College MS 61', *English Manuscript Studies*, 1100–1700, 6 (1997), 52–69.

Harvey, Patricia A., 'ME. "Point" (*Troilus and Criseyde*, III, 695)', *Notes and Queries*, 15 (1968), 243–4.

Havely, Nicholas (trans.), *Chaucer's Boccaccio* (Cambridge, 1980).

Hazelton, R., 'Chaucer and Cato', *Speculum*, 35 (1960), 357–80.

Helmholz, R. H., *Marriage Litigation in Medieval England* (Cambridge, 1974).

Hoepffner, E. (ed.), *Oeuvres de Guillaume de Machaut*, Société d'anciens textes français (3 vols.; Paris, 1908–21).

Hoffman, R. L., 'Ovid's Argus and Chaucer', *Notes and Queries*, 210 (1965), 213–16.

Hornsby, Joseph Allen, *Chaucer and the Law* (Norman, OK, 1988).

Houston, Mary G., *Medieval Costume in England and France: The 13th, 14th and 15th Centuries* (London, 1965)

Howes, Laura L., *Chaucer's Gardens and the Language of Convention* (Gainesville, FL, 1997).

Hoy, J., 'Chaucer and Dictys', *Medium Aevum*, 59 (1990), 288–91.

Huber, John, 'Troilus' Predestination Soliloquy: Chaucer's Changes from Boethius', *Neuphilologische Mitteilungen*, 66 (1965), 120–25.

Hutson, Arthur E., 'Troilus' Confession', *Modern Language Notes*, 69 (1954), 468–70.

Isaacs, N., 'On Six and Sevene: *Troilus* IV, 622', *American Notes and Queries*, 5 (1967), 85–6.

Jefferson, Judith A., 'The Hoccleve Holographs and Hoccleve's Metrical Practice', in Derek Pearsall (ed.), *Manuscripts and Texts: Editorial Problems in Later Middle English Literature* (Cambridge, 1987), 95–109.

Jennings, Margaret, 'Chaucer's Troilus and the Ruby', *Notes and Queries*, 23 (1976), 533–7.

Kaske, R. E., 'The Aube in Chaucer's *Troilus*', in Schoeck and Taylor 1961: 167–79.

Kaylor, Noel H., 'Boethian Resonances in Chaucer's "Canticus Troili"', *Chaucer Review*, 27 (1993), 219–27.

Kellogg, Alfred E., 'On the Tradition of Troilus' Vision of the Little Earth', *Mediaeval Studies*, 22 (1960), 204–13.

Kelly, Henry Ansgar, *Love and Marriage in the Age of Chaucer* (Ithaca, NY, 1975).

—, 'Shades of Incest and Cuckoldry: Pandarus and John of Gaunt', *Studies in the Age of Chaucer*, 13 (1991), 121–40.

—, *Ideas and Forms of Tragedy from Aristotle to the Middle Ages* (Cambridge, 1993).

—, *Chaucerian Tragedy* (Cambridge, 1997).

Kerkhof, J., *Studies in the Language of Geoffrey Chaucer* (2nd rev. edn, Leiden, 1982).

Killough, G. G., 'Punctuation and Caesura in Chaucer', *Studies in the Age of Chaucer*, 4 (1982), 85–107.

Kittredge, George Lyman, *The Date of Chaucer's Troilus and other Chaucer matters* (Chaucer Society; London, 1909).

—, 'Chaucer's Lollius', *Harvard Studies in Comparative Philology*, 28 (1917), 47–133.

Kölbing, E. (ed.), *The Romance of Sir Beues of Hamtoun*, EETS, e.s. 46, 48, 65 (London, 1885–94; repr. 1973).

Kornbluth, A. F., 'Another Chaucer Pun', *Notes and Queries*, 204 (1959), 243.

Krochalis, J. (ed.), *The Pierpont Morgan Library MS M.817* (Norman, OK, 1986).

Langlois, E. (ed.), *Le Roman de la Rose*, Société d'anciens textes français (5 vols.; Paris, 1914–24).

Levine, Robert, 'Pandarus as Davus', *Neuphilologische Mitteilungen*, 92 (1991), 463–8.

Lewis, C. S., 'What Chaucer really did to *Il Filostrato*', *Essays and Studies*, 17 (1932), 56–75.

—, *The Allegory of Love* (Oxford, 1936).

Lindsay, W. M. (ed.), [Isidore of Seville] *Etymologiae* (2 vols.; Oxford, 1911).

Longo, Joseph A., 'The Double Time Scheme in Book II of Chaucer's *Troilus and Criseyde*', *Modern Language Quarterly*, 22 (1961), 37–40.

Lowes, John Livingston, 'The Date of Chaucer's *Troilus and Criseyde*', *PMLA*, 23 (1908), 285–306.

Lumiansky, R. M., 'The Story of Troilus and Briseida according to Benoît and Guido', *Speculum*, 29 (1954a), 727–33.

—, 'Calchas in the Early Versions of the Troilus Story', *Tulane Studies in English*, 4 (1954b), 5–20.

McCall, John P., 'Chaucer's May 3', *Modern Language Notes*, 76 (1961), 201–5.

McCall, John P. and Rudisill, George, jun., 'The Parliament of 1386 and Chaucer's Trojan Parliament', *Journal of English and Germanic Philology*, 58 (1959), 276–88.

Macaulay, G. C. (ed.), *The Complete Works of John Gower* (4 vols.; Oxford, 1899–1902).

—, *The English Works of John Gower*, EETS, e.s. 81, 82 (London, 1900–1901).

McKinley, Kathryn L., 'Chaucer's Flexippe', *English Language Notes*, 30 (1992), 1–4.

McKinnell, J., 'Letters as a type of the formal level in Troilus and Criseyde', in Salu 1979, 73–89.

McLean, Teresa, *Medieval English Gardens* (London, 1981).

McNeillie, Andrew (ed.), *The Essays of Virginia Woolf, Volume IV: 1925–1928* (London, 1994).

Magoun, Francis P., jun., '"Himselven Lik a Pilgrym to Desgise": *Troilus* V.1577', *Modern Language Notes*, 59 (1944), 176–8.

—, 'Chaucer's Summary of Statius' *Thebaid* II–XII', *Traditio*, 11 (1955), 409–20.

Maguire, John B., 'The Clandestine Marriage of Troilus and Criseyde', *Chaucer Review*, 8 (1974), 262–78.

Malarky, Stoddard, 'The "Corones Tweyne": An Interpretation', *Speculum*, 38 (1963), 473–8.

Manzalaoui, M., 'Roger Bacon's "In convexitate" and Chaucer's "In convers" (*Troilus and Criseyde*, V.1810)', *Notes and Queries*, 11 (1964), 165–6.

Marti, B. M. (ed.), *Arnulfi Aurelianensis glosule super Lucanum* (Rome, 1958).

Martin, G. H. (ed. and trans.), *Knighton's Chronicle* (Oxford, 1995).

Mary, A. (ed.), *Oeuvres de François Villon* (Paris, 1970).

Mathew, G., *The Court of Richard II* (London, 1968).

Matthews, Lloyd J., 'Chaucer's personification of Prudence in Troilus (V.743–749): Sources in the Visual Arts and Manuscript Scholia', *English Language Notes*, 13 (1976), 249–55.

—, '*Troilus and Criseyde*, V.743–749: Another Possible Source', *Neuphilologische Mitteilungen*, 82 (1981), 211–13.

Meech, Sanford B., 'Chaucer and an Italian Translation of the *Heroides*', *PMLA*, 45 (1930), 110–28.

—, 'Chaucer and the *Ovide Moralisé*: A Further Study', *PMLA*, 46 (1931), 182–204.

—, *Design in Chaucer's Troilus* (Syracuse, NY, 1959).

Meek, M. E. (trans.), *Historia Destructionis Troiae* (Bloomington, IN, 1974).

Meister, F. (ed.), *Daretis Phrygii de excidio Troiae historia* (Leipzig, 1873).

Metlitzki, Dorothee, *The Matter of Araby in Medieval England* (New Haven, CT, 1977).

Mieszkowski, Gretchen, 'The Reputation of Criseyde 1155–1500', *Transactions of the Connecticut Academy of Arts and Sciences*, 43 (1971), 71–153.

—, 'Chaucer's Pandarus and Jean Brasdefer's Houdée', *Chaucer Review*, 20 (1985), 40–60.

Migne, J. P. (ed.), *Patrologia Latina* (Paris, 1844–).

Mills, Maldwyn (ed.), *Six Middle English Romances* (London, 1973).

Minnis, A. J., 'Aspects of the Medieval French and English Traditions of the *De Consolatione Philosophiae*', in M. Gibson (ed.), *Boethius: His Life, Thought, and Influence* (Oxford, 1981), 312–61.

Minnis, A. J. and Scott, A. B. (eds.), *Medieval Literary Criticism c. 1100–c. 1375: The Commentary Tradition* (rev. edn, Oxford, 1991).

Mirrer, Louise (ed.), *Upon My Husband's Death: Widows in Literature and Histories of Medieval Europe* (Ann Arbor, MI, 1992).

Moland, L. and d'Hericault, C. (eds.), *Nouvelles françoises en prose du XIVe siècle* (Paris, 1858).

Moore, E. and Toynbee, P. (eds.), *Tutte le opere di Dante Alighieri* (4th edn, Oxford, 1924).

Murphy, J. J., 'A New Look at Chaucer and the Rhetoricians', *Review of English Studies*, 15 (1964), 1–20.

— (ed.), *Three Medieval Rhetorical Arts* (Berkeley, CA, 1971).

Muscatine, Charles, 'The Feigned Illness in Chaucer's *Troilus and Criseyde*', *Modern Language Notes*, 63 (1948), 372–7.

Mustanoja, Tauno F., *A Middle English Syntax, 1: Parts of Speech* (Helsinki, 1960).

Newton, S. M., *Fashion in the Age of the Black Prince* (Cambridge, 1980).

North, J. D., *Chaucer's Universe* (Oxford, 1988).

Norton-Smith, John, *Geoffrey Chaucer* (London, 1974).

O'Connor, John J., 'The Astronomical Dating of Chaucer's *Troilus*', *Journal of English and Germanic Philology*, 55 (1956), 556–62.

Offord, M. Y. (ed.), *The Book of the Knight of the Tower, translated by William Caxton*, EETS, s.s. 2 (London, 1971).

Olson, Donald W. and Laird, Edgar S., 'A Note on Planetary Tables and a Planetary Conjunction in *Troilus and Criseyde*', *Chaucer Review*, 24 (1990), 309–11.

Panofsky, E., *Studies in Iconology* (Oxford, 1939).

Parkes, M. B. and Beadle, Richard (eds.), *The Poetical Works of Geoffrey Chaucer: A Facsimile of Cambridge University Library MS Gg.4.27* (3 vols.; Cambridge, 1979–80).

Parkes, M. B. and Salter, Elizabeth (eds.), *Geoffrey Chaucer, 'Troilus and Criseyde': A Facsimile of Corpus Christi College, Cambridge, MS 61* (Cambridge, 1978).

Pauly–Wissowa: A. F. von Pauly (ed.), *Real-Encyclopädie der classischen Altertumwissenschaft*, rev. G. Wissowa et al. (46 vols.; Stuttgart, 1894–1972).

Pearsall, Derek (ed.), *Chaucer to Spenser: An Anthology of Writings in English 1375–1575* (Oxford, 1999a).

—, 'The Weak Declension of the Adjective and its Importance in Chaucerian Metre', in G. Lester (ed.), *Chaucer in Perspective: Middle English Essays in Honour of Norman Blake* (Sheffield, 1999b), 178–93.

Pollock, F. and Maitland, F. W., *The History of English Law* (2nd edn, Cambridge, 1898).

Pratt, Robert A., 'A Note on Chaucer's Lollius', *Modern Language Notes*, 65 (1950), 183–7.

—, 'Chaucer's "natal Jove" and "Seint Jerome . . . agayn Jovinian"', *Journal of English and Germanic Philology*, 61 (1962), 244–8.

Purdie, Rhiannon (ed.), *Ipomadon A*, EETS, o.s. 316 (Oxford, 2001).

Raynaud, G. (ed.), *Les Cents Ballades*, Société d'anciens textes français (Paris, 1905), 203–4.

Riedel, G. (ed.), *Commentum Bernardi Silvestris super Sex Libros Eneidos Virgilii* (Greifswald, 1924).

Rigg, A. G., 'Calchas, Renegade and Traitor: Dares and Joseph of Exeter', *Notes and Queries*, 45 (1998), 176–8.

Riley, H. T. (ed.), *Liber Albus: The White Book of the City of London* (London, 1861).

— (ed.), *Historia Anglicana* (2 vols.; Rolls series; London, 1863–4).

Robbins, R. H. (ed.), *Secular Lyrics of the XIVth and XVth Centuries* (2nd edn, Oxford, 1955).

Robbins, R. H. and Cutler, J. L., *Supplement to the Index of Middle English Verse* (Lexington, KY, 1965).

Roberts, G. (trans.), *The Iliad of Dares Phrygius* (Cape Town, 1970).

Robertson, D. W., jun., 'The Probable Date and Purpose of Chaucer's *Troilus*', *Medievalia et Humanistica*, 13 (1985), 143–71.

Robinson, F. N. (ed.), *The Works of Geoffrey Chaucer* (2nd edn, London, 1957).

Rollins, Hyder E., 'The Troilus–Cressida Story from Chaucer to Shakespeare', *PMLA*, 32 (1917), 383–429.

Root, Robert K., 'Chaucer's Dares', *Modern Philology*, 15 (1917), 1–22.

— (ed.), *The Book of Troilus and Criseyde* (Princeton, NJ, 1926).

Root, Robert K. and Russell, Henry N., 'A Planetary Date for Chaucer's *Troilus*', *PMLA*, 39 (1924), 48–63.

Rowland, Beryl, *Blind Beasts: Chaucer's Animal World* (Kent State University Press, OH, 1971).

Sadlek, Gregory M., 'To Wait or to Act?: *Troilus*, II, 954', *Chaucer Review*, 17 (1982), 62–4.

Salu, Mary (ed.), *Essays on 'Troilus and Criseyde'* (Cambridge, 1979).

Salverda de Grave, J. J. (ed.), *Roman d'Eneas* (Paris, 1925–9).

Sams, Henry W., 'The Dual Time-Scheme in Chaucer's *Troilus*', *Modern Language Notes*, 56 (1941), 94–100; repr. in Schoeck and Taylor 1961: 180–85.

Samuels, M. L., 'Chaucerian Final -E', *Notes and Queries*, 217 (1972), 445–8.

—, 'Chaucer's Spelling', in J. J. Smith (ed.), *The English of Chaucer and his Contemporaries* (Aberdeen, 1988), 23–37.

Saul, Nigel, *Richard II* (New Haven, CT, 1997).

Schibanoff, Susan, 'Argus and Argyve: Etymology and Characterization in Chaucer's *Troilus*', *Speculum*, 51 (1976), 647–58.

—, 'Criseyde's "Impossible Aubes" ', *Journal of English and Germanic Philology*, 76 (1977), 326–33.

Schmidt, Dieter, 'Das Anredepronomen in Chaucer's *Troilus and Criseyde*', *Archiv*, 212 (1975), 120–24.

Schoeck, Richard J. and Taylor, Jerome (eds.), *Chaucer Criticism, ii. 'Troilus and Criseyde' and the Minor Poems* (Notre Dame, IN, 1961).

Schofield, John, *Medieval London Houses* (New Haven, CT, and London, 1994).

Scott, Forrest S., 'The Seventh Sphere: A Note on *Troilus and Criseyde*', *Modern Language Review*, 51 (1956), 2–5.

Scott, Kathleen, *Later Gothic Manuscripts 1390–1490* (2 vols.; London, 1996).

Seymour, M. C. (gen. ed.), *On the Properties of Things: John Trevisa's Translation of Bartholomaeus Anglicus, 'De Proprietatibus Rerum'*, vol. 1 (Oxford, 1975).

Simmons, T. F. (ed.), *The Lay Folks' Mass Book*, EETS, o.s. 71 (London, 1879).

Singleton, Charles S. (ed. and trans.), *The Divine Comedy* (3 vols.; Princeton, NJ, 1970–75).

Skeat, W. W. (ed.), *The Complete Works of Geoffrey Chaucer* (6 vols.; Oxford, 1894).

— (ed.), *Chaucerian and Other Pieces* (Oxford, 1897).

Slocum, Sally K., 'How Old is Chaucer's Pandarus?', *Philological Quarterly*, 58 (1979), 16–25.

Smalley, Beryl, *English Friars and Antiquity in the Early Fourteenth Century* (Oxford, 1960).

Smith, Sarah Stanbury, '"Game in myn hood": The Traditions of a Comic Proverb', *Studies in Iconography*, 9 (1983), 1–12.

Smyser, H. M., 'The Domestic Background of *Troilus and Criseyde*', *Speculum*, 31 (1956), 297–315.

Southworth, John, *Fools and Jesters at the English Court* (Stroud, 1998).

Spearing, A. C., *Criticism and Medieval Poetry* (2nd edn, London, 1972).

—, *Chaucer: 'Troilus and Criseyde'* (London, 1976).

Stahl, W. H. (transl.), *Macrobius: Commentary on the Dream of Scipio* (New York, 1952).

Stanbury, Sarah, 'Women's Letters and Private Space in Chaucer', *Exemplaria*, 6 (1994), 271–85.

Steadman, John M., *Disembodied Laughter: Troilus and the Apotheosis Tradition* (Berkeley, CA, 1972).

Steele, R. and Day, M. (eds.), *The English Poems of Charles of Orleans*, EETS, o.s. 215, 220 (London, 1941; repr. 1970).

Stevens, Martin, 'The Royal Stanza in Early English Literature', *PMLA*, 94 (1979), 62–76.

Stillinger, Thomas C., *The Song of Troilus: Lyric Authority in the Medieval Book* (Philadelphia, 1992).

Stockton E. W. (trans.), *The Major Latin Works of John Gower* (Seattle, 1962).

Sundwall, McKay, 'Deiphobus and Helen: A Tantalizing Hint', *Modern Philology*, 73 (1975), 151–6.

Tatlock, J. S. P., 'Notes on Chaucer: Earlier or Minor Poems', *Modern Language Notes*, 29 (1914), 97–101.

—, 'The Date of the *Troilus* . . .' *Modern Language Notes*, 50 (1935), 277–96.

Thundy, Zacharias P., 'Chaucer's "Corones Tweyne" and Mathcolus', *Neuphilologische Mitteilungen*, 86 (1985), 343–7.

Tinkle, Theresa, *Medieval Venuses and Cupids* (Stanford, 1996).

Tout, T. F., 'Literature and Learning in the English Civil Service in the Fourteenth Century', *Speculum*, 4 (1929), 365–89.

Utz, Richard J., ' "For all that comth, comth by necessitee": Chaucer's Critique of Fourteenth-Century Boethianism in *Troilus and Criseyde* IV.957–8', *Arbeiten aus Anglistik und Amerikanistik*, 21 (1996), 29–32.

Vitto, Cindy L., *The Virtuous Pagan in Middle English Literature*, Transactions of the American Philosophical Society, 79: 5 (Philadelphia, 1989).

Wack, Mary F., *Lovesickness in the Middle Ages: The 'Viaticum' and its Commentaries* (Philadelphia, 1990).

Walcutt, Charles Child, 'The Pronoun of Address in *Troilus and Criseyde*', *Philological Quarterly*, 14 (1935), 282–7.

Walker, Sue Sheridan (ed.), *Wife and Widow in Medieval England* (Ann Arbor, MI, 1993).

Wallace, David, *Chaucer and the Early Writings of Boccaccio* (Cambridge, 1985).

Walsh, P. G. (ed. and trans.), *Andreas Capellanus on Love* (London, 1982).

Webb, C. C. J. (ed.), [John of Salisbury] *Policratici sive De nugis curialium et vestigiis philosophorum* (2 vols.; Oxford, 1909).

— (ed.), [John of Salisbury] *Metalogicon* (Oxford, 1929).

Welsford, Enid, *The Fool, His Social and Literary History* (London, 1935).

Wentersdorf, Karl P., 'Some Observations on the Concept of Clandestine Marriage in *Troilus and Criseyde*', *Chaucer Review*, 15 (1980), 101–26.

—, 'Pandarus's *Haselwode*: A Comparative Approach to a Chaucerian Puzzle', *Studies in Philology*, 89 (1992), 293–313.

Wenzel, Siegfried, 'Chaucer and the Language of Contemporary Preaching', *Studies in Philology*, 73 (1976), 138–61.

Wetherbee, Winthrop, *Chaucer and the Poets: An Essay on 'Troilus and Criseyde'* (Ithaca, NY, 1984).

Whiting, B. J., 'Troilus and Pilgrims in War Time', *Modern Language Notes*, 60 (1945), 47–9.

Wilkins, Nigel (ed.), *La Louange des dames, by Guillaume de Machaut* (Edinburgh, 1972).

Wilson, Edward, 'The Sense of "Directe" in Chaucer's *Troilus* V.1856: A Correction', *Notes and Queries*, 45 (1998), 24–7.

Wimsatt, James I., 'Guillaume de Machaut and Chaucer's *Troilus and Criseyde*', *Medium Aevum*, 45 (1976), 277–93.

Windeatt, Barry, 'The Text of the *Troilus*', in Salu 1979: 1–22.

—, '"Love That Oughte Ben Secree" in Chaucer's *Troilus*', *Chaucer Review*, 14 (1979b), 116–31.

— (ed.), *Troilus and Criseyde: A New Edition of 'The Book of Troilus'* (London, 1984; 2nd edn, 1990).

—, '*Troilus* and the Disenchantment of Romance', in D. Brewer (ed.), *Studies in Medieval English Romances* (Cambridge, 1988), 129–47.

—, *The Oxford Guides to Chaucer: 'Troilus and Criseyde'* (Oxford, 1992).

Witlieb, Bernard I., 'Chaucer's Elysian Fields ("Troilus", IV.789f.)', *Notes and Queries*, 16 (1969), 250–51.

—, 'Chaucer and the "Ovide Moralisé"', *Notes and Queries*, 215 (1970), 202–7.

—, 'Chaucer and a French Story of Thebes', *English Language Notes*, 11 (1973), 5–9.

Wood, Chauncey, *Chaucer and the Country of the Stars* (Princeton, NJ, 1970).

Wright, N. (ed.), *The Historia Regum Britannie of Geoffrey of Monmouth* (Cambridge, 1985).

Wright, T. (ed.), *Concordia Facta inter Regem Riccardum II et Civitatem Londonie* (London, 1838).

Yager, Susan, '"As she that": Syntactical Ambiguity in Chaucer's *Troilus and Criseyde*', *Philological Quarterly*, 73 (1994), 151–68.

Youmans, Gilbert, 'Reconsidering Chaucer's Prosody', in C. B. McCully and J. J. Anderson (eds.), *English Historical Metrics* (Cambridge, 1996), 185–209.

Young, Karl, *The Origin and Development of the Story of Troilus and Criseyde* (Chaucer Society, 2nd series, 40; London, 1908).

Glossary

This glossary aims to explain words and phrases in *Troilus and Crise-yde* which are used in ways unfamiliar in modern English, and to provide references, by book and line number, to typical instances. Words with the same meaning and the same or very similar forms in modern English are not generally recorded, but familiar words are included where they have a different range of senses than in modern English or form part of phrases and idioms now unfamiliar. Where words are included on account of meanings no longer current, the modern meaning has not necessarily been noted. Although some overlap is unavoidable in the interests of helpfulness to the general reader, this glossary and the on-page glossing are designed to be complementary, with the glossary providing information on the part of speech of a word and its possible range of senses. Not all words used only once, or rarely but with the same meaning, and for which a page gloss has been provided at each occurrence, are included in the glossary.

Glosses are arranged within the entries in approximate order of frequency and importance in *Troilus* rather than as a record of a word's historical or semantic development. Variant spellings, regular verb inflections, noun plurals, etc., are not specifically entered, but forms likely to cause difficulties of identification are recorded, both under their own form and under the headword to which they belong. Verbs are generally entered in the infinitive form, unless it is only the inflected form(s) that occur in *Troilus* or are likely to cause difficulty. Otherwise, a headword for an inflected form is followed by a reference to the infinitive form, where glosses will be found. Where a verb has special forms to be recorded, these are generally placed at the end of an entry, as in the case of strong verbs (which form their past tense and past participle by a change in the vowel of the stem). In passages quoted within entries, a tilde (~) represents the headword in its form in that passage, except where a special form is given in full.

Parentheses are used to indicate forms that appear both with and

without final -*e* or -*n*. Parentheses are also used in entries for words –
abo(o)d, ap(p)ayed – where a vowel or consonant is variously written
with a single or double letter, or in the case of minor variants such as
-*a(u)nce, -cio(u)n*.

Abbreviations

1, 2, 3, first, second, third person
adj adjective
adv adverb
auxil auxiliary
comp comparative
conj conjunction
contr contracted, contraction
dat dative
dem demonstrative
fig figuratively
gen genitive
imp imperative
impers impersonal
infin infinitive
intens intensifier
interj interjection
intrans intransitive
n noun
num numeral

pl plural
poss possessive
pp past participle
pr present tense
prep preposition
pron pronoun
prp present participle
pt past tense
refl reflexive
rel relative
sg singular
s.o. some one
s.th. something
subj subjunctive
superl superlative
trans transitive
v verb
vbl n verbal noun

a *prep* in; **a-temple** in the temple
1.363
abaist, abaysed *pp* abashed 3.94,
3.1122; frightened 3.1233
abedde *adv* in bed 1.915; to bed
3.1679
abet *n* incitement, urging
2.357
abide(n, abyde *v* stay, remain
1.474, 3.1432; delay 5.1202;
wait, be patient 1.956, 2.1158,
4.1328; await, wait for 4.156,
5.1175; *3 pr sg contr* **abit**
1.1091; *imp* **abid** 2.985; *pt sg*
abo(o)d 1.127, 4.156

able *adj* deserving 2.207;
inclined 2.903
abod *n* delay 3.854, 5.1307
abo(o)d *pt sg of* **abide(n** *v*
aboughte *pt pl* paid for, suffered
5.1756
aboute *adv* about, around 1.149,
268; **bryngen ~** cause 4.1275
aboute *prep* round, around; in
attendance on 2.215; **ben ~** be
engaged in 5.1645; **gon ~**
occupy oneself with 1.863,
1091
above(n *prep* above 1.154,
4.1679

abregge *v* abridge, shorten
3.262, 4.426, 925

abreyde, abrayde *v* wake 5.520;
regain consciousness 3.1113,
4.1212; start up 1.724

abusioun *n* absurdity 4.990;
falsehood 4.1060

accesse *n* sudden illness, fever
2.1315, 1543, 1578

accident *n* occurrence 3.918; ines-
sential attribute 4.1505

accusement *n* accusation 4.556

accusour *n* revealer, betrayer
3.1450

acord *n* accord, agreement
3.1750

acorde *v* agree, consent 4.1109,
1519, 5.1310; ~ to concern
3.1409; arrange 4.808; be in
harmony 5.446

acorse *v* curse 3.1072, 4.839; *pp*
acorsed accursed 3.1452, 4.251

acoye *v* soothe, coax, entice
5.782

acuse *v* blame 2.1081

adawe *v* awake 3.1120

a-day *adv* by day 1.1075, 2.60

adieu *interj* goodbye, farewell
1.1041, 4.630

adorneth *3 pr sg* ornaments 3.2

adoun, adown *adv* down, down-
wards 1.110, 2.407, 515

adrad *pp adj* afraid 2.115

adversaries *n* enemies 2.1435

adverse *adj* contrary, hostile,
unfavourable 4.1192

adversite(e) *n* misfortune, hard-
ship, adversity 1.25

advertence *n* attention, concern
4.698, 5.1258

advocacies *n pl* charges, accusa-
tions 2.1469

afer *adv* afar 1.313, 2.516

a-fere *adv* (*see also* afire) on fire
1.229

afered *pp adj* afraid 1.974,
2.606, 3.482

affeccioun *n* affection 1.296;
emotion, feeling 4.153

affectis *n pl* desires 3.1391

afferme *v* affirm 2.1588

affile *v* file, polish 2.1681

afire, a-fyre *adv* on fire 3.24,
856, 4.509, 5.720

aforyeyn *prep* opposite 2.1188

after *adv* afterwards 1.4, 2.1746;
right ~ just as 3.175

after *prep* after, following 1.293;
for 1.619

after *conj* after; ~ that in the
manner which 2.1347

a-game *adv* in jest 3.636, 648

agaste *v* frighten 2.901; *pp* agast
afraid 1.715

agayn, agayns *see* ayein, ayeyns
prep

age *n* age, time of life 5.826,
1836; old age 2.395; era,
period 2.27

ago(o)(n *pp* departed, gone
2.410, 4.1090; ago 2.722

agree(n *v* agree 3.131; suit,
please 1.409

agreveth *3 pr sg* harms 5.783

agrief, a-grief *adv*: take it not ~
do not take it hard, be
annoyed, upset 3.862, 1621,
4.613

agrise *v* shudder with fear, be
frightened 2.1435; *pt sg*
agroos 2.930

agylt(e) *v intrans* do wrong
4.261, 5.1684; *trans* wrong,
offend 3.840, 1457

ail(l)eth *3 pr sg* afflicts 1.766;
what ~ yow what's the matter
with you 2.211, 4.331

ake *v* ache 2.549; *n* 3.1561; *vbl n*
akyngge aching 1.1088

al, alle *adj and n* all 1.100,
2.139; ~ **and/or some** one and
all 1.240, 3.607, 5.883; **in** ~
entirely 1.396

al *adv* entirely, completely
1.316; ~ **right** exactly 1.99;
(introducing a concessive
clause, with subject-verb order
inverted and verb in subjunc-
tive form, e.g. **al sholde I**)
although, even if 1.17, 3.87

alday *adv* all the time, continu-
ally 1.106, 217; constantly
4.1563

alderbest(e *adj* best of all 3.1597;
adv best of all 1.1008

alderfirst, aldirfirst *adj* very first
3.97; *adv* first of all 1.1069,
4.74, 832

alderlest *adv* least of all 1.604

alderlevest *adj* very dearest
3.239, 5.576

aldermost, aldirmost *adv* most of
all 1.152, 248, 1003

alderwisest *adj* wisest of all
1.247

aleyes *n pl* alleys, garden paths
2.820

algate(s *adv* at any rate 2.964,
5.1071; especially 3.24

alighte *v* alight, dismount; *pt sg*
5.189; *pt pl* 5.513; descend
5.1017

allegge *v* cite, adduce 3.297

alliaunce *n* association, bond of
friendship, trust 3.1746

allied *pp* joined 1.87

aloes *see* **ligne aloes** *n*

alofte *adv* (*see also* **o-lofte**)
above, on top 1.922; in the air
3.670

along *adj*: ~ **on** owing to,
because of 2.1001, 3.783

alose *v* commend 4.1473

als *adv* as 2.726

also *adv conj* also 1.327; as
1.523, 3.1633; (introducing
asseverations) 3.1378

altered *3 pt sg* changed 3.1778

alway, alwey, alweies *adv*
always, continually 1.782; pro-
gressively 3.242; any way, in
any event 5.298

am *1 pr sg of* **be(n** *v*; **it am I** it is I
3.752

amayed *pp* dismayed, amazed
1.648, 4.641

ambages *n pl* ambiguities 5.897

amende(n *v* improve, improve
upon 2.854, 3.422, 1287,
5.829; mend, make better
2.1731; put right 5.692, 1613,
1741; relieve 5.138; make
amends 2.245

amendes *n pl* amends, rec-
ompense; **maken** ~ (**of** 'for')
2.342

among *adv* mixed in 3.1816

amonges *prep* amongst 1.900,
2.1175

amorous *adj* enamoured 3.17; ~
daunce love-making 4.1431

a-morwe *adv* in the morning
2.405; next morning 2.1521

amphibologies *n pl* ambiguities
4.1406

amydde *prep* in the middle of
1.417

amys *adj* amiss, wrong 2.313;

adv amiss, wrongly 4.1410;
    don ~ 3.270; **fare ~** 1.491; **seye**
    ~ 2.1048; **take ~** 2.229
and *conj* and 1.14; if 1.125,
    2.289
angre *n* anger 1.563, 5.1535
angwissh *n* anguish, distress
    4.155, 844
angwissous *adj* painful, distress-
    ing 3.816
anhonged *pp* hanged 2.1620
ano(o)n *adv* at once, immedi-
    ately 1.75, 116
anon-right, anonright *adv*
    immediately 1.389, 2.1551
anoy *n* trouble, vexation 4.845
answerd(e) *pt* answered 1.737,
    1037
answerynge *prp* corresponding
    1.282
apaisen *see* **apese** *v*
ap(p)ayed *pp* pleased, satisfied
    3.421, 5.1249; **yvele ~** dis-
    pleased 1.649, 4.642
ape *n* ape, monkey 2.1042;
    goddes apes born fools
    1.913
apeired *pp* injured, damaged,
    harmed 1.38
aperceyve *v* perceive, realize
    4.656
apese *v* appease, assuage 3.22,
    110, 887, 5.117; *pp* **apesed**
    1.250, 940
apoynte *v* decide 3.454; specify
    5.1620; *refl* decide, settle 2.691
appaire *pr subj pl* should perish
    2.329
appetit *n* desire 4.1677; appetite,
    craving 5.1851
aproche *v* approach 3.1696, 5.1,
    1549

aquayntaunce *n* acquaintance,
    companionship 5.122
aquite *v* repay, reward 2.1200
arace *v* uproot, tear out 3.1015,
    5.954
ar(r)ay *n* dress, gear 2.1264; dis-
    play, splendour 4.1670; prep-
    arations 3.536; behaviour,
    conduct 3.1798
ar(r)ayed *pp* dressed 1.167,
    3.423; decorated 2.1187;
    located 2.680; destined 2.200
arede *v* interpret, explain 2.132;
    guess 2.1505, 4.1112, 1570
argu(w)e *v* debate, dispute
    2.694, 4.497, 5.772
argument *n* reasoning 1.466,
    2.1025; sign 4.1179; **maken ~**
    reason, assert 4.477
argumented *pt sg* reasoned 1.377
aright *adv* correctly 3.199; prop-
    erly 2.1261; straightaway,
    directly 3.462; **faren ~** be suc-
    cessful, do well 1.878, 2.999
arise, aryse *v* stand up, get up
    2.221, 1059; *pt sg* **aros** 2.598;
    pp **arise** 2.1462
armes *n pl* armour 3.1773; deeds
    of arms, warfare 1.470,
    5.1556
armonye *n* harmony 5.1812
arn *pr pl of* **be(n** *v*
aros *pt sg of* **arise** *v*
art 2 *pr sg of* **be(n** *v*
arten *v* urge on 1.388
artow *contr of* **art thow** 2 *pr sg*
    of **be(n** *v*
arwe *n* arrow 2.641, 4.44,
    4.1548
as *adv and conj* (with *subj*) as if,
    as though 3.64; (in assever-
    ations) as, so 3.790; **as help me**

5.999; (introducing impera-
tive; no modern equivalent)
5.523; (*as intens, with adv*) as
faste very quickly 2.898; as
now just now, for the present
3.190; as paramours passion-
ately 5.158; as who seith as if
to say 1.1011
ascaunces *adv conj* as if to say
1.205, 292
ascry *n* outcry, alarm 2.611
ashamed *pp adj*: for pure ~ out
of very shame 2.656
aske(n *see* axe(n *v*
asonder *adv* asunder, apart
3.660, 1339, 1763
aspectes *n pl* aspects, disposition
(of planets) 2.682, 3.716
asp *n* aspen tree; *gen sg* 3.1200
aspie *v* (*see also* espye(n) descry
2.649; discover, notice 2.1507,
3.573; *pt sg* aspide 2.1252;
tyme ~ find an opportunity
5.556
aspre *adj* bitter, sharp 4.827,
847, 1501, 5.265, 1326
assaile *v* attack 1.607, 4.1595
as(s)ay *n* trial, test; putten in ~
test 4.1508
assaye, asay *v* try, attempt 5.783,
788; test 5.1760; investigate
4.639, 1104; experience 1.646,
3.1447
asse *n* ass 1.731; asses ass's
2.1042
assege *n* siege 1.464, 2.107, 123,
4.62, 1480, 5.857
assegeden *pt pl* besieged 1.60
assembled *pt sg* came together
2.1567; *pp* come together
4.1258
assent *n* consent 4.165; opinion

4.535; will, intent 4.554; by
oon ~ with one accord, by gen-
eral agreement 4.346; of oon ~
of one mind 4.933
assente *v* agree, consent 1.391
asseuraunce *n* confidence 5.1259
asshen *n pl* ashes 2.539, 4.119
assigne *v* offer, allege 5.1302
assoilen *v* resolve, solve 5.1453
assure *v* grow confident 5.870;
trust 1.680, 5.1624; *pp adj*
assured confident 1.182,
3.1395
asterte *v* escape; *pr sg* asterte
1.1050, 3.97, 1070; *pr subj sg*
5.1343
astoned *pp adj* stunned, stu-
pefied 1.274, 2.427, 3.1089;
bewildered 2.603; dumb-
founded 5.1728
astrologer *n* astronomer, star-
gazer 3.1415
astronomye *n* astrological divi-
nation 4.115
asure *n* lapis lazuli 3.1370
aswage *v* lessen, diminish 4.255
a-swowne *adv* in a swoon, uncon-
scious 3.1092
a-temple *see* a *prep*
atempre *adj* moderate, restrained
1.953
athynken *v* displease 5.878;
impers with dat m'athenketh
I am displeased 1.1050
atir *n* attire, dress 1.181
aton *adv* at one, in agreement
3.565
atones, attones, at-ones, atonys
adv at once, immediately
2.939, 5.41; at the same time,
together 1.90, 804, 4.841
atrede *v* outwit 4.1456

atrenne *v* outrun 4.1456

atte *contr of* at the (in set phrases): ~ fulle squarely 1.209; ~ laste finally 1.1047, 2.145; ~ leeste at least 2.362

attendaunces *n pl* attentions 1.339

attricioun *n* regret, imperfect remorse for sin, short of contrition 1.557

atwixe(n *prep* between 4.821, 5.472, 886

a-two *adv* in two 3.1475, 5.180, 530

atwynne *adv* apart 3.1666, 4.1614

auctorite *n* authority 1.65

auctour *n* authority 1.394, 2.18, 49, 700; creator 3.1016, 1765; writer 5.1088

audience *n* hearing; yeven ~ listen (to) 4.70, 545, 5.235

aught, ought *n* anything 1.578, 1035; for ~ I woot/kan aspien for all I know/ can see 3.447, 1135, 4.1469; for ~ that may bitide whatever may happen 3.1736, 5.59; in ~ as far as 4.1285; in any way 3.524; for ~ so far as 4.1164

aught, ought *adv* at all, in any way 1.123, 383, 633, 864

aughte *see* oughte *v*

augurye *n* augury, divination by omens 4.116, 5.380

aungelik *adj* angel-like, angelic 1.102

auter *n* altar 5.1466

autour *n* (*see also* auctour) author, source authority 3.502

availle *v* avail, be effective 4.937,

5.1850; be of use to 1.604, 3.520, 5.449; help, benefit 1.756, 2.1439; *pr subj sg* availle 1.20

avale *v* come down 3.626

avaunce *v* advance, promote, further 1.47, 518, 3.1386, 5.1435

avaunt *n* boast 1.1050, 3.289; maken ~ boast 2.727

avaunte *v refl* boast 3.318

avauntour *n* boaster 2.724, 3.308, 314

aventaille *n* chain-mail neck-guard on helmet 5.1558

aventure *n* chance 1.568, 4.388; fortune, lot 1.1092, 2.742, 5.1540; misfortune 1.35; (good) fortune 1.368, 2.224, 281, 4.324; opportunity 2.1519; event, experience 4.1329; *n pl* 1.3; in ~ uncertain 1.784; on ~ in case, to provide for the event 5.298

avise *v* look at, contemplate 1.364, 2.276, 5.1814; consider 2.1701; decide 4.1262; instruct, advise 2.1695; *refl* consider 2.1124, 1730; *prp* avysyng deliberating 3.157; (with of) considering 5.1657; *pp* avysed (having) considered 2.1177; informed, aware 3.328; resolved, determined 3.1186

avowe *v* vow, affirm 3.855

avys *n* advice 1.620; judgement, deliberation 3.453, 4.416

avysement *n* deliberation 2.343, 4.936, 1300; with ful ~ clearly 5.1811

avysiouns *n pl* dreams, visions
5.374

await *n* watchfulness, caution
3.457; delay 3.579

awe *n* fear; **han in ~** fear 1.1006;
for any ~ despite any fear 4.620

a-wepe *adv*: **breste ~** burst out
weeping 2.408

awey(e *adv* gone 4.357; out of
the way 2.1194; over, finished
2.123; **falle ~ fro** leave 3.1306;
exclam go away 3.1321,
5.1525

awhaped *pp adj* confounded
1.316

awook *pt sg of* **awake** 3.751

axe(n *v* ask 2.147; need, require
2.227

ay *adv* always, ever 1.44, 449;
every time, ever 2.483; all the
time 2.643; **~ newe** always
1.440; **~ wher** wherever 2.200

ayeyn *adv* back 2.1141; again
2.52; in return 2.391; in reply
5.1589

ayein *prep* again 1.280; **~ the
moone shene** in the moonlight
2.920; **~ the sonne** in the sun-
shine 5.1285

ayeyns, ayens *prep* against, con-
trary to 1.228, 603, 902

ayeynward *adv* back again
3.750, 4.1581; on the other
hand 4.1027

bad, badde *pt sg of* **bidde** *v*
baiten *v* feed 1.192
bak *n* back 2.639, 3.1247,
5.811
bakward *adv* backwards 4.1553
balaunce *n*: **in ~** at risk 2.466,
4.1560

bale *n* suffering 4.739

bane *n* death 4.774, 907; destruc-
tion 2.320, 5.602; destroyer
4.333

bar *pt sg of* **bere(n** *v*

barbe *n* wimple, woman's head
dress 2.110

bare *adj* bare, naked 2.110,
4.226; uncovered 3.1099,
4.1522; unsheathed 4.1225;
deprived 4.1168; inadequate,
useless 1.662

baroun *n* nobleman 4.33,
190

bataille *n* battle 2.630

bathe *v* bathe, bask 1.22, 2.849,
4.208

baude *n* bawd, pimp 2.353

bauderye *n* (act of) procuring,
pandering 3.397

bawme *n* balm, balsam 2.53

be(n *v* to be 2.1056; 1 *pr sg* am
1.10; 2 *pr sg* art 1.555, (*with
suffixed pron*) artow 1.731,
(with unstressed *pron*) arte
5.1161; *pr pl* arn 1.1006, be
2.113, ben 2.235; *pr subj sg* be
1.890; *pr subj pl* be 2.584; *imp
sg* be 4.651; *imp pl* beth 2.302;
1 *& 3 pt sg* was 1.2; *pt pl*
were(n 1.283, 455; *pt subj sg,
pl* were 1.51, 2.353; *pp* ybe
4.1108

beaute, beute *n* beauty
1.102

be(e)de *v* offer 4.1105, 5.185

beele *adj* fair, lovely 2.288

been *n pl* bees 2.193, 4.1356

be(e)ne *n* bean; as something
valueless: **nat (worth) a ~**
3.1167, 5.363

beer(e *n* bear 3.1780, 4.1453

beere *n* bier 2.1638, 4.863,
    1183, 1208
before *see* **biforn** *adv*
behelden *pt pl of* **biholde** *v*
bekke(n *v* nod 2.1260
bemes *n pl* beams 2.54, 3.1,
    1418, 5.9, 643
ben *pr pl of* **be(n** *v*
benched *pp* furnished with
    benches 2.822
bende *v* bend 2.1378; turn, go
    2.1250; *pt pl* **benten**: in ~ his
    bowe tried it, experienced
    (love) 2.861; *pp* **bente** strung
    4.40
bendiste, benedicite *exclam* (the
    Lord) bless you 1.780, 3.757,
    860
benigne *adj* kind, gentle, con-
    siderate 1.431, 3.26, 1802; gra-
    cious 3.1261, 5.1869
benignite *n* goodness, gracious-
    ness, kindness 1.40, 2.532,
    3.39, 1285
bente: in ~ **moone** quarter, cres-
    cent moon 3.624
benten *pt pl of* **bende** *v*
berd *n* beard; in the ~ face to
    face 4.41
bere(n *v* carry 1.650; have, keep
    5.460; give birth to 4.763; *refl*
    behave, conduct o.s. 2.401,
    1498; ~ **the belle** come first
    3.198; ~ **lif** live 2.835; ~ **on**
    hond accuse 3.1154, accuse
    (falsely), persuade 4.1404; *pr*
    sg **berth** 5.460; *pt sg* **bar**
    3.488; *pp* **bore** born 2.1412
beset *pp* bestowed 1.521 (*see*
    also **bisette** *v*)
beste *adj as n*: my (oure, thi *etc.*)
    ~ my (our, your *etc.*) best

course 1.597, 1028,
    2.382
bestes *n pl* beasts, creatures
    3.620
bestialite *n* animal nature, con-
    dition 1.735
besy *see* **bisy** *adj*
besynesses *see* **bisynesse** *n*
bet *adj comp* better 1.257; *adv*
    comp better 1.275
bete(n *v* (1) beat, strike 3.1416;
    (of heart, *etc.*) beat 4.910; *imp*
    sg **bet** 1.932; *pt sg* **bet** 4.752;
    pp **ybete(n** beaten 1.741,
    2.940
bete(n *v* (2) cure, assuage 1.665,
    4.928
beth *imp pl of* **be(n** *v*
bettre *adj* better 2.177; *adv*
    2.1215
bewaille *see* **biwaille** *v*
bewared *pp* employed, applied
    1.636
bewreye *see* **bywreye(n** *v*
beye *v* (*see also* **bye(n**) redeem
    5.1843
biblotte *v* blot 2.1027
bicome(n *v* become 1.434; *pt sg*
    bicom 1.1079; *pr subj sg*
    bycome 2.1151; **wher** ~ **it/he**
    what becomes of it (him)
    2.795, 1151
bidde *v* command, tell 1.357;
    ask, beg 1.1027; pray 2.118,
    3.875; wish, desire 3.1249;
    imp sg **bid** 3.342; *pt sg* **bad**
    1.112; *pp* **boden** 3.691
bide, byde *v* wait 1.1067,
    2.1651; await 2.1519; stay
    4.162; 5.496; *imp sg* **byd, bid**
    2.1519, 3.740; *pt sg* **bood** 5.29
bifalle, byfalle *v* befall, happen,

occur 1.236; *pt sg* **bifel** (*with omission of subject*) it happened 1.155, 271; **byfallynge** *vbl n* happening 4.1018, 1076

biforn, byfore, before *adv* before, previously 2.966, 4.977

biforn, byforn *prep* before, in front of 1.110

bigete *pp* begotten 1.977

bigge *adj* strong 4.40

bigile, bigyle *v* deceive 2.270, 4.3; delude 5.881; trick (out of) 1.716; wile away (time) 5.404

bigon, bygon *pp* (*see also* **wo-bygon**) beset, overwhelmed; **wel** (**wo, sorwfully** *etc.*) ~ in a happy (sad, sorrowful, *etc.*) situation 1.114, 2.294, 597, 3.117, 4.464, 5.1328

biheld *pt sg of* **biholde** *v*

bihe(e)ste *n* promise 2.359, 423, 3.315, 5.1431, 1675

bihete *v* promise; *pr subj pl* **byheete** 1.539; *pt sg* **bihighte** 5.510; *pt pl* **bihyghte** 3.319; *pp* **bihyght** 5.354

biholde *v* see, look at, gaze on 1.275; observe, consider 5.533, 1748; *pt sg* **byheld** 2.275; *pt pl* **behelden** 1.177; *pt subj sg* **byhelde** 2.378

bihovely *adj* useful, needful 2.261

bihoveth: in to hym ~ it behooves him, he must 1.858; ~ **it** it is necessary 4.1024, 1054

bileve *v* believe 2.1502

bille *n* letter 2.1130

bilynne *v* cease 3.1365

bi-path *n* short-cut 3.1705

biseche, biseke *v* beseech, pray, beg 2.1674; *pt sg* **bisoughte** 2.1354

bisegede(n *pt pl* besieged 1.149, 5.1496; *pp* **biseged** 1.558, 802

bisette *v* employ 3.471; bestow 3.1552; *pp* **beset, biset** bestowed 1.521, 905

biseyn *pp* in appearance 2.1262

bishet *pp* shut up 3.602

bisily *adv* earnestly 1.771, 3.1153, 4.669; diligently, zealously 2.1357, 4.486, 941; anxiously 5.452

bisoughte *pt sg of* **biseche** *v*

bisy, besy *adj* busy, active 1.355; anxious 3.1042

bisynesse *n* activity, employment 2.1174; diligence 3.165, 1610; attention 3.1413; task 1.1042; **don** (one's) ~ strive, endeavour 1.795, 2.1316, 3.244, 363, 4.1488

bithynken *v* consider, think of 1.982, 3.1694; *pt sg* **bythought** 1.545; *pp* **bithought** 2.225

bitide(n, bityde(n *v* happen, come about 2.623; *3 pr sg* **bitit** 2.48, 5.345; *pt sg* **bitidde** 2.55; *pp* **bitid** 3.288

bitokneth *3 pr sg* means, symbolizes 5.1513

bittre *adj* bitter 1.385; *as n* torment, suffering 3.179

bitwene, bytwene *adv* in between 2.823; in the meanwhile 5.1086

bitwixe(n *prep* between 1.135, 417

biwaille, bywaille, bewaille *v* bewail, lament 1.755, 5.639,

1556; lament the loss of 4.272;
prp **bywayling** 1.547, 4.1251

blame *n* reproach, censure 2.15;
have ~ be blamed 4.551; dis-
grace, scandal 3.265; fault,
guilt 5.1068; **in ~** at fault
4.594; **~ have I** I am at fault
2.210

blame(n *v* reproach, censure,
find fault with 4.527; **ben to ~**
be at fault 2.287; *2 pr sg (with
suffixed pron)* **blamestow**
1.841

blase *n* fire 4.184

blast *n* gust of wind 2.1387

blaunche *adj* white; **in ~ fevere**
'white fever', i.e. love-sickness
1.916

blede *v* bleed 1.502; *pt* **bledde**
2.950

blende *v* blind, deceive, delude
2.1496, 3.207, 4.5, 648, 1399,
1462, 5.526; *pt sg* **blente**
5.1195; *pp* **blent** 2.1743

blesse *v* bless 3.1595; protect
1.436

bleve(n *v* remain, stay 3.623,
4.539, 1357, 1484, 5.478,
1180

blew(e *adj* blue 2.51, 3.885

bleynte *pt sg* turned 3.1346

blisful *adj* blissful, happy
3.1317; blessed 1.1014, 3.705;
beneficent 2.680; fortunate
2.422; fair, beautiful 3.1

blisfully *adv* happily 5.570, 1808

blisse *n* happiness 2.849; **in ~** in
heaven 3.342; **hevene ~**
heavenly bliss 3.704, 1322

blissed *pp adj* blessed 1.308

blithe *adj* happy, joyous 3.1318,
1682, 5.1383

blody *adj* bloody, blood-stained
2.203, 3.724

blood *n* lineage, family, race
5.600; kin, relative 2.594

blosmy *adj* flowery 2.821

blyve *adv* quickly 1.595, 2.1605,
3.225; **bylyve** as soon as poss-
ible 2.1513; **as/also ~** at once
1.965, 2.137, 208, 4.174

boden *pp of* **bidde** *v*

bok *n* book 3.1818, 5.1786

bole *n* bull 3.723, 4.239; the
zodiacal sign Taurus 2.55

bon(e *n* bone 1.805, 2.926; **fel
and bones** skin and bones, com-
pletely 1.91, 3.591

bo(o)ne *n* request, prayer
1.1027, 4.68, 5.594

bond *n* band, chain, fetter 2.976,
3.1358, 1766; binding force
3.1261; constraint, confine-
ment 3.1116

bonde *adj* unfree, enslaved, in
slavery 1.255, 2.1223; *n* serf,
slave 1.840

bood *pt sg of* **bide** *v*

bo(o)r *n* boar 3.721, 1780,
5.1238, 1449

boot *n* boat 1.416, 2.3

bo(o)t(e *n* remedy, relief 1.352,
763, 2.1379; **do ~** do good,
help, heal 2.345, 3.61, 5.672;
find a remedy 4.614

booteles *adj* without remedy
1.782

bore *n* chink 3.1453

bore *pp of* **bere(n** *v*

born *pp* born 1.904; by birth
4.332; living 5.155

borneth *3 pr sg* polishes 1.327

borugh, borwe *n* surety, one leg-
ally responsible for another's

fulfilling a pledge 1.1038,
2.134; **to** ~ as a pledge 2.963,
1524, 5.1664

borwe *v* borrow 1.488, 5.726

bost *n* boast, boasting 3.248,
298

bothe *adj; gen* **oure** ~ of us both
1.972; **youre bother** of you
both 4.168; *as n* **booth** 2.329

botme *n* bottom 1.297, 2.535

botmeles *adj* without founda-
tion, groundless 5.1431

bought *pp of* **bye(n** *v*

bounde *pp of* **bynde** *v*

boundes *n pl* boundaries, limits
3.1272

bounte *n* goodness, kindness
2.1444, 3.882

bountevous *adj* bountiful, gener-
ous 1.883

bowen *v* bend 1.257, 2.1387

brak *pt sg of* **breke** *v*

brast *pt sg of* **breste** *v*

braunche *n* branch 4.227, 5.844;
species 3.132

brede *n* breadth 5.1657; space
1.179; **on** ~ abroad 1.530

brede *v* breed, arise, grow
3.1546, 5.1027; *pt sg* **bredde**
1.465

breke *v* interrupt 2.1600,
5.1032; be interrupted 3.1403;
~ **feith, biheste, heste** break
one's word 1.89, 3.315, 5.355;
pt sg **brak** 2.1600; *pr subj*
breke 5.1032

breme *adv* fiercely 4.184

brenne(n *v* burn 1.91; be
inflamed 4.704; *pt sg* **brende,
brente** 1.440, 2.1337; *pp*
ybrend 5.309; **brennynge** *vbl n*
burning, cremation 5.1499

brennyngly *adv* ardently 1.607

breste *v trans* break 3.1434; *v
intrans* break, burst 1.599,
3.1637; burst out 2.408,
4.373, 5.1078; *3 pr sg* **brest**
1.258, 3.1637; *pt sg* **brast**
5.180; *pt pl* **breste** 2.326; *pt
subj sg* **brest** 2.1108; *pp*
brosten 2.976

breth(e)ren *n pl* brothers 1.471,
2.1438

breyde *v* start, wake 5.1243; ~
out of (one's) **wit** go mad, out
of one's mind 4.230, 348,
5.1262

brid *n* bird 3.10; **briddes** *gen sg*
2.921; *n pl* 4.1432

bridel *n* bridle, reins 1.953,
3.1762, 5.92, 873

bridlen *v* bridle, control; *imp sg*
bridle 3.1635; *pt sg* **bridlede**
4.1678

bright *adj* bright, shining 1.175;
(of women) radiant, fair,
beautiful 1.166

bringe *v* bring 1.560; ~ **of lyve**
kill 2.1608, 5.1561; **out** ~ utter
3.99, 107; ~ **to preve** put to the
test 3.307; ~ **to meschaunce**
destroy, ruin 4.203; *pt sg*
broughte 3.586; *pt pl* **broughte**
2.914; *pp* **brought** 1.424

broch(e *n* brooch 3.1370,
5.1040

brode *adj* broad, wide 5.1017

brosten *pp of* **breste** *v*

brotel *adj* brittle, fragile, un-
certain 3.820

brotelnesse *n* fickleness, un-
dependability 5.1832

brother *n* brother; *gen sg* 1.678

brought(e *pt & pp of* **bringe** *v*

broun *adj* dark 1.109
browe *n* eyebrow 1.204
burgeys *n* burgess, citizen 4.345
burthe *n* birth 4.839, 5.209
busshel *n* bushel (measure or
   weight of corn) 3.1025
but *conj* but, except 1.1038,
   3.232; unless 1.383; ~ if unless
   1.413, 4.221; **I nam** ~ I am as
   good as 5.706, 1246; *adv* only
   1.223
by *prep* by, beside 2.1228;
   through, over 5.1144; towards
   5.1193; at 5.1491; during
   1.452; **by the morwe** in the
   morning 2.961; **by this** by this
   time 3.793; with respect to
   1.225, 3.936; in comparison
   with 1.889; according to
   2.1341
bycause *conj* because 3.991,
   4.223; (with **that**) 4.717; *adv*
   (with **of**) 4.1341; (*also as two
   words*)
bye(n *v* buy, pay for; ~ **dere** pay
   dearly for 1.136, 4.291, 5.965,
   1801; redeem 3.1165; *pt pl*
   boughten 1.136; *pp* **bought**
   4.291
byhalve *n* behalf 2.1458
byjaped *pp* fooled, deceived
   5.1119; mocked 1.531
byleve *n* belief, faith 5.593
bynde *v* bind, tie 1.237; hold
   2.359; *imp sg* **bynd** 3.1750; *pp*
   bounde 1.859
byquethe *v* bequeath 4.786
byreve *v* take away, remove
   4.225, 277; deprive 2.1722,
   4.228; prevent 1.685; *pr subj
   pl* **byreeve** 2.1722; *pp* **byraft**
   4.228

byreyned *pt* showered 4.1172
bytyme *adv* early, soon 2.1093;
   in good time 4.1105
bytraise *v* betray 5.1783; *pp*
   bitraised 4.1648, 5.1780
bytrent *3 pr sg* encircles 3.1231,
   4.870
bywepe *v* lament, weep over
   1.762; *pp* **bywopen** in tears
   4.916
by-word *n* proverb 4.769
bywreye(n *v* reveal 2.537, 1370

ca(a)s *n* case, situation, circum-
   stance 2.422; **(as) in this** ~ in
   this situation 3.283, 4.668; **for
   no** ~ in no circumstances
   4.635; event, occurrence
   4.420; chance, fate 2.285,
   4.388; **in** ~ in the event that, if
   2.758, 4.1509; **upon** ~ by
   chance 1.271, 4.649; **sette** ~
   put the case, assume for the
   sake of argument 2.729
cache *v* catch 1.214; seize, take
   hold of 2.291, 448; recover
   1.280; come by, receive 5.602;
   ~ **an hete** become hot 2.942; ~
   his lyves ende meet his death
   5.1554; *pt* **caughte** 5.602,
   1554; *pp* **ikaught** 1.534;
   caught 1.557
calkulynge *n* calculation 1.71,
   4.1398
cape *v* gape; ~ **after** seek, look
   for 3.558, 5.1133
care *n* grief, sorrow 1.505, 550,
   587; **maken** ~ grieve, lament
   5.336; anxiety, concern
   1.1023, 5.54; **have no** ~ don't
   worry 3.1066; *pl* (esp. **colde** ~)
   miseries 1.264

care(n *v* be anxious, worry
3.670, 1645
carte *n* chariot 5.278, 665
cast *n* throwing 2.868
caste(n *v* throw 2.513, 615; ~
forth utter 2.1167; turn, direct
5.927, 1825; consider, deliber-
ate 1.749, 2.659, 1485; decide
1.75; plan 1.1071; calculate
2.74; *pp* cast felled 2.1389
casuel *adv* due to chance 4.419
caughte *pt of* cache *v*
cause *n* cause, reason 2.727; ~
why the reason (was) 3.795;
by the ~ because 5.127, 1342;
by that ~ because 4.99; case,
condition 1.20, 5.1230; maken
~ further one's purpose 5.80;
pretext 3.1162
causeles *adv* without cause 1.779
causyng *prp adj* original,
primary 4.829
caytif *n* captive, prisoner 3.382;
wretch 4.104
cedre *n* cedar tree 2.918
celestial *adj* heavenly 1.979,
4.1541
cerclen *v* encircle, encompass
3.1767
certein *adj* fixed, settled 3.532,
1431, 4.1012; a ~ a certain
number (of) 3.596; sure, firm
3.1030; for ~ certainly 4.120;
in ~ certainly 4.908; in noun ~
in uncertainty 1.337
certes *adv* certainly, to be sure
1.572, 773
certeyn *adv* certainly, indeed
1.492, 2.724
certeynlich *adv* certainly 5.100
cesse(n *v intrans* cease 2.692; *v*
trans stop, cause to stop 1.445;

pr subj sg cesse 2.483, 1388;
pt subj sg cessed 1.849; *pp*
cessed 2.787
chace *v* in: ~ at attack 1.908; har-
ass, persecute 3.1801
cha(u)mbre *v* room, bedroom
1.358, 547
champioun *n* defender (of one of
the parties) in a judicial dual
2.1427
chaunge *n* change, alteration
2.22; exchange 4.665
cha(u)nge(n *v* change, vary
2.1470, 4.485, 5.122, 1683;
exchange 4.553; *pp* ychaunged
4.865
chaungynge *n* exchange 4.231
char *n* chariot 3.1704
charge *n* burden 1.651; respons-
ibility 1.444; task, duty 2.994,
4.180
chargen *v* trouble 2.1437; be
important 3.1576
char-hors *n pl* chariot horses
5.1018
charitable *adj* benevolent, gra-
cious 5.823
charite *n* charity, the Christian
virtue of love; loving kindness,
benevolence 1.49, 3.1254
charme *n* charm, magic spell
2.1314, 1580
chartres *n pl* documents, deeds
3.340
chastised *pp* admonished 3.329
chaunce *n* event, occurrence
5.1668; fortune, luck 2.464; *pl*
winning throws at dice
2.1347, 4.1098
che(e)re, chiere *n* (facial)
expression 1.14, 280;
manners, behaviour 1.181;

manner, bearing 2.1507;
spirits, mood: **be of good** ~ be
glad, confident 1.879, 3.332;
make (sorwful, good *etc.*) ~ be
sorrowful, cheerful, *etc.* 5.416,
913; hospitality, friendly atten-
tion: **make ~, doon** ~ treat in a
friendly way 2.360, 578
chek: in ~ **mat** check mate 2.754
cheke *n* cheek 4.130
chep *n* bargain; **as good** ~ **as**
profitably 3.641
cherice *v* cherish, hold dear
1.986, 2.726, 3.175
cherisynge *vbl n* love 4.1534
cherl *n* man, fellow 1.1024
chese *v* choose 4.189; **for to** ~ to
be chosen 2.470; *imp sg* **ches**
2.955; *pt sg* **ches** 5.1532
cheterynge *v* twittering 2.68
cheyne *n* chain 1.509, 2.618
chide, chyde *v* reproach 3.1433,
1464, 5.1093
childissh *adj* childish, child-like
3.1168
childisshly *adv* in the manner of
a child 4.804
chiste *n* receptacle 5.1368
chivalrous *adj* brave, chivalric
5.802
chois: in **fre** ~ free will 4.971,
980
chymeneye *n* fireplace 3.1141
circumscrive *v* circumscribe,
encompass 5.1865
cite(e *n* city 1.59
cladde *pt sg of* **clothen** *v*
clause *n* stipulation, condition
2.728; particular, brief passage
5.1301
clawen *v* scratch, rub 4.728
cledde *pt sg of* **clothen** *v*

clene *adv* completely, clean 4.10,
5.1054, 1198
cle(e)ne *adj* pure 2.580, 3.1166;
free, unpolluted 3.257
cle(e)r *adj* bright, shining 3.1;
unimpeded 4.991; free, un-
encumbered 3.526, 982
cle(e)re *adv* brightly 4.1575;
clearly 2.825, 5.578
clepe *v* call, name 1.8; *pp* **clepid**
1.66, 4.762
clere *v* become clear 2.2, 806;
dawn, become light 5.519
clerk *n* scholar, writer 1.961,
1002, 3.41
cleve *v* split 3.375
cleymen *v* claim 5.1487
clippe *v* embrace 3.1344
cloke *n* cloak 3.738
clomben *pp* climbed 1.215
cloth *n* garment 3.733; *pl* bed-
clothes 2.1544
clothen *v* clothe, dress 5.1418; *pt
sg* **cladde, cledde** 4.1690,
3.1521
coghe *v* cough 2.254
cok *n* cock 3.1415
col *n* coal 2.1332
cold(e *adj* chilling, painful, in:
cares ~ 1.264, 3.1202, 5.1747
colde(n *v* grow cold 3.800,
4.362, 418
coler *n* collar 5.811, 1660
collateral *adj* subsidiary,
subordinate 1.262
combre-world *n* burden, encum-
brance to the world 4.279
combust *adj* burnt, obstructed
(in astrological influence)
3.717
comende *v* praise, commend
3.217, 1692, 5.761, 1151

commeve *v* move, influence 3.17,
5.1783

committe *v* commit, entrust 5.4,
1542

compaignie *n* company 1.450;
companionship, friendship
3.396

compassioun *n* sympathy 3.403;
have ~ of sympathize with
1.50, 467

complet *adv* perfectly 5.828

complexiouns *n pl* humours,
characteristics, temperaments
5.369

compleyne *v* lament, mourn,
complain 1.415, 2.1499

compleynt(e *n* lamentation, com-
plaint 1.541, 2.1583

comporte *v* endure 5.1397

comprende *v* contain 3.1687

comune *adj* common, shared
1.843; in common 4.392;
public 3.1415

conceyte *n* conception, idea,
notion 1.692, 996, 3.804

conceyved *pp* understood
5.1598

concord *n* harmony 3.506

concordynge *pp adj* harmonious,
agreeing 3.1752

condicioun *n* state, circum-
stances, situation 3.817,
5.831; character, quality
5.967; *pl* 2.166

conferme *v* confirm, ratify
2.1526, 1589

confounde *v* destroy 4.245

confus *adj* confused 4.356

confusioun *n* destruction, ruin
4.123, 186

congeyen *v* send away, dismiss
5.479

conjectest 2 *pr sg* suppose, con-
jecture 4.1026

conjure *v* charge, urge 2.1733,
3.193

connyng *n* ability, skill 2.4,
3.999 (*see also* konnynge)

co(u)nseil *n* counsel, advice
1.627, 2.1044, 4.1114; secret
1.743, 992; purpose 4.1325

conserve *v* preserve, keep
4.1664, 5.310

conseyte *see* conceyte *n*

considered *pp* considering,
taking into account 2.1290,
3.923, 985, 4.1271, 5.1348

consistorie *n* council 4.65

constellacioun *n* horoscope, pos-
ition of planets at one's birth
4.745

constreinte *n* distress 2.776,
4.741

constreyne *v* compel, force
2.476, 1232; control, govern
3.1759

construe *v* explain, understand
3.33

contek *n* strife, contention
5.1479

co(u)ntena(u)nce *n* look,
expression 3.1542, 5.539;
fond his ~ assumed an attitude
3.979; make a ~ assume an
appearance 2.552; make thi ~
upon give your attention to
2.1017

contene *v* take up, fill 3.502

contraire *adj* contrary, opposite
1.212

contrarie *n* contrary, opposite
1.637; in ~ in opposition
1.418

contre(e *n* country 2.42, 5.1471

contrepeise *v* counterbalance
3.1407

convers: in in ~ on the reverse
side 5.1810

converte *v* change, convert
1.308, 999; change one's mind
2.903, 4.1412

cope *n* cape, cloak 3.724

copie *n* copy, transcript 2.1697

corage *n* heart, spirit, disposition
1.892, 3.897; courage 1.564,
4.619

corageous *adj* courageous, brave
5.800

corde *n* string (of musical instru-
ment) 5.443

cordeth *3 pr sg* agrees 2.1043

corones *n pl* crowns 2.1735

cors *n* corpse 5.742

corse(n *v* curse 3.896, 1701,
5.207

corsednesse *n* wickedness
4.994

corteys *see* curteys *adj*

cost *n* expense 3.522

coste *v* cost 5.438

cote *n* tunic 5.1653; cote-armure
tunic embroidered with her-
aldic device 5.1651

counseillen *v* advise 1.648

counte *1 pr sg* account, value (at)
5.363

co(u)ntrefete *v* imitate 3.1168;
simulate, pretend 2.1532; pass
oneself off 5.1578

cours(e *n* course, path 1.140,
2.1385; orbit 2.907, 5.661

courser *n* war-horse, charger
2.1011, 5.85

couth(e *pt sg of* konne *v*

coveitise *n* covetousness, avarice
3.261, 1389

covenable *adj* suitable, fitting
2.1137

covered *pp* hidden, concealed
3.31

coveyteth *3 pr sg* desires 4.1339

coveytous *adj as n* a covetous
person 3.1373

coward *adj* cowardly 1.792,
4.1409, 1573

coye *v* cajole 2.801

craft *n* skill, art 1.379, 665,
3.1634; cunning, trick 1.747

craftyly *adv* artfully 2.1026

crampe *n* spasm, agony 3.1071

crave *v* request 2.1455

crede n creed 5.89

crepe(n *v* creep, move slowly
3.1069, 1505, 5.1214; *pp*
cropen 3.1011

crepel *n* cripple 4.1458

crie(n *v* shout, scream 1.753; cry
out 4.1225; invoke 2.436;
applaud 2.646; beg for
2.1076; weep 1.806; ~ after
beg for 4.753; ~ (up)on cry out
against, condemn 2.865,
3.1022; *pt sg* cride 4.585,
1213; *pp* cryd 4.587

crois *n* cross 5.1843

crop *n* top, growing tip (of
plant); ~ and roote everything,
whole 2.348, 5.25, 1245

cropen *pp of* crepe(n *v*

crowne *n* crowning, finest
example 5.547

cruelich *adv* cruelly 4.1304

cruelte(e *n* cruelty, heartlessness,
severity 1.586, 1083

cruwel *adj* cruel 1.9, 4.266

curacioun *n* cure 1.791

cure *n* cure, remedy 1.707, 5.49;
effort, diligence 5.1539; do

(one's) ~ apply oneself 1.369;
in (one's) ~ in one's power
2.741; **out of alle** ~ beyond
remedy 5.713; **take** ~ **of** pay
attention to 2.283
curteisie *n* courtliness, good
manners 2.1486, 5.64
curteys *adj* courteous, chivalrous
1.81, 3.26
curtyn *n* bed curtains 3.60

dampned *3 pt sg* condemned
5.1823
dar, darst, darstow *see* **durre** *v*
darte *n* spear, javelin 4.771;
(Love's) arrow 4.472
daun *n* lord, master (as title of
respect) 1.70, 3.1808
daunce *n* dance: **the olde** ~ the
ancient practice, all the old
tricks 3.695; **th'amorouse** ~
love-making 4.1431
daunger *n* disdain, reserve (of a
lady to a lover) 2.384, 1243,
1376; 3.1321
daunteth *3 pr sg* tames, subdues
2.399; dominates, overpowers
4.1589
dawyng *vbl n* dawn 3.1466
day *n* day 1.452; dawn 3.1450;
(appointed) day 5.84
debat *n* quarrel, dispute 2.753
debonaire *adj* meek, submissive
1.214; gracious, gentle 1.181;
as n gracious one 3.4
debonairly *adv* meekly 2.1259;
modestly 3.156
declamed *pt pl* discussed 2.1247
declare *v* tell, explain, make
known 1.637, 2.1680
de(e)d *adj* dead, lifeless 1.723,
4.235; dead looking, deathly

pale 4.379, 5.559; **for** ~ **in a**
swoon 4.733; **I nam but** ~ I'm
as good as dead 5.1246
de(e)d(e *n* action, deed, act 1.93;
with the ~ immediately 3.1301
dede, dedest *see* **do(o)n** *v*
dedly, dedlich *adj* agonizing,
grievous 4.871, 898; deathly
5.536
deef *adj* deaf 1.753
de(e)l *n* share, part, bit: **every** ~
completely, entirely 2.590; **al
or any** ~ entirely or in part
2.1214; **ech a** ~ in its entirety
3.694; **no** ~ not a bit 1.1089
de(e)le *v* have dealings, have to
do 2.706, 1749, 3.322, 5.1595
dees *n pl* dice 2.1347, 4.1098
de(e)th *n* death 1.411, 799;
?plague 1.483
deface *v* disfigure 5.915; mar,
spoil 4.804; obliterate 4.1682,
5.1335
defamen *v* slander 2.860; dis-
grace 4.565
defaute *n* deficiency 5.1796
defence *n* means of defence
4.287; **breken** ~ disobey pro-
hibition 3.138
defende *v* defend 1.511; forbid,
prohibit 2.1733; *pr subj* **God** ~
God forbid 4.1647
defet *adj* changed for the worse
5.618; disfigured 5.1219
defouled *pp* defiled 5.1339
degree *n* rank 1.244; extent,
standing 5.1360; **in no** ~ not at
all 1.437, 5.836; **in
som** ~ to some extent 1.844
deignous *adj* haughty 1.290
deite, deyte *n* deity 4.1543; god-
head 3.1017

deliberacioun *n* deliberation, consideration 3.519

delibere(n *v* decide 4.169, 211

delicious *adj* delightful 5.443

delit *n* pleasure, delight 1.762, 2.709; (sensuous) pleasure, desire to have or enjoy sth 4.1668, 1678

delite(n *v* please 4.1435; take pleasure 4.1433; *refl* 2.256

deliveraunce *n* release 4.202

delivere(n *v* release, set free 4.100, 196; be rid of, freed from 3.223, 1012

deliverliche *adv* deftly 2.1088

demaunde *n* question 4.1295, 1694; request 5.859

deme(n *v* judge 1.347, 2.371; think, suppose 1.799, 2.461, 3.763

denye *v* refuse 2.1489

dep(e *adj* profound, heartfelt 1.298, 2.151, 5.675, 1259; *adv* deep, deeply 1.272; fervently 2.570; profoundly 4.589; *comp* depper further 2.485

depardieux *interj* by God 2.1058, 1212

departe(n *v* depart 1.78; separate, part 2.531, 3.1666, 1709; divide into parts 1.960; differentiate 3.404

depeynted *pp adj* stained 5.1599

derk *adj* dark, gloomy 2.1307, 5.640

derknesse *n* darkness, obscurity 1.18, 3.826; gloom, despair 4.300

derre *adv comp* more dearly, at a greater cost 1.136; more highly, as worth more 1.174

descende(n *v* descend 1.216; be descended 5.1480; ~ (down) proceed, pass 5.859, 1511

descente *n* falling, lighting (of censure upon a person) 1.319

descerne *v* discern 3.9

desdayn *n* scorn, disdain 2.1217; indignation 4.1191

desertes *n pl* merits, what is deserved 3.1267

desgise *v* disguise 5.1577

desirous *adj* eager 1.1058, 2.1101

desolat *adj* deserted 5.540

despeired *pp* in despair 1.36, 5.713

despise, dispise *v* disdain 2.720; speak ill of 3.1699, 4.1478

despit, dispit *n* anger, resentment, scorn 2.1246, 3.1037, 5.1243; for ~ through resentment 1.207, 2.1049; as an insult 1.909, 5.1693; han in ~ scorn 3.1787, 4.1675, 5.135; bear a grudge against 2.711; holden ~ of scorn 3.1374; in ~ of out of hostility towards 3.1705, 4.124

despitously *adv* cruelly 5.1806

desport, disport *n* pleasure, delight 1.592, 4.309

desteyned *pp* stained, sullied 2.840

destine *n* destiny 1.520, 3.734

desto(u)rbe *v* prevent, hinder 2.622, 4.573, 1103, 1403

destreyne *v* constrain, compel 1.355, 5.596; afflict, oppress 3.1528

determyne *v* come to an end 3.379

devise(n *v* arrange, contrive

3.612; imagine 3.56, 5.1363;
compose 2.1063; describe
4.259; relate, set out 2.31,
3.41, 160; converse 2.1599;
think of 4.543; discuss 4.1423;
advise, suggest 2.388

devocioun *n* inclination,
devotedness 1.187; piety,
devoutness 1.555

devoir *n* duty; **for my ~** for my
sake 3.1045

devoute *adj* sacred, holy 1.151

devyn *n* soothsayer 1.66

devyne(n *v* foresee 4.389; be sus-
picious 2.1745, 3.765; **~**
(upon, of) suspect 2.1741,
3.458; speculate, ponder
4.589; conjecture, suppose
5.270, 288

devyneresse *n* prophetess
5.1522

dewete *n* what is due, as a matter
of duty and courtesy 3.970

deye(n, dye(n *v* die 1.573; **(for)**
to ~ in the peyne on pain of
death by torture 1.674,
3.1502; *pt sg* **deyde, deide**
1.56, 460, 875; 2 *pt sg* **deidest**
3.263; *vbl n* **deyinge** death
1.572

deyne, deigne *v* grant 3.139,
1435; condescend 1.435,
3.1281, 1811

deynte *n* delicacy, fine food or
drink 3.609; **holden it ~** con-
sider it honourable 2.164

diffame *see* **defamen** *v*

diffence *see* **defence** *n*

diffusioun *n* diffuseness, loquac-
ity 3.296

diffyne *v* define, describe 5.271;
conclude 3.834, 4.390

dighte *v* dispose 4.1188; prepare,
array 3.1773; *refl* go 2.948

digne *adj* worthy, honourable
1.429, 968, 3.23; **~ to** worthy
of 5.1868

directe *v* send, address, dedicate
5.1856 (Wilson 1998)

dis- *see also* **des-**

disavaunce *v* repulse, repel 2.511

disaventure, dysaventure *n* mis-
fortune 2.415, 4.297, 755,
5.1448

disblameth *imp pl* exonerate,
excuse 2.17

disclaundre *n* slander, reproach
4.564

discomfort *n* distress, dismay
4.311, 848

disconsolat *adj* cheerless 5.542

discordable *adj* inclined to
discord, inharmonious
3.1753

discordant *adj* dissonant 2.1037

discoveren *v* betray, give away
1.675

discrecioun *n* judgement, dis-
crimination 3.894, 1334;
4.206

discret *adj* circumspect 3.477,
943

discryve(n *v* describe 2.889,
4.802, 5.267, 1367

disese *n* distress, discomfort
2.987, 1360, 3.1043, 5.109;
do yow ~ annoy you 2.147

disese(n *v* distress 1.573, 3.1468,
4.1304; make uncomfortable
2.1650; **disesed** distressed
3.443

disesperaunce *n* despair 2.530,
1307

disespeyr *n* despair 1.605, 2.6

disfigure *v* disfigure, mar 2.223

disjoynte *n* difficulty, straits 3.496; stonden in ~ be in a predicament 5.1618

dispende *v* spend 4.921

dispitous(e *adj* cruel 2.435, 3.1458; fierce, pitiless 5.199

displese *v* displease 1.27; offend, annoy 4.275

dispone *v* order, regulate 4.964; *pr subj sg* dispone dispose 5.300

disposed *pp* inclined 2.682, 4.230

disposicioun *n* disposal, arrangement 2.526, 5.1543; power to control 5.2

dispute *v* argue, reason 3.858, 4.1084

disserve *v* deserve 3.175, 387

disseveraunce *n* separation; make ~ of separate 3.1424

dissimilen *v* dissemble, pretend 3.434; conceal 1.322

dissymelyng *vbl n* dissimulation 5.1613

distille *v* flow or fall in drops; in teris ~ weep profusely 4.519

distreyne *see* destreyne *v*

disturne *v* avert, turn aside 3.718

divers(e *adj* various, sundry 1.61; unfavourable, hostile 4.1195

diverseth *3 pr sg* varies, changes 3.1752

diversite *n* distinction 3.405; variety 5.1793

dok *n* dock 4.461

do(o)m *n* judgement 4.1188; (as) to my ~ in my opinion 1.100, 4.402

donne *adj* dun, grey-brown 2.908

do(o)n *v* act 2.318; perform 2.75; commit 2.1510; cause, make s.o (to) do s.th 2.327; cause 2.763; put 4.1643; put on 2.954; ~ awey remove 5.1068; ~ wey put away 2.110; no more of this! 2.893; (*as auxil, with infin*) 2.54; *2 pr sg* do(o)st 2.1510, 3.1436, (with *pron*) dostow 4.515; *imp pl* do(o)th 3.975; *2 pt sg* dedest 3.363; *3 pt sg* dede 1.369; *pt pl* diden 1.82; *pp* ido 3.386, (y)doon 2.789, 1245

dorst(e, dorstestow *pt & 2 pt subj sg of* durre *v*

double *adj* double, twofold 1.1, 54; duplicitous 5.898

doubleth *pr sg* doubles 4.903

doughter *n* daughter 3.3; doughtren *n pl* 4.22

doutaunce *n* uncertainty 1.200; out of ~ without a doubt 4.963, 1044

doute *n* anxiety, fear 5.1453; uncertainty 4.1277; without-oute(n ~ 4.404; out(e of ~ certainly 1.152

doutele(e)s *adv* doubtless 2.414

doute(n *v* fear 1.683

doutous *adj* unreliable, uncertain 4.992

dowe *v* dedicate, give 5.230

dowve *n* dove 3.1496

dradde *pt sg of* drede(n *v*

drat *3 pr sg contr of* drede(n *v*

drawe *v* draw, pull, drag 1.224, 3.674, 1704; draw out 2.262; draw (breath) 3.1119; tear apart 1.833; *refl* go, withdraw

2.1186, 3.978; turn 3.177; *pt
sg* **drow, drough** 3.978,
5.1558

drecche *v* delay 2.1264, 4.1446;
trouble 2.1471

drecchyng *vbl n* delaying 3.853

drede *n* fear 1.180, 499; anxiety,
worry 1.463; uncertainty,
doubt 1.529; **out(e of ~, with-
oute(n any ~** doubtless, with-
out doubt 2.672, 746

dred(e)ful *adj* fearful, apprehen-
sive 2.776, 1101, 1258,
5.1331; frightening, terrible
2.426, 5.590; *superl* **drede-
fulleste** most frightening 5.248

dredeles *adv* doubtless, without
doubt 1.1034, 1048

drede(n *v* fear 1.1019; be afraid
2.455; avoid, abhor 1.252; **to
~** to be feared 1.84; *3 pr sg
contr* **drat** 3.328; *pt sg* **dredde,
dred, dradde** 2.874, 3.1647,
5.1570; *pt pl* **dredde(n** 1.483,
4.56; *pp* **ydred** 3.1775

dredfully *adv* fearfully 2.1128

drenche *v* drown, inundate
3.1761; **~ in teris** be drowned
in tears 4.510; *pt sg , pt pl*
dreynte 1.543, 4.930; *pp*
dreynt 5.1503

drery *adj* sad 1.13

drerynesse *n* sadness, dejection
1.701, 971

dresse *v* arrange 4.1182; *refl* pre-
pare, get ready 2.71, 5.279;
attire, arm oneself 2.635; **on
hors ~** mount 5.37; **~ hym
upward** raise himself up 3.71

dreye *adj* dry 3.352, 4.1173

dreynt(e *pt sg, pl, of*
drenche *v*

drif, drifth *imp sg, 3 pr sg contr*
of **drive** *v*

drinke, drynke *v* drink 1.406,
3.1214; (*fig*) endure 2.784,
3.1216; *pt sg* **dronk** 5.1440;
pp **dronke(n** 3.674, 1390

drive *v* drive 2.1535; compel
2.576; drive (vehicle) 5.665;
go 3.227; banish, expel 4.427,
5.913; **~ forth** pass (time)
5.389, 394, 628; endure
5.1101; **~ awey** pass 2.983; *3
pr sg contr* **drifth** 5.1332; *imp
sg* **drif** 4.1615, 5.359; *pt sg*
drof 3.994; *pp* **dryven** 2.983

drof *pt sg of* **drive** *v*

dronk(e *pt sg & pp of* **drinke** *v*

dronkenesse *n* drunkenness
2.716

drough, drow *pt sg of* **drawe** *v*

drye *v* suffer 1.303; endure, bear
up under 1.1092, 2.866,
4.154, 5.42, 1540

drynkeles *adj* without, lacking,
drink 2.718

dul *adj* dull, stupid 1.735, 2.548;
heavy 5.1118

dulle(n *v* be satiated, become
bored 2.1035, 4.1489

dure(n *v* endure, last 1.468,
4.295, 1680; *prp* **durynge**
enduring, lasting 3.1754

duresse *n* suffering, distress
5.399

durre *v* dare 5.840; *1 pr sg* **dar**
1.16; *2 pr sg* **darst** 1.768, (with
suffixed *pron*) **darstow** 5.1279;
pl **dar** 2.1747; *1,3 pt sg, pt pl*
dorste, durste dared 1.98,
3.455 (sometimes used in a pre-
sent sense, as a substitute for
pr subj, 1.767, 3.377, 5.1169);

2 *pt subj sg* **dorstestow** 1.767;
3 *pt subj sg* **dorste** 1.27
durryng *vbl n* daring 5.837
durste *pt of* **durre** *v*
dwelle *v* continue 1.789; remain
2.314, 3.651, 4.1449, 5.615;
delay 2.1595, 1614, 5.1394;
detain 1.144; reside, dwell
3.590; wait 3.201; *pr subj*
dwelle 1.789; *pt subj* **dwelte**
5.910
dygnelich *adv* haughtily 2.1024
dymynucioun *n* reduction, dimin-
ishing 3.1335

ebben *v* recede, decrease
4.1145
ec(c)h *pron* each (one) 1.1078;
adj every 1.510
eche(n *v* increase, add 1.705,
3.1509, 5.110; *pp* **eched**
3.1329
echone *pron* each one, everyone
4.218
e(e)re *n* ear 1.106, 2.195
eet *pt sg of* **ete(n** *v*
effect *n* consequence 1.212; out-
come 4.144; substance,
essence, point 2.1220, 1566,
3.346; matter 5.1629; **grete ~**
main point 3.505; **in ~** in fact,
naturally 1.748, 3.1149; essen-
tially 5.1423
eft *adv* again 2.301, 3.251;
another time 1.137; likewise
1.360
eftsone(s) *adv* again 2.1468;
another time 2.1651; in reply
4.181
egal *adj* equal 3.137; *adv* equally
4.660
egge *n* edge (of blade) 4.927

egle *n* eagle 2.926, 3.1496
eiled *pt sg* was wrong with 4.331
(*see also* **ail(l)eth**)
eise *see* **ese** *n*
ek(e) *adv* also 1.32, 642
elde *n* old age 4.1369; ageing,
advancing years 2.393
element *n* one of four primary
substances (earth, water, air,
fire) 3.1753; one of the celes-
tial spheres 5.1810
elles, ellis *adv* otherwise, else
1.345, 371
elleswhere *adv* elsewhere 4.698,
1521
em *n* uncle 1.1022, 2.162
emforth *prep* to the extent of
2.243, 997, 3.999
emprise, enprise *n* undertaking,
enterprise 2.73, 1391, 3.416,
4.601
encens *n* incense 5.1466
enchaunten *v* enchant, bewitch
4.1395
enchesoun *n* cause, reason
1.348, 681, 5.632
enclyne *v* be inclined 2.674
encrees *n* increase, augmenting
3.1776, 4.1257
encresse(n *v* increase 2.1337; *pr
subj sg* **encresse** 5.1359
ende *n* conclusion 2.260, 5.499;
outcome 2.1235
endeles *adj* without end 2.1083;
adv perpetually 4.23
endite(n *v* write, compose 1.6,
2.13, 257, 700
enforce(n *v refl* strive, labour
4.1016
engyn *n* contrivance, trickery
2.565, 3.274
enhabit *pp* devoted 4.443

enlumyned *pp* illuminated 5.548

enquere(n *v* enquire 3.1684, 4.1010

ensa(u)mple *n* example 1.232, 3.872; illustrative story, exemplum 1.760; model, exemplar, pattern 5.1590; ~ why for example 1.1002

enseled *pp* ratified 4.559; sealed up, left unopened 5.151

enspire *v* inspire, move 3.712, 4.187

entecched *pp* endowed 5.832

entencioun *n* intention, purpose 1.211; will, disposition 1.52, 345

entende *v* intend 5.469; be inclined 2.853, 3.27; perceive, expect 4.1649; listen 4.893; attend 3.424

entendement *n* intellect 4.1696

entente *n* intention, purpose, aim 1.61, 738; plan, design 5.1305; mind, disposition 2.524; meaning 5.150; in (with, of) good ~ with good will or intention 1.935, 3.1188, 4.853; seyen ~ speak (one's) mind 4.173

ententif *adj* diligent 2.838

ententiflich *adv* diligently 1.332

entrechaungen *v* exchange 3.1368; *pp* entrechaunged reciprocal 4.1043

entrecomunen *v*: ~ yfeere have dealings with one another 4.1354

entree *n* entrance, entering, threshold 2.77

entremete *v*: ~ (of) concern oneself (with) 1.1026

entreparten *v* share 1.592

entune *v* sing 4.4

envie *v* contend, vie with 5.1789

envious *adj* envious 3.838; malicious, ill-willed 2.857; *as n* malicious person 2.666

envye *n* envy 3.1805; ill will, spite 4.275; hostility 5.1479

epistel *n* epistle, letter 3.501

er *adv* before, formerly 3.763

er *prep* before 2.245

er *conj* before 1.56; er that before 1.5

erand *n* mission 2.72

ernest *n* seriousness 2.452; in ~ genuinely 2.1529; in ~ greet very seriously 2.1703; bitwixen game and ~ half in jest 3.254; for ~ ne for game in any event 4.1465

ernestful *adj* serious 2.1727

erratik *adj*: ~ sterres wandering stars, planets 5.1812

erre(n *v* err, be wrong 3.1774; do wrong, transgress 1.1003; break the law 4.549; wander 4.302

errowr *n* error 4.993; heresy 1.1008; misunderstanding 4.200

erst *adj superl* first: at ~ for the first time, only now 1.842

erst *adv superl* before, earlier 1.299, 3.1683

eschaunge *n* exchange 4.146, 158, 559, 878

eschu(w)e(n *v* avoid, shun 1.344, 634; escape 4.1078

ese *n* comfort, well-being 2.1659, 5.1376; success 3.19; pleasure, joy 3.1304; don ~ please, gratify 2.1225, 3.633; benefit, advantage 4.86; relief

4.726; **don** ~ relieve 4.703;
ease 1.28

ese(n v ease, soothe 3.950; com-
fort, relieve 2.1400, 3.1790;
imp pl **eseth** 3.197; *pp* **esed**
cheered 1.249; relieved (from
suffering) 1.447, 943

esilich *adv* slowly 1.317, 2.988;
gently 3.156

espye *n* spy 2.1112

espye(n, aspye v notice, descry
1.193, 2.649; discover 2.1507,
3.573; find 5.556; **espide**
pt sg 5.539; *pt subj* 4.1388

est *n* east 2.1053; **(by)** ~ **or west**
in one direction or another,
anywhere 5.751, 1432

est *adj* eastern 5.1109

estat *n* state, condition 2.465;
rank, social status, dignity
1.287, 2.881, 4.584; class,
social condition 5.1749

estatlich *adj* dignified 5.823

estraunge *adj* distant, standoffish
1.1084

estward *adv* eastwards, towards
the east 3.1419, 5.277

esy *adj* easy, gentle 3.1363; com-
pliant, tractable 1.1090; **an** ~
pas at a slow pace 2.620

esyng *vbl n* comforting 2.1287

ete(n v eat; *pt sg* **e(e)t** ate 5.1216,
1440; *pt pl* **ete** ate 2.1184

eternalich *adv* eternally
4.1540

eterne *adj* eternal, everlasting
3.11, 375; **from** ~ from etern-
ity 4.978; ~ **on lyve** immortal
5.1863

ethe *adj* easy 5.850

eve(n *n* evening 2.1301; **at** ~ in
the evening 3.560, 5.481;

bothe ~ **and morwe** all day
long, constantly 1.487, 5.725

ever(e *adv* ever, always 1.9, 236,
5.756; ~ **in oon** constantly,
invariably, continually 1.816,
4.1602, 5.451

everemo, evermore *adv* continu-
ally, constantly 4.284, 1110;
for ~ forever 3.1426

everich *pron* every one 5.170;
adj every, each 3.1496, 1806,
4.1518

everichon(e, everychone *pron*
everyone, each 1.154, 3.412

excellence *n* surpassing qualities,
perfection 3.215, 1274

excesse *n* excess of feeling,
despair 1.626

excusable *adj* pardonable 3.1031

excuse(n v make excuses for,
exonerate 3.1025, 5.1097; *refl*
1.112, 3.810; pardon 3.1036;
refl beg pardon 2.12; beg to be
excused 3.561; **han excused**
pardon 2.1079

execucioun *n*: **putten in** ~ carry
out, perform 3.521; **don** ~ per-
form 5.4

execut *pp* carried out 3.622

executrice *n* (female) adminis-
trator 3.617

expert *adj* learned, skilled 1.67

expounde(n v interpret 5.1278,
1456

ey *interj* ah! 2.87

eye, ye *n* eye 1.272, 453; *pl*
eighen, eyghen, eyen, yen
1.192, 305, 2.142, 534

eyr *n* air, breeze 5.671

faille *n*: **withouten (any)** ~ for cer-
tain 2.629, 4.1596

faille(n, faylen *v* prove unsuccess-
ful, ineffective 1.217, 4.1452;
lack 2.1440; be lacking 1.764,
3.523; miss 5.642

fair *adj* fine, beautiful, good
1.101; favourable 1.907,
2.224; dear 2.1670; *as n* fine
thing 3.850

faire *n* fair, passing show
5.1840

faire *adv* well 2.328; beautifully
2.886; courteously, hand-
somely 3.1556

falle(n *v* fall 5.258; fall down
2.770; ~ aswowne faint
3.1092; ~ on knowes kneel
3.1592; fall, sink (fig. into con-
dition or state) 1.813, 3.794; ~
aton agree 3.565; ~ awey turn
aside 3.1306; ~ forth engage
2.1191, 5.107; ~ in attain, win
1.370; ~ to belong to, be appro-
priate to 1.142; decrease
1.563, 4.430, 469; befall, hap-
pen 1.212; ~ foule or faire turn
out badly or well 4.1022;
(*impers*, with *dat* of *pers*): hem
fel they happened 3.1401;
foule falle may bad luck befall
4.462; *pt sg* fel, fil 1.64, 110;
pt pl felle(n 1.3, 145; *pt subj sg*
fille 1.320; *prp* (*as adj*) fallyng
felling, causing to fall 2.1382;
pp falle 1.555, 3.859; *vbl n*
fallynge befalling, occurrence
4.1021, 1061

fals *n* deceit, falsehood 3.298

fals *adj* untrue 1.593; wrong, in
error 5.1526; spurious 3.814;
disloyal, treacherous 1.93;
unfaithful 4.616; untrust-
worthy 5.1832

false(n *v* betray 3.784, 5.1053

falsly *adv* unjustly 1.38; treacher-
ously 1.89, 4.1193

falsnesse *n* treachery 1.107

fantasye *n* imagination 2.482;
imaginings 3.1032, 5.261;
delusion 3.1504, 4.1470; in-
clination, desire 3.275; caprice
5.461

fare *n* behaviour, conduct
1.1025, 2.1144; frendes ~
friendliness 3.605; business,
ado 3.1106, 1566; com-
motion, fuss 5.335; condition,
state 5.1366; yvel ~ misfortune
2.1001

fare-carte *n* cart for transporting
merchandise 5.1162

fare(n *v* go, depart 3.1529,
5.359; behave 1.739, 4.1087;
~ (bi) act towards, treat 4.463;
get on, fare 1.666, 2.92; ~ wel
prosper, be successful 2.163,
3.248; ~ aright do well 1.878;
~ amis feel unwell, suffer
1.491, 2.1007; it fareth/ ferde
it (of, by) it turns/turned out
(regarding) 1.225, 963; *imp sg*
far 1.878; *pt sg* ferde 1.491; *pt
subj pl* ferde 2.39; *pp* yfare,
ferd 3.577, 5.1358

farwel *imp* goodbye, good luck
2.1524

fast(e *adj* dense 5.1235

faste *adv* firmly 1.534, 969;
swiftly 2.906; as ~ very quickly
2.657, 898, 3.1094; ~ by close
by, close at hand 2.1275,
4.117; *as intens*: closely 2.276;
copiously 4.130

fatal *adj* predestined, fated 5.1; ~
sustren the Fates 3.733

fate *n* destiny 5.1550, 1552; individual lot, destiny 5.209

faukoun *n* falcon 3.1784

fawe *see* **fayn** *adj*

fawny *n pl* fauns 4.1544

faylyng *vbl n* failure, lack of success 1.928

fayn, feyn *adj* glad, pleased 4.1321, 5.425; *adv* gladly, willingly 1.691; **fawe** eagerly 4.887

feble *adj* weak 5.1222

febly *adv* feebly, half-heartedly 1.518

fecche *v* fetch 3.917, 5.485; take away 5.322

fecches *n pl* vetches, beans (valueless things) 3.936

fecchynge *vbl n* abduction, seizure 5.890

feeblesse *n* weakness 2.863

fe(e)le *v* experience, sense 1.400, 4.706; comprehend, realize, perceive 2.1283, 3.960, 4.984; find out 2.387; suffer 4.840; *pr subj sg* **feele** 2.856; *pt sg* **felte** 1.306; *pp* **felt** 1.25; **feled** 4.984

fe(e)re *n* (1) fear, fright 1.726; **have ~** be afraid 3.753; cause of fear, danger 3.583, 1144

fe(e)re *n* (2) companion 1.13, 224; mate 3.1496; wife 4.791

feffe *v* enfeoff (invest s.o. with fief), endow, present 3.901, 5.1689

feith *n* faithfulness, loyalty 1.89, 2.410; trust 3.1751; pledged word 2.963, 5.1675; *in asseverations*: **in (good) ~** 1.336, 2.169

feithed *pp* in faith, belief 1.1007

feithfully *adv* faithfully, devot-

edly 3.1672; loyally 2.263, 5.1076; truthfully 4.114; convincingly, sincerely 2.1577

felawe *n* friend, comrade 1.696, 4.524, 5.1488

felawshipe *n* friendliness, amity 2.206, 3.403

feld *n* field of battle 1.1074, 2.195, 4.42; **~ of pite** Elysian fields 4.789

feldefare *n* thrush 3.861

fele *adj* many 4.512

felicite(e *n* happiness 3.814, 1691, 5.763

fell(e *adj* terrible 1.470; deadly 4.44; violent 5.50

felle(n *pt pl of* **falle(n** *v*

feloun *adj* sullen, angry 5.199

felyng *n* feeling 3.1090; understanding 3.1333

fend *n* devil, fiend 2.896, 4.437

fer *adv* far, at a distance 1.18

ferd(en *pt & pp of* **fare(n** *v*

ferd(e, fered: in **for/of ~** because of fear 1.557, 4.607, 1411

ferforth *adv* far 2.960, 1106, 5.866; **as ~ as** as much as (if) 1.121

ferforthly *adv* insofar as 3.101

ferfulleste *superl* most timid 2.450

ferme *adv* firmly; **holden ~** keep resolutely 2.1525

ferne yere *n* yesteryear 5.1176

ferther *adv comp* further 3.281, 949

ferventliche *adv* earnestly, eagerly 4.1384

fery *adj* fiery 3.1600

fe(e)ste *n* feast, entertainment, banquet 3.1159, 1312; ceremony 5.304; religious festival

1.161, 3.150; rejoicing, plea-
sure 2.421, 3.344, 5.524;
maken ~ pay attention, pay
court 2.361, 3.1228, 5.1429

festey(i)nge *n* festivity, entertain-
ment 3.1718, 5.455

fetered *pp* fettered, shackled
4.106

fethered *pp* covered with
feathers 2.926

fette(n *v* fetch, bring 3.609, 723,
5.852

fevre *n* fever 2.1520, 3.1213

fey *n* faith; **by youre ~** upon your
honour 2.1103

feyne(n *v* dissemble 2.1558,
4.1463; pretend 1.326, 354;
refl pretend 1.494, 2.1528,
5.846; hold back, hesitate
2.997, 3.167; *pp* **feynede** pre-
tended, unreal 5.1848

feynte *v* become exhausted, grow
faint 1.410

fieblesse *n* weakness 2.863

fierse *adj* fierce, bold 1.225; fero-
cious, violent 3.22, 5.1806

fiersly *adv* violently 3.1760

figure *n* person 1.366; **in ~** as a
symbol, symbolically 5.1449

fil, fille *pt sg, pt subj sg of* **falle(n**
v

filthe *n* filth, foulness 3.381;
infamy 4.1578

final *adj* ultimate 1.682; **for ~**
finally 4.145

finaly *adv* eventually, at last
2.1324, 5.1635; **for good**
3.1006

finde(n, fynde(n *v* find, discover
2.641; invent, create 4.1408;
fond his contenaunce assumed
an expression 3.979; find in

writing, read 1.399, 5.834,
1758; **~ writen** read 4.1415; **2**
pt sg **fownde** 3.362; *pt pl*
founden 1.137; *pp* **ifounde**
4.594, 5.834

fir *n* fire 1.445, 449; (of passion)
3.484

fisshe(n *v* fish (for) 5.777; **a
cause ~** invent a reason
3.1162; **fisshed fayre** made a
fine catch 2.328

fixe *adj* fixed, unchangeable
1.298

flat: *as n* flat (of a swordblade)
4.927

flaumbe *n* flame 4.118, 5.302

fle(n, flee(n *v* (1) flee, go away
1.747, 2.194, 4.868; pass
away 3.828; shun 3.1806; **2** *pr
sg* **fleest** 3.1435; *imp sg* **fle**
2.1254; *pt sg* **fledde** 3.350; *pp*
yfled, fledde 4.661, 1.463

fle(n, flee(n *v* (2) fly 4.306, 1356;
pt sg **fleigh** flew 2.194, 931

flemen *v* banish 2.852

flemyng *n* banishment 3.933

flesshly *adj* well rounded,
shapely, plump 3.1248

flete *v* float 3.1221, 1671; *prp*
fletyng overflowing, suffused
with 2.53

flighte *n* act of fleeing, flight,
escape 2.613, 766, 1239

flikered *pt sg* fluttered 4.1221

flitted *pp* moved, transferred
5.1544

flod, flood *n* river 3.1600; *pl*
waters 3.1760; **on a ~** flooded
3.640

flour *n* flower 1.158, 2.51,
5.792, 1317

floureth *pr sg* flourishes 4.1577

flowen *v* flow, overflow
3.1758

fo(o *n* foe, enemy 1.837, 874; *pl*
foos 1.1001, 2.1428; **foon**
5.1866

fol, fool *n* fool 1.532, 618; jester
2.400; *gen* **foles** of fools 3.298;
~ **of kynde** born fool 2.370;
singe a ~ a masse use flattery
3.88; ~ **of fantasye** victim of
delusions 5.1523

fold *n* fold in a cloth, pleat 2.697

folde *v* fold; **folden** folded 4.359;
in armes ~ embrace 3.1201,
4.1230, 1689

folie *n* foolishness, stupidity
1.532, 4.1504; foolish act
3.762; madness 3.838, 1382;
wrongdoing 3.394; **don ~**
behave foolishly 2.1510

fol(o)we(n *v* follow 1.259,
3.1062; (a source) 2.49

fomen *n pl* enemies 4.42

fonde(n *v* try 2.273, 5.352; test
3.1155

foon, foos *see* **fo(o** *n*

for *conj* because 1.12; ~ **that**
3.1667; since 3.934; ~ **that**
4.1031, 5.1768; ~ **as muche as**
in as much as 5.1352

for *prep* for the purpose of
4.413; in exchange for 4.149;
as, as being 1.987; as though,
as if 4.733; in response to
4.1633; notwithstanding
4.1462; ~ **which** therefore, on
account of which 2.1113; ~
why because 4.1496; ~ **al** not-
withstanding 4.1397; ~ **aught**
so far as 4.1164

forbar *pt sg of* **forbere(n** *v*

forbe(e)de *v* forbid 2.113; *3 pr sg*

contr forbet 2.717; *pr subj sg*
forbede 2.716, 1690

forbere(n *v* refrain from 3.173;
forgo 2.1660; *pt sg* **forbar**
spared 1.437; refrained from
3.365

forbise *v* instruct by examples
2.1390

forby *adv* past, by 2.658, 5.563

fordo(n *v* destroy, ruin 4.851,
1091; break 1.238; *pp* 1.74,
525, 5.1687

forgo(n *v* lose, be without
3.1384, 1442, 5.63; give up
2.1330, 4.195; *pt sg* **foryede**
2.1330

forknowynge *prp* foreseeing
1.79

forlong *n* furlong; ~ **wey** time
taken to walk a furlong, short
while 4.1237

forlore *pp* lost, forfeited 5.23

forlost *pp* utterly lost 3.280,
4.756

forme *n* form, shape 5.300;
appearance 2.1243; manner
3.160, 4.78, 1579; style, usage
2.22; substance, essence
5.1854; **holde the ~** preserve
proper usage, propriety
2.1040, 3.1674; **in ~** formally,
with decorum 2.41

forme(n *v* create; *pp* **formed** mod-
elled, mirrored 5.817; **han**
yfourmed be endowed with
4.315

formely *adv* correctly 4.497

forncast *pp* planned, pre-
meditated 3.521

fors *n* power; **of fyne ~** by sheer
necessity 5.421; **no ~** it does
not matter (about) 2.1477,

1717; **what** ~ what does it matter 2.378

forseynge *vbl n* foresight 4.989

forshapen *pp* transformed, metamorphosed 2.66

forshright *pp* exhausted with shrieking 4.1147

forso(o)k *pt sg* abandoned, deserted 1.56, 4.15

forsothe *adv* (*also two words*) in truth, indeed 2.883, 4.1035

forth *adv* forth, onwards 2.688, 1020; **dryven** ~ **a day** pass a day 5.628; **moot** ~ must leave 5.59; **tellen** ~ tell on 5.196; afterwards 5.6; (*as intens*, emphasizing continuation): 1.1092, 5.194

forthby *adv* past 5.537

forthere(n *v* help, advance 2.1368, 5.1707

forthi, forthy *adv* therefore, for this reason 1.232, 445, 691

forthynke(n *v* displease, grieve 2.1414

fortunat *adj* favoured by fortune 2.280

forward *n* agreement, promise 5.497

forwhi, for-why *adv and conj* why 3.1009; because 1.714, 3.477; wherefore 2.12

forwoot *3 pr sg* knows in advance 4.1071

foryaf *pt sg of* **foryive** *v*

foryat *pt sg of* **foryete(n** *v*

foryede *pt sg of* **forgo(n** *v*

foryete(n *v* forget 2.375; *pt sg* **foryat** 5.1535

foryive, foryeve *v* forgive 3.1178; spare (o.s. sth.) 5.387; *pr subj sg* **foryive** 1.937; *imp*

sg **foryeve** 3.1183; *pt sg* **foryaf** 3.1129; *pp* **foryeve(n)** 2.595, 3.1106

foughles *n pl* birds 1.787

foul(e *adj* vile, bad 1.213; wretched 2.896; shameful 5.383

founde *v* build, erect 1.1065

fourtenyght *n* fortnight 4.1327, 5.334

fowel *n* bird 5.425; *pl* 1.787, 5.380

fownes *n pl* fawns, any animals' young 1.465

frame(n *v*: **in** ~ **up** to join or frame, to build a timber house 3.530

frape *n* company 3.410

fre(e *adj* of free, not servile, condition 1.840; gracious, noble 3.1522, 5.1362; *as n* noble one 3.128; generous, magnanimous 1.958, 5.823

free *adv* freely 2.1121

frely *adv* generously 3.1719

fremde *adj* distant, reserved 2.248; ~ **and tame** wild and tame (i.e. every creature) 3.529

frenesie *n* madness 1.727

frenetik *adj* frantic 5.206

fressh *adj* lovely, blooming 1.166; vigorous, tireless 2.636, 5.830; joyous, gay 2.552, 3.611

fresshly *adv* joyously 5.390; ~ **newe** anew 5.1010; starting afresh 4.457; unfailingly 3.143

frete(n *v* eat, devour 5.1470

freyne(n *v* ask 5.1227

frote(n *v* rub 3.1115

ful *adv* quite, completely, very 1.378, 5.506

ful, full *adj* full, sated 2.1036, 3.1661; ~ **a strete** a streetful 4.929; complete 3.436; ~ **frend** true friend 1.610; **ten dayes** ~ 5.239; **took purpos** ~ firmly resolved 1.79; *as n* **atte** ~ squarely, hard 1.209; **unto the** ~ fully, unreservedly 3.213

fulfelle *v* complete 3.510

fulfilled *pp adj* full 2.632, 4.1191

fullich *adv* fully 1.316, 680

funeral *adj* of or pertaining to a funeral 5.302

furie *n* rage, fury 3.1037, 4.253, 1429, 5.212

fy *interj* (expressing scorn, outrage, impatience) 1.1038, 1046

fyn *n* end, conclusion 1.952, 5.1828; purpose, aim 2.425, 757; **for** ~ to this end 4.477

fyn(e *adj* fine, excellent; sheer 5.421

fynder *n* originator 2.844

fyne *v* end, finish 4.26; desist 2.1460, 5.776

fyne *adv* fully, well, thoroughly 1.661

gabbe(n *v* talk foolishly, lie 3.301, 4.481

galle *n* bitterness, sorrow 4.1137, 5.732

game(n *n* pleasure, joy, happiness 2.38, 4.1563, 5.420; sport, entertainment 1.868, 2.647; amusement 2.1110; joke, jest 3.650; scheme, course of action or events 3.250, 1494, 4.562; conduct, part, role 3.1126; **for ernest ne for** ~ in any event 4.1465;

bitwixen ~ **and ernest** half seriously, half in jest 3.254

gan *pt sg of* ginne *v*

gat *pt sg of* gete(n *v*

gaude *n* trick 2.351

gaure(n *v* (with **on**) stare at 2.1157

gayned *pt sg* availed 1.352

geant *n* giant 5.838

ge(e)ste *n* story, history 2.83, 3.450; *pl* histories, exploits 1.145, 5.1511

gemme *n* gem, jewel 2.344

general *adj* universal; *as n* **in** ~ in one body 1.163; not specifically 1.900; in general terms 1.926; without exception 3.1802; in all respects 5.822

generaly *adv* everywhere 1.86

gentil *adj* noble (in character, in conduct), gracious, refined, sensitive 2.331, 3.5, 904, 4.1674; *superl* **gentileste** 1.1080, 5.1056

gentilesse *n* nobility (of birth, of character), graciousness, kindness 1.881, 2.160, 662; **don** ~ behave nobly, graciously 3.882

gentily *adv* courteously 2.187

gere *n* armour 2.635; apparel, clothing 2.1012; goods, possessions 4.1523

gerful *adj* changeable 4.286

gesse *v* guess, suppose, imagine 1.286, 656; suspect 3.984

gest *n* visitor 2.1111

gete(n *v* get, win 2.376; *pt sg* **gat** 1.1077, 2.679, 3.1803

gide(n, gyde(n *v* guide, lead, direct 1.183, 630, 2.77

gilt, gylt *n* guilt, offence, fault

3.1177, 5.1257; **as in my ~** by
my fault 2.244

gilt(e)le(e)s *adj* guiltless, inno-
cent, blameless 2.328, 1372,
5.1084

giltif *adj* guilty 3.1019, 1049

ginne *v* begin 1.266; (with *infin*)
2.2, 5.1; (with **for to/to**)
1.189, 218; (*as auxil with
plain infin or* **to** *and infin* = do,
does, did*) **gynneth wepe** does
weep 5.1286, **gan multiplie** did
multiply 1.546; *pt sg* **gan**
1.139; *pt pl* **gonne(n** 2.99, 194

gynnynge *vbl n* beginning 1.377,
2.671

gise *n* manners, style 5.861; way
4.1370; custom 5.1650

glad *adj* glad, happy, joyful
1.300, 592; *comp* **gladder**
1.884, 3.357

glade(n *v* make happy, cheer,
comfort 1.116, 173, 2.979,
1545; *refl* take comfort 1.897,
5.1184; *pp* **gladed** 1.994

gladly *adv* joyfully, willingly
3.642; *comp* **gladlier** 5.1777

glaze(n *v* glaze; **his howve to ~**
provide delusive protection
(i.e. mock) 5.469

gle(e)de *n* ember, glowing coal
2.538, 4.337, 5.303

glee *n* music 2.1036

glente *pt pl* glanced 4.1223

glide *v* drop, slide 4.1215

glorifie *v* exult, boast 3.186; *refl*
be proud 2.1593

glose *v* interpret 4.1410; cajole,
induce 4.1471

glotonye *n* gluttony 5.370

gnawe(n *v* gnaw 1.509; feel a
gnawing pain, suffer 5.36

gon, goon *v* go 1.53; depart
4.1276; pass (of time) 5.1142 ;
proceed (to) (with *infin*)
3.313; **go we** (with *infin*) let us
2.615, 5.402 ; (*intens imp*)
2.396; *pt sg* **yede** 5.843; *pt pl*
yeden 2.936; *vbl n* **goynge**
4.934

gonne *pt pl of* **ginne** *v*

good *n* goodness; advantage,
benefit, something useful 2.97;
goods, property 3.1108;
konnen ~ know how to behave
2.1178; **konnen (one's) ~**
know what is good for oneself
5.106

good *adj* (*as n*) good friend
1.1017, 4.1660; (*as adv*) well
1.119

goodlihede *n* excellence, virtue,
beauty 2.842, 3.1730, 5.1590

goodly *adj* excellent, beautiful,
pleasing, gracious 1.173, 277;
as n 1.458; *superl* **goodlieste**
most excellent 2.747, 880

goodly *adv* pleasantly, amiably
2.1606; beautifully, finely
5.578; intently, eagerly
3.1345; with propriety 2.946;
may nat ~ can hardly 1.253

goosissh *adj* silly 3.584

goost *n* spirit 2.531, 3.464; soul
4.302

gospel *n* absolute truth (i.e. as
true as the gospel) 5.1265

gostly *adv* truthfully, with truth
of spirit 5.1030

goter *n* gutter, eaves trough,
drain 3.787

governaunce *n* rule, control
3.1744; guidance 2.467, 1442,
3.481, 945; behaviour, con-

duct, manner 3.216; business, way of life 2.219; self-control 2.1020, 3.427

governe *v* control, regulate 1.746, 3.373; *refl* 3.475; conduct 2.375

grace *n* favour, good will 2.1070; grace, divine benevolence 1.933; fortune 1.713, 907, 2.266; providence 1.896; **do ~** allow 5.694; **of ~** out of kindness 3.719; **stonden in ~** find favour 2.714

graceles *adj* out of favour 1.781

gracious *adj* well-disposed 1.885

grame *n* grief, pain 1.372, 4.529; anger, hatred 3.1028

gramercy *interj* thank you 3.1305

graspe *v* grope 5.223

graunte *v* grant, allow 1.41; agree, consent 1.785

grave(n *v* carve, engrave 2.47, 3.1462; make an impression upon 2.1241, 4.1377; bury 3.103; *pp* **grave** 3.103, 1499

gredy *adj* eager, voracious 3.1758

gree *n* favour, good will: **in ~** favourably 2.529, 4.321

gre(e)ne *adj* green 2.821, 918; vigorous 1.816; pale, sickly 2.60, 4.1154, 5.243; *as n* greenery, green leaves 1.157, 4.770

gre(e)t *adj* big 5.1469; *as n* great part, substance 5.1036; great (in qualities, accomplishment) excellent 1.66; high in status, important 2.881, 5.1025; chief, most important 3.505

gres *n* grass 2.515

grete(n *v* greet, salute 3.1258,

1556; *pt* **grette** 3.955, 1588, 5.293

grevances *n pl* hardships, afflictions 1.647

greve(n *v* harm, injure 1.1001; be harmful 5.783; cause pain, distress 2.237, 3.1642; offend 5.590; be angry, take offence 1.343; *refl* 3.1004

grevous *adj* grievous, painful 4.904, 1492; serious, grave 5.1231

greye *adj* grey; *as n* greybeard, old man 4.127

greyn *n* seed, speck 3.1026

grief *n* trouble, distress 2.1632

grisly *adj* grim 2.1700; terrible 4.155

grote *n* groat, fourpenny piece 4.586

ground *n* ground 1.856; soil 1.946; foundation 2.842, 3.982, 1304

grounded *pp adj* based 4.1672

groyn *n* groan 1.349

grucche *v* grumble, complain 3.643

gruf *adv* face down 4.912

gruwel *n* gruel, soup 3.711

guerdo(u)n *n* reward 1.818, 5.594, 1389, 1852; *v* reward 2.1295

guerdonynge *vbl n* rewarding 2.392

gydyng *vbl n* guidance 5.643

gye *v* guide, direct 3.1747, 5.546

gyle *n* guile, deception 3.777

habit *n* clothes 1.109, 170, 2.222

habounde *v* abound 2.159

habundaunce *n* abundance, plenty 3.1042

half *n* side; **on my halve** on my
part 4.945

halt 3 *pr sg of* holde(n *v*

halten *v* limp 4.1457

halve *see* half *n*

halvendel *n* half 3.707, 5.335

halwed *pp* held sacred, revered
3.268

hameled *pp* hambled, crippled,
lamed 2.964

han *infin, 3 pr pl of* have(n *v*

hap *n* chance, fortune, luck
1.896, 3.1246; chance event
2.1696

happe *v* happen 1.625, 2.29

happy *adj* lucky, fortunate
2.621, 1382

harde *adv* violently, intensely
3.1531

hardely, hardily, hardyly *adv*
assuredly, certainly 2.304,
1012, 1425

hardinesse *n* boldness,
daring 1.566, 2.634,
3.1776

hardnesse *n* resistance 2.1245

hardy *adj* bold, brave 2.1074,
4.601, 5.802, 830

hardyment *n* boldness, daring
4.533

harm *n* wrong, injury 1.347,
3.861; pain, grief, suffering
1.333, 409; a matter for regret,
a pity 2.350; defamation
2.801; *pl* misfortunes 1.614;
evils 2.470

harpour *n* harpist 2.1030

haselwode *n* hazel wood 3.890;
5.505, 1174 (*see* nn.)

hastif *adj* hasty, rash 4.1567

hastiliche *adv* soon 4.1318

hatte *pr sg or pp of* hote(n *v*

haukyng *vbl n* hunting with
hawks 3.1779

haunteth 3 *pr sg* makes a prac-
tice of 5.1556

have(n, han *v* (*auxil*) have 1.197;
have, possess 1.120; ~ **here my
trowthe** take my word 1.1061;
show, feel 3.1173; hold 3.864;
infin han 1.13; 2 *pr sg* hast
1.557 (with suffixed *pron*) has-
tow 1.276; 3 *pr sg* hath 1.83;
pt sg hadde 1.89; 2 *pt sg* (with
suffixed *pron*) haddestow
4.276; *pt pl* hadde(n 2.24

hawe *n* haw, hawthorn berry
(i.e. something valueless)
3.854, 4.1398

hayis *n pl* hedges 3.351

hed *n* head 2.540; source 2.844

hede *n* heed, notice 3.639; **take ~
(of)** pay attention (to) 1.501,
2.747; **take ~** take care 5.1048

he(e)le *n* health, well-being
1.461, 2.707

heet *pp of* hote(n *v*

he(e)te *n* heat (of passion) 1.420,
978, 4.511; **cachen an ~**
become hot, fevered 2.942;
rage 5.1761

hegges *n pl* hedges 3.1236

heleles *adj* without health,
healthless 5.1593

helmed *adj* helmeted 2.593

help(e *n* helper 1.1010; *pl* assist-
ance 2.1455

helply *adj* helpful 5.128

helpynge *vbl n* aid 1.853; sup-
porter 2.1550

hem *acc and dat pl of* 3 *pron*
them 1.29; (*refl* with *v*) them-
selves 2.256; (*in impers constr*)
2.1598

hemself, hemselven *pron pl* them-
selves 1.922

hemysperie *n* hemisphere 3.1439

heng *pt sg of* honge *v*

henne *adv* hence, from here
2.209, 3.630; from now
4.1246

hennes *adv* hence, from here
1.572; fro ~ from here 5.607

hente *v* seize, grasp, take 2.1154,
3.21, 4.5, 5.90; take hold
1.1045, 2.924, 3.1187; catch
4.1371; *pp* hent 1.509

heped *pp* accumulated 4.236

herbe *n* plant 3.10; medicinal
plant, herb 1.661, 2.345

herber *n* garden 2.1705

herde *n* shepherd 3.1235; *n pl*
hierdes shepherds 3.619

herdesse *n* shepherdess 1.653

here-ayeins *adv* against this, in
reply 2.1380

herebyforn *adv* before this
2.296, 1271

heretofore *adv* before this 5.26

herie, herye *v* praise 3.951,
1672; *pp* yheried 2.973, 3.7,
1804

herke(n, herkne(n *v* listen (to),
hear 1.164, 602, 624; 2.95;
5.1812

herof *adv* about this 2.108,
3.565, 939

heroner *n* falcon for hunting
herons 4.413

herte *n* heart 1.228; deere ~
2.871; swete ~ 3.69; ~ blood
2.445; *gen* hertes; ~ lif 2.1066;
~ queene 1.817; ~ reste 3.1045

herteles *adj* dispirited, disheart-
ened 5.1594

hertely *adv* earnestly 2.1277;

cordially 2.1677; sincerely
5.941

herto *adv* to this 3.520, 4.1072

heryinge *vbl n* praise 3.48

heste *n* behest, command 3.419,
1157, 1745; promise 4.1439,
5.355, 1208

hette *3 pr sg of* hote(n *v*

heve(n *v* heave, lift, raise 5.1159;
exert oneself 2.1289

heven *n* heaven 1.31, 878; the
heavens, sky 3.626; sphere 3.2;
as adj hevene blisse 3.704,
1322, 1657; *gen* hevenes
4.1594

hevenyssh *adj* heavenly 1.104;
celestial 5.1813

hevy *adj* weighty 1.651; gloomy
3.1139

hevynesse *n* sadness, unhappi-
ness 1.24, 655, 970

hewe *n* colour, complexion
1.441, 487, 2.60, 4.663;
chaunge ~ change colour,
grow pale or red 2.303, 1470,
3.1698; of ~ in appearance
4.379, 736; hele and ~ health
and looks 1.461, 5.1403; *pl*
hewes complexion 3.94; hewis
colours 2.21

hewed *pp* coloured 2.1198

heynous *adj* hateful 2.1617

hider *adv* hither, here 4.932,
1360

hie, hye *v* hurry 3.157, 1441,
4.320

hierdes *see* herde *n*

hight(e *see* hote(n *v*

hire *n* payment, wages 4.125;
ransom 4.506; quite (s.o.'s) ~
repay s.o. 1.334

hir(e *pron acc* her 1.679; *dat* to

her 3.570; (*in impers constr*)
1.985; *refl* 2.812

hir(e *adj poss* her 1.127; their
1.63

hir(e)s *pron poss* hers 1.889,
3.1608

hireself, hir(e)selven *pron* herself
1.112, 2.651, 1223

ho(o) *interj* stop! 3.190, 4.1242;
as n ceasing 2.1083

ho(o)l *adj* whole, complete
1.961; healthy, unhurt, well
2.976, 1670; *adv* completely
1.1053; al ~ completely
4.1641

holde(n *v* hold, grasp 2.203;
hold up 3.184; keep, maintain
3.29; retain 4.1628; observe
1.161; consider, believe 2.164;
~ hym consider himself 3.421;
~ in hond cajole, encourage
with false hopes 2.477, 3.773,
5.1615; *3 pr sg contr* halt
2.37, 3.1007; *pt sg* held 1.126;
pp holde(n beholden, obliged
2.241, 3.1259, 4.417, 5.966

holder up *n* defender, supporter
2.644

holly, hoolly *adv* wholly, com-
pletely 1.366, 3.145

holpen *pp* helped 2.1319, 1441,
3.1270

holsom *adj* healthful, beneficial
1.947, 3.1746

holtes *n pl* woods 3.351

houlghnesse *n* concavity, inner
surface 5.1809

holynesse *n* piety, devotion
1.560

hom *n* home 2.187; *as adv*
to (one's) home 1.126,
2.596

homly *adv* familiarly 2.1559

homme *v* hum 2.1199

hond *n* hand 1.433; beren on ~
accuse 3.1154, accuse or con-
vince (falsely), persuade
4.1404; have on ~ be occupied
with 2.217, 3.937; holden in ~
deceive, play along, encourage
with false hopes 2.477, 3.773,
5.1615

honeste(e *n* honour, reputation
4.1576; in ~ honourably 2.706

honge *v* hang 1.833; remain
undecided 2.1242; *pt sg* heng
2.639, 689

honte *v* hunt 3.1780

hoor *adj* white-haired 5.1284

horn *n* (of creature) 1.300; (the
material) 2.642; (of crescent
moon) tip 3.624

horned: in ~ newe the new cres-
cent moon 5.650

horrible *adj* appalling 5.250

hot(e, hoot(e *adj* hot 1.445;
heated, passionate 5.507; *adv*
hotly 3.1390; have ~
experience intensely 3.1650,
4.583

hote(n *v* be called 1.788, 3.797;
promise 2.1623, 5.1636; *3 pr
sg* hette 5.319, hatte 3.797; *pr
pl* highten 1.788; *pt sg* hyghte
5.1636; *pt pl* highten 2.1623;
pp heet 1.153, ihight 5.541,
hight 2.492, 4.445

hove *v* hover 3.1427; wait, linger
5.33

howne: in here and ~ everybody
4.210

howve *n* hood (in expressions
meaning 'hoodwink, delude')
3.775, 5.469

humblely *adv* humbly 2.1719,
5.1354

hust *pp* hushed 2.915, 3.1094

hye *n* haste 2.88, 4.1385

ibete *pp of* **bete** *v*; beaten 2.940

iblowe *pp* make known, spread
abroad 1.384, 530, 4.167

iborn *pp of* **bere** *v*; borne, carried
5.1650

ibounden *pp of* **binde** *v*; bound
4.229

ibrought *pp of* **bringe** *v*; brought
2.1638, 4.96, 5.11

ich *pron* I 1.406, 678, 864

icleped *pp* called 1.654

iclosed *pp of* **close** *v*; closed up
2.968

icomen *pp* come 3.1668

idarted *pp* pierced 4.240

ido *pp of* **do(o)n** *v*; done 3.386

ië *see* **eye, ye** *n*

if, yif *conj* if; **but if** unless 5.897;
if that if 4.1633

ifounde *pp of* **finde** *v*; found
4.594

ifourmed *pp of* **forme** *v*; **han ~** be
endowed with 4.315

igrounde *pp* sharpened 4.43

iheryed *pp of* **herie** *v*; praised 3.7

ihight *pp of* **hote(n** *v*; called
5.541

ijaped *pp of* **jape** *v*; joked, made
fun 1.318

ikaught *pp of* **cache** *v*; caught,
captured 1.534

ilaft *pp of* **le(e)ve** *v*; left 4.227

ilke *adj* same, very 2.1262, 1706

illusioun *n* delusion, fancy
3.1041, 5.368

ilost *pp of* **lese** *v*; lost, wasted
2.1749, 3.896

imagine(n *v* imagine, conceive
2.836, 4.1695; fancy, suppose
mistakenly 5.617, 624; con-
sider, wonder about 5.454;
devise, plan 4.1626

imedled *pp* mixed, mingled
3.815

impossible *adj as n* impossibility
3.525

impresse(n *v* imprint 2.1371,
3.1543

impressioun *n* mental impres-
sion, image 1.298, 2.1238,
5.372

in-comynge *n* entrance, coming
in 2.1308

in-fere *adv* together 2.1266 (*see
also* **yfe(e)re**)

influences *n pl* astrological influ-
ences, emanations 3.618

infortune *n* misfortune 3.1626,
4.185, 297

infortuned *pp* ill-fortuned,
unlucky 4.744

inhielde *v* pour in, infuse 3.44

injure *n* injury 3.1018

inly *adv* inwardly 1.640;
entirely, greatly 3.1606

instaunce *n* request, urging
2.1441

inward *adv* inwards 2.1725; pri-
vately 2.1732

inwardly *adv* closely, penetrat-
ingly 2.264

inwith *prep* within, inside 2.508,
3.1499, 5.1022

ire *n* anger, wrath, bad temper
1.793, 3.22, 1805, 5.36

iren *n* iron 2.1276

ironne *pp of* **renne(n**; run 3.84

iset *pp of* **sette(n** *v*; set, fixed
3.1488, 4.184, 674

iseye *pp of* **se(e)(n** *v*; seen 5.448

isought *pp of* **seche, seke(n** *v*; sought for 3.1317

issen *v* issue, go out 4.37

issue *n* outlet, vent 5.205

isworn *pp* sworn 2.570

itake *pp* taken 3.1198

iwis, iwys *adv* certainly, indeed, to be sure 1.415, 425

iwryen *pp of* **wrye(n** *v*; hidden 3.1451

iyolden *pp of* **yelde(n** *v*; yielded, submissive 3.96

jalous *adj* jealous 3.899; *as n* jealous person 3.1168

jalousie *n* jealousy 2.753

jangle *v* chatter, gossip 2.666, 800

janglerie *n* gossip 5.755

jape *n* trick 2.130; joke 1.911, 937, 1083, 2.1167, 3.408

jape *v* trick, deceive 5.1134; joke, jest 1.929, 2.943; mock 1.508

japer *n* jester, trickster 2.340

jaspre *n* jasper 2.1229

jo *v* come about, turn out 3.33

jolite *n* merriment, cheerfulness 1.559

joly *adj* merry, cheerful 2.1031; high-spirited, gallant 2.1099, 1105; ~ **Robyn** (typical shepherd figure) 5.1174

jompre *v* jumble 2.1037

jouken *v* roost (as a falcon), lie up, rest 5.409

juparten *v* endanger 4.1566

jupartie, jupertie *n* danger, risk 5.916; **in** ~ in jeopardy, at risk 2.465, 772

just *adj* just, fair 2.527; ~ **cause** good reason 2.727, 3.1227

kalendes *n pl* first day, beginning 2.7, 5.1634

kan *pr sg of* **konne** *v*

kankedort *n* ?predicament, *see* 2.1752n.

keene *adj* sharp 2.58

ke(e)pe(n *v* keep 1.627; care 1.763; observe, hold to 3.419; take care of 5.1048; protect, preserve 5.1077; ~ **tonge** hold one's tongue 3.294; *imp sg* **kep** 3.332

kep: in take ~ take notice 1.486, 3.1410; *vbl n* **kepyng** retention 1.200

kerve *v* cut 2.325; *prp adj* **kervyng** cutting 1.631

keste *pt sg* kissed 3.1129, 1519

kevere *v* recover 1.917

kidde *pt of* **kithe** *v*

kiste *pt* kissed 1.812, 2.250, 3.1252

kithe *v* show, make known 4.538, 619; *pt* **kidde** 1.208

knette *v* draw together, join 3.1748; *pt sg* **in** ~ restrained, contracted 3.1088

knotteles *adv* smoothly, without impediment 5.769

knowe *n* knee 3.1592; **sitten on** ~ kneel 2.1202

knowe(n *v* know 1.240, 340; recognize 3.1419, 5.1117, 1404; *pp* **knowe, yknowen** 1.638, 2.792

knyghtly *adj* gallant 2.628

konne *v* know, understand 1.647, 3.83; ~ **good** know what is proper, have good

sense 2.1178, 3.638; ~ (his)
good see (his) advantage
5.106; ~ thank be grateful (to)
2.1466; (as auxil with infin)
can, know how to 3.377; be
able to 5.1404; can do 1.776,
2.175, 1078, 1673; I kan no
more 3.390, 1193; pr sg kan
1.11; 2 pr sg kanst 1.511,
(with suffixed pron) kanstow
1.757, 4.460; pr pl konne
1.776; pr subj sg konne 2.49,
1497; pt sg koude 1.193;
kowthe 1.984; couthe 1.629,
660; kouthe 3.958; 2 pt sg
koudest 1.622; pt pl koude
3.1358; pp couth 4.61
konnyng adj clever, knowledge-
able 1.302, 5.970; superl
konnyngeste 1.331
konnynge n ability, skill, under-
standing 1.83, 662, 2.4, 1079,
3.101, 999, 5.866
koude, kouthe, kowde see konne v
kynde n nature 1.238, 2.1374; of
~ by nature, naturally 2.1443
kynrede n family, birth 5.979

labbe n tell-tale 3.300
labour n work, effort, exertion
1.199, 955, 1042
laboure(n v make an effort, take
pains 1.458, 3.1265; refl
4.1009
lad pt sg of lede(n v
lade v load 2.1544
lady n lady 1.45; gen 1.99, 2.32
laft pp of le(e)ve(n v
laiser, layser see leiser n
lak n want, lack 2.909, 959;
fault, flaw 2.1178, 5.814
lakken v be lacking, wanting

4.945; impers hire (me, us etc.)
lakketh (something) is lacking
to her (me, us, etc.), she lacks,
I/we lack 1.522, 3.531,
4.1523, 5.745, 824; find fault
with, disparage 1.189
lambyc n alembic 4.520
lame adj lame, halting 2.17
langage n words, speech 3.1336
langour n suffering, distress
4.844, 5.42, 245, 268, 397
languisshe(n v suffer, grow weak
1.569, 3.241
languisshyng vbl n languishing,
suffering 1.529
lappe n fold, edge (of garment)
2.448, 3.59, 742
large adj large, extensive 1.185;
ample, full 1.109, 5.205; free,
lavish 5.804
largely adv fully 2.1707
largesse n generosity 3.1724,
5.436
lasse, lesse adj less 2.1532,
4.578; lesser 2.470, 4.478;
thinner 5.618; adv less 1.284,
4.616
lat, late imp sg, pr sg, pr subj pl
of lete(n v
laude n praise 3.1273
laurer n laurel 3.542, 727,
5.1107
lay n (1) song 2.921
lay n (2) belief, faith, religion
1.340, 1001
leche n doctor, physician 1.857,
2.571, 1066
lechecraft n medicine 4.436
lede(n v lead 1.527; (a life)
2.832; govern, control 2.527;
conduct 5.16; carry, take
4.1514; 3 pr sg contr let 2.882;

pt sg **lad, ladde, ledde** 1.184,
5.714, 3.59; *pp* **led** 1.872,
2.553

ledere *n* leader, keeper 4.1454

le(e)f *imp sg of* **le(e)ve(n** *v*

le(e)f, leve, lief *adj* dear, beloved
2.251, 1693, 3.460; **ben ~** be
pleasing 3.1619; **have ~** hold
dear, love 3.864, 869; *pl* **leeve**
4.82; *as n* dear one, love
4.611; desired object 4.1585;
comp **levere** preferable: **have ~**
value more highly 4.570; **me
were ~** I would rather 1.1034,
2.352; **hadde I ~** I would
rather 2.1509; *superl* **levest**
most preferable: **me were ~** I
would most like 2.189

le(e)ne *adj* lean, thin 1.553,
5.709, 1221; feeble, slender
2.132

le(e)re *v* learn 3.406; teach 2.97,
1580; **to ~** to be instructed
5.161

leese *n* pasture 2.752

le(e)st *adv* least 1.516, 2.840

le(e)st(e *superl adj* least, smallest
3.1320; **atte ~** at least 2.362,
5.525

leet *pt sg of* **lete(n** *v*

lefull *adj* permitted, legitimate
3.1020

leigh *pt sg* lied 2.1077

leiser *n* leisure 3.516; opportun-
ity 2.1369; **at bettre ~** at
greater length 5.945

lered *pp as n* learned persons
1.976

lese(n *v* lose 2.472; *pt sg* **loste**
1.441; *pp* **(y)lorn** 1.373,
4.1250; **(y)lost** 1.201, 4.1283;
vbl n **lesyng** losing, loss 3.830

lessen *v* decrease 5.1438

lessoun *n* lesson, something
learned 3.51, 83

lest *n* (*see also* **list** *n*) pleasure,
delight 1.330

leste *see* **list(e** *v*

lete(n, late(n *v* let, allow 2.650,
5.351; **~ be** give up 1.701,
2.248; abandon, give up
4.1585; consider 1.302;
refrain, desist 2.1500; pretend
2.543; *1 pr sg* **late** 1.133; *pr
subj pl* **late** 2.323; *pt sg* **leet**
2.650, **lete** 5.226; *pt pl* **leten**
4.1135; *pt subj sg* **lete** 3.1762;
imp sg **lat** 2.1401; *prp* **letyng**
leaving behind 5.1810

lette *n* delay, stopping 3.235,
699, 4.41; hindrance 1.361

lette(n *v* prevent 2.732, 4.1301;
hinder 3.545; obstruct 3.717;
refrain from 1.150; desist
2.1089; *imp sg* **lette** 3.725;
imp pl **letteth** 2.1136; *pp* **let**
2.94, 3.717

lette-game *n* spoilsport 3.527

letuarie *n* medicine, remedy
5.741

letyng *prp of* **lete(n, late(n** *v*

leve *see* **le(e)f** *adj*

le(e)ve *n* leave, permission; **by
youre ~** with your permission,
if you please 2.1634; **biside
(one's) ~** without (one's) con-
sent, permission 2.734, 3.622;
take (one's) ~ take leave to
depart 1.126

leve *v* (1) allow; **God ~** may God
grant 1.597, 2.1212

le(e)ve(n *v* (2) leave 4.87; give up
4.896; leave off, desist 1.686,
4.1335; *imp sg* **le(e)f** 4.852,

5.1518; *pt sg* lefte 2.560; *pp*
(y)laft 4.227, 281

le(e)ve(n *v* (3) believe, trust
1.342, 2.420, 5.1637; to ~ to
be believed 3.308; *imp sg* leve
5.378

levere, levest *see* le(e)f *adj*

lewed *adj* stupid, ignorant 1.198,
3.398

libertee *n* freedom 2.773, 1292

licour *n* liquor 4.520

lief *see* le(e)f *adj*

lif *n* life 1.95; bere ~ be alive
2.835; bring of ~ kill 2.1608,
5.1561; on lyve alive 2.138;
(my/his *etc.*) lyve during (my/
his *etc.*) life 2.205, 1056; *gen
sg* lyves: lyves ende death
3.392, 5.1554

ligge(n *pr subj sg, pr pl of* lye(n
v (1)

light *adj* light in weight 2.1238,
5.1808; easy 4.484, 1570;
cheerful 5.352, 684

lighte(n *v* (1) illuminate 4.313;
brighten 1.293

lighte(n *v* (2) lighten, relieve
3.1082; cheer, gladden 5.634

lightles *adj* without light 3.550

lightly *adv* easily 2.289; quickly
2.1239; readily 2.1388; frivol-
ously, without good reason
2.668, 3.804

ligne *n* lineage 5.1481

ligne aloes *n* aloes 4.1137

lik(e *adj* like; similar 2.1040; *as
n* the same, alike 2.44; *comp*
likkere more like 3.1028

lik(e *adv* like 1.103

like(n *v* please, give pleasure
1.289, 431; take pleasure
3.354; hym (hire, *etc.*) liketh it

pleases him (her), he/she likes
2.1266, 5.631

likkere *comp of* like *adj*

likynge *prp adj* pleasing 1.309

line, lyne *n* straight line, plumb
line 1.1068, 2.1461, 3.228

lisse *n* comfort 3.343; joy 5.550

lissen *v* relieve, alleviate 1.702,
1089

list *n* (*see also* lest *n*) pleasure,
delight 3.1303

list, listow 2 *pr sg contr of* lye(n
v (1)

liste, leste *v* (*impers*) (hym, hire,
etc.) ~ it pleases him/her, s/he
wishes; be pleased, wish 1.518,
671, 707; *pr pl* listen 3.1810;
pt sg leste 1.189, liste 2.949

litargie *n* lethargy, sleeping sick-
ness 1.730

lite *n* little 5.176; *adj* little, small
2.1646; *adv* 1.826

litel *adj* little 3.601; *adv* 1.216;
as n into ~ nearly 4.884

lode-sterre *n* guiding star 5.232,
1392

lok *n* look 1.446

loke(n *v* look, gaze 1.1078; look,
appear, seem 1.206; see, try
5.1113; consider 3.316; *vbl n*
lokyng appearance 1.173

longe *adv* long, for a long time
2.1127, 3.1536

longen *v* (1) long, desire 2.546,
5.597; *impers* me longeth
I long 2.312

longen *v* (2) befit, suit 2.1346,
5.837

lo(o) *interj* look! see! 1.205, 302

lo(o)re *n* teaching 1.645, 745;
advice 1.1090; learning, know-
ledge 3.243

lo(o)th *adj* displeasing, hateful
2.808, 3.732, 1339; reluctant,
unwilling 3.154, 369, 5.21; *as
adv* unwillingly 2.1234; *superl*
lothest 2.237

lordship *n* power, authority
3.1756; patronage, protection
3.76

lorn *pp of* lese(n *v*

lough *pt sg* laughed 1.1037,
2.1163, 1592

loute *v* bow 3.683

lowe *adj* humble 2.528; heigh
(and/or) ~ in all respects 3.27,
418

lowe *adv* low 2.689, 3.683;
humbly 1.178

lowely *adv* humbly 2.1072,
1122, 5.174

lufsom *adj* lovely 5.465, 911

lust *n* pleasure, delight 1.326,
2.844; desire 1.407, 443,
2.830; sexual desire, lust
4.1573; inclinations 2.476

lustinesse *n* pleasure 3.177

lusty *adj* delightful, full of life,
gallant, brave 1.165, 560;
pleasant 2.752; cheerful 1.958,
2.1099, 5.393; *as n* vigorous,
lively person 3.354

lustyly *adv* cheerfully 5.568

lye(n, ligge(n *v* (1) lie 1.752,
3.660; remain 5.1207; *2 pr sg
contr* list 1.797, 2.991
(with suffixed *pron* listow
4.394); *3 pr sg* lith 2.465; *pr pl*
liggen 3.669, 685; *pr subj sg*
ligge 5.411; *pt pl* laye(n 3.749;
pt subj sg lay(e 4.1560; *imp sg*
ly 2.1519; *prp* liggyng 1.915

lye(n *v* (2) tell lies 3.880; *pt sg*
leigh 2.1077

lyere *n* liar 3.309, 315

lyme *v* lime, catch with birdlime
1.353

lymes *n pl* limbs 1.282, 4.1158,
5.709

lyves *adj* living 3.13, 4.252

maad *pp of* make(n *v*

mace *n* club, often with spiked
metal head 2.640, 4.44

madde *v* be mad, rage 1.479

mafay *interj* by my faith 3.52

maille *n* mail-armour 5.1559

maisterfull *adj* masterful, domin-
eering 2.756

maistow *contr of* maist thow, 2
pr sg of mowe(n *v*

makeles *adj* matchless 1.172

make(n *v* make, build 4.121;
compose 2.878; make, cause
to be 5.684; make (with *infin*)
2.677, 5.1126; *pt sg* made
1.312; *pt pl* made(n 5.1802;
pp maad 1.553, ymad 5.1537

makere *n* creator, author
3.1437, 5.1787

makyng *vbl n* composition,
poetry 5.1789

maladie *n* illness, sickness 1.419,
2.483

malapert *adj* presumptuous 3.87

malencolie *n* melancholy, depres-
sion, black bile (of the four
humours) 5.360, 622, 1646

malice *n* ill-will 3.326

malt *pt sg of* melte *v*

maner(e *n* way, manner 1.291,
742; in (som, this, no) ~ 1.33,
1059, 3.1412; kind of 1.495,
844; manners, conduct 1.880,
3.216; bearing 1.182, 313; cus-
tom, habit 1.1021, 5.809

manhod *n* manly qualities 2.676, 3.428, 4.1674; manly courage 4.529, 5.1476

manly *adv* like a man 4.622

mannes *gen of* **man**: human, of human beings, man's 2.417, 3.820, 1098

mannyssh *adj* like a man, unwomanly 1.284

mansuete *adj* meek 5.194

marcial: in **torney** ~ tournament 4.1669

martire *n* martyrdom 4.818

mat *adj* exhausted, dejected 4.342

matere *n* (physical) matter 5.1322; matter, business, affair 1.265, 1062; subject matter 1.53

maugre *prep* despite, in spite of 4.51

may, mayst, maystow *1 & 3 pr sg, 2 pr sg of* **mowe(n** *v*

mayde *n* girl 2.880, 3.305; virgin 5.1869

mayden *n* girl 1.166, 2.119

maze *n* delusion, puzzle 5.468

mede *n* meadow 1.156, 2.53

mede *n* reward 3.415; fulfilment 2.423; **to medes** in return 2.1201

medled *pp* mingled 4.339

medlynge *n* meddling, interference 4.167

meeltid *n* mealtime 2.1556

meene *n* means, intermediary 3.254, 5.1551; mean, middle way 1.689

me(e)ne(n *v* mean 2.133; signify 2.171; portend 1.552, 5.364; mean, intend 2.581, 5.1150; say 4.433; *pt sg* **mente** 1.320

meeste *adj* highest in rank 1.167; **at the** ~ at the most 5.947

me(e)te(n *v* dream 3.1344, 1559; *impers with dat pron* 2.925; *pt* **mette** 1.362, 2.90

melte *v* melt 3.1445, 4.367; *pt sg* **malt** 1.582; *pp* **molte** 5.10

men *pron indef* (with *sg v*) one 4.866

mende *v* put right 5.1426; profit 2.329

mene *adj* average 5.806; middling 1.167

merie, mery(e, mirye, mury *adj* merry, cheerful, pleasant 2.1746, 3.230, 952, 1563

merites *n pl* merits, rights and wrongs 4.965

merveille *n* marvel, wonder 1.476, 3.189

meschaunce *n* misfortune 1.92, 2.1019, 3.290; *as interj* confound it! 4.1362; **with** ~ with bad luck 1.118, 3.691

meschief *n* misfortune 1.755, 3.1622, 4.614

messager *n* messenger 3.1417

mesure *n* moderation 2.418, 715

meve *v* move 1.472

mevynge *vbl n* movements 1.285, 289

me-ward: in **to** ~ to me 4.1666

mewe *see* **muwe** *n*

meyne *n* household, servants 1.127, 2.614, 5.526

milnestones *npl* millstones 2.1384

mirour *n* mirror 1.365; model, paragon 2.266, 842

mis- *see also* **mys-**

misacounted *pp* miscalculated 5.1185

misericorde *n* mercy 3.1177

misse *v* feel lack or absence of 3.445; come to grief 3.1624

mo *n* more, others 1.613; without ~ alone 4.1125; *adj* more 3.234; *adv* more, any longer, again 5.158, 1263

mocioun *n* inclination, desire 4.1291

moeble *n* possessions, movable goods 4.1380, 1460, 5.300

mokre *v* hoard, rake in 3.1375

moleste *n* trouble, distress 4.880

molte *pp of* melte *v*

mone *n* complaint 1.696, 2.558; maken ~ lament, complain 4.950, 5.250

montance, mountance *n* amount 3.1732; length 2.1707

mo(o)t *v* must 1.216; may 2.90; *pt* had to 4.216; *pt* in sense of *pr* must 3.1214; *1 & 3 pr sg* mo(o)t 1.573; *2 pr sg* most 4.648; *pr pl* mote(n 1.846; *pr subj sg* mote 1.341; *pt sg, pl* moste(n 2.1507, 3.1214

moote *n* particle, speck 3.1603

morneth *pr sg* longs for 5.793

morter *n* float-wick lamp 4.1245

morwe *n* morning 1.951; dawn 3.1469; next day 4.1617; a/by the ~ in the morning 2.405, 961; on the ~ next day 1.965

moste, mot, mote *see* mo(o)t *v*

motre *v* mutter 2.541

mowe *n* grimace 4.7

mowe(n *v* be able, have power, may, can; *1 & 3 pr sg* may 1.253; *2 pr sg* maist, mayst 1.600, 1052 (with suffixed *pron* maistow, maystow 1.673, 2.1016, 4.265); *pr pl*

mowe(n 4.1330; *pr subj* mowe 1.1015; *1 & 3 pt sg* myghte 2.451; *2 pt sg* myghtest 5.1527 (with suffixed *pron* myghtestow 4.262); *pt pl* myghte(n 2.1624

muable *adj* mutable, changeable 3.822

mucche *v* munch, eat 1.914

muchel *n* much 2.1659; *adj* much 2.1071

multiplie *v* increase 1.486, 546

mury *see* merie *adj*

muse *v* ponder, reflect 3.563

mutabilite *n* changeableness 1.851

muwe *n* cage, coop, pen 3.1784; in ~ in (a) hiding (place), in secret 1.381, 4.496, 1310

muwe *v* change 2.1258

muwet *adj* mute 5.194

myght *n* power, ability 1.33, 2.175; strength 3.436; don his ~ exert himself 2.1340, 3.512

myghte(n *1 & 3 pt sg, pt pl of* mowe(n *v*

myghtyly *adv* greatly 5.262

myn *poss pron* my, mine; *as n* my goode ~ my own good one 3.1009

myne *v* mine, undermine (as in a siege) 2.677, 3.767, 4.471

myrthe *n* joy, gladness 3.715

mys *adj* amiss 4.1267, 1348, 5.1426

mysaunter *n* misfortune 1.766

mysbyleved *adj* misbelieving, infidel 3.838

mysconstruwe *v* misconstrue, misunderstand 1.346

mysforyaf *pt sg* misgave 4.1426

myslyved *adj* wicked 4.330

mysmetre *v* spoil the metre, scan wrongly 5.1796

mysspak *pt sg* said something amiss 1.934

myswent *pp* gone wrong 1.633

myte *n* small (Flemish) coin (used to express worthlessness) 3.832, 900, 4.684

nad, nadde (= ne hadde) *pt sg contr* had not 3.1319, 4.1233

nam (= ne am) *1 pr sg contr* am not 4.689; ~ **but** am as good as, no more than 5.706

name *n* name 1.99; reputation 1.251, 880

namely, nameliche *adv* especially 1.165, 743

namore *adj* no more 1.713; *adv* no more 1.753

narwe *adv* closely, tightly 3.1734

nas (= ne was) *pt sg* was not 1.101

natal *adj* presiding over birthdays 3.150

nath (= ne hath) *pr sg contr* has not 2.777, 5.1199

natheles *adv* nonetheless, nevertheless 1.19, 170

natif *adj* natural, inborn 1.102

nativitee *n* horoscope, astrological conditions at one's birth 2.685

naught, nought *n* nothing 1.444, 894; *adv* (*emphatic*) not, in no way, not at all 2.46, 574, 930

nay *adv* no 1.657

necessaire *adj* necessary 4.1021

nede *n* need, necessity 1.886; business, affair 1.772; hour of

need, crisis 3.546; **ben** ~ be necessary 1.128; **the ben** ~ you need 5.336; **comth to the** ~ becomes necessary 3.1225; **at the** ~ when necessary 4.1106; *pl* affairs 1.355

ned(e)ly *adv* of necessity, necessarily 4.970, 1006

nedes *adv* necessarily 1.573, 2.439, 536

nedeth *3 pr sg impers* (it) is necessary 3.1676; ~ **it** 2.176, 917; **it** ~ **me** I need 2.462; (**me/us** *etc.*) ~ (**I/we** *etc.*) need 2.11, 3.1463; **what** ~ what is the need of 2.497; what need is there 2.1541

nedfully *adv* of necessity, necessarily 4.1004, 1054, 1074

neigh *adv* nearly 1.60, 543; **wel** ~ very nearly, almost 1.108; *prep* near 1.180, 2.68

neighen *v* approach, draw nigh 2.1555

ner *adv comp* nearer 1.448

nere (= ne were) *pt subj sg* were not

nerf *n* sinew 2.642

nevene *v* name, mention 1.876

newe *v* renew 3.305

newe *adj* new 1.157; **of** ~ recent 2.20; *adv* newly 1.222; anew 5.650, 1333; **ay** ~ continually 1.440, 5.1572; ~ **and** ~ again and again 3.116

next *prep* next to 1.948; *adj* next 2.1273; nearest, most direct 1.697; *adv* the next time 2.982; next 3.1256

noblesse *n* nobility (of character, conduct) 1.287, 5.439, 1831

nobleye *n* nobility 4.1670

noise *n* rumour 1.85; outcry 4.183; voice 4.374

nolde (= ne wolde) *pt contr* would not, did not want to 1.77, 150; 2 *sg* (*with suffixed pron*) **noldestow** 3.1264

nome(n *pp* taken 3.606, 5.190, 514

nones: in for the ~ for the occasion, purpose 1.561, 4.428; purposefully, indeed 2.1381; at that time 4.185

no(o)n *adj* no 1.465, 3.415; *pron* none 2.502; *adv*: in or ~ or not 1.132

not, noot (= ne wot, woot) *1 & 3 pr sg contr* (I/he) know(s) not 1.410, 426

noriture *n* nourishment 4.768

nost (= ne wost) 2 *pr sg contr* you do not know 4.642, 1101

notifie *v* take note of 2.1591

nought *see* **naught**

noumbred *pp* (with **unto**) included among those enjoying 3.1269

nouncerteyn: in in ~ without certainty 1.337

nouther *conj* neither 4.1264

novelrie *n* novelty 2.756

nowthe *adv* now 1.985

nyce *adj* foolish 1.202, 625

nycely *adv* foolishly 5.1152

nycete *n* foolishness 1.913; scrupulosity 2.1288

nygard *n* miser 3.1379

nyghte *v* grow dark, become night 5.515

nyl, nil (= ne wyl) *1 & 3 pr sg contr* will not, am/is not willing 1.758, 777; 2 *pr sg* **nylt**
2.1000; (*with pron*) **nyltow** 1.792

nys, nis (= ne ys) *3 pr sg contr* is not 1.203, 684

nyste (= ne wiste) *pt contr* did not know 1.96, 356, 3.1351, 4.349

o *adj* (*see also* **oon**) one 3.1026; *prep* on 3.552; **o poynt to** about to 4.1153, 1638, 5.1285

obeisaunce *n* respectful submission, deference 3.478

oblige *v* pledge 4.1414

observaunce *n* observance, ceremony 1.160, 4.783; (lover's) observance, attentions 1.198, 337, 2.1345; respectful attention, homage 3.970; **don ~** perform a ceremony (in honour of) 2.112

occupie *v* take up 5.1322; take possession of 4.836

offence *n* transgression, wrongdoing 1.556, 3.137; harm, injury 4.199

offende *v* attack, assail 1.605; displease 2.244

office *n* function, role 3.1436

ofter *adv comp* more often 1.125, 2.496

oft-tyme (*also as two words*) *adv* many times, frequently 4.1324

o-lofte, on-lofte *adv* above 1.950, 4.1221, 5.8, 259; high 5.348

o-morwe (*see also* **morwe** *n*) in the morning 3.1555, 4.1443

o(o)nes *adv* once 1.472, 549

onfolde *v* unfold 2.1702

onliche *adv* only 4.1332, 5.677

on-lyve *see* **lif** *n*; (with or with-

out hyphen) alive 2.138,
4.1237, 5.885

ook *n* oak 2.1335, 1380

oon, on *adj* one 2.1740; the
same, constant 2.37, 3.309;
united 2.1740; one thing
4.1453; alone, unique 3.782;
pron one 1.350; (*as intens*) ~
the beste (etc.) the best,
etc. 1.1081, 5.1056; **aton** at
one, in agreement 3.565

oost *n* host, army 1.80, 4.29

oother *adj* other 1.702, 2.81;
pron 5.1764; *pl* 2.818

opned *pt* opened 3.469, 1239

oppresse *v* distress, overcome
3.1089, 5.177; suppress,
repress 5.398

oppressioun *n* wrong, injury,
harm 2.1418

or *conj* or 1.39

or *prep* before 4.1685

ordal *n* ordeal 3.1046

ordeyne *adj* well-ordered 1.892

ordinaunce *n* arrangement,
decree 4.964, 5.1605; prep-
aration 3.535; plan 2.510; **by**
~ in due order 3.688

ordre *n* order 4.1017; (religious)
order 1.336, 4.782

ordure *n* rubbish, nonsense
5.385

orisonte *n* horizon 5.276

oth *n* oath 2.299, 3.1046

ought *see* **aught** *n, adv*

oughte *v* ought to; **the aughte**
you ought 1.649; **2** *pt sg* ogh-
tist 1.894 (with suffixed *pron*
oughtestow 5.545)

oure *pron gen* ours 4.539

out(e *adv* out; (*with v of motion
omitted*) go out 4.210, 1437;

to the end 3.417; ~ **and** ~
altogether 2.739

oute(n *v* go, come, out 5.1444;
pr subj sg oute 3.1498

outher *conj* either 2.416, 857

outrely, outrelich *adv* utterly,
completely, entirely 1.382,
2.710, 3.1486, 4.955

overal *adv* everywhere 1.928

over-go(n *v* pass away 1.846,
4.424

over-haste *n* over-hastiness
1.972

over-nyght (*also as two words*)
the night before 2.1513, 1549

overraughte *pt sg* reached over
5.1018

oversprede(n *v* spread over,
cover; *pr sg contr* oversprat
2.767; *pt* overspradde
2.769

overthwart *adv* opposite 3.685

ow(e)n(e *adj* own 1.407, 442

ownded *pp adj* wavy 4.736

pa(a)s *n* step 3.281; course
2.1349; pace, speed: **a** ~ at a
walk 2.627; apace 4.465; **an
esy** ~ slowly, at an easy pace
2.620; **a ful good** ~ rapidly
5.604; **sorwfully a** ~ at a sad,
slow pace 5.61

pace *see* **passe(n** *v*

paillet *n* pallet 3.229

palays, paleis *n* palace 2.76, 508;
~~**ward** towards the palace
2.1252

palestral *adj* athletic 5.304

paramour *n* lover 2.236

paramours *adv* (with love)
passionately, by way of
passionate love 5.158, 332

paraunter *see* **peraunter** *adv*

pardc(e, pardieux *interj* by God, indeed, to be sure 1.717, 197, 2.366, 759

paregal *adj* fully equal 5.840

parfit, perfit *adj* perfect 1.104, 2.891

parlour *n* private chamber 2.82

parodie *n* period, lifetime 5.1548

passe(n, pace *v* go, proceed 2.80; go by 1.847, 5.681, 1085, 1791; depart 4.1153; pass over 2.1595, 3.1576; surpass 4.1698, 5.838; pass for 1.371; *pt* passed, paste 1.456, 2.398

passioun *n* passionate feeling, emotion, suffering 3.1040, 4.705

paumes *n pl* palms 3.1114

payed *pp* made favourable 2.682

paycns *n gen pl* pagans' 5.1849

paynted *pp adj* painted, adorned, coloured 2.424

peere *n* equal 5.1803

pekok *n* peacock 1.210

pcnaunce *n* suffering, misery 1.94, 201

pencel *n* token, pennon 5.1043

pens *n pl* pence 3.1375

peraunter, paraunter *adv* perhaps 1.619, 668, 2.711

peraventure *adv* perhaps 5.991

percede *pt sg* pierced 1.272

perfit *see* **parfit** *adj*

perfourme *v* carry out 3.417

permutacioun *n* change, alteration 5.1541

perseveraunce *n* continuance 1.44

perso(u)n(e *n* person 2.168; physical appearance, figure, body 2.701, 1267; **in (his/my)**

propre ~ in person 2.1487, 4.83

perturbe *v* disturb 4.561

peyne *n* pain, suffering 1.9, 34; **in the** ~ under torture 1.674, 3.1502; effort, endeavour 1.63; **don** (one's) ~ devote one's efforts 2.475, 3.1118, 5.115

peyne(n *v refl* take pains, make an effort 1.989, 2.1574

peynte *v* paint, adorn 2.262, 1041

peyntour *n* painter 2.1041

philosophical *adj* learned, expert in philosophy 5.1857

phisik *n* medicine 2.1038

pie *n* magpie 3.527

piete(e *n* pity 4.246, 731, 5.1598; sense of duty 3.1033

pietous *adj* pitiful 3.1444, 5.451

pike *v* (1) pick, pull out 2.1274

pike *v* (2) peek, peer 3.60

pil(o)we *n* pillow 3.444, 5.224

pyne *see* **peyne** *n*

pite(e, pyte *n* pity, mercy, compassion 1.23, 522, 899

pitous *adj* piteous, pitiful, sad 1.111, 422; merciful, compassionate 1.113, 4.949

pitously, pitouslich *adv* piteously, pitifully 2.1076, 1353; compassionately 5.1424

plat *adv* flatly, bluntly 1.681, 2.579

platly *adv* flatly, bluntly 3.786, 881; plainly 4.924

pleinly, pleynliche *adv* fully, frankly 1.395, 2.272; unreservedly, simply 2.1623

plesaunce *n* pleasure, delight 1.46, 3.4; **don (s.o.)** ~ give

pleasure, do favour to s.o.
3.971, 5.314

plete *v* go to law, sue 2.1468

pley *n* game 5.304; amusement
2.705; contrivance 4.1629; *pl*
games 5.1499

pleye(n *v* play, amuse oneself
1.671, 2.812; *refl* 2.1514; be
cheerful 1.1013; jest, be play-
ful 1.267, 3.1368; play (instru-
ment, game) 3.614, 4.460; act
2.462; act the part of 1.1074,
2.1240; *pt sg* pleyde 1.1013

pleyinge *adj* playful 1.280

pleyn *adj* full, complete 2.1560,
5.1818

pleyne(n *v* complain 1.11, 409; ~
on make complaint, bring
accusation against 3.1020;
lament 1.534

pleynte *n* complaint, lament
1.408, 544

plight *pp* pledged 4.1610;
yplight 3.782

plighte *pt* plucked 2.1120

plit *n* plight, condition 2.1731;
position, situation 2.74, 712,
3.246, 1039

plite *v* fold 2.1204; turn over
2.697

plukke *v* pluck, tug 4.1403

plye *v* handle, touch 1.732

poeplissh *adj* vulgar 4.1677

poesye *n* poetry 5.1790

point *n* essence, purpose 3.604,
701; bit, small amount 3.1377,
1509; detail 1.338, 3.1544;
?note of music 3.695; o ~ to
about to 4.1153, 1638, 5.1285

port *n* bearing, manner 1.1084

pose *v* suppose, put the case
3.310, 571

possed *pp* tossed 1.415

possessioun *n* goods, possessions
2.1419

possibilite(e *n* something poss-
ible 3.448; of ~ possibly, per-
haps 2.607

post *n* prop, support 1.1000

potente *n* crutch 5.1222

poudre *n* dust 5.309

poure *v* look closely, gaze
intently 1.299, 2.1708, 3.1460

pous *n* pulse 3.1114

power: in ben of ~ to be able to
5.166

poynte *v* describe in detail 3.497

preche *v* preach 4.1472; speak
about 2.59; exhort 2.496

preciously *adv* over scrupulously
4.590 (Ph+ variant)

predestyne *n* predestination
4.966

prees *n* crowd 1.173, 2.1643

pregnant *adj* cogent, telling
4.1179

preise *v* praise 1.189; *vbl n*
preisynge praise 2.1589

prenten *v* imprint 2.900

prescience *n* foreknowledge 4.987

presse *n* cupboard; leye on ~ put
aside, shelve 1.559

presse(n, preesse *v* push forward
1.446, 2.1341, 5.1011; exert
pressure 2.693

prest *adj* ready, prompt 2.785,
3.485, 917, 4.162

presumpcioun *n* arrogance, over-
confidence 1.213

preve *v* prove 4.969; test 3.1048,
4.1401; prove true 1.239; be
clear, evident 3.1637

preye, praye *v* pray 1.48;
beseech, beg 1.760

prie, prye *v* peer 2.404, 3.1571;
  spy out 2.1710
priken *v* incite, urge, goad 1.219,
  4.633
prime, pryme *n* canonical hour
  of prime (6.00 a.m.), the
  period 6.00–9.00 a.m.,
  9.00 a.m. 2.992, 1095, 1557;
  beginning 1.157
pris *n* praise 2.181, 376, 1585;
  esteem 1.375; value, currency
  2.24
prive *adj* secret 3.787, 921
privetee *n* secrecy 3.283; inmost
  recess 2.1397, 4.1111
procede *v* proceed 3.455; origin-
  ate 5.360, 370
proces *n* course of events 5.583;
  business, undertaking 2.485,
  3.334; story, discourse 2.268,
  292, 424, 3.1739; suit, case
  2.1615; by ~ in course of time
  2.678, 4.418
profre *v* offer 3.1461
prolixitee *n* longwindedness
  2.1564
pronounced *pp* stated, declared
  4.213
proporcioun *n* proportion;
  relation, shape, form of body
  parts 5.828
propre *adj* own; in ~ persone in
  person 2.1487, 4.83; usual
  4.1152
propretee *n* ownership 4.392
protestacioun *n* avowal, dec-
  laration 2.484, 4.1289
proverbed *pp* spoken in proverbs
  3.293
prow *n* profit, advantage 1.333,
  2.1664, 5.789
pryvely *adv* secretly, discreetly

1.80, 380, 2.1115; **priveliche**
  4.1601
punyce *v* punish 5.1707
purchace *v* acquire, gain 2.33,
  713, 4.557; ~ yow provide
  yourself 2.1125
pure *adj* very, mere 1.285,
  4.1620; *adv* for ~ ashamed for
  very shame 2.656
purpos *n* purpose 1.5; argument,
  point 2.897, 5.176; to ~ to the
  point 3.330, 5.1460, 1799;
  fallen to ~ be pertinent 1.142,
  3.1367; take ~ decide 1.79,
  5.770; was in ~ grete fully
  intended 5.1576
purposen *v* propose 4.1350
purpre *adj* purple 4.869
pursuyt(e *n* perseverance 2.959;
  prolonged entreaty 2.1744
purtraynge *prp* picturing, imagin
  ing 5.716
purveiaunce *n* providence, fore-
  sight 2.527, 4.961; prepara-
  tion, arrangement 3.533
purveye(n *v* foresee 4.1066; pre-
  pare 2.504; provide 2.426,
  1160
purveyinge *vbl n* foresight, provi-
  dence 4.986, 1015
put *n* pit 4.1540
pyk *n* pike 2.1041

quake *v* shake, tremble 1.871; *pt*
  quook 3.93, 5.36, 926
qualitee *n* nature, quality, con-
  dition 3.31, 1654
qualm *n* croak 5.382
quappe *v* pound, palpitate 3.57
quelle *v* beat, dash 4.46
queme *v* please, gratify 2.803,
  5.695

quenche *v* quench, extinguish
3.846, 1058, 4.511; *pp* **queynt**
4.313, 1430, 5.543

queynte *adj* strange, curious
1.411; ingenious, clever
4.1629

quik *adj* alive 2.52, 3.79; living
1.411

quod *pt sg* said 1.551

quo(o)k *pt of* **quake** *v*

quyken *v* quicken, kindle 1.295,
443; keep alive 3.484; revive
4.631

quysshyn *n* cushion 2.1229, 3.964

quyt *adj* free, rid 1.529, 3.1019,
1226

quyte *v* requite, repay, reward
1.808, 4.1663; *pt* **quytte**
released 4.205; *pp* **quyt** 2.242;
~ (s.o.'s) **hire** repay 1.334

racle *see* **rakel** *adj*

radde *pt sg of* **rede(n** *v*

raft *pp of* **reve(n** *v*

rage *n* frenzy, passionate anger
or grief 3.899, 4.253, 811, 892

rakel *adj* rash, hasty 1.1067,
3.429, 1642

raket *n* (the game of) rackets
4.460

rape *n* abduction 4.596 (Ph+ vari-
ant reading)

rascaille *n* rabble 5.1853

rathe *adv* early 4.205; quickly
2.1088, 5.937

rather *adj* former 3.1337,
5.1799; *adv* sooner 1.835, 865

raughte *pt of* **reche** *v*

ravysshe *v* abduct 4.530, 637,
5.895; carry away 4.1474

ravysshyng *vbl n* abduction 1.62,
4.548

real *adj* royal 3.1534, 5.1830

rebell *adj* rebellious 2.524

rebounde *v* return 4.1666

reche *v* reach for, fetch; *pt*
raughte went 2.447

recche *v* care, mind 3.112; ~ (of)
care about 1.797, 2.338; *pt*
roughte 1.496

recoma(u)nde *v* commend
1.1056; *refl* commend oneself,
submit 2.1070, 5.1323

reconforte *v* comfort, encourage
2.1672, 5.1395

recorde *v* remember 5.445, 718;
refl 3.1179; go over, memorize
3.51

recours *n* recourse, resort 2.1352

recovere *v* recover 3.1406; help,
save 1.383; get in return
3.181, 4.406

recreant *adj* cowardly, admitting
defeat 1.814

rede(n *v* read 2.83, 1176; inter-
pret, understand 2.129; tell,
say 3.1383, 4.980; advise
1.83; *3 pr sg contr* **ret** 2.413;
pt sg **radde, redde** 2.1085,
5.737; *pt pl* **redden** 2.1706; *pp*
red 3.192

redempcioun *n* release from cap-
tivity 4.108

redere *n* reader 5.270

redresse *v* redress, set right
3.1008, 5.139; *refl* recover
2.969

redy *adj* ready 1.988; resourceful
5.964

reed *n* advice 2.389; assistance
1.661; plan 2.1539; **to** ~ to do,
as a course of action 4.679

re(e)d *adj* red 3.1570; *as n* ?gold
3.1384

rees *n* rush, hurry 4.350
refere *v* return 1.266
refiguryng *prp* representing to
the mind 5.473
refreyde *v* grow cold 2.1343,
5.507
reft(e *pt & pp of* **reve(n** *v*
refus *adj* rejected 1.570
refut *n* refuge 3.1014
regne *n* kingdom, realm 3.29
regne *v* reign 5.1864; prevail in
2.379
reherce(n *v* repeat, go over
2.572, 917; recount, relate
3.493
reise *v* exalt 2.1585
rejoie *v refl* rejoice 5.395
rejoissen *v* rejoice 2.1391,
5.1165
rekenynge *n* calculation 2.1640
religious *adj* in a religious order,
a nun 2.759
relik *n* relic, sacred object
1.153
remembraunce *n* memory 3.968,
1533; memento 5.315
remenant *n* remainder 4.1376
remeve *v* remove 1.691
remorde *v* afflict with remorse
4.1491
remuable *adj* changeable 4.1682
rende *v* rend, tear 4.1493; *pt*
rente 2.928, 3.1099
renne(n *v* run, hasten 1.1066,
5.485; approach 2.1754; *2 pr
sg* **rennest** 4.1549; *imp sg* **ren**
5.656; *pp* **(y)ronne** 2.907,
1464
renoun *n* renown, fame 1.481,
2.661; reputation 2.297
rente *n* income 4.85; **to ~** as trib-
ute 2.830

repaire *v* return 5.1837; resort
3.5, 5.1571
repeled *pp* revoked, rescinded
4.294, 560
repentaunce *n* regret 3.1308
repente *v* repent 1.933, 2.525;
regret 1.392
repeyreth *imp pl of* **repaire** *v*
reprehencioun *n* reproach 1.684
reprehende *v* reproach 1.510
repressioun *n* restraint 3.1038
repreve *n* reproach 2.419, 1140;
v reproach 1.669
requere *v* ask, ask for, request
1.902, 3.483; ask of 2.473;
require, need 3.405
rescous *n* rescue 1.478, 3.1242
rescowe *v* rescue 3.857, 5.231
resigne *v* resign 1.432; renounce
3.25
reso(u)n *n* reason, sense 1.764,
3.1121, 4.572; **of ~** reasonable
2.366; argument 1.796, 4.589;
pl speeches 3.90
resort *n* resource, source of aid
and comfort 3.134
respect: in **to ~ of** in comparison
with 4.86, 5.1818
respit *n* respite, delay 5.137
resport *n* regard 4.86, 850
reste *n* rest 1.600, 3.925; peace,
tranquillity 1.188; **to ~** to bed
2.911; **hertes ~** peace of mind
3.1045; **sette at ~** settle, fix
2.760; *pl* times of repose
2.1722
restreyne *v* restrain 1.676; *refl*
4.940; check, hold back 4.708,
872
ret *3 pr sg contr of* **rede(n** *v*
retornyng *prp* turning over
5.1023

reulen *v* govern, control 2.1377;
  refl behave, conduct oneself
  5.758
reve(n *v* deprive of 1.188,
  2.1659, 4.285, 468; *pt sg, pl*
  refte 1.484, 4.249, 5.1036; *pp*
  raft, reft 5.1258, 1260
reverence *n* reverence, veneration
  3.1273; respect, deference; **at ~**
  of in honour of, out of respect
  for 3.40, 1328; **don ~** show
  respect (to) 3.212, 4.69;
  holden in ~ respect 1.516
revesten *v* clothe anew 3.353
revoken *v* recall (to conscious-
  ness) 3.1118
reward *n* regard 2.1133, 5.1736
rewe(n *v* repent, regret, feel sor-
  row 2.455, 5.1070; have pity
  on, feel pity for 1.460, 3.1770;
  feel sorry 3.114; cause to
  regret 4.1531; *imp pl* **rueth**
  4.1501
rewfully, rewfullich *adv* pit-
  eously, sorrowfully 3.65,
  4.1691, 5.729
reyne *v* rain 3.551, 4.299; (of
  tears) 4.873, 5.1336; *pt* **ron**
  3.640, 677; **reyned** 3.1557
richesse *n* riches, wealth 4.1670,
  5.438; abundance 3.349
ride(n *v* ride; *3 pr sg contr* **rit**
  2.1284; *imp sg* **ryd, rid**
  2.1013, 1020; *pt sg* **rood**
  2.627; *pt pl* **riden** 1.473; *pp*
  riden 2.933, 5.68
right *n* justice, right 3.1282;
  right, prerogative 1.591; **by ~**
  justly 4.396; **by alle ~** in all jus-
  tice 2.763, 4.1280; **of ~** right-
  fully 3.984, 1795, 4.571,
  5.1345

right *adj* straight 3.228; correct,
  proper, true 3.998; rightful,
  true 2.851; true, own 2.1065,
  3.1663; (*following n*) 3.134,
  981, 1472
right *adv* precisely, exactly, just
  2.286, 1064; **al ~** exactly 1.99;
  ~ after just as 3.175; **anon ~**
  immediately 2.1551; **~ nowthe**
  just now 1.985; (*intens, with*
  adjs and advs) 1.368, 2.264
rise(n *v* arise, get up (from bed)
  3.756; get up 1.695, 2.1597,
  4.1243; stand up 2.1302,
  3.594; *refl* **~ up** stand up
  2.812, 4.232; arise 1.944,
  5.1479; rise (of heavenly
  bodies) 3.1418; *3 pr sg contr*
  rist 1.944, 2.812; *imp sg, pl*
  ris, rys 2.944, 1716; *pt sg*
  ro(o)s 2.88, 3.1521
rist *3 pr sg contr of* **rise(n** *v*
rit *3 pr sg contr of* **ride(n** *v*
roche *n* rock 3.1497
rode *n* cross 5.1860
rollen *v* turn over in the mind
  2.659, 5.1313; *pp* talked
  about 5.1061
romaunce *n* romance 2.100,
  3.980
ron *pt sg of* **reyne** *v*
rong *pt sg of* **rynge** *v*
rood *pt sg of* **ride(n** *v*
roore *n* uproar, confusion 5.45
ro(o)s *pt sg of* **rise(n** *v*
rosy *adj* rose-coloured 2.1198,
  3.1755, 5.278
roughte *pt of* **recche** *v*
route *n* company 1.271, 2.620;
  host 2.613
route *v* roar 3.743
routhe *n* pity, compassion 1.582,

2.349; han ~ (of, on, upon)
1.769, 2.523, 1270; for ~ out
of compassion 5.1099; a pity
2.664; distress, grief 5.1687
routheles *adj* pitiless 2.346
rowne *v* whisper 3.568, 4.587
rudenesse *n* lack of cultivation,
boorishness 4.1489, 1677
ruyne *n* descent from a state of
well-being, prosperity 4.387
ryme *v* versify 1.532, 2.10
rynge *v* ring, resound 2.233,
3.1237; sound (a bell) 2.805;
proclaim 2.1615; *pt sg* **rong**
2.1615, 3.1725; *pp* **ronge**
2.805, 5.1062
rysshe *n* rush (valueless thing)
3.1161
ryve *v* stab, pierce 5.1560
ryvere: in **for ~** for hawking
waterfowl 4.413

saigh *pt sg of* **se(e)(n** *v*
salu(w)e *v* greet, salute 2.1016,
1257
saluynges *n pl* greetings 2.1568
salvacioun *see* **savacioun** *n*
salve *n* salve, cure 4.944
sapience *n* wisdom 1.515
satiry *n pl* satyrs 4.1544
sat(t)e *pt subj sg of* **sitte(n** *v*
sauf: in **myn honour ~** preserv-
ing, without prejudice to, my
honour 2.480, 3.159; **vouche**
~, *see* **vouche** *v*
saufly *adv* safely, confidently
4.1320
saugh *pt sg of* **se(e)(n** *v*
savacioun *n* salvation (of soul)
2.381, 563; safety, security
1.464, 4.1382; saving 2.486
save *prep* except (for) 1.395,

5.210; *conj* except (that) 2.156
save-garde *n* safe-conduct 4.139
savory *adj* pleasant 1.405
savour *n* delight 2.269
sawe *n* speech 2.41, 4.1395,
5.38
say *pt sg of* **se(e)(n** *v*
scapen *v* escape 5.908
scarmuch(e *n* skirmish 2.611,
934, 5.1508
scarsly *adv* scarcely 2.43
scathe *n* harm 4.207, 5.938
science *n* knowledge 1.67,
5.1255
sclave *n* slave 3.391
scole *n* lesson, source of instruc-
tion 1.634
scorne *v* scorn 1.234; jeer 1.576;
mock, treat disrespectfully
5.982
scornynge *vbl n* scorn, mockery
1.105
scripture *n* inscription 3.1369
scrit *n* writing 2.1130
scryvenyssh *adj* in a formal
hand, like a professional scribe
2.1026
se(e)(n *v* see, look at 2.301;
observe 3.1063; **for to ~** to be
seen 3.1093; **God yow see** may
God watch over you 2.85; *2 pr*
sg contr (with *pron*) **sestow**
3.46; *1 pt sg* **saugh** 1.114; *3 pt*
sg say, sey, **saigh** 1.351,
2.1355, 5.165; *pt pl* **seigh**
4.720, **syen** 5.816; *prp* **seyng**
4.363; *pp* **yseene** 1.700, **iseye**
5.448; *vbl n* **seynge** 4.423
seche, seke(n *v* seek, look for
1.704, 763; search 5.1855; *2*
pr sg (with pron) **sekestow**
3.1455; *pt sg* **soughte** 1.388;

pt pl **soughten** 2.937; *pp*
isought 3.1317
secre(e) *adj* secret 1.744, 3.286,
312, 759
secret *adj* secret 2.1664; discreet
3.142, 478
seigh *pt pl of* se(e)(n *v*
selde *adv* seldom 2.168, 377
selve *adj* same, self-same 3.355,
4.1240, 1425
sely *adj* happy 4.503; poor, piti-
able, unfortunate 1.871,
2.683, 5.1093; hapless 3.1191;
insignificant 1.338
selynesse *n* happiness 3.813,
825, 831
selys *n pl* seals 3.1462
seme(n *v* seem, appear 1.703; **me
semeth, him semed** it seems/ed
to me/him 3.188, 4.1424
semynge *n* appearance 1.284
sentement *n* emotion, feeling
2.13, 3.43, 1797; sensation
4.1177
sentence *n* meaning, sense 1.393;
purport 3.1327; opinion
4.1063; maxim 4.197
sepulture *n* tomb, burial 4.327,
5.299
sermoun *n* discourse, speech
2.965, 1115, 1299, 4.1282
serve(n *v* serve 1.15; be the ser-
vant of love in, be lover of
1.426, 817; be of service, use-
ful 3.1078, 1136, 4.279; serve
(with food) 5.437
service *n* service 1.82; (religious)
service 1.164; service in love
1.430, 958; **don ~** 3.133
sesed *pp* in possession 3.445
sestow *contr of* seest thow, 2 *pr
sg of* se(e)(n *v*

sette(n *v* set, place, put 1.643,
2.585; set, fix, settle (heart,
intention) 2.760; arrange
3.334; fix, assign (time) 3.340;
postulate 2.367; **~ a caas** put
the case 2.729; *refl* sit down
1.359, 2.600; **~ on knees** kneel
3.953; estimate, value, reckon:
~ at nought count as nothing
1.444; **~ lite of** think little of
2.432; **~ (at) a myte, a grote**
(coins of small value) 3.832,
900, 4.586
seur *adv* surely 3.1633, 4.421
seurte, suerte *n* security 2.833,
3.1678
sexte *adj* sixth 5.1205; **sexti** *num*
sixty 1.441
seye(n, seyn *v* say 1.396; 2 *pr sg*
seist 1.939; 3 *pr sg* **seith** 1.694;
pr pl **seyen** 5.1639, **sygge**
4.194; *pr subj pl* **seye** 2.801; 2
pt sg **seydest** 1.916 (with suf-
fixed *pron* **seydestow** 1.919);
pt sg **seide, seyde** 1.117, 597;
pt pl **seyde(n** 1.90, 5.1265; *prp*
seyng 4.363; *pp* **seyd** 1.611
shadewed *pp* shaded 2.821
shal *v* owe 3.791, 1649; *(auxil)*
(obligation) must, have to
1.870, 3.1474; am/is to
2.1757; *(auxil)* (futurity)
4.771; *(with ellipsis of infin)*
4.1680; *(infin of motion under-
stood)* 4.264; ought to 5.1825;
should, were to 1.17, 3.81; 2
pr sg (with suffixed *pron*) **shal-
tow** 1.349; *pr pl* **shul** 1.122;
pt sg **sholde, shulde** 5.14;
2 *pt sg* (with suffixed *pron*)
shuldestow 5.351; *pt pl*
sholde(n 1.73

shame *n* dishonour, disgrace
1.107; modesty 2.645, 1286;
confusion, embarrassment
1.867, 3.80, 1570; do ~ harm,
dishonour 2.763, 3.777; for ~
you should be ashamed
3.1127; ~ it is it is shameful
3.249; *gen sg* shames 1.180

shap *n* appearance, figure 2.662,
5.473, 807

shape(n *v* shape, create, fashion
3.411, 734, 4.252; arrange,
devise 2.1363, 3.196, 4.652;
refl prepare 3.551, 4.1273,
5.1211; plan, intend 1.207;
destine, decree, ordain 2.282,
3.1240; happen 2.61; *pt sg*
sho(o)p 1.207, 2.1557; *pp*
shapyn, yshape 2.1092, 3.411

shawe *n* wood 3.720

she(e)ne *adj* bright, shining
2.920; fair, beautiful 2.824;
adv brightly 4.1239

sheld *n* shield 2.640, 5.308; pro-
tection, defence 2.201, 532,
3.480; cover 2.1327

shende *v* destroy, ruin 1.972,
4.79; injure, harm 2.357; spoil
2.590; blame, reproach
5.1060; *pt* shente 5.1223; *pp*
shent 2.38

sherte *n* shirt 3.738, 1099; in
(hire/oure) ~ wearing only a
shirt 4.96, 1522

shette(n *v* shut, close 3.749; shut
in 1.148; *refl* 3.726; close up
(letter) 2.1090, 1226; *pt sg*
shette 2.1090; *pt pl* shetten
1.148

shethe *n* sheath, scabbard
4.1185

shewe(n *v* show, reveal 2.110;

declare, make known, express
1.33, 286; appear, be revealed
1.487; observe 1.159

shilde *v* protect 2.1019, 4.188

shof *pt sg* pushed 3.487; shove
pp laid 3.1026

sholde(n *pt sg & pl of* shal *v*

sho(o)p *pt sg of* shape(n *v*

shorte *v* shorten 5.96; *adv* with
quick breaths 3.58

shortly *adv* to put it briefly, in
brief 3.176, 4.671; quickly
3.1436

shotes *n pl* arrows 2.58

shour *n* assault, battle 1.470,
3.1064, 4.47

shove *see* shof

shrewednesse *n* wickedness 2.858

shrichyng *vbl n* screeching 5.382

shright *pp* shrieked, screeched
5.320

shrinke *v* draw in 1.300

shryve *v* confess, make con-
fession 2.440; *pp* shryven
revealed 2.579

shul, shulde *pr pl, pt sg of* shal *v*

sighte *pt of* syke(n *v*

signal *n* sign, token 4.818

signe *n* token, indication 4.1164,
5.1652

signifiaunce *n* signification
5.362; sign 5.1447

sik, syk *n* sigh 2.145, 463

sik(e *adj* sick, ill 1.575, 2.1516;
as n sick person 2.1572

siker *adj* safe 1.927, 2.1370,
3.921; certain 1.673; *adv*
surely 2.991; confidently
3.1237

sikerly, sikirly *adv* certainly
2.520, 4.652, 5.1122; soundly
3.746

sikernesse *n* security, safety
2.773, 843
siklich(e *adj* sick, ill 2.1528,
1543
sikynge *vbl n* sighing 1.724
singynge *vbl n* song, singing
3.1716
sit 3 *pr sg contr of* sitte(n *v*
sith, sithen *conj* since 1.253,
941; ~ that 1.998
sithe, sythe *n* times 3.1595,
4.753, 5.472, 1381
sithen, sith *adv* since 3.244; gon
~ longe while since a long time
ago 1.718; afterwards 1.833
sitte(n *v* sit 2.783; ~ on knowe
kneel 2.1202; affect, pain
3.240, 4.231; *impers* befit, suit
1.12, 246, 2.117; 3 *pr sg contr*
sit 1.12, 2.935; *pr subj sg* sitte
4.1023; *pt sg* sat 1.362; *pt pl*
sete(n 2.1192, 1251; *pt subj sg*
sat(t)e 1.985, 2.117; *pp* sete(n
2.81
sittyng *adj* suitable, fitting 4.437
skile, skylle *n* reason; ~ is is
reasonable 2.365, 3.646
skilful *adj* reasonable 2.392,
3.287, 938
skilfully *adv* with reason, reason-
ably 4.1265
skippe *v* jump, leap 1.218, 3.690
slake *v* fail, abate 2.291
sle(e)n *v* slay, kill 2.459, 665;
overcome 4.1583; 2 *pr sg*
sleest 4.455; *pt* slough 4.364;
pt subj sg slowe, slowh 4.506,
5.1272; *pp* slawe 3.721,
4.884; slayn, sleyn 1.608,
5.227
sleighe, slye *adj* cunning, subtle,
artful 4.972, 5.898

sleighly *adv* cunningly, adroitly
2.462, 1185; secretly, privately
5.83
sle(i)ght(e *n* craft, cunning, trick-
ery 4.1459, 1461; ingenuity,
shrewdness 5.773; ingenious
plan, trick 2.1512, 4.1451
slide *v* slip (by, through) 5.351,
769; slydynge *prp adj* change-
able, wavering 5.825
slomberynge *vbl n* slumber 2.67,
5.246
slough *pt of* sle(e)n *v*
slouthe *n* sloth, indolence,
inaction 2.286, 959, 1008
slynke *v* creep 3.1535
slyvere *n* sliver 3.1013
smale *adj* little 3.1462; slender,
slim 3.1247; minor 2.1191
smert *n* pain 4.373, 5.417
smerte *adj* bitter, painful 4.248,
5.1326; *adv* sharply, painfully
4.243
smerte *v* hurt, give pain 1.667,
2.1097; me, hym ~ I/he suf-
fer(ed) 3.146, 4.1186; feel pain
1.1049, 3.1182, 4.1448; *pt*
smerte 2.930; *pr subj* 5.132; *pt
subj* 4.1186
smyte(n *v* smite, strike 2.1276,
4.243; hit (upon) 1.273; ~
adown lower, hang (head)
2.540; *pt* smot 1.273; *pp*
smyten 2.1145
smytted *pp* disgraced, sullied
5.1545
snowissh *adj* snow-white 3.1250
so *adv* (*as intens, introducing
imp and subj*) 3.1470, 4.1652;
(*introducing exclamation*) how
3.82, 1380; *conj* provided that
2.1162, 4.798

sobre *adj* grave, serious 1.1013,
2.1592; demure 5.820

sobrely, sobrelich(e *adv* seri-
ously, gravely 3.359, 954; mod-
estly 2.648

socour, socours *n* succour, help
2.1354, 4.131

socouren *v* succour, aid 3.1264

sodeyn *adv* sudden 2.667;
impetuous, forward 5.1024

softe *adj* soft, tender 3.1247;
soft, quiet 5.636; weak, yield-
ing 1.137

softe *adv* gently 3.72; comfort-
ably 1.195, 3.442; quietly
1.279, 3.566

softely, softeliche *adv* quietly
2.519, 5.506; slowly
2.627

sojo(u)rne *v* stay, dwell 5.483,
598, 1350; continue, remain
1.326, 5.213; stop 1.850

solas *n* joy, solace 1.31, 5.607;
comfort, consolation 2.460

som *adj* one, a certain 1.33, 500,
538; *pron* one 1.916; a part
5.854; *pl* some 4.995; **alle and
~ one** and all 4.1068

somde(e)l *adv* somewhat 1.290,
1088, 2.603

somer *n* summer; *gen sg* **someris**
3.1061

sommes *n pl* sums (of money)
4.60

sonded *pp* sanded 2.822

sondry *adj* various, differing
1.159, 440

sone, soone *adv* soon 2.1517; at
once 5.847; *comp* **sonner**
2.686

sonnyssh *adj* sun-like, golden
4.736, 816

so(o)nde *n* message 3.492,
5.1372

so(o)r *adj* wounded, grieving
3.1421, 5.639

so(o)re *adv* intensely 1.95; bit-
terly, sorely 1.751; grievously,
painfully 1.1087

soote *adj* sweet 5.671

so(o)th *n* truth 3.1212, 4.47;
true saying, thing 2.1137,
4.1407; **in ~** truly 5.143, 371;
(the) ~ (for) to seyn to tell the
truth 1.12, 591

so(o)th *adj* true 4.1597; *as adv*
truly 3.1357

sore *n* wound, affliction 4.944

sort *n* fate, lot 2.1754; casting of
lots, divination 1.76, 4.116,
1404

sorted *pp* assigned, allotted
5.1827

sorwe *n* sorrow, grief 1.1

sorwen *v* sorrow 4.394, 1106;
prp **sorwynge** 1.9

sorw(e)fully, sorwfullich *adv* sor-
rowfully, sadly 1.114, 5.1633

sorwful, sorowful *adj* sorrowful,
sad, 1.10, 2.64

sory *adj* sad, sorrowful 1.14;
sorry 2.94

sothfast *adj* true 3.30, 4.870

sothfastnesse *n* truth 4.1080

soupe *v* take supper 2.944, 3.560

sourmounteth *3 pr sg* over-
comes, exceeds 3.1038

sours *n* source, fountainhead
5.1591

sovereigne *adj* most excellent,
supreme, ruling 4.316, 1070

sovereignete *n* sovereignty,
dominion, mastery 3.171

sowne(n *v* make a sound 3.189;

sound (like) 5.678; repeat
2.573; play (an instrument)
2.1031; tend to, incline to, be
consonant with 1.1036,
3.1414, 4.1676
space *n* space of time, while
2.767, 5.942; time, opportu-
nity 5.1704; respite 1.505;
extent 5.1630; room 1.714
span-newe *adj* brand-new
3.1665
spare *v* refrain from 5.51;
restrain 5.204; spare, have
mercy on 1.435
speche *n* speaking, talk 1.327,
2.497, 3.1710; **withouten
more ~** briefly, in short
2.1421; **fallen in ~** begin talk-
ing 2.1191, 5.107, 855; conver-
sation 2.1600; talk, gossip
2.1291, 3.584; language 2.22;
manner of speech 2.34, 4.128;
power of speech 4.249, 1151
spede *v* succeed, prosper 1.774,
865, 4.75; help, cause to pros-
per 1.1041, 4.630; *refl* make
haste 2.949, 4.220; *pt* **spedde**
1.482
speed, spede *n* success 1.17,
1043; help 2.9
spe(e)re *n* sphere, orbit 3.1495,
5.656, 1809
spere *n* spear 3.374, 4.40
spered *pp* barred 5.531
sperhauk *n* sparrow-hawk
3.1192
spete *v* spit 2.1617
spices *n pl* spiced cakes, sweet-
meats 5.852
spien *v* spy 3.1454
spille *v* destroy 5.588; *pp* **spilt**
4.263

spir *n* shoot 2.1335
sponne *pp* spun 3.734
spore *n* spur 2.1427
sporne *v* stumble, trip 2.797
spot *n* speck 5.1815
spotted *pp* stained 4.1578
sprede *v* spread 2.54; (of heart)
swell 1.278, 2.980; (of
flowers) open 2.970; *pp*
spradde wide open 4.1422
sprynge *v* spring, leap 1.745,
4.239; appear 5.657; grow
5.719
square *adj* thick-set 5.801
stable *adj* abiding, unchanging
3.1751
staire, steire *n* stairs, staircase,
steps 1.215, 2.813, 1705; *gen
sg* **steires** 3.205
stak *pt sg* pinned, fastened
3.1372
stal *pt sg of* **stele** *v*
stant *pr sg contr of* **stonde(n** *v*
starf *pt sg of* **sterve(n** *v*
steere *n* pilot, helmsman 3.1291;
helm, rudder: **in ~ astern** 5.641
steere *v* steer, control 2.4, 4.282
steire *see* **staire** *n*
stele *v* steal 3.1451; carry off
5.48; go quietly 4.1503; *pt sg*
stal 1.81; *pp* **stole** 3.1451
stente *pt of* **stynte(n** *v*
steppes *n pl* footprints 5.1791
stere, stire *v* stir, disturb, move
1.228, 3.910; bring up, pro-
pose 3.1643, 4.1451; *prp*
steryng stirring, moving 3.692,
1236
sterelees *adj* rudderless 1.416
sternelich *adv* violently 3.677
sterre *n* star 1.175
stert *n* start 5.254

sterte *v* leap, spring 2.447,
3.1497; rush, move quickly
2.1094, 1634, 4.242; move
suddenly 3.949; give a start
5.253; *pt sg* sterte 4.1411

sterve(n *v* die 1.17, 427; *pt sg*
starf 2.449

stevene *n* report, talking
3.1723

stewe *n* small room, room with
fireplace 3.601, 698

steyre *see* staire *n*

stiel *n* steel 3.480, 4.325, 5.831

stille *v* silence 2.230

stille *adj* still, quiet 4.521; *adv*
still, quietly 2.542; as ~ as
(any) sto(o)n 2.600, 1494

stokked *pp* put in the stocks
3.380

stonde(n *v* stand 1.292; be
placed 3.247; be situated
2.1146; be (in a condition)
2.712, 714, 3.496, 5.171; be
(of circumstances) 3.923;
remain 3.851; *impers with* it
the situation is 3.785; ~ with
(s.o.) s.o.'s condition is 1.602;
3 pr sg contr stant, stont
2.1188, 3.1562; *pt sg* stood
1.172; *pt subj sg* stood 1.1039;
pp ystonde 5.1612

storie *n* history, story, narrative
2.31, 3.297

stounde *n* time, while, short time
1.1086, 3.1695; *pl* seasons
3.1752

stoundemele *adv* hour by hour,
gradually 5.674

stoupen *v* droop 2.968

straunge *adj* unusual, surprising
2.24, 5.120, 860; not of the
family 2.1660; distant,

reserved 5.1632; *as n* strangers
2.411; *comp* straunger 4.388

straungely *adv* distantly, coldly
2.1423, 5.955

straw *interj* (*expressing con-
tempt*) ~ for 5.362

strecche *v* extend, reach 1.888,
903; be adequate, suffice 2.341

stree *n* straw (i.e. valueless thing)
2.1745

streght *adj* straight 3.1247; *pp*
outstretched 4.1163

stre(i)ght *adv* straight, directly
1.53, 606, 2.1461; immedi-
ately 2.599; ~ o morwe first
thing in the morning 3.552

stremes *n pl* ray, beam (from
eyes) 1.305, 3.129

streyne *v* clasp tightly 3.1205,
1449; grip, constrict 3.1071,
1482

strif *n* strife, contention 2.780,
837; maken ~ quarrel 5.341

stryve *v* struggle, contend, vie
3.38; ~ ayeyns oppose 4.175,
5.166; *pt sg* strof 5.819

studye *n* reverie 2.1180

stynte(n, stente(n *v* stop, cease
1.60, 273, 2.1361; cease speak-
ing of 1.1086, 2.687; bring to
a stop 2.383, 5.686; *imp pl*
stynte 2.1242; stynteth
2.1729; *pt subj sg* stynte
1.848; *pt sg* stente 1.736; *pt pl*
stente(n 1.60; *pp* stynt 3.1106

subgit *n* subject, servant 2.828;
adj subject, submissive 1.231,
5.1790

substaunce *n* essential quality,
reality 4.1505; means, pro-
vision, money 4.1513; the
majority 4.217

subtile, subtyl *adj* clear, pure, ethereal 1.305; ingenious, intricate 2.257

subtilte *n* guile, cunning 5.1254, 1782

sucre *n* sugar 3.1194; **sucred** *pp* sweetened, softened 2.384

suerte *see* **seurte** *n*

suffisaunce *n* sufficiency 5.763; fulfilment 3.1309, 4.1640; contentment, satisfaction 3.1716

suffise(n *v* suffice, be sufficient 1.610, 3.849

suffrant *n* patient person 4.1584

suffre(n *v* permit, allow 1.755, 3.154; endure, suffer 1.978, 3.105; 2 *pr sg* **suffrest** 3.1021, 1467; *imp pl* **suffreth** 4.1204

supprised *pp* seized, overwhelmed 3.1184

surplus *n* remainder, remaining group of people 4.60

surquidrie *n* pride, haughtiness 1.213

sustene *v* support 2.1686; bear, withstand 4.795, 5.242

sustren *n pl* sisters 3.733, 1809, 5.3

suwe *v* pursue 1.379

swapte *pt sg* dashed, struck 4.245

sweigh *n* momentum 2.1383

swelte *v* grow faint, be overcome 3.347

swev(e)ne *n* dream 5.358, 362

swich *adj and pron* such 1.34; ~ **oon** such a one 1.369, 521

swithe *adv* quickly 4.751; **as ~ as** as soon as 5.1384

swo(o)te *adj* sweet 3.1231; *as adv* sweetly 1.158

swough *n* swoon, faint 3.1120, 4.1212

swoune *v* swoon, faint 2.574, 3.1190

swynke *v* toil, labour 5.272

syde *n* side (of a person) 3.1248, 5.1705; **on every ~** everywhere, in all directions 1.185, 4.1391, 5.699

sye *v* sink down 5.182

syke(n *v* sigh 1.192, 751; *pt* **siked, sighte** 3.972, 1056; *pp* **siked** 5.738

sykernesse *see* **sikernesse** *n*

synke *v* enter, penetrate 1.734, 2.650, 902, 3.1538, 4.1494

t' (= to), -o elided before *infin* beginning with a vowel, e.g. **t'endite** 1.6

tale *n* conversation, talk 2.218, 267, 3.1403; *pl* 2.149, 498, 1566, 3.224, 4.702, 5.178; stories 4.671; **taken first the ~** begin to speak 2.1605

talent *n* desire, inclination 3.145

tame *adj as n* tame animal 3.529

tarie(n *v* tarry, delay 2.1019, 1622, 3.1195; *pp* **taried** wasted 2.1739; *vbl n* **taryinge** delay 2.1642, 5.774

teche(n *v* teach, instruct 1.698; *pt sg* **taughte** showed 5.1016

tecches *n pl* faults 3.935

tempestous *adj* stormy, turbulent 2.5

temporel *adj* transitory 4.1061

tendernesse *n* sensitivity 5.242

tendreliche, tendrely *adv* in a heartfelt way, pitifully 1.111, 4.950

te(e)ne *n* vexation 1.814,

4.1605; affliction, trouble
2.61, 3.1226, 5.240

terme *n* period of time 5.1090;
appointed time 5.696, 1209;
(technical) term, expression
2.1038

tery *adj* tearful 4.821

testif *adj* headstrong 5.802

th' (= the), -e elided before noun
beginning with vowel

than *conj* than 1.532

thanke(n, thonke(n *v* thank
2.1415; *pp* ythonked 4.2

than(ne, thenne *adv* then 1.409,
498

thar 3 *pr sg impers* it is neces-
sary; **hym ~** he need 2.1661; *pt
subj sg* thurste 3.572

that *rel pron* that, which, who
1.15; that which, what 1.744,
1033; *conj* so that, in such a
way that 1.807; **for ~** because
4.998

the *pron* thee, you 1.511, 569,
2.1394

thee *v* prosper, thrive, succeed
1.341, 4.439

thef *n* wretch, villain 1.870,
3.1098

theigh *see* **tho(u)gh** *adv*

thenke(n, thynke(n *v* think, con-
sider 1.818; think of 1.476;
intend 1.263; *imp pl* thynketh
1.26; *pt* thoughte 1.276; *pp*
thought 4.554

thenne *see* **than(ne** *adv*

thennes *adv* thence, from there
3.1145, 4.734; absent
4.695

ther(e, theere *adv* there 5.1358;
(*introducing wish, curse or
blessing; untranslated*) 2.588,

3.947, 1437, 5.1525; *conj and
rel* where 2.333

theraboute *adv* about it 2.1393

therafter *adv* afterwards 4.174,
546; for any 4.861

theras *adv* where 2.272

ther-ayeins *adv* in reply to that
2.369

therby *adv* by that, this 1.383,
447

therfro *adv* from that 1.627

therin *adv* in that 2.269, 3.695;
inside, within 4.785

therof *adv* from that 1.333;
about that 4.1277; through
that 5.374

theron *adv* about that, concern-
ing that 2.1197, 1289

therto *adv* to it/that 1.266; for it/
that 1.1064; also 2.377

ther-while *adv* whilst 3.538

therwith *adv* by it/that 1.243;
because of that 1.274; with
this 3.884, 4.1212; thereupon
1.278; whereupon 3.199

therwithal *adv* with it/that
2.349, 3.1330; thereupon
2.877, 3.1350

thewes *n pl* (personal, moral)
qualities 2.723

thiderward *adv* towards there
2.1250

thikke *adv* thickly, densely
4.1356; frequently 2.456

thilke *dem adj* that (same), the
1.185, 946

thin, thyn *possess adj* thy, your
(before vowel or *h-*) 1.509;
pron yours 3.1458

thinke *v* (*with dat*) seem 1.405;
impers (me, hym, yow *etc.*)
thinketh (it) seems to (me, him,

you, *etc.*), (I, he, you) think(s)
1.403, 2.207, 401, 3.380,
5.120; **thoughte hym** 1.294; **us
thinketh hem** they seem to us
2.25

thirled *pp* pierced 2.642

tho *dem pron pl* those 1.931,
1085; *dem adj pl* those 4.193,
631; *adv* then 1.300, 1058;
er ~ before that time 5.448

thonder-dynt *n* thunder bolt
5.1505

thonk, thank *n* thanks, gratitude
1.803, 1015, 1060; **han ~** be
thanked 1.21, 803

thorugh *prep* through 1.86; by
means of 1.39

thorugh-darted, -girt, -shoten *pp*
transfixed, pierced 1.325;
pierced through 4.627; shot
through 1.325

tho(u)gh, theigh *adv* though,
although 1.221; ~ **that** 1.148,
677

thought *n* thought, idea 2.745;
anxiety, care 1.579

thoughte *pt of* **thinke** *v*

thral *n* servant, slave 1.439

thraldom *n* slavery, servitude
2.856

thralle *v* enslave 1.235, 2.773

threste(n *v* push, thrust 3.1574;
press upon, oppress 4.254; *pt
sg* **thraste** 2.1155, **threste**
4.254, **thriste** 3.1574

thrie *adv* thrice 2.89, 463, 1285;
thries 5.9

thrift *n* success, welfare; **by my ~**
if I succeed, upon my word
2.1483, 3.871, 4.1630;
good ~ 2.582, 847, 1687,
3.947

thrifty *adj* fitting, decorous
1.275; *superl* most admirable,
worthiest 1.1081, 2.737

thriftily *adv* properly, becom-
ingly 3.211

thringe *v* press 4.66

thriste *pt sg of* **threste(n** *v*

throwe *n* (short) period of time,
while 2.687, 4.384

thurste *pt subj sg of* **thar**

tirant *n* tyrant, absolute ruler
2.1240

tiren *v* tear, rend 1.787

tit *3 pr sg contr of* **tyde(n** *v*

titeryng *n* vacillation, hesitation
2.1744

title *n* name 1.488

tobreste *v* be shattered 2.608

tocleve *v* split in two 5.613

todasshed *pp* shattered in pieces
2.640

toforn, tofore *prep* before; **God ~**
(I swear) before God, in God's
sight 1.1049, 2.431, 992,
1409

to-hepe *adv* together 3.1764

tohewen *pp* hacked to pieces
2.638

tokenyng *n* sign 4.779, 870

tolis *n pl* tools 1.632

tomelte *v* melt away, disappear
3.348

tonge *n* tongue 2.1681; speech
5.804; language 2.14, 5.1794

torende *v* afflict 4.341; *refl* suf-
fer, torture oneself 2.790; *pt*
torente 4.341

torne(n, turne(n *v* turn 1.848,
2.688, 5.85; (toss and) turn (in
sleep) 1.196, 3.444, 5.211; *refl*
turn round 4.855; go 5.482;
return 1.324, 5.245; ~ **ayeyn**

return 3.1516; change (into), transform 2.798, 3.179, 1074, 1400

torney *n* tournament 4.1669

tosterte *v* burst 2.980

tother *contr of* the other 4.434

totorn *pp* distraught 4.358

touche(n *v* touch 2.1033; touch upon, treat 5.996; involve, concern 1.265, 744, 1033; suit, befit 2.1662

tough: in make it ~ show off, put on airs 2.1025; be pressing 3.87, 5.101

to-yere *adv* this year 3.241

traitour *n* betrayer 3.273

transmewen *v* transmute, transform 4.467, 830

trappe *n* trap-door 3.741; **trappe-dore** 3.759

traunce *n* state of abstraction 2.1306; unconscious state, swoon 4.343

travaille *n* effort, labour 1.21, 3.522, 5.184; han ~ take trouble 2.1437; **don** ~ exert oneself 1.475; suffering 1.372; difficulty 2.3

travers *n* curtain, screen 3.674

trays *n* traces 1.222

traysen *v* betray 4.438

tremour *n* palpitation 5.255

tresoun *n* treason, treachery 1.107, 2.793

tresour *n* treasure, wealth 3.874, 4.85, 1514

trespace *v* transgress 3.1175

tresses *n pl* plaits, braids 4.816

tret *3 pr sg* treads 2.347

trete(n *v* tell 1.742; discuss 1.975; negotiate 4.58, 1346;

treat 5.134; **hireselven** ~ behave 4.813

tretys *n* document 2.1697; treaty 4.670; negotiation 4.64, 136

trewe *adj* true 1.593; loyal, steadfast 1.957, 2.306; *as n* faithful servant 3.141

trewely, trewelich(e *adv* truly, indeed 1.246, 985; loyally 2.493, 5.174

trewe *n* truce 3.1779, 4.58, 1312; *pl* 5.401

tribulacioun *n* distress, anguish 5.988

trist, trust *n* trust, reliance 3.941, 1305; loyalty, fidelity 3.403, 5.1259; object of reliance 1.154

triste(n, truste(n *v* trust 1.690, 692; ~ to 1.601; ~ (up)on 3.587, 916

trone *n* throne 4.1079

trouth(e *n* loyalty, constancy 1.584, 2.160; faithfulness 2.1084; troth, pledged faith, word 1.770, 2.1686; by my ~ on my word 1.676; have (here) my ~ take my word for it 1.831, 1061

trowe(n *v* believe 4.383, 1547, 5.1298; ~ in/on 5.383; trust (in) 2.956, 5.327; ~ on 5.736; suppose, think 1.240; (as) I ~ 1.640

tweye, tweyne, twaye *adj* two 1.494, 2.620, 5.1307

twighte *pt sg* pulled 4.1185; *pp* **twight** torn, pulled apart 4.572

twiste *n* tendril 3.1230

twiste *v* wring 4.1129; *pt* wrung 4.254; *pt subj sg* would constrain, press 3.1769

twyes *adv* twice 2.1399, 3.98,
  5.889
twyne *v* twist, spin 5.7
twynne *v* part, leave one another
  3.1711, 4.904, 1270; separate
  4.1197, 5.679
twynnyng *vbl n* separation
  4.1303
tyde *n* time 2.1739; time (of
  occurrence) 4.1077; occasion
  5.700; (propitious) time
  1.954
tyde(n *v* befall, happen to: **hym ~**
  befall him 1.333; **(yow/me) is**
  tid has befallen (you/me)
  2.224, 464; **the . . . han tid**
  have befallen you 1.907; *3 pr*
  sg contr **tit** 1.333; *pp* **tid**
  1.907, 2.224
tydynge *n* piece of news 2.951;
  pl news 2.1113
tyssew *n* band of rich fabric
  2.639

unapt *adj* not disposed 1.978
unavysed *pp adj* unaware 1.378
unbodye *v* leave the body 5.1550
unbore *pp adj* unborn 3.269
unbridled *pp adj* uncontrolled
  3.429
unbroiden *pp adj* unbraided,
  loose 4.817
unbynde *v* untie 3.1732
uncircumscript *adj* boundless
  5.1865
unespied *pp adj* undetected
  4.1457
unfelyngly *adv* insensitively,
  without understanding from
  experience 2.19
unfettre *v* unshackle, unchain
  2.1216

unfeyned *pp adj* unfeigned, sin-
  cere 2.839
ungiltif *adj* guiltless 3.1018
unhap *n* misfortune 1.552,
  2.456
unhappy *adj* ill-fated 4.1341
unhappyly *adv* unfortunately
  1.666, 5.937
unholsom *adj* corrupt 4.330
universe: in **in ~** universally 3.36
unkist *pp* without having been
  kissed 1.809
unknowe *pp* unknown 1.616,
  4.168
unkonnyng *adj* ignorant, unskil-
  ful 5.1139
unkouth *adj* unfamiliar 2.151;
  novel, striking 3.1797
unkynde *adj* unnatural 3.1438;
  4.266, 1440
unkyndely *adv* cruelly 1.617
unlik *adv* differently from what
  2.1656
unliklynesse *n* unsuitableness
  1.16
unloven *v* cease to love 5.1698
unmanhod *n* unmanly act 1.824
unmyghty *adj* unable, incapable
  2.858
unneste *v* leave the nest 4.305
unnethe(s *adv* hardly, scarcely
  1.301, 3.1034; with difficulty
  2.4; **wel ~** 1.354
unpreyed *pp adj* unsolicited
  4.513
unpynne *v* unfasten 3.698
unreste *n* distress, (emotional)
  turmoil 4.879, 5.1567, 1604
unresty *adj* distressing, causing
  discomfort 5.1355
unright *n* offence, wrong 2.453,
  4.550; *adv* wrongly 5.661

unsely *adj* unhappy, unfortunate
1.35

unshethe *v* unsheathe, draw
4.776

unsittynge *prp adj* unsuitable,
unfitting 2.307

unskilful *adj* unreasonable 1.790

unsought *pp* not striven for, unre-
quested 1.809

unstable *adj* impermanent 3.820

unswelle *v* become less full
4.1146

unteyd *pp adj* untethered, free
2.752

unthonk *n* reproach, blame
5.699

unthrift *n* nonsense, foolishness
4.431

unthrifty *adj* profitless, foolish
4.1530

untormented *pp* free of torment
1.1011

untrewe *adj* unfaithful 3.1053,
4.446; faithless, treacherous
2.786; false 3.306

untriste *adj* distrustful 3.839

untrouthe *n* faithlessness 3.984,
5.1098

unwar *adj* unaware 1.304,
5.1559; *adv* unexpectedly
1.549

unwery *adj* without weariness
1.410, 2.839

unwist *adj* unknown 2.1294,
1509, 3.603; undetected
3.770; unaware 1.93, 2.1400

unworthi *adj* undeserving
3.1284, 4.329

unworthynesse *n* undeserv-
ingness 2.1081

unwre *v* uncover 1.858

up-born *pp* exalted 1.375

upbounde *pp* concluded, tied up
3.517

upbreyde *v* reproach 5.1710

uprist *3 pr sg* rises 4.1443

usage *n* custom 1.150, 2.28

use(n *v* use, employ 2.1038; prac-
tise 2.11; be accustomed, used
3.1023, 4.182, 681

vanite(e *n* folly 4.536; futility
4.703, 729; vain pursuits
5.1837

vapour *n* influence, emanation
3.11

variaunce *n* variation, variety (of
possibilities) 4.985, 5.762;
changeability 5.1670

varien *v* be otherwise 2.1621

Veer *n* spring 1.157

venym *n* venom, poison 3.1025

vermyne *n* vermin 3.381

verray *adj* true 3.6, 825; loyal,
faithful 3.141; pure, sheer
3.92, 4.357; real, veritable
1.202

verraylich *adv* truly 3.1545,
4.1424

verre *n* glass 2.867

vers *n* line 1.399; *pl* **vers** lines 1.7

vertu *n* power 3.1766; (moral)
excellence, virtue 1.1085,
2.844; usefulness 4.315;
maken ~ of make the best of
4.1586

vertulees *adj* without power
2.344

vertuous *adj* virtuous 1.254, 898

veyn *adj* futile, idle, worthless
3.817; **in ~** in vain, fruitlessly
3.1412

veyne *n* vein 1.866; **every ~** every
part 4.943, 5.417

viage *n* enterprise, undertaking
2.1061, 3.732; **don ~** under-
take a project 2.75

vice *n* vice 1.252, 2.173; fault
1.687, 987

vigile *n* wake 5.305

vigour *n* force, energy 3.1088

vilanye *n* shame, dishonour
1.1033, 2.438; reproach, dis-
grace 4.21; discourtesy 5.490

visage *n* face 4.862, 5.899; atten-
tion, concern 5.1838

voide *n* nightcap of spiced wine
3.674; *adj* devoid 2.173

voide(n *v* depart, withdraw
2.912, 3.232

vois *n* voice 1.111; (favourable)
report, esteem 3.1723;
decision, judgement 4.195

volturis *n pl* vultures 1.788

voluptuous *adj* tending to, occu-
pied with, sensual pleasure,
gratification 4.1573

vouchesauf (*or as two words*) *v*
agree, grant 2.1691, 5.922; be
content 4.90

vulgarly *adv* in the ordinary
sense, in common parlance
4.1513

wade *v* **~ in** proceed into 2.150

waggyng *vbl n* waving, move-
ment 2.1745

waken *v* waken (s.o.) 2.547,
3.764; remain awake 1.921,
3.341, 1560; keep vigil, watch
3.540; wake up, rouse 5.928;
pt **wo(o)k** 1.362, 5.289, 928

walwe *v* writhe 1.699, 5.211

wan *adj* pale, sickly 2.551, 4.235

wantrust *n* distrust 1.794

war *adj* aware 2.275, 1181; **be(n**

~ beware, take care 2.1018;
be(n ~ by be warned by (the
example of) 1.203, 635; *v*
ware hym let him beware
2.868

wardein *n* guardian 3.665;
guard, porter 5.1177

warie *v* curse 2.1619, 5.1378

warly *adv* prudently, cautiously
3.454

warnynge *vbl n* summons 3.195

wasten *v* consume 2.393; dimin-
ish 3.348

wawes *n pl* waves 2.1, 5.1109

wax *pt sg of* **wexe(n** *v*

wayken *v* weaken, lessen 4.1144

waymentynge *vbl n* lamentation
2.65

wayte(n *v* watch 1.190; expect
3.491; **~ on** attend, await 5.24;
pay attention to, observe
3.534

wede *n* clothing, apparel 1.177,
3.1431, 1719

weder *n* weather 2.2, 3.657, 670

weep *pt sg of* **wepe(n** *v*

we(e)te *adj* wet 5.1109

we(e)x *pt sg of* **wexe(n** *v*

weilaway, wailaway, welaway
interj alas! 3.304, 1695, 4.972

wel, weel *adj* well, favourable, as
desired 3.528, 652, 710; **~ was
hem** they were happy 3.231; **~
is/was hym** he is/was fortunate
1.350, 3.612; *adv* (*with adjs*)
very much 1.578; (*with advs*)
very 1.108

weldy *adj* vigorous, active 2.636

wele *n* joy, well-being, prosperity
1.4, 2.866

welfare *n* happiness 4.228,
5.1359

welk *pt sg* walked 2.517, 5.1235

welle *n* well 2.508; source, well-
spring, fountainhead 1.873,
2.841

welle *v* well up, gush 4.709,
5.215

wel-willy *adj* benevolent 3.1257

wende(n *v* go, travel 2.220; *refl*
2.812; leave, depart 3.208; *3
pr sg contr* went 2.36

wende(n *pt of* wene(n *v*

wendyng *n* departure 4.1344,
1436, 1630

wene *n* doubt 4.1593

wene(n *v* think, imagine, sup-
pose 1.575; expect 1.217;
intend 4.88; *pt sg* wende
1.227; *pt pl* wenden 4.683; 2
pt subj sg wendest 1.1031; *prp*
wenyng 4.88; *pp* ywent 5.444;
wende (*with infin*) 3.83, 4.683;
vbl n wenynge understanding
4.992

wepe(n *v* weep 1.7, 699; *pt sg*
wep 3.115, 5.1046; weep
4.1138, 5.725; wepte 2.562; *pt
pl* wepten 5.1822; *pp* wepen
5.724; wopen 1.941

werbul *n* tune 2.1033

werche(n, werke(n *v* work, act
1.380, 1071; perform, do
5.861; cause 3.1354, 5.1236;
make, create 2.577; *pt sg*
wroughte 3.261; *pt pl*
wroughte(n 1.63, 3.463; *pp*
wrought 1.578

wereye *v* make war upon 5.584

werk *n* work, task 1.1066;
deeds, actions 1.265; (literary)
work 2.16; business 2.960; suf-
fering 4.852; workmanship
5.1658

werne *v* refuse, deny 3.12, 149

werre *n* war, conflict 1.134,
5.234

wers *comp adj* worse 2.862; *as n*
3.1074, 4.840

werst(e *superl adj* worst 2.304,
3.278; *as n* 1.341

wery *adj* weary 2.211, 4.302,
1142

wesshen *pt pl* washed 2.1184

westren *v* move westwards 2.906

wete(n *v* dampen, moisten
3.1115

wexe(n, waxe(n *v* grow, become
2.908, 1578; *pt sg* wax, we(e)x
1.229, 231, 1011; *pp*
(y)woxen 5.275, 708, 827

wey *adv* away 1.574; **do** ~ put
aside 2.110; enough! 2.893

wey(e *n* way 1.219, 1062; **by no**
~ 1.495

weyve *v* neglect 2.284; forsake
4.602; turn aside 2.1050

whan(ne, when(ne *adv and conj*
when 5.1428; whenever
5.1417; after 4.587; since
1.404

what *pron, conj, adj, adv*; what
1.419; whatever 1.320; ~ **so**
whatever 3.1799, 4.442; who
1.765, 862; whosoever 1.679;
why 1.813; how 2.464, 862; as
much as 4.35; *interj* what!
1.292

whennes *adv* whence 1.402,
408

wher *conj* (*contr of* whe(i)ther)
whether 2.1263; ~ **so** 1.270;
(used to introduce a question;
not translated) 4.831

whereas *conj* where 4.1358

wherby *adv* why 3.778

wherfore *adv* why 1.311; for which reason 1.430, 988

wherfro *adv* from which 1.436

wherof *adv* of which 3.1647; why 4.641, 1365; from what 5.1224

wheron *rel adv* on which 5.1199

wherso *adv* wherever 2.847, 3.1046

wherto *adv* why 1.409, 2.302

wherwith *adv* with which 1.942, 4.1112

wheston *n* whetstone 1.631

whette *pp* whetted, sharpened 5.1760

whi *adv* why; *as n* reason 2.777

which *adj and pron* which; ~ that which 4.176; the ~ 5.391; *exclam* what a 1.803

whider *adv* whither, where 3.391, 4.647

whiderward *adv* where 4.282

whielen *v* wheel, turn 1.139

while *n* time; every ~ constantly 1.328; in this ~ at the same time 3.776; gon sithen longe ~ for a long time past 1.718; naught gon ful longe ~ recently 2.507; weylaway the ~ alas for the time! 3.1078

whilom *adv* once, formerly 1.508, 4.740

whit(e *adj* white 1.158; fair 2.887, 1062; fair-seeming, specious 3.901, 1567; *n* silver 3.1384

whiten *v* whiten, become white 5.276

who *pron* who; whoever 3.49; ~ that he who 2.867; as ~ seith as one might say 1.1011, 3.268; *gen* whos whose 1.532,

4.973, the whos 5.1359;

whom whom; whomsoever 1.189, 2.1717; whom that whom 1.717

whoso *pron* whoever 1.147; whomso whomsoever 5.145

wierdes *n pl* Fates 3.617

wif *n* wife 1.678; woman 3.106, 1296

wight *n* creature, person, man 1.13, 2.195; a litel ~ a little bit 5.926

wike, wyke *n* week 2.430, 5.499

wikke *adj* bad, evil 1.403; noxious 1.946; *as n* bad 3.1074, 4.840

wikked *adj* wicked 1.93; malicious 1.39

wilfull *adj* self-willed 3.935

wilfully *adv* purposely, wilfully 2.284

wilfulnesse *n* perversity, obstinacy 1.793

wil, wille *n* will, desire, intention 1.125, 3.623, 4.639

wilne *v* wish, desire 3.121, 295

wir *n* wire, thread 3.1636

wisly *adv* certainly 3.1653; (*in asseverations*) so/as ~ 2.1230, 3.790

wisse *v* inform, guide 1.622

wist, wiste *pp & pt of* wite(n *v* (1)

wit *n* mind, reason 4.348; understanding, judgement, intelligence 2.662; emforth my ~ to the extent of my understanding 2.243, 997; cunning 5.1782; opinion 5.758; intent 4.1104; idea, notion 4.1425; *gen sg* wittes: ~ ende 3.931

wite *n* blame, reproach 2.1648,
3.739

wite(n, wete(n *v* (1) know 2.226,
238; *1,3, pr sg* wo(o)t 1.195,
2.1440; *2 pr sg* wo(o)st 1.633,
3.256; (*with pron*) wostow
1.588; *imp pl* witteth 1.687; *3
pt sg* wiste 1.76; *2 pt sg* (*with
pron*) wystestow 3.1644; *pp*
wist 1.57

wite(n *v* (2) blame on 5.1335;
impute to 2.1000; to ~ to be
blamed 1.825, 2.385

withal, with alle *adv* as well
5.820; indeed 1.288

with(h)olden *v* retain, keep back
4.597; restrain 5.76

withoute *adv* outside 2.611;
of ~ from out of town
1.270

withseye *v* oppose 4.215

withstonde *v* withstand, resist
1.839, 1008; oppose 4.160,
1298; *pt subj sg* withstoode
were to oppose 4.552; *pp*
withstonde 1.253

wo(o *n* woe, sorrow, misery 1.4,
34; me (hym, *etc.*) is ~ I am
unhappy 1.356, 3.1698; wher
me be ~ whether I am unhappy
3.66; do(o)n ~ cause sorrow
2.1360; ~ worth a curse upon
2.344; lamentation 5.1509;
maken ~ lament 4.855

wo-bygon (*see also* bigon *pp*)
sad, beset with sorrow 3.1530,
4.822

wodebynde *n* woodbine, honey-
suckle 3.1231

wo(o)dnesse *n* madness 3.794,
1382

woful *adj* woeful, sorrowful, sad

1.7, 519; *superl* wofulleste
4.303, 516

wo(o)k *pt sg of* waken *v*

wol, wil *v* wish, desire; require,
demand 3.988; (in formation
of future tense) will; wolde: in
conditional sentences; in
describing habitual actions
('would', 'used to'); in forma-
tion of the future in the past;
modal uses ('would like to');
wolde God would that God
(would grant) 1.459; *pr sg*
wol(e 3.1262; *pr pl* wol(e,
wollen 2.311, 3.768; *2 pr sg*
wilt, wolt 3.412, 2.955, (with
suffixed *pron*) wiltow, woltow
1.1018, 5.1157; *pt sg* wolde; *2
pt sg* woldest; *pt pl* wolde(n

wolken *n* sky, heavens
3.551

wommanhod, wommanhede *n*
womanliness 1.283, 3.1302,
1740; womanly ways 4.1462

wommanly *adv* in womanly,
feminine fashion 2.1668,
5.577

wommanliche *adj* (quintessen-
tially) womanly 1.287, 3.106,
1296

wommanysshe *adj* woman-like,
feminine 4.694

wonder, wondre *n* marvel, object
or cause of amazement 1.403,
2.1143; (feeling of) amazement
5.981; *adj* amazing, marvel-
lous, strange 1.419, 621; *adv*
marvellously, amazingly 1.288

wonderlich *adv* amazingly
3.678; incredulously 1.729

wonderynge *vbl n* wonder 2.35

wondren *v* be amazed 3.753,

5.162; be curious 2.141, 3.32,
4.647

wone *n* wont, custom, habit
2.318, 5.647

wone *v* dwell 1.276, 4.474; *pp as
adj* wont accustomed 1.183,
510

wood *adj* mad 1.499, 2.1355,
1554

woon *n* resource 4.1181

wo(o)st, wo(o)t 2 *pr sg, 1 & 3 pr
sg of* wite(n *v* (1)

wopen *pp of* wepe(n *v*

word *n* word; promise, vow
4.1550; good ~ approval
5.1081, 1622; at o ~ briefly
3.1308; with that ~ at that,
thereupon 2.91, 3.978; ~ and
ende beginning and end, all
2.1495, 3.702, 5.1669; at
shorte wordes briefly 2.956,
4.636; withouten wordes mo
immediately 2.1405, 3.234,
4.219, 500

worship *n* honour 1.46, 82

worth *adj* of value 2.866, 3.14

worthe(n *v* remain 5.329; *imp sg*
worth mount 2.1011; *pr subj*
wo ~ woe be to, a curse on
2.344, 4.747, 763; wel ~ good
luck to 5.379

worthi *adj* noble, distinguished
1.226; excellent, having worth
1.895; deserving 1.91; fitting
3.1169; *comp* worthier 1.251;
superl worthiest 1.244

worthynesse *n* excellence,
honour 1.567, 2.161

wowe *v* woo 5.791, 1091

wowke *n* week 4.1278, 5.492

woxen *pp of* wexe(n *v*

wrak *pt sg of* wreke(n *v*

wrat(t)h(e, wreththe *n* anger
1.940, 3.110, 5.960

wratthe *v* be angry with 3.174

wre, wreigh *see* wrye *v*

wrecche *n* wretch, miserable,
despicable person 1.708, 777;
villain 5.705

wrecched *adj* wretched, unhappy
2.782; cowardly 3.736, 4.621;
miserable, despicable 5.1817,
1851

wrecchednesse *n* misery, wretch-
edness, despicable behaviour
2.286, 3.381, 1787, 5.39

wreche *n* vengeance 5.890; tor-
ment 2.784

wreke(n *v* avenge 1.62; make up
for 3.905; *pt sg* wrak 5.1468;
pp (y)wroken 1.88, 207, 5.589

wreste *v* constrain, force 4.1427

wreththe *see* wrat(t)h(e *n*

wreye *v* reveal 3.284

wringe *v* wring (hands, fingers)
4.738, 1171; wring, wrench
(the feelings) 3.1531; *pt sg*
wrong

write(n *v* write; 3 *pr sg* writ
1.394; *pr subj sg* write should
write 5.1293; *imp sg* write
2.1026; *imp pl* writeth 5.1399;
pt sg wro(o)t 1.655, 2.1214

writhe *v* turn 4.9; wriggle, escape
4.986; 3 *pr sg* writh encircles
3.1231

wroken *pp of* wreke(n *v*

wrong *pt sg of* wringe *v*

wro(o)th *adj* angry 1.349, 2.300;
at odds 1.140

wroughte(n *pt sg & pl of*
werche(n *v*

wrye *v* (1) cover 2.539, 3.1569;
~ hymself cover himself, dis-

semble 1.329; **wre yow** cover
yourself 2.380; conceal 3.620,
4.1654; *pt sg* **wreigh** 3.1056;
pp (i)**wrie(n** 3.620, 1451,
4.1654
wrye *v* (2) go, turn 2.906
wy *interj* why 3.738, 842
wyd(e *adj* wide 2.615, 4.627,
1336; *adv* widely 1.384,
2.175; far 1.629
wyde-wher *adv* far and wide
3.404
wyke, wike *n* week 2.430
wylde *adj* violent, passionate
2.116; fierce 4.239
wyle *n* guile, trickery 1.719,
2.271, 3.1077
wyn *n* wine 3.671, 5.852
wynde *v* clasp 3.1232; turn over
(in mind) 2.601, 3.1541; bend
1.257; go 3.1440
wynke *v* close one's eyes 1.301,
3.1537
wynne(n *v* win, gain 1.504, 698;
conquer 2.1376; get away
(from) 5.1125; ~ **on** get the
better of 1.390; *pp* (y)**wonne**
2.1743, 4.1315; *vbl n*
wynnynge obtaining 1.199
wys *adj* wise, prudent 1.233,
635; *as n* wise man 1.79, 694;
adv certainly, surely 2.474,
887; (*in asseverations*) **so/as** ~
2.381
wyse *n* manner, way 1.61, 159
wyt(t)ynge *vbl n* knowledge
2.236, 4.991
wyvere *n* snake 3.1010

yaf *pt sg of* **yeve(n** *v*
yate *n* gate 2.615, 3.469
yave *pt pl of* **yeve(n** *v*

ybe *pp of* **be(en**; been 4.1108
ybete(n *pp of* **bete(n**; beaten
1.741, 3.1169
yblowe *pp* made known 1.384
yborn *pp of* **bere(n**; born, living
1.382, 2.298
ybought *pp of* **bye(n**; paid for
1.810; bought 3.1319
ybrend *pp of* **brenne(n**; burnt
4.77, 5.309
ybrought *pp of* **bringe**; brought
3.1599
ychaunged *pp of* **cha(u)nge(n**;
changed, altered 4.865
ycleped *pp of* **clepe(n**; called,
summoned 4.504
ycome(n *pp* come 4.366, 5.71,
512
ydel *adj* in on ~ in vain 1.955,
5.94, 272
ydoon *pp of* **do(on**; done 4.789;
maintained 2.1245
ydrawe *pp of* **drawe(n**; drawn
3.853
ydred *pp of* **drede(n**; feared
3.1775
yë, yën *see* **eye** *n*
yede *pt sg* went 5.843; *pt pl*
yeden 2.936
ye(e *adv* yes 1.775; indeed, to be
sure 2.92, 3.932
yef *imp sg of* **yeve(n**; 1.1042
yelde(n *v* surrender, give up
4.212; give back 4.347; *refl*
submit 3.1208; ~ **up breth** die
1.801; **God** ~ **the** God reward
you 1.1055; *3 pr sg* **yelt** 1.385;
pp **yolde** yielded, surrendered
3.1211; **iyolden** submissive
3.96
yelpe *v* boast 3.307
yerd *n* garden 2.820

yerd(e *v* rod, staff 2.1427;
scourge 2.154; bough, sapling
1.257; **under yowre** ~ subject
to your authority 3.137

yerne *v* desire, seek 3.152; **to** ~
to be desired 4.198

yerne *adv* in **as** ~ soon, quickly
3.151, 4.112, 201; **late or** ~
ever 3.376

yesternyght *adv* last night 5.221

yeve(n *v* give; *pt sg* yaf 2.651; *pt
pl* yave(n 2.1323, 4.710; *pt
subj sg* yave would give 2.977;
imp sg yef, yif 1.1042, 2.293,
5.308; *prp* yevyng 5.685; *pp*
yyeven, yyive 3.1376,
1611

yfare *pp of* fare(n; gone 3.577,
4.1169

yfe(e)re *adv* together 2.152, 168,
5.813

yfled *pp of* flee(n; fled 4.661

ygraunted *pp of* graunte; granted
4.665

yheere *v* hear of 4.1313

yheried *pp of* herie; praised
2.973, 3.1804

yif *imp sg of* yeve(n; 2.293

yif *conj* if 2.1297

yiftes *n pl* gifts 4.392

yis *adv* yes (*more emphatic than*
ye) 1.1054; (*in response to
negative question*) 2.278, 1424

yit, yet *adv* yet 1.239

ykaught *pp of* cache(n; caught
2.583

ykist *pp* kissed 4.1689

yknet *pp of* knette; tied 3.1734

yknowe *pp of* knowe; known
2.175, 792

ylike *adv* equally, invariably
3.144, 485

ylissed *pp of* lisse(n; relieved
1.1089

ylorn *pp of* lese(n; lost 4.1250

ylost *pp of* lese(n; lost 4.1283

ymad *pp of* make(n; made
5.1537

ymage *n* image, likeness 4.864,
5.1839; statue 4.235

ymagynen *v* imagine, form a men-
tal picture, conceive 2.836,
4.1695; suppose mistakenly,
fancy 5.617, 624; believe,
deduce 1.372, 5.1441; devise,
plan 4.1626; consider, wonder
(about) 5.454

ymasked *pp* enmeshed 3.1734

ymet *pp* met 2.586

ynome *pp* taken 1.242

ynorisshed *pp* brought up 5.821

ynowe *adj* enough 3.299, 4.107

yolden *pp of* yelde(n

yond *adv* yonder, over there
2.1284, 4.1023

yonder *adj* yonder, over there
2.1237; **the/that** ~ 2.1188,
5.575, 580

yo(o)re *adv* formerly 4.1497,
5.55, 324; ~ **ago** long ago
5.317; **of** ~ formerly 5.1734;
for a long time 4.719

youre *pron gen* of you: ~ **bother**
love the love of you two 4.168;
yours 2.587; **youres** 1.423

ypassed *pp of* passe(n; past
5.746

ypleyned *pp of* pleyne(n; com-
plained, lamented 4.1688

ypleynted *pp* filled with laments
5.1597

yplight *pp* pledged 3.782

ypreysed *pp* praised 5.1473

yput *pp* put 3.275

yred *pp of* rede(n; read 4.799

yronne *pp of* renne(n; run
2.907

yse, ysee *v* see 2.354, 1253,
4.1048, 5.1299; look 4.838

yseene *pp of* se(en; seen 1.700,
4.1607

ysent *pp* sent 5.471

yserved *pp of* serve(n; served
5.437, 1721

yset *pp of* sette(n; placed, set
3.1731

yseyn *pp of* se(e)(n; seen 2.168

yshape(n *pp of* shape(n; formed
3.411; ordained 3.1240

yshette *pp of* shette(n; shut 3.233

yshewed *pp of* shewe(n; shown
5.1251

yshore *pp* shaven 4.996

ysonder *adv* asunder, apart
5.983

ysonge *pp* sung 4.799, 5.1059

ysounded *pp* penetrated, sunk
2.535

yspoke *pp* spoken 4.1108

ystonde *pp of* stonde(n; stood
5.1612

ysuffred *pp of* suffre(n; suffered
5.415

ytaken *pp* undertaken 5.1765

ythe *v* prosper 2.670, 4.439

ythonked *pp* in ~ be thanks be to
4.2

ythrowe *pp* thrown, cast down
4.6, 482

ytressed *pp* in tresses, plaits
5.810

ytwynned *pp of* twynne(n; separ-
ated 4.788

yvel *n* evil, ill 1.782; **non ~ mene**
intend no harm 2.581, 3.1164;
for ~ take take amiss 4.606,
5.1625

yvel *adj* bad, evil; **~ fare** misfor-
tune 2.1001; **~ wille** reluctance
5.1637

yvel(e *adv* badly; **~ appayed** dis-
pleased 1.649, 4.642; **~ faren**
get on badly, suffer 1.626,
5.238

ywar *adj* aware 2.398

ywent *pp of* wene(n; supposed
5.444

ywis, ywys (*see also* iwis)
certainly, indeed 1.657,
893

ywonne *pp of* winne(n; won,
gained 2.1236, 3.280,
4.1315

ywoxen *pp of* wexe(n; grown,
become 5.275, 708

ywriten *pp* written 5.1059

ywroke *pp of* wreke(n; avenged
5.589

ywrye *pp of* wrye(n; hidden
4.1654

yyeven, yyive *pp of* yeve(n; given
3.1376, 1611

zeles *n* zeal 5.1859

PENGUIN (Ⓟ) CLASSICS

The Classics Publisher

'Penguin Classics, one of the world's greatest series' JOHN KEEGAN

'I have never been disappointed with the Penguin Classics. All I have read is a model of academic seriousness and provides the essential information to fully enjoy the master works that appear in its catalogue' MARIO VARGAS LLOSA

'Penguin and Classics are words that go together like horse and carriage or Mercedes and Benz. When I was a university teacher I always prescribed Penguin editions of classic novels for my courses: they have the best introductions, the most reliable notes, and the most carefully edited texts' DAVID LODGE

'Growing up in Bombay, expensive hardback books were beyond my means, but I could indulge my passion for reading at the roadside bookstalls that were well stocked with all the Penguin paperbacks ... Sometimes I would choose a book just because I was attracted by the cover, but so reliable was the Penguin imprimatur that I was never once disappointed by the contents.

Such access certainly broadened the scope of my reading, and perhaps it's no coincidence that so many Merchant Ivory films have been adapted from great novels, or that those novels are published by Penguin' ISMAIL MERCHANT

'You can't write, read, or live fully in the present without knowing the literature of the past. Penguin Classics opens the door to a treasure house of pure pleasure, books that have never been bettered, which are read again and again with increased delight' JOHN MORTIMER

CLICK ON A CLASSIC

www.penguinclassics.com

The world's greatest literature at your fingertips

Constantly updated information on over 1600 titles, from
Icelandic sagas to ancient Indian epics, Russian drama to
Italian romance, American greats to African masterpieces

•

The latest news on recent additions to the list, updated
editions and specially commissioned translations

•

Original scholarly essays by leading writers: Elaine Showalter
on Zola, Laurie R. King on Arthur Conan Doyle, Frank
Kermode on Shakespeare, Lisa Appignanesi on Tolstoy

•

A wealth of background material, including biographies
of every classic author from Aristotle to Zamyatin, plot
synopses, readers' and teachers' guides, useful web links

•

Online desk and examination copy assistance for academics

•

Trivia quizzes, competitions, giveaways, news on
forthcoming screen adaptations

•

eBooks available to download

READ MORE IN PENGUIN

In every corner of the world, on every subject under the sun, Penguin represents quality and variety – the very best in publishing today.

For complete information about books available from Penguin – including Puffins and Penguin Classics – and how to order them, write to us at the appropriate address below. Please note that for copyright reasons the selection of books varies from country to country.

In the United Kingdom: *Please write to* Dept EP, Penguin Books Ltd, Bath Road, Harmondsworth, West Drayton, Middlesex UB7 0DA

In the United States: *Please write to* Consumer Services, Penguin Putnam Inc., 405 Murray Hill Parkway, East Rutherford, New Jersey 07073-2136. *VISA and MasterCard holders call 1-800-631-8571 to order Penguin titles*

In Canada: *Please write to* Penguin Books Canada Ltd, 10 Alcorn Avenue, Suite 300, Toronto, Ontario M4V 3B2

In Australia: *Please write to* Penguin Books Australia Ltd, 487 Maroondah Highway, Ringwood, Victoria 3134

In New Zealand: *Please write to* Penguin Books (NZ) Ltd, Private Bag 102902, North Shore Mail Centre, Auckland 10

In India: *Please write to* Penguin Books India Pvt Ltd, 11, Community Centre, Panchsheel Park, New Delhi 110017

In the Netherlands: *Please write to* Penguin Books Netherlands bv, Postbus 3507, NL-1001 AH Amsterdam

In Germany: *Please write to* Penguin Books Deutschland GmbH, Metzlerstrasse 26, 60594 Frankfurt am Main

In Spain: *Please write to* Penguin Books S. A., Bravo Murillo 19, 1°B, 28015 Madrid

In Italy: *Please write to* Penguin Italia s.r.l., Via Vittoria Emanuele 451a, 20094 Corsico, Milano

In France: *Please write to* Penguin France, 12, Rue Prosper Ferradou, 31700 Blagnac

In Japan: *Please write to* Penguin Books Japan Ltd, Iidabashi KM-Bldg, 2-23-9 Koraku, Bunkyo-Ku, Tokyo 112-0004

In South Africa: *Please write to* Penguin Books South Africa (Pty) Ltd, P.O. Box 751093, Gardenview, 2047 Johannesburg